AUTISM SCHOOL DAZE
TRILOGY - 1

STORIES OF ADVERSITY, FAMILY, LOVE & TRIUMPH

DR. SHARON A. MITCHELL

CONTENTS

AUTISM GOES TO SCHOOL

Chapter 1   5
Chapter 2   19
Chapter 3   29
Chapter 4   34
Chapter 5   52
Chapter 6   64
Chapter 7   81
Chapter 8   102
Chapter 9   109
Chapter 10   122
Chapter 11   132
Chapter 12   143
Chapter 13   163
Chapter 14   175
Chapter 15   183
Chapter 16   194

AUTISM RUNS AWAY

Chapter 1   205
Chapter 2   216
Chapter 3   224
Chapter 4   232
Chapter 5   242
Chapter 6   247
Chapter 7   254
Chapter 8   258
Chapter 9   262
Chapter 10   266
Chapter 11   270
Chapter 12   280

Chapter 13   289
Chapter 14   298
Chapter 15   306
Chapter 16   311
Chapter 17   316
Chapter 18   325
Chapter 19   333
Chapter 20   342
Chapter 21   354
Chapter 22   358
Chapter 23   362
Chapter 24   366
Chapter 25   368
Chapter 26   373
Chapter 27   376
Chapter 28   378
Chapter 29   383

AUTISM BELONGS

Prologue   391
Chapter 1   393
Chapter 2   394
Chapter 3   399
Chapter 3   403
Chapter 4   407
Chapter 5   414
Chapter 6   417
Chapter 7   427
Chapter 8   432
Chapter 9   447
Chapter 10   456
Chapter 11   462
Chapter 12   468
Chapter 13   474
Chapter 14   491
Chapter 15   500
Chapter 16   506
Chapter 17   511

Chapter 18   517
Chapter 19   527
Chapter 20   536
Chapter 21   543
Chapter 22   553
Epilogue   561
Dedication   565

EXCERPT FROM AUTISM TALKS AND TALKS

Excerpt from Autism Talks and Talks   571

GONE: A PSYCHOLOGICAL THRILLER

Part I
MONDAY

Chapter 1   583
Chapter 2   587
Chapter 3   594
Chapter 4   600

AUTISM GOES TO SCHOOL

SCHOOL DAZE: BOOK ONE

Autism
GOES TO SCHOOL

Dr Sharon A Mitchell

CHAPTER 1

*B*en grabbed for Kyle's hand as they approached the front of the school. As usual, Kyle cringed and pulled away.

"All right, all right, just come on already. We're late. You have to get to school." I hate being late, Ben muttered to himself. He pulled on the door handle. Nothing. He heaved. "Shit!" Nothing. Kyle, who had remained silent for the last half hour, repeated, "Shit! Shit, shit, shit, shit, shit."

"No. You can't say that." Ben so badly wanted his son to talk to him, but did the kid have to repeat the one taboo word Ben had uttered so far today? He searched for another door, spotted one farther down the building and again reached for Kyle's hand. The sound Kyle let out made him drop it. "Kyle, come on," Ben told his son, "we have to get in there." Kyle came, but, "Shit, shit, shit" came faintly from his mouth. Ben sighed.

It took three doors and more expletives before Ben found one that would allow them to enter the building. He had no idea what was wrong with this place. A school was a public building, wasn't it?

Once in the school, Ben stopped. He had not thought this far. Did he have to find the room for five year olds on his own? He spotted a sign telling visitors to report to the office and an arrow pointing down the beige hall. Without thinking, Ben put his hand on Kyle's shoulder to steer him in the right direction. Predictably, Kyle pulled away, rubbing the shoulder that Ben had touched. Ben winced. "Well, just come then, if you don't want me touching you." Whatever Kyle might be thinking didn't register on his face, but he followed Ben anyway.

In the distance, screaming started up. Ben instinctively stepped in front of his son. He stopped. Where was that coming from? Was a child in danger? What kind of a school was this anyway?

They continued cautiously, Ben ready to grab Kyle and run. The screams became louder as they came to an open door. Inside Ben glimpsed some kids sitting around tables, one in a rocking chair, others standing in front of easels and one little boy writhing on the floor as a woman knelt beside him, about to lay a blanket over him. What the hell were they doing to that child to cause him to scream like that?

Ben glanced at Kyle to make sure he was safe, then stepped into the doorway, ready to intervene. As he watched, the woman spoke softly to the screaming child and laid the blanket over him. She pressed it down firmly around him but the blanket didn't mold to the child's body the way a blanket should. As she continued to press down with the blanket, the screams lessened to whimpers. The woman then reached for a large plastic ball and started running it up and down the little boy's body, pressing harder than Ben would have thought advisable. This was a small child, after all.

"Hey," Ben called. "What are you doing to that kid? Is he all right?" All eyes turned to him. The wailing momentarily eased then started up again. With a nod to a younger woman, the teacher or whoever she was rose to her feet, keeping pressure on the ball until the other woman came to take her place. Then her calm expression changed as she came toward Ben with purpose.

"Please leave my room. You're disturbing my students," she said when she got to the doorway where Ben stood.

Ben looked at her. "I'm disturbing your students?" he asked

6

incredulously. "It looks like you're torturing that poor kid." The kid in question, calm now, looked out at him with big eyes.

"Does he look disturbed?" the teacher asked. "Don't answer that," she added. "This is my classroom and these are my students. Kindly carry on with your own business. If you're new here, the office is that way." She pointed in the direction Ben and Kyle had been going.

"I don't know what your problem is, lady, but I heard a kid screaming and thought he might need help." Ben backed out the door, shaking his head. His heart settled back into its normal pattern after the fright of hearing the child's screams. He'd never let anyone like that near his son.

THE OFFICE RESEMBLED a jungle with green plants everywhere. They were greeted by a welcoming, grey-haired woman, half-hidden by the counter. She stuck out her hand. "Good morning, you two. I'm Mrs. Billings."

Ben shook her hand. "Ben Wickens and this is my son, Kyle". Kyle neither looked at them, nor showed any sign he noticed the smile and hand extended his way. "Ah, Kyle's a little stand-offish at first," he explained.

"Well, I'm sure we'll become firm friends in no time. How may I help you?"

"Kyle is new to the area and needs to be in school."

"Let me introduce you to Dr. Hitkin, our principal. She'll get you registered and in the right classroom."

BEN SANK INTO THE CHAIR, fidgeting and expecting a long wait. Bureaucrats did that sort of thing, of course. They'd show him how important they were by keeping him waiting. He hated it, but he'd suffer through it for the sake of his son.

Pulling back his sleeve cuff to check his watch, Ben then glanced at Kyle. Shirt was clean; pants looked all right. He'd remembered to rub the milk off Kyle's mouth. Yep, he looked pretty typical.

The realization hit him once again that yes, he indeed did have a son. The kid was actually quite cute, even if he was biased. Kyle stood at the side of the room, his little body swaying in rhythm to the asparagus fern blowing in the breeze coming through the open window. Ironic. Of all the houseplants in the world, this was one of the very few Ben could actually name. And, this was one his son obviously was attracted to. As he watched, he noticed his son's lips moving, keeping time to the swaying. What was he saying? Ben got up and moved closer.

"Shit, shit, shit, shit," Kyle said. Quietly, at least, thank god.

"Kyle. Shhhh. Don't say that. It's not a nice word." Kyle turned to look at his dad. His eyes actually met Ben's momentarily, before sliding away. Whoa. When was the last time Kyle had looked at him, even briefly?

"Kyle, that's a bad word. Daddy should not have said that. I was frustrated, is all. No, that's not an excuse. I'm sorry you heard that, but please don't say that word."

"Shit, shit, shit, shit," Kyle intoned.

Ben was about to try again when the inner door opened and a middle-aged woman came out smiling, with her hand ready to take Ben's.

"Hi. I'm Dr. Delora Hitkin, principal of Madson Elementary School. What can I do for you?"

Ben introduced himself as he shook her hand. He then pointed to Kyle. "This is my son, Kyle. He needs to start school, but at the moment he seems fascinated by your plants."

"He's not the only one. I love them as well." She turned to Kyle. "Hi, Kyle. Welcome to our school."

Ben started to apologize for his son's behavior. Kyle was so intent on the swaying plant that he did not seem to even notice the principal's presence. Dr. Hitkin waved her hand at Ben's consternation. "Don't worry. We're used to kids here and all are welcome."

She went to the plant and ducked underneath it. She swayed her head in time with the plant, smiling at Kyle. Ben held his breath, waiting for Kyle to explode.

Kyle froze. Ben stepped forward to interfere but Marie, the secretary gave him a warning look.

Kyle's gaze shifted from the plant to the person who dared interfere with his pleasure. Eventually, he met Dr. Hitkin's eyes. She grinned and said, "Boo!"

Ben was amazed and relieved to hear Kyle's giggle. Phew! A crisis averted. He so didn't want Kyle to create a scene even before he'd been accepted into the school.

This brought Ben back to the dilemma that kept him up all night. Should he pass Kyle off as just a typical five year old? Or did he let the cat out of the bag and admit that Kyle had autism? If he told them, what if they would not let Kyle enter the school? What if there was a special school just for morons or kids who had things like autism? What if they didn't want Kyle?

"Mr. Wickens, would you like to come into my office with me?" Ben hesitated. Dr. Hitkin continued, "Kyle will be just fine here with Ms. Billings. She's a great fan of all kids and they adore her." What could Ben say? Should he tell her that Kyle's not like other kids? Before he could decide, Dr. Hitkin ushered him into her office. His last glimpse of Kyle was of Ms. Billings dragging out a tub of chunky, wooden building blocks and getting onto the floor beside Kyle.

"Don't worry, they'll be fine," Dr. Hitkin assured him. "We'll leave the door open so he can see you."

"Now, we have some paperwork to fill out. Will your wife be joining us?"

Ben thought he'd stepped into it already. How to explain the situation without making either he or Deanna sound like a horse's ass?

"No. I'm a single parent. "The words sounded strange to his ears. "Kyle lives with me."

"School started two weeks ago. Why didn't you register him earlier?"

There was no easy way to get around this. He didn't want this new school to be prejudiced against Kyle because of his wacky parents.

"Kyle has only been living with me since yesterday. Prior to that he was with his mother and her husband in California. I now have custody."

"I see. I'll need to retain a copy of the legal custody agreement for the school records."

Ben stared at her. He had no such thing. Damn Deanna. Why had she not mentioned these details? Kyle had been in school before, so surely she must have known.

"Ah, that is still in the works. His mother just sent him to me yesterday and in the rush of exchanging information and Kyle's things, we didn't get to the legal parts. I'll contact her today and get this straightened out. I'm sure there will be no problem."

"Are there any other problems you want to tell me about?"

Ben tried not to squirm. "What do you mean?"

"Let me get one thing straight." Ben's heart filled with dread. Dr. Hitkin had sensed something different about Kyle and was going to say he didn't belong in this school. She continued, "Madson Elementary is a public school. Here we welcome all students. We respect the different learning styles of all children. Do you have any questions or concerns?"

This was obviously the opening for Ben to talk about Kyle's autism. But, he didn't know how to do that, hardly had any idea what autism was all about, other than the quick website search he'd done after Kyle went to bed yesterday. What he read left his mind boggling. The stories! Surely, they did not fit Kyle. Ben didn't know if he could cope, but he sure could not function if Kyle was not in school all day. He had a business to run.

A good defense is a good offence in the business world, Ben believed, so he launched in. "I have certain requirements for my son. I want him in a safe environment. I want him to learn. I want him to have good role models."

Dr. Hitkin nodded.

"I do have some concerns," Ben launched in. "First, you said that this is a public school. As such, I would think that it's a public building. I'll have you know that I had to try three doors before I could find one that let us in. What if there was a fire? How would all these children get out?"

Again, Dr. Hitkin nodded. "And did you notice which one opened for you?" She didn't wait for his reply. "The main door, the one that leads directly to the office. We keep all other doors locked during the day. The one you used is monitored by camera at all times. When the door opens, we're alerted in the office and Marie or I watch the monitor. This is for the safety of our students. We need to know at all times who is in our building and if anyone leaves. And, for your information, in case of a fire alarm, all the other doors are automatically unlocked. Does that answer your question?"

Ben was a little ashamed, but had more. "As we walked along the hall, we came across this one room, not the kind of place I would like any child of mine."

"What exactly do you mean?"

"This little boy was screaming. He was just a small child. A woman, I presume his teacher, threw this big blanket over him and held it down. Then she took this huge ball and put in on top of him. I could see the muscles in her arms working as she pressed down on it!"

"And, what did the child do?" Dr. Hitkin inquired.

"Ah, well, he got quieter, or at least he seemed to."

"And what about the rest of the children in the room?"

"What do you mean?" Ben asked.

Dr. Hitkin clarified. "What were they doing while this was taking place?"

"I didn't pay a lot of attention to them; my concern was all for that one boy," said Ben.

"Think back. Did they look sad? Distressed? Unhappy? Shocked?"

"I don't know them well enough to say, but no, come to think about it, they seemed to be carrying on their business."

"Could you describe the teacher to me?" Dr. Hitkin asked.

Ben gave a brief description of the teacher and the room's location.

"That is Ms. Nicols room. Melanie Nicols is a stellar kindergarten teacher, one of the best you will ever come across."

"I'd have to object to her methods or at least those I witnessed." Ben thought a minute. "Kindergarten? Isn't that for five year olds? Kyle's five. Is that where you think you're going to place him? Oh, no. That's not the place for my son. He's delicate and impressionable. I don't want him exposed to kids who scream or get thrown to the floor."

"Did you see Ms. Nicols or anyone else throw that boy to the floor?" the principal asked.

"Well, no, but...."

"I can assure you that his teacher did not throw him or any other student to the floor." She watched Kyle and Marie through the open door for a minute. "Mr. Wickens, can you honestly tell me that Kyle has never screamed?"

Ben told her, "Come on. He's a child. No child is perfect."

"Exactly. But there is a range that we normally think of as typical for children of a certain age. Then, there are other children of the same age who may do some of the things just like others their age, but may have some, shall we say, quirks. Do you ever see that in Kyle?"

"He's my son. He's the only five year old I know. I don't really have anything to compare him to."

"Mr. Wickens, I presume that you were once a five year old boy yourself. And surely you've seen children in parks and malls and on television. Can you honestly say that Kyle is just like the everyday, typical little boy?"

Ben bristled. "Are you saying there's something wrong with my son?"

"Not at all. I would never suggest that there is anything wrong about any child. Different, yes. Wrong, no. There's a difference."

Ben sighed. He was new at this parenting thing. This crafty old lady was not going to let things slide by. As Ben hesitated, he heard a giggle in the outer office. His head whipped around. Yes, it was Kyle! It was his son. He was actually giggling. Ben watched in amazement.

He had not known Kyle had it in him. He was pleased at the sound of the childish delight but saddened that it took a stranger to bring out that glee. Kyle would barely even look at his own father, let alone play with him.

His gaze came back to Dr. Hitkin who was watching him intently. "You're new to this, aren't you Mr. Wickens?" she asked.

Ben wanted to squirm like a little boy sent to the principal's office. "Yes, ma'am," he said reflexively. "Kyle just came to live with me yesterday."

She smiled at him. "I don't mean just new to parenting. I meant that you're new to autism, aren't you?"

Ben stared at her. How the hell did she know? Did Kyle have a big "A" stenciled on his forehead? Or did he himself? Could she tell already that he was the kind of father who would create a kid with autism? Would they turn them away if they thought Kyle had autism?

Ben's back was up again. He needed to defend his son. "Kyle's a good kid, really he is. He's just new to me and to Madson. It's normal to have a period of adjustment. He'll be fine. I'll be fine. I'll support the school and help out and join the PTA or whatever it is you have these days."

Dr. Hitkin grinned. "Good to know. We'll hold you to that."

He blanched; she smiled as if she was enjoying this.

"You're in luck. Kyle has autism and we just happen to have an autism specialist in the building - Ms. Nicols."

"Not that teacher, that woman who held the kid down and pounded on him with a ball? That lady is not getting anywhere near my son. I will not have him treated that way."

"That woman is a highly trained teacher with a Master's degree in autism. She was not, nor would she ever "pound" on a child. What she was doing was calming him down. You heard his screaming as you came in. You witnessed him calm down under the gentle pressure of the weighted blanket and the ball. Many kids with autism react positively to weight and pressure. You ought to try it with Kyle."

"Let's get one thing straight. There is nothing wrong with Kyle. He's just a little boy. He does not talk much but it's coming. Yeah,

Deanna said that when he was younger some doctors said he had autism. But we spent thousands of dollars on treatment over the last three years; pretty much a normal person's salary in a year went to just Kyle's ABA treatment. They said it would cure him and that if we did this intensely, he'd be typical by the time he went to school. Well, he's school age now and I want him in school."

"Certainly he should be in school and he is welcome here. In fact, he can either start tomorrow or spend the rest of today with us. He will be in Ms. Nicols room. It's the ideal spot for him. I guarantee you'll be pleased at his progress. Both he and you will learn a lot."

"Me? I finished school a long time ago."

"True, but now that autism has come into your life, there is suddenly a lot more to learn, isn't there? Don't worry. We'll help."

THE PRINCIPAL EXCUSED herself to get the paperwork started and left Ben alone with his thoughts. Unfortunately. That damn principal had said the word "autism". How did she know? He hadn't mentioned it.

Usually he was pretty good at paperwork. He was, after all an accountant and dealt in papers much of his waking life. But he'd never before registered a little boy in school. What sort of questions might he be asked? He already failed the test about custody papers. What else didn't he know about his son?

Actually, a lot. He thought back to last night, his first night alone with Kyle. His son; he actually had a son.

He remembered the shock when he first learned that he had a child. But back then, it had still been an abstract concept. Sure, he'd stepped up and supported him financially as soon as he learned of his existence, but that was about it. Deanna would not allow him to meet their son, saying it would be too confusing for Kyle. And, to be honest, Ben had not protested too hard. He had his own life, far, far away from where Kyle and Deanna lived in California His conscience told him it was enough to send money. Lots of money, considering the size of the child.

He had not given much thought to what it would have been like to live with Kyle day by day. Sure, Deanna had said that Kyle had autism and therefore needed all this expensive treatment in order to be cured. But what must life have been like for Deanna before treatment if this was the way Kyle was AFTER treatment?

Last night had been hell, just hell and Ben finally fell into bed exhausted. Then, he thought about it from Kyle's point of view. Maybe it had not been so nice for him either.

Kyle was just a small boy. The kid didn't know him from any stranger on the street. He'd never had such a long car ride before.

There'd been the hysterical call from Deanna saying that she couldn't take it anymore. She and her new husband, Neil, were expecting their first baby together. She had morning sickness, was exhausted and just could not cope with Kyle any longer. She had to concentrate on this new life she was creating and on her marriage. Kyle was just too much for her - for them. It was now Ben's turn.

Before Ben could marshal his arguments and tell her how ridiculous this was, Deanna had hung up, sobbing. Ben assumed he'd hear from her next with apologies, saying she hadn't meant it and all their lives would return to normal.

Instead, just after supper last night there was a knock at the door. A car idled at the curb. In front of him stood a woman and a small boy. If Ben hadn't just talked to her on the phone, he would not have recognized Deanna. Her face was drawn and haggard. She'd aged considerably in the short six years since he'd last seen her when she moved to California, after amiably breaking it off with him.

That had been no big shock or heartbreak. While they'd had a good run briefly, their ardor had paled quickly and they remained buddies with separate lives. He'd wished her well and not thought about her again until the phone call three years ago. Again, Deanna had called him sobbing. She'd told him they shared a son. Kyle had been born eight months after she left for California. Ben didn't question if Kyle was his; Deanna had sobbed on.

Kyle was not a normal child, she said. What? He had autism. He spent his days screaming. He'd been just diagnosed and the treatment - THE treatment was ABA, Applied Behavior Analysis, the only proven treatment for autism, or so they told her. He needed this treatment if he even had a hope of being normal. Whatever normal was, Ben thought.

So, get it for him, Ben said. What's the problem? Well, it seemed the problem was money. The treatment did not come cheap. It required forty hours a week of one on one treatment with a trained therapist. The cost was exorbitant.

Ben had paled when he heard the cost. But, this was his son, even if this was the first he had heard of him. An errant thought entered his mind. Was this really his son? How did he know? He pushed that notion away. His son, his responsibility.

For some time now, Ben had been squirreling away money for a down payment for a house. Sure, this condo was handy, right in the same building as his office, but it was more a place to crash than a home. While he didn't imagine picket fences, he still had an image of a house in his future one day.

The money in his house fund would cover about a year and a half of Kyle's fifty thousand a year therapy. He'd worry about the rest later. Then another thought hit him. How had Deanna managed when she was pregnant? Who had looked after her? How had she handled money when she was unable to work?

Deanna admitted to dipping into her savings. She insisted she had been all right. Since it had been her choice to have a child alone, she had not wanted to ask anything of him.

How had this happened, Ben wanted to know. Well, it wasn't quite the accident he'd assumed. The idea of being a mom had blossomed in Deanna's mind. She knew that her relationship with Ben was more friendship than marriage material. She decided to have a child on her own. Ben was a nice guy, good looking and intelligent; he seemed an acceptable sperm donor, a father she could look back on fondly. She'd stopped taking her birth control pills and assured Ben that his condoms were not necessary.

And you didn't think about letting me in on these plans, Ben had asked, his anger rising. He tamped it down. What's done was done and now Kyle was his responsibility. Deanna should have been as well, if only he'd known about the pregnancy. He quickly calculated what it might have cost to feed and clothe a baby. Maybe five hundred dollars a month? Hell, he didn't know. That worked out to six thousand dollars a year and Kyle was now two and a half years old. That meant he owed Deanna fifteen thousand dollars in back child support. She must have had to take time off work as well. He had sent her a check for twenty-five thousand dollars the next morning and began the monthly installments of two thousand for the part of the treatment costs insurance didn't cover, plus another five hundred for Kyle's keep.

His thoughts were interrupted by the return of Dr. Hitkin with her papers.

"MOST OF THIS is just basic information like your address and contact numbers in case we need to reach you during the day. Then we need his medical information."

"Medical?" Ben asked. "He's a pretty healthy kid." His voice broke on the word healthy. Was Kyle actually healthy? Is autism a disease? Was he sick? And, apart from the autism, how was his health? Had he had those things kids get like measles and mumps? Ben had no idea about his own son.

"By medical, for now I just mean his doctor's name and contact information."

Well, he wouldn't get parent of the year award yet again. Ben had no clue who Kyle's doctor was or if he'd ever seen a physician. Ben didn't even have the name of a doctor or one of his own he could use to fake it.

There was so much he didn't know about this little man who was his son. Best 'fess up and try to maintain as much dignity as possible. "Kyle has only just moved to town and I have not yet had time to set him up with a local doctor." Nor had he even thought about it, Ben admitted to himself. "I'll get you this information as soon as possible, but Kyle's healthy and I'm sure calling his doctor won't be necessary."

"I see you left the section on custodial care blank. That is required information. In this era of non-traditional families, we need to know who has legal access to the child, who to send reports to and that sort of thing," Dr. Hitkin explained.

"I have full custody, "Ben replied.

"I don't dispute that but I'm sure you'll understand that for our records we require a copy of the legal custodial order."

Damn Deanna for not mentioning this. "I'll get that to you as soon as possible as well. Can Kyle start school without it?"

"Is there any way you can prove that you have custody and the right to enroll this child in school?"

Ben thought a minute. "What if you phoned his mother? Could she confirm consent over the phone?"

"It's not the usual process but for now it could do," Dr. Hitkin said as Ben pulled out his phone to find Deanna's number.

The ensuing conversation between the principal and Deanna was brief. It sounded like Deanna was trying to get off the phone, while Dr. Hitkin attempted to probe for more information and asked for copies of previous reports.

"Well," she said, "his mother certainly does not dispute that she wants you to have full say and responsibility for your son." She looked at Ben compassionately. "I think she will be sending you copies of medical reports and treatment notes. It would be helpful if you'd be willing to share them with us."

"Those are from when Kyle was much younger. He's better now and ready for school." Again, he received that look but this time it almost showed pity.

"Shall we collect Kyle now and proceed to the classroom? I'm sure you'll want to meet the teacher."

CHAPTER 2

*A*s Ben followed Dr. Hitkin out of her office, he stopped to stare at his son. Kyle was no longer playing with the blocks on the floor but was back staring at the swaying plant. He stood on his tip toes and his little body moved in time with the plant. As Ben watched, Kyle's hands rose to his sides. His hands flapped. A sound came out of his mouth but Ben could not make out what it was. What would Dr. Hitkin think of Kyle if she saw him pulling this kind of stunt?

Ben turned to find her watching him, not Kyle. "Um, he's…," Ben tried to explain.

The principal interrupted. "He's just fine." She planted herself directly in front of Kyle, moved the plant aside and told him to come with her and his dad now. They were going to meet his new teacher.

To Ben's surprise and relief, Kyle lowered himself back down to his heels, turned and followed the principal. Ben trailed behind, adding, "Just as long as it's not that room where the kid was screaming. I don't want Kyle upset by seeing things like that going on."

Dr. Hitkin just looked over her shoulder at him and continued down the hall. She stopped before that very doorway and without waiting for Ben, rapped twice on the open door, placed her hands firmly on Kyle's shoulders and moved him into the classroom.

Ben was about to warn her to get her hands off Kyle because he hated to be touched, when he noticed his son standing quietly with the principal's palms firmly on his shoulders. "Kyle, Mr. Wickens, I'd like you both to meet Kyle's new teacher, Ms. Melanie Nicols. Ms. Nicols, I'm pleased to bring you a new student, Kyle and his dad, Mr. Ben Wickens."

That woman, the one who had crushed the little boy under the blanket then squashed him with a ball, approached Kyle with a smile. Her hair was pulled back into a tight, low pony-tail. Her clothing suited her hair, plain and practical. She knelt in front of him and held out her hand. Kyle stared out the window.

"Hi, Kyle," she said. "I'm Ms. Nicols. I'm your teacher. Will you look at me?" She remained perfectly still, waiting. And waited. And waited. Ben grew uncomfortable and started to intervene. One look from Ms. Nicols and he froze. After an eternity, Kyle shifted his gaze from the window to his new teacher. "Hi," she repeated. "In this room you are free to explore. Go ahead and take a look around."

Ben tried to apologize. "Look, he doesn't talk much."

"Oh, really?" Ms. Nicols raised her eyebrow at him.

Ben felt his temper rising. "Yes, really. He's just a little boy who's been uprooted and brought to a new home, a strange city and..." He stopped himself. He'd almost said "and to a strange father". That was too much information.

Ms. Nicols repeated that they were welcome to wander around and explore the classroom. Without even glancing back at Ben, Kyle took off, dragging his hand along the wall of the classroom.

"Kyle. Kyle, come back here," Ben called.

"He's fine, just let him go," Ms. Nicols interrupted him. Kyle ignored his father anyway.

Ben glared at her, not feeling good about relinquishing control of his son to a stranger - to this stranger in particular. Dr. Hitkin motioned to the younger woman who was talking with some children. When she came up to them, Dr. Hitkin said, "Mr. Wickens,

I'd also like you to meet Ms. Lori Nabaku. She's the EA in the room." Seeing Ben's perplexed look, she explained, "That stands for Educational Associate. Kyle is lucky; there are two adults in this room rather than just one teacher." She continued, "Lori, this is Mr. Ben Wickens. His son's name is Kyle and he'll be joining your classroom." They all turned to look at Kyle.

As they watched Kyle, a little boy approached the group of adults. He walked close to Ben, stared him up and down, and then walked in a circle around him. The circling became faster and the look on the boy's face changed. His breathing hitched, and then he backed away from Ben with a look of terror on his face. He opened his mouth and these awful noises came out. Ben felt as if he was strangling a kitten.

"What? What? I didn't do anything. What's the matter with him?" Ben asked.

"Lose the aftershave," Ms. Nicols told him.

"What"

By this time she had the boy slung across her arms and was carrying him toward a bean bag couch at the side of the room. The child's eyes never left Ben, and the look of terror remained. Ms. Nicols sat on the bean bag with the child, holding him close. Gradually the child's noises subsided and tears ran down his cheeks. Ms. Nicols got up and returned with a flat, stuffed animal that she placed on the boy's lap. His hands immediately went to the tufts of hair and his fingers pulled at the strands over and over. But, at least he was calm.

Ben looked at the principal. "What just happened here?"

"Some children are extremely sensitive to things like sounds and smells. Daniel there reacts intensely to smells. Your aftershave, as Ms. Nicols pointed out, can seem overpowering to one with such sensitivities. Daniel was curious about you and likely would have struck up a conversation with you once he had determined that you were safe, but then he smelled your cologne and that took over any other thoughts or plans he might have had."

"Jeez. I didn't know. Sorry. Should I go apologize to him or would that set him off again."

"I think it best you not go anywhere near him right now. His system is just starting to calm down. There are reasons that this is a scent-free building. A number of our children have similar sensitivities. Surely you saw the notice when you came in the front door? It's also posted in all the hallways."

"I might have seen it but would not have known what it meant," Ben admitted.

"This is something to keep in mind now that Kyle is living with you. I don't know if it's the case with him but many children with autism spectrum disorders have these sensitivities."

Ben looked at her. "That's the second time you've made reference to the word autism about Kyle. I never said he still has autism. What makes you think that?"

They both turned to look at his son. Kyle was standing with his body angled to the sun streaming through the windows. Dust motes were visible. Kyle had his hands up and his fingers danced through the sun's rays. He was standing on his toes and a delighted smile marked his face. He truly seemed to be enjoying the way his fingers moved through the sun light.

Ben sighed. The principal quirked an eyebrow at him.

"All right. I still have trouble believing this, but when Kyle was two, this team of doctors diagnosed him with autism. They said he was delayed in many areas and didn't speak. But we got him all the treatment they said he needed. They said if he had this early and intensive treatment that he'd be cured and ready for school by age five. We paid for forty hours a week of ABA for three years. Well, he's five now. But look at him!" Ben ran his hand over his face.

"Mr. Wickens, Kyle *IS* ready for school. He's here now and here he shall stay. He'll be fine. He will learn and progress. Autism is not a dirty word. It's a different way of viewing the world. There are challenges involved in autism, for sure. But, there are also strengths."

Ben looked at her. "Right now, I'm not seeing a lot of those strengths."

"You will and we'll help both you and Kyle to learn and appreciate those strengths. The other things we'll work on together." Strange, but Ben felt somewhat reassured by this steady woman.

NOW THAT THE crisis seemed over and the teacher rejoined them, Ben apologized. "I'm sorry. I didn't know. I didn't mean to upset anyone.

Ms. Nicols ignored that and asked, "Do you have any questions about our program here?"

"Actually, I do. Just what kind of a place is this? I know that economic times are hard, but can't the school district even afford desks for kids? Or real furniture instead of this mishmash of plastic whatevers?" He gestured to the eclectic seating arrangements in the room. There were rocking chairs – adult and kid sized. While there were a few regular chairs, some of the kids actually had to sit on big plastic balls. They looked more solid than beach balls, sort of like ones he'd seen at his gym. A couple other kids sat on plastic stools that looked like mushrooms but the bottoms were not flat, forcing the children to rock slightly and shift their weight to balance. Then another poor kid was forced to perch on a stool that had only one leg in the middle of it.

"I can assure you, Mr. Wickens, that there is a reason for everything you see in this classroom and for everything we do here."

"I mean, I know this is only kindergarten, but there's not a blackboard in sight. How do you teach kids without a blackboard?"

Ms. Nicols directed his attention to the front of the room where three children were gathered around a white screen on the wall. At first Ben thought it was just a projector screen and said, "Hey, look what he's doing," as he saw a kid pick up a marker and draw on it.

"I take it you're not familiar with interactive white boards, Mr. Wickens?" Then, to the students, "Gracie, Mack, James, please show Kyle's dad how you use that program." The kids proceeded to touch the screen, circle objects, drag objects, then capture the image before moving on to the next page.

"Wow. That ain't your mama's blackboard."

Up to now, the principal had stood watching this interaction with a twinkle in her eye. At Ben's next statement, she stiffened.

"Since you asked if I have questions, yes, I do have more. Why are those kids here?" Ben nodded his head at two children in wheelchairs with half-moon tables pulled over the armrests of their chairs. One kid seemed to be laboring away at some paper task, while another painstakingly moved a game piece around a board as two other students eagerly awaited their turn at the game.

"Just what do you mean?"

"I mean, what kind of a classroom is this? You seem to have all sorts of kids in here."

"Exactly."

"Well, my son's not like that. He doesn't talk much, but he needs good role models and a place to learn." He looked over at Kyle who was still entranced by the dust motes visible in the sunlight streaming through the window. Kyle had his hand up and was watching the sunlight play on his fingers. Ben sighed. The teacher looked at Kyle then at Ben.

"You were saying?" she prompted.

This was not easy and she was not cutting him any slack.

The principal intervened. "Why don't you take a look around the room Mr. Wickens and get a feel for the class."

Ms. Nicols left him. To Ben's amazement, she picked up a book and crawled into a tent at the back of the room. Quickly two students joined her in the tent. Ben could hear her voice reading them a story. Kyle edged closer until he could peek inside. Ms. Nicols invited Kyle to come listen and to Ben's surprise, his son crawled in. Once the story was over, the kids left the tent and went back to their odd seating arrangements. Kyle checked out the displays on the back counter.

Ben watched a little girl swivel in her seat, pick up some metal contraptions, fit her arms through leather straps then heave herself to her feet, relying on the crutches for support. This ungainly walk took her near the back of the room where Kyle was. Ben held his breath, waiting for Kyle to react in fear. The girl flashed Kyle a smile, reached for a bucket of crayons and returned to her table. Kyle showed far less discomfort than Ben.

He tried again with Ms. Nicols. "Look. Kyle is a normal little boy. I'm not sure he belongs here. He's not like these kids."

Just then there was a huge wail from the back of the room. Kyle. As Ben watched, Kyle's voice ramped up an octave and his wail became a scream that went on and on and on. He was staring at an ant farm. No one was near him. Ben couldn't see any blood or any sign that his son was hurt. Kyle just kept staring at the ant farm, screeching and flapping his arms.

Ben was frozen to the spot, but not Ms. Nicols. She brushed past him, muttering as she went, "Oh no, he's not like these kids. None of them is screaming over an ant farm."

Ben clenched his teeth and strode after the teacher. She had already turned Kyle around so he was no longer facing the ants. She was speaking softly to him but Ben couldn't make out the words. She put her hands on Kyle's shoulders and pushed down. Hard.

"Hey!" Ben protested.

He reached to interfere, but something amazing happened. Kyle stopped. His screeching actually stopped at her touch. After a few more seconds, he sort of melted into his new teacher, allowing her to stroke his hair. He never let Ben touch him like that.

The principal turned to Ben. "You were saying...?"

Ben had not gotten as far as he had in business without holding his ground. Something about this Ms. Nicols got under his skin. "I'd really prefer my son be in another class, a normal one. And one with a different teacher. Aren't kindergarten teachers supposed to warm and nurturing? While I'm sure Ms. Nicols has her good points, warm and fuzzy she isn't."

Ben and the principal both turned to look at the teacher. As she walked toward the carpet area in the corner of the room, two children ran up to her, each hugging her from a side. She wrapped an arm around each child, smiling down at them as they walked.

"Well, she certainly wasn't warm to me," Ben complained.

. . .

"JORDAN," Ms. Nicols called, "please get Mr. Wickens something to sit on. The Hokki™ behind my desk would work."

A grinning five year old half dragged, half-carried a bright green stool across the room towards Ben. Ben moved to reach for it, but the boy twisted his body between Ben's and the stool, saying, "I can do it." Ben let him. The child proudly placed it in front of Ben who stared at it. He was sure it would crumple under his weight, plus there was obviously something wrong with it. Where it should be flat on the ground, it wasn't, well flat on the ground. It listed seriously to one side. Ben tried righting it, but the stool swayed to its other side. The little boy giggled.

Ben asked, "What am I supposed to do with it?"

"You sit on it, silly!" The child thought his question preposterous. "Like this." He swung his hip over the top and tried perching on the too tall stool, without either foot hitting the ground, the hopped off.

Cautiously, Ben lowered his bottom to the chair, keeping most of the weight on his feet. It was uncomfortable and awkward. The other woman in the room, Ben forgot her name, took pity on him and assured him that it would hold his weight. Ben tried. There was no cracking sound of breaking plastic and he was not flat on the floor. So far, so good. He cautiously allowed himself to relax and found that he swayed a bit himself. After the first few minutes, it wasn't so bad. He could actually rock back and forth or side to side.

Ben felt eyes on him. A tiny girl in torn jeans watched him. "Are you afraid when it wobbles?" she asked.

"Ah, well, not really afraid. I wasn't sure it would be strong enough to hold me. It's not so bad, though." Then he noticed what she was sitting on. What in the world?

"I like my chair better than a Hokki™," she informed him.

"What exactly is it you are sitting on?"

The child looked at him like he was daft. "It's called a stool."

It was not like any other stool Ben had ever seen. Sure, it had a round piece of wood to sit on, but the thing had only one leg. He looked closer. The single leg was in the middle, so it was doubtful it had simply lost its other three legs. As he watched, the child wiggled on the stool, humming to herself as she drew with crayons.

"Why does your teacher make you sit on that?" he asked.

"Make?" she looked puzzled. "She doesn't make us sit on anything. We choose which way we want to sit. Molly, my best friend always likes a peanut and Jaden likes the disc."

"Why? Why don't you just sit on regular chairs?"

Another little girl came bouncing by. She made her way across the floor bobbing up and down, sitting on a ball. Actually, a ball with feet and a handle. As she scooted by, she said, "Because it makes my engine run just right."®

DR. HITKIN CAME to his rescue. His head was boggling.

"It looks like Kyle is settling in. Do you want to leave him here for the day or would you prefer he start school tomorrow? If you want my opinion, I'd say that we should dive right in and begin today. Otherwise he might get the idea that he comes here just for a half hour or so then goes back home."

Ben cast a guilty look at his son. In the last five minutes, he had not given Kyle a thought. He'd just tried to assimilate what was happening in this strange classroom. "I do need to get to work," he said. "Do you really think Kyle will be all right if I leave him?"

"Spoken like a first time parent. Yes, he'll be fine. We have your contact numbers, so if there is any problem we'll be in touch with you. Where is Kyle's lunch?"

"Lunch?" Cripes. Packing a lunch for his son had not even entered his head.

"Don't worry. We have plenty we can give him today, but you'll need to get him a lunch kit so he can bring his lunch tomorrow."

Ben walked over to Kyle, hesitant to disturb him when he seemed so engrossed in the wooden blocks. He also wasn't sure what to say to him. It's not as if Kyle would miss him when he left; he hardly even knew his father. Ben tried to get Kyle's attention but Kyle did not look up from his blocks. Ben crouched down beside his son and tried to get in his field of vision. He was self-conscious with both Dr. Hitkin and Ms. Nicols watching him, and judging his every move, he felt. So, he spoke to the top of Kyle's head, saying, "Dad's going to work now. You'll be fine here with your teacher and the other kids. I'll come get you after school." No response. With as much of his dignity intact as Ben could muster, he retreated to the door.

When he was almost there, a little voice said, "Bye. See you soon raccoon."

Ben whipped around, but Kyle's head was once again focused on his blocks. But Dr. Hitkin and Ms. Nicols had heard the words and were both smiling at him. Both. This was the first time Ms. Nicols had directed anything but a scowl in his direction. She was actually quite pretty when she smiled.

CHAPTER 3

*H*aving a kid was certainly different. He had heard expecting couples say how having a baby was not going to change their life style. The baby would fit into their lives. Huh. Maybe that was true with babies, but it certainly was not true with five year olds. Or, maybe it was just his five year old, or maybe, it was just him. Once he got the hang of this fatherhood thing, it might be better and he'd have more time.

How did the time get away from him? Usually Ben saw himself as an organized guy, working six, often seven days a week with ten or twelve hour days. He got a lot done. He'd actually liked his life.

As a hand moved a piece, Ben's attention returned to the chess board in front of him. Kyle watched the board intently. Son of a ..... Kyle had just blocked Ben's queen. Bested by a five year old?

"Nice job, little man. But that's it for now. I have to get some work done." Usually Sundays were spent at the office. He motored through paperwork when it was quiet and there were no distractions. This was his first weekend as a father and Ben found that small boys, even ones who didn't talk, took up a lot of time. Exhausting time. Ben had fallen into a doze on the couch when he felt a weight fall into his lap. He woke with a start as the onyx chess men dropped onto his legs.

Somehow Kyle had managed to carry the heavy, carved set from its display case across the room to the couch. That set had cost him a fortune. Was he going to have to childproof his home?

"Kyle, no. That's for adults only. You have your own toys; this is daddy's." His words had fallen on deaf ears as Kyle, ignoring him, set the marble board on the coffee table and one by one, fished the fallen pieces off the couch and placed them in their correct places on the board. Ben's irritation turned to wonder as he watched this small boy. How old had he been when he first learned how to play chess? Ten? Twelve? Is this something five year olds did nowadays?

Ben had read how some people with autism had strong visual memories. Maybe that was it and Kyle remembered the positions of the chessmen and was replicating what he'd seen.

Then Kyle turned the board so the white men were by Ben. He folded his hands and waited, staring at the board. Could the kid actually be expecting them to play a game? Ben moved his rook, just to see what would happen. Kyle hesitated only a couple seconds then made his counter move. Correctly. They each took another turn. The kid did seem to know what he was doing. Just to test it out, Ben moved his bishop straight ahead rather than on a diagonal line. Kyle's hands came up. He flapped. "No, no, no!" he said, with his voice rising with each word.

"Sorry. My mistake." Ben took the bishop back and made a different move. Kyle's shoulders relaxed and they carried on. Is this really what five year olds did these days? Shouldn't Deanna have had Kyle out kicking a ball or playing in a sand box rather than teaching him chess?

IN HIS NORMAL, orderly life, Ben was at his desk each morning by eight at the latest. But, he had to take Kyle to school. The earliest he could do this was at 8:30, as he'd been informed by a grouchy Ms. Nicols when he and Kyle showed up in her classroom at eight o'clock one morning. What was the problem? She was obviously there already. Her frosty voice had told him that she was Kyle's teacher, not his babysitter. She was at work early to prepare for the day. What's to prepare, Ben thought. These are just five year olds. They played all day, didn't they? Boy, she certainly was not a morning person, or perhaps just not a Ben kind of person. She had not warmed up to him, and reserved her smiles only for his son.

So, Ben did not arrive at work until nearly nine o'clock these days. Losing an hour or two out of his morning each day was taking a toll. It's a good thing he had no boss to answer to, that was the beauty of owning your own company. The drawback was that he was in charge and the work still needed to get done.

When he had first realized that he would be spending less time at the office now that Kyle was his responsibility, he thought he'd simply carry his work home and do it there. Kyle kept to himself and they'd each do their own thing, right? Little did Ben know. There was always some crisis. A kid needed to eat on time and good food, not just any old thing he could rummage from the fridge. Although Kyle seemed self-sufficient and self-absorbed, he still needed attention and watching. The hours slipped away and little work got done.

Small children slept a lot, didn't they? If Kyle was in bed early, that would leave hours each night for Ben to get caught up. But putting Kyle to bed and getting Kyle to sleep were two different things. Last night's bath was an example.

Personally, Ben preferred showers. They were quick and efficient. He tried the same thing with his son.

The first night he'd carefully set the shower's water temperature, making sure it would not be too hot for a child. Then he'd steered Kyle into the bathroom and told him to get in. Ben then left to get some work done. His concentration was interrupted by a rhythmic bang, bang, bang. He checked the bathroom, only to find Kyle, fully dressed, pulling the sliding shower door back and forth along its runners. Each time he opened it, water spilled out on the floor and on Kyle, who seemed oblivious.

"Kyle, quit it. Can't you see the mess you're making? Look at this floor." Kyle continued opening and closing the door as if Ben wasn't even there.

"Kyle!" Ben's hand stopped the door and pulled it closed. "Look at me. Kyle, get into the shower while I clean up the floor."

Ben reached for towels and bent to mop up the spreading flood. The shower door opened. Ben felt water on his back and turned. "Now what, Kyle?"

Kyle was standing in the tub, fully dressed, and scrunched into a corner, cowering from the water flow. "Oh, for...." Ben began. He shut off the tap and regarded his son, trying to hold in his temper. Then he remembered. He'd read that people with autism tended to take things literally. Ben had told Kyle to get in. Had he told him to take his clothes off first? Doubtful. Ben sighed.

He hauled his son out of the shower but at least Kyle didn't scream at his touch this time. Ben stripped the sodden clothes off his son, no easy task as each garment clung to the little body. Kyle stood still, not helping but not resisting either.

Ben debated skipping the whole business but as he pulled off Kyle's socks, his nose was near Kyle's head. His hair didn't have that clean, little boy smell, but more of a sweaty overtone. He needed a scrubbing. For that matter, so did Ben.

What the hell. He'd kill two birds with one stone. Guys showered beside each other in locker rooms all the time. Ben stripped, then turned on the shower again. He stepped into the water flow then reached for Kyle. As usual, Kyle went stiff, holding his body as far from Ben's as he could. Obviously this child was not exactly warming up to his father yet. He plunked Kyle in front of him, under the full force of the water. Ben felt Kyle take in a big breath. Ben knew this routine - Kyle was preparing to let out one of his horrendous screams. Ben grabbed Kyle under the arms and spun with him, settling him near the back of the tub where Ben's body would shield Kyle from most of the water flow.

Not knowing what else to do, Ben massaged Kyle's shoulders the way he had seen Ms. Nicols do. As Kyle tensed, he remembered how firmly she'd pressed, not the light touch he thought you'd use with a small child. As he pressed harder, he felt Kyle relax. Ben stepped to the side so the edges of warm water flow touched Kyle. Ben relished the quiet, the warm water and steam and a few peaceful moments with this little man. His son.

Then, he remembered his duty as a father. Nice as this moment was, he needed to get his son clean before the hot water ran out. He reached for the shampoo, warmed it in his hands then began massaging Kyle's scalp. He rubbed gently, softly, watching the suds. Out of nowhere, Kyle stiffened then let out this blood-curling scream.

"What, what?" Ben cried. He could not see anything wrong. He turned Kyle to face him and saw the shampoo suds flowing down Kyle's forehead and into his eyes. Kyle's balled fists punched at his eye sockets. Frantic, Ben pulled Kyle's hands from his face and held them. How the hell would he get the shampoo out of the kid's eyes? Didn't he know enough to shut his eyes when his hair was being washed?

Ever tried to pry a child's eyes open? Wet eyelids and cheeks are slippery, no less slippery with a hysterical, soapy child. Ben tugged the squirming ball of boy under his arm, stepped out of the shower and held Kyle's head under the sink's tap. He turned the water on and tried to fit the boy's head under the flow. Not going to work. He sat Kyle on the vanity and reached for a glass. Holding his head over the sink, he carefully poured water across his eyes. Gradually Kyle stopped howling. Ben had no idea if the crying had washed the shampoo from his eyes or drenching them with water had worked. Either way, this crisis seemed over. Ben let the tension in his shoulders relax. As he turned around, his feet squelched in water. Only then did he notice the steady stream of water running from the shower faucet onto the floor. "Son of a ...."

CHAPTER 4

*I*t all came down to money, didn't it? As an accountant, that belief framed the basis of his work life and his personal life. That was part of the reason he wanted no part of his father's bakery. The thing had been leaking money for years.

Money came easy to Ben. At thirty-three, he worked hard, lived simply and didn't have a lot of needs, with just one real indulgence - the sound system set up in his living room. His business was flourishing. There was no way it shouldn't with the hours Ben put in. Even in tough economic times, accounting firms were still in demand.

Ben's bank account had looked healthy until that call came from Deanna about Kyle. But that certainly changed after he paid Deanna for back child support since Kyle's birth, and put another ten thousand into a registered education plan for Kyle's college. Then, each month he put money into the college fund and two thousand for the ABA treatments. He would have been able to handle that on top of his condo fees and payment, if it wasn't for that damn bakery. It was bleeding him dry. There had to be a doorway out of this.

Even worse, it had to remain a secret. His father, a Polish immigrant and the technical owner of the bakery had no head for books and no idea that what he took in did not cover what needed to go out each month. Some months were better than others, but Ben always had to contribute something, whether for employee salaries or bills left over at the end of the month. If only the old man would listen or admit that he could no longer run the place and let his daughter, Ellie, take over formally. Hell, she had run the place for years with their father there only as a figurehead.

You can only whittle away at your savings so long until the word savings was an oxymoron. Prior to Kyle coming to live with him, it had not been such a worry. When Ben needed to make more money, he just worked more. Simple. Maybe it wasn't much of a life, but it was his life and it had seemed to work for him and those around him.

With Kyle to look after, it was not so easy to put in all those work hours. For one small boy, he certainly took up a lot of time. Since his office was in the same building as his condo, Ben was used to slipping back to the office after supper and at any hour to get more work done. Now, he couldn't leave Kyle alone in the condo to go to the office. He'd tried taking Kyle with him last night, but ended up spending more time looking at Kyle than at his ledgers.

Then he'd tried packing up his files to work on them at home. After all, kids slept a lot, didn't they? Apparently Kyle had not read that book because he sure as heck didn't seem to sleep the way Ben imagined kids were supposed to. But there did come a time each night when Kyle was in bed and asleep. That was when Ben thought he'd get work done. Last night he'd come to with his head on his desk and drool on his papers. Having a kid around was exhausting.

Now, the crunch was on. The bakery's mortgage was due next week. Actually, it's second mortgage. Neither Ben nor his sister knew why their father had re-mortgaged the bakery when surely it had been almost paid off. But, he'd done it and there was no money to make this quarterly payment. Ben to the rescue, he thought, mocking himself. Only this time, there was no money in Ben's account either. So, he'd need to work like a demon this week to finish these contracts and get the payments in his account so he could get the funds to his sister. That meant long hours, the kind of hours he'd been used to putting in pre-Kyle.

Kyle was at school and Ben was at his desk. He thought about it. Four little words - Kyle was at school. That sounded so simple but hell, it was not. Getting one small boy up, ready and to school took more organizational skills than Ben certainly possessed. He ran a business with ten employees, handled million dollar accounts, but could not manage one small boy.

They'd been late for school today. The frosty Ms. Nicols certainly let him know what she thought of that. At least she had smiled at Kyle and welcomed him even if she did block his father at the door. But, he was safely at school now and Ben could concentrate on his business.

He worked through lunch, focusing and motoring through the files on his desk. He checked the work of his subordinates, lined up meetings with potential new clients and ploughed through the reports. Lucky for Ben, when he was in the zone he could really work. The rest of the world dropped away from him.

His phone rang and he glanced at the caller ID. Beside the ID was a clock. Son of a.... It was three thirty. School was over at three fifteen and he should have been there to get Kyle. This call was about a merger he was brokering, one that would net him a nice chunk of change.

Ben rubbed his hands over his face. Well, the priority was Kyle. He phoned the school secretary to see if Kyle was all right. Her normally cheery voice was a notch colder than usual. If he'd hang on, she'd find out. Yes, she came back on the phone; Kyle was waiting in his classroom. All the other children had been picked up. There was censure in her voice. Ben apologized and said someone would be right there. He hung up on her voice.

What to do, what to do. Send his secretary after Kyle? Kyle didn't know her and might freak out. Didn't they teach kids about stranger danger or some such thing?

Millie! It came to him. Millie was the perfect answer. Kyle had already met his cleaning lady and today was Millie's day to be at his condo, cooking and cleaning.

Ben called his home. "Millie, I need a big favor. Kyle is still at school and I can't get away to go pick him up. Would you be able to go to the school and get him for me? Then stay with him till I get home around say six thirty?"

There was a pause. What was wrong? Millie was always so accommodating.

"Mr. Wickens, I'm sorry but I don't think that's possible."

"What? Why not? It's just this one time. Kyle's a little boy and he's left at school waiting for someone to get him."

"I understand that and I feel for the tyke but I'm afraid I have other commitments."

"Other commitments? What do you mean?"

"I mean that when I'm finished with your place I have another job. I was just packing up to leave. If I don't go right away, I'll miss the bus and not get this next job done before dark."

"Ah, Millie, look. I'll pay you double if you'll just do this for me today."

Millie sounded miserable, but remained firm in her refusal.

Ben hung up, rubbed his face some more, then picked up his car keys and headed out the door.

HOW DID parents do this day after day? Ben was late again, twenty-five minutes late to be exact. Honestly, today he hadn't forgotten about picking Kyle up from school, not like the other day. And, he would have been on time, too, if he had not picked up the ringing phone just as he was leaving the office. The phone call actually hadn't taken that long, but then traffic had been detoured and it all added up to him being late.

He strode quickly into the office, needing to leave his completed registration form with Marie, the secretary. Marie glanced at him then at his side. Not seeing his son, she asked, "Where's Kyle today?"

"Still in his classroom. I was late getting here."

Marie's welcoming smile faded. "Oh, dear. That's not good. Kids thrive on routine and things like this can really throw them off."

Thanks for that, Ben thought. Then, something about the way Marie was looking at him, something about the way she tilted her head reminded him of something. Or someone. "Have we met before?" he asked her, "I mean before this week."

"No, I don't think so. I might remember you, but I usually don't forget kids once I've met them."

"It's just that you remind me of someone, but I can't think of where we might have met. But, I'd better go collect Kyle now."

At least all was quiet as he approached the kindergarten classroom. There was a murmur of voices. Not wanting to disturb them, Ben poked his head in the doorway. There, nestled on the bean bag chair were Kyle and Ms. Nicols. She was reading him a book and their heads were close together as they studied the pictures. Kyle rested trustingly against her.

Ben felt a jab of resentment. Why was Kyle so relaxed with her when he was so jumpy around him, his father? Why did Kyle snuggle willingly against her, yet tense when Ben came close. He was trying, wasn't he? What did it take to open the door and win this kid over?

As Ben watched, the teacher tussled his son's hair and Kyle leaned into her. Ben's teeth clenched. He wanted that kind of closeness with Kyle but it didn't seem that the kid shared his wishes. Why did Kyle relish this closeness with a virtual stranger when he couldn't stand his own father's touch?

Ben spoke more sharply than he intended, his annoyance and hurt clear in his voice. His intrusion into the cozy scene startled Kyle. This earned a glare from Ms. Nicols. Figures. That's all he ever seemed to get from her.

The teacher looked toward Lori, the EA or Educational Associate in the room. Ben had gathered that she had some training in education but not as much as a teacher and definitely not as much as Ms. Nicols. But, the two operated as a seamless team in the room. In fact, if you didn't know for sure who the teacher was and who the assistant, it would be hard to tell. Sometimes Ms. Nicols stood at the front of the room directing the whole group; sometimes Lori took that role while Ms. Nicols worked with an individual or small group.

Now, Lori walked with Kyle toward the cubby where his coat and backpack hung. She talked with him while he put his belongings in his back pack.

Ms. Nicols rounded on Ben. She crooked her finger at him, beckoning him back into the hall and shut the door.

"Do you know what time school is out?"

Ben figured this was a rhetorical question, but she didn't give him time to answer anyway.

"Do you have any idea how it felt to Kyle to watch everyone else's family pick them up? To be the only student left behind?"

Ben had not thought of it that way. He'd assumed that the teacher was mad that she'd had to look after Kyle for a few extra minutes. He couldn't see what the big deal was since she was obviously there anyway. Now, with a few words, she put a different take on his tardiness. She was right.

Maybe his thought process showed on his face because her tirade softened.

"Routine is so important to kids like Kyle. Look. When you have autism, the world can be a scary place. It can seem that things come at you from all sides. You're contending with the sensory issues when every touch, every sound, every light can feel like just too much."

Ben listened intently, his defensive anger fleeing.

"Then, there's the whole language issue. We live in a talkative world. People with autism spectrum disorders have trouble with auditory processing."

Ben's face showed that he had not a clue what she was talking about.

"What I mean is that while the child can physically hear all right, he will have trouble making sense of what he hears. Remember that teacher in the old Charlie Brown movies? The one who went, 'Wa, wa wa wa wa' and we had no idea what was said? That's how it often is for kids with autism. And, for some, they not only have trouble understanding what is said to them, but they also have trouble letting us know their wants and needs."

Some of this made sense to Ben, but it was a lot to take in.

"There's more. Most of us automatically see patterns and

connections in the world and our daily lives. Not so with many kids who have autism. They have to be directly taught that there are patterns and consistencies and you can predict what is going to happen. When you can do that, the world is not quite as scary a place."

Ben tried to follow her words.

"In this classroom we work hard to make it a safe place to come to. To do that, we create routines and make it predictable so that the children don't need to feel on edge all the time, wondering what's coming next and what might be expected of them."

That made sense. Ben liked order himself.

"We have a morning routine and an end of the day routine. You, Mr. Wickens, ruined your son's end of the day routine." She glared at him and continued without mercy. "You should have seen his little face when all the kids were picked up but him. He has not been with you long and he needs to feel secure with you, that he has a place with you and can count on you."

She was right. What could he say?

BEN WENT to the back of the room where the children's belongings were hung. He took Kyle's coat from its hook and approached his son. Kyle stood passively while Ben awkwardly worked his son's arms into the jacket. He then knelt to do up the zipper.

Melanie called out, "Mr. Wickens, would you please come here a minute."

Ben looked up to see her frowning at him. "In a minute," he said. "I just need to do this for Kyle."

"Now, please." Annoyed, Ben looked back at her. While his attention was diverted, Kyle squirmed, letting the coat dangle off the ends of his arms. Ben sighed at the thought of having to do this all over again.

When he reached her desk, Melanie launched into him, keeping her voice low. "What do you think you're doing?" she asked Ben.

"I'm putting my kid's coat on since we're already late, as you kindly informed me."

"Make him do it himself."

"I'm just getting to know my son. I like doing things for him. Look, I missed his earlier years; I have a lot to make up for."

"This isn't about you, Mr. Wickens. It's about Kyle and what's best for him."

"Are you saying I don't have my own kid's best interests at heart? Besides, he can't do it. He hasn't once put on his own coat since he's been with me."

Melanie turned from Ben to look at Kyle, standing beside a grinning Lori. Kyle's jacket was on and zipped. His shoes were on and done up. His back pack was on and he stood waiting by the door with Lori, the EA. Lori, grinning, assured them that Kyle had done it all by himself.

LATE YET AGAIN.

Ben had learned something. The words, "Hurry up, we're late!" caused a small boy to dig in his heels and not move. At least this small boy. When you looked at the size of him, what made him take so long to get ready in the morning? Since he bathed before bed, he didn't need to shower in the morning. He didn't have to make breakfast; all he had to do was sit down and eat it. He didn't clean up the kitchen afterwards. He didn't even brush his own hair or figure out which clothes to put on. Ben did all that for him and still Kyle dragged his heels and made them late in the mornings. They both left the house angry and disgruntled.

Now, he half walked, half pulled Kyle down the hallway towards his classroom. He could just imagine the look on Ms. Nicols sour face when they entered, late once again. Since the classroom door always seemed to be open, perhaps he could slip Kyle in quietly without her noticing.

Fat chance. Her eagle eyes were everywhere. She was standing right by the door when they approached. Ben tried to push Kyle into the room, hoping to slip out without having to talk with his son's teacher. Kyle entered the threshold then stopped. Ben's gentle push between his shoulder blades made Kyle cry out. His little body tensed and Ben braced himself for a screaming fit.

Kyle's eyes were on his classmates all sitting in a loose circle on the floor around Lori, the education assistant. Ben could not see what the problem was. He knew Kyle had participated in circle time before. Lori held up a book as she read to the kids. Ben could not even see any scary pictures in the book. What was his problem?

But Ms. Nicols was right there. She knelt in front of Kyle, putting her face in his line of vision, blocking out the sight of circle time. She spoke softly and brought her hands up to rest firmly on his shoulders. Ben could see her hands pressing down.

"Kyle, it's all right. This is circle time. What do you do when you come into the class?"

Kyle gave no reaction, but at least he wasn't screaming.

Ms. Nicols reached for a plastic thing on a string around her neck. It was a pouch holding four pictures. The first was a photo of Kyle at the doorway of the classroom. The second picture was of Kyle hanging up his backpack in his cubby. The third was of his son hanging up his coat. The last one was on Kyle sitting at a table. Ms. Nicols held the pictures in front of Kyle's face and prompted, "What is our morning routine?"

It took a few seconds, but Kyle's eyes ceased their frantic perusal of the room and focused on the pictures in front of him. Ben watched some of the tension leave his little body. He pointed to each picture in turn, then walked toward the cubby that had KYLE written above it. He removed his backpack, then his coat, placing them on the hooks. He then went to sit at a table where the name KYLE was taped in big letters. He stared straight ahead.

Ms. Nicols gave a glare Ben's way and as she walked to Kyle said, "Wait right there."

Again, the frostiness was missing from her voice as she knelt by Kyle and showed him another strip of pictures. Craning his neck, Ben could see that that the top picture was of children sitting in a circle on the floor. Kyle stood up and went with Ms. Nicols to the circle. He sat on the edge of the group with almost two feet between him and the nearest child, but at least he was with the rest of the kids and was not screaming or flapping or any of those things that made Ben cringe.

After watching a few minutes to make sure Kyle was all right, Ms. Nicols turned her icy gaze to Ben once more. She marched past him into the hallway, beckoning for Ben to follow her. After checking again to make sure Kyle was all right, Ben complied. He felt like a small boy being sent to the principal's office.

"Just what do you think you're doing to Kyle?" She launched her attack.

How should he respond to that? "I'm bringing him to school," Ben replied as evenly as he could.

"You're late!"

As if he didn't know. "I'm aware of that Ms. Nicols. I can assure you it's not intentional. I'm not used to being late for anything. We start out early, but have you ever tried to get a little boy ready and out the door on time?"

Ms. Nicols' face softened just a tad. "Look. I know you're new to this. Do you want some help?"

Was she offering to come get Kyle up in the mornings? Doubtful. But yeah, he could certainly use any help he could get. Ben nodded for her to continue.

"How do you handle things in the morning? What do you do?"

Ben's defenses came up again but he tried tamping them down for the sake of his son. What they were doing was not working obviously and it made both him and Kyle upset.

Ms. Nicols launched in. "Did you see what happened to Kyle when he came in? He froze at the door. You upset his routine. What was going on in the class was not what he expected to see when he arrived. We can't hold up the program because one child does not arrive on time. We work hard to get our children settled in to a pattern, to make life predictable for them. Predictable means safe in the mind of a child, especially a child who has an autism spectrum disorder."

Ben interrupted, "But I never said he had..."

The teacher cut him off. "If it looks like a duck and quacks like a duck.....Look. The medical reports have arrived. Remember you gave your wife permission to send them to us?"

"I don't have a wife."

"Your ex-wife, then."

"I don't have an ex-wife, either."

That gave Ms. Nicols pause. Then she carried on. "Whatever. The reports clearly state that your son has autism." Another pause. "He is your son, isn't he?"

Ben's teeth clenched. "Yes, he's my son."

"Your son has autism - the big "A". That's neither the end of the world, nor a death sentence. It simply means he has a different take on the world. He will need to learn strategies to help him make his way. Right now we have no idea just how far he will go. But, you can play a big part in helping him."

"How? I'll do anything I can to help Kyle."

Just the opening the teacher wanted. "To start with, get him to school on time." She paused to let that sink it. "It's not just for my convenience. It throws Kyle when he gets here late; you saw that yourself. It takes time to get him settled in. If he just arrived when all the other children do, it will be easier for him."

"I get that," Ben admitted, "but how? I try. We start early but getting him ready and out the door is not easy, short of dragging him."

"How do you get him ready?"

Ben looked at her.

"Tell me what your morning routine looks like."

"Routine? Well, there's not much of a routine. I used to have a routine when I lived alone, but Kyle, well, he's not much of a routine kind of guy."

"That's where you're wrong," Ms. Nicols informed him. Figures, Ben thought. She continued, "Kyle right now may be unable to establish a positive routine on his own, but he'll flourish with routine. You have to create the structure and impose it". She let him ponder that a moment.

Then, she looked up at him. "I bet you talk a lot, don't you?"

Ben stared at her.

"Tell me what you say to Kyle in the morning."

Ben's frustration showed in his words. "I have to tell him over and over to do every little thing. I know he can dress himself, yet he'll have one sock part way on, then spy some toy and start playing. It's the same thing with breakfast. It should take him five minutes to down a bowl of cereal but it can take forty-five minutes. I feel like I have to rag on him all the time to get the simplest thing done." Ben warmed to his subject. "I know it gets on Kyle's nerves and it damn sure gets on mine. It makes him late for school and me late for work. I'm already at my desk an hour later than I used to. I tell him and tell him and tell him but he doesn't listen."

Ms. Nicols nodded. "Look. I'll try to explain. People with autism spectrum disorders, and yes, including Kyle, take in information that they see much better than things that they hear. He's a visual learner, rather than an auditory learner." She waited to see if Ben was following her. He was watching her, but hard to tell how much was sinking in.

She tried again. "Did you see what I did when Kyle came in? Did I talk to him or at him? How many words did I use?"

She carried on before Ben could think of an answer.

"I could tell that he was feeling overwhelmed and close to a melt-down So, I didn't talk or give all those verbal explanations I could have. Instead, I showed him. Remember that he learns more easily visually? I showed him pictures of what he needed to do. Did you see how he reacted?"

"Yeah. He followed along and did what he was supposed to. But, he's a little kid and you're his teacher. At his age, teachers are gods and he'll do what you say."

"The key is, I didn't say anything. If I had talked at him, the likelihood of him melting down would have been high. You could see that he was on the verge, couldn't you?"

"Oh, only too well do I know the signs and what happens."

"It's nice that you think I have some marvelous bag of tricks being a teacher, but no, Kyle did not follow the routine because I'm his teacher. He followed because he could understand what was expected of him because I showed him the visuals. This is not the first time he's seen those particular pictures. Look around - they are all over the room."

Ben looked and she was right. He'd not paid attention before, but yes, similar pictures were all over.

"Our classroom runs on routines. These routines are taught using pictures. If you tried this at home, it would make your mornings run more smoothly."

Ben looked skeptical.

"Do you want a hand with this? Are you willing to try?"

Ben's back was up again. What did she think he was? "Despite what you think of me, if it'll help my son, I'm game."

A smile crept out. That was the first time she'd actually smiled at Ben. He stared at her and caught a glimpse of why the kids gravitated to this woman.

"I have to get back to my class, but here's some paper. Make a list of the things you want Kyle to do in the morning. Leave it on my desk and I'll try to have some visuals ready for you when you pick him up this afternoon. And remember, when you use them, if you use them, stop nagging. Show him, don't tell him." She turned her back on him and the kids made room for her in their circle.

SHE REALLY DID RUB him the wrong way, Ben thought. It was a while since he'd met a woman who had such a lousy opinion of him, without even knowing him. He looked around for someplace to sit. The only options close to her desk seemed to be a gigantic beach ball or another of those Hokki™ stools he'd tried that first day. If he'd worried about that holding his weight, the ball looked even more precarious. He'd be damned if he'd fall on his butt in front of her. He gingerly lowered himself to the Hokki™ and wiggled to get comfortable. He looked up and caught Ms. Nicols watching and suppressing a smile. Lori, the EA did not even attempt to hide her grin. Ben sighed and got on with his assigned homework.

. . .

"HOW'D IT GO THIS MORNING?" A less antagonistic Ms. Nicols approached Ben when he came to pick up Kyle after school several days later. They had made it on time this morning and Kyle had easily slipped in with the other kids, without freezing at the door.

"Not perfect, but better, certainly better. Thanks. Your cards helped."

Ben had remembered her admonishment that the cards were not miraculous and Kyle would not automatically know what they meant. Ben would first have to teach him. Ben had wanted to tell Ms. Nicols that she was his teacher, that Ben did not have time to teach. But since she'd gone to all this work for him, he should keep his mouth shut and just give it a try. It couldn't be worse, could it?

And, it actually had helped. Surprise, surprise. After supper Ben had taken out the cards. Ms. Nicols had given him a length of cardboard. Running the length of the page was a strip of Velcro. On the back of the card was an envelope and in the envelope were cards, each with matching Velcro hooks. After sorting through them, Ben had shown each to Kyle. He started with the pictures of socks, underwear, pants and shirt, explaining to Kyle that this was how he was to get dressed. Keeping in mind that Ms. Nicols had said not to overwhelm Kyle with a list that was too big, he started first with the things Kyle would need to do to get dressed.

Overseeing the process, Ben had removed each picture as Kyle completed that job and placed it in the envelope. When he was dressed and Ben told him, "All done," Kyle had actually replied. It was not loud, but Ben was sure he heard Kyle say, "Good job."

Encouraged, they had moved on to the bathroom. There Ben placed on the card the pictures of a toilet, hands washed, a face being washed, and teeth brushed. Again, it worked, with only a minimum of coaching from Ben. He saw Kyle looking over at the cards to see what came next. And, the last picture Kyle removed himself and placed it in the envelope.

Then, on to the kitchen and breakfast. Again, it worked but not quite as slickly. There were distractions and Kyle would rather play with his cereal than eat it. Still, they did not end up mad at each other as they had the other mornings. Instead of ragging on Kyle to get moving, Ben just tapped the appropriate card to draw his son back to the task at hand. It worked! There was actually something to this shut-up-and-show business.

But, Ben needed to learn more. He had not quite gotten the order correct. Tomorrow, he would not have Kyle get dressed and washed before he ate. By the time most of the cereal was inside Kyle, a fair bit was on his outside as well. His face needed washing again and he needed a change of shirt. Kyle protested. Ben could see his point. According to the visual schedule, he had already done those things and put their pictures away in the envelope. Kyle might be learning, but Ben obviously needed to learn more as well.

BEN WATCHED as the kids formed a line and one by one trailed past their teacher. Ms. Nicols addressed each child as they went out the door. "High five or hand shake or a hug?" she asked each. This intrigued Ben.

"Why do you ask them that?"

"I want to make a connection with them as they leave for the day. You may have noticed that some kids are naturally more physically affectionate than others. Some want a hug. Others don't like that kind of contact and may not even want to touch hands. But shaking hands and some degree of physical contact is part of our culture, so we teach them to do one of these at the end of each day. Some stick with one choice; others vary it day to day."

"I notice that you hug like you mean it."

"Are you suggesting that I'm not gentle?" Ms. Nicols grinned at him, knowing she was putting him on the spot.

The smiling Ms. Nicols was a far cry from the stern, condemning Ms. Nicols Ben had met only a week or so ago. He squirmed a bit. "Well, these are just small children and you do seem to squeeze them rather tightly."

"There's a reason for that. Have you noticed how we touch your son?" Ben nodded and she continued. "Many kids with autism spectrum disorders have sensory sensitivities. To them, running hand gently down their arm may feel to them what fingernails on a chalkboard may to you. But if your touch is firmer, it can have a calming effect. Haven't you experienced that with Kyle?"

"Yeah, I have. The first night he was with me, when I touched him I did it with kid gloves. He pulled away and that could be just enough to start up his screeching." Ben grimaced at the memory. He'd been convinced his kid hated him and could not stand his touch. "But if I put my hand firmly on his shoulder to guide him somewhere, he allows it."

From the look Ms. Nicols gave him, he expected to be patted on the head or given a gold star. But he did feel proud of himself. Maybe he could get the hang of this parenting this after all. And, he had been wrong about Ms. Nicols. Her students liked her, his son liked her and he was starting to himself.

BEN MADE it on time to pick up Kyle. Well, almost. It truly was hard to get out of the office at precisely the right time each day. He should never have answered that last phone call.

As he approached the kindergarten room, he heard screams. He stopped. Kyle! Those were Kyle's cries. What was that woman doing to him? Had Ben's first impression been right and she should not be allowed near his son?

Rushing into the room, he spied his son on the floor. Kyle was tossing his head back and forth, kicking his heels and screaming. Ms. Nicols stood beside him placidly as if nothing was wrong. Lori was also nearby, but tidying a book rack rather than attending to his son. Three other kids were putting on their coats and one mother waited nearby.

"What the hell's going on here?" Ben yelled. "What's wrong with my son?"

"Nothing, Mr. Wickens. And, please keep your voice down," said Ms. Nicols.

"Why aren't you helping him? What's wrong with Kyle?"

"He's mad."

"Mad? At what? Did someone hurt him?"

"He wants Jordan's Dora book," the teacher explained.

"Then give it to him," Ben said. What was wrong with these women?

"Excuse me? Give it to him? It doesn't belong to him."

"So?" Ben said. "I'll buy the kid another one. Or two if he wants. Just give that one to Kyle."

Ms. Nicols turned on him. "This isn't about buying anyone anything. Money can't fix everything. This is about Kyle throwing a tantrum to get what he wants."

"If you just give it to him, he'll stop this god awful screaming," said Ben.

"It's not his book. He didn't ask to borrow it; he didn't want to share. He snatched it out of Jordan's hands. We don't tolerate that behavior in this class."

Kyle had quieted for a minute, listening to the exchange between his father and his teacher. On hearing Ms. Nicols' last words, he squirmed sideways and tried to kick her.

"Kyle!" Ben was horrified. He started to apologize to the teacher but she held up her hand to stop him. They watched as Kyle leapt to his feet, ran to the front of the room and attempted to tear the papers from the wall. Lori, the EA was there and effectively blocked him before he did too much damage. He raised his foot to kick her. She said his name firmly and crouched down in front of him, placing her hands on his shoulders. Looking him in the eye, she pressed firmly. It took a few seconds, but before their eyes, they could see the tension drain out of his little body.

"Now, shall we clean up these papers?" Lori asked him.

Kyle bent and picked up the scraps he'd torn and carried them to the waste basket.

BEN WAS DRAINED. Kyle seemed to be recovering faster than he was. Ben turned to Ms. Nicols. "What just went on here? Why weren't you helping him? I've seen you do things for other kids when they were upset?"

"What you just witnessed was a tantrum. Kyle was mad because he didn't get his way. Remember how he reacted the first time he saw the ant farm at the back of the room that first day?"

Ben nodded.

"Well," she continued, "that wasn't a tantrum. Your son was genuinely upset then. That was what we call a meltdown. He was feeling overwhelmed for whatever reason. We used some sensory techniques and they helped him to calm down. That's quite different from what just happened here.

Ms. Nicols continued her explanation. "If you or I or anyone had given in to his tantrum and given him what he wanted just because he raised a fuss, then we would have taught him that tantrums are a good way to control others. Pitch a fit and people will give in. Is that the way you want your son to think?"

"I get it," said Ben. "It's just hard to see him like that. And, he almost kicked you. God, I'm sorry."

She put a hand on his arm and actually smiled. "I'm fine and its fine. He's just a little boy and he's still learning how to navigate his world. He's already doing better and will continue to do so."

CHAPTER 5

The next day he was late. Again. Only this time he made it on time for school both morning and after school. He, who always considered himself Mr. Punctual and hated lateness in others, was actually late for an important meeting with a new client. A woman Ben had been training, a new hire, was giving her first pitch to a potential client. The firm needed this client, Ben's wallet needed this client and Bonita needed the confidence boost she'd get when her first pitch produced results.

He should not have taken any time to chat with Ms. Nicols when he picked up Kyle, but the time had just flown. Funny how that could happen with that woman, as annoying as she could be. Now, he was once again in the position of hurrying Kyle along, this child who did not like to be pushed. Ever.

It had briefly crossed Ben's mind to get Kyle settled in the apartment with his toys, and then run the three floors downstairs to his office for the presentation. But that thought was fleeting. He could not leave a small boy alone, even if he was in the same building.

"Come on, Kyle. We're late!" Ben regretted the words even as he said them. When had the words "hurry" or "late" even made Kyle move faster? In fact, they seemed to put him firmly into balking mode. Yep, it was happening again. Kyle's feet stuck to the floor. Ben took his arm to move him along faster. Kyle's "No, no, no..." voice started to rise. All right. Deep breath. Try this again.

"Kyle, we're going to daddy's office. There'll be a meeting around a big table. Some important people will be there. See? We've brought your toys. I'll make you a spot in the corner and you can play while the grownups talk. All right? Daddy needs you to be real quiet while we meet."

Kyle neither looked at him nor gave any response. Ben could only hope he'd gotten through.

When they reached his board room, the others were all present. Bonita looked nervous but relieved to see him. Ben entered, holding Kyle's arm, but felt resistance. Kyle was frozen at the doorway. His gaze took in all the strange faces then the floor to ceiling windows overlooking the cityscape outside. Ben felt Kyle tense. When Ben tugged on his arm, Kyle leaned backwards and his mouth opened. No, no not now, not in front of all these people. Please don't pitch a fit.

Ben's anger rose. All he needed the kid to do was to sit quietly and play with his toys for half an hour. Was that expecting too much? He'd just turned his own life upside down to accommodate his son; couldn't the kid do at least a little bit for him?

Ben squatted down to put his face near his son's. Maybe he could reason with him. Too bad he didn't have some visuals in his back pocket this time, but he hadn't thought of it.

Then he looked, really looked at Kyle. This was not a child being stubborn and uncooperative. This was a child who was terrified. His little body was rigid and with such a look of fear on his face. Ben's heart broke. What a bastard he was to be thinking awful things about his son, when the child was clearly scared to death of something.

But what? Yeah, there were strangers here but Kyle had never shown such fear of people before. What was he staring at? Ben followed Kyle's line of sight to the windows. What was there? The glass was clear; there were no birds or planes going by. What was the matter with the kid?

All eyes were on them. If Ben couldn't control his own son, what would the new client think of him? How could he trust Ben with his business if Ben obviously couldn't manage one little boy? His eyes returned to Kyle and all thoughts of business fled his mind. His son was scared, just plain afraid.

Without thinking about those around them, he gathered Kyle close and squeezed tight. He hid Kyle's face against his shirt to blot out whatever it was that frightened him. He rocked him back and forth, brushing firmly up and down his back the way he'd seen Ms. Nicols do with upset students. Gradually Kyle's steel rod of a spine started to relax. His little body shuddered as he surrendered his weight to Ben's arms. Despite the situation and all the eyes on them, Ben felt a thrill. *My son trusts me. I was able to calm him down. Maybe the kid likes me, even a little.*

Someone above him cleared a throat. Ben raised his head to meet Bonita's gaze. She was nervous about interrupting him but probably anxious to get her meeting underway.

"I'll just get Kyle settled. You go ahead and start and I'll be right in."

Ben lifted Kyle into his arms and turned back into the hallway. What to do, what to do?

"Are you feeling better now, buddy? What was it that bothered you?" There was no response. This was worse than charades because then at least your partner tried to give you some clues to work with.

Maybe if Kyle just sat on Ben's lap, they could get through this. Ben started through the door with Kyle in his arms. He made it only a couple steps when Kyle raised his head, saw the windows and let out a god awful shriek. Bonita, who had just started her power point presentation dropped the remote with a clatter to the table. That sound though, was hardly heard over the cries coming from Kyle. He began writhing in Ben's arms making it difficult to hold onto him. God, Ben thought, if I drop him, he'll really have something to howl about. How could one forty pound child be so difficult to hold?

Ben sat down across from the windows and placed Kyle on his lap facing him. He wrapped Kyle's legs around his waist and again tucked his son's face into his shirt. He held on tight to the little boy. The shrieks started to subside once again, and then became whimpers.

Ben raised his head to find all eyes on them. What to say, how to explain? Damned if he should have to apologize about his son. This was his company and everyone in the room was either his employee or a potential client. If they didn't like his son, they could leave. He and Kyle weren't going anywhere.

Some of the eyes looked at him with sympathy. Some showed censure. They probably looked down at him for not being able to control his kid. Or for raising a spoiled brat. But not all the eyes had that look.

Mr. and Mrs. Bower, the new or hopefully new clients didn't look at him that way. Mr. Bower spoke up.

"Is he afraid of heights? I hate these picture windows in sky scrapers myself. I never look out of them."

Was that it? Was Kyle afraid of heights?

Mrs. Bower was the next to speak. "Our grandson has autism. He hates shiny surfaces and anything that reflects the light. I wonder if that's what bothered your little boy."

Ben looked at her. These two strangers, these people who had no blood connection to Kyle and had never met him before, in five minutes had come up with two possible explanations for Kyle's behavior. Ben had been clueless as to what the problem might be.

He looked gratefully at the Bowers. "I'm sorry about the ruckus. I have no idea what set him off, but he was really upset." He thought a second. "You know about autism?"

"Oh, yes. We've learned a lot since our grandson was diagnosed - had to learn. There's a little boy down the street who has autism as well. More than one in every hundred children in our country has autism now."

"Actually, it's now one in eighty-eight," Mr. Bower corrected.

Ben looked at them. He had not known that. One in a hundred? One in eighty-eight?

Bonita looked at him pleadingly. Ben nodded at her to continue. As she talked, Ben again felt Kyle's little body gradually relax. Ben let the tension drain out of his own body. Maybe they'd get through this yet.

Ben whispered to Kyle, "All right now, bud? Do you want to get down and play?" If he set Kyle on the floor by his chair, the center support of the table would block his view of the window. It should be safe.

Ben set Kyle down and opened the backpack of toys. Kyle brought out his little cars and lined them up. There seemed to be some exact order to this that only Kyle knew. But at least it was a quiet activity.

He was concentrating on Bonita's presentation, so the sounds didn't register at first. They were coming from near his feet. It was Kyle. He was singing:

"Do-do-do-do-do-Dora!

Well, even if it was nonsense he was singing, at least it was quiet and he wasn't screaming.

Kyle continued, getting a little louder all the time.

"Do-do-do-do-do-d Dora! Do-do-do-do-do-Dora!" Ben tried shushing him. "Sh! Kyle! Quietly, please."

"Dora dora dora the explorer!

Boots that super cool exploradora!"

"Kyle, hush. Keep it down," Ben said, his own voice rising

"Need your help!

Grab your backpacks!

Let's go!

Jump in!

Vámanos! "

Ben's patience was slipping away. "Kyle, stop that right now."

Kyle's voice rose above Ben's, singing, "You can lead the way!" Ben, his face red, apologized to the group, saying he had to take his son out of there. He grabbed Kyle in one arm, the backpack in the other and took long strides to get out of the conference room. Kyle had started his song over again,

"Do-do-do-do-do-Dora!"

But the last "Dora" changed to a shriek as Kyle stiffened in his arms. His arms flailed and Ben had trouble not dropping the squealing, squirming little boy. What now? He turned with Kyle in his arms to survey the spot where they'd been moments before. He's left two of the cars. Ben clenched his teeth together to keep all the bad words in his head. They should not be uttered in a business meeting or in front of a small boy, no matter how trying he was.

Ben stooped with Kyle in his arms swinging Kyle's hands so they could pick up the delinquent cars. Kyle grabbed them and held them to his collar bones. The two of them left the room hurrying toward the elevators and the safety and privacy of their home.

IT WAS NOT good to resent your kid. Kyle was just being a child, a child with autism and getting by the best he could. Kyle did not intend to ruin Ben's business meeting. It was Ben's fault for subjecting his son to such a situation.

But how did people do it? How did they hold down a job and care for a child? There had to be a better way.

WHEN BEN and Kyle unlocked the door of their condo, tantalizing aromas came from the kitchen. Kyle made a beeline for that room. Ben followed. There they found Millie, his housekeeper. Millie came twice a week to tidy up his place, clean and to cook meals. She was a wonderful cook. She made up two or three meals, kept one warming in the oven and froze the others with instructions on how to heat them up. Weekends he was on his own, but Ben appreciated this amount of help, especially now that he had Kyle to think about.

"You sit yourself right down here, little man. I just baked some chocolate chip cookies for you." Kyle plunked himself down in anticipation. Ben did the same. He may not be that little, but he certainly craved Millie's cooking.

Once Kyle finished and went off to watch another Dora the Explorer™ video, Ben planned what he'd say to Millie.

"Thanks for the cookies and the meals. They're great and Kyle loves them." There. How was that for easing in? Millie regarded him steadily, guessing that more was coming.

Ben rubbed his hands over his face. "Millie, I'm in a bind. I'm not doing well at all and I need to do better for Kyle's sake. Today after I picked him up from school I had to take him back to the office with me for a meeting. It did not go well. I should have known that you can't expect a little boy to sit and play quietly through a dry business meeting. I had to leave early and have one of my assistants carry on without me." He paused with a sigh. Bonita had done just fine and pulled off the deal, no thanks to him.

"This is Year End for some of our biggest clients. In the accounting world, that's a big deal. I can pass some things off to my associates, but other things I just can't. Tomorrow I have to be at a meeting from one to five. I can't get out of it and I can't subject Kyle to that. Or them to him, if it went anything like it did this afternoon. "

He looked at Millie. "I'm asking if you would consider coming in tomorrow afternoon to stay with Kyle." Before she could say whatever she was going to say, he rushed on. "I know, I know. This is not in the realm of the housekeeper duties that you do so well. But you're also good with Kyle. Hell, you're a lot better with him than I am. It would just be until five o'clock. There's still plenty of daylight left then." He remembered that she didn't like being out after dark.

He could see that she was struggling with this. She was truly a nice lady and seemed to care for Kyle.

"What would it take? I'll pay double your regular rate. Or if you'd rather come Saturday and not one of your usual days next week."

Still Millie hesitated. She hated to admit that the extra money really appealed. But there was that long bus ride home and she did so hate to walk that last little bit in the dark.

"Please Millie. I really need your help."

"Are you sure I'd be free to leave by five o'clock?"

"I promise."

That would leave her about an hour and a half of daylight to get home. Plenty of time. "All right," she said.

"Oh," the relief on Ben's face was palpable. "Thank you. And Kyle thanks you. It means a lot to us that you'd do this."

. . .

LATER THAT NIGHT when Deanna called to see how Kyle was doing, Ben was honestly able to tell her that things were working out all right. Kyle had little interest in talking to his mother on the phone and set the receiver down to return to his video. Ben started to apologize to Deanna but she said she understood. After they hung up, Ben thought that the one thing he didn't understand was how someone could live with Kyle for five years, turn him over to a virtual stranger, and then only call once to check on her son's well-being.

ONE THING BEN had going for him was his ability to focus. That skill had helped to build his business into the enterprise it was today. Today, he fully gave his attention to the client in front of him and to his assistants at his side. So far the afternoon had been productive as they weeded through the troubles the client put before them. The client stretched and said he needed to take a break.

"How long have we been going at it anyway," he asked Ben.

Ben was wading through a file so one of the others called out the time. Almost half past six. It took a few minutes for that to register, to break through Ben's focus on the task at hand. "What did you say?"

"Six-thirty."

Ben leapt up from his chair. "Six-thirty! My babysitter was only free until five. I completely forgot the time." He threw files into his briefcase. "Bonita, would you mind shutting down for me? I have to go get Kyle."

He left without waiting for a response. He didn't wait for the elevator, but flew up the three flights of stairs to his condo, thankful that at least he lived in the same building. Breathlessly he raced into the kitchen, his tie hanging over his shoulder and his jacket on only one arm.

"Millie, Millie, I'm sorry. I completely forgot the time. I'm sorry. This will never happen again."

Kyle and Millie sat watching a video of Dora the Explorer. She had a crossword puzzle by her side. Millie accepted his apology but she was not happy about it. Ben cursed himself. How could he have done something like this to such a nice woman? And, he'd promised her she could leave by five. Thank god she had stayed with Kyle.

Millie was putting her coat on, a worried look on her face.

"Hold on a minute," Ben told her. "Kyle and I will walk you to your car. It's dark out now."

"I'm quite aware that it's dark out and I don't have a car."

"Then how did you get here?"

"On the bus," she replied.

"Is your car in the garage?"

"I don't have a car."

"Then how do you get here each time? A taxi?"

"Mr. Wickens, do you think I could afford a taxi every time I want to go out? I doubt that. The bus is fine but I do always try to be home before dark." She started out the door.

"Hold on, Millie. Wait a sec. We'll drive you home, but you have to wait until I get Kyle's coat."

"That's not necessary. I'll be fine."

"No. It's my fault you're so late. I apologize, but we will take you home. I don't want you out at some bus stop alone this time of night. Come on bud; let's go give Millie a ride."

With Kyle strapped into his booster seat in the back, they drove through the darkness. The drive took half an hour; how long must it take on the bus? Just how long must this woman take getting to and from her jobs?

"Where are the other places you work? Near my building?"

"One is not too far away, but the other is on the other side of town. That one I still do, but the Gibsons moved away last week. I'm now down to just two contracts - yours and that other one."

"Is that good or bad?"

"Well, it gives me a bit more free time this week but I'll need to find another contract pretty quickly."

They drove in silence as Ben thought.

He needed some more information. "Is the reason you wouldn't stay with Kyle after school because you'd have to take the bus home in the dark?"

"Yes. I don't mind the bus in the daylight, but I don't fancy it after dark. The bus doesn't go far enough and I have to walk the last five blocks."

Ben considered this some more. "What if I asked you to pick Kyle up from school each day and stay with him until half past six, then we drove you home?"

It was Millie's turn to think. "Well, I wouldn't mind on the days I'm working for you, but I need to find work for the other three days. I wouldn't be able to get my cleaning finished on the other side of the city and be at Kyle's school in time to get him."

"Millie, do you really like those cleaning jobs?"

"What do you mean? It's a living and I'm good at it."

"I'm not denying you're good at it. I know only too well how good you are. Look. What do you think about working for me - just me? What if you were at my place Monday to Friday, full-time? Or just afternoons if that's what you want? I'd take you home every night so you wouldn't have to worry about the bus in the dark."

Millie did not know what to say. Some of the clients she'd cleaned for had been slobs. Some were not as nice as Ben and going between houses was tiring. It would be nice to have just one place to think about, one system to remember... one little boy to mother.

She looked at Ben.

Ben thought she needed more convincing. "Look. I'll be out of your way during the day. I get Kyle ready and to school in the mornings. You could come in whenever you wanted as long as you picked Kyle up from school, fed him and stayed with him until I got home. If you were still willing to do the cooking and cleaning you do, or any part of it, I'd be grateful."

She still didn't say anything, but thoughts whirled through her head.

Ben tried again. "I have no idea what the going rate is for child care like this. Name your pay. You're probably more up on these things than I. I need someone and it's you we want. Kyle likes you and trusts you. He doesn't feel that way about many people. Hell, you're better with him than I am, but I'm getting better..."

"Yes." Millie interrupted him.

"What?" Ben said. He didn't think he'd heard it correctly. "Did you say yes?"

"Yes." Millie smiled at him. "I'll take the job."

"Hey, did you hear that bud? Millie's going to be with us." He smiled at her. "Thank you. When can you start?"

"I'll need to give two weeks' notice to the Shermans, but I only go there once a week. So for the next two Wednesdays I can't be at your place or get Kyle, but other than that I can start Monday."

Ben followed Millie's directions the rest of the way, feeling that knot in his stomach release now that he knew he had someone trustworthy to help with Kyle. He started paying more attention to the quiet neighborhood he was driving through. This was a place where families lived. There were shrubs and hedges and bikes on the lawn, hockey nets in the driveways and a lived-in feel to the area.

TWO MORE TURNS took them to Millie's street and her house. Ben pulled into the double driveway and just looked at her home. It was huge, a beautiful old Victoria with wrap-around porches stretching as far as he could see to the side. "Wow," he said, "what a house!"

Millie got defensive. "I know it needs work. Bill and I bought it so many years ago. We'd hoped to fill it with children but that just never happened. We loved the place anyway."

Ben continued staring and now he picked out more details. One of the steps leading to the front door was missing. The porch roof sagged under the upstairs bay window. The roof shingles he could see from the glow of the streetlight seemed to be more curled than straight as their edges pointed skyward.

Millie watched him take that in. "I know. It needs work. It was easier when Bill was alive; he took care of those sorts of things. He was handy and did them himself. Now everything costs so much."

Ben agreed with her that repairs were costly. He had first-hand knowledge of that with his parents' bakery. "How many bedrooms does this place have?"

"Five, plus an extra one that we turned into a study."

Ben got out and unbuckled Kyle's booster seat. "Come on, bud. We're going to see Millie to the door and make sure she gets in all right." To Millie, he asked, "Don't you leave a light on when you're gone?"

She raised one eyebrow at him. "I thought I'd be home before dark today," she reminded him.

Ben ducked his head in apology. "Yeah, it was my fault. Again, I'm sorry." Then he grinned at her. "But maybe it all worked out since you'll come work for me now." He grabbed Kyle's hand. "Let's go, quick, before Millie changes her mind."

Millie laughed as she said, "Good night Mr. Wickens. See you Kyle."

"Good night and the name's Ben. Right?"

CHAPTER 6

This week had been better than the last. Yesterday when he picked Kyle up from school, Ben had complained to Mel and Lori that it was so hard to get Kyle to let him in. His efforts to bond with his son were showing few results. He wanted even some small sign that the door was cracking open just a bit and he was making progress.

Discouraged, he called to Kyle that it was time to go. Without making eye contact, Kyle walked to the door then stood with his hand out, waiting for his dad to take it. Lori grinned and imitated the sound of a door creaking open.

THE WET SPOT on his chest woke Ben. What the hell? The weight against his left side and under his arm registered. Kyle. He's fallen asleep on him and the wet was Kyle's drool. Funny, but that should have been a turn off. Instead, it seemed part of being a dad. A dad. Who would have thought?

He'd never understood his married friends who went all gaga when they had children. Sure, you might expect their wives to do so, but these guys, these rugby players? They changed when they had kids. Now Ben had entered that world that had seemed so far out there before. And you know, it wasn't half bad. He could get used to this warm, heavy weight at his side. Maybe the door to the mystery that was Kyle was cracking open bit by bit.

Wait! What was he doing? This was Kyle's second nap within a few hours. Ben remembered what it was like to try to get Kyle to bed when the kid wasn't sleepy. Ben had been exhausted those first few days with Kyle and had needed to hit the bed, whether Kyle wanted to or not.

"Wakey, wakey." No response. "Come on, Kyle, time to wake up. Let's go, let's go to the, to the...." What was he going to do with this kid? But they had to do something and preferably something that would wear him out. In a good way, of course. What did kids do? Ah, they played in the park.

"Up. Now, let's go. We're heading to the park to play."

"Play?" a groggy voice asked.

"Let's wash your face, take a..., well, use the bathroom and get on our way." He led Kyle down the hall.

What was it like out? That was the trouble with a condo. With air conditioning and heating and windows with a fifth floor view, he had little idea of what it was really like outside. When he was a boy, they'd just look outside or open a door or run into the backyard to see. What kind of a life was this for a little kid in a condo?

While Kyle was in the bathroom, Ben checked the weather on the internet. Cool enough for jackets.

"Kyle, go grab your jacket." No response. "Kyle. Your coat." No response. Ben sighed and went to find him.

Kyle was in the den, kneeling in front of the couch looking at a Dora the Explorer book. A nice quiet activity, but that's not what Ben was after right now. "Let's go. Grab your coat." Kyle ignored him. Ben's temper, never too far under wraps, rose. "Kyle!" he said sharply. "Now!" Still no response. Ben strode the few feet and took Kyle's arm. The child started and looked at Ben. Ben's annoyance deflated. Kyle acted like he had not heard him, had been engrossed in his book. Who could get mad at a kid who liked books? Maybe he'd inherited Ben's ability to totally focus on what he was doing. It had worked all right for Ben.

But now, he wanted his kid doing things like running around in the fresh air, playing with other children, kicking through piles of leaves. They needed to get moving to hit the warmest part of this fall day.

Just as he opened his mouth to tell him once again to get his coat on, Ben remembered Ms. Nicols admonishment - show, don't tell. Ok. He had a picture of a coat some place. Ben got his own coat then showed Kyle the picture. Kyle looked from Ben's jacket to the picture and went to the low hook that Ben had installed in the hallway. He struggled into the jacket, doing up the snaps on his own with painstaking concentration. There. They were finally ready.

On the way out the door, Ben reached for his ball cap. The sun looked bright. Kyle stood there watching, and then as Ben went to shut the door, he moved with a wail. What, what now? Ben hadn't touched him. What was the kid's problem? Back in the condo, Kyle raced from room to room, frantic. Ben trailed after him telling him to come. Again, Kyle ignored him. Like what else was new? The den was a mess. Kyle's suitcase contents were strewn all over the floor. Finally Kyle, raking through the piles grabbed something and stood. On his head he placed a miniature ball cap then strode to the door. I'll be damned, Ben thought, following his son into the hallway.

The park was a pleasant five block stroll. Actually, it took much longer to get there than usual as Ben matched his steps to his son's much shorter stride. He was tempted to swing Kyle to his shoulders or give him a piggyback ride, but that hadn't worked so well the last time he tried it.

Once at the park, the noises of the city faded away. It was like a world apart, this oasis of grass and shrubs and trees. Along the west side was a playground with a few older kids. Kyle glanced at them but seemed to have little interest in them or their games. Ben took a seat on a bench. "Go on. Go on Kyle and play," he urged. Kyle stood beside Ben and didn't seem to know what to do with himself.

Maybe he's shy and doesn't want to go by himself. Ben took his hand and walked towards the other kids. When he stopped, Kyle stopped without seeming to notice the older kids playing on the slide. The swings were empty so Ben led him that way. He lifted Kyle onto a swing, admonished him to hold tight and walked behind to give him a push. Kyle stiffened and Ben recognized the signs of an impending howl. He quickly retraced his steps until he was facing him again.

"What's the matter buddy? This is fun. You like the swings, all kids like swings. Look, it's like this. I'll push you gently." He remained facing Kyle and, holding the chains, gently rocked the swing. Kyle slowly relaxed his shoulders. As the gentle back and forth movement continued, Kyle closed his eyes and seemed to fully relax. So did Ben. Crisis averted. But what kid didn't love the playground?

Watching him, Ben was afraid that Kyle was going to yet again be lulled into a snooze. He brought him here for exercise and fresh air to tire the kid out, not send him into napville again.

Ben grabbed his hand and set off at a brisk walk, well aware that Kyle had to hustle to keep up. That was the idea. There were few people in the park, only one woman and her dog over yonder. As their feet trod the leave-strewn path, Ben recalled autumn when he was a kid and all the fun they'd had with leaves. He dropped Kyle's hand and quickly used his feet to scoop leaves into a pile. Then he stepped back and ran through the pile, kicking his feet at he went. He remembered from childhood the brittle crunching as the dried leaves cracked beneath his feet, releasing aromas of soil and sun. He rebuilt the pile, then taking Kyle's hand, pulled the child through the pile. Kyle, looking startled, just ran. Then Ben stopped, turned him around and ran him through again. This time Kyle got it. He kicked his feet as he'd seen Ben do.

This time Ben squatted and used his hands to make a pile. Kyle watched for a second, then made his own pile. Ben said, "Ready? One, two, three!" and he jumped in, kicking leaves everywhere. Kyle laughed. He actually laughed! "More," he said.

Ben raised his head in surprise. It was rare to hear Kyle laugh and even rarer for him to speak. Yes!

"Okay, again, bud. First make your pile." Then, "Ready? One, two, three!" With an echoing, "Three!" Kyle mimicked his dad and they both jumped, scattering leaves everywhere.

The next time, after Ben said, "Ready?" Kyle counted with him. The anticipation was almost as much fun as the jumping and the scattering. Ben felt like a kid himself.

He was glad they were in a secluded part of the park and no one was watching. Whoa. There was that lady and her dog again, coming closer. Well, the hell with what she thought. He was having fun with his son. "Ready? One, two, three!"

The next time, Ben thought he'd mix it up a bit. Just before he said three, he reached down and scooped up a handful of leaves. As soon as they jumped into their piles, Ben added to the fray by throwing the leaves over Kyle's head.

There was silence. Oh, shit, Ben thought. Have I ruined it now? So focused was he on his son that Ben had not noticed the woman drawing up to them. She said, "Sit" to her dog, then reached down into Kyle's pile of leaves, grabbed two handfuls and threw them over her own head.

Kyle stared at her as she laughed. Then he lunged for her, wrapping his arms around her legs. It was Ms. Nicols! She gave Kyle a hug while she laughed, then threw more leaves at him. Then she smiled at Ben. A real smile. There was nothing cynical or dismissive about this one. It was the kind of smile she shared with the kids in her room, but somehow different. It warmed Ben and at the same time froze him to the smile. God. She was beautiful. He'd seen her how many times and never noticed before?

"Can I play, too?" she asked.

"By all means," Ben said and stepped back to give her room to make her own pile of leaves. They each yelled their "One, two three" in unison and jumped and threw leaves at each other.

After a few turns, Ben's attention was drawn to the dog. It was huge to his eyes, at least an eighty pound German Shepherd. Ben knew that not all were the family pet type and not all were used to small children. He edged his body between Kyle and the dog, not taking his eyes off the creature. Obviously he was well-trained because he had not moved since receiving that one "Sit" command. But the dog's body was quivering, either with the desire to play or to attack.

Ben couldn't take any chances with his son. "Shouldn't your dog be tied up or something?"

"Why?

"Well, do you think he's safe? Kyle's pretty small and the dog doesn't know us."

"Are you afraid of dogs, Mr. Wickens?"

Ben grimaced. "No, I'm not afraid but I've got a kid to take care of. And the name's Ben."

Ms. Nicols backed down and smiled. Her crusty parts seemed close to the surface or maybe it was just him that brought that out in her.

"Kyle, come with me," she told his son. Ben tensed and moved to interfere." Trust me, Mr. Wickens. I know what I'm doing."

She led the child by the hand to the great dog whose head was level with Kyle's. His son didn't show the same trepidation Ben felt. Ben stayed at Kyle's side, ready to defend his boy if need be.

"Kyle, this is Max. Max, this is Kyle. Shake hands with Kyle." Max lifted a paw and held it there as Kyle didn't move. He didn't look afraid, more as if he didn't know what to do. Ms. Nicols grasped her dog's paw, shook it twice then let go. "Now you're turn, Kyle. Max, shake a paw"

The dog again held up his paw and this time Kyle grabbed it with his free hand. He shook it up and down forcefully and Ben prepared to lunge, but the only sign that this wasn't according to the script was that the dog wiggled slightly backward. His grin didn't leave his face.

Ms. Nicols continued. "Now hold out the back of your hand so Max can sniff it." Kyle obeyed. After a few sniffs, the dog licked Kyle's hand and Kyle jerked back then giggled. He slowly offered his hand once again and again, got his hand washed.

Without taking his eyes off the dog's massive head, Kyle groped for Ben's hand. When he found it, he thrust his dad's hand towards the dog's mouth. Ben's hand got a thorough washing as well. Between giggles, Kyle offered his own hand then his dad's and Max responded to the game as if he, too, enjoyed it. Over their heads, Ben's gaze met Ms. Nicol's. He mouthed, "Thanks."

She gave one of her smiles again and mouthed, "My pleasure."

And Ben thought she meant it.

MAX CIRCLED KYLE, straining for a better lick at his hands. His tail swished a pile of leaves, reminding Kyle of the previous game. He leapt into a pile, grabbing an armful of leaves and tossing them. Max's front feet left the ground as tried to catch leaves in his month. Max and Kyle romped through the leaves, both with huge grins on their faces.

Ben and Ms. Nicols watched the two frolic. Ben mused, "Kyle's playing. He's actually playing."

"Yes," Ms. Nicols agreed. "It's lovely to see." Then, she added, "You're doing a good job with him."

Ben turned to her in surprise. She'd given him exactly the opposite opinion last week and he said so.

"I might have been a bit hard on you at first. Sorry. I thought you were another uninvolved parent and these kids really need their mothers and fathers behind them one hundred percent. I was wrong about you, though. You do care."

"Damned right I do. But I have no idea how to do this."

"Who does? Kids don't come with a rule book, especially kids with autism."

Ben let that last bit go. "But you're right. I was an uninvolved father." He told her how he'd only learned of Kyle's existence when the child was two, when Deanna had called asking for money. He remembered cradling the phone in one ear, listening to her, while he used his computer to search for flights to LA to go meet his son. Deanna had heard the tap-tapping through the phone lines and asked what he was doing. In no uncertain terms she told him he was not welcome to visit them in LA. Kyle was just starting to adjust to her boyfriend who had recently moved in. Having one father was all Kyle

could cope with now. Meeting Ben would only confuse and
upset him.

"I'm ashamed to say that I took Deanna's word for that and did not
push a face-to-face meeting. Instead, I just sent money. Some father,
huh, Ms. Nicols?"

"It's not what you did then, but what you're doing now that counts.
And my name's Melanie."

"Yeah? That suits you. Melanie." They smiled at each other.

Ben reached out and brushed some leaves from Melanie's hair,
leaves put there by an exuberant Kyle. Or, maybe they were from Max
who was spreading almost as many leaves around as his playmate
with two hands. The button on Ben's coat snagged the covered elastic
holding Melanie's ponytail, pulling it most of the way out. Her hair
tumbled around her face. Ben stared. Her hair was gorgeous and
framed a face that was lovely in the sunshine.

She reached to repair her ponytail. Ben impulsively stayed her
hand. "Don't. It looks nice like that." Uncertain, Melanie complied.

They watched the boy and dog a few minutes more but gone was
that easy camaraderie between the two of them. Ben thought Kyle
showed signs of tiring. Melanie thought he showed signs of getting
too wrought up. Time to switch activities, she thought.

But that's as far ahead as her brain thought. The next words out of
her mouth surprised even her. "Who wants hot chocolate?"

"Kyle. Kyle wants hot chocolate," Kyle said, referring to himself.
"And Max. Max wants hot chocolate."

Ben looked around. He didn't remember seeing a restaurant or a
take-out stand around here.

Now Melanie's face was reddened, but not from the sun or wind.
"I meant at my place. I don't live far from here and I have hot
chocolate." She rushed on, "I didn't mean to impose. Of course you're
busy. Don't feel obligated...."

Ben studied her. "What do you say, Kyle? Want to go have hot
chocolate with Ms. Nicols and Max?"

"Yeeees!"

"Kind of hard for you to back out now." Ben grinned at Melanie.

71

. . .

MELANIE'S HOUSE was three blocks the other side of the park. Max was now on a leash, walking beside Kyle, while Ben and Melanie brought up the rear. Kyle walked with one fist bunched in Max's ruff; both seemed content. The adults were not quite so peaceful with each other.

"Are you regretting your offer? We can just walk you home then leave if you want. I'll make up an excuse to Kyle." Ben sensed that Melanie wished she had never opened her mouth.

"No, it's not that." Melanie paused, and then being forthright, said what was on her mind. "It's just that we're not friends."

Ben raised an eyebrow at her.

"I don't mean we can't be friends. Well, we can't really. I'm your son's teacher. I have a policy about not dating in the workplace and certainly not a student's parent." Her face was again red.

"A date is usually something I plan. We had no idea we'd run into you at the park. You didn't know either."

"True, but..."

"So, we're just acquaintances being social and sharing a warm drink on a fall day."

By then they were in front of Melanie's house. It was the quintessential white picket fence bungalow, although small. Tiny, in fact.

"How many bedrooms does this place have? Half of one?"

Melanie gave him a mock glare. "Two, if you must know. Or more like one and a half. There's my room then a small room I use as an office for my school stuff."

As soon as the gate was opened and Melanie unsnapped the leash, Max took off, spinning circles in the front yard, running back and forth in front of Kyle, trying to get him to play.

"Is it all right?" Ben asked, but was too late as Kyle tore around the side of the house after the dog. In the fading distance, they could hear the dog's glad bark and Kyle's answering giggle.

"Is Max safe?"

"I'd stake my life on it. And Kyle's," she answered. "Come on in."
She turned the key in the lock, then pushed on the door with her
shoulder. It didn't budge. She stood back, and then tried again. Ben
placed his hand flat on the door above her head and pushed with her.
"The front door's a bit tricky," she explained.

ONLY A FEW STRIDES took them right through the house to the back
door. Melanie unlocked the knob, opened the door and called out to
Kyle to come right in when he wanted.

Ben leaned against the kitchen counter as Melanie got out a pot
and the ingredients. Soon the kitchen felt cozy with the smell of the
warming milk. The place suited Melanie. It was homey but
uncluttered, everything in its place. Ben smiled to himself as he
thought that at least her hair was not in place.

Melanie caught Ben's frequent glances out the back door window
to check on Kyle. She liked that his son was never far from his mind.
She suggested, "Why don't we take our mugs and sit outside where we
can watch them".

They relaxed on the wide Adirondack chairs. In the lee of the wind
with the late afternoon sun shining on them, the weather was just
right. So was the company, Ben thought in surprise. Around them, his
son and Melanie's dog bounded with endless energy. Ben could not
tell which of the two was having the most fun. Periodically Kyle
swooped by for a slurp of his hot chocolate then charged off again
with Max in pursuit.

As it began to grow chillier, Ben called Kyle over to finish his hot
chocolate. Feeling the back of Kyle's hand, Ben thought he was getting
a bit cold, so he sat him on his lap and shared his jacket with his son.
Kyle snuggled in and drank his cocoa. When he put the cup down, he
sank back down into his dad's arms and relaxed. In about a minute he
was asleep. Ben gazed at his slumbering son, then remembered where
they were.

He started to apologize and to rouse Kyle.

"No, no, he's fine. Just stay there. He's had a big day and looks worn out. Let him recharge his batteries a few minutes."

"Well, if you're sure," Ben told her.

They sat in companionable silence, Max collapsing at their feet and shutting his eyes as well. Ben relaxed, loving the feel of a warm boy in his arms and the sun on his face. It was nice to sit here with his son, a friendly dog and an attractive, pretty amazing woman. The sun was warm and so far it had been a good day.

Melanie watched as Ben drifted off, joining his son and her dog in sleep. What did that say about her company, she wondered? But this did give her an opportunity to study Ben. His face looked softer, younger in sleep. He showed a vulnerable side he'd never allow to sneak out when he was awake.

She'd misjudged him. She chided herself for making snap judgments, but she was not usually wrong. She'd had him pegged as an uncaring suit, a businessman who had little time for anything other than work, and certainly no time for his son. At first she figured his wife had roped him in for some child care time. Then when she learned that he was a single parent, she assumed he was one of those dead beat dads, only now being called to task to take some responsibility for his child. But, take responsibility he had. Oh, there had certainly been some glitches and he still had a lot to learn, but he was trying. You could see the difference in Kyle.

And today, today had been an eye-opener for her. When she spied them across the park, she instantly dismissed them as just people who only resembled Kyle and Ben. The Mr. Wickens she knew would never risk getting his suit rumpled or his clothes dirty by roughhousing with his son. He'd never risk losing his dignity by playing in the leaves with a child. Actually, like a child. But Ben had seemed to be having just as much fun as Kyle and when he recognized her, he didn't stop in embarrassment. Yes, there was more to this Ben Wickens than she had thought.

As she gazed at him, she did not like the direction her thoughts were heading. This was the parent of one of her students, after all. To distract herself, she got up and went into the kitchen. Might as well make herself useful and create a treat for Kyle. Living with a single dad, he might not get many homemade treats. She smiled at her own admittedly chauvinistic thoughts.

"ANYONE FOR PEANUT-BUTTER COOKIES?"

Ben came to with a start. Where was he? Oh, shit. Now he remembered. Had he actually fallen asleep on his son's teacher's deck? And what was that heavenly aroma?

Melanie stood at the door, delectable smells drifting over the two snoozing Wickens men.

Kyle woke up. "Cookies," he yelled and just like that he was off Ben's knee and into the open kitchen door.

Ben could hear Melanie instructing him to first wash his hands then have a seat at the table. It took Ben longer to gather his wits, then he followed his son back inside the house. He saw that the table was set for three. A glass of milk was in front of one place setting. A bottle of beer stood by each of the two other plates. Ben smiled. The end to a perfect afternoon.

BY THE TIME they walked home, Ben was ready for supper. Unfortunately, with a son to look after, he needed to provide healthy meals. No more calling for pizza delivery and having a cold brew in front of the television. So he got Kyle settled with his building blocks and went to work on supper.

What guy didn't know how to fry a couple steaks or chops? Ben was no different.

He put some water on to boil for pasta and heated the oil in the frying pan.

The phone rang. It was Ellie, Ben's sister. Ben was her go-to person when it came to finances and their family's bakery. Balancing the books was always an issue with that bakery. Ben kept the books for them and the ledgers were in his desk.

Ben sat behind his desk to search for the answer to Ellie's pressing question. Their conversation got involved as they weighed options.

KYLE WANDERED INTO THE KITCHEN. He stared, mesmerized by the swirling pattern of smoke rising from the pan on the stove. Moving closer, he poked at the smoke, liking the way his finger dispersed the pattern. He pushed his finger closer to the pan, but drew back sharply when some grease sputtered and burned him.

Watching some more, Kyle noticed a dish towel hanging over the oven door handle. He grabbed the towel and used that to poke at the smoke. The tail of the towel floated close to the gas burner. At first there was just a spark and the edges turned black. Then flames burst onto the edge and rapidly spread up the towel. Kyle watched, fascinated.

In no time, the flames reached his hand. The sensation didn't register for a second, and then it did. Kyle screamed! He tried to shake the towel off of his hand, but part of it stuck. Kyle waved the towel, fanning the flames. He dropped the flaming towel into the hot pan of grease. More flames burst forth.

From the den, Ben heard Kyle's screams. Throwing down the phone, he raced to the kitchen. At first he couldn't see his son due to the grayish smoke making swirling patterns in much of the room and covering the stove with a smoke like dense fog.

Ben peered through the smoke frantically and found Kyle. Part of a flaming towel was on his son's hand. Flames erupted on the sleeve of Kyle's shirt. Ben threw the child to the floor, fell with him, smothering the flames with his own body. He used his hands to bat at the flames still on the towel, while trying to grab Kyle's hands and press them between their bodies.

Mindful of his own greater weight, Ben quickly rolled off his son, eyes alert for any further signs of flames on the little boy's clothes. Although Ben could not see any more fire on him, Kyle continued to scream.

Then the condition of the rest of the room penetrated Ben's panic.

Flames were rising higher on the stove. Remnants of the dish towel still smoldered. Leaving Kyle momentarily, Ben grabbed a box of salt in one hand, the box of baking powder in the other. He hesitated before throwing either on the fire. Grease, grease, grease. Which did you use for a grease fire? He couldn't remember and couldn't take a chance. He threw both boxes to the ground and pulled the drawer off its runners to the floor in his search for a lid for the pot. Ah, he found it and slammed the lid onto the pot. The hiss of the smoke and grease was now smothered but smoke still billowed out from the edges. Shit! The burner was still on.

There. The fire was out. While the smoke wasn't dying down, at least the amount pouring out was less.

He heard Kyle coughing on the floor behind him. Ben picked up his son, cradling him in his arms and ran to the bathroom to look at the damages.

Kyle's screaming had subsided to whimpers and coughs. Ben tore the remnants of Kyle's shirt away. Miraculously, despite the flames he had seen, the harm to Kyle seemed slight. He must have let go of the towel soon enough, or only the outside parts of the damp towel had burned, the wetter areas shielding the kid from the worst of the flames. Although the sleeve of his shirt was scorched and full of holes, Kyle's arm looked okay. Ben stood Kyle on the vanity and ran his hands over his jeans. They looked fine in the front. He turned him around, careful to balance him with one hand. No, he had not been burned on the back of his legs either. There were no marks at all on Kyle's back and only a slight redness on his arms. The most injured part Ben could see was a burn on Kyle's right index finger.

With his heart still beating a staccato tempo Ben asked Kyle over and over if he was all right, if he hurt anyplace. Kyle didn't reply; Ben had to reassure himself by checking over every inch of Kyle's skin.

Thank god the child was all right. What kind of a father was he to have let such a thing happen to his son? Kyle'd only been with him such a short time and look, he'd almost been killed. Well, not quite killed, but he could have been in just a couple more minutes.

Ben fished under the bathroom sink for first aid supplies. He held

Kyle's finger under the cold, running water. At first Kyle yelled and fought him, not heeding Ben's words that this would make him feel better. Slowly it sank in, that his finger was actually hurting less now. Ben instructed Kyle to leave his finger under the water while he sorted out the bandages and burn salve. After gently wrapping the hurt finger loosely in gauze then surgical tape, Ben lifted Kyle off the vanity. He held his son in his arms tightly, apologizing for not paying attention and allowing Kyle to get hurt. Then his voice rose as he told Kyle to never, ever, touch that stove again. Ben crushed Kyle to him once again and carried him in his arms to the couch, where he sat rocking him.

As Ben's heart rate slowed, the rest of the world started to enter his senses. There was the smell of little boy hair and sweat against his face. He could smell the ointment he'd just applied. In the background was the smell of smoke and singed material. While the smoke had been concentrated in the kitchen, some tendrils had drifted down the hallway and into the living room. The mess in the kitchen and airing the place out would all need to be attended to but for now, Ben just wanted to sit and hold the miracle that was his precious little boy.

WHAT WAS THAT? What could he hear? It was kind of tinny and sounded far away. Ben did not want any more surprises tonight so he set Kyle down to go investigate.

The sound got louder as he went down the hall. He paused in the doorway to his den. Yes, he could hear it louder in here. It sounded like a voice. He walked to his desk and looked underneath. There on the floor was his cordless phone and the noise was coming from it. He put it to his ear and listened.

"Mom?" he asked.

He had to move the phone away from his ear when she screeched her frantic reply. This didn't make sense. Before the fire, Ben had been on the phone with his little sister. He didn't think he'd hung up but couldn't remember what he'd done in his panic when he heard Kyle's scream.

Gradually his mother's words lowered in volume and stridency, making them easier to understand. Yes, Ben had been on the phone with his sister. Through the phone Ellie had heard Kyle's screams then a thud. That would have been when Ben threw the phone. Ellie had remained on the phone, frantically calling to Ben to learn what was happening. Did he need help? Was he all right? Why was there a child screaming in the background?

Ellie had held on for several minutes. She'd yelled for her mother to come hold that phone while she scrambled for her cell to call Ben's cell. No answer. Desperate, not knowing if they should call the police or 911, Ellie paced with the phone in her hand. The screams subsided. Straining to hear, Ellie thought she could hear her brother's voice low in the distance but not yelling. So maybe it wasn't a 9-1-1 situation.

But Ben had always been there for Ellie and it was not often he needed something from her. So, while their mother stayed on the line, calling out to Ben to return to the phone, Ellie grabbed her jacket and car keys. She'd drive over to Ben's to check it out, while their mother remained on the phone, hoping to be able to talk to Ben.

"Sorry, mom, sorry to have worried you. We're all right," Ben explained. "There was a little fire, a grease fire on the stove, but it's under control now."

"What was all that screaming Ellie said she heard? She thought it sounded like a child"

Ben sighed. This was so not the way he wanted to break the news about Kyle to his parents.

"It was a child. A little boy. His name is Kyle, and he's staying with me."

There was silence on his mother's end of the phone. What the hell, he might as well just plunge in now.

"He's my son, mom. I know this will come as a shock to you. He's been with me this past couple weeks. I wanted to give him time to get used to being here before I introduced him to the rest of my family." Silence. "Mom? Mom, are you there? Are you all right?

"Look, it's a long story. I was going to tell you this week anyway. I can't get into it right now. I have to go check on Kyle. I'll call you later and tell you everything. Okay?"

"You'd better. You have a lot of explaining to do, young man."

Ben grinned despite the situation. Those were the exact words his mother had used on him when he was growing up and found himself in trouble. This time, she was right, oh so right. He really did have a lot of explaining to do.

CHAPTER 7

The bell rang. Ah, that had to be Ellie. Much as Ben loved his sister, he so did not want to have to deal with her or anyone for that matter, right now. He'd had enough for the day, enough fun and enough sun and enough drama. Cripes. He's had more crises in the past week since Kyle had come into his life than for years put together. But, today's fire was not Kyle's fault. It was Ben's responsibility as a dad to look after his son. He'd failed. Maybe Kyle would be better off back home with his mother.

Ben's gut clenched at the thought. He'd begun by accepting Kyle as his responsibility. But somehow, sometime, it had grown to be much more than that. The kid had gotten under his skin and as much as his days had been thrown into a spin, he could hardly imagine life now without Kyle in it.

Delaying it would not make this any easier. From the repeated and ferocious ringing of the doorbell, Ellie was not going to wait much longer. As that thought left his brain and his foot took that first step towards the door, that bell was joined by a pounding fist and a kicking foot. His sister could be a feisty thing and had been since she could barely toddle around chasing after her big brothers.

Kyle, who had calmed after the excitement, again tensed. This pounding was the last straw. Ben now knew the signs of an incoming storm. He pressed firmly on both of Kyle's shoulders and crouched down to his level. Over his shoulder, he yelled towards the door. "Hang on a sec, El. I'm coming. We're all right."

"Ben?" The muffled voice came through the heavy door. "Ben, are you all right? Who's we?"

"Kyle, it's your aunt Ellie come to visit us. She wants to know that we're not hurt from the fire. It'll be all right."

Still pressing firmly, he led the boy toward the door and held him to his side as he opened the door. Knowing his sister, he made sure Kyle was safely out of the way of the swinging door.

On cue, Ellie burst in. She looked like she might have been in some sort of crisis herself. Her wavy black hair was tousled, either from a wind storm or from obsessively running her fingers through it. Her pale blue eyes were wild as they scanned Ben from head to toe. Her hands grabbed at him.

"You're all right? You're OK?" she demanded.

"We're fine. The place smells a bit badly and there's cleaning to be done, but we're all right."

"We?" Ellie's eyes drifted to the little boy half hidden by Ben's legs. Kyle's face peeked out but his eyes were on her shoes.

And well they might be, thought Ben. Ellie must have been relaxing at home because she still had on her plush, grey hippopotamus slippers - a gag Christmas gift from their youngest brother many years ago. Although they looked decidedly the worse for wear, she forsook all other footwear when lounging at home. In her haste to check on Ben's situation she had obviously given no thought to her appearance. Ben smiled. Ellie really was a good kid and not at all the girly-girl type their dad believed.

"Come in, El. Have a seat. There's quite a bit to tell you."

"I'm not budging an inch until I learn who this is and what's going on here."

Ben's shoulders dropped and he let out a breath. In this mood, there was no point in arguing with Ellie. He'd tried in the past and it never worked.

"Ellie, I'd like you to meet your nephew, Kyle. Kyle Wickens." He squatted beside Kyle, lifting the child onto his one knee. "Kyle, this is your aunt Ellie. She's my sister," he added, then wondered if a five year old, only child had such a concept.

Kyle remained silent, his eyes on those slippers.

Ellie, bless her heart, lowered her volume and the stridency. She, too, crouched down, her face almost level with Kyle's. "Hi," she said. "I'm very pleased to meet you. I'm El." She put out her hand.

"Kyle, can you shake hands with Aunt Ellie?" Ben said.

No response. Ben repeated his words, careful to use the exact phrasing. Ellie raised her eyes to Ben's and he warned her with a look. Thankfully, Ellie caught on and just waited quietly. In his head, Ben counted to ten, then to fifteen, as Ms. Nicols - no, Melanie, he remembered with a smile - had instructed him to do. It was this wait time thing and something to do with auditory processing being slower in kids with autism. Autism. How was he going to explain that one to his sister? His sister, hell, she was going to be the easy one. Wait till he tried to tell his father, the guy who had never understood even one of his three children. Nor, had he put much effort into that, Ben reflected.

"Will you shake hands with me, Kyle?" Ellie asked, mimicking Ben's words, bless her.

"Handshake, hug or high five," Kyle repeated. Ellie looked quizzically at Ben.

"That's what his teacher asks each kid as they leave her room at the end of the day. They all get the choice," Ben explained.

"Ah, makes sense," Ellie said, as if this was all part of normal life. For Ben, it sure wasn't. Or hadn't been, he reminded himself.

"Which should we do, Kyle? A handshake, hug or high five?" Ellie asked then waited.

Without raising his eyes to hers, Kyle replied, "Hug." He moved off Ben's knee and put his arms around Ellie's neck. She squeezed him back, tightly. Her eyes meeting Ben's were moist. Ben was as proud of his son as if he had taught Kyle these social graces himself.

Kyle pulled away, his eyes returning to Ellie's feet. He said, "Dora the Explorer. Diego's Hippo Adventure." While Ben had thought he'd learned more this week than he had ever wanted to know about Dora, this stuff about a Diego and some hippo was new to him. However, Ellie didn't seem in the dark.

"Ah, so you know about Dora, too. Do you have a book about Diego and the hippo? Or the video?" she asked Kyle. Kyle didn't answer but turned and headed down the hall towards the living room. Ellie followed, her nose like a dog sniffing the air, giving Ben a look over her shoulder. It was a WTF kind of look.

Ben surveyed the mess in the kitchen. This was going to take a looong time to fix. He started by opening the window and turning on the fan over the stove. Grabbed a pot holder and tossed the ruined frying pan and remnants of the towel into the sink. He needn't have bothered with the pot holder and the pan was barely warm now. But as it hit the sink, the bottom of the pan separated from the sides. Sheesh, it must have gotten hot. When he thought of what could have happened... How could he have left a pan of oil heating on the stove? And, most important, how could he have forgotten he was no longer just fending for himself but had a child to consider?

The child. Cripes. Once again, Kyle had slipped his mind. It was only for a few moments, but look what could happen in just minutes. The nightmare wreck of his kitchen reminded him. Ben went to open the door to the condo hallway, thinking to air the place out still more. When he opened the door, faint smoky patterns drifted by him into the hallway. As he watched the smoke curl, he hastily shut the door. What if the wafting smoke set off the building smoke detectors? Or worse, the sprinkler system? No telling what damage that would do.

Smoke detectors. Why hadn't his gone off? With the amount of smoke, they certainly should have. There was one in his hall, right outside the kitchen door, wasn't there? Yep. Oh. Then, Ben remembered. One night, months ago, the stupid thing had started beeping in the night, low on batteries. While he had an assortment of batteries in a drawer, none were the right size. To stop the infernal thing from beeping he had unhooked the inside wires, then forgotten all about it. First thing in the morning he was replacing the batteries in every smoke detector. And, he was buying two fire extinguishers - one for the kitchen and one to go beside the fireplace.

What else did parents do? The fire department might have suggestions on their website. And, hadn't he seen some advertisement on television about having a safety plan, an evacuation drill that you practiced with your kids. He'd need to get on that. Maybe Melanie knew about this stuff; she seemed to know everything there was to know about kids. There really was a lot to this parenting stuff.

Parenting. He'd done it again, forgotten about Kyle for minutes more. At least there were no screams. Instead, there was the low murmur of voices, or at least one voice - Ellie's.

In the den, Ellie sat on the couch, with an opened book in her lap. Another one of Kyle's endless Dora books. That chick Dora really got around, Ben thought. There was a story or video about her and her friends in almost every part of the world, or so Ben had experienced so far from reading and watching with Kyle.

As Ellie read aloud with Kyle beside her, Ben watched Kyle edge closer. Soon, there was no space between their bodies. Ellie, still reading, glanced at Kyle out of the corner of her eye. She paused, asking him to point to something in the picture. As he did, she put her arm around him, snuggling him close. Rather than pulling away or howling as he had the first time Ben tried to tentatively touch Kyle that way, he relaxed against his aunt, naming the objects in the background of the picture.

It had taken days for Kyle to let him touch him, Ben thought with chagrin, and within a half hour of meeting Ellie, he allowed her touch. Here Ben thought he and his son had bonded over the course of this past week, when Ellie had accomplished as much as he in just a fraction of the time.

What would Ms. Nicols - Melanie - say about that? It was nice to think of her now as Melanie and perhaps not just Melanie, his son's teacher but possibly, Melanie a friend. He had certainly come to trust her advice on Kyle.

Okay. She said not to take things personally, especially with kids with autism. The child's reactions might have nothing to do with you, she had said. Instead, it might be more to do with something going on inside him, some sensory sensitivities, some reaction to the environment, fatigue or overload.

Look at how Ellie held him. Firmly. She seemed to know instinctively how Kyle liked to be held, while Ben had struggled to treat the kid like spun glass. His initial touches had been tentative and light, in his efforts to be gentle and not startle this little man. Melanie had explained that to some kids light, feathery touches on their skin were akin to finger nails on a blackboard for other people. The light touch might send his nerve endings jangling, while a firmer touch could be calming. In fact, she'd said to press much harder than you would think you would have to for a child of that age.

That's why she used a weighted blanket in the classroom when kids were upset. That's why they had bean bag chairs that kids could sink into. That's why they had weighted lap pillows or tube "snakes" to drape around their shoulders and big cushions to crawl under. Weight and pressure could have a soothing effect. Once Ben learned to use pressure, rather than a light touch, his son actually gravitated to him, rather than shied away from his touch. Much more gratifying to a new father.

It was also gratifying to see his son so cozy with his aunt. Ah, families. Somehow, cozying up brought an image of Melanie. He'd certainly never be that close to her, but what might it be like?

"EVERYTHING OKAY HERE?" It certainly looked that way to Ben, but it didn't hurt to check.

"Why don't you do something about your disaster zone? We're fine," said Ellie.

"We're fine," echoed Kyle. He gave his dad a smile. God that kid could get to him, Ben thought.

Ben grabbed some garbage bags and tackled the worst of the kitchen. He went through two sponges, trying to scour the stove and sink. The smell still lingered. Next, he mopped the floor and took the garbage to the trash can out back. Still, there was the smell of smoke.

On television ads, some woman would come in and spray some stuff in the air and everyone would sniff and smile. Somehow, Ben thought it would take more than that to solve this problem.

He went around the condo opening all the windows, despite the chill of the evening air. He didn't want Kyle getting cold, so he lit the fireplace in the den, and then threw a heavy comforter over both his son and his sister. They snuggled in.

"That was supposed to be dinner and I don't fancy trying to cook anything else in that room now. Would you be all right with Kyle if I ran out for some pizza?"

"We're fine. Go ahead. Make my side double cheese, don't forget. And no anchovies," Ellie said.

A little head peaked out from under the blanket. "No anchovies!" Ellie and Ben laughed, both doubting that the kid had any idea what an anchovy even was. But, he was certainly taking to his new aunt, and Ben would take any words his son uttered. Was it his imagination, or was Kyle actually speaking more?

THE AROMA of pizza preceded Ben into the condo. He set the extra-large pizza box on the coffee table in front of his two favorite people. Next he brought out three plates and tore a bunch of paper towels off the kitchen rolls for napkins. He brought extras, having experience now with the way a young boy eats.

Ben served while Ellie wrapped up what must be her fourth book, judging from the stack beside Kyle. He gave Kyle a plate with a large slice. He handed Ellie a piece from the double cheese, no meat or veggies side. Kyle stiffened when he looked at his plate. Ben, knowing the signs asked, "What is it bud? Don't you like pizza?" Kyle held the plate out at arm's length and looked ready to throw it. "What, what's wrong?" Ben said.

"He doesn't like it, there's something about it he doesn't like," said Ellie. "While you were gone, we talked about pizza and I think he was looking forward to it."

"Quick, grab it," she said, sensing Kyle was about to throw or thrust the plate away from him. Ben complied.

Kyle whimpered. "What's wrong?" Ben repeated. "What do you want?"

"It's touching. No, no, no!" came from Kyle.

Ben and Ellie looked at each other. What's touching? He and Ellie were touching and had been for some time now. What was bugging the kid?

Kyle reached for Ellie's plate and took it from her hands. He grabbed her pizza slice and started eating.

"Hey," his father yelled. "Kyle, that's rude. Put that back."

Kyle looked like he was about to cry, but gave Ellie back her plate. He just sat there, staring at the pizza box.

Ellie studied Kyle, her plate and the pizza. Then it hit her. "Ben, don't you remember Samuel when he was little? Remember what a picky eater he was? He hated the foods on his plate to touch each other. Mom had that little kid's divided plate that he used for years so it would keep the different foods separate. Maybe Kyle doesn't like his things touching either."

Maybe Ellie was on to something. Ben remembered words, "Don't take it personally. Odds are it's not about you." Okay, if he looked at it like that, maybe Kyle was not just being rude. Ben studied Kyle's plate and Ellie's. Ellie's looked bland, all one color with just melted cheese on her crust. The pizza slices on Ben and Kyle's plates were colorful with a variety of meat and vegetables poking out from the cheese. It was worth a try.

"Kyle, do you like this one better?" Ben pointed at the all-cheese side of the pizza pie. Kyle just looked at the cheese side.

Ben placed Kyle's slice onto his own plate then put a cheese only slice onto Kyle's plate. His son rewarded him with a smile and reached for the plate. Why he hadn't just said something, Ben wondered. He met Ellie's gaze and read the question in them. "Later," he mouthed.

· · ·

KYLE'S EYES drooped by the end of the meal. Ellie asked if Kyle usually had a bath before bed. When Ben nodded, she became almost shy, unusual for her. She asked, "Would it be all right if I gave him his bath and put him to bed?" At Ben's nod, she turned to Kyle. He stood up and held out his hand to her.

When Ben checked in on them a while later, they were both making motor noises with their mouths as they drove bars of soap through the water. Folding his arms and leaning against the door jamb, Ben asked Ellie, "What made you give him a bath instead of a shower?"

Ellie looked at him like he was a moron. Probably only because of Kyle's presence did she not tell him so. "Ben, he's a little kid. What did you think? How old were you when you switched from baths to showers? Don't you even remember being a little boy?"

Come to think of it, she was right. They had always had baths when they were children. It was only in his teen years that Ben could remember showering. Just one more example of why he wouldn't be getting any Father of the Year award.

After Ellie read Kyle yet one more Dora the Explorer book and they both tucked him into bed, then Ben and Ellie each nursed bottles of stout in front of the fire.

"So, come on, big brother. Give. I want all the details." Ellie continued, "But first, when are you gonna buy that kid a bed? Just how long are you going to have him sleep on the couch in your office?"

Ben had actually forgotten that that might be a problem. Kyle's first night with him, it had seemed like a huge problem. He'd had no idea where to put the kid, until he spied the fold-out couch in the den.

Ben's condo had two bedrooms. Since he lived alone, he'd turned the smaller room into a den. His desk took up most of the middle of the room, one wall was solid book case and a leather fold-out couch took up another wall. When it was folded out for Kyle at night, there was barely room to get between the desk and the wall. Kyle's suitcase was open in another corner of the room, with clothes and toys and books strewn over almost every square inch of visible floor space. Ben had been meaning to clean it up, but had gotten distracted numerous times. It was a daunting task, because just where was he going to put things? His desk drawers were full. The book shelves were filled and there wasn't room for a dresser in the room.

Ellie wasn't finished. "And, did you watch how close Kyle's head came to the corner of this coffee table? Several times, in fact, when he was sitting on the floor." Ben looked at the offending table. It had come with the place when he hired a decorator to furnish it for him. The half inch sheet of beveled glass sat on a molded ceramic base, sculpted to resemble something or other. Ben had never figured out just what. It was a table to put stuff on and doubled as a foot rest when he watched television. Looking closely now, he noticed the dozens and dozens of little finger prints all over the glass surface. He guessed that Millie had not been here for a few days. She must be the one wiping and polishing its surface.

Was that fair to Millie? Perhaps this wasn't the most kid-friendly sort of table. Looking closer, neither was the white Berber carpet its base sat on, nor the white leather sofa. Actually, when did this room get so white? Ben knew it had been the same since he moved it, and had never given his decor any thought. Who in their right mind wants to live in an all-white room? And who was expected to keep it clean? Wouldn't something dirt-colored be more practical?

ELLIE WATCHED him steadily as these thoughts flittered through his mind. She would wait no longer for her answers, so Ben plunged in.

He told her how he and Deanna had dated years ago, but parted amicably when she accepted a job offer in California. He'd not heard from her again until she called one night, upset. Honestly, when she identified herself as Deanna, it had taken a second for him to place her. Ellie's face mirrored Ben's initial shock when Deanna told him he had a son.

"Did you question if it really was your kid?" Ellie asked.

Ben paused and looked at her. If Deanna said he had fathered the child, he had no reason to doubt her. The timing fit. Roughly. Ben dismissed that thought from his mind.

"So, if she hadn't needed money, would you ever have known you had a kid?" Ellie said.

"I'm not sure. I'd like to think she'd have let me know, but she didn't when she was pregnant and she didn't for Kyle's first two years of life. God, am I that unapproachable of a bastard?"

"No. You said that she said she wanted a child. You were likely an acceptable sperm donor."

Ben just looked at her.

"You may be my big brother, but I'm not blind. I've seen women look at you. Don't let it go to your head, but you are good looking. And, at least most of the time, you're an okay guy."

"Thanks. At least I think."

Ellie made carry on motions with her index finger.

Ben continued, telling her the reason Deanna called was that she needed money. Ellie rolled her eyes. Ben felt the need to defend Deanna. After all, she had never asked him for anything for the previous three years, when she certainly could have. She'd gone through the whole pregnancy and baby thing without any help at all from him, the father, the one who should have shouldered the responsibility.

There was more to it, he told her. Kyle had not been an easy child and by age two he wasn't talking. Deanna had taken him to doctors and therapists for help and to figure out what was wrong. They gave Kyle a diagnosis. Autism.

Ben watched his sister. She didn't look shocked or surprised. Was he the only one who didn't know about autism? She nodded at him to continue.

Kyle needed treatment. The therapists Deanna went to told her that the only proven treatment for autism was something called Applied Behavior Analysis or ABA for short.

"Okay, so what's the problem?" Ellie asked.

Money, he explained. The treatment was expensive.

"Well, you have insurance. She probably has insurance through her job as well."

It was not that easy, Ben told her. Insurance would only cover a part of it and the rest had to be dredged up by the families.

"Just how much are we talking?" Ellie asked.

It was hard to give an exact figure, depending on how the child responded, but it usually worked out to about sixty thousand a year.

"Dollars?" Ellie's eyebrows rose.

Ben nodded. A year. It cost so much because the treatment was individual and required a trained therapist.

"Hokey. That therapist must be raking it in for a few hours office visit a week."

Ben shook his head this time. "There aren't office visits. The therapy is done in the home and it takes up to eight hours a day, five days a week. Then on the weekend and evenings, the parents are supposed to carry on using the same methods."

Ellie was incredulous. "That's forty hours a week, the same as an adult works. When's the kid supposed to play? To nap? To just be a kid?"

Deanna had been told that this was necessary if she wanted to have a good outcome for Kyle's life. If he had this therapy, early intervention, they called it, then Kyle would be cured and ready for regular education when he hit school age.

"How did she come up with the money for it?" Ellie queried. Then, before Ben could reply, she said, "You. Of course. That's just like something you would do. No wonder you've been putting in the hours you do these last few years."

They sat in silence a minute. Ellie, not usually tactful with him, asked, rather hesitantly, "But, does he seem cured to you?"

Exactly Ben's thoughts. And those of Melanie and even the school principal had seemed to recognize autism in Kyle within just a few minutes of meeting him.

"No." His word hung in the air.

"So that's why he doesn't talk much." She waited a few moments.

"But I wonder what he was like before? Maybe he'd be a lot worse if he had not had that ABA. Who knows?"

After a few minutes, Ellie apologized. "Sorry for ragging on you about this condo and Kyle's bed. You have bigger worries at the moment."

ELLIE LEANED FORWARD to grab a remote off the coffee table. She looked at the three remotes laying there, each with more buttons than any one of hers. "Which one turns on the TV?" she asked. "Sheesh. What does anyone want with all these buttons?"

Ben reached for the right one and turned on the news. It was a family tradition to watch the eleven o'clock newscast.

"That's another thing. Kyle. That kid is amazing," he told his sister.

She grinned at him. "I see you're already a doting dad. Nice to see, bro.

Ben turned a bit red and carried on. "That first night I got hardly any sleep. Sheesh, this was just dumped on me. I knew nothing about being a father. So, I guess I slept in a bit the next morning and heard noise in the place. I thought someone had broken in.

"I grabbed my pants and went down the hall, trying to be silent until I saw what was up. There was Kyle, sitting beside the pointed end of that coffee table, watching TV. At least at first I thought it was a television show but it turns out he was watching a DVD - one of his DVDs. A Dora one." His sister gave a knowing grin.

Ben continued. "You know how I am about my electronics equipment."

"Boy, do I ever. You chased me all the way down the block once when we were kids when I'd touched your precious stereo system. And, you've only gotten worse over the years."

"Yeah, well, this stuff's expensive and I put a lot of time into getting exactly the right components.

"Just now you had trouble with the remotes and couldn't even turn the TV on. Would you be able to load and play a DVD? No, I know you wouldn't. I'm not sure most people would, if they weren't familiar with my system.

"I had certainly not shown Kyle how to do this. In fact, I had told him not to touch anything along this wall." Ben pointed to his elaborate shelving system of electronic components. "But here he was. He's five years old, had woken up in a strange place and instead of crying, coming to get me, howling or any other kid thing, he came in here, figured it out and was watching his movie. Yet, he can hardly talk. The kid's a strange mixture of can and can't do things."

"From what I gather, that's autism," Ellie said.

"How would you know that?"

"Because I'm from this planet, you dork? Don't you listen to the news? Read? You hear about autism all over the place nowadays. I think Time Magazine had named Temple Grandin one of the one hundred most influential people of our times."

"Temple who?"

"Oh Ben, you are clueless sometimes. Temple Grandin. She's probably the most famous person with autism. She's a prof at Colorado U, world famous for her innovative cattle handling systems, plus she lectures and has written books on autism. She has autism."

"She has autism and she can do all that?"

"Ben, get with it. There are all kinds of people with autism. Silicon Valley is full of them. Some people with autism need full care all their lives, others are independent."

"So, maybe there's hope for Kyle?"

"Jeez, Ben. You obviously have a lot to learn."

"Thanks for that reminder, little sister." He grabbed for her foot, long years of practice reminding him how much she hated having her feet tickled.

With three brothers, Ellie was adept at avoiding their torments. She rescued her foot then made herself comfortable, snuggling in with the comforter from the arm of the couch.

"It's late and the bakery's closed tomorrow," she told him. "I think I might just crash here for the night, if you don't mind."

"Even though you're a brat, you're welcome to my bed and I can take the couch."

"Thanks, but I'm comfy right here. You're white couch might be impractical, but it's just made to sink into."

THAT RETURNED Ben's thoughts to the impracticality of this condo for a family, even a family of two. "I wish Kyle could live in the kind of place we had growing up. He needs more room and a yard and an actual neighborhood."

"Well, why don't you move?"

"This place is so handy to my work, just two floors above the office. It was fine when there was just me. But, you're right. The kid can't grow up without any space of his own, living out of a suitcase and crashing on my spare couch."

"I thought you were saving up for a house deposit."

"I was, but I had to give all that to Deanna for Kyle's therapy. I also had to start a college fund for him when I heard I had a kid."

"But you rake in a ton of money. You're always working; you put in more hours in a week than anyone else I know."

"*Did* put in more hours. That's had to stop now that I have Kyle. Who's going to look after him while I work, and I think I need to spend some time with him. Jeez, I'm just getting to know my son after missing the first five years of his life."

Ellie looked at him, mulling over these problems. She dreaded that she was about to add to them.

Ben continued, "I've got a bit of the problem cased now. Remember Millie? The woman who comes in twice a week to clean and cook?"

Ellie nodded.

"Well, she's agreed to give up her other cleaning jobs and work just for me. She'll be here every day until 6:30 when I get home from work. And, she'll pick Kyle up from school, which solves a real problem for me."

. . .

"Out with it, El. What's bugging you?" He knew her too well.

"I hate to add to your problems," she said.

"Out with it."

"Okay. I know you have a lot on your plate, but it's the usual. Money and the bakery."

No surprise there, thought Ben. "Anything special this time?"

"No, just dad and everything. We won't be able to make payroll again this month." This was not new although it didn't happen every month, usually just when the bakery's quarterly mortgage payments were due.

The bakery was, in the parents' words, a family business. The trouble was, the majority of the family had nothing to do with it and, more importantly, wanted nothing to do with it. Sure, they'd all worked there as kids - it had been expected. But of all four children in the Wickens family, only one had an actual interest in the bakery - Ellie.

But, of all four kids in the Wickens family, only one was deemed unacceptable by their father to take over the bakery from him - Ellie. And the reason? Because she was female.

Yes in this day and age, there were still a few chauvinists around. Their father was at the head of that list. Sure, Ellie was good enough to work in the bakery, but to run it? Impossible, their father said. Forget the inhuman hours that Ellie put in. Forget the fact that she virtually ran the place.

Well, the last fact wasn't exactly forgotten; it had never been recognized by their father. For some reason, he believed that he still ran the bakery when everyone else knew differently. In a way though, you could see how their dad could have the wrong take. He still went into the bakery some days. He still threw in supply orders. He still gave orders to the staff.

The problem was that all these things he did harmed the bakery. Truly. He still lived back the way things were twenty years ago. If he saw the invoice of an incoming shipment, he'd be aghast at the prices and refuse to accept the order. Then the bakery not only lost the product but had to pay restocking fees.

He'd pop in, look at the shelves and order new supplies, not considering that Ellie might have done this just that morning. When customers asked for a latte or espresso, he'd tell them that they served coffee, just plain coffee and refused to use the bistro machines. Although the bakery ran smoothly on the days he was absent, he would still come in and give the staff orders that conflicted with their usual, efficient way of doing things.

THERE WAS no talking to the senior Mr. Wickens about these things. He refused to acknowledge Ellie's role in managing the bakery. The only way he would discuss the running of the bakery was if one of his sons agreed to take over. His sons, not his daughter.

The oldest son had fled to New York. Their father still held out faint hope that Jonathan might uproot his children from school, his wife from her law practice and himself from his job to return to take over the bakery. Since he was a chef, he was already in the food business. Right, their dad reasoned. It all fit. Everyone but their father knew this would never happen. Jonathan had even used words about hell and freezing over the last time he was asked.

Their youngest brother, Samuel, had joined the armed forces to escape their father and the bakery. Of all of them, he had hated the most the hours he'd slaved over making dough and waiting tables. He craved a life of outdoors and action and physical activity.

Then there was Ben. Since he was the only son remaining in the city, their father made it clear that it was now up to him. He said it was Ben's responsibility to take over and to provide for his parents in their old age. Rather than taking up the reins and apprenticing (read slave labor) with their father right after high school, Ben had left for college. But, his choice of major won grudging approval from their father. After all, accounting skills were needed in the bakery, just like any other business.

But Ben had absolutely no interest in the bakery. Instead, over time, he'd started his own accounting firm. Perhaps his early work training in the bakery contributed to his overzealous work ethic, but the long hours had paid off and his accounting firm was thriving. Not that it didn't require constant care and attention on his part, but it was doing well.

So well, in fact, that Ben had propped up the bakery for years. Like many small businesses, it struggled. Under Ellie's guidance, it had limped into the twenty-first century. But whenever their father spied any hint of this change and progress, he'd in no uncertain terms stomp on it. This back and forth cost money in terms of waste and staff. Staff would quit, unclear who their orders should come from. They'd get used to doing things one way, and then Mr. Wickens would pop in and change it all. In the past year, they'd lost two baristas, both fired by Mr. Wickens as needless frivolities. The customers who had come to look forward to the creations served up by these people stopped dropping by. When Ellie introduced low-fat alternatives and soy milk, her father threw out the stores, and ran the products down vocally in front of both staff and customers.

Maybe the bakery could have weathered these storms. Maybe. But the worst hammer that hit their books was the mortgage payments. The second mortgage payments to be exact.

Their parents had purchased the bakery thirty-five years ago. By every estimate that Ben and Ellie could guess at, the bakery property should have been paid off ten years ago at the latest. But, it wasn't and five years ago, their father had taken out a second mortgage on the property.

No one had any idea why or where the money went. No one, that is, except their father and he refused to say. The bakery was his business, he told them and since Ben wouldn't take it over, then the finances were none of his business. And Ellie, well, their father just discounted her entirely. They'd asked their mother numerous times, but she seemed to know no more than her children did about the financial end. Her husband had always handled the money in the family, as fitting a man's role, she told them.

But the quarterly payments for this second mortgage were killing Ellie and the business. Fearing that they'd lose the place, Ellie made these payments above all other bills. But that left a gaping hole every three months for staff salaries and often for suppliers as well.

Step in, Ben. Yes, he had, out of obligation to his sister and to his parents. After all, he was making all right money and what did he have to spend it on? True, he wanted a house - a house with a yard and in a neighborhood where people actually knew each other. As a kid he'd hated when it was his turn cutting the grass but now at the ripe age of thirty-three, owning grass that needed cutting had appeal.

But, his house down payment savings account was now barren, given to Deanna for Kyle's ABA treatment. He didn't resent that, not one bit. For the past few years when he needed to come up with extra cash for the bakery, he'd simply worked longer hours and taken on more clients. Now, his ability to do that was seriously impeded. He had Kyle to look after and needed to spend time with him.

Ben vowed not to be the kind of dad his father had been to him. There was never time for his kids - looking after children was women's work. Never once could Ben remember his father coming to a Little League game or a school play or graduation. Always, the bakery came first.

When he was not at the bakery, their father was home in front on the television with a drink in his hand. When their dad was home, everyone else in the house tiptoed around. They could not disturb their father and that included trying to talk to him. Often the kids would see their dad passed out in his recliner when they went to bed at night and rise in the morning to see him still there, snoring, with unwashed, unpleasant odors emanating from the chair. No one else ever sat in that chair, partly because it was their father's place and partly because no one else wanted to go anywhere near that grubby fabric.

The unwashed part and the hangover/ drunken part had then and still did cause the bakery staff turnover. He was not a pleasant man to work for. Maybe he had been at one time, but not as long as either Ellie or Ben could remember. When they asked their older brother, Jonathan, he replied, "Why do you think he's there and I'm all the way up here in New York?"

Ellie was desperate to save the bakery. Without her constant effort and running interference every time their father showed up, they would have lost the place to foreclosure several years ago. Even Ben's infusion of cash would not have saved the place from mismanagement.

Ellie had a plan, one she pleaded with Ben to accept. But, he wouldn't. While he didn't mind handing over money without their father's knowledge, he refused to be underhanded enough to go along with her plan.

What Ellie wanted was for Ben to take over the business. This was exactly what their father wanted. Except, in Ellie's mind, Ben would head it in name only. He could leave all the day-to-day work and management to Ellie and their father would never have to know. In Ellie's mind, this was the only way she was ever going to get the bakery and make all the changes that needed to be done.

But, to Ben's mind, this was dishonest and deceitful and he refused to lie to their parents in that way. He was willing to argue all he could with their father to get him to change his mind and pass on the business to Ellie. He'd back his sister all the way. But he would not lie and pretend that he was the owner. They'd been back and forth on this so often each knew the other's arguments by heart, but Ben would not budge. His hope was that their father would be forced to come to his senses and he worked on their mother, trying to get her to help out.

In the meantime, it fell on Ben's shoulders to come up with the money to keep the damn bakery afloat.

"What do you need, El, and when?" he asked her.

"I'm three thousand and a bit short next week's payroll and delivery bills."

Ben tried not to let Ellie see him wince. At one time that would not have been impossibility. He could have written a check for that amount from his savings, then replaced that money by doing a couple extra contracts that month. But now, his savings were no longer flush. Any spare funds he had would now go to the extra money he would be paying Millie to come in every day and be with Kyle, money well spent.

But what to do? In the past, he'd simply spend every night working. He was home alone, so it was no problem. But now he had to spend those evenings with his little son and he wanted to, he really did.

Kyle went to bed ideally by eight o'clock so that should give Ben time to get more work done then, but cripes, it certainly had not worked out that way so far. He had no idea how other parents did it, but by the time he had Kyle in bed, tidied up the place a little and prepared Kyle's lunch to take to school, he was whipped. Working twelve hour days at his accounting firm was a piece of cake compared to spending less than half that much time with one little boy. And to think, some people actually had twins.

CHAPTER 8

*H*e studied the chess board and moved his rook to cover his
castle. At first he thought he'd have purposely let his son
win these games, because it would hardly be fair to trounce a five year
old time after time. But the more they played, the more Ben had to
actually think to keep up. His kid was no slouch at chess. Ben could
never have imagined that someone so young could be so skilled at this
game.

Sunday at home. Ben often took half of Sunday off to just relax or
be with his parents and sister, although those latter two things rarely
went together – relax and his family. But for today, Ben would not
think about those things, but focus just on his own, new family of two.

Waiting between moves gave Ben time to think and sip his coffee.
They'd come a ways these past weeks, the two of them. Calling them a
unit would be stretching things, but they were on their way to neutral
ground and some level of understanding. He thought they'd each
given in, just a little. Well, a lot on Ben's part, he reflected but even a
little was a lot for a kid with autism, he realized.

Now that Ben had read some more, yeah, his son did seem to have
autism. Some of the stuff he read on the internet was downright
terrifying – parents in physical battles with their grown autistic

children, violence, fear, tears, frustration. But then you read the other stories of kids with autism who were in college, or adults with jobs and families. How could you ever predict which of these outcomes would be Kyle's? Ben squared his shoulders. He knew which were in line for Kyle. Kyle would make it. He would be successful and hopefully independent. And if not, then he'd still have his dad in his corner.

There was this pat, pat, pat on his knee. Ben looked. Yep, his king was cornered. Yet again. He looked more closely and could discern no viable move. A look at his son confirmed his fears. The kid had got him yet again.

Ben grabbed him under the arms for a tickle. Kyle's giggles were music to his ears. It was getting near lunch time, so he picked him up and perched him on his shoulder to head into the kitchen. Instantly Kyle's sounds of glee turned to terror. He clutched at his father's hair, clinging to life.

"Whoa, whoa, little man. Easy. Easy. You're safe." Kyle's cries did not diminish. Ben couldn't set him down because of Kyle's grip on his hair. It was making his eyes water. "Kyle, it's all right. I've got you. I won't let you fall." In desperation, he sat himself back onto the couch, rolled to his side to put Kyle there as well. Inadvertently, he partly rolled on Kyle. As he pressed the little boy into the cushions, Kyle's cries notched down some decibels and the grip on Ben's hair lessened. Ben started to roll off the child, fearful of crushing him. As his weight shifted, Kyle's grip tightened and his cries rose again. Ben lowered himself back onto Kyle and again, the cries became less strident. Ben remained that way for several minutes, feeling the tension leave Kyle's body. They remained pressed together for five more minutes before Ben dared move again. By then, Kyle's hands were loose at his sides and the noises changed to the light sounds of a sleeping child.

Ben looked at his son. How could the kid go from hysterical to sleeping? Ben's heart was still pounding and he felt ready to jump out of his skin. Yikes. What had he done to the kid? He'd ruined what had been a good moment with Kyle, one of the few times when he felt they were truly bonding and having fun together. Then he had to go and hoist the kid in the air, scaring him.

How was he to know what Kyle liked and what would scare him? This parenting business was all trial and error. He so did not want to screw things up, but it looked like he was doomed to just that. Poor Kyle to be stuck with such a parent. He hadn't exactly lucked out with his mother either.

Ben covered Kyle with a heavy comforter, a thing his grandmother had made when he himself was just young. Kyle slept on. Ben went to the kitchen to make some grilled cheese sandwiches for them.

When they were ready, he brought a tray with lunch into the living room. Although he'd assumed Kyle was still sleeping, he was sitting on the floor, his head precariously close to the sharp corner of the thick glass coffee table. His eyes were fixed on the TV screen where Dora the Explorer gets a puppy. Kyle seemed unaware that Ben had entered the room or set down the lunch tray. Ben called Kyle's name three times, each with no response, each with rising frustration. The television wasn't on that loud. What was the matter with the kid? Where did he get off thinking he could ignore his father like that?

Again, reason asserted itself and he remembered what Ms. Nicols had said. Show, don't tell. Well, he had no pictures on him, but he did have the sandwich. He moved it in front of Kyle's face. Kyle reached for it. Ben held it back, waiting. Kyle reached again. Ben prompted, "What do you say?"

"Please," Kyle responded.

Ben gave it to him. Well, at least they were getting somewhere. He corrected himself. It was obvious that Kyle had learned basic manners long before he came to Ben's house. Ben just needed to learn how to prompt his son to use them. He was getting better at it; they both were.

They ate their lunch in silence, watching the adventures of Dora. Kyle continued to watch; Ben dozed. He was startled awake by movement beside him. Kyle had left his spot on the floor and crawled onto the couch beside Ben. He snuggled in and didn't stir when Ben moved his arm to put it around his son. His weight felt warm. His hair smelled like little boy. Ben drifted back to sleep thinking that Kyle had forgiven him for that ill-advised air toss. Maybe he could make it as a father after all.

MEL SAT IN HER CAR. "BREATHE," she told herself. "In through the nose; out through the mouth. Practice those calming breaths." How could she teach her students calming strategies? How could she handle any crisis her class threw at her, yet could not get through one dinner with her family in peace?

Once upon a time, they had weekly family dinners. Mel would spend Sunday afternoon and evening with her parents and brother. But these last few years, the tension had grown so thick; she could only bear to come once a month at the most. Come to think of it, they no longer invited her any more than that. Well, at least they were all on the same page on this one point.

She slipped out of the car, more pressing her door shut than slamming it, hoping no one heard the sound. She felt guilty trying to sneak in, but it was the only way. She walked on the grass, muffling her footsteps, around to the side door. No one used this door, but her brother.

Grinning, she picked up the miniature oil can she had left under the steps several months ago. She squirted a few drops on each of the hinges, replaced the can, then carefully opened the door. No squeaks.

Inside, she avoided the middle of the old steps and made her way down the stairs. Once at the bottom, there was no need for stealth. The basement suite had been well sound-proofed so her parents upstairs would not be disturbed by Jeff's activities. Her older brother still lived at home and spent almost twenty-four hours each and every day within these basement walls.

Picking her way across the room, Mel avoided the piles of dirty (or maybe they were clean - who could tell?) clothes on the floor. Jeff wouldn't care if she stepped on them, but his acute hearing would immediately tell him if her foot trod on a CD case or any of the electrical components strewn around in what Jeff insisted was an organized fashion.

Stopping within a foot of him, Jeff was oblivious to her presence. His gaze was intent on the computer screen in front of him. He focused on just the one, ignoring the programs flashing on the other two. Mel's heart sank as she recognized his avatar.

Jeff was playing Second Life™. The online game advertised itself as the place to connect, to work, to explore, to be different and to be yourself - all the things Jeff wasn't good at in the real world. For Jeff, this game was his world. It made Mel's blood boil. What a waste. What a crime. And, she placed the blame squarely on her parents.

Knowing better than to startle him, Mel moved into Jeff's peripheral vision. No response. She moved closer, calling his name and pressing into his side.

"Yeah, yeah, I'll be with you in a minute. I can't stop right now," Jeff told her.

Melanie sighed. She wondered how long he'd maintained that stiff posture, head and shoulders tilted toward the screen. She looked at his hair. It was clean, and he didn't smell so likely he'd not spent all night doing this, although it had happened before. Often.

"Okay. I'm good now. I just had to finish that part," Jeff explained. "How are ya, Mel?" He gave her shoulders a quick hug, carefully keeping only his arm in contact with her body.

In return, Mel put both arms around her big brother and gave him one quick, hard squeeze. He tolerated it.

"I'm good," she said. "What's new with you?"

That started Jeff into a detailed monologue about some new activity he was into on Second Life. Once he got going on a topic, it was hard to derail him. From experience, Jeff recognized her signal. Mel held up one hand between them, in a stop motion. Since they were kids that had been their signal that he was talking too much and needed to let her have a turn.

"Oh, sorry, Mel. It's just so neat that...."

"Stop!" Mel told him. That's not what I meant when I asked you what was new. I meant in the actual world, not on the computer.

"Are you going to start that again? Geez Mel, you just got here."

"I'm sorry Jeff. It's just that I worry about you. You're my big brother; you're way smarter than me and you're stuck here in this basement."

Jeff's shoulders turned away from her. His eyes returned to the computer monitor where a screen saver flashed his avatar. She was losing him.

She tried again. "Didn't you tell me you were going shopping last week?"

"Yeah. The latest version of...." and he was off and telling her about the newest game he had bought. Mel sighed. Jeff played computer games. Jeff created computer games. He taught himself programming languages to enhance the games he had. And he did all this with no formal training.

JEFF HAD two passions - computers and cooking. As he was growing up their parents let him do the former but not the latter. The kitchen was their mother's domain and rare was the occasion when she'd allow Jeff to "mess it up". So, any cooking Jeff did, he did at Mel's house.

"Are you spending the weekend at my place? If you give me your list, I'll get the groceries."

Jeff rummaged through the papers scattered on his desk and produced a coffee-stained print-out. "Remember to get exactly what I wrote down," he reminded her. "Is there anything there you don't understand?"

From experience, Melanie knew it would take her days to scour the city for all the ingredients on Jeff's list. He took his inspiration from the food network on television, and some of the items were not exactly the staples found in normal households. But, when she tasted his creations, the shopping efforts were worth it.

She had something specific on her mind. "Would you make me something special this time? There's a new kid in my class. He and his dad came over to play with Max. He's kind of a lost kid and doesn't have a mother. I tried to make him some chocolate chip cookies, but they were nothing like yours. I'd like to have some on hand in case he comes again."

"Since when do your students come to your house?"

"Oh, never mind. Is supper ready? I suppose I should go say hi to the folks."

"Yeah, I'll be with you in a little bit. I just have to do some more here..." and Jeff was back into the world of Second Life. Watching him, Mel didn't know if she was more mad or sad at what his life had become.

HER MOTHER LOOKED over her shoulder when she heard the basement door open. She stirred the sauce on the stove. "Hi, honey. Nice to see you," she began. Then she looked closer at her daughter's face. "Oh. You're not going to start that again, are you?"

"God, mom, how can you stand to see Jeff just sit there day after day when there's a big, wide world out there and he has all this talent?"

"He's doing what he wants."

"How does he even know what he wants? He's never had the chance."

"No, he didn't have the same chances you had. It's different. You weren't born with autism; he was."

CHAPTER 9

little after ten the next morning, Ben dropped in at the condo to welcome Millie. She was pouring herself a cup of coffee.

"Any regrets, Millie? Is this arrangement going to work for you?" he asked.

"I'm looking forward to spending time with the little one, but right now, I'm relishing the peace and quiet of your place. Then I'll start picking up around here and...."

"Yeah, sorry about the mess. We had a bit of excitement last night. Actually, more than a bit.

"I did something really stupid," he confessed. I was going to fry us some steaks so I heated the oil in the pan. Then the phone rang and I got caught up in talking with my sister, Ellie. You've met her before."

Millie nodded.

"While I was on the phone, I guess Kyle came into the kitchen and saw that the pan was smoking. I can only guess what happened next, but I heard him screaming and came in to find the pan on fire, and a tea towel on fire, wrapped around Kyle's arm. I panicked."

"Oh the poor little lamb. Is he all right? Is he here?" Millie got up to go to Kyle.

"I don't know how, but he's all right, just one burn on a finger. His shirt was trashed but I think I got to him in time and all that happened was his skin was a bit reddened on his arm. When I think of what could have happened, what almost happened...Kyle deserves a better father than me. I almost caused a fire and he could have been killed."

"Do you think you're the first parent who has ever forgotten a pan on a burner?"

"It's inexcusable. A parent is supposed to take better care of his kid."

"Yes, you're right. But all of us do the best we can at the time. Kyle's okay, you said."

"Yeah."

"Did he seem traumatized by the whole thing?"

"No. That's a funny thing. I certainly was, but he seemed okay. Ellie came over and she was less shaken by it than I, but then, she wasn't here and it's not her kid."

"When I arrived this morning, it smelled faintly of smoke. I looked around but couldn't find anything wrong."

"Well, if you look, you'll find one less frying pan in the cupboards."

"We'll survive that, I imagine. But these walls look a bit dinghy. It takes a special compound to wash away the traces of smoke. I'll bring some with me tomorrow."

"You don't need to do that. Tell me what to get and I'll pick it up. It's my mess you're cleaning up."

"And it's my job to be the cleaning lady."

"Thanks. Millie, I don't mean to be rude, but you look a bit tired today. Are you all right? Is this job going to be too much for you?"

"I may be almost old enough to be your mother, but I'm not that old. In fact this job and working at just one place and looking after a little boy all seem like less work than I've been doing these past few years. I love Kyle already and you've always been good to work for."

"But...?"

"It's nothing to do with you and this job. My nephew, my late husband's brother's eldest son is living with me. His boss relocated him here just for six months to oversee the opening of their new branch. He's a dear fellow. So are his wife and four children. They couldn't find a house big enough for them all that didn't require a one year lease. He didn't want to spend that kind of money when they're only here for six months.

"My house is huge, as you saw and there's just me in it, so I told him they could move in with me. I can use their rent money to get started on some of the repairs that need doing. I know you noticed them; I could see it on your face."

"Sounds like a good arrangement."

"It is. And, I shouldn't complain. It's just that I'm used to being alone even though I do get lonely and complain about how quiet it is in that rambling house. Now, it's not quiet. Oh, no. Two more adults and four kids certainly fill up a place. There is always noise, music playing, the television on, someone running up and down the stairs, kids bickering, the fridge opening.

"Listen to me. I sound like a cranky old woman. I can see that they are trying, really trying not to be intrusive, but I'm the one who feels like she's intruding on their space."

"Sounds rough," Ben said. "At least it'll be quiet here as soon as I shove off and before Kyle gets home from school. Even then, he's a pretty quiet kid. When he's not screaming, that is." Then he added, "But I think the screaming happen less often now and maybe doesn't last as long. Either I'm getting used to it or getting better at heading things off."

Ben put his cup in the dishwasher, picked up the mail and headed back upstairs to work.

Unusual for him, he had trouble getting his mind back into his files. Sorting through the mail, he spied the monthly condo board newsletter. Ah, that should either put him to sleep or make him eager to get back to work.

The newsletter included a list of the number of people waiting to purchase condos in this building. Good to know in case he ever wanted to sell. The newsletter also included a listing of any condos for sale at this site. Ben saw that the penthouse was available. Hmm. Those things didn't come up often. The owner had to leave the country temporarily and was looking for a tenant for eight months, beginning next week. Ben winced when he looked at the rent they were asking. Other than the price, maybe that's where Millie's nephew should have moved his family, leaving Millie to the peace of her own house. But then, the penthouse only had three bedrooms. Three bedrooms plus three bathrooms and a small den.

Ben paused. Could this be the answer to his problem about Kyle not having a room of his own? Three bathrooms for just the two of them might be a bit much, but it was more space and still in the same building so he was close to work. Maybe it would take him five seconds more in the elevator, that's all. Ben continued to read the description. This suite came with a wrap-around balcony, each eight feet by ten feet long on two sides of the condo. A concrete balcony wasn't quite the same as a backyard for a kid to play in but at least it would offer some fresh air without having to go outside the building.

Ben did some calculating, something accountants were good at, naturally. He'd bought his condo when prices were in a slump and things had risen considerably. Judging by others for sale in the building, he could get almost double what he'd paid for it. And, thanks to his fanatic work hours and hoarding of money, pre-knowing about Kyle, the condo was well on its way to being paid off. Putting in double the required payment every month paid off. Actually, considering what he paid into his mortgage, he could just about swing the penthouse rent. And that would give him a few months to figure out where he wanted to live.

Three bedrooms, three bathrooms. I wonder, Ben mused. The timing was right. He called the building manager.

Ten minutes later, he and the manager shared an elevator ride to the penthouse. The owners had already left for Europe, putting their belongings in storage. Ben prowled the empty place, thinking about possibilities. Yes, if he and Kyle took the two smaller bedrooms and offered the master suite to Millie, she'd have her own bedroom/sitting room and bath. He wondered if she might even remotely consider moving in with them, being a live-in housekeeper. That would solve her problem of living with her nephew's family and certainly solve Ben's child care problem. She'd be getting free room and board plus her present salary, in exchange of looking after the house and Kyle.

He'd need to be careful about giving her her own space and any time off she wanted, but it just might work. It would certainly free up more of Ben's time to work. The den was small, but if he organized it properly, it would be a fine place to work at home, without needing to run back to the office in the evenings. The den opened off the living room, without even a door to mar his view of Kyle playing.

"Millie, will you come with me a minute? I'd like your opinion on something." On the ride up in the elevator, he told her of his frustrations over his condo being too small. While it had been fine for one man alone, having Kyle changed things. Millie had noticed, boy had she noticed, she said.

Ben showed her the master suite last. As she exclaimed over its spaciousness and view on two sides and how the furniture could be arranged, Ben worked up his courage to present his idea.

"Listen, no obligation at all. I want your honest opinion. If you don't like the idea, we'll stick to our original arrangement. I just thought that it might be a solution to both our problems, at least temporarily."

"Okay, Mr. Wickens - Ben, get on with it."

When he outlined his proposal, she was quiet, too quiet. Ben started to back pedal, fearing he might lose Millie all together.

"No, you have it wrong. I can hardly imagine living in such a grand place and yes, this seems like an answer to my prayers. Are you sure about it? This seems a hasty decision."

"The paperwork might take a bit of time but I could put in an offer today. We'd need furniture and I'd need to list my place, but I don't think there will be a problem selling it. It was a show home and I could sell it with all the original furnishings."

"It's a deal, then. My nephew and his family, dear as they are, will be pleased to have my house to themselves."

· · ·

NOW THAT MILLIE was fetching Kyle from school in the afternoons, Ben found that he missed that job. It was the few extra minutes he had with his son, Ben told himself, nothing to do with passing the time of day with Melanie. If he did enjoy seeing Melanie, it was for the tips about managing his son that he looked forward to.

It was Friday and over a week since he'd seen his son's teacher. It was time to probe her for more hints. Millie was heading back to her house to have dinner with her nephew's family and to pick up a few more of her things. The family's van had fold-down seats that would transport some of the furniture Millie wanted to use in her new room in the penthouse. Ben was heading to the school for Kyle.

HE CAME HALF an hour early - not a tardy father, he thought. That gave him time to slip into the back of the room to watch. Watch his son, of course, not his son's teacher. His timing was good, giving him a chance to watch a lesson in *How Does Your Engine Run?* ®, part of the Alert Program®. It was always the way Melanie started off the school year. That way the kids all used the same terminology and were on their way to learning ways to manage themselves.

Ben leaned against the back counter, after waving to Kyle, and listened. The children were giving Melanie examples of when it was all right for their engines to run high, like at recess, when they should be low, like before falling asleep at night and when their engines should be in the middle, like right now. On the white interactive board at the front of the room was displayed a gauge that resembled a car speedometer. Kids pointed to various places on the gauge to show where they felt their engines were right now.

Then the discussion changed to things the kids could do to alter their engine speeds. They gave a number of examples, many of the children pointing to things they used in the classroom, like the different seating options and the weighted products. One kid talked about Theraband™, something new to Ben. He watched as the little boy said, "See?" and demonstrated with his feet. Attached to the front legs of his table was a stretchy band. The student put his feet on it and pushed back and forth. Well, if he seemed to think it worked for him, at least it was a quiet activity that wouldn't bother anyone, Ben thought.

Jordan, the child who had given Ben the Hokki™ to sit on that first day of school kept watching Ben. His steady gaze made Ben squirm. He hated to think that he wasn't comfortable with people in wheelchairs and likely that wasn't it. The kid just kept staring.

Jordan called out, "Ms. Nicols, Kyle's dad is wiggling too much. His engine is running high and he needs to do something about it." All eyes turned to regard him, making Ben fidget even more. Melanie grinned at him, enjoying his discomfiture.

Lori weighed in. "What would you suggest he try?"

Answers popped up from all around the room. "Eat something crunchy. Sip water through a straw. Chew gum. Sit on a ball. Sit on a wiggly cushion. Use a lap weight."

Melanie looked at Ben. "So, you've heard the suggestions. Which do you think might work for you?"

"Would running out the door work?" he asked.

The kids giggled. Kyle got up and dragged over Melanie's Hokki™ stool. Jordan said, "It worked for him before."

Ben planted himself on the wobbly stool and tried to find his balance. He so did not want to fall on his butt in front of Melanie and Lori and all these little kids who were expertly perched on all kinds of contraptions. He got the hang of it, continuing to wiggle, just a little.

"Feel better?" Melanie asked.

Ben gave her a sardonic look of thanks. In a few minutes, actually, he did feel better.

As the kids filed past their teacher, each pausing for their, "hug, high five or handshake", Ben waited just outside the door. He wanted to talk to Melanie before taking Kyle home. He looked up to find Lori watching him, amusement on her face. He looked away quickly. What did she know? A father would do a lot for his son, wouldn't he and it certainly didn't hurt that the source of his advice was not bad on the eyes.

But as the last child left the room, Melanie hustled off down the corridor. He called after her and she gave the one minute signal with her hand, but kept going. Ben and Kyle stepped back into the room, Kyle heading for the beanbag chair and bookshelf area.

"She'll be back soon," Lori told him, "She has a lot to battle right now."

"What do you mean?"

"You haven't heard the controversy? About how some parents are trying to shut this classroom down?"

"Why would anyone do that? Even I can tell that the kids are happy here and progressing. Just look at Kyle. She's a fantastic teacher. Why would anyone want her fired and what can I do about it?"

"It's not Melanie they're trying to get rid of, but this classroom. It's the whole integration concept they don't like."

Ben looked blank.

"Look," Lori continued. "Haven't you noticed how small this room is, how there aren't very many kids in it? Most kindergarten classes would have half a dozen more kids. And most schools would have a class for typical students then another room for only those with special needs."

"Like Jordan?" Ben asked about the most easily identifiable child.

"Kids like Jordan and like Kyle," Lori corrected. "In this room we have eight kids with special needs and eight typical kids. Plus me, the educational assistant."

"Eight kids with special needs. Which ones are they?"

"Hah! The point exactly. You can't tell. That's the point of integration and from students learning together. Life is not a segregated affair, they're all going to have to learn to live together and learn from each other.

"But some parents don't see it that way. They fear that the special needs kids will take up so much of the teacher's time that their precious baby won't receive enough attention and progress at the proper rate. I could tell them that their kids are going to end up further ahead than those who are in a straight K room."

"K?" Ben asked.

Lori smiled. "Kindergarten. Sorry – school lingo." She continued. "The other issue is money, of course. The parents' group complain that this program is too expensive, having two adults in the room for just sixteen students. But they're getting a bargain. My salary is half of what they pay a teacher. If this room wasn't here, they'd still be paying Mel to teach the Special Ed class. I'd be out of a job, or at least this job, but they'd probably end up putting me in the room the eight typical kids get moved to because thirty K kids all together is too much for one teacher to manage. So, there would be no money savings, just one crowded classroom and one half empty one."

"So what's Melanie doing about it?"

"She's meeting with the principal right now. Dr. Hitkin supports this room and she's a staunch supporter of Mel, but this goes farther than her power. Parents have gone to the school board and there's a meeting tomorrow night."

"What happens if things don't go the way you want?"

"Then come Monday or at least the following Monday, this classroom will look very different. It might have just the eight special needs kids in it and the other students will be dispersed into the other classroom. That would make that room overcrowded and the parents' precious children would get even less attention than they fear they're receiving now."

"What can I do?"

"Well, if you really want to help, show up here tomorrow night at half past seven, in the gym. Just the moral support of parents coming out will help Mel, even if things don't go the way she's fighting for."

A YOUNG MAN came to the door of the classroom. Ben moved aside and the man drew Lori, the EA, toward the back of the room. Something about the guy made Ben take another look, but Lori smiled as the guy kissed her cheek lightly, so Ben withdrew, giving them some privacy.

Several minutes later, he poked his head in again, hearing raised voices. After all, his son was still in the room. He didn't like the look on Lori's face; her usual, open grin was missing along with her confidence. The guy had a grip on her arm. As Ben watched, Lori pulled back but didn't get far as the guy tightened his hold on her. He heard Lori tell the guy to leave her alone; she didn't want to go with him tonight.

That was enough for Ben. He was about the guy's height, but had twenty pounds and ten years on him. It might not be his business but he could not stand to see Lori intimidated by this dude.

"I heard the lady tell you to leave her alone. Step back, please," Ben said.

The guy looked him up and down but didn't loosen his grip on Lori's arm. "Who are you?" he asked.

"A friend." He put threat into the words. "Now, step back and let her go."

"Ben, please, it's all right," said Lori, although her eyes didn't tell him to go away. Ben stood his ground. "I told you to let her go," he reminded the man.

The guy eyed the two of them, weighing his options. He released her arm, giving it a shake. He retreated with, "I'll see you later."

Ben asked Lori, "Is that all right? Do you want to see him later?"

"It's all right. We used to see each other but I've been kind of backing off lately and he isn't taking it that well."

"He looks like someone you might want to be careful of. Are you sure you're okay?"

"Yeah, thanks. You know, we weren't sure at first, but Mel's right. You are a nice guy." Before Ben could ask what she meant by that, she was gone. Had Mel actually said he was a nice guy?

MELANIE RETURNED TO THE CLASSROOM, walking too fast. Lost was the relaxed air she had around the children. She stopped short, surprised to see Ben still there. Was he that forgettable, he wondered? Apparently so. The look on her face worried him. "Are you all right?" he asked.

"I am, or I will be. It's just that some people are so short-sighted. What we're doing here is good and it's right. All the kids are benefitting."

"You don't have to sell me."

Melanie looked at him skeptically. "I thought you didn't want your son in a classroom with those kids?"

Ben sheepishly remembered the things he had said that first day. Well, when you're wrong, you're wrong. So, he said, "I was wrong. I didn't know. Kyle is exactly where he should be and he's already doing so much better. I'm doing so much better. Thanks to your help and your ideas, my son and I are all right. I gotta tell you, those first few days I didn't know if we were going to make it."

Melanie relaxed and smiled at him. "You would have been all right. I didn't know about you at first, and wondered if you were the sticking around kind. It's not easy to raise a child with an autism spectrum disorder and some parents bolt or fold under the pressures."

Ben looked offended that she would think he'd be like that. Then he remembered that that's exactly what Kyle's mother had done. Well, Kyle was his for good now and nothing could pry them apart. Ever.

Watching the expressions flit across Ben's face, Melanie had the impression that this guy really was a keeper. For Kyle, of course, she meant.

"That brings me to why we're still here. You've already helped me so much with Kyle and I appreciate the time you've taken. But I'm going to ask another favor of you, if you have the time. I know this is a lot to ask but I don't know who else to turn to." He hesitated.

"Go on."

"Look, the place we're living in is awful. It's not actually an awful place and it wasn't for a bachelor who's hardly ever at home. But for a child it's just not right. We're living in a two bedroom condo, but the second bedroom is my office. Kyle's sleeping on a fold-out couch in that office. The room's small and already full with book shelves, a desk and the couch. There's no room for Kyle's things, he's living out of a suitcase and there's no room for him to play."

He had her full attention, so went on. "The living room looked okay to me, prior to being a father. The furniture is all white leather. There's a white carpet and in the center of the carpet is this glass monstrosity of a coffee table, perched on some kind of sculpted base. The glass is about a half inch thick with pointed corners. I've cracked my shins on them a number of times but I'm worried Kyle will knock his head on one. When he plays on the floor, his head is close to those corners."

Okay, he was babbling. Get to the point. "So, I'm going to sell the condo. We're moving into the top floor condo in my building. It has three bathrooms, three bedrooms and a small den off the living room. Millie, the woman who used to cook and clean for me twice a week has agreed to move in with us to help with Kyle. She'll have the master suite and space of her own. She's a widow with her own house, but her nephew and his family moved in with her for six months and she's finding it crowded."

This was way, way too much information. Something about this woman made him nervous. "So. I'm going to sell my condo as is, with all the furnishings. It was a show suite that some big deal decorator did up. But the new place is empty. I need furniture and I need it fast."

He looked appealingly at her, hoping she'd sifted through all this and figure out what he was asking. Obviously not, because she just looked at him. Try once more. Why was this so hard? She'd either say yes or no and what did it matter? It's not like he was asking her on a date.

One last try. "Will you help us?"

"Help you what?"

God, she must think he was an idiot. "Help us furnish the place. I have no idea what a kid needs and you seem to know so much about kids in general and Kyle especially. I want a home that's comfortable for a child, not some designer show piece that even I'm not comfortable with." He tried to grin. "Please?"

She grinned back. "When?"

When? It was that easy? Why did it take him a huge monologue when all it would have taken was one sentence? "Tomorrow." He hastily added, "If that's all right with you. I thought we could go shopping and have lunch or something. To pay you back for helping us, of course."

"Sure." They grinned at each other until Kyle's weight leaned against Ben's leg. He was tired of waiting.

CHAPTER 10

*K*yle and Ben were in the park near where they'd agreed to meet Melanie the next morning, indulging in some more leaf-jumping, leaf-throwing while they waited. Across the way they spotted Melanie, sitting on a bench overlooking the pond, her back turned to them.

He had an idea. Signalling to Kyle to keep quiet, he grabbed an armful of leaves, gesturing for Kyle to do the same. Then he pantomimed tiptoeing and the two Wickens men advanced stealthily towards the unsuspecting woman. When they were close enough they each let out whoops and threw their leaves over Melanie's head. Too late, Ben at the last minute remembered that women didn't like getting their hair messed up and Melanie might be mad at them. What if she hated having bits of dirt and crawly things on her head? What if she refused to go shopping with them? What if she refused to hang out with them ever again?

Melanie turned around, looking at one then the other of them. Then she grabbed her own handful of leaves and tore off after Kyle, mashing leaves all over his head. They fell to the ground laughing together. Then Mel whispered to Kyle and they both turned to look at Ben. He backed up with both arms outstretched as they advanced on him. Not paying attention to where he was going, the back of his knees hit the bench and he sat down, hard. Instantly, Melanie was on him from behind, holding his shoulders down as Kyle threw leaves all over him, all over all of them.

Well, at least she didn't seem mad.

Brushing themselves off, they headed back toward Ben's condo, so Melanie could take a look at the space they were going to furnish. Kyle walked between them, reaching for each of their hands. Ben glanced over to see if Melanie minded, but she was relaxed, probably far more relaxed about holding the hand of a child than he was. Every so many steps, both he and Melanie would raise their hands, giving Kyle a swing in the air. Unlike the time Ben had raised him toward the ceiling, Kyle liked this ride.

No, Melanie wasn't mad. She even seemed to be having fun with them. Like a family. Now, where did that thought come from?

As THEY ENTERED THE LOBBY, Kyle led the way to the stairs. Ben tensed. He'd totally forgotten.

The first time he tried to get Kyle into the elevator, it had been fine until the car started to move. Kyle totally freaked. Totally. Ben had been unprepared and even if it happened again now, he'd have no idea how to cope. He had solved the problem by forsaking the elevator for the stairs from then on. Or, at least whenever Kyle was with him. Climbing three flights of stairs would keep him in better shape anyway. Right? And although it might seem like a lot of steps to an adult, a five year old seemed to handle them no problem.

But what now? The penthouse was on the fifteenth floor. There was no way they were going to trudge up all those stairs. Ben looked helplessly at Melanie, fresh out of ideas. He seated Kyle in a lobby chair and pulled Melanie to the side to explain the problem and how he'd gotten around it so far by taking the stairs. Melanie threw him a disapproving look, as if this was his fault. Well, what was he supposed to do? And how were they going to get Kyle to the penthouse now? He had not thought about that at all when he signed the papers to lease the new condo or when he'd signed to put his present condo on the market. What had he done to them now?

"Do you have any paper? A pen?" Melanie asked?

"What?" Ben didn't understand.

"Pen? Paper? You know that stuff we use to write?"

Ben sighed. He reached in his pocket and gave her his pen and a small notebook.

"Huh. Moleskin. Nice," she said.

Quickly Melanie sketched out stick figure drawings of the three of them standing close together in a little box. She drew an arrow pointing up. "I'm making Kyle a social story," she told Ben. This did not seem like a social moment to him, but whatever. She did seem to know how to handle Kyle.

She explained to Kyle what an elevator did and gave him far more details about the pulleys and operating systems than Ben thought any small child should have to hear. He was surprised that Kyle listened intently. She then showed him her drawing and hurriedly made another one.

"Kyle, today you have a choice. Today, you have a choice. You can ride in the elevator two ways. Remember in class when we read that book about the monkeys and how the baby monkey clung to its mother?"

Kyle looked at her unblinkingly. Melanie seemed to think he was following her.

"You have a choice. You can ride in the elevator standing between your daddy and me, holding our hands. Or you can ride hanging on to the front of your dad, just the way the little monkey did to its parent. And, any time during the ride you can change your mind and ride standing or with the tight hug.

"Then when we get out of the elevator we're going to see the new condo. We'll measure it to see how big the stuff we buy should be. I will need your help holding the tape measure."

She stood, took his hand and led him to the elevator door. He tensed and started to pull away. She shoved the picture she'd drawn in front of his face and repeated her story, pointing out Kyle, Ben and herself in her drawing. Having averted crisis number one, she engaged Kyle's attention with the elevator buttons. She had him push the up button.

"Now watch it. Watch closely and you'll see it change color. When the color changes we'll hear this little ding sound. Right after that the doors will open and we'll get in. Once inside, we turn around and will see more buttons. I'll tell you which one to push. Now watch that button closely, please and tell us when it changes color."

Through her machinations, they actually got inside the elevator. She instructed Kyle about which button to push; Ben had to lift him up to reach the P for penthouse. They were fine even when the doors closed, but not when the elevator started moving. Kyle tensed and put back his head to howl.

Melanie got on her knees, so her face was level with Kyle's and placed her hands firmly on Kyle's shoulders, pressing down. His eyes were wide with fright. "Kyle, Kyle," she said. "What is your choice - standing with us or monkey ride?"

Kyle couldn't seem to form any words. Melanie repeated the choices. Kyle turned to his dad and raised his arms. Ben reached down, and enfolding the little boy in his arms, stood. Melanie arranged Kyle's legs around Ben's waist and his little arms around Ben's neck. Kyle's face was buried between Ben's chin and collar bone. Breathing was a problem for Ben, part from the squeeze of Kyle's arms, part from being overcome with emotion himself. His son was terrified, yet trusting Ben to protect him. What a responsibility. What an honor. Over Kyle's head, Ben's eyes met Melinda's. "Thank you," he mouthed.

MELANIE INSPECTED what seemed like every visible inch of the condo, approving of Millie having the master suite and taking measurements of the living room, den and Kyle's room. Ben's room he could do himself, she told him. It needed his personal touch. What would she say if he told her he'd like her personal touch in that room? Banish that thought, he told himself.

. . .

WHAT KYLE ENDED up with was not what Ben had imagined. The pieces Melanie chose were of good quality, sturdy but not overly pricey. She bypassed the bright-colored shiny pieces, saying that Ben wanted Kyle's bedroom to be a quiet retreat, a place conducive to relaxing and sleep. But there were fun pieces and plenty of places to hide. His bed looked like a circus tent, albeit a taupe big top. No gaudy colors. The bed section was reached by scaling steps at the end - nothing like the ladders from bunk beds of Ben's childhood, but these ones were an actual set of stairs running along the end of the structure. There were handrails and the steps were enclosed on the sides so Kyle wouldn't fall off. As a bonus, each step was a storage box with a pull-out drawer. Nice touch. The top bunk was draped with a circus high top curtain. Melanie insisted that Ben climb atop with Kyle. When he protested that it might not bear his weight, Mel said then they'd better find out now before they bought it. Gingerly Ben climbed the stairs and stretch out on the bed, testing its solidity before allowing Kyle to join him. Once inside, it felt cozy like they were in a tent. There was a clear window so Kyle could look out and the drapes could be pulled back if he didn't want them.

Under the bed was a walk-in area that contained a child-sized desk, chair, lamp, book shelves and storage areas. Again, this area had curtains that could be opened or closed, depending on the child's mood. And, best of all, the side of one curtain had a flap that could be opened if they wanted to put on an old-fashioned puppet show.

The closet would have built-ins with an adjustable hanging rod at Kyle's height now that could be raised as he grew. Instead of a chest of drawers, clear pull-out bins would hold the rest of his clothes, clear so Kyle could see what was in each container.

For reading and lounging, Melanie selected an adult sized bean bag couch, big enough for two cuddly adults, an adult and a little boy or several children. Melanie chose storage bins, all again in that same taupe color that would hold Kyle's blocks and puzzles and toys. There were similar ones in bright oranges and reds and greens but Melanie vetoed them in favor of dull colors that didn't stand out. "Trust me," she said, "You'll thank me later." Ben certainly did have a lot to thank her for.

The living room ended up with leather again, but not white. These were butter soft brown couches that invited you to sink in and cuddle up. A flick of the levers at either end of the couch turned that seat into a recliner with foot rest. Ah, what a way to watch the game.

There would be a coffee table, yes, but no more glass with sharp edges and nothing precariously balanced on a base. Solid wood with rounded corners and inset tile on the top. Easier to maintain than wood when small children spill their milk and juice, Melanie explained.

Ben's stereo equipment would have a safe home with components that Kyle would use easily within his reach. There was no point in putting them higher because Kyle would just climb to reach them. He was going to use them anyway and had already shown his proficiency.

The rest of the condo furniture came together quickly. The den was furnished as a work space for Ben, yet with space for Kyle. Mel explained that since Ben would likely be spending a lot of time in there, Kyle would want to be with him and Kyle would want to mimic his dad. So there was a big desk and a child-sized desk. There were storage shelves for Ben's books and shelves for Kyle's books. Ben had a matching filing cabinet and Kyle had a not-quite-so-matching storage cabinet with pull-out bins instead of drawers.

This place was going to have such a different feel than his present condo. It would feel like a home, something that was currently missing. Ben hadn't really noticed before since he spent little time at home anyway and even less time thinking about his surroundings. In fact, he gave so little thought to decorating that when it had come time to furnish his offices, he hired the same decorator that had done his apartment. He did this not because he was particularly enamored with her style, but because she was the only decorator he'd heard of and her business card happened to be posted in the lobby.

Much as Ben thought he hated shopping, this had been fun. They'd actually played in the stores, bounced their butts on countless sofas and pretended they were sitting on the couch eating pizza and watching TV. Cheese pizza only Ben had remembered, earning him a grin from Kyle and a head on his arm. Ben hid his face hoping no one would see just how much this gesture from Kyle meant to him. Melanie saw, though, but didn't comment. She kept her thoughts to herself, grateful that no one knew how watching Ben with his son affected her.

Lunch had been gyros at a mall food court. Glorious, messy gyros they enjoyed, Kyle especially getting as much on him as in him. The adults did not escape the sauce and Melanie reached with a napkin to wipe some off Ben's cheek, before drawing back embarrassed. He said, "No, go ahead. I can't see it there." She continued, not meeting his eyes, his not leaving hers. She made a show of cleaning up their tray and saying they needed to get going if Kyle didn't want to end up sleeping on the floor.

At one point Ben had become so used to Kyle holding each of their hands that he automatically reached for a hand when they left the store. To his surprise the hand enfolded in his own was Melanie's. Kyle appeared on his other side and took his hand, grinning at both of them. Ben grew red and started to apologize. Melanie squeezed his hand but didn't withdraw. She didn't meet his eyes but left her hand there. Ben didn't know how the day could get better. His son's teacher was really something. A good sport, smart and practical. And beautiful. The kind of woman a guy could get used to.

He stole a glance at her. What was she thinking? Was she just doing her duty for one of her students, one of her more needy students, considering what a dud his father was? Of course that's what it was. This woman was a true teacher, dedicated to her profession and to the kids in her charge. Look how she'd lit into him each time he screwed up with Kyle. Yes, she was doing this for Kyle since the poor kid had such a clueless dad.

Melanie herself wondered what in the world she was doing. She had a firm policy to keep her professional life and personal life separate. She never dated anyone she worked with. And, she most definitely never dated the parent of one of her students. That would be unprofessional. She could not recall any school board policy against it or anything in the teaching code of ethics, but certainly it just made sense.

Plus, this meant nothing to Ben, she was sure. He had asked for her help because he didn't know where else to go. Obviously he could not rely on the decorator who had furnished his sterile, impractical condo. She shuddered, remembering how it had looked. Definitely not the environment for a young child or anyone for that matter who wanted to be comfortable.

Yes, Ben had been right to ask for her help. She knew Kyle and she knew kids and she knew autism. That combo was what he needed. That's all this was. She should not delude herself into thinking there was any more to it than that. Sure they'd had fun. Why not? Why make shopping drudgery. Yes, they'd had fun in the park. Why not? Didn't even harried businessmen need a chance to unwind and play sometimes? That's all there was to it. He'd been playing with his son and she just happened to be nearby. The whole day felt so good just because she'd been under stress with this whole school board thing. That's all there was to it.

THE PLAN WAS for Ben and Kyle to drop Melanie off at her home so she could get ready for the school board meeting that evening. But the adults had not counted on one little boy and one big dog. Max was waiting for them when the car drove up and he was wild with excitement to get at Kyle. Kyle was just as anxious to get out and romp with Max. So, Melanie and Ben ended up sipping glasses of wine on the back deck while boy and dog raced up and down the enclosed yard, indulging in a game with rules that were a mystery to all but the two of them.

The sun was losing ground on the horizon. The leaves were tinged with autumn colors. The two lounging in the chairs were mostly quiet. But, it was a good quiet, the kind where companions didn't need to fill the space in order to be comfortable and content in each other's presence. Ben didn't know when he last felt this relaxed. Well, yes he did - the last time he and Kyle were here at Melanie's. In fact, he'd felt so relaxed that time that he'd acted like a jack ass and fallen asleep on her. Smooth move, dude.

He asked her, "Have you forgiven me for passing out in this chair last week?"

She laughed at him. "You looked cute while you slept."

Hmm. Was that how he wanted her to remember him? Cute? What about handsome or manly or even hot? Cute was a long way from any of those adjectives. He'd need to work on his approach some more.

What was he thinking? Work on it? Why? Did he actually care what she thought of him? Well, of course he did. She was his son's teacher and they'd become friends of sorts. Did it matter that all she thought of him was that he looked cute sleeping and he was Kyle's dad? Yes, it did, it certainly did seem to matter.

"What?" Melanie asked. "Why are you looking at me like that, like you're sizing me up?"

"I'm thinking about what you said and I'm not sure I'm happy with you thinking I'm cute."

Melanie was embarrassed. "It's just a figure of speech. I didn't mean anything by it. I'm not coming on to you or anything."

"Why not?"

"Why not what?"

"Why aren't you coming on to me?"

"Jeez, Wickens, what are you talking about? We had a nice afternoon. Let's just relax and not spoil it."

Ben continued to watch her. "Would doing anything more spoil it? Or could it make it even better?"

"This is not the time or place. Kyle's watching." As she said those words, Kyle and Max raced around the side of the house. They could hear his squeals and laughter from the front yard now. "Thanks, kid," Melanie muttered.

Ben grinned. "I don't see you running away after him." He leaned towards her. She didn't move. Ben took Melanie's wine glass and placed it on the floor between them, along with his own. "I think we'll hear those two coming before we see them." He leaned closer, giving her time to pull away if she chose to do so. She didn't. In fact, she seemed frozen in place, staring at him. His hand reached behind her head, caressing the back of her neck, while looking into her eyes. Still, she didn't move. Ben put pressure on her neck, drawing her head closer. He lowered his own head then closed his eyes as his lips met hers.

Oh, thought Melanie. Oh. This was better than she had imagined and yes, she had imagined what this would be like if it ever happened. His lips were warm, his cheeks slightly chilled from the air, the taste of the Riesling on his tongue.

Wait! This wasn't right. She was a teacher with ethics and principles to uphold and this was the father of a student. She couldn't do this.

"Melanie?"

"Y-y-es," she stammered.

"Don't."

"Don't what?"

"Think. Don't think. Just quit it." And he went back to kissing her. Melanie, never one to take orders willingly, obeyed. And enjoyed.

CHAPTER 11

*B*en was early. Ellie was staying with Kyle and he had wanted to make sure he got a seat with a good view of Melanie.

He was certainly not into these kinds of meetings, or meetings in general that weren't absolutely needed for his business. He had almost not come, thinking it wasn't a big deal. When he'd said as much, Melanie had looked at him like he'd lost his mind.

She'd said that if it did not go the way she wanted, come Monday, Kyle's school world would look different. The classmates he'd come to know would be gone, or at least half of them. Lori would be gone. Mel would be there, hopefully, although even that was not a foregone conclusion. She might be sent elsewhere and a new teacher would take her place. Other special needs kids from around the district might be imported into the room. Maybe their exact room would shift and the remaining kids would be put elsewhere in the school or even in the district. Life as Kyle knew it would most definitely change.

THE GYM WAS NOT full but there were certainly more people there than Ben anticipated. He'd thought since there were sixteen kids in the room, maybe thirty parents would come, tops, then a couple school board people, the principal and Melanie. Instead there had to be at least four times that many people. The buzz of conversation was electric. Maybe this wouldn't be quite the boring Parent Teacher Association meeting he'd thought it would be.

In a row of chairs along the front were a handful of men and women in suits, board members he assumed, plus Dr. Hitkin the principal and Mel. Actually, the description that came to mind first was his Mel. A day ago he would have knocked that thought out of his head fast, before it had time to take root. But today, considering the afternoon they'd spent together, maybe, just maybe, it was not so wrong to let his thoughts drift in that direction.

Ben had always assumed he'd have a wife and family one day. Even the white picket fence bit didn't scare him off. But all that seemed so far away, a one day dream. It might have moved closer toward that dream if the right person had come along, but that had never happened. Hell, what chance was there of meeting someone when all he did was work twenty-four seven? Nah, his work wasn't to blame. That was his choice and he liked it, the challenge, the drive, the hours and the feeling of success.

Then Kyle had burst into his life. Well, he had part of the dream now, just not in the order he'd thought and not in the manner he'd wanted. A planful person, Ben liked to be in control. He thought things out, made a plan, took charge and followed the path he'd laid out. It worked, always had for him. Then, Kyle. Nothing about Kyle was planned. Well, perhaps his conception was planned by Deanna, but not by Ben.

Ben was not in control with Kyle. In fact, the little man had blown into his life and taken over control. Did that mean he was a chip off the ol' block? Ben smiled to himself. The kid certainly did have a will of his own. No, Ben was not in control but that feeling was not as scary as it was a month ago. Although he knew that as the parent, he had to ultimately make the rules, his household was evolving into more of a shared power place where it was not all about Ben anymore, but life flowed around a pint-sized person. And, that was not so bad, he was discovering.

Mel was a lady who also liked to be in control; that was evident in her classroom. His original opinion of her had been wrong. The opinion had been honestly earned, the way she had glared at him at first and told him off each time he screwed up. He had deserved some of that, maybe more than just some. What he had seen as just bitchiness had really been her fierce protectiveness of the children in her charge. She truly cared and not just about their progress as students in her class, but cared about them as people and how they'd get along after they finished their year with her.

She cared. That was one of the first things you noticed about her. She even cared enough about Kyle and how he'd settle into his new life with his stranger father, that she'd offer assistance from how to run their home to how to furnish it. She really did go over and beyond what any teacher should have to do.

That was why she'd agree to go shopping with them, wasn't it? Or could there be anything more? Did she do this for all her students? Doubtful. But then, most kids wouldn't have such clueless parents.

Ben detested shopping - always had, always would. But, today had been fun. Rather than impatience with the waiting and the crowds and the time it took, he'd had fun. Honest fun. Why? It's not like children's furniture stores were exciting places to be, nor was a mall his idea of a hang-out place on a Saturday afternoon. But, the company had been good - great, in fact. Spending time with Kyle and Mel, what more could a guy ask for?

The meeting was called to order, just in time. His thoughts were heading in a strange direction best left uninvestigated.

LISTENING, Ben learned that Kyle's classroom was not usual - it was an experiment, the brain-child of master teacher, Melanie Nicols. It was her belief that students with special needs learned best in the company of their age peers, not in secluded classrooms without typical role models. On top of this, she also believed that typical students would also benefit from being with their counterparts who had extra challenges.

She said that while in our grandparents' generation, different may have been seen as wrong or needing to be hidden away, society has changed. Not only are we multi-cultural, but multi-ability. People with physical and intellectual handicaps are living and working with us. Kids with special needs who spend their entire school life in segregated classes will be less equipped to manage in the adult world. Typical kids who have grown up rubbing shoulders with those who have more challenges will be comfortable with differences. They will have learned to lend a helping hand when needed. Even more importantly, they will have learned to see past what lies on the surface and see the abilities that may be less obvious.

As the meeting progressed, research citing the benefits of integration for all students was explained and written copies were ready for anyone who wanted in-depth reading.

One father stood and asked just how much this experiment was costing them.

Dr. Hitkin, responsible for budget matters, talked about the economics. It was a given that all children deserved and must be provided with an education. That included all the children of the adults in this meeting, whether the child had a special need or not. It was the law. All these students would receive a free, public education.

In a school that had a segregated classroom, there would be a teacher, an educational assistant and a small number of special needs children. The number was set by state law; the adult/pupil ratio was small. For example, in Madson School, there would be a teacher such as Ms. Nicols, and an educational assistant with eight children.

The other eight students currently in Ms. Nicols room would have been with the other kindergarten class, bringing their total number to thirty-two - a lot of little ones in one room.

Being well aware of these numbers and having spent her Masters of Education work studying service delivery models, Ms. Nicols proposed combining classes. In addition to the eight special needs kids assigned to her room, she offered to take an additional eight students. There would still only be a total of sixteen children, far less than the anticipated thirty-two. This would also bring the numbers in the other classroom down to just twenty-four. The cost was still the same to outfit the two rooms and pay the salaries.

The benefit was to the students in the smaller classroom - all the students. Teachers like Ms. Nicols go through the traditional training common to any educator. But on top of this, Ms. Nicols had a specialization in exceptionalities. Her studies included disabilities of all sorts, on top of master teaching techniques, the kinds that benefit all children. Her training looked at methods of assessing an individual child's strengths and challenges. And, make no mistake; all children had strengths and challenges, just as did every adult in this room. Ms. Nicols was especially suited to looking at each child as an individual, designing and providing individualized programs to move each child along as far as possible. In her arsenal were far more than the usual range of teaching methods. These were extra sets of skills possessed only those taking advanced training in exceptionalities. All the children in her room this year benefited from her individualized approach.

Dr. Hitkin pointed out that no two of us learn alike. We all have strengths and weaknesses, ways that appeal to us and approaches that cause us struggles. Ms. Nicols took each of these facets into account and designed lessons tailored to the way your child learns best, and at the same time exposing them to other ways. While we have many talented teachers in our building, none has as much training as the teacher nurturing your children right now.

SOME PARENTS initially opposed to this classroom and wanting it shut down, became quieter. Still others adamantly demanded changes for their kids. They worried that their children were not receiving the attention they deserved. They worried that the curriculum would be watered down to a level far below their child's skill level. They worried that the kids with special needs would demand all the teacher's time and attention. What would happen to their kids in the next grade if they had not covered the kindergarten program?

To address this concern, test scores were projected on the screen. While names were removed, the audience could see where students were in September in the basic areas covered by the tests. Then overlaid on top of this were the mid-year scores. Everyone could see that every child had progressed. For some, the progress was slight; others had moved leaps and bounds. The lines were rarely even. Each child seemed to be moving at their own pace, some gaining half a year or more in the two months, others gaining the expected two months while a few moved only a couple weeks' worth.

Despite this evidence of progress, some nay-sayers still muttered.

BEN WAS NOT A PUBLIC SPEAKER, far from it. Although he'd make his opinions known in a meeting when warranted, his preference was to gather behind closed doors with his subordinates, debate and hone their collective thoughts, then let his staff present the consensus at client meetings. He'd found it worked well, built their confidence and skills and it certainly did his firm no harm to have him remain in the background unless needed.

But, this was different. He'd had no closed door meeting to prep ahead of time. And the way this gathering was going, things would go downhill for Kyle, for Melanie and for the other kids. Not only for the sake of his son, but for the other kids in the class, Ben felt he must offer his two cents to the discussion. He rose.

"At the beginning of the year, I shared many of your opinions. I took one look at the classroom they were putting my son in and said that I didn't want him in with those kids." People turned to look at Ben, a couple applauded. Dr. Hitkin frowned at him; Melanie glared.

He continued, "I was put off by the mixture of students in the room. I didn't even notice the low number; I was so out of touch with school systems that I didn't even know it was unusual to have just sixteen kids in a kindergarten room. I thought the economy had hit this school hard because kids didn't even get their own desks - they had to share tables. And, I thought the school couldn't afford proper chairs because the kids were perched on all sorts of things like one-legged stools, wobbly plastic stools, balls, cushions - all strange things to my eyes.

"The first time I observed, this kid - a little kid in a wheelchair kept staring at me. It made me uncomfortable, and I guess I was restless. The kid finally told the teacher that the man in the back was squirmy and needed a Hokki™, whatever that was. The teacher said, 'Good idea'. I ignored him. Then there's the sound of an electric motor and the kid somehow propels himself to this larger plastic stool that's tilted to one side. This little kid leans way out of his wheelchair to grasp the stool in his arms because he didn't seem able to lift with his hands. No one helped him. I thought that here's this poor little handicapped boy struggling and no one helps him. The kid got the stool onto his lap and wheeled it over to me. He made it obvious he wanted me to sit on it. I did. You know, the kid was right. I did need that crooked, wobbly stool. When I sat on it, I was less restless and my attention focused on what was going on at the front of the room. The kid watched me a few minutes then returned to the lesson. The others just carried on as if all this was normal. I didn't even thank the kid, something I still regret.

"That's the way this classroom operates. They observe each other and help each other. All of their contributions are considered and appreciated. They all have something to offer.

"I watched another lesson, one the kids call "How Does Your Engine Run™" from the Alert Program®. The language and concepts the students used were far more sophisticated than I'd dreamed of from five year olds. They were talking about keeping their engines or their attention at just the right level, revving high when they were out for recess, low when it was time for bed and in the middle when working in school. They offered each other suggestions for how to raise or lower their engine speeds. I saw five year olds, barely more than babies, getting things, doing things to help themselves work better. More importantly, they were not just following the teacher's directions, but figuring out for themselves what they needed to do and then just doing it. Oh that some of my employees would exercise that judgment." That brought a laugh.

"I'M new to this world of special needs and I came with lots of preconceived notions. I thought normal kids did stuff and other kids should do other things. I had limits in my mind of what certain children could or should do.

"My son has autism. I consider myself a bright enough guy, and like many of you, I have a college education. I'm a businessman and own an accounting firm. My son is five. We play chess. Try as I might, I rarely win. That kid whomps my ass." Some in the audience laughed, others turned to look at him. Ben didn't care.

"My ideas of what certain kids can and can't do were wrong. I set limits. I assumed that since my son does not talk much, he does not think much. I was wrong. I thought that because a kid was in a wheelchair that he couldn't think, or that he'd have nothing to offer me. I was very wrong.

"In my company, there are certain things I look for in employees. I want self-starters. I want people who can think independently. I want people who can work as part of a team, who can problem-solve, who can work their way through conflicts and present ideas. These are the sorts of things I see happening in Ms. Nicols classroom and to a degree that blows my mind."

"I see the beginning of these things in your children when I visit their kindergarten classroom. The door is open and any of you would be just as free to observe.

"We live in a multi-cultural world now days. This includes multi-abilities, as Dr. Hitkin said. Even more than we do, your children will need to understand and get along with all sorts of people.

"What do we want from a school? I think that we want our kids to become educated and to have the skills to find a job afterwards. These are the things our kids are learning in Ms. Nicols' inclusion classroom. I would not want my child anywhere else." Ben sat down.

There was silence. And silence. Then in the far corner the sound of a clap was heard. Then another, a second later, followed by another after the same wait. That lone clapper was joined by another, and then another until much of the crowd clapped along, the pattern long since lost. Some parents stood, and soon a standing ovation filled the room. While not all parents stood or clapped, the critical mass tipped and the class was safe.

Ben slipped out the back door as the meeting broke up and the panel at the front surrounded Mel.

MEL PUTTERED in her kitchen feeling lighter than she had in months. She had not realized just how heavily it was all weighing on her. The thought of losing her class was too hard to bear. She'd feared that they wouldn't understand the progress the kids had made - all the kids. They'd become a community together, learning together, helping each other, playing together. Each and every one had progressed. Some were farther ahead than their counterparts in the regular kindergarten class down the hall. An integrated classroom, with the proper supports, did not hold anyone back. It was a win-win situation.

But she and Dr. Hitkin had worried about how to get that across to the public and to the school board. The kids had been tested up the wazoo and yes, they had the proof on paper that the students were learning at least at the expected rate. But how to demonstrate that without putting the audience to sleep with statistics, comparisons, graphs and test scores?

Inviting parents and board members to visit the classroom hadn't worked. Few actually came. Few that is, except Ben.

Ben. Help had come from an unexpected quarter. Ben had saved the day with his speech tonight. Who woulda thunk it? she said to herself.

Boy, had she misjudged him. Her first impression had been of a dead beat dad. The mom had gotten tired of single parenting and tried to make Ben own up to some of his responsibilities, dumping Kyle on him for a change. She'd assumed he was the kind of guy to take no interest in his child, to leave the hands-on child care to others.

Well, she was right in her assumption that he knew nothing about his son. That much certainly was obvious. He had not known his son, but as she later learned, that was through no fault of his own. Still, could he not have made more of an effort to be involved in his son's life? Perhaps he was telling the truth when he said he'd stayed away at Deanna's request so as not to confuse Kyle with two daddies. Maybe. And, he had said he supported them financially once he learned of Kyle's existence.

She smiled to herself. Ben. He'd looked uncomfortable at the parent-teacher meeting, certainly not a place he'd envisioned for himself. But when he spoke, people listened.

A part of her wanted to think that he'd stood up to defend her. That would have been nice. But realistically, why would he bother? She was his son's teacher and yes, she'd given him advice about Kyle, but it wasn't anything more than that. Couldn't be.

So, why was she conflicted? One part of her was proud professionally that Ben had defended her class and her teaching because she was good at what she did. He liked the changes he'd seen in Kyle and attributed them to Mel's teaching. He spoke so definitely and so eloquently that he'd swayed the crowd and her room was safe. Yes, he'd done it for his son's sake. Surely that was it. It only made sense.

A small part, a teeny, tiny part, buried way down deep in her heart wanted Ben to have done that for her. Not for any philosophical belief, not for the sake of his son, but for her. Because he cared and wanted to support her.

Okay, get rid of that thought.

She took her tea and snuggled back against the pillows. What kind of reading was she in the mood for? She had a new Janet Evanovich book on her bedside and a new John Locke book on her Kindle ereader. Hmmm.

Locke it was. There was always some vague romantic thread running through Evanovich's books; less so with Locke. Any hint of romance might make her examine her own life too closely and that would make her think of the afternoon she'd spent with Kyle and Ben.

That must be what it felt like to be a family. Kyle was such a sweetie. She grew close to all her students, felt like they were part her own. But it was different with Kyle; he was special. Maybe it was because he came to her such a lost soul, dumped by one parent and faced with this second parent who was a stranger. A stranger with no idea what to do with a child. They'd needed her. Her advice, that is.

Ben had actually listened, listened far more than she'd ever expected. He'd not only listened, but he took her advice, trying out each approach, reporting back on how it worked, and asking for help in refining it. On top of that, he'd researched and read on his own. When he came with fresh questions, they were intelligent and thoughtful. He really wanted to learn and he really wanted to help his little boy. It showed.

He was also not the stuffed shirt in a suit she'd first assumed. Watching him cavort in the park with Kyle had opened her eyes. There was more to him than a stiff businessman. He took his responsibilities to his company seriously, and he took on the responsibility of fatherhood just as seriously. But he was more than just serious. He knew how to have fun and play with his little boy.

He knew how to have fun with her, as well. Yes, the three of them had definitely had fun shopping today. Ordinarily she was an in and out kind of gal when it came to shopping but they'd dawdled and browsed and enjoyed the day. Who would have thought an uptight guy like Ben could unbend and have fun?

Drats! Her mind had wandered back to Ben again. Enough. Relax with some chamomile tea, find out how Donovan Creed was doing in the Locke book, and then have a good sleep. Her class was safe and that worry, the constant need to prove herself, was over.

Although Creed's adventures and misadventures usually held her rapt, not so much this night. Her mind wandered to lunching with Ben and Kyle, bouncing on mattresses as they tested out beds for Kyle, the pillow fight he'd had with his son. Yes, her thoughts were about Kyle and Ben as she nodded off.

CHAPTER 12

*E*llie gabs too much; she always was a pest. That's the thought that went round and round in Ben's mind. It had been a busy week, then a big day shopping plus the meeting at the school tonight. The tension in the gymnasium had been palpable and now Ben was tired. He just wanted to go to bed.

Kindly, Ellie had stayed with Kyle while Ben attended the meeting. She'd bathed and put her nephew to sleep. There was silence in the condo, or at least there would be if Ellie quit talking.

She was pestering him with questions, questions to which he had no answers. And, he didn't even want to think about such questions. She wanted to know about Mel, Kyle's teacher.

It seemed that Kyle had been unusually eloquent that evening, telling Ellie about their shopping spree, having lunch with Ms. Nicols, throwing leaves with Ms. Nicols, playing with Max, going to Ms. Nicols' house and on and on and on. All this information had Ellie honing in on Mel and Ben, wanting to know what was going on, what there was between them, and where this was headed - all questions Ben could not answer.

Luckily, siblings can be blunt with one another and Ben finally told El that he was going to bed. She was welcome to stay over or leave but he was tired and had had it for the day. Being the little sister, one who had learned the art of self-preservation while growing up with older brothers, Ellie knew when to pull back and regroup, waiting for another day to come at Ben again with her probing. She decided to go home but in her parting shot, said she was leaving so things would not be awkward if Mel came over the next morning. Ben sighed.

SLEEP DIDN'T COME AS EASILY as he'd hoped. Ben tossed and turned. Damn his sister. Her probing had struck a nerve and made it impossible for his thoughts to turn away from Mel. Every time he closed his eyes, there she was. His mind had a snapshot of her standing in the tree-dappled sunlight with her hair full of the leaves Ben and Kyle had thrown on her, her head thrown back laughing. Then there was Mel bouncing on a mattress in the store with Kyle. She lifted Kyle high in her arms so he could bonk his dad on the head during their pillow fight. Mel holding Kyle's other hand as they swung him along the sidewalk. Mel offering them warm cookies. Mel watching his son play with her dog. Mel leaning back in her lawn chair, her eyes watching his as their lips met. Yes, these were not the sort of thoughts destined to lull a man into sleep.

Ben woke with a start, his legs tangled in the sheets, his bed a wreck. What woke him up? There it was again. What had he heard? There. That noise. And movement. Someone was in the apartment. Kyle! He had to protect his son.

Hurrying out of bed took more work than usual, with his covers wrapped around his limbs. But he got out and searched the floor for his sweat pants. He felt vulnerable enough with a small child in the apartment; he didn't fancy facing an attacker stark naked.

Thankful for the thick hallway carpet, he crept towards the faint sounds. The kitchen was dark but there was enough illumination from the streetlight to show him that the kitchen was empty. The study with Kyle on its fold-out bed had its door still closed, just as it had been when Ben checked on Kyle before he went to bed himself.

Next, the living room. There was a faint glow and yes, the sounds were louder now. At least he was now in between the sleeping child and whatever he might find in the living room. Ben flattened himself against the hallway wall and peered into the room. No, nothing at eye level. But, looking lower, the glow came from the television. It was on. Someone was watching his TV.

Peering closer, Ben watched an animated little girl with a big head and monkey pal dancing across the screen to the music. Faintly, he could hear, "D-D-D-D-D-D-D-Dora..." Kyle! That was one of Kyle's shows.

Approaching the back of the couch, Ben could see not see the top of anyone's head - the couch was empty. Looking down, the flicking images on the television showed a small shape on the carpet beside the coffee table, that glass monstrosity the decorator had so raved about. There was Kyle, out of bed at two-thirty in the morning watching his Dora the Explorer™ DVD.

Disconcerted to see him, but relieved that they had no intruder, Ben bellowed, "Kyle!"

Kyle, engrossed in his show, had not heard his father's approach and was startled by the yell. His head swiveled around quickly, so quickly that his left temple whacked the sharp corner of the glass coffee table. There was silence for the space of three seconds, then either the pain of the bump or the surprise of Ben's yell caused Kyle to let out his own bellow. Just as that sound began to die down, Kyle noticed the blood.

Oh, the blood was everywhere. Ben had heard that head wounds bled profusely but surely no one meant like this. Maybe the white of the carpet made the growing stains more glaring. Maybe the widening pool spreading on the surface of the glass table made it worse. You could see the blood both on the table and in the pool beneath it. Worse though was the crimson soaking the little boy's purple dinosaur pyjamas and the worst was the rivers of blood coursing down the side of Kyle's tiny face. He screamed as one trickle of blood flowed into his eye, stinging him. Ben didn't know if the child was crying from pain or fear.

But, to Ben, it looked like his son was dying. He felt like wailing right along with Kyle. No. He had to keep it together. He had to get help for Kyle. He had to save his son.

He scooped the small boy up in his arms and cradled his head. Kyle clung to him, sobbing and bleeding until they were both covered in blood. As Kyle wiggled, Ben had more and more difficulty holding him snuggly as they became slick from the blood.

Right. First he had to get help. Nine-one-one. No, he could not stand waiting here until the ambulance came. They weren't far from the hospital, he'd take Kyle there himself.

First aid. What were you supposed to do with bleeding wounds? Cripes, he couldn't think. Ben had always considered himself calm and efficient, a cool head in a crisis, but all that had deserted him now, now when it mattered the most.

To the bathroom. He ran with Kyle in his arms and sat him on the bathroom vanity. A quick rummage brought out bandages. Bandages. How do you put one on when the skin is flowing with blood? Quick, think. What to do, what to do? Okay, pressure. Yes, that's what you're supposed to do. Apply pressure to help stop the bleeding. But how do you press on a little boy's head, especially when there is a gaping wound on that same head?

A towel. Ben's brain slowly started to function and he grabbed the damp towel off the nearby rack. He balled it up and pressed it gently to the cut, holding Kyle's head steady with his other hand. Kyle leaned against him, crying softly. Ben's heart rate slowed just a notch, enough for him to let out the breath he'd been holding and raised his eyes to the mirror.

What he saw ratcheted everything back into overdrive. Both he and Kyle looked like something out of a war-ravaged conflict. Ben's chest, shoulders and face were smeared with blood, some spots drying, others glistening in the bright vanity light. And Kyle, Kyle looked worse. His new pyjamas, selected by Kyle and Mel that very afternoon were unrecognizable. They were sodden and stiffening and dark red. His hair was matted with blood. There was so much blood on the right side of his face that a first horrifying glance would make you think he'd lost an eye.

Okay. Deep breath. Don't show your panic or you'll frighten Kyle even more. Think. What to do next. Try to stop the bleeding with pressure. He was doing that. Elevate the wound. Well, he had the kid sitting right side up, so that was as elevated as he was going to get. What else? Oh, right. Keep the wound clean.

What was he doing? How many times had he showered and used this towel, the very one he now held to the open wound on his son's head? He could at least have grabbed a clean towel.

"Hold on, Kyle. Sit right here little man and press this to your head. I have to grab another towel." With a steadying squeeze to Kyle's shoulder, Ben ran to the linen closet to grab a handful of clean towels. Returning, he threw the used one into the tub, folded a new one and gently pressed it to Kyle's temple.

As Kyle calmed and Ben calmed, Ben had Kyle hold the towel himself while he wet a face cloth with warm water and tried to wash the worst of the blood off the rest of Kyle's face, his neck and body. Gingerly he unbuttoned Kyle's pyjama top and rinsed off the drying blood.

"Are you all right to sit there a minute bud while I get you some fresh clothes?" Kyle nodded and Ben raced to the den. Once again he cursed the fact that his son was living out of a suitcase. It was too hard to find things in. Frustrated, Ben upended the suitcase, spilling the contents in a half circle around his feet, rummaging until he found a fresh top for Kyle. He grabbed his jacket as well.

Kyle had not moved and his crying had all but stopped. He watched Ben with big, trusting eyes that made Ben's heart break. How had he let this happen to his son?

He lifted him off the vanity onto the floor. Then he changed his mind and picked him up in his arms. He was not going to let this child out of his grasp.

Carrying Kyle into his bedroom, he set him on Ben's bed while he grabbed the first shirt he could find to put on his bare, bloodstained chest. Okay, they were ready for the hospital.

Picking Kyle up again, he walked with him to the closet where their coats were kept. As he removed the towel to help Kyle into his jacket, the bleeding began again in earnest, starting to soak the clean shirt. This was not working. How was he going to drive and hold this towel to Kyle's head, especially when Kyle was supposed to sit in the back seat in his booster seat where it was safest? Ben couldn't do it all. He needed help.

Mel. The name came immediately to his mind. He needed Mel. Oh, it was so true; he really did need her, in every way.

Would she come? If he called her, would she come to help him and to help Kyle? It was iffy if she would actually come out in the middle of the night for him, Ben, but she just might do it for Kyle. She was a devoted teacher and really did seem to care for the kid.

He tore his cell phone off the charger and dialed with one hand. His other held the uninjured side of Kyle's head firmly to his side with the towel pressed against the gash. He moved the towel slightly to take a look. Yes, the bleeding might be easing off again.

Come on, come on, Mel. Answer the damn phone.

"Hello?" came the sleepy question. "Who is this?"

"It's Ben. We need your help. Kyle's cut his head and it's real bad and we have to get to the hospital. Would you meet us there?"

"I'm on my way," was the reply, and then there was just dial tone in his ear. Despite the situation, Ben smiled to himself. His panic felt cut in half with just hearing those four little words.

Now, how to keep the towel firmly in place while he drove. Ben's eyes roved the kitchen searching for answers. His gaze lit on the junk drawer. Ah, ha. He eased Kyle that way and opened the drawer. Yep, he had some. He carefully folded a fresh towel and held it in place. He got out the scissors and handed them to Kyle, showing him how to hold them. Wait. This wouldn't work. They'd never get the stuff out of Kyle's hair.

He remembered seeing a cap when he dumped out Kyle's suitcase. He picked Kyle up and ran back to the den. Yes, there it was. Nope, that wouldn't work. With the cap on, there was no room for the towel. He threw the now bloody cap on the floor.

Back by the door was a cap of Ben's. Yep, it was big enough. Carefully holding the folded towel in place, he gently placed his hat over top of Kyle's head, towel and all. It fit. Sort of. Kyle turned to look at him, knocking the hat sideways, then half off. Not going to work.

Deep breath, try again. Back to the original idea. Towel in place. Dad's hat on. Kyle wielding the scissors, Ben the roll of tape. Round and round and round he rolled the tape around Kyle's head, holding both the towel and hat in place. Just for good measure, he wound more tape across the top of Kyle's head, down across his shoulders, under his armpits and back up the front side to meet on the top of the hat. Goofy looking? Perhaps. But would it hold things in place during the ten minute drive to the hospital? Probably.

"We're ready, bud. Let's go." Kyle resisted the pull of Ben's hand. Now what? This was not the time for the kid to get stubborn. Kyle tried to remain rooted to the ground. When Ben bent down to pick him up, Kyle told him, "No."

Ben bit back a curse. The kid had been through a lot. This was not the time to lose his patience with him. Kyle struggled to get out of Ben's grip. Ben let him for a second and ran his hands over his face in frustration. Kyle bent into the closet and returned with his shoes. He then threw Ben's out as well. Ben just looked at him. They were both in bare feet and it was late autumn outside. Which of them had kept their head? Kyle grinned at him. And, off they went.

BEN PULLED up to the emergency room door, parking alongside an ambulance. He unstrapped Kyle from his seat, lifted him into his arms and ran through the sliding glass doors. He paused only momentarily, deciding which way to go. A passing nurse, spotting the copious amount of blood once again covering both Ben and Kyle pointed him in the right direction, saying, "Go, go!"

Ben ran, Kyle's uninjured temple pressed hard into his dad's shoulder, Ben's one hand cradling the bleeding side, pressing on the hat and towel. Kyle, whose crying had pretty much stopped, whimpered in the bright lights and the unfamiliar smells. A passing intern's rubber soled shoes squeaked on the freshly washed floor, making Kyle struggle to free his hands to cover his ears. He buried his face in his father's shirt.

Just as Ben again hesitated, unsure where to go next, there was Mel. She stood waiting for them. One step behind her was a nurse, obviously alerted to their arrival. Mel half turned to her and beckoned towards Ben, confirming the nurse's guess that this was the case Mel had told her would be arriving soon.

Thanks to Mel's intervention, there was no sitting in the waiting room. They went right in, laying Kyle on a gurney draped with a thin, light blue sheet. Overhead was a light enclosed in a two foot diameter dull metal casing with handle grips on either side.

The nurse leaned over Kyle and smiled. "What have we here?" she said.

"He cut his head on the side of the coffee table. It's heavy and sharp and has no business being in a room where a little boy plays. This is entirely my fault."

The nurse just looked at him.

"Too much information," Melanie muttered. Ben started to speak but she shook her head at him.

The nurse ignored them both. "Let's take a look. Hmmm. How do we get this hat off of you?"

Mel looked from Kyle's head to Ben. "Duct tape?" she asked. "All you could think of was duct tape?"

"Well, it worked, didn't it? And, I was pressed for time." Ben said, his posture defensive.

Kyle stayed still, with only the odd tear on his cheek until the nurse murmured that she'd need to cut the hat to get it off. Kyle let out a yell.

"It's okay, bud. She's only cutting the hat, not you or your hair. It's okay, sh, sh, sh," Ben soothed. His words had no effect.

Mel thought a minute then stepped up. She asked the nurse for just a minute and pressed her hands firmly on each of Kyle's shoulders. "Are you worried about your dad's hat?" she asked.

Kyle quieted and looked at her. Someone had understood.

She continued. "It's your dad's old hat. He was going to throw it out anyway. He has other ones, better ones. And, I think he was planning on buying a new one, a special hat that comes in your size and his size so you can both wear the same hats when you go out.

Kyle's gaze zoomed in on his father's face. Ben nodded and confirmed that what Mel had said was true, even if this was the first he had heard of it. It did not sound like such a bad idea, anyway. "And maybe we could find one for Ms. Nicols, too."

Kyle smiled at his teacher and held his head still. The nurse started cutting and cutting and cutting, glancing up at Ben several times as she did so. "You didn't want this to fall off, did you?" she commented.

Ben would have defended himself again but he caught Mel ready to laugh at him. He smiled sheepishly in return then moved his gaze back to Kyle. His hand hovered close to his son's head as if he was ready to snatch the scissors from the nurse's hand if she so much as harmed a hair on the child's head. Mel, noticing Ben's jumpiness, reached over and took his hand. The gesture startled Ben, causing him to look at her in surprise. She kept her gaze on Kyle, but squeezed Ben's hand reassuringly. He squeezed back then folded his fingers around hers. It felt good, almost like they were in this together.

As the nurse cut through the layers enough to unearth the towel, she gently tried to pull it from Kyle's temple. He moved his head away, resisting her attempt and clamped both his own hands to the makeshift bandage.

Mel looked at Ben. "Did you tell him to keep that towel on his head?"

"Yes. I needed his help to keep pressure on it. I had to drive, you know."

"Kyle, you did a good job of helping your dad. But he only meant that you had to hold it until you got to the hospital. You're here now so it's okay to let go. The nurse needs to take a look. She'll help you."

With the towel relinquished, all three adults leaned in for a closer look. Ben felt sick. It was so much worse than he thought.

To Melanie, it was not as bad as she had feared. Ben's voice on the phone had sounded on the verge of panic, like this was a life and death situation. That's the way she had prepped the triage nurse, expecting the worst.

The nurse tut-tutted a bit then bustled about finding swabs and disinfectant. "We'll just wash this up a bit so we can have a better look. The bleeding's almost stopped now."

Almost stopped, Ben thought. He could clearly see it still seeping out the cut and running back through Kyle's tousled hair. Some lodged in the whorls of Kyle's ear; some ran on behind and onto the thin pillow.

The nurse moistened a swab then began dabbing at the cut. Her dabs were swift and sure and firm. Too firm, in Ben's opinion. He moved to grab her hand. Again, Melanie interfered, scowling at him. "Look at Kyle," she hissed in his ear. "Does it look like it's hurting him? Don't make him any more scared than he is."

Ben looked. No, Kyle was relatively relaxed; certainly more relaxed than Ben himself felt. He shifted his gaze to what the nurse was doing. Now that the area was cleared of dried and drying blood, the edges of the gash were clearly seen. Then the nurse wiped directly on the cut. The edges opened up and she wiped right inside! Ben stiffened and Mel stiffened the arm of her hand that grasped Ben's hand. She held more firmly and turned her body so that it was partially in between Ben and the gurney.

She was blocking him! How dare she? Ben thought. How dare she think that she or anyone else could get between he and his son. Did she think she could stop him from protecting his child? Ben could feel his ire rising. The adrenal that had shot through his body when the accident first happened had not subsided yet and those old adrenal glands were ready to pump out more at a moment's notice. Ben felt his breath quicken. Mel inched slightly more in front of him.

Not that she blocked much. He could see right over her shoulder, over her head for that matter. He looked at Kyle and the nurse's current handiwork. She was still dabbing right on the cut in short, firm bursts. The blood welled, the edges of the wound gaped, the blood spilled, the insides of the skin were visible, the blood flowed....

The next thing Ben knew he was sitting in a chair on the other side of the room. Mel had one arm across his shoulders, the other on the back of his head pushing hard. He was staring at the floor and his head hurt right behind his ear. An orderly or someone or other in hospital scrubs hovered nearby staring at him.

The guy asked, "All right now, fella?"

Who was he talking to, Ben wondered? Why was he asking about Kyle but looking at Ben? Kyle! Where was he? Ben started to get up. Both Mel and the guy pushed him back into the chair. Maybe that was just as well because the room sort of swam when he tried to get up. The guy roughly shoved Ben's head down between his knees again. Ben's heart rate gradually slowed and he lifted his head just a bit.

Mel was kneeling on the floor beside his chair. "Are you all right?" she asked.

Why was everybody asking if he was okay? It was Kyle who got injured, not him. "Why am I over here?" Ben asked.

"Because you fainted."

"What? You've got to be kidding. I don't faint," protested Ben.

From the bed a little voice said, "Daddy fell down. He looked funny."

The nurse agreed with Kyle. Mel tried not to smile. "Can I leave you now and go to Kyle?" she asked.

Just what kind of an idiot did she think he was? Did he need a nursemaid?

"Stay," Mel said, looking at him sternly as she left his side and returned to Kyle's bed.

Now Ben was mad. How dare she talk to him that way? He made to get up. The guy in scrubs warned him, "You better take it easy, buddy. You don't want to take another tumble. They're too busy taking care of your kid to have to look after you again."

Did they all think he was some kind of pantywaist? Sheesh.

Ben glared at the guy and got to his feet. Slowly. They may have a point, he thought. He really did not feel all that steady. He felt the side of his head, surprised to find it tender and a lump starting. He shuffled to the gurney, using the wall at the head of the bed to partially prop himself up.

"Hey, bud," he greeted his son.

"Daddy fell down. You went..." and Kyle gestured with his hands.

The nurse reminded Kyle to lay still.

Just then the doctor walked in, bustling to the sink to wash his hands then slip on sterile gloves. "Now, what do we have here, little man?" he asked Kyle.

"I hit my head. I bled all over me and daddy."

"It looks like you did but it's stopping now. The area looks clean now. What's that hanging off your shirt?"

"Duct tape," Kyle, Melanie and the nurse said in unison. The doctor looked at Ben, the only person who had not spoken. "It's a long story," he told the doctor.

"Head wounds always bleed a lot but most look far worse than they actually are. This one will only need a few stitches and a tetanus shot. In a couple weeks you'll be good as new, with a shiny new scar to show off to your friends."

Kyle was doing remarkably well, obviously better than he himself had done, thought Ben. The doctor explained that he'd numb the area with a salve first so Kyle would not feel the needle going in when he froze the area prior to putting in the stitches. The nurse pulled out the salve, dousing the swab with it. The scent filled the room.

Kyle tensed. His gaze went from adult to adult, trying to figure out where that offensive smell came from. The nurse approached with the swab and Kyle honed in on the culprit. No way was that stuff coming any place near him. He could hardly stand it in the same room let alone on his head. He tensed, ready to let out one of his shrieks.

Mel stepped up fast. She placed both palms firmly on Kyle's shoulders and pressed. That got his attention. She waited until his gaze rested on her face before speaking.

In soothing tones she repeated over and over that he was all right. It just smelled bad but would not hurt him. The bad smell would go away quickly and after his head would feel better. She motioned for Ben to come forward and take her place pressing firmly on Kyle to keep him calm. Kyle gazed frantically from Melanie to Ben, before his eyes settled on his dad.

Mel stepped back and motioned to the doctor. In quiet tones she explained that Kyle had autism and sensory sensitivities. She asked if their x-ray room was nearby. Yes, it was. Was there an x-ray apron they could borrow, one of the heavy, lead-lined ones used to protect patients or technicians? Yes.

In a couple minutes one arrived and Mel draped it over Kyle's body. Quickly, his tenseness drained away and Kyle lay quiet and compliant again. Ben looked at Mel with gratitude.

"Remarkable," the doctor said. He looked at the nurse. "We'll have to remember that trick".

Kyle obviously still didn't like the smell but he made no more protest. The numbing took affect almost right away. The nurse gestured Ben and Mel to the other side of the bed and turned Kyle's head toward them. "Talk to him," she urged.

Mel pulled a children's book out of her purse. Ben looked at her in amazement. Where did that come from? She didn't even have kids of her own, yet she just happened to have a kid's book with her? Anyway, it worked. While they kept Kyle's focus on them, the doctor hid the needle in the palm of his hand, out of Kyle's line of sight. He pressed the tip of the needle against Kyle's skin, watching his face for any reaction. None. Good, the freezing had done its job. He injected the site in several places, handed the spent needle to the nurse to dispose of and readied his materials. By the time he turned back and again made a test prick, the freezing had fully taken affect and he began the stitching.

Ben, watching, felt sick again. But this time he wondered if he was going to throw up, not just pass out. Not that he was admitting he'd actually passed out but he had felt queasy.

Mel again shifted her body, trying to block Ben's view. She put the book in his hands, saying, "Here. Read. It's your turn."

Ben started to refuse, but the steel in her eyes brooked no argument. He read.

"Just one more thing left. Keep reading," she instructed Ben. The nurse pulled down the elastic of Kyle's pyjama bottoms just a bit and swabbed a spot with antiseptic. Then she flicked at the skin.

"One little poke," the doctor explained. Before Kyle realized what was happening and could get out a yell, the tetanus shot was done.

Then, it was over. They said Ben could pick Kyle up and he gladly held the little body tight in his arms. Kyle wanted to see the bandage so Ben carried him to the mirror above the sink.

"Wow!" Kyle said.

"Yep, it's a doosey," the nurse told him. "Better than your dad's."

"Yeah," Kyle agreed. Ben stifled a tiny feeling of hurt. He thought he'd done a pretty good job under the circumstances. He caught Melanie grinning at him.

THEY MOVED to the waiting room where they were told to have a seat while the doctor made out a prescription for antibiotics. There were more people waiting there now than when Ben and Kyle had come in. Or, at least Ben thought there were; he really couldn't be sure. It had been all a blur when he was in such a panic.

But now his little boy was all right, or at least he would be soon. Ben sighed. It had been a long, harrowing night. He vowed to take better care of this precious child who trusted his father to look out for him. Kyle shifted on his lap.

Maybe he was over tired, but Kyle certainly was squirmy. He couldn't seem to get comfortable sprawled either on a chair of his own or with a body part on Ben, part of one on Melanie. Initially Ben had apologized to her when his son used his teacher as a chair but she had not seemed to mind.

The small space between Ben and Melanie's bodies seemed to cause Kyle problems. He could not get comfortable. He squirmed to get to his feet and stood surveying the two adults. Then he climbed back into Ben's lap, kneeling. "Careful, guy," Ben reminded him.

Kyle knelt and, making himself taller, grabbed Ben's left arm. He raised it high in the air and brought it down over the back of Melanie's chair. Ben glanced apologetically at Mel. Kyle climbed back down to the floor and surveyed his work. Not quite right yet. Leaning over Mel, he grabbed Ben's hand and put it on Melanie's shoulder. Then he pulled Ben's hand harder, drawing the two adults close together. The space between their bodies disappeared. This must have been Kyle's goal because he climbed back up, laying his head in Melanie's lap and dangling the rest of his body over his father's legs. Within what seemed like seconds, he relaxed and fell asleep.

Ben looked at his son, then at Mel. She looked tired. He brought his hand up to the side of her head and pressed gently to bring her head to his shoulder. At first she put up slight resistance, then gave in and lowered her head. Ben gathered her closer. This felt all right. Definitely all right.

BY THE TIME the orderly brought over the filled prescription, Kyle was sound asleep across their laps and Mel's breathing had slowed and evened. Ben guessed that she, too, had dropped off. It felt so good and so right holding the two of them that he hated to disturb them. But, they were sitting under the glaring lights of a noisy emergency room on hard, plastic seats. Only Kyle seemed truly comfortable.

"Hey, guys," Ben gently shook them. "It's time to get going."

Mel came awake, her hair askew from rubbing on Ben's shirt. Kyle turned over but that's about it. Ben hoisted him into his arms and started for the door. Melanie stumbled along beside him. Watching her, Ben thought she was in no shape to drive. Although she'd pulled through when they needed her most, she looked done in now.

"How did you get here?" he asked.

"I drove. My car's in the lot. How'd you get here?"

"We drove. My car's right over..." His voice trailed off.

His car that he hurriedly parked beside the open back doors of an ambulance was no longer there. It was not anywhere in sight. Ben felt his pockets. Neither were his keys anywhere in sight or feel. "Son of a ...." He stared at the spot where he'd last seen his car.

"Maybe it's not stolen. Maybe they towed it away since you parked in an emergency vehicle only spot."

"It was an emergency," Ben retorted.

"I'm not sure the powers that be would see it that way. Let's go back in and see if anyone here knows what may have happened to it. Do you know your license plate number?"

Ben looked at her. "I may have bonked my head a little but not that hard."

When he described his vehicle to the clerk at the night desk, she confirmed that yes indeed his car had been towed. He could claim it from the city compound after eight-thirty next morning, or rather this morning. And pay the two hundred dollar fine.

Kyle was starting to stir. Ben adjusted him so his head rested more firmly on Ben's shoulder. He asked the clerk if there was a taxi phone around.

"Come on, my car's just in the lot. I'll drive you guys home."

"Are you sure? You've already done enough for us tonight. We really appreciate your help. I really appreciate your help. We needed you."

They were quiet on the drive home. Ben broke the rules since there was no child's seat for Kyle and cradled him in his arms while Mel drove.

When they were almost there, she asked, "What were the doctor's instructions again?"

Ben repeated the doctor's warnings. They were to watch Kyle for any signs that the bleeding was starting again and to check for signs of a concussion. Every two hours Ben was to wake Kyle up. If it was impossible to rouse him at all, they were to return to the emergency room. It was not always easy to tell with young children as they often slept deeply. But if he didn't even stir when Ben tried to wake him, bring him back.

Mel hesitated, let out her breath, and then spoke. "I've been thinking. Kyle's had a rough night but so have you. And you're not going to get much more sleep tonight if you have to keep checking on Kyle. It's my guess that your place might be a mess and there are things to clean up. I don't want to impose, but how about I crash on your couch? We could take turns with Kyle and I could give you a hand with the cleaning."

"You'd do that for us?"

She was slightly embarrassed. "Well, yeah. I really care about Kyle."

"And?"

"And, you could probably use a hand tonight."

Ben let it go at that. There would be time to investigate where this might be going later. "Thanks. We'll take you up on that offer."

They drove in silence a few more minutes. Then Mel looked over at Ben. "Duct tape?"

AN HOUR later the soiled towels were soaking in a washing machine full of cold water and salt. "Salt?" Ben had asked. Melanie assured him that just washing the towels with detergent would set the stain and the blood would never come out.

"So? We'll throw out the towels and get new ones."

Mel's look said what she thought of such wastefulness. And, the towels ended up soaking in half a box of salt.

Ben had rummaged in this drawers and closet for something for Mel to wear to sleep in. All the sweat pants he found were far too huge on her. An old, worn t-shirt was stretched and hung to Mel's knees.

"It's decent enough," she told him.

"Well, it never looked that good on me," he replied. He didn't have words to tell her how it made him feel to see her padding around his condo, barefoot, wearing just his old shirt. He kept drawing his imagination away from what she might or might not have on under that shirt. She'd done so much for them tonight. He should not have lecherous thoughts about this angel who was his son's teacher. One thing he did know for sure - that t-shirt would never, ever be thrown out. He was not even sure he'd ever wash it again.

. . .

THEY ARGUED OVER SLEEPING ARRANGEMENTS. Mel insisted she would be just fine on the couch. Ben insisted she take his bed. In the end, Mel relented, probably seeing that this was one time Ben would not be moved.

IT TOOK some time for Mel to lose her grip on consciousness. It had been a taxing day. The first half had been fun, although novel. She'd never before shopped with a man and a little boy and it was not at all what she expected. She'd never spent so much prolonged time in a mall before. And, it had actually been fun. She'd enjoyed the company of both Wickens men.

Her heart had nearly stopped when she awakened from a deep sleep to hear Ben's voice. The near panic had sounded so un-Ben-like that at first she didn't recognize his voice. Then she came fully awake immediately, and threw on the nearest clothes. She raced through the nearly deserted streets, reaching the hospital before Ben and Kyle. She had time to apprise the staff that they were coming with a child bleeding from a head injury.

Then, Ben had fainted. She shouldn't laugh at the guy, but he'd struggled so to be in control then just face-planted.

Boy, had she misjudged him at their first meetings. He really did care about his son, even if he was new to this whole parenting thing. He was willing to turn his life upside down for the child, selling this condo, moving to a place with more room for Kyle, buying new, kid-friendly furniture. He'd talked about his "monstrosity" coffee table and how he constantly banged his shins on the sharp edges. He'd told her how he was always telling Kyle to sit further away from it so he wouldn't bump his head.

And, look what had happened. His worst fears about it. Mel smiled when she recalled Ben's reaction to the white Berber carpet under the table, now stained with blood, likely ruined. He'd hoisted the heavy table onto its side, separated the glass top from the suction cups holding it to the base, stashed the table on its side wedged between the door and another chair, moved the base to the side of the room, then balled the thick carpet up, carried it downstairs and threw it in the dumpster. By the time he got back, Mel had mopped up the blood stains from the hardwood under where the carpet had stood.

Yes, he was a good guy. Far from being a high pressure business man only concerned about his company's bottom line, he had his priorities right. His son came first. Although his apartment was beautifully furnished, the possessions meant little to him. He was prepared to sell them with the condo and buy all new stuff, stuff that would suit a little boy.

Thinking about Ben was not helping her fall asleep. She was in his bed. This was the pillow where he had laid his head only hours before. She turned her face into the pillowcase and sniffed. Ah. It held his scent.

Jeez. What was she doing? Anyone would think she'd lost her mind sniffing a pillow and smiling. Get a grip.

She heard his bare feet on the hardwood as he went yet again to check on his sleeping son. Yes, a good guy all right. She fell asleep holding that thought.

IT'S NOT easy to sleep with your head propped high on the rolled arm of the couch and your knees bent over the other arm. When Ben tried sleeping on his side with his legs bent, he perched precariously on the edge of the couch, his legs more off than on. It didn't matter. He did not have much opportunity for sleep anyway, jumping up every half hour to go check on Kyle. Even though he told himself not to and felt himself every kind of a heel for doing so, he also checked on Mel. She'd left his bedroom door half ajar and slept sprawled in his bed. Her hair was loose from its perpetual ponytail and it spread across his pillow. He already knew how soft it was, how the strands felt in his hands when he'd pulled leaves from her hair in the park. Her face was relaxed in sleep, softer, gentler than the Mel he frequently saw. She could be stern, she could really lace into him, and she could laugh and play with the kids. She was many things, his Mel.

His Mel? Where the hell did that come from? He was obviously overtired and needed to get back to his couch.

BEN WOKE TO A WHISPER THEN A "SHHHH". Instantly, he thought "Kyle!" He lifted his head, and then regretted it. Oh, his neck. Sleeping at that angle was so obviously not a good thing. The whisper came again, then a giggle. Kyle sounded fine. Then Ben's senses woke up and he smelled the coffee. And, was that bacon?

He unfolded himself from the couch and leaned against the kitchen doorway, watching the domestic scene. Mel was making pancakes, or rather Kyle was. Ben watched him ladle batter onto the hot pan, or rather ladle some batter into the pan and some on the stove top. Melanie didn't seem upset with the mess.

Kyle turned and spotted his dad. He launched himself at Ben, with the total confidence of a child that his father's arms would be there to catch him. And, they were.

Breakfast was a domestic affair, the three of them around the small round table, bumping knees, getting sticky from maple syrup, both adults focusing their attention on Kyle, studiously avoiding each other's gaze. Neither knew what to do with the forced intimacy of the situation.

Well, Ben did. But it seemed too much, too fast. They might really have something here, the three of them and he didn't want to move too quickly or make any wrong moves that might scare Mel off. He had plans for her if only he'd be able to convince her how right they were.

CHAPTER 13

The move was on. Once Ben made up his mind about
something, he wasted little time. The instant the penthouse
became vacant, he planned his move.

It was a matter of faith that his current condo would sell. It had to.
He'd committed that money to help pay the rent on the penthouse,
plus the sale of the condo would give him a cushion he could use to
help Ellie and the bakery. Plus, add to Kyle's college fund and maybe,
just maybe build towards a house down payment.

Ben's condo had been the show home of the building. He'd moved
in as is, with all the appliances and furnishings the decorator had used
to showcase the place. Since he actually did little living there, it was
still in pristine condition, largely thanks to Millie's efforts. The only
thing that had really changed was the area rug that had stood under
the coffee table. That was toast and hauled away to the dumpster. So,
he was hopeful that his place would sell quickly and had the realtor's
assurances on that. He'd been afraid to list his condo too soon in case
it sold before he and Kyle could move upstairs. And Millie. He was
really looking forward to the addition of Millie to his household, and,
he believed, so was she. When he asked her about how things were

going with her nephew and his family, she'd shake her head and ask how soon he thought the penthouse would be ready for them.

Now. Now, was when it was ready. As of today, they could move in. So as not to create any further delays, Ben hired a moving company to pack and move them. As soon as he left to drop Kyle at school, the movers would arrive, begin packing and moving boxes up the freight elevator to the penthouse. Millie would arrive by nine o'clock to direct the move and tell the movers where to place their things. Ben felt comfortable letting Millie make all such decisions. She seemed to care about such things, while he didn't. Besides, she likely knew more about organizing a household than did he. Especially a house with a small child.

The furniture that he, Mel and Kyle had chosen weeks ago was to be delivered right after lunch. By the time Kyle got home from school, everything should be in place.

Millie was a godsend. When Ben was unable to take Kyle to school, she would be able to do it. When Ben could not make it to the school at three thirty to pick up his son, Millie said she would be glad to. As much as he appreciated that offer, he found himself more and more often making an excuse to leave work mid-afternoon to go to the school. He liked going to get Kyle, even going a bit early so he could watch his son in action in the classroom.

He had improved. Ben was astounded at the rate with which Kyle had grown and changed. Already, he was becoming more social. Ben saw him talking to kids, playing with kids and even better, solving problems with them. That was a big part of Mel's room - problem solving. She didn't teach so much as she let them discover. Watching, Ben realized that this did not happen by accident. The activities and the problems were carefully staged, set up so that the students would have to think and to discover and try and work together.

Ben could see the similarities to what he did in his company. Mel was actually training these kids to be future employees, working together, solving problems together. It was amazing to watch and so different from what Ben remembered of school.

For him, much of school was a torturous bore. Endless days of remaining seated in a hard wooden chair, chairs that were made for only one size body - the size Ben never was. School days varied between listening to the incessant drone of a teacher, and doing page after page of monotonous, repetitious, meaningless question after question that had little connection to the real world.

He was not sure he remembered kindergarten. If he did, he could not have been anything exciting like the room that Mel ran. His earliest school memories were of sitting in rows of desks, having knuckles rapped for talking, standing in the corner for not responding fast enough and longing for recess. It's not that Ben didn't like learning - he did. He actually did. It's just that he wanted to learn what he wanted, when he wanted and how he wanted. Those traits certainly did not fit school the way he remembered it.

But things must be different now, or at least they were for Kyle in Mel's room. And, not just for Kyle, but for all the children. From what Ben could gather Mel set up work or explore stations or gave the kids problems, then let them have at it. Some of their attempts at solutions worked out, some didn't. That did not seem to matter to Mel or to the kids. The goal seemed to be to explore and to learn and to work together.

IT WAS ALMOST time to go for Kyle and Ben was bracing himself. The ride up in the elevator was still shaky. Shaky, but getting better. On Mel's instruction, Ben had practiced with Kyle over and over, anticipating moving day when riding the elevator would become a necessity. Kyle was getting more comfortable but it still was not his favorite thing.

From clinging to Ben's neck like a desperate monkey facing imminent death, with practice Kyle had loosened his grip. Slightly. Ben's neck no longer bore the marks of Kyle's nails and his little fingers. Quickly Ben had learned to cut his son's finger nails short enough so they were no longer lethal to his father's jugular. Kyle's little body no longer shook in Ben's arms as they suffered the ride up or down.

He still made the trip in Ben's arms but the little boy's grip was not as much a stranglehold and breathing not as frantic. He seemed to recover a bit sooner after each trip, even opening his eyes at the sound of the elevator door opening. He could now bear to wait as his father placed him on the ground, rather than scrambling down Ben's legs, coming close to unmanning his dad each time.

Yes, even in this, his son was making progress.

A thought struck Ben. It was one thing for him to carry Kyle up and down in the elevator that way, but how could he ever expect Millie to cope? She didn't have Ben's strength and while she might be able to lift Kyle for a couple seconds, she could not bear his weight long enough for the elevator to make it to the top floor. Nor could Ben run the risk that Kyle might hurt Millie in his panic.

It looked like he needed Mel's advice, yet again.

Mel. What would they have done without her? He hated to think of where he and Kyle might have been. He reflected back to those first few days of him and Kyle on their own, their tentative approaches, and their suspicion of each other and lack of understanding. They were strangers, literally and figuratively. While they shared blood, that was it. Neither had laid eyes on the other, ever before.

Now that he had a taste of what it meant to be a parent, Ben could not believe that he'd allowed himself to miss any part at all of his son's life. Certainly he'd not even known of Kyle's existence for his first two years, but once Deanna told him he was a father, nothing should have stood in his way of getting to know this little boy.

In fact, when Deanna first called him, while she spoke on the phone, Ben had been on the computer, booking a flight to Los Angeles. His first instinct had been to fly out immediately to see this new life. But Deanna told him no. She didn't want him to come, saying it would confuse Kyle to suddenly be confronted with two daddies. She was recently living with Neil and didn't want anything to interfere with the budding relationship between her fiancé and her son.

Out of respect for her wishes, Ben had complied and cancelled his flight. He had believed that Deanna, as the mother, knew what was best for their child. It hadn't entered his head that Deanna might not have had Kyle's best interests foremost in her mind.

He still wasn't sure. Really, she'd abandoned their son. Sure, she had brought Kyle to his natural father, but to let him go? The thought was inconceivable. And how many times had she called to check on him in the months since. Twice? Maybe three times? Now that Ben knew Kyle and had a taste of what parenthood was all about he could not imagine his life without Kyle. Ever. If someone tried to take him away he would fight with every fibre of his being to keep Kyle with him.

Yes, life with this child could be difficult and downright frustrating at times. But whose life runs smoothly? Certainly not his. And, the difficult moments were so worth it when the little guy threw his arms around Ben's neck. Or when he settled in beside him for a cuddle as they watched a Dora the Explorer DVD.

Yes, life with Kyle was good.

A GLOOMY, rainy day, Mel thought as she glanced out of her classroom window. One of those days where the natural light coming in those windows was not enough. She rarely used the overhead fluorescent lights as their barely perceptive flicker bothered some kids who had visual sensitivities. Although economical to run, if Mel had her way, she'd ban fluorescents from all schools. On sunny days, the windows provided most of the illumination in her classroom. But on days like today the halogen task lights gave a cozy glow scattered throughout the room. Mel and Lori found that the lower light levels had a slight soothing effect on the kids.

Mel's eyes settled on Kyle, bent over the fort he was creating out of wooden blocks. Although he played alongside, rather than with the boy nearby, it was coming. His interactions with other kids were increasing as was his tolerance of their ideas into his games.

Her goal for Kyle today was to keep everything as calm and routine as possible because he was in for a big change after school. Today was moving day for him and Ben.

She went over in her mind the plans she'd helped Ben with so far and how she'd assist after school. She was doing this for Kyle, she told herself. The more settled her students were in their personal lives, the smoother the classroom ran; a win-win for all concerned.

Her conscience gave a twinge. There were ethical boundaries between teachers and students. Although her job often took her in close proximity to the home lives of her kids and she learned more than she might have wanted to know about the personal lives of their parents, still there were boundaries.

For a while, she'd felt that she was going too far over that line and tried to pull back. It was hard though when Ben kept showing up in her room near the end of the school day. Worried, she talked to her principal.

"It started when I ran into them in the park. Kyle was chilled so I invited them back to my place for hot chocolate; I live just down from the park. You should have seen how Kyle opened up to my dog, Max. That was the most verbal I've ever heard him."

"That sounds fairly innocuous," Dr. Hitkin said.

"Well, there's more. Kyle's dad is new to parenting; he's quite clueless in fact, but is trying. His present condo was no place for a child, so he's moving them to a bigger place. Although initially he complained about the furniture in our classroom, he's seen the difference it can make and wanted furnishings suited to Kyle in their new place. He asked my advice on what to get."

"Yes, you'd certainly have some suggestions to offer."

Melanie nodded. She felt guilty not detailing just how involved she had been with her suggestions but couldn't bring herself to talk about their shopping day together. It's a good thing the school year was almost over. In just a few weeks Kyle would be assigned to a new teacher and she would no longer need to feel guilty about her involvement with him. And the rest of his family.

FAMILY. Families were strange things. Melanie thought back to her dinner with hers last Sunday. She cringed recalling her argument with her mother. It was though just a variation of the same fight they'd had over and over and over again.

"No, Jeff didn't have the same chances you had. It's different. You weren't born with autism; he was," her mother said.

"So?" Melanie replied. "So what if he has autism? That's one part of him. What about all the other things that make up Jeff?"

"Melanie, you know he's not strong like you. Life is harder for him. It's my job as his parent to protect him."

"Oh, for...." Melanie blew out a breath. "Look. He has a diagnosis of autism. No one will deny that. But autism does not have to define his life. That's one aspect of it and with it comes challenges and strengths.

"He's smart - smarter than me. Despite having autism, his grade 12 marks were higher than mine and he put in far less effort than I had to. But then life all just stopped for him."

"Well, life is hard for him. He's doing what he likes now. He's fine."

"You call it fine when a thirty-three year old man spends his life in a darkened basement with his face plastered to a computer screen? His only interactions are with made up characters in a computer program."

"No, he spends time with his father and me. He eats one meal a day with us, usually."

"And you think that's enough of a life for my brother? And what's going to happen when you and dad are no longer around?"

They broke off their argument as Jeff came up the stairs.

As they ate the meal their mother had prepared, Melanie had an idea.

"Hey Jeff, I need a favor. Some friends of mine are moving Friday and I'm helping them after school. They're going to be in a big mess and won't feel like cooking supper. Would you make something for us?"

Before he could answer, their mother said, "No. You know how I hate a mess in my kitchen and I need to be getting our own meal ready." Their father kept his eyes on his plate and shovelled the mashed potatoes into his mouth.

As if their mother had never spoken, Jeff said, "How many people?"

"Five adults, counting you and one child."

"No!" from their mother.

"What do they like to eat?"

"I don't think they'll care. But Kyle, the little boy, does not like different foods touching each other."

Jeff grinned. "Well, who does?"

"No. It's out of the question," continued their mother.

"Five, counting me. You want me to eat with you?"

"Yes, definitely," said Mel.

"No, that is going too far. Melanie, I insist you stop taking advantage of your brother right now."

Mel looked at her mother. So far, she'd ignored her. Jeff's ability to hyper-focus worked in his favor in times like this. He'd hardly been aware that their mother was even there. Now both siblings turned to look at her.

"I'm simply asking my brother for his help," Melanie said.

"Well, I think it's unfair of you to even think of asking him to do such a thing. He has his own things to do."

"Like what?" Melanie asked.

"Yeah, like what? Jeff echoed. "I have nothing to do on Friday. Or most other days either."

Their mother raised her other argument. "And just where do you think he's going to do this? You know I hate a mess in my kitchen. I like everything in its place. And these people will hardly have their kitchen ready for Jeff to use."

"He can cook at my place," Mel said.

"And how's he going to get there?"

"Mom, I'm right here. You don't have to talk about me. Mel, I'll take the bus or walk. I'll get there. "

"You still have your key to my place, right?"

"Yeah. I'll call you with the ingredients you'll need to have ready for me. You can add it to the stuff I'll need for the weekend." With that, Jeff left the table and headed for the basement.

"Where are you going, son?" their mother called.

"Gotta plan the menu." And that was the last they saw of Jeff that evening.

"Now look what you've done," her mother chided Melanie. "You've gotten his hopes up and he could get hurt. What if they don't like what he makes? You're expecting him to sit down with strangers and eat? Make small talk during the meal?"

"Yep. It's just a single father named Ben, his housekeeper Millie and his five year old son, Kyle." At Melanie's explanation, her father looked up from his plate.

"Single, you said?" he asked.

Melanie didn't meet his eyes. "Yes. He's new to parenting, just got custody of his son this fall. He's needed some help. Kyle's one of my students. He has autism."

Her mother looked shocked. "He's not going to upset Jeff, is he?"

"Mother!" Melanie tried not to grind her back teeth.

DRIVING HOME, Mel regretted fighting yet again with her mother. She reminded herself that most parents do the best they can at the time. But, time worked against her brother. He had not moved on with his life for the past fifteen years, since he finished high school. School had provided a structure to his life and got him out of the house each day. Once that was over, nothing had taken its place. Her parents could not bear the thought of Jeff going out into the world, to further education or to a job. What if people didn't understand him? What if he felt overwhelmed? What if he got scared? What if he didn't know what to do? No, he was safer at home with them where they could look after him.

Partly, her parents went into protection mode because they didn't know what else to do or how to help. It was true that Jeff could become anxious and new situations were difficult for him. Rather than figuring out ways to help him cope or problem solve, their parents hovered and protected, doing everything for their son.

They were not the only ones. An alarmingly small percentage of young adults with high functioning autism and Asperger's Syndrome lived independently. Many suffered from learned helplessness, having been over-helped all their lives. Well, see where this had gotten Jeff so far. Melanie was determined to help Jeff make a better life for himself. And, she was determined that this would not happen to Kyle.

What? Where did that thought come from? Kyle was not her child, not her responsibility. No, but he was her student, at least for a few more weeks. And she strove to help each child in her class to be as independent as possible.

UNDER MEL'S INSTRUCTIONS, Ben and Millie went to work. The plan was for Millie to play in the park with Kyle while Mel and Ben got ready for Kyle to come home to the penthouse.

They used the digital camera voraciously. They took pictures of everything imaginable in the new place. Mel kept talking about something called a social story. Ben didn't get it and said that over and over. Mel pretty much told him to just shut up and take the pictures. So, he did.

The pictures were of everything in their new place. He started at the outside door and took pictures of the entrance, the lobby, the elevator button, elevator doors and the open elevator. Then he took a picture of the elevator buttons with a finger pushing P for the penthouse floor. He gave these all to Mel, both printed out and in digital form. She used them to make a social story about Kyle coming home and going in the building. She taped Kyle's name in big block letters beside the P button in the elevator to show him which one to push that first day he was to go in the elevator. Even though Kyle could not reach that high and had to be hoisted up by Ben or Mel, Mel still insisted that Kyle getting to push the button would give him some semblance of control over his environment. He would feel less like things were being done to him and that he had a part in what was happening. If he could feel that he had control and could make things happen, he'd be less fearful.

Next, they took pictures of leaving the elevator and the hallway to the penthouse. Ben took a picture of the door to their new place and a picture of his hand turning the key in the lock.

Then, they were inside. The day before he'd taken pictures of the bathroom and the kitchen and given them to Mel, but not before placing their own towels on the bathroom racks at Mel's insistence. They had to be towels that Kyle used often so he would feel that they were his and that this was not a totally strange place.

Mel made him go back to the store to take pictures of the furniture they'd bought. Ben put his foot down at that and refused unless Mel went with him and Kyle. He'd feel less a fool that way and besides, he just plain enjoyed her company. Any excuse to get her to spend time with them was fine with him. To be honest, it didn't seem to take a lot of arm twisting to get her to come. Maybe, just maybe, she'd had fun, too.

Kyle loved revisiting the furniture store. He remembered what they'd done there last time and raced for a pillow to use to attack his father. He bounced gleefully on the mattress with Mel. While she insisted that they take pictures of the living room furniture and the bed set Ben would use, she spent the most time on the furniture meant especially for Kyle. In the store, she had Ben take detailed photographs of everything that would be in Kyle's room, even though Ben felt like a fool. When they had entered the store, Mel spent a few quiet minutes with the manager and after hearing her explanation, they had not been disturbed.

Mel must have spent the rest of the weekend on her computer, judging by the books she created for his son. What kind of a teacher did that? Didn't teachers spend their evenings marking assignments and grading papers and planning lessons? How did she find the time to do all this work for his son? And, why did she do it?

When he asked her, she said that it was to her benefit to have each of her students as calm and settled as possible because that helped the other kids in the room. Ben had quirked an eyebrow at her. "So, you're telling me that you go to the home of your other students and take pictures, choose furniture and make books for them?" Mel had blushed and mumbled something about that she probably would if asked. Ben just looked at her and she would not meet his gaze.

It gave Ben hope. Maybe as drawn as he felt to Mel, maybe, just maybe she was not reciprocating just for the sake of a poor motherless new student in her class. Yes, she truly did seem to care for Kyle but maybe there was something more as well.

CHAPTER 14

"Are you all set, Jeff?" Mel was in Ben's new penthouse, calling her home number. She had not been one hundred percent sure her brother would pull through and was relieved to hear his voice answer her phone.

"You said you would be here to pick up the food and me at 6:15. It's only 6:07 now. Of course I'm not ready. You won't be here for another seven and a half minutes."

"Okay, okay. You're right. I was just checking. I'm leaving Ben's place now to come get you. I'll be there in five or ten minutes."

"Seven and a half minutes," repeated Jeff.

"Oh," Ben groaned. "Oh, this roast beef sandwich is wonderful. Where'd you find this beef?"

"On the roast," Jeff answered.

"I mean, which deli do you use?"

"I guess you could call it Chez Mel," said Jeff.

"Chez Mel? Our Mel? Have you been holding out on us and you own a deli, Mel?" Ben asked.

"Jeff's referring to my house," explained Mel. "Knowing him, he seasoned and cooked the roast. And, I'd guess he also made the Panini bread. Right, Jeff?" Jeff nodded.

"Is this all you can make?" Ben asked him.

"No, I can make...." Jeff began.

Mel cut him off, knowing that Jeff would give a complete itemized list of every dish he made and that list would go on and on and on. She tried summarizing for Ben the gourmet skills her brother possessed even though he did not have as many opportunities to use them as he'd like.

Ben grew pensive. "Have you worked in a restaurant?" he asked Jeff. Jeff shook his head no.

"Ever thought about it? Ben continued. "I'm thinking more of a deli and bakery rather than a restaurant."

Again, Jeff shook his head.

Mel was her mother's daughter, she realized, and some of her mother's trepidation filled her. What was Ben thinking? Would he suggest something that would be too much for Jeff? Then she sat back. This over-protection was what she accused her mother of. Jeff was a thirty-three year old man. He could make his own decisions.

"My sister runs a bakery. She's run off her feet trying to do everything. She has a couple of kids who help wait tables, but Ellie finds it hard to do all the baking, ordering and managing on her own. And, she's trying to introduce new things in the bakery, things to get more people in there. Food like this sandwich would be ideal."

Jeff listened intently but didn't say anything. Ben waited, getting uncomfortable with the silence.

"Well, if you don't like the idea, that's fine. It was just a thought," Ben said, his eyes not meeting anyone's.

"What idea?" Jeff asked.

Ben stared at him, and then looked at Mel. He caught on. "I guess I didn't say what was in my mind. Would you be interested in meeting my sister? In seeing the bakery? Maybe the two of you could talk about the possibility of you helping her out."

Jeff stood up and left the room. No one else moved. He returned a few minutes later with his coat on. "Well," he said, "aren't we going?"

"Going?" Ben asked.

"To meet your sister." Jeff was impatient. "Did you forget what you just said?"

Mel intervened. "Jeff, I don't think Ben meant right now, but some time. Right, Ben?"

"Yeah. What if I call Ellie and set something up for this weekend? Would that work for you?"

Jeff nodded and sat back down to finish his meal.

LIFE MOVED ON. They settled into the penthouse more or less all right. With Mel's help, they prepared Kyle for the changes. Even though they had showed him the space, he had not seemed to recognize that it had anything to do with them. Telling him did not seem to make it so.

"YOU TALK TOO MUCH," Mel said.

"What the hell is that supposed to mean?" Ben asked Mel. Attractive as she was, she could really push his buttons.

"When you're frustrated with Kyle, you talk too much. That confuses him even more and gets you more frustrated."

She tried to be patient with Ben and explain. She talked about something she called auditory processing.

See, Kyle could hear all right. Ben knew that for a fact because Deanna had told him she'd had Kyle's hearing checked twice when he was younger. They had thought that perhaps he wasn't talking because of a hearing impairment that made it difficult for him to hear then repeat words.

But no, that was not it. His hearing tested fine both times. And, Ben was sure he could hear all right. He must to be able to have memorized huge dialogues from his Dora videos.

Something must be wrong with Ben's hearing because he had trouble following some of what Mel tried to explain to him. She said that there was a difference between hearing and understanding what

177

was said. Hearing the words was only the very first step. The words had to go into the child's ears, and then the child had to begin to make sense of them. That was where communication often broke down. Then there was yet a third step, where the child had to determine how to respond to what he had heard and understood. This making sense of what he heard was called auditory processing.

And, Kyle's ability to process what he heard varied. Sometimes it was easier than under other circumstances. Take noise for instance. Background noise could make a big difference and his ability to process would go way down. This auditory processing weakness was part of the reason Mel was so big on using visuals – visual schedules, pictures, and pictorial stories. Show, don't tell. Use pictures, not just oral words. And Ben had seen that it did actually make things easier for Kyle.

MEL EXPLAINED MORE. For kids with autism spectrum disorders, everything in the environment came at them with the same intensity. For most, especially most adults, our brains automatically filtered out extraneous, background noise. While our senses might register the humming of a fan or the flickering of the fluorescent lights then tune them out, a child with autism would not be able to do such things automatically. If he blocked out all those background noises and concentrated on a voice, it would be through a conscious decision on his part and require concentration. When a skill was not automatic, it required more effort. That is why kids with autism often tire readily. It's taking them so much effort to handle a normal day, far, far more effort than for other typical kids their age.

Ben's heart hurt at the thought of how hard all this was for his son. Mel sharply reprimanded him for any pity he felt.

"Understand it, feel it, but don't pity," she said. "This is the hand the child has been dealt. He knows no different. It's your job as Kyle's father and my job as his teacher to help, to train him and guide him towards independence."

Mel was adamant that there would be no "poor me" or "poor Kyle" under her watch. No siree. Sure, Kyle had challenges, but he also had strengths. They would build on those and teach Kyle how to use his strengths to prop up his challenges and find other ways to do the things that were difficult for him. Isn't that what everyone did?

Yes, Mel had no sympathy for him, Ben. Ben often felt that she was hard on him. She did not cut him any slack, or at least only rarely. Ben had the feeling she was teaching and training him just as much as she was training and teaching and guiding his son. To be honest, though, he needed it. He'd been like a babe in the woods when he first met this kid and again, being honest, without Mel's guidance, he and Kyle would not be where they were today - a team.

BEN'S THOUGHTS turned to Mel, as they often did. In fact, it did not seem to take much to make him think of Mel. She had become an integral part of their lives.

Take the move, for instance. Without Mel's instruction, Ben did not think he would have ever gotten Kyle into the elevator. Mind you it was still not smooth, but it was better.

Some of what Mel suggested he didn't get.

"This seems excessive – pretty much useless. Besides, who has time for all this?" Ben asked her.

"Well, you're welcome to try it your way then," Mel retorted.

When he did, usually the result was not what he'd hoped and sometimes it was actually a disaster. He now avoided disasters whenever possible because not only were they hard on him and his ego, but they were hard on Kyle. It was not fair to his son when he did not heed Mel's advice.

How did she seem to know his son so well when she'd met him only a couple days after Ben did?

SUNDAY AFTERNOON, Ben and Kyle picked up Melanie and Jeff at Mel's house. They drove to the bakery.

As they entered the door, they were met by the tantalizing smells of warm yeast breads. Kyle stopped and went up on his toes, his nose in the air, sniffing with a smile of pleasure on his face. Ellie came from behind the counter, wiping her hands on a towel. She bent down and held out her arms to Kyle. "Come here, Munchkin."

As soon as he spied her, Kyle began a headlong run for his aunt, but at her words stopped short and looked behind him. Nope, no other kid was there. He looked back at Aunt Ellie. She was still crouched, arms outstretched toward him. He checked again behind him, then asked, "Who's Munchkin?"

"You are," Ellie told him.

"I'm Kyle."

"But I'm going to call you Munchkin."

"Why?" he wanted to know.

"Just come here anyway," his aunt told him.

After giving Kyle a hug and a cream puff, Ellie turned to Ben and Mel. "You usually don't bring girls home, big brother. In fact, the last time was like hmmm, well never. What's the occasion?"

"Can it, brat, or I won't introduce you," Ben told her.

"Mel, this is my little sister, Ellie. El, this is Melanie Nicols, Kyle's teacher. We came so that you could meet her brother."

As the women shook hands and chatted a few minutes. Ellie glanced all around, not seeing the brother. Then she spied a strange man fiddling with things behind her counter. "Hey," she yelled. "Get away from there. You're not allowed behind the counter."

The man ignored her. Then they all heard the whoosh of the latte machine steaming milk.

"That thing hasn't worked for weeks! What are you doing back there? How'd you make it do that?" Ellie asked.

"Oh no," said Mel. "Don't ask how. Just accept that he fixed it."

"What?" Ellie didn't get this.

Jeff grinned. "Afraid I'll give too much information, sis?"

"Exactly," Mel agreed. "Don't ask him how he fixed it unless you want the full - and I mean full - explanation. Ellie, I'd like to introduce my brother, Jeff Nicols. Jeff, this is Ben's sister Ellie and the owner of this bakery."

Ellie nodded, but her attention was more on her coffee machine. "Do you think we can actually use it now?"

"If you want a coffee," Jeff told her.

"How the hell did you do that? We worked at it, and had the repair guy out twice. He said it was toast."

"I see why he couldn't fix it," said Jeff. "Anyone who would confuse a coffee maker with a piece of toast does not know what he's doing."

Ellie stared at Jeff. Ben thought this a good time to display what was in the cooler he carried. "Hungry, El?" he asked his sister. Let's have a seat and try the food Jeff made for us.

They joined Kyle and his cream puff while Ben brought out the array of deli sandwiches Jeff had created. They were cut into small slices, made for sampling.

"Oh, this is so luscious," Ellie told Jeff. "I thought I was up on most of the delis and bistros in town but I've never had anything like this. Who do you work for?"

Ben told her that Jeff was not working in any restaurant right now. Melanie shot him a look. He gave her a look back. What he said was technically true.

"Between jobs, eh?" Ellie asked. Without waiting for a response, she rushed on, "Any chance you'd consider working here? Don't worry - no long term commitment if that scares you off. But, we really could use food like this here; our clientele would go for it big time. We'll take any amount of your time you can give us. We can even offer lattes again now, thanks to you. How about it? Interested in helping out here? I can't pay you a lot but we could work something out."

"El, if you'd shut up a minute, Jeff might be able to give you an answer," Ben told her.

"What would I have to do," Jeff asked.

"Make sandwiches like these. Make coffee. Help with the baking. Anything you feel like doing around here."

"Okay."

"Pardon?" Ellie asked.

"Okay. I'll work here," Jeff said.

"That's it? It was that easy? Don't you need to think about it?" Ellie wanted to make sure.

"I already did." Jeff said.

"Did what?"

Jeff looked at Ellie strangely. "Think about it. I already did think about it. Yes, I'll work here."

Although Mel had hoped for something like this, she now had second thoughts. "Wait a minute. What's mom going to say?"

Ellie looked confused. "Your mother? Is that why you're not working right now, because you have to look after her?"

"Not exactly," Mel explained.

"Then, I don't get it. What does your mother have to do with you working here?" She asked Jeff.

"I don't know what she has to do with it," said Jeff.

"Nothing," agreed Mel.

"Nothing," echoed Kyle.

CHAPTER 15

"All right, class. What's our lining up routine?" Ms. Nicols asked.

"One table at a time."

"Arm's length from the person in front of you."

"Hands down at your side."

"Arms crossed over your chest," offered various students.

"Very good. But I'm confused. How do I cross my arms over my chest and put my hands down at my side at the same time?" Melanie hoped for the right answer.

"That's a choice," explained Jordan. "Put your hands at your side or across your chest."

"Excellent." They really did get it, thought Melanie. It had been a good year and now was time to help her students move on to the next teacher.

"There are two grade one classrooms in this school. You will be with some of your friends from this class and you will be making some new friends next year.

"Right now, those who will be in Mr. Johnson's grade one room will come with me for a tour. When I say your name, please line up."

She called out the names of about half her class and they headed down the hallway.

"THIS IS MR. JOHNSON. He'll be your teacher for grade one next fall," Ms. Nicols told the boys and girls. She pulled out a digital camera and took a picture of Mr. Johnson standing in the doorway waving hello to his future students, then a few of the classroom. These would be added to the booklet each child would receive before summer vacation. Some children like Kyle, who found transitions difficult would have a number of introductory sessions like this one.

WHEN BEN SHOWED up after school for Kyle, Mel took the two of them to meet Mr. Johnson. She took pictures of the cubby where Kyle would hang his coat, the desk where he would sit, the inside and outside of the washroom he'd use and where the schedule was kept on the wall. While Mr. Johnson chatted with Ben, he encouraged Kyle to explore the room, check out the view from his desk and generally get a feel for the room. Kyle would have the chance to do this several times this month to help prepare him for next fall.

"ISN'T THIS OVERKILL?" Ben asked when Melanie presented him with Kyle's book of pictures.

"In my experience, it helps. But, suit yourself," Melanie replied. Ben sighed.

THAT NIGHT as he tucked Kyle into bed, Ben opened up Kyle's Grade One book. While he read the captions, Kyle studied each picture. Even though Melanie had suggested they go through this every night, Ben was sure Kyle'd have it memorized within a couple days.

. . .

"GOOD MAN," Ben told his son several weeks later.

"Good man," echoed Kyle, his voice small and tentative.

Ben settled his hands more firmly on Kyle's shoulders. Although it was still far from perfect, Kyle's comfort level with riding the elevator increased daily. He'd graduated from enduring the ride with his limbs plastered around his father's torso and his face buried in Ben's neck to now standing on his own feet. To feel secure he needed to be pressed firmly into an adult, with pressure on his shoulders. His little body tensed but no longer trembled during the ride. Together, he and Ben counted off the floor numbers as each lit up. Ben faithfully followed Mel's instructions to practice the elevator ride so that Kyle would be able to do it with Millie. Once again, her advice worked.

"Someday champ, you'll be taking this ride all on your own," Ben told his son.

WITH MILLIE AROUND, Ben was able to get more work done in the evenings. As Mel had predicted, Kyle liked to sit at his own little desk while Ben worked. Tonight he was looking over his Grade One book. He brought it over to Ben and squeezed between the desk and chair until he could perch on his dad's lap. Kyle pointed to the book. Ben stifled his impatience at the interruption; this was important to Kyle and the work could wait. Still, he thought....

Bye now, Kyle repeated the words with Ben.

"This is Mr. Johnson, Kyle's teacher. This is where Kyle will hang his coat. This is Kyle's desk..." and so on until Ben thought they had covered every possible aspect of a grade one child's life. But, day after day, Kyle stared intently at each photograph.

As Ben lifted Kyle down from his knee, he thought the little boy felt heavier. "I think you've grown, Kyle. You're getting to be quite the little man, getting bigger every day. Soon you'll be doing so many more things on your own. I'm so proud of my big boy Kyle."

Kyle wandered out of the room. Soon Ben could hear one of the endless Dora DVDs playing. He'd long since gotten over his nervousness at Kyle using his equipment. The kid could probably teach him a few things about the components. Millie was in the kitchen preparing dinner.

A WHILE LATER, the meal was ready and Millie called them to the kitchen. Ben went to wash his hands and called for Kyle to do the same. When Kyle didn't appear in the bathroom, Ben assumed his son had gone to use the kitchen sink.

When Ben entered the kitchen, Millie asked, "Where's Kyle?"

"I thought he was in here with you. He must be engrossed in his DVD. I'll go get him."

Millie said, "No, you sit down and I'll go fetch him."

She returned a minute later with a frown. "He's not in the living room or in his bedroom."

"He must have dozed off somewhere. Let's take a look."

It didn't take long for them to scour the whole place, looking in most spots twice. There were only so many spots for a little boy to hide. Ben called out to his son but there was no reply. He yelled louder, hoping to wake Kyle up if he'd fallen asleep. The silence was deafening. Ben's and Millie's steps got faster as their voices raised. On his way to check the hall closet yet again, Ben noticed that the condo's door to the outside hallway was ajar. He was positive he'd shut it when he came home.

With a sinking feeling, Ben opened the door and peered into hall, hoping to spy his son. No such luck. With his heart in his throat, Ben checked the hooks beside the door, the ones he'd put at the just right height for a small boy to hang his coat. Empty. Kyle's jacket was missing.

He wouldn't. He couldn't. Kyle would not leave the condo. Why would he? There was no place to go in the hallway. It was small with only two doors - the one to their condo and the one for the elevator. Kyle hated the elevator, so he certainly would not go there. But, he had been getting better at riding it. No, he would not do that; he'd never wander off on his own.

Is that what all parents of lost children said, Ben wondered? No.

Kyle was not lost. He had just fallen asleep someplace in the condo. You know how deeply children can sleep. He'd not heard them calling; that was it. That had to be it.

Ben returned to the condo, and with Millie's help searched every last inch of the place again. No Kyle.

"Millie, will you stay here, please? I'll check the elevator just in case Kyle did go in there. He could be huddled in the corner, scared to death. He was too small to push the button for the penthouse, so he wouldn't be able to get back home."

Ben had a long wait for the elevator, indicating that it must have been on the ground floor. He rode down, trying to talk himself calm. No Kyle.

The doorman was snoozing behind the counter. Ben's voice woke him. "Have you seen a little boy go by here by himself? This would have been in the last half hour or so," Ben told him.

"No, I haven't seen anyone come in or out in the last while and definitely not a kid alone."

"My son. I thought he was in the living room but when we called him for supper there was no answer. We live in the penthouse and can't find him anywhere. He's only five."

"Did you check the stairwell?"

Damn. How could Ben have forgotten about that? There were three doors in his hallway, not just two. He'd never taken the stairs since they moved to the penthouse, but Kyle had been used to the stairs when they lived on the third floor.

"Thanks. I'll go up that way and check."

"All fifteen floors?" the doorman's question was spoken to thin air as Ben dashed for the stairwell.

Ben paused on the seventh floor landing. How could he have let himself get this out of shape? He took a few deep breaths and continued up three more floors. He paused there to use his cell phone to call Millie. Maybe she'd found Kyle.

"Millie, any luck?" Ben asked.

"No. I was hoping you were calling to say you found him."

"The doorman hasn't seen anyone go out for the past half hour but asked if I'd tried the stairwell." Ben huffed as he plodded up. "I'm four floors down from you now. Maybe we'll find him on the landing of our floor. See you in a minute."

Ben had only made it up one more floor when his cell rang. "You found him?" he asked.

"No, but the doorman called. He checked the videotapes. I didn't know but the elevator is on video camera. He can see Kyle. He wants us to come down to his desk."

Ben opened the door to the nearest hallway and pressed the elevator button. When it came, Millie was already in it. Together they counted the seconds until the car landed in the lobby.

The doorman was ready for them with a freeze frame on the monitor. "There. See?" he pointed. There, in grainy black and white was Kyle, alone in the elevator. He pushed the L button for lobby and rode down, his arms rigidly at his sides, concentration on his face. When the doors on the lobby, Kyle hesitated as if he was going to leave the car, then went back in. They watched as he jumped and jumped, trying to hit the P at the top of the panel, the button that would send the elevator car back up to Kyle's home. Try as he could, Kyle was too short.

Next, he put his backpack on the ground. Ben grimaced. He had not even noticed that it was gone. Some father he was. Kyle stood on his back pack, trying to gain some height. Still not enough. Kyle sat in the corner, with his knees drawn up under his chin. He clutched the back pack to him. Ben's heart broke watching his son. When a tear slid down Kyle's cheek, Millie grabbed Ben's arm and her own tears began.

Ben put his arm around Millie as they watched. Kyle stood and pressed the button to open the elevator door. The last the video showed of him was one little boy leaving the elevator.

"Where'd he go? Where's the rest of the video?" Ben demanded.

"That's all there is," explained the doorman. There's only a camera in the elevator, then one outside the front door."

"Can you pull that one up?"

"Just give me a minute."

"We don't have a minute! My son could be out there. He's only five and he's alone and it's getting dark and he has autism and he hardly talks! He'll be scared out of his mind and anything could happen to him. I need that video now!"

"Ben," Millie patted his arm. "It's here."

They could see Kyle on the screen now, his dark jacket fading in with the growing shadows outside. It took him several tries but he finally got the outer door opened and went through. He hesitated just an instant then turned left down the street.

Ben snarled at the other man. "I thought you said no one went in or out for the past half hour?"

"Honest. I didn't see anyone enter or leave. I do remember the door making some noise but I thought it was the wind blowing it. You know how it's been gusting. Besides I was sitting behind the counter. I can certainly see any adult coming or going but your little boy's head would have been below counter height, so I would have missed him."

Ben wanted to turn on him. He needed to take this out on someone. But the important thing right now was Kyle.

"Call 9-1-1 will you?" Ben said to the doorman. "When he has them on the line, would you give them a description, Millie?"

"Yes. Are you calling Mel?"

"You bet."

Both the cruiser and Mel pulled up at about the same time, both parking diagonally and part on the sidewalk.

WHILE MILLIE RETURNED to the penthouse to get the officers copies of Kyle's school pictures and Kyle's Grade One book, Ben tried to think of where Kyle might have headed. Nothing came to mind.

"We sometimes go to the park off that way. Yes, that's the direction Kyle went, but it's almost dark. He never wants to play with other kids there, just with me."

"He doesn't play with other kids? Who are his friends and where do they live?"

Melanie stepped in. "Kyle's friends are mainly the kids in his class but he only sees them during school time. Right, Ben? He doesn't play with them other than at school, right?" Ben nodded.

Melanie explained that Kyle had autism. She told them that when they called, he might not respond to his name. Sirens and flashing lights might spook him, making him feel the need to hide from strangers looking for him.

"But would he come if you call?" they asked Ben.

Ben hesitated. What kind of a father did this make him?

Again, Melanie helped. "People with autism are sensitive to sound, lights and touch. What might not bother you at all could seem like fingernails on a blackboard to someone like Kyle. It's hard to predict how he will react in an unusual situation. He's not used to being out at night alone."

Ben's panic was rising. "Why are we standing around here yakking? My son's out there somewhere. He's alone. He could be cold and scared. What if some creep picks him up? Shit, he's only five. He doesn't know about all the weirdoes in the world. So far he's only met people who help him. We need to get our asses in the saddle and find him!"

"Mr. Wickens, as we speak there are two patrol cars and four officers at his school. They're scouring the ground looking for him. There's a call in to the school principal to meet us there to unlock the doors just in case he found a way to get in. They'll turn on all the lights in the school and the principal and an officer will stay there just in case Kyle makes his way there.

"Two other officers are in the park checking for him. They've just started their sweep. Now, if you could tell us where else you think he might have gone...."

A policeman came up to them. "Your housekeeper said you wouldn't mind if we used your scanner and computer. Your son's picture has now gone out to all our officers. While I did that, Millie ran off copies of his photo on your printer. We'll sweep the blocks surrounding your place then hand out pictures at any businesses that are open."

He continued. "Now, we need someone to stay in your apartment in case Kyle returns on his own. Your housekeeper volunteered. The doorman will stay on alert here and notify us if he sees your son. Do you two want to stay here and wait? If you're up to it, given that this kid has autism, it might help if you would check the park as well. Maybe he'll come to you even if he won't respond to an officer. Do you have cell phones on you?"

Ben and Mel nodded and gave him their numbers. "Wait right here while I patch your numbers through to dispatch so we can call you right away if we see him."

Mel wrapped her arms around Ben. It was hard to tell if she was giving or receiving comfort, but it didn't really matter anyway. She was the one thing Ben could hang on to in the middle of this whole mess.

They were given the go-ahead and started for the park, calling Kyle's name as they went. They entered the park and passed the swings and slide. They passed the spot where Ben and Kyle had made piles of leaves and jumped through them. They passed the bench when Melanie had waited and they threw leaves on her head. Everywhere they went, they called Kyle's name but there was no response.

They came to the other end of the park, Ben's despair growing. He turned to retrace his steps, but Mel was rooted to the spot, looking off down the street.

"He wouldn't," she said. "No, it's too far and he wouldn't remember the way."

"What way? What are you talking about?"

"Ben, you don't think he'd walk all the way to my place, do you? Remember that day in the park? He had such a good time, and then afterwards you came to my place for hot chocolate, Kyle played with Max."

"Shit, he's only five years old. He's only been to your place a few times and the last time we drove, not walked. That's a long ways for a small kid alone and in the dark."

"He had fun at my place. He probably felt safe and secure there."

"I have no better ideas, so we might as well go look." Ben checked his cell just in case there was a message and he for some reason hadn't heard it ring. No such luck.

They continued in silence for a block, holding hands.

"First thing tomorrow morning, I'm calling Deanna. No. As soon as we find Kyle I'm calling her. She can come and get him in the morning, "Ben said.

Melanie stopped walking to search Ben's face in the light from the street lamp. "But, why? Why would you want to give him up?"

"Why? WHY? Because I'm a goddamned unfit father, that's why. Because I can't look after my own kid. I can't keep him safe. Look at all the things that have happened to him since I've had him. He almost dies in a fire. He cracks his bloody head open. And now, I can't even keep track of one little kid and here he's lost in the dark all alone." Ben's voice cracked.

Melanie just held him. There was nothing she could say right now that would help him see all the good things that had happened to Kyle this past year.

"Come, on. Let's go check out your place. I can't figure out what else to do." Ben's shoulder's stooped. His head was down. As he berated himself in his mind, he momentarily forgot to scour the bushes they passed but Melanie watched for him.

As THEY APPROACHED Melanie's house, Ben could see that her lights were off. For some reason, he had hoped to see all her lights blazing with Kyle cozily ensconced in her living room. But, how could he be? She would have locked her doors when she left, of course.

Melanie stopped as they entered the front gate. "That's funny," she said. "Usually Max hears me coming down the street and by the time I get to the yard he's here waiting to greet me."

"Did you leave him locked in the house?"

"No. I definitely remember leaving him outside. Let's go around the back way and see what's going on."

As they walked around the side of the house, flashes of Kyle and Max tearing around the yard came to Ben's mind. He'd have to get the kid a dog. Kyle really enjoyed Max and dogs were good protection. It would have to be a big dog, one like Max.

Melanie grabbed Ben's arm. "Shhh," she said and pointed. There on the chaise lounge was Max, his head in the air pointed towards them, his tail thumping on the chair pad. His body was curled around a small shape. Although Max's tail continued to wag, his head went back down and he would not meet Mel's eyes. "He knows he's not allowed on the chairs," she explained.

But she'd forgive him this time. For in between his big paws was the head of one little boy. As they hustled up, they could see Kyle's chest rising and falling, one arm draped over the big German Shepherd.

"God," was all Ben could say. He fell to his knees beside the sleeping boy and placed one hand on his son's tousled hair and the other on the dog's shoulder. Steak every day. Caviar. Anything this dog wanted, it was his. He had stayed and protected his son. Kyle was safe. He was safe.

Safe! Holy shit. The city was full of policeman out looking for his son. He turned to hear a low voice. Mel was on her cell, letting the police department know that they'd found Kyle. She clicked off and dialed another number. Now there were tears in her voice as she told Millie that Kyle was fine and where he was. They'd be bringing him home soon.

Meanwhile, Ben nudged Max out of the way and picked up his son in his arms. He just stood there holding him, his head bowed and his eyes closed. Melanie rested her head on Ben's other shoulder and held them both close.

Kyle stirred. His half-awake gaze rested on his father's face. "Max and me had a sleep," he told Ben.

"I can see that, bud. We'll have you back home in bed in no time. Just rest. I've got you."

CHAPTER 16

"*B*en, come back to bed. Kyle's all right now." Mel was dressed in Ben's bath robe. Through the glow of the night light in Kyle's room, she could see the deeply sleeping little boy. Ben sat on a child-sized bean bag chair, his chin on his fists, staring at his son.

He looked up at where Mel stood, silhouetted in the doorway. "I take that back about calling Deanna. I'm a selfish bastard, but I can't imagine my life without him. God, I can't believe how close I came to losing him."

"But you didn't. He's not the first kid to ever wander off. Lots of parents get scares like this. We'll just have to teach Kyle more, show him more rules and work on what to do if he gets lost."

Ben looked over his hands at Mel. "We?" he asked.

It was too dark for Ben to see her blush. "Sorry. I meant you. I guess I was thinking that I'm his teacher and we could do more of this at school. But I'm not his teacher anymore, so my official involvement is over."

"It doesn't have to be."

"What do you mean?"

"I mean that you can have as much involvement in Kyle's life as you want. And in my life. We need you. I need you."

Melanie didn't know what to say. But, as always, she was direct. "What are you saying?"

Ben rose and came towards her, pulling Kyle's door partially closed. "I mean I need you and want you. I think I've been showing you that for months now. I may have used Kyle as an excuse to get you close but it was not just for Kyle's sake that I kept calling you. And tonight, in my room, didn't I show you how I felt about you?

"I love you, Melanie Nicols. I want to be with you; I want you to be with Kyle and I. Would you marry us? I'll take you anyway I can have you. If I'm going too fast and you don't want to get married, you could live here with us or we could get another place. Or you could stay at your place and we could take this a little slower if you need to."

"I thought accountants were cautious, careful planners, not the impulsive types."

"This isn't impulsive. I've thought about it for a long time now, just wasn't sure how to bring it up. Well, actually, my first goal was to get you in my bed, but now I want longer term." He peered down at her, trying to make out her expression in the darkened hallway.

Melanie took his hand and pulled him back toward his bedroom.

"Wait," Ben said. "Don't I get an answer? Even an 'I'll need to think about it'?"

"Yes, if you want a formal answer. Now, get in here. This calls for more action than for talk."

MILLIE MADE waffles while Mel turned the bacon. Kyle seemed none the worse for his adventure. Melanie and Ben glowed as they teased one another and touched often. Millie was the quiet one of the bunch.

It took a while for Ben to notice Millie's withdrawn mood, but finally Mel's pointed looks made him pay attention.

"Millie, are you feeling all right?" he asked. "Is anything wrong?"

"No, I'm fine. I wondered if I might have the rest of the day off. I have some things to do and would like to visit my nephew. I presume Mel will be sticking around? She'll help with Kyle, I'm sure."

"Sure, I can stay," Mel assured her, a question in her voice. "Is there something you'd planned for supper that you'd like me to make?"

"No. I'm sure you have your own ideas," she said as she left the room.

Melanie and Ben looked at each other. This was not like Millie.

"Just let me get my keys and I'll give you a ride," Ben called.

THE FIRST HALF of the ride to Millie's house was silent. Millie stared out the window. Ben did not know what to say. Well, obviously guessing was not going to work, so he'd better just ask her. But ask what, he wondered.

Millie spoke first. "So, it looks like you and Melanie are an item."

"I'm not sure I would have put it that way, but yes, we are together. Definitely together now." He grinned at Millie. "Last night she agreed to marry me. Marry us - Kyle and me."

Millie smiled back at him, but her enthusiasm didn't reach her eyes. "Congratulations. I'm very happy for all of you. She'll make a lovely mother to Kyle. She's a wonderful young woman."

Ben felt the but coming.

And, it did. "But I guess this changes things. Kyle will have a mother now to look after him. You won't need a housekeeper."

Ben looked at her then laughed. "I'm not marrying Mel to get a housekeeper. Nothing's changed that way. We still need you. In fact probably more than ever. Who will stay with Kyle this summer if you're not there?"

"Well, teachers don't work in the summer. Mel will be home with Kyle."

"Some teachers don't work in summer, but not Mel. Ever heard of extended school year? Mel begins next week teaching at the middle years school; she'll be there four days a week all summer."

Millie had more worries. "Some women like to be mistress of their own home. They don't want another female mucking around their place."

"Does that sound like Mel to you? You can ask her yourself, but as far as I can see, she thinks it's a real boon that Kyle and I come with a housekeeper. And, she likes you, she really does."

"I'd better talk directly to her about this. I don't want to interfere or stay where I'm not wanted."

Ben thought a minute. "There is a problem. We can't stay where we are. I can hardly stand the thought of keeping Kyle in that condo another minute after what we went through last night. A condo is no place for a child. We have to get a house, a house with a back yard where we can have Max."

They pulled into Millie's driveway. They sat and took in the views of the house.

"God, you have a lovely place, Millie. A fenced yard, the verandas, the dormers, and look at this neighborhood. It's a place where families live."

"I love it, but I'm aware of all the repairs it needs. Once my nephew and his family leave I hope to get started on some of them. If I keep renting the place out, I should be able to afford to fix up a few things now and then. Really, I should sell it but I have such good memories of the place that I hate the thought of strangers living here."

Ben looked at her. "When does your nephew leave again?"

"In just a few weeks now."

"And how many bedrooms did you say are in this place?"

"Five."

There was a pause. "Mel's accused me of being impulsive. That's a strange thing to say to an accountant. And to think my life was so orderly this time last year." Ben took a big breath. "Millie, would you consider selling to me? Then we could all live here together, you, Kyle, Mel and me. Or, if you don't want to sell, we could rent from you. Either way, we could work something out."

Millie said nothing. Then, Ben remembered. "Of course, I'd have to check it out with Mel first. I think she'll like the idea, in fact I bet she'll be excited. We were talking last night about how we need to find another place to rent, or buy a place with room for Kyle and Max."

Still, Millie was silent. Then a tear trickled down her cheek. Shit, thought Ben. Why didn't I keep my big mouth shut? And, where's Mel when I need her? Looks like I have to do this on my own.

"Okay, Millie. Bad idea, I guess. Sorry. Just forget it. We'll work something else out. It's just that your house really appeals to me - has since the first time I saw it."

"No. Don't forget it. I'm just overcome. I've missed my house. To think of living back here with you and the little one and Melanie and maybe more little ones to come."

Ben had not really thought about that last part, but yes, a smile spread across his face. He could see it. "Let's go talk to Mel. Oh, but wait. Do you need to think about it some more?"

"My head's too full to think of details right now. I imagine there's a lot to work out."

"We get the place appraised to find the fair market value. That would tell us the price either way, if I was to buy it from you or just rent. And we could get a lawyer to work out the details about how you'd always have a place here, even if I bought it."

"Bless you. But we're getting a little ahead of ourselves. Go on home and see what that bride-to-be of yours thinks of your impulsive offer."

MEL, it turns out, was ecstatic, especially after she toured the place. Kyle didn't really get what all the excitement was about, but when Ben said, "Where shall we go to celebrate?" Kyle had an answer.

"To the bakery! Yeah!"

The smells of strong coffee and yeasty dough greeted Millie, Mel, Ben and Kyle when they entered the bakery. Kyle yelled, "Munchkin's here!" It was a good thing his yell warned Ellie before he launched himself at her. Jeff waved a hand at them, but didn't turn his attention from the mocha latte he was building.

Ellie settled them at a table to take their orders. "Why don't you have Jeff waiting tables?" Ben asked her.

"I found that his talents really lie behind the counter. He might be a whiz at cooking, but customer service isn't exactly his forte." She and Melanie exchanged a grin. "Business has picked up since he's been here. We're in the black and it looks like we'll stay there. His sandwiches are a big hit."

"That's great news, little sister." Ben gave her a hug. "We have some news of our own."

"Well, give," Ellie said.

"Ms. Nicols lives with us only I don't have to call her Ms. Nicols, only if I want to. I can call her Mel or I can call her Mom, too."

Ellie's eyes rose. She looked questioningly from Ben to Mel.

"Yes, that's true," said Mel."

The door to the bakery opened and in walked Mel's and Jeff's parents. Since Jeff had started work there they had become regular patrons. At first they came to hover and worry but gradually they'd relaxed as they saw their son blossom. He was a competent, contributing member of the bakery team.

The door from the kitchen opened and Ben and Ellie's parents came out. Ben raised his eyebrows at Ellie. "Yeah dad dropped in, but mom has been coming with him lately, keeping him in check and they don't stay long. Everything's good," she assured him. "And now we're in for one big family adventure. Time to spill your news, big brother."

"Adventure?" asked Kyle. He began singing, "Dora, the explorer..."

***

Would you like a free story?
Anything For Her Son is a tale about a mother's love for her autistic child. Grab your free copy at https://dl.bookfunnel.com/a27d9uzou0

If nonfiction plus autism is your preference:

Autism Questions Parents Ask & The Answers They Seek
Autism Questions Teachers Ask & The Answers They Seek

∽

Young Anna (short story free at https://dl.
bookfunnel.com/xrj0h5wef9)

∽

AUTISM RUNS AWAY

Autism
RUNS AWAY

Dr Sharon A Mitchell

CHAPTER 1

Shrieks split the air. Ellie froze. She could make out the words, "No, no, no, no," but not much else. Then the screams came again.

Ellie hurried down the hall and broke into a run. The office, where was it? She should know this. Ben and Mel had told her to check in there before getting Kyle. Besides, she had no idea which room he was in.

The screams died down then rose to a new crescendo, accompanied by bangs and bumps, objects striking hard surfaces. Kyle!

The sign saying Office was just ahead. Ellie raced in and grabbed the counter. "Kyle. Kyle Wickens. I'm here to collect my nephew. Is he okay? Where is he?"

A placid gaze met hers as an older woman rose from behind a desk and approached the counter. "May I help you?" she asked.

Ellie gaped at her. "Help me?" What was with this woman? "Yes, you can help me. What's going on here? I want my nephew right now!"

The woman peered at her, the calm not leaving her face. "Have we met before?" she asked. "Your face looks familiar."

Was she dense? Or deaf? Couldn't she hear the ruckus down the hallway? Who cared about social niceties? Something was clearly wrong here. Some kids may be in danger, including her nephew. Couldn't this strange woman see that?

There was a commotion in the hall and Ellie retreated to the doorway, ready to snatch Kyle and run if need be. A group of small children lined up against one wall of the hall. With the door open, the yells and thumping were louder. The kids, however, did not seem perturbed, at least not nearly as perturbed as Ellie felt.

She turned her head back to the woman in the office. "What's going on?" she asked.

"I imagine they're doing a room clear."

"A what?"

"A room clear. That's what we call it when for safety's sake we bring the other children out of the classroom when one of their classmates is particularly upset."

"Upset? Upset! Is that what you call all this screaming?"

Before the woman answered, Ellie spotted her nephew in the line of children. Her breath whooshed out and her shoulders came down from their hunched position. He was safe. She didn't know how she'd ever explain to her brother and sister-in-law if Kyle was hurt the very first time she was entrusted to pick him up from school.

"Kyle," she called. "Kyle, come here."

The child turned his head and stepped slightly out of line to see who was calling him. His face lit up when he saw her. "Auntie Ellie!" He waved and waved a grin on his face. "Hi, Auntie Ellie."

"Kyle, come here."

Kyle's grin faded, and he didn't move other than to lower his hand.

"Get over here now." Ellie spoke more sharply than she'd intended.

Still Kyle's feet didn't move. But his hands, both of them now, rose. Instead of waving this time, his arms went out from his sides and his hands started to flap.

Oh, great, Ellie thought. Here it comes now. She spoke more softly this time. "Kyle, please come here now. We need to get out of here."

Kyle's eyes got wider. His hands flapped harder, and his gaze shifted from Ellie to the open doorway and back again.

A girl beside Kyle put her hands on Kyle's shoulders and pushed.

"Hey!" called Ellie as she stepped forward. Was this girl the source of the screams? Was she about to turn her attack on Kyle?

But, Kyle didn't appear fearful, and the girl was not screaming. She continued to push on Kyle's shoulders. As Ellie got closer, she saw Kyle's arms lower and the flapping motions slowed. The little girl looked relaxed, but determined. As Kyle's hunched shoulders lowered, and he took in then let out a big breath, the girl released his shoulders, turned away and began chatting to the girl in front of her.

Ellie took Kyle's face in her hands. "Are you okay?" she asked him.

"Hi, Aunt Ellie," he said as his arms came around her.

Ellie hugged him back. "Hiya, Munchkin. Are you all right?"

Kyle nodded.

"What are you doing in the hall?"

"Ethan got upset."

"Ethan?"

Kyle nodded. Well, that didn't tell her a lot.

"Let's go. Grab your things and let's get out of this place."

Kyle froze. She reached for his hand but he pulled back.

"What's wrong?"

Kyle stared at her. The boy behind him said, "We're supposed to stay right here."

"Yeah, well, I've come to get Kyle and I say we're leaving now."

"The rule is wait for the all clear," Kyle recited under his breath.

"What?"

The other boy explained. "After a room clear, we're supposed to wait here until we get the all clear."

A deeper voice behind her spoke up. "They're right, you know. When we've had to clear the room, the other students are to wait against the wall until a teacher tells them it's all right to return to the room. The kids have not received their all clear yet, so Kyle is doing exactly what he's supposed to do."

"And who exactly are you?" Ellie's eyes blazed.

"His teacher."

"Oh."

He held out his hand. "My name is Rob Sells. And who are you?"

"I'm Ellie Wickens. Kyle's father is my brother. He and Mel are both out of town today and they asked me to pick up Kyle for them. I guess I'm a bit early but I didn't want to be late." Then she noticed the hand that was still outstretched. "Sorry," she apologized as she accepted his firm handshake.

"Ah, you're Mel's sister-in-law. She told us you'd be coming. Welcome to Madson School."

Was this place surreal or what? How could they stand here having a social conversation when just moments ago it had sounded like a child was being hacked to pieces in this very classroom?

"Is everything all right? What's been going on here?" she asked him.

"One of our students became a bit upset."

"A bit?

Mr. Sells flashed a grin. "Well, maybe more than a bit, but he's okay now. In fact, we were just about to go back into the classroom. Care to join us for a few minutes before it is home time?"

Without waiting for her answer, he turned to the children. "It's all clear now. Head back to your seats." The students turned toward the doorway and walked quietly into the room and to their desks.

Well, "desks" was using the term loosely. Ellie had never seen such a rag tag collection of furnishings in a school. Where were the desks of her childhood, those heavy wooden things with a seat attached to a side bar welded to the desk top?

Kyle perched atop a grey plastic mushroom-looking thing. Its round top had a slight depression, which narrowed to a thinner stalk. On the bottom was another disk. As she watched, he squirmed. The poor kid had to wiggle to keep his balance because the stool or whatever it was, was warped. The bottom was not flat. Kyle didn't seem perturbed though. Kids could get used to anything, she thought.

Gazing around the room, she saw other, similar stools, in different sizes. They were the lucky kids, she guessed. One poor kid didn't even have a stool; he was standing at a tall desk, a box of crayons out, his tongue protruding between his lips as he labored away at something.

A couple students sat not on chairs or stools at all but on balls. Looking closer, Ellie thought they looked a lot like the therapy balls she used at the gym, only smaller. Some seemed to have rubber protrusions on the bottom. Maybe to keep them from rolling away? A girl sat reading in a child-sized rocking chair.

There seemed to be an awful lot of movement in this classroom with kids rocking and wiggling and moving but there was surprisingly little noise. The kids had returned to the classroom and had taken up where they left off with their work. Even Kyle. Ellie was amazed at the calm in the room. Her heart rate was just now approaching normal after the horrid screams that had come from this very room.

A VOICE SPOKE BEHIND HER. "So, what do you think?"

She just looked at Mr. Sells. She didn't know what to say.

"It's a bit much, isn't it, when you're not used to it? Today's classroom does not look like the ones we used when we were in school, does it?"

Ellie looked at Kyle's teacher. Mr. Sells was close to her age, possibly a bit older. He was pleasant-looking, with scuffed runners, cargo pants and a polo shirt. He did not look like any grade one teacher she remembered.

Without thinking, she said, "What are you doing teaching first grade?"

"I'm good at it."

"But don't usually women teach the elementary grades."

"Yeah. Actually, I trained for high school English, but needed a job as soon as college was out in April. The only teaching jobs open at that time of year were for substitute teachers. I spent a couple days in a high school then the next call I got was for an elementary school. I accepted, expecting to feel like a bull on a lily pad. But I loved it. And, the kids responded well to me. So, here I am."

She was sounding like her father who believed only men should be in charge of businesses. She knew how much it galled her that her father didn't believe she could run the bakery simply because she was female. Now she was making the same sort of assumption about a guy who wanted to teach little kids.

"Sorry," she apologized. "It's just different. But, different is okay," she hurried to assure him.

Mr. Sells nodded, then moved to the front of the class. He circulated up and down the rows, checking work and exchanging comments with his students.

There was a light knock at the open door. A woman stood there, her brow furrowed, her shoulders sagging as if the weight of her hand bag was dragging her down. As Mr. Sells approached, her hushed voice asked, "Is Ethan here?"

"Hi, Mrs. Fellows. Come on in. He's right here, reading a book." He turned to Ellie. "Mrs. Fellows, this is Ms. Wickens, the aunt of one of our students. Ms. Wickens, this is Mrs. Fellows."

As the women said hello, a little head peaked out from the opening of a tent Ellie hadn't even noticed. It blended into a nook by the book shelves, a taupe, kid-sized tent with the door flaps tied open. The floor of the tent held scattered pillows, some hand-sized soft balls, a couple bean bags and one small boy.

The child crawled out of the tent with a book in his extended hand. He gave the woman no hello, no hug or any other sign of recognition. His expression did not change. But, he held the book out to her, launching into a detailed explanation about the giant sawfly butterfly and how in its pupa stage, the caterpillar looked like bird poop. The woman tried to shush the child with a hand over his mouth and pressed him to her side, but he resisted and continued on with his spiel. The next page of the book covered buckeye butterfly, whose larva exactly matched the color of toadflax, its favorite meal. Ellie was impressed with the kid's knowledge, but the corners of his mother's mouth drooped. In fact, everything about her seemed to sag.

Ignoring what Ethan was saying, the woman looked to Mr. Sells. "He seems all right now," she said.

"Yes, he's calmed. The quiet of the tent helped settle him. We'll work on this some more tomorrow."

"Tomorrow? You mean he can come back tomorrow?"

Mr. Sells looked confused. "Didn't I understand that you had moved to our area and Ethan would attend school here now?

"Well, yes, but I thought that after this afternoon you might not want him back."

The teacher looked concerned. He gave her a warning glance and knelt in front of Ethan. When he placed his hand covering the page of the book, the child's mother took in a sharp breath and tensed. Mr. Sells ignored that and continued.

"Ethan, it's time to go home now with your mom. But you'll be back tomorrow and we'll start a new day. I'm giving your mother a copy of our visual calendar. Will you explain it to her? She's new to this so you must help her. Please go get the copy off my desk."

As Ethan walked to his desk, Mr. Sells turned back to Mrs. Fellows. "This was your son's first day and new experiences are hard. It will get better each day.

"It will help if he knows what he'll be doing during the day. Actually, that helps all of us, including you and I. Ah, here it is. Thanks, Ethan."

He spread the page on a nearby table and the three of them hunched over it. Mr. Sells explained that the pictures in this list represented the overview of the activities they would do the next morning. On the back of the page was the schedule of afternoon activities. Each picture depicted another subject or assignment. "Let's tell your mom what these pictures mean."

One by one he pointed to each line drawing and Ethan said the word associated with the picture. He only stumbled once, needing Mr. Sells help with the picture for music period. His teacher beamed at Ethan. "After only one day you already know these so well. Good job, Ethan." Again, Ethan's face didn't change in response to the praise, but he didn't look upset either.

"Why don't you show your mom where you hang your coat and you can get ready to go home."

Ethan and Mrs. Fellows were almost out of the door. "Wait," the teacher called. "We have a routine in this room." Mrs. Fellows stood hesitantly by the door; Ethan stood impassive.

Mr. Sells turned to the students. "Class, Ethan is leaving now. What do we say to him?"

Not quite in perfect unison, the kids said, "Goodbye, Ethan. See you tomorrow." The last tomorrows echoed.

Mrs. Fellows' eyes brimmed. Ethan turned to go through the door.

"Not so fast," his teacher said. "Wait. What do you say back to the class?"

His mom put a hand on her son's shoulder and tried to hustle him into the hall. "Oh, that's all right. You know what he means. Thanks for the sentiment and all."

Mr. Sells stood firm. "No. We have rules here. No student leaves for the day without saying goodbye." He stood waiting, his gaze locked on Ethan's. "Ethan, the class said goodbye to you. Now, what do you say?"

"But he's not into the social stuff much. You *know* what he means. We need to get going."

Mr. Sells was unmoved. His eyes never left Ethan's face other than to give Mrs. Fellows one warning glance. He looked like he was ready to wait there all day. The class waited calmly as well. Only Mrs. Fellows looked uneasy. And Ellie. Ellie definitely did not want a repeat of that god-awful caterwauling Ethan had produced earlier. How could this teacher risk starting that up all over again?

As everyone waited and his mom squirmed, a small word came from Ethan's mouth. "Bye."

His teacher beamed as if Ethan had delivered the valedictory address. He waved. "See you tomorrow."

From Kyle's seat a voice said, "See you soon raccoon."

Ethan turned his back as he said, "After a while crocodile." Then they were gone.

. . .

ELLIE LET OUT HER BREATH. "Well, that was risky. What would you have done if he'd started screaming again?"

Mr. Sells shrugged. "I don't know. Wait it out, I suppose, like we did the last time. He left to continue his walk up and down the rows of students. Despite the strange seating, the kids worked well, most on their own, some conferring with neighbors.

Ellie thought about what the teacher had said. Wait it out. She shook her head. She knew how things might go, having witnessed some of Kyle's upsets.

When the teacher's path took him back to where she was standing, Ellie asked, "Don't you worry about impressionable young children seeing such things? God, I'd do anything to prevent Kyle from having one of these upsets."

"Is that good for Kyle?"

Ellie didn't know what to say. "He's my nephew. I love him and can't stand to see him upset."

"I'm glad he has you for a champion but are you doing him any favors if you tiptoe around him? Look. Life is full of challenges and frustrations. Part of growing up is in learning how to handle them and how to handle ourselves."

"Yeah, but you don't get it. Kyle's just a kid, and he's different. He has autism - an official diagnosis and everything."

"Yes, I understand that. But, so what?"

"So what? Autistic kids are different. They don't get the sorts of stuff that come naturally to other people."

"Yes, all true. But what are you doing to help him?"

"I try to keep his life as calm as possible. Have you ever seen Kyle in a meltdown?"

"I have," his teacher admitted.

"And what did you do?"

"I waited it out. Then when he was calm, we went over what happened, what his choices would be the next time and what was expected of him."

"Yeah, right. You make it sound so simple. I'm ready to crawl into bed and put the covers over my head when one of these is over. Or have a good stiff drink," said Ellie.

"I can't say I've never felt the same way but that wouldn't help the kids."

"Maybe not, but it would help me," muttered Ellie.

"I admit that watching a meltdown can be draining."

"No shit, Sherlock," came out of Ellie's mouth before she could stop it. She put up a hand, too late, to cover her face. Her fingers partly obscured her eyes, so she missed the grin the teacher turned away to hide.

A chime that sounded from the hallway, rescuing Ellie. In a minute she heard the sound of children's voices and movement of many sneakered feet. She looked at her watch and saw that school was over for the day.

"Sorry. Looks like I'd better get out of the way before I get trampled." She remembered the end-of-the-day mass exodus from her own childhood.

"There is no trampling in my classroom. Watch. You'll see. We have a routine for everything."

To the class he said, "Time to get ready to go home. Jenny, please bring up on the SMART Board the picture that shows what our desk should look like at the end of the day."

A little girl rose from her seat and walked to the screen at the front of the room. She looked at the little pictures on the bottom, then put her finger on the one she wanted. The screen filled with a picture of an organized desk, pencils in the slot at the front, books neatly stacked along the side, crayons, scissors and glue in their plastic container. The kids busied themselves at their desks, some glancing often at the picture on the board, others tidying up without that visual reminder.

Mr. Sells gave the next instruction. "Put your hand up when your desk matches the picture on the board."

The teacher checked each child's desk with an approving word or smile, then had them get their things from their cubicles at the back. Each child lined up with their jackets on, their back packs over their shoulders. Ellie watched as each child approached the back of the line, with one arm held in front of them. When he was an arm's length from the child in front, he lowered that arm and crossed his arms in front of his chest. The teacher waited at the door, saying to each child, "Tell me in one sentence something you learned today?" After each response, he asked "Handshake or high five?" After Kyle's turn, he waited just outside the door with Ellie.

With the last handshake or high five exchanged, Ellie asked Mr. Sells, "What was that all about? I thought it was supposed to be a hug, handshake or high five?"

He grinned at her. "Maybe it's part of that gender thing you were referring to earlier. I don't like it, but it's probably better for me career-wise to keep some physical distance from my kids. A couple students in the room have witnessed spousal abuse and have not always had positive associations with men. Plus, some of these kids, like those with autism, need years to get used to certain rules. I'm safe and it would be okay to give me a hug but not all children have a sense of stranger danger and would over-generalize, thinking it's all right to hug any man. It's a sad comment on my gender, but that would not be a safe habit to get into. It was different in kindergarten but now they're a whole year older and we're working on behaviors that will carry them through the next years. We practice high fives or handshakes because that's a cultural norm they need to get used to."

"There's more to all this than meets the eye," Ellie said, but she thought that there was actually more to this guy than met the eye. Interesting. She'd ask Mel about him.

CHAPTER 2

No matter how many times she made them, cream puffs were still Ellie's favorite. Who didn't love the fresh whipped cream oozing out the middle of the rich, golden, puffed pastry? The sprinkling of powdered sugar with a mere hint of cinnamon was the crowning glory.

Layered on top of that were the smells of Jeff's cooking. Corned beef and herbed chickens roasted in the oven, ready for their part in his deli lunch creations. Yes, the bakery had taken off since Jeff joined the crew, taking them from a struggling neighborhood bakery to a full-fledged bistro. Baristas no longer quit weekly because now Jeff was here to keep the coffee equipment functioning. Plus, the extra revenue allowed Ellie to buy needed upgrades.

Best of all was her dad. Although he would never admit out loud that Ellie now ran the family bakery, he'd stopped interfering, giving conflicting directions to staff, mixing up orders and the other things that used to contribute to the business running in the red.

Oh, there were still problems. Having an employee with Asperger's Syndrome was new to her, especially an employee who had never held down a regular job before in all of his thirty years. But he was talented, oh so skilled on many fronts. They were learning to work together and once they'd hammered out the ground rules, combining flexible rigidity, if you'd believe it, they rolled along with less conflict than she'd had with previous employees.

JEFF WAS NOT A MORNING PERSON. Well, neither was Ellie, but it came with the territory of running a bakery, so she got used to it. She enjoyed working alone in the early morning, relishing the peace and solitude as she prepared for the day's baking.

There was no need for Jeff to arrive as early as she, but he needed to get there in time to start the meat roasting to create his tantalizing deli sandwiches. Theirs was not a large kitchen and Ellie needed all the ovens for the baking first thing in the morning.

At first, Jeff arrived when he wished and commandeered the ovens for his meats. He seemed oblivious to the fact that Ellie had loaves rising, soon ready for the oven. Jeff was honestly perplexed when a perturbed Ellie found her oven racks taken up with beef and chicken and pork and complained. Jeff replied, "But I thought you wanted fresh deli sandwiches. How can they be fresh if I don't roast the meat before lunch?"

When Ellie countered with, "How can you make fresh deli sandwiches if I can't bake the bread?" Jeff saw her point.

Now, they had a system. By coming in only thirty minutes earlier, half of Ellie's baking was finished before Jeff's meat was seasoned, prepared and ready for the ovens. The temperature of oven A read 350° and oven B was at 400°. Neither temperature perfectly suited Ellie nor Jeff but they each had to deal with it, adjusting recipes in line with this. With the middle two racks in each oven reserved for Ellie and Jeff had use of the rest. He also got full oven use once Ellie's bread finished baking. Those were the rules. When Ellie overstepped them, Jeff let her know, even when that meant she had to get up an hour earlier to bake the Easter breads. Rules were rules. Besides, how could El complain when Jeff's cooking brought in so much extra business?

. . .

THE TINKLE of the bell signaled the arrival of another customer. Ellie didn't glance up; her staff would take care of the orders.

When she'd finished icing the last of the donuts and arranging the cheese cakes in the display case, Ellie took a breather. She noticed the brimming coffee pots, telling her that someone had made new batches and customers would be ready for refills. She took a pot of decaf in one hand and Arabic dark in the other and made her rounds to the tables.

A lone woman glued to her phone caught Ellie's attention. The woman would scroll through her screen, read, and set the phone down, only to pick it up again moments later. Compulsive smart phone use was nothing new with her customers, but usually people looked more content, especially when wooed by the bakery concoctions and smooth, dark roast coffee. Besides, this woman looked familiar.

She was not one of their regulars. Ellie puzzled over where she might have seen her before. Stopping in front of the table with pots in hand, it came to her. Ethan's mother. Ellie recognized that look, the walking on egg shells, waiting for the next bomb to fall look this woman had worn when she picked up her son from Kyle's class last week.

Ellie had a few minutes. The customers seemed happy, her staff productively occupied. She asked, "Mind if I join you for a couple minutes? I could use a cup of coffee myself." Before the woman had time to plan her refusal, Ellie left for a mug of her own.

"Hi," she said upon returning. "We met yesterday. I was at the school picking up my nephew and you were there for your son." She held out her hand, "I'm Ellie Wickens, aunt to a grade one Munchkin and owner of this bakery."

The woman's social skills forced her to accept the handshake even though her shoulders partly turned away from Ellie and her eyes made contact only fleetingly.

"I'm Sara Fellows. Mother to a grade one boy."

"Pleased to meet you. Is this your first time to our bakery?"

"Yes. We're new to this area." There was a pause. Ellie waited. Sara continued, "You have a nice place here. This cranberry walnut bran muffin is wonderful."

"Wait until you taste our deli sandwiches."

"Oh, I doubt I'll be here that long. I'll probably have to head to the school any minute now."

Ellie turned her head to the side. "Why? Is this a short day, teachers' meetings or something?"

"No, nothing like that. It's just that I'm on call in case I need to go get Ethan."

"Why?"

"Why what?"

"Well, my brother and sister-in-law have a kid in school and I guess they're always on call like any parent. I'm pretty sure the school would be good about phoning parents if their child has an accident or something. But Ben and Mel don't act like they're on call all day long."

"It's different for us." Her eyes welled with tears. "Our son has autism."

"So does my nephew."

Sara gaped at her. Ellie nodded, confirming that yes, Sara had heard correctly.

"And he's in Ethan's class?"

"Yep. This is his second year at Madson School and he's in first grade now."

"I didn't know. I never noticed."

Ellie laughed. "Well, Kyle doesn't exactly have a big A painted on his forehead."

Sara's cheeks tinged with red. "No, I didn't mean that. It's just that whenever I've been to the school, I've never seen any other student in the room act like Ethan."

"What do you mean, act like Ethan?"

Sara's face changed. "Oh, god. It's dreadful. He has these terrible meltdowns."

"Tell me about it. I've seen a few of Kyle's, even though they're happening less and less now."

"Less often? Ethan's have gotten worse over the last years." It all came out in a rush. "Our lives are awful, just awful. Every waking minute is ruled by either Ethan's tantrum or the threat of a tantrum or doing everything in our power to prevent the next one.

"I can't work anymore. I got called to pick him up so many times when he was in kindergarten that I lost my job. This fall, it was even worse in grade one. The school didn't understand what to do with him. He kept pitching these fits, throwing things, screaming and creating so many disturbances that the other kids couldn't work. They feared that he was going to hurt someone, and he almost did several times.

"We moved to try a new school. Maybe a fresh start. Maybe a place where they don't know his past, maybe new kids who aren't afraid of him would help. But, it's started again, the same thing all over again and I have no idea what we're going to do."

Ellie handed Sara more napkins to mop up her tears.

"I don't know a lot about this autism stuff and even less about teaching. But, I've seen my nephew make great strides since he's been at this school. It's not perfect, don't let me mislead you, but it's gotten better and better. Part of it is that my brother has learned more about parenting in general and especially about parenting a kid with autism. It's not rocket science if even *he* can learn." She grinned. "It helps that he married Kyle's old teacher. Mel has her master's degree specializing in autism."

Sara hung on her every word.

"I've only met Kyle's grade one teacher, Mr. Sells, once, but Mel thinks highly of him."

"He seems to stay calm and at least he's not furious with me and with Ethan, or at least not when I've been there." Sara's voice showed hope that her face dared not acknowledge.

Ellie studied her and decided to be frank. "I might have witnessed one of Ethan's meltdowns. I was there to pick up Kyle when his parents were not able to. I arrived early and heard the screeches."

Sara winced.

"I admit, they unnerved me," said Ellie. "But I seemed to be the only one upset, well apart from Ethan. The other kids waited in the hallway, then went back into the classroom when Mr. Sells told them to. They got right back to work. *I* was still vibrating but everyone else seemed to take it in stride."

Sara tried to apologize. "I'm so sorry you had to witness that and sorry that he disturbed the class and even sorrier that this happens to my son. Honestly, we try; we really do. We love our son. We're not bad parents, at least we try not to be, but we must be if our kid acts like this."

"Hmmm. Most of what I know about this, I've learned from my sister-in-law. I don't think she holds with that bad parent theory or even a bad teacher theory. She explained that many kids with autism are simply wired differently."

Sara brow furrowed like these were new concepts. "What do you mean?" she asked.

"OKAY. I can't do this nearly as well as Mel does, but I'll give it a try. You should meet her someday, by the way. You'd like Mel.

"Kids with autism can be hyper-sensitive to some things, things the rest of us would hardly notice or dismiss them if we did notice. Like a thread from your sock lying across your toe. Or the swishing sound of rain pants or the hum of fluorescent light."

"I didn't realize lights made any noise."

"I believe it's only fluorescents," Ellie explained.

"Yes, they sure do," came from across the room. Jeff.

"Who's that?" Sara asked. "Was he talking to us? How did he know what we're talking about?"

"That's Jeff. He's in charge of the deli part of the bakery and our chief fixer-upper when anything breaks down. Oh, you should sample his sandwiches. You must bring your family here for lunch someday."

"We don't go out much and certainly we can't bring Ethan to eat in public."

"Why not?"

"You never know what might set him off and how he might act."

Ellie raised an eyebrow as she looked at Sara. "This is a pretty casual place and you're welcome anytime."

"Thanks, but I can't see us chancing it anytime soon. A lot would have to change before we'd be able to eat out as a family."

Jeff's back was to them, but they could hear him add, "You need to look at the situation from the kid's point of view."

Sara turned to regard Jeff's back. "How does he do that? He's on the other side of the room. How can he tell what we're talking about?"

"That's Jeff." Ellie's smile took in both Sara and Jeff. "He's a man of many talents beyond sandwich making. He has hearing like you'd never imagine. It may appear that he's not paying attention, but he's likely aware of everything going on in this building."

"You bet your sweet patootie I am," said Jeff.

"Jeff! That's probably not appropriate to say in a place of business."

"Probably?" he echoed. "Well, is it or isn't it? Make up your mind. And, not everything is meant literally. Didn't anybody ever tell you that? It's like an idiom. Besides, maybe your patootie's not sweet. I have no personal experience with it."

"Can it, Jeff." Ellie laughed; Sara looked shocked. "Did I mention that Jeff is my sister-in-law's brother?"

"Oh, so you know each other well. He's not just your employee."

"No, we're friends and relatives of a sort." Ellie continued. "And, did I also mention that he has autism?"

From Jeff, "Get it right, El. For those purists among us, my diagnosis is Asperger's Syndrome, still within the autism spectrum, but a subset characterized by no lag in communication, cognitive or self-help skills. Should I go on?"

"Not right now, Jeff, but thanks for offering. Likely we've overwhelmed Sara enough."

"Okay. I know what it's like to feel overwhelmed." Jeff retreated to the kitchen to remove the corned beef from the oven.

Sara leaned forward and lowered her voice. "What's he doing working here if he has autism?" she asked.

A voice from the back yelled, "I heard that. Want me to answer it, El?"

"No. Thanks, but I've got it," answered Ellie.

Mortified, Sara whispered, "God, I'm sorry. I didn't think he could hear me from the back room. What must he think of me?"

There was no reply from Jeff.

Sara waited a minute. "Could my son ever be like Jeff? Have a job? Be around people?"

"That's me. Role model to the masses or at least the masses with autism," came from the kitchen.

Ellie raised her voice to be sure it would carry to the kitchen. "Are you sure you'd *want* your kid to be like Jeff?"

"Yep, as soon as she tastes my corned beef on rye, she'll be sure," Jeff yelled back.

CHAPTER 3

$\mathcal{M}$el looked up at the knock on her open classroom door. "Ellie, hi. What brings you here?"

"Hey Mel. I wanted to talk to you about something and thought this would be a quiet place without the interruptions of the Munchkin."

"He does demand your attention whenever you're around. He thinks a lot of his Auntie El. Come on in. Let me introduce you to Lori Nabaku. Lori's the EA, Educational Associate, in our room. Lori, this is my sister-in-law Ellie Wickens."

Mel continued. "And, I'd like you to meet Kyle's teacher, Rob Sells."

Rob nodded, and Ellie said, "Good. I'm glad you're here. You're part of what I wanted to talk to Mel about."

"This sounds interesting," Mel said. Rob's expression went from open to guarded.

He turned to Mel. "You know I can't talk about Kyle to anyone other than you or Ben without written consent."

"It's not Kyle I want to talk about. It's Ethan."

"Whoa. That's even worse. If it was about Kyle at least I could have obtained verbal consent from his step-mother. But I definitely cannot and will not discuss someone else's kid with you or in front of you."

"I get that," Ellie said. "So what if I talk in generalities about how you're handling things in your classroom?"

The book she was holding rose to cover the lower half of Mel's face as she stifled a laugh. Lori's twitter escaped, before she said, "Guess that's my cue to get out of here before the fireworks start. See ya. Mel, at least you have that desk to take cover behind." With that, she was gone.

Rob looked like part of him wanted to be gone too, but the rest of him wanted to put this annoying, intrusive woman in her place. His initial thoughts of Ellie had been that she was smart, attractive, a bit mouthy but worth getting to know. Now, the first three still applied but he changed his mind about the last bit. Damned if he was going to run from her, though. He crossed his arms, leaned his shoulders back against the wall, bent one knee and rested the toe of his shoe against the wall. The picture of nonchalance, or so he hoped.

When Ellie didn't say anything, he extended an index finger horizontally and waved it in a circular motion to signal her to go on.

"Thanks. Glad I have your permission." Ellie's tone dripped sarcasm. She turned to her sister-in-law. "Mel, I think this guy needs lessons on autism and on how to treat kids. I spoke with Ethan's mother."

That got Rob off the wall. "You what? How dare you seek out one my kid's parents? That's like stalking. What business is it of yours? How could you invade that family's privacy?"

"Keep your shorts on," Ellie reassured him. "I didn't seek anyone out. Sheesh. What do you think I am?" Then she added, "Don't answer that.

"Sara Fellows came into my bakery. I remembered seeing her with Ethan that day I came to pick up Kyle. You know, Mel, the day you and Ben were both away and Millie had that appointment?"

Mel nodded.

"Other people in the bakery might text and read messages on their phone but they don't cling to it the way Sara was. She couldn't relax but kept checking to see if she had a message. It was a slow morning, and I had some time so I started talking with her. She told me that she couldn't stay long. She was waiting for a message from the school to come for Ethan. No, she didn't have an appointment and no, he wasn't sick. She was just used to the school calling her constantly to take her son home."

Ellie turned to Rob. "Did you know that she got fired from her job because she had to take so much time off work to get Ethan? The woman has no friends, no life and can't get one because she's constantly waiting for a call from the school. From *you*."

Rob started to speak but Ellie rushed on, giving him no chance.

"Have you no idea how to handle kids? If that's the problem, Mel here could help you. She's great with kids, especially kids with autism. She's taught us a lot - I mean my brother and my parents and me. We're all much better with Kyle than we used to be. Look, there are strategies you can use, things that really help."

"Like listening more and talking less," Mel said wryly.

"Well, yes. I don't remember the listening more, but I did learn to talk less and show more, and all that whole visual stuff."

"Tell me more about this visual stuff you mentioned." Ellie missed the glint in Rob's eyes as he spoke, but Mel didn't.

Mel thought it was time to referee. "Look, Ellie. I think you mean well, but you don't know what you're talking about. You're way off base with Rob...."

"No," Rob interrupted, "let her speak. I'd like to hear what else she has to say. Who knows? Maybe I'll learn how to teach grade one from her."

"Rob," Mel started.

Ellie jumped in. "I'm not trying to tell you how to teach grade one. I'm sure you know more about that than I do."

"Well, thanks for that much anyway," Rob told her.

Ellie gave a half smile, the sarcasm going over her head.

"Look, I get that you can't have a kid screaming in your classroom. I heard Ethan that day. I don't know how anyone could stand that noise; the students certainly couldn't get any work done with that going on. And, it sounded like he was throwing things or beating something - that could be dangerous for the other kids.

"But it doesn't have to be like that. Mel could show you ways to get Ethan calmed down and ways to keep all this from happening. Just look at Kyle. He went from being one big tantrum to only having a couple a week and even these aren't such a big deal anymore."

"I'm happy to hear that Kyle and his family have benefited from Mel's wisdom," Rob told her.

Encouraged, Ellie nodded. "Sure, and you could, too."

Mel tried again to stop her. "Ellie, listen. You don't know what you're talking about..."

"But, I do. Don't be so modest, Mel. What you've done is miraculous. Without you Ben would still be floundering." She paused a second. "Hey, I don't mean that he married you just for the help with Kyle. I mean, well you know what I mean."

"Yeah, I get it. But you're not in possession of some facts."

Ellie turned back to Rob, earnestly trying to convince him.

"What I'm trying to say is that things can get better. If you'd just try some strategies, I'm sure Ethan will get calmer. Then his poor mother can get some peace.

"And what is school about, anyway? Aren't kids here to learn? Maybe the stuff Ethan needs to learn first isn't written in the textbook on reading or math."

"Actually, the things he needs to learn all *are* in the curriculum in one form or another," Rob said.

"If he's ever going to learn, Ethan has to be in school and be in school consistently. Mel told us over and over to be consistent with Kyle. That means he has to be here every day like other kids."

She was not done. "And his mother deserves a break. She needs to know you can handle her kid and that he'll be in school every day. This might be her kid, but she needs a life, too."

She paused for breath.

Rob waited. "Are you done?" he asked.

Ellie nodded. "For now, anyway."

"I'll anxiously await your next installment. Do I get to say a few things now?"

Again, Ellie nodded.

"Do you have a child in grade one or soon to be in grade one?"
Ellie shook her head no.

"Good. Two points. One - my teaching methods are none of your business. I will and do explain my teaching to my students, their parents and to my principal. I don't need to explain myself or defend myself to you. Two - if you ever do decide to have a child, let me know before he or she is ready for grade one and I'll ask for a transfer out of here." He unfolded from his spot on the wall and headed out the door with a wave of his hand, adding, "Have a nice evening, Mel."

ELLIE WATCHED him leave then turned to Mel. "That wasn't much of a discussion, was it?"

"Are you talking about your diatribe to him or his parting comments?"

"The least I thought he'd do was defend himself. Or ask for your help," Ellie replied.

"El, just what did you hope to accomplish with this? You come in here knowing nothing about the situation, proceed to criticize a good man, accusing him of things you know nothing about."

"I do know about them. Sara Fellows told me all about what she's been through with the school and Ethan. She's a woman on the edge, hanging on by her toes. Her son needs help. She needs help, the kind of help you give people.

"I've seen what you did for Kyle and my brother; you turned their lives around and gave them a shot at normalcy. Ethan and his family deserve the same kind of help."

"How do you know they're not going to get it from Rob?" Mel asked.

"Well, it sure hasn't happened so far. That woman has been through hell with the school and her son. How many kids do you know who get kicked out of kindergarten? That happened to Ethan last year."

"Where did he go to school?"

"I'm not sure. She didn't say. But she did talk about his year and how she can't go anywhere or do anything because she just gets started and there's a call to come get him from school."

"And did she say who calls her?" Mel asked.

"No. No, she didn't. But it must be Rob or maybe he gets the school secretary to do it."

"Ellie, did anyone ever tell you that you should get your facts straight before launching into attack mode?"

"What? What? I wasn't in attack mode. Sheesh. I was just trying to help out, to point out to that teacher some things he might be missing. And, I did get my facts straight. I got them right from the kid's mother. How much more accurate can you get? You should have seen that woman. It's not everyday someone blubbers in my bakery."

"Sometimes when people are under stress they need to talk, sure. But their story might not come out in a coherent sequence. They may remember incidents and feelings they've had for a while."

Melanie continued. "Did it ever occur to you that some of what she said does not apply to Rob and this school? Didn't she mention that they had moved and were new to this area?"

Ellie paused. "Well, yes, she did, but I thought she meant they were in a new house."

"They likely are, plus...."

"Plus what?" Mel didn't reply, just continued to look at Ellie. Then she got it. "Mel, are you saying that Ethan is new to *this* school?"

Mel nodded.

"How long has he been here?"

"The day you came for Kyle was Ethan's first day in Rob's grade one room."

"Oh, shit. And all those phones calls to come get him were not from this Rob guy but from their previous school?"

Mel nodded her head yes.

"But I saw her coming for Ethan. And I heard his tantrum just a bit before that. Surely the teacher must have called her."

"What were you doing when you saw her?"

"I was picking up your son, remember?"

Mel looked pointedly at her sister-in-law.

"Oh, double shit. I owe someone an apology, don't I? I have made a fool of myself, big time. He must think you have such an idiot for a sister-in-law and a loud-mouth one at that.

"Do you think he's still here? I'd better go apologize."

"Wait! You might want to let him cool off before...." It was too late. Ellie was out the door and down the hall. Mel shrugged and grinned. Ellie had met her match in Rob. She was sure they could both hold their own with each other. Each other - that thought flitted through her mind. Well, if there had ever been a glimmer of a chance for anything to develop between the two of them, Ellie had likely doused those flames well and good.

THE DOOR WAS CLOSED but not latched and the lights were on. Peering through the door's window, Ellie could see Rob at his desk reading. She could only see part of the thin paperback he held in his hands, something about Journal... of Psychol.... Well, at least he was alone so she was not interrupting anything too crucial, as far as she could see.

She knocked.

Rob's head lifted, and he looked out the window. He eyes met hers then his hand re-adjusted their grip on his book and his gaze returned to the page.

Hmm. Not very friendly, Ellie thought. But then, she may not have given him reason to feel warm and fuzzy towards her.

She rapped again.

"I'm working here and don't wish to be disturbed," he said to the door.

"I just want to apologize."

"Good for you, but I'm busy."

Ellie was getting annoyed. What was with this jerk? She was trying to apologize. Couldn't he cut her a break?

"Look. Can I come in? Just for a minute?" Was he going to make her speak through the door?

"Go away. School's out and I'm on my own time here."

Not exactly the chummy sort. "Mr. Sells, I'm sorry. I was out of line. I didn't have my facts straight, and I blamed you for things that were not your fault."

He looked pointedly at her then back to his journal.

"Mel says you're a good guy and a great teacher. I'm sure she's right. It's just that I was so worried about Sara and her son. I was only trying to help. I've seen what Mel has done for Kyle and wanted stuff like that for Ethan's family. From what Mel's told me, I'm now sure that you do know how to teach Ethan."

"Well, thank you for that vote of confidence. Now, if you don't mind...."

"Can't you just open the door and we'll talk face to face? I'd like to apologize properly."

"Ms. Wickens, I've had a long day, I have work to do and frankly, you have nothing to say that would interest me. Please leave."

"But..."

Rob got up and walked to the door. Oh good thought Ellie. Finally. Now I can tell him how sorry I am and maybe we can even talk about autism things I've learned from Mel. Besides, Mel liked him and he really wasn't a bad-looking guy. They'd just gotten off on the wrong foot.

Then, he was in front of her. "Goodbye," he said. The door shut in her face and Rob returned to his desk, rearranging his chair so that his back was to the door.

Well. What a rude, arrogant man. The least he could have done is let her apologize. What a jerk! He was not worthy of her apology or her time.

Ellie stormed down the hall to tell Mel what Rob had just done. She stopped; Mel's lights were out, and it looked like she'd gone home. Maybe that was just as well since Mel had not seemed too pleased with Ellie anyway.

CHAPTER 4

Sneakers squeaked along the floor, the swish of backpacks rubbing, and squeal of little voices contributed to the excitement in the air. Milling small bodies heralded the arrival of another school day.

Mr. Sells greeted each child at the door. Some received a handshake, some a pat on the back, others a squeeze to the shoulder and others had a picture schedule placed in their hands. Rob Sells believed they all needed a personal touch to begin the day but how that touch should look varied depending on the current needs of each child. He strove to know his kids well and to give each what they needed to have a good day.

One head towered above all the others in the hallway. Mrs. Fellows. She approached the room holding on to the hand of Ethan. He was the only child to arrive at the classroom door with a parent and the only child whose hand was attached to an adult. Well, they'd only been at the school a week and there was time to help Mrs. Fellows let go. But that would not happen until she was more relaxed and trusted Rob with her son.

He greeted Ethan with a, "Hey, bud. Nice to see you," and a raised hand ready for a high five. To his satisfaction, Ethan met his hand, even if his eyes did not glance his way. As always, Rob marveled at how this could happen, a kid accurately places his hand without his eyes obviously following the progress of the end of his arm. But it happened. Rob himself was neither that skilled nor that coordinated and knew his high five would look more like a flail if he tried it that way. "

Once inside the room, Sara Fellows knelt to remove her son's backpack and jacket. Ethan stood impassive as she went to work. Rob sighed inwardly. Time to intervene.

"Mrs. Fellows, I have something to show you, some of Ethan's work that is quite good. Would you mind coming over here a minute? Ethan can hang his coat up himself."

"Yes, I'll be there but first I need to help Ethan." While her head was turned toward the teacher, Ethan had stepped away. His coat was mostly down his arms already and as they watched, he shook it off, picked it up and hung it on the hook marked "Ethan".

Sara gaped. "He never does that at home on his own."

"No? Well, you see now that he can, can't he?" Rob hoped the point was made and he could move on to other things.

"Have a seat over here, please." He handed her a strip of paper. "This is a copy of Ethan's visual schedule. It lets him know what we'll be doing during the day. I've found that it helps when the kids know, and then there are no surprises for them. If you look you'll see that his schedule ends here at lunch time. That's *not* because that is the end of his day, but because just looking at the morning activities is enough at once. Just before lunch starts, he receives his new schedule which covers between noon and when it's time to go home.

"If you look around, you'll see that everyone here uses a schedule, but that they may look differently for different kids. We all share one big one on the wall over there," he pointed," then another one will appear on the SMART Board. For some of my students, that's all they need. For others, it's better to have a schedule of their own on their desk or attached to their book. If you look over there, you can see that Ethan has his on his desk.

"Some kids have visual schedules that cover the entire day, some for just a half day, like Ethan's and for some students even that is too long. Theirs is broken into four parts, separated by recesses and lunch."

He held the schedule strip out to Sara. "Here, this is your copy and the afternoon strip is on the back. It often helps if the parent goes over the next day's activities at home the night before or over breakfast in the morning before school. It won't take up a lot of your time. Ethan's starting to know our routine, so just point to each picture in turn and he'll tell you which subject the picture stands for." Rob beamed at her. "Can I count on you to help by going over this with Ethan at least once a day? I can assure you that it will help make your son's life easier at school."

Rob watched Sara's face carefully to judge her reaction. Was she ready for more? No, not quite yet. She still didn't look comfortable in the classroom which meant she didn't truly trust him enough with her son.

He invited Sara to sit and watch for a while.

"Why, is Ethan causing problems?"

"No. Oh, no, nothing like that. It's just that you're new to this school and I thought you might want to see how we operate in this room and how your son is fitting in. He *is* starting to fit in, you know."

"After the fuss he made last Friday, I wasn't sure you'd let him back."

Rob looked at her curiously. "Your son is a part of our class. Why wouldn't we have him back? He went through a rough spell that day, yes. But have you noticed that those incidents started to decrease as the week went on? Keep in mind that he's only been here just over one week and that's not much time to learn our ways. But, I can assure you that he will learn and he'll flourish here."

Sara looked like she didn't dare hope for that. "I'm really sorry that he's so much of a bother."

Rob stopped her there. "Stop. Your son is not a bother. He's a small child in a new situation. He's not sure of what's coming next or what's expected of him. His system is on high alert. It's my job, or rather *our* job together," his finger moved back and forth between himself and

Sara," to help Ethan settle in and feel safe here. His mind won't be available for learning until he feels more secure. That's part of what that visual schedule is all about and why it's crucial for you to help by going over it at home daily with your little guy."

Sara's hands wrapped around the laminated strip. "I will, I will. Anything to help my son. He was so unhappy in his last school and they weren't happy with him. I just want him to fit in and be like a regular little boy." Then her face fell. "But I guess that won't ever happen. He has autism."

"Yes, he has autism. So do three other kids in this room. Can you tell which ones?"

Sara's eyebrows rose, and her mouth formed a little oh. Even her shoulders seemed to sit up and take notice. "Really? You mean he's not the only kid with autism in this school? In this classroom? Which ones? Who? I can't tell."

"That's the point." Rob smiled at her. "You can't tell which students in this room have an autism spectrum disorder.

"Wait," Sara said. "Is it that one with the Educational Assistant beside him right now?" Even as she said those words, Lori Nabaku pressed her hand down on Kyle's shoulder then moved on to the girl ahead of him. She was making the rounds, speaking to each child and offering assistance where it was needed, not lingering long with any one student.

"What's she doing?" Sara asked.

"She's helping the students in the room."

"Isn't she assigned to just one child? If there are four kids with autism in this class, shouldn't there be four aides? What is Ethan going to do when he needs help? That's what I asked your principal that first day. Just who is going to help my son?"

"We are," was Rob's reply. "Mainly me - that's my job. Often Lori, Ms. Nabaku, is here and she circulates around the room with me. Between us, we get to all the kids. And, the kids help each other."

"But Ethan gets frustrated, he gets so frustrated. If he has a question or gets stuck you would not believe the meltdowns he has if someone isn't right there to help him."

"I know. We're working on that."

"But in the meantime, what's he going to do?"

"Pretty much what you're seeing him do right now."

As they watched, the little girl in front of Ethan turned with her paper and pencil in hand. She asked Ethan a question; he pointed to something on the girl's paper, said a few words and wrote something. The girl nodded, smiled, and turned back around.

Sara wasn't satisfied. "It doesn't look like she helped him at all. If I didn't know better, I'd say that Ethan helped her."

"Exactly," was Rob's reply. "Ethan's a competent kid. Sometimes he needs help; sometimes he gives help. That's our way in this classroom and in this school."

"Why don't you stay and watch for a bit? We'd love to have you."

"Oh, well, I have some errands to run and things I have to get done." Sara looked decidedly uncomfortable.

Rob studied her face a moment. "You know, I'm not asking you to stay so that you can help out or be responsible for Ethan. That's my job while he's here. You might like to watch to see how he's adjusting and to get to know our ways. Sit back and relax."

"Okay, I might be able to stay for just a little." Sara agreed to stay but she didn't comply with Rob's request to sit back and relax. She remained on the edge of her seat, her eyes on her son's back.

As the lesson progressed Rob watched Ethan's tension level rise. His shoulders were hunched. His feet swung faster beneath his chair. Time for some low level intervention.

Before he could move in, he saw Mrs. Fellows react. She got up from her chair to make her way to her son. Rob raised his hand in a stop gesture, wanting her to wait a few moments and to let him handle this. On the plus side, she seemed in tune with her son.

"Let's review a few of our strategies," he told the class. "Who is using their TheraBand® right now?" A few hands went up. "Let's all try it for a minute. Jerome, would you please explain to Mrs. Fellows what TheraBand® is?"

The child nearest to Sara's chair pointed to the Theraband, a thick, rubbery band tied between the front legs of every desk. He put his feet on it and pushed, relaxed, then pushed again several times. "See?" he asked Sara. "Sometimes I work better when I do this."

The rest of the class returned to their work, some pushing on their TheraBand. Rob noted that Ethan was trying this, and his tension level decreased enough that he picked up his pencil. Still, his arousal level didn't seem quite regulated, so he'd keep an eye on this student.

From the back counter, Rob snagged a weighted cushion, a square about a foot long, made of brown corduroy and filled with material that added weight. He approached Ethan's desk. "Here, bud. Want to give this a try? Put it here on your lap and tell me what you think. Some kids find that it feels good and they can concentrate on their work better when they use one. I'd like your opinion, please. I'll be back in a minute to hear what you think about it." Then he walked away.

With his head turned slightly in another direction, Rob observed Ethan. First Ethan ran his hands over the surface. Then he flipped the cushion over several times, rearranging it on his legs. Then he settled his butt more firmly into the back of his seat, picked up his pencil and went back to work.

IT WAS time to change topics. Rob flicked the lights two times, the signal that he wanted the class's attention. "Let's take a look at our visual schedule." He brought the pictures up on the SMART Board. "Follow along on the board or on your own copy if you wish. Notice that we're just finishing math. Next on the list is circle time on the carpet. I'll start the time timer on the board and when the red color has all run out, I want you all in your places on the carpet." He started the timer and five minutes showed bright red in a gradually diminishing slice.

Some of the students put their books away and sat in their places on the carpet. Others first wrote a little more on their papers before putting that work in their basket. Ethan looked uncertain.

"Class, what do we do if we don't quite get finished some work?"

Several little voices said, "We put it in our red folder."

"What clue does the red folder give us?"

"To stop and look in here for any work we need to do."

"Right," Mr. Sells approved. "Anyone who is not finished, go put that paper in your red folder and there will be time to complete it later." He saw Ethan standing with his paper in hand, his eyes wide as he glanced around. Another student was close by who could help. "Doug, Ethan's new and hasn't used his red folder very often. Will you please show him where it is?"

"This way," Doug said to Ethan, who followed him to the shelf under the window.

Rob saw Sara's shoulders slump with relief. Likely she'd thought a meltdown was imminent. Well, so had he, but Ethan kept it in control. Good for him. Now for the hard part.

Although circle time had many benefits socially and academically, it could be a trying time for many kids. The opportunity to leave their desks and move to another area was a good thing. But sitting in close proximity to others on the floor could be tough for anyone sensitive to touch and also anyone who didn't have a good sense of where their body was in space.

Sitting in a circle looked deceptively simple. First it meant a change in activity and transition times were hard. Then each child had to sit near to his neighbor but without touching. Arms, legs and feet must be kept under control and out of other kids' spaces. There wasn't a lot of wiggle room when little bodies were seated close.

So, Rob had masking tape boxes drawn on the floor, one for each child. The ones in the outer ring were a little larger. Those were reserved for those children who needed even more spatial reminders. Two kids sat on child-sized rocking chairs, rockers with stops on the runners, preventing them from moving backward or forward too far. A couple of kids sat on plastic chairs with arm rests. One used a bean bag chair, the smaller one borrowed from the reading corner. Jerome brought along a weighted vest, knowing that would help him remain focused during their circle discussion. Several students sat on small, inflated cushions designed to allow some wiggle motion. Jerome picked up the lap weight Ethan had left behind on his chair. "Hey, Ethan," he asked. "May I borrow this?"

"Yeah," came the reply. Rob reminded the boys that there were more weighted products on the shelf if anyone wanted one.

As they started the lesson, Rob could see that Ethan was not comfortable. He wasn't the only one; Kyle was showing signs of anxiety as well. Best nip this in the bud before anyone became too upset. Especially with Mrs. Fellows sitting on the edge of her seat, ready to leap into action if Ethan looked on the verge of a tantrum.

"Before we go any further, Dr. Hitkins needs some help in the office. She needs some paper for the photocopier. Will a couple of you take her some, please?" Hands went up. "Kyle, would you carry two reams of paper and Ethan would you take two as well, please? Kyle, you'll need to show Ethan where we keep the paper and how to get to the office."

He turned to Jerome, seated nearest his desk. "Would you please give Kyle and Ethan each an iPod then bring one to me?" He had planned to stay in his seat in the circle but could see Sara's growing tension. She'd left her chair and was enroute to her son. Before Rob could get there, she had her hands on Ethan's shoulders, bracing him against her.

This might take a while, Rob thought. He signaled to Lori to take over circle time for him.

"Where are you sending my son," Sara asked. "He's new and he's only six. He doesn't know his way around this building. You can't ask him to leave the room, to run errands for you. Don't you have people who do that kind of thing for you?"

"It's fine and they'll be fine. The office is just down the hall and Kyle's been there before. He knows the way, don't you, Kyle?" Kyle didn't look as confident as Rob had hoped. But, that's what the iPods were for.

Rob took the three iPods from Jerome with a thank you and

draped the lanyard of one around his neck. He then held out one each to Kyle and Ethan. Kyle placed a lanyard around his neck and turned the iPod so the screen was facing out. Ethan watched Kyle, and then copied.

This didn't make Sara feel any better. "What are you doing? These are only small boys. They can't handle expensive electronics like this. What if they break them? What if they drop them?"

"That's why we have them on lanyards so they don't get dropped. Watch. You'll see how we use them."

Turning to Kyle, Rob said, "Do you remember how we use FaceTime?"

Kyle pressed the Home button and soon Rob could see Kyle's grinning face on Rob's own iPod. "Good. Now show Ethan what you did to get into FaceTime."

Ethan, like most kids was a quick study and soon the boys were Face Timing each other, even though they were standing only arm's length apart.

"Now, Kyle, do you remember when to FaceTime me?"

"At the corner."

"Right. There's a table there where you can set down the paper while you FaceTime me to let me know where you are. Do you think we should let Ethan's mom in on this, too?" He handed her another iPod. She was hesitant, so he had Jerome show her how to start the FaceTime app.

"Okay. Kyle how many reams of paper should you each take?"

"Two."

"How many will you take to the office all together, between you?"

The boys conferred a minute but were able to come up with the number four.

"Show Ethan where the paper is, each of you pick up your two reams, then head to the office. Don't forget to FaceTime us when you get to the corner."

Sara was clearly still unsure about her son venturing into the bowels of the school without an adult. While the boys gathered their packaged paper stacks, Rob motioned Sara to the door. He pointed down the hallway so she could see the sign marked Office not too far away. Then he asked her to step back from the doorway. It wouldn't do the boys' confidence any good to see them hovering, unsure if the kids could carry out this task on their own.

As the boys left, carefully carrying their weighty loads of two reams each, Rob pulled the classroom door mostly closed. Sara started to protest but Rob cut her off. He flicked the intercom button quickly two times and explained that this was the sign to the school secretary to watch for students coming to the office with an errand. She would be watching for them and contact the teacher immediately if the kids didn't appear in a few minutes.

Before Rob could begin to explain to Sara the benefits of heavy work and the calming effects from carrying something heavy, there was Kyle's voice over FaceTime. Sara snatched up her iPod to see her son's grinning face. "How are you doing, little man?" she asked him.

Using his iPod, Kyle told his teacher that they had made it to the corner and were now going to the office to deliver the paper. Sara could see the tiny image of her son's face nodding in agreement to Kyle's message.

"I did it, mom!" were Ethan's first words when the boys returned to the classroom. Sara gazed at her son. Rob hoped she was seeing a different Ethan, a child capable of tackling new things and succeeding. Kyle gathered the iPods and put them away. He and Ethan rejoined the circle and sat calmly for the rest of the time.

CHAPTER 5

"Sara! What are you doing here?"

Oh, no, Rob thought he recognized that voice. Blast. What was that darned woman doing here? Again. And in his classroom no less.

Ellie continued without waiting for Sara's reply. "I was bringing my sister-in-law a sandwich for lunch when I noticed you as I walked by the room. Hey and there's Munchkin." Ellie's nephew, Kyle launched himself at her, evading the other kids who were getting their lunches out of their backpacks. "Hey, big guy. I brought your mom a yummy sandwich from the bakery. And, there's something special waiting for you at home."

Ellie turned warily to Rob. "Hi," she said. "Sorry to intrude."

He just bet she was sorry. Intrude seemed to be one of the things she did best. He crossed his arms. Sara looked between the two of them. Despite her pressing errands, she'd ended up staying the entire morning in the grade one room, looking more relaxed as the hours passed without major incidents.

When Rob didn't say anything, Ellie said, "All I ever seem to say to you now is sorry."

Rob waved his hand. He didn't want to talk about her being sorry or about anything else with this woman. "I'm sure Mel is eagerly awaiting her sandwich. Her room is just down the hall." He could not get her out of here fast enough. Something about her made him antsy.

Sara complied with a request for help opening a child's thermos and was soon busy with her son's classmates. Ellie stepped closer to Rob, rather than out the door as he would have preferred.

"Mr. Sells, I really am sorry, you know. I'd like to apologize properly."

Not now, not in front of his kids, in fact, not ever was Rob's preference.

"Look, let's just call it a day. We might bump into each other if you're visiting Mel or come for Kyle, but that's it. We can be civil to each other for those few minutes. Other than that we'll stay in opposite corners of the city if I have my way. Now, I need to see to my class."

Ellie couldn't see what urgently needed his attention in the classroom. All the kids were eating in their desks and chatting. "Here," she said. She reached into her back pocket and pulled out a slightly crumpled bakery coupon, good for one coffee and a muffin or dainty. She handed him the slip of paper. "At least accept this as my apology."

He couldn't very well refuse the paper when his students might be looking. He took it, muttered, "Thanks" and turned away.

MEL WAS QUITE an all right person, Rob thought. Her husband, Ben seemed okay and their son, Kyle, was a great kid. How did she ever end up with a sister-in-law like Ellie? They sat in the staff room after school chatting.

"How's your boys' group coming along?" asked Mel.

"Fine but some of the sports games we had planned aren't to everyone's liking. They need some physical activity, but a bunch of these guys are more into computer gaming than soccer games. You can tell just by looking at a couple of them just how much time they must spend plastered in front of a screen.

"I know I'm not going to change that, but if I could channel their computer interest into something productive, we might be getting somewhere."

"What do you have in mind?" Mel asked.

"Well, in my ideal world, I'd teach them programming. Not that I know a lot about it but surely there are some kid-friendly programs out there that could help these guys create their own games. That might be a skill they could turn into a job one day, turn an obsession into an occupation or at least a skill that could lead to an occupation."

Warming to his subject, he continued. "And, if I somehow run into buckets of money, I'd like to take it further. I'd like to teach these kids how to refurbish computers or even better, to build computers from the ground up.

"I don't know a lot about this, but I think I could learn enough to get the kids started. They're so smart - if I give them just the basics, I think they'd take it and run. Buying a new computer is prohibitive for many of their families but you know, I've heard of this other operating system that's free and there are lots of open source software options that would not cost a thing."

"That operating system you're talking about is probably a version of Linux. There are lots of Linux distros, most free but some cost just a bit to buy the disc. Some forms of Linux are pretty complex, others easier than Windows."

"How do you know all this? Did you used to teach computers?"

"Never. And I sound better than I actually am. The little I know I learned from my brother who can talk ad nauseum about all things computer related. He's a big fan of Linux distros and believes everyone should have that running their computers rather than Windows."

"Why?"

"He says that Linux is more stable, less prone to error messages, freezing up and that sort of thing. And, you get away from the worry about computer viruses and malicious software invading your machine. It's also free or nearly free as compared to hundreds of dollars for the common operating systems."

"But don't most programs run on Windows?"

"Yep, most do. But a lot of them will also run on many Linux distros."

"Distros?"

"Distributions. We think *we* use jargon in the education field, but you haven't seen anything like the lingo techs and programmers use."

"Is Linux something kids could use?"

"Some versions, as far as I know. Jeff's told me that some forms of Linux are favored by programmers and are heavily command oriented, sort of like the old DOS computers. But some other Linux versions are no brainers that even I can use.

"In fact, my home machine runs on Linux. My old computer was gasping its last breath and Jeff offered to build me a new one for under $300. I didn't think it could be done, but this computer is faster and more powerful than any I've had before."

"What can you do on it if it runs on Linux?"

"I don't have huge computing needs. I'm not a gamer. I use it for researching on the Internet, emails, managing my music, accounting and word processing."

"So, you can run Microsoft Word® on a Linux computer?"

"I'm not sure about that," Mel replied. "I've never tried. I use something similar, except that it's free. And, stuff I work on at home opens up in Microsoft on my work laptop and vice versa. Files convert just fine."

"Free?"

"Free. Like Microsoft Office®, Apache's Open Office® has a word processor, spread sheet, database, presentation maker and stuff like that."

"Free. Do you know how much I paid to have Office on my home computer?" Rob asked.

"Yep."

"How do I learn about all this stuff? Did you take a course? Do online stuff?"

"My brother. If you ask him, he'll tell you more than you ever possibly wanted to know. The problem will be in getting him to *stop* explaining."

"Do you think he'd be willing to talk to me? Maybe even help with my boys' group?"

"Talk to you, for sure. I'm positive. About the boys' group, well, you'll have to ask him. I don't know how good he is in front of groups, but you never know. He loves sharing his interest with people."

"Is there a way I can contact this guy?"

"He's not big on keeping his phone on. But he hangs out at this bakery on 21st Street. Drop by there almost anytime and you'll find him puttering about."

"Do they have computers there?"

"Their Internet cafe part was pretty much just decoration until Jeff came along. Now those machines are in tip top shape."

CHAPTER 6

$\mathcal{H}$e stood outside and pulled the crumpled piece of paper from his back pocket. Yep, this was the same bakery that woman Ellie had given him the coupon for. He might as well make use of it. Even if he didn't like *her*, he did like good coffee.

The bell jingled as Rob pushed open the door. A young woman behind the counter smiled and said, "Be right with you in a moment." The smells of sweet dough, cream and sugar mingled with roasted chicken and beef. Rob paused just to take in the aromas, getting sidetracked from his mission.

He perused the counter windows and placed his order. Then he asked, "Would you know if there's a guy named Jeff here?" He was pointed to a man prying the back off one of the computers along the wall. Ah, that fit with what Mel had told him about her brother.

"Hi. Are you by any chance Jeff?" he asked.

"Yes." The man replied but kept his back to Rob, intent on the bowels of the computer.

Rob tried again. "Ah, can I talk to you a minute?"

"Yes." Well, at least that was a reply but still no eye contact.

"Have I caught you at a bad time?"

"No."

Well, this wasn't going very well. Rob stood there, uncertain of what to do next.

Then Jeff spoke. "Are you shy?"

What? "No, not particularly," he replied.

"I thought you said you wanted to talk."

"I did. I mean I do, but you looked busy and I thought I was interrupting you."

"Oh, did I forget to make eye contact? Observe the social niceties?" He turned to face Rob and stuck his hand out. "Hi. I'm Jeff. How are you today?"

This was weirder and weirder but rather intriguing. "I'm Rob Sells. Mel suggested I come here to ask you some computer questions. I teach with your sister at Madson Elementary School."

Jeff's face widened into a grin. He thumped Rob on the shoulder with more force than Rob thought warranted. Rob studied Jeff's face, but he seemed open and delighted to see him now.

"Any time, any time. Any friend of Mel's can drop by anytime. And computers are my favorite subject. What do you want to know, or should I just talk about the most recent fascinating bits?"

"No, no." Rob held up his hand. It was dawning on him. Hadn't Mel once said something about her brother having autism? Now it made sense and he was more comfortable. "There are some specific things I want to know, if you've got a minute."

Rob explained about the boys' group he ran Friday evenings and how some of the kids were more interested in computers than sports. He wanted to steer them away from just playing games to maybe building games and to learning more about the inner workings of computers. But they were on a really tight budget, so he needed to do things cheaply.

"You've come to the right place, my man. You might need a bit of cash, but we can do this thing on the cheapo, scrounging parts and picking the right distros."

"Do you think you could give us a hand? Steer me in the right direction?"

"Sure. When?"

"Well whenever it's convenient for you. I work during the week, but this is Saturday and I'm free for the rest of the afternoon."

"Okay."

"Okay?"

Jeff nodded his head toward the door. "Let's go. I can show you some of the stuff at my place and you can see what you might be getting into."

As they started to rise, there was a grinding sound, a sound different than the one of grinding coffee beans. This one sounded metallic. There was a yell.

"Jeff, it's doing it again."

Jeff was already on his way over to the espresso machine. Soon it was apart, Jeff's hands in its innards, Rob forgotten. Rob sat down to finish his coffee, which was excellent, by the way. He hoped that when Jeff was done, he'd remember their plans.

A woman whirled out from a doorway, put her hand on Jeff's shoulder, gave it a squeeze, and said, "Thanks. We don't know what we'd do without you." She returned to the back of the shop, without once looking into the customer area. Rob thought there might be something familiar about her, but it all happened so fast he didn't pay much attention. His gaze was fixed on the display case. While he waited, he might as well sample another of the bakery's delectable offerings.

Rob was just wiping the last of the powdered sugar off his face and the front of his shirt when Jeff appeared in front of him. "Ready?" Jeff asked. He didn't wait for Rob's answer but headed for the door.

Rob scrambled to catch up. "Sorry," he said as he jostled a table, almost upsetting a woman's latte.

JEFF'S HAND was pushing open the door when a female voice said, "Where do you think you're going?"

The men turned and there she was. That blasted woman turned up everywhere, Rob thought. Ellie, Mel's sister-in-law. And, what was she wearing? All white might be in fashion but those baggy pants and stained, stiff, high collared cotton shirt certainly weren't the latest thing in haute couture. And why was her hair plastered to her head? Was that a net thingy over her hair? Ellie stood with her hands on her hips glaring at Jeff.

Rob looked at Jeff, who appeared unconcerned. Maybe this was normal mode for Ellie; she's certainly not been warm and fuzzy whenever Rob had seen her. Well, maybe that wasn't quite fair. Obviously, her nephew adored her and Mel seemed fond of her. Maybe Rob and Ellie just rubbed each other the wrong way.

She repeated herself. "Where do you think you're going, Jeff?"

"Home. I gotta show this guy some stuff. He wants to teach kids to build these Linux boxes then design games."

"Now?"

"Yeah." What was her problem, Jeff wondered? Oh, now he remembered. "Sorry, Ellie. Are you feeling left out? That's not polite. I wasn't thinking of your feelings. Why don't you come with us? We'd like your company, wouldn't we, ah...?" He looked at Rob. "What did you say your name was?"

Rob and Ellie spoke at the same time.

"Rob. My name is Rob Sells and I teach with your sister."

"Now? Now? The bakery doesn't close for another half hour. Look around. We still have customers here."

Rob couldn't see what that had to do with either him or Jeff. But Ellie's get-up was starting to make sense. "You work here?" he asked her.

"Do I *work* here? Yeah, I'd say so. I'm here every morning by five and close the place up twelve hours later. I guess I do work here. In fact, I own the place."

Rob's head went up. He looked at Ellie and around at the obviously flourishing business. "Nice place you have here." Maybe there was more to this pesky woman than he'd thought at first. Then he remembered. "Oh, so that's why you had that coupon you gave me hanging around in your pocket. I thought you were just passing on to me something that had been given to you."

"You really don't think much of me, do you?"

This was not the time to get into it, Rob thought, not with customers around. Actually, not anytime. Avoiding each other would solve a lot of problems.

"So, are you coming or not?" asked Jeff. He was shifting his weight from one foot to the other.

"No and neither are you," Ellie started, but was interrupted by Rob.

This annoying woman was seriously interfering in his life and trying to run Mel's brother's life to boot. The guy obviously had time on his hands since he was just picking away at the computers when Rob walked in. "Why don't you cut the guy a break?" he asked Ellie. "He's just trying to give me a hand; Mel told me Jeff would likely be willing to help. And, geez, it's for a boys' group." He was starting to get ticked. First, she'd tried to tell him how to run his classroom. Now she was riding this Jeff guy. She should just return to her kitchen, manage away back there and let him and Jeff get on with their own things.

"I'll give him a break all right; right after his shift is over. Right now, he's on my dime and I've not gotten any work out of him since you appeared."

"Your dime?" What did she mean, Rob wondered?

Jeff shifted his feet and looked down. "I'm not standing on your dime, Ellie. Yours or anyone else's."

Ellie rolled her eyes. "That's an idiom, Jeff. I didn't mean it literally."

"You mean he works for you?"

"Yes."

"Does he like fix those computers?" He pointed to the side wall.

"Among other things. Yes, he fixes stuff but he's also responsible for many of the smells in this place. You should come for lunch sometime and taste the deli sandwiches Jeff creates."

Jeff launched into a detailed explanation of the meats he planned to cook for the rest of the week, in far, far more detail than Rob ever wanted to hear about any culinary effort.

Ellie approached, holding her arm out and palm up, facing Jeff. "That's TMI, Jeff. The short version would do."

"TMI?" asked Rob.

"That's what she says when she's too lazy to say, 'too much information'," explained Jeff. "She probably shouldn't butcher the language that way, but she uses it as a signal to tell me when customers don't want the full story. It's not always easy to know how much to tell them. If they ask things like, "Where did this delicious meat come from?" I tell them. Sometimes I'm only part-way through the explanation and they stop making eye contact. Did you know that some people have short attention spans? They ask a question then can't remain focused long enough to get a proper answer. It's not just eye contact you have to watch for. Sometimes they stop eating and stare at the table. Shoulders give you clues as well. Their shoulder may drop down or it'll turn away from you. You gotta watch for things like that, even when it doesn't make sense. I mean, if someone asks, isn't it only polite to give an answer?"

The temptation to shake his head was strong in Rob's mind; shake it to see if his brains would rattle. Following this conversation was hard. He glanced at Ellie to see if she was having the same trouble.

Blast that woman. She was grinning. At him. Was she actually trying not to laugh at him? Ellie turned her gaze to Jeff and the two of them exchanged broad smiles.

"I did it again, didn't I, Ellie?" Jeff asked her.

"Yep." Neither of them seemed to mind, though. The only one uncomfortable was Jeff. But then, when had he not been uncomfortable in this woman's presence? Ellie and Jeff must have known each other a long time to be this relaxed together. Or, maybe they had a thing going on. He looked more closely at the two of them. He wasn't getting any back-off vibes from Jeff, but then again, he likely didn't see him as any threat. It was pretty obvious that Rob and Ellie rubbed each other the wrong way.

Anyway, they needed to get rolling. He turned to Jeff. "What time do you get off work?"

Ellie replied for him. "In about twenty minutes."

"Ellie, your watch is off again," Jeff told her after checking the time on his own watch. "In exactly seventeen minutes and forty-six seconds we close down."

Was Ellie that much of a task master boss that Jeff needed to be absolutely precise, Rob wondered?

Jeff continued. "I told you that you should get an atomic watch like mine. It corrects itself to a fraction of a second, so you never need to wonder about the time." He turned to Jeff. "Some people have problems with time, you know. They try to say 'about' or 'roughly'. There actually is no 'about' with time. Time either is or it isn't. It's measurable. If we all used atomic watches there would be no confusion over this 'about' stuff. What does that even mean, anyway? If you say 'about twenty minutes' do you mean eighteen minutes or twenty-two minutes? There's a difference, you know."

Ellie cut him off. "And we've just lost another four of those precious minutes talking about it. Let's get this place shut down, and then you're free to go." They stood back out of the way as the last customers went out the door.

"Anything I can do to help?" Rob asked, and then wondered where that had come from.

"Sure," said Ellie. "You can empty the coffee machines and rinse them out. I'll bus the tables and get the dishwasher going. Jeff needs to get his stuff ready for the morning and put that espresso machine back together."

CHAPTER 7

*O*nce again, Rob found himself standing at the door to the bakery with Jeff, but this time Ellie was beside them. She looked different, younger, softer and better out of her starched whites and in a t-shirt and jeans.

Once on the street they loitered a minute, then Ellie said, "Well, I'd better let you guys get on your way. See you tomorrow, Jeff."

Jeff remembered his manners. "Why don't you come with us, Ellie? It's not good to feel left out. Three is an okay number. I don't know how much this guy knows so maybe you can help us. You know, interpret or explain stuff to him if I get too technical."

The laughter came out of Ellie's mouth. Rob thought it was probably at his expense but her laughter was infectious. He couldn't be mad, at least not this once.

"Sure," he echoed. "Why not come along? You've never been shy about giving me instructions before, so I don't see why you should start now."

Ellie was unsure how to take this and was prepared for a fight. "Jeez, Louise. How many times do I have to apologize for that? I was wrong, all right? I jumped to some conclusions in my attempt to help Sara and her kid. Cut me some slack, why don't you?"

She stopped as she checked out Rob's face and caught his grin. Was he having her on? Did this guy actually have a sense of humor? She slowly returned his smile and suddenly it was all right.

"Sure. I've got nothing better to do right now. I was going to go home and nap, but you can sleep when you're dead, right?" Ellie took an arm of each guy and they started off toward Jeff's place.

"Well, you can't actually liken death to sleeping. Our culture has a lot of euphemisms for death, but sleep isn't one of them unless you add an adjective like permanent sleep," Jeff explained.

Ellie grinned at them both and sauntered down the street arm in arm as Jeff continued his discourse on society's illogical views on death.

"Do you walk to work every day?" Rob asked Jeff.

"Yes."

Jeff's home was *not* close by. When they had started walking from the bakery, Rob assumed that they'd be going a few blocks, half a dozen at most. But they were still walking forty-five minutes later.

Ellie sensed his unease and squeezed his arm. "It's not much farther now," she said.

"Twenty-three more houses to be exact," Jeff said.

"If it's this far, why didn't we take my car?" Rob wondered.

"You have a car? Did you drive to the bakery?" Jeff asked.

"Yes, I parked around the corner."

"Why didn't you say so?" questioned Jeff. "I can't read your mind, you know. You didn't say anything about a car, so how would I know? You have to tell people things, or they can't guess. We'd have been in front of the computers by now if you had suggested we drive instead of walk."

"Yeah, Rob, yeah. What was the matter with you? We could have been there already." Ellie could hardly contain her grin. If she wasn't ripping into him, she was ribbing him.

Rob sighed. "Sorry, guys. I didn't know. I assumed you lived close by."

"Close is a relative term. If you think nationally or globally, then yes, I do live close to the bakery. If you're an arachnid making the trek, then I do not live close and it would be a long, long walk."

Rob just looked at him. Jeff thought that Rob was unfamiliar the word. "Arachnid is the proper term for what you might know as a spider," he explained.

Rob then looked from Jeff to Ellie. She was having the time of her life. Why was she so relaxed around this guy? Then it came to him. Mel had told him about her brother, her brother with Asperger's Syndrome. Asperger's was on the autism spectrum. This must be the same fellow. Ah, that explained some things - like his precise language, conspicuous use of social niceties and tendency to deliver speeches when he was on a topic he enjoyed.

Changing the subject, Rob asked, "How long have you two known each other?"

"We met some time after Ben and Mel started seeing each other, so it's been less than a year, right?" Ellie asked Jeff.

There was a slight pause, and then Jeff said, "ten months, one week and three days."

Embarrassment washed over Rob. What was the matter with him? Look how at ease Ellie was with Jeff. She was a baker, just a lay person, while he was the one with the post-graduate special education training. He'd taken classes in working with students with autism spectrum disorders. He'd taught these kids for years now. How could he get on their wavelengths and do so well with them, but not be comfortable with an adult with autism? What was different?

He thought about it as they cruised by the houses, Jeff counting them off as they walked. When he got a new group of students, Rob knew in advance which kids had autism or any other learning difference. He made sure to read the cumulative files and any reports in those files. Did that give him preconceived notions about those kids? About what they could do? What to expect from them? He did it so he'd be prepared, have ready the things that each child needed to feel comfortable and be successful. There was very little the kids did that could throw him.

But Jeff, this man of about his own age, was a different story. Rob had lost that at-ease feeling he usually had around kids with unique styles. Rob was not sure this said anything good about himself. Did he feel superior and in charge around kids? That he had a lot to offer them?

But Jeff it seemed had something to offer Rob - maybe a whole lot of somethings. He certainly seemed like a smart guy, talented on many fronts.

Rob thought about Ellie, relaxed walking between these two men, holding their arms, joking with Jeff. It's not as if they had known each other forever, ten months or so as Jeff had informed them, but Ellie accepted Jeff like an old friend. Their banter was companionable, their trust obvious. Jeff actually seemed to like Ellie and Rob was beginning to see why.

When she wasn't attacking him, she was, well, nice. Attractive even. She had an easy acceptance of people. And, to her credit, when she'd launched into him at the school, she had been trying to help a couple people who were almost strangers to her. Watching her out of the corner of his eye, there was that grin on her face that hinted at mischief now that he had gotten to know her better.

Know her better? What was up with that? This was the woman he'd sworn to avoid at all costs just last week. Was he actually thinking of ways to spend more time with her to get to know more about her?

CHAPTER 8

The three of them clomped down the stairs to the basement of Jeff's parents' home. Rob looked around in the dim light. "You live here?" he asked.

"Sure. Well mostly. I have a bedroom over there," he gestured behind them," but it's not used very much. Usually I bunk down there," pointed at a futon messed with a quilt and a pillow. Hard to say what color the quilt might have once been but the colors on the pillow were clearer - the middle had a large yellow stain, probably where Jeff's head had lain many, many times. The whole basement had that funky smell that went along with heavy use, closed windows and questionable cleaning practices.

"You live here alone?" he asked Jeff.

"Yeah, but my parents live upstairs. I mostly eat with them. My Mom insists. She's positive I can't feed myself properly even though I'm a way better cook than she is."

Rob could understand Mrs. Nicol's misgivings. On the other hand, he'd sampled some of Jeff's cooking when Mel brought in extra lunch and it had been without a doubt stupendous. He really could cook.

"I think I'll go say hello to your parents," said Ellie.

"Why? Jeff asked her.

"To let them know we're here."

"They know. Do you think that we tip-toed in? They heard us, I'm sure. Mom says she always listens for comings and goings as she calls it."

"It's still polite for me to go say hello to Mr. and Mrs. Nicols."

"Oh." This surprised Jeff. "Well, say hello to them for me, too." Jeff looked expectantly at Rob.

"Ah, yeah, and for me, too," echoed Rob uncomfortably.

Ellie stifled her laughter and said, "Sure." Rob could tell that she was smirking as she retreated back up the stairs. She really did like having a laugh at his expense, didn't she?

JEFF STARTED in on their plans. He didn't offer Rob a seat, something to drink or tell him where the bathroom was. He was all business.

"So," Jeff asked. "Do you want to jump right in along with your boys' group or do you want to practice ahead of time?"

"What do you suggest?"

"That depends on how smart you are. How technical you are. Have you done much programming? Built many computers?"

"Neither."

Jeff looked disappointed. "Well, what *do* you know? You at least do your own upgrades, don't you - replace the hard drive, add RAM, swap out drives...?"

"Yeah, I know how to do stuff like that, just basic things the average guy can do."

"Average? I don't have much concept of average. I've found that what I think is common, basic knowledge everyone should have is not that common at all. You shouldn't be allowed to have a computer if you don't know how to take care of it. If you don't understand how a thing runs, you don't deserve to have it."

"I'm not sure that's fair. The typical person can use a computer for years without having to know those things. Besides, they can pay people to fix it when things go wrong."

"What a cop out." Jeff shook his head. He continued. "I don't have time to figure out all that you know or more likely, don't know," Jeff told Rob.

Rob tried to get the conversation back on to what he needed, rather than on his personal deficiencies, which he's sure would be numerous in Jeff's estimation. "Mel told me that that I should look at Linux for an operating system if I wanted the kids to build computers on a shoestring."

"On a shoestring? Why would she say that? I can't think of any use for a shoelace in a computer. Tying components in would not be stable enough." Jeff shook his head. "Sometimes Mel doesn't make a lot of sense."

Before Rob could explain or even try to follow this train of thought, Jeff went on. "She's right about choosing Linux instead of a Mac OS or a Windows box, but you can't just say Linux. Linux is an operating system, sure and many versions are free or close to free, but there are all kinds of Linux distros, some for newbies, some for home, some for professional use, some for servers and some for programmers. Which do you want?"

"How should I know?"

Jeff rolled his chair over to another computer. He woke it up with the touch of a mouse, and called up a website. His fingers flew faster than Rob could read the letters that appeared on the screen.

"Here," Jeff told him. "Take this online test. It'll assess your knowledge level, what you plan to do on the computer then suggest which Linux distro might be best for your needs."

"You keep saying distro. What's distro mean again?" Rob asked.

"Distro is short for distribution. Really, it means who you get it from, the copy of your Linux operating system, I mean. Now, take this test and we'll see which distro it recommends for you."

Rob turned his attention to the Linux Distribution Chooser test (http://www.zegeniestudios.net/ldc/index.php?lang=en).

. . .

"OKAY, I'm finished. And based on the answers I chose, the program narrows it down to four different Linux operating systems." Now that he'd gotten this far, Rob had no idea how to proceed.

"Did you read through them? Choose one?"

"Yeah, I read through all the descriptions but that didn't help. Half of this is like reading Greek to me."

"So, what did you do next? Did you look any of them up? Compare the pros and cons?"

"Well, no. I was sort of hoping you'd help me with that."

Jeff sighed. "I can only hold your hand so far. You're going to have to do some of the work yourself. You're the person who's going to live with this distro, so you should tailor it to you needs."

"I don't know where to begin."

Jeff's chair slid over again, and his fingers flew over the keys. "Maybe we'd better start at the very beginning." To himself he muttered, you'd think Mel wouldn't have sent me someone this green. She knows I have no patience with people too lazy to learn. "Here," he said as if Rob would not have been able to hear what he just said. "Read through this," and he pulled up a website called, *What is Linux and Why Is It So Popular?*.

CHAPTER 9

*T*he light evening breeze beckoned, and Sara couldn't stand the thought of staying cooped up. It was the weekend and what did it matter if Ethan's bedtime was extended a bit. The fresh air might even help him sleep better. The park a few blocks away awaited them. She zipped Ethan into his new blue jacket and perched the grey, knit cap on his head.

The park bordered a residential area, then stretched into the hills and wooded areas surrounding the edge of the city. It was a calm place, an oasis for urban-dwellers. Sara wished she knew what sorts of birds were singing; one day when she had time, she'd find out.

She headed for a bench, not too far from the swings and climbing equipment. There were a couple kids playing and she assumed Ethan would go join them. The thump against her back told her otherwise. Ethan pushed up against her side.

"Go on, son. Go play with the kids. Doesn't it look like fun?"

Ethan shook his head back and forth.

"Sure, it'll be fun. Look. See that little girl on the swing? She looks like she's having fun." Ethan didn't budge. Sigh. This was not going to go well. She took his hand. "Come on. I'll go with you." It took a little tug, but Ethan trailed behind her, over to the swing set.

With some encouragement and coaxing, Ethan clambered onto the swing and submitted to his mother's pushes. But her bench and her book beckoned, so Sara instructed Ethan to swing himself now.

From time to time, Sara would glance up. Ethan propelled himself in a desultory fashion, never seeming to achieve that graceful coordination of leaning into the swing's forward arc and pushing back with his legs.

The next time Sara glanced up, she tensed when she didn't see her son on the swings. Oh, there he was. He'd followed the little girl to the slide. Good. She went back to her story.

The giggles caught her attention as the other child spread her arms wide and zoomed down the slide. Sara smiled. Ethan stood at the bottom of the ladder, ready for his turn, but hesitating. The girl ran around and stood behind Ethan. She waited, and then poked him in the back. "Get going," she said.

Sara could see Ethan stiffen. She rose to intervene, knowing what could come next. But she sat back down when Ethan stepped out of the way to let the girl have another turn. He stood watching her. He'd take his turn next, she was sure.

The next noises Sara heard voices deeper than those of the couple children around Ethan. Three boys several years older than Ethan milled around the swings now. Sara stood to see over them to spy Ethan. His bright, blue jacket should stand out. No, she couldn't see him. Since there was an assortment of climbing equipment in the playground, she wasn't worried; he could be playing on any on it. She sauntered around the area, looking in all the small spaces. No Ethan.

She turned toward the older boys. They were loud and laughing and posturing the way of wannabe punks. What were they saying? They were laughing about the little dweeb. One slapped his buddy on the back as they chortled and pointed in the distance. Sara followed his point and off in the distance, on the hill's upward slope was a blue jacket, moving steadily away.

Ethan! She screamed his name. All activity in the play area stilled. Sara pointed toward the rapidly retreating figure. "Get him," she yelled. "He's running away. Help!" She took off after him.

The older boys looked at one another, then took off after Sara. They had youth and excess energy on their sides and quickly overtook her. Much of Sara's breath was taken up with calling Ethan's name.

Was he slowing? Maybe. As he climbed the rise of the hill, he glanced over his shoulder. He stopped as he saw the three boys pounding after him, and then took off again, faster than ever.

But a frightened six-year-old is no match for almost-teenaged boys who were enjoying the thrill of the chase. As Ethan passed the crest of the hill, just out of Sara's sight, the boys caught up with him. Now that they'd achieved their goal, they didn't quite know what to do with him. No one had given them instructions. Uncertain, they surrounded Ethan. As he tried to escape their circle, one grabbed him by the arm. "Hey. That lady told you to stop or come back."

Ethan struggled in his grip and when he would have slid away, a second boy grabbed the back of his jacket and held on. "Settle down, kid. We're not going to hurt you. We'll just take you back to that lady. Is she your mom?"

There was no response. The kid shook the back of Ethan's jacket. "Kid. I'm talking to you. Is that lady your mom?" He looked at his friends. They'd all had the lectures about stranger danger when they were younger. Was something like that going on here? Were they supposed to give the kid back to the lady or protect him from her? The same thoughts went through all of their minds.

Puffing and calling, Sara made her way up the last part of the hill. "Oh, thank god," she huffed between sucking breaths. "Thank you!" She fell to her knees in front of Ethan and held out her arms. Ethan threw himself into her embrace and held on and held on. After several seconds, she raised her eyes to take in the young men around them. "Thank you for catching him. He was so scared. When he gets overwhelmed, he just takes off, but he doesn't know where he's going and could get lost or hurt. You saved him." She released Ethan and rose to her feet but kept firm hands on her son's shoulders. To the boys she said, "You are heroes and might have saved Ethan from harm. You should be proud of yourselves."

The youth puffed up, their cockiness ratcheted up several notches as they sauntered back down the hill, making up the stories they'd tell their buddies.

CHAPTER 10

*R*ob and Jeff still labored on in the basement, sometimes Jeff patiently explaining, sometimes not. Every so often Ellie would chime in, "He wants the short version, Jeff. He's never going to be a programmer. He just wants to use the system and show kids how to use it."

"I know, I know," Jeff would reply, "but the beauty of this is that there is so much more to it. Sure, you can just use Linux the way you would a Windows box. But don't you want to take a look under the hood?"

He'd get a resounding, "No!" from both Ellie and Rob. To Rob's surprise, Ellie knew a fair bit about this. Initially, she'd been intrigued by the concept of a free operating system, given the cost of buying the popular systems on the market. She was astounded to learn that hundreds of extra dollars were tacked onto the cost of a new computer just for the operating system when there was an equivalent free or for under twenty-five dollars.

Too chicken to try it out on her main computer, she had an older one in her closet that had been owned by one of her brothers before he left home. She crossed her fingers and wiped that hard drive clean. Then, having downloaded a Linux distro called OpenSuSE (http://www.opensuse.org/en/) onto a DVD and inserted it into the computer. After clicks and whirls and waiting, it worked! She had an up and running computer without paying hundreds of dollars on an operating system. After playing with it for a few months, Ellie became so comfortable with its speed and ease of operation, not to mention its stability, that she removed the operating system that had come with her laptop and installed Linux as its operating system. She avoided the programming geek versions of Linux and kept to those which were kind to inexperienced users. What she looked for in an operating system was one that allowed her to carry on as if it was not even there. To her mind, the job of operating systems was to work away in the background without any input from her, letting her just plain use the computer as she pleased.

FOR A GUY who used to think he wasn't bad with computers, Rob felt left out. Humbled as he was, he still saw a problem. "So, I collect old computers and even if I get Linux thrown on them, or help the kids do it themselves, then what? It's not enough to say we have computers with operating systems. We have to be able to use them. Part of the point is in helping the kids learn the skills of building a computer, then letting take them home. For most of these kids there is no computer at home when they need to do homework. We don't have the budget to buy software any more than we do to buy operating systems."

"So, use Apache's Open Office®."

"What's Open Office®?"

"It's what I use to make the menus at the bakery and to keep inventory and send invoices," said Ellie. It's a complete suite of tools, pretty close to Microsoft Office®, but it's free. It has a word processor, spread sheet, database and presentation software. And, if I create something in Open Office® then go somewhere where there's only Microsoft Office® available, my Open Office® stuff opens in the other program and reads it just fine. And oh, did I mention that it's free?"

"Free as in legally free? I can't be doing anything against the law with these kids," worried Rob.

"Take a look," Jeff said as his fingers on the keyboard too them to http://www.openoffice.org/.

Ellie surfed the web while Rob read, and Jeff tapped away on his own computer. There was no shortage of computers in this basement; they could have had three other people here, each with a machine of their own to use. When he shut down the website, Rob looked through files until he found that Open Office® was indeed installed on this computer. He started it and played around a while.

"Okay, I'm convinced about this part of it. Open Office® would definitely work for these kids' needs throughout high school and college, too. But they need to use a computer for more than just word processing and the stuff that Open Office® does. Email is a part of our lives. How are they going to search the internet? I looked, and I don't see anything that looks like Internet Explorer®."

"They'll do it the same way you were just using the internet," said Jeff. "Internet Explorer® is only one example of a browser. I think the machine you're on uses Safari®." He slid over and looked. "Yep. Again, it's free and will work fine with Linux."

"Then what about email? I don't see any form of Outlook® here."

Jeff gave him a few examples of free, web-based emails he could use.

Rob was not quite sold on this "free" stuff yet. "But what about viruses, spyware and other malicious software we have to protect ourselves from online?"

"That's the beauty of Linux. It's really rare for anyone's Linux machine to be attacked or get hacked."

"Why's that?"

"Think about it."

Rob had been trying, truly trying to think for the past two hours but was coming to his limit, Ellie could tell. She took over from Jeff. "Those nasty beasties who create viruses and worms and those things program them to attack the largest number of computers they can reach. What's the most common operating system?"

That Rob knew. "Windows, like Windows Vista® or 10."

"Right. And who gets almost all the viruses and stuff - Windows users. At one time MAC users felt fairly immune but now they have some trouble as well. But Linux users, well it's extremely rare for them to be bothered."

"But just to be sure," Jeff added, "there are lots of free anti-virus programs you can install." He was about to launch into a list of them when Rob put up his hand.

"Enough. My mind's boggling. I believe you, but I think I've learned enough for tonight. I'd better head out now, but can I give you a call when I have more questions?"

"No," was Jeff's answer.

"NO? Oh, sorry, I realize I've taken up a lot of your time and I appreciate all your help. You've steered me in the right direction and I'll try to take it from here." He stopped, because Jeff was scribbling on a paper, paying no attention to Rob whatsoever.

Jeff swiveled his chair back to face Rob, handing him the paper. "Here. I hardly ever use a phone. Email me or if you really need the face-to-face thing, use Skype®. Other than that, I'm at the bakery every day. Bye." Then he turned back to his computer and became lost in his typing.

Ellie said, "I guess that's our cue." As they walked toward the stairs, she said, "See you tomorrow, Jeff."

A slight lifting of his hand from the keyboard indicated that Jeff had heard them and responded.

CHAPTER 11

"So, did you learn what you needed to?" Ellie asked Rob.

"That and then some. If you had the time to just sit and soak up his knowledge, it would be amazing. I thought I wasn't bad with computers but now I see that I know nothing compared to him. Sometimes I thought he was good at bringing things down to my level but at others he'd go on and on, way over my head. I had had this faint hope that he might be willing to help the kids with this project but now I doubt it. He'd lose them within the first few minutes."

"Don't be too sure about that. With you, he was trying to find your comfort level. Once he knows that, he can tailor what he says to fit your needs. With the kids, if he knew they were rudimentary gamers but had no experience with the insides of what makes a computer tick, he could teach them a lot. He's pretty systematic and could lead them along. I wouldn't rule it out."

They were standing in the driveway of the Nicols` home, under the reflection of a street light. Rob looked down the street in the direction they'd taken to get here. "I really wish I'd brought my car."

"Do we want to get into *that* again?" Ellie teased as she started walking.

"No. I've had enough of having my short-comings throw into my face for one night." When they got to the end of the driveway, he asked, "Where do you live?"

"A few blocks the other side of the bakery. It's not a bad jaunt to work in the mornings, just enough to wake me up."

"I'd offer to drive you home if I had my car here. Once we get back to my car, I can give you a ride from there. Or would you prefer that we call a taxi?"

"It's a nice night. Let's walk," and she took his arm again, just like she had with he and Jeff on the walk here. They continued in companionable silence, something Rob could never have imagined even earlier this day. Feeling relaxed around Ellie? Choosing to walk somewhere with her? Letting her touch him and actually liking it?

Ellie was not one to let things lie. "So, is this a good time to try to apologize again?"

Rob sighed. "It's a peaceful evening. Can't we just let things be?"

"No! You never did let me tell you how sorry I was for misjudging you. I hate injustice and I tend to jump in, sometimes without waiting to gather all the facts. I didn't know you at that time. If I had known you, I'd have realized that you would not be out to get Sara or her son."

Rob pulled back his head, raised one eyebrow and looked down at her. "Out to get them?"

"You know what I mean. The stuff that happened at their other school. What was going on there, by the way? I don't get it."

"Hard to speak for someone else, but the 'don't get it' you mentioned might have been happening there. When you're working with kids on the autism spectrum it really helps if you can 'get it'. By that, I mean put yourself in their shoes. If you can imagine what it might feel like to be them, then you can put things in place to help them become more comfortable."

"What do you mean?"

"Take time for instance. Time is a very hard concept for most kids with autism. It's not exactly easy to grasp for any little kid, but it seems especially elusive for those on the spectrum as well as kids with other sorts of difficulties like attentional issues, learning disabilities, fetal alcohol syndrome, to name a few.

"See, most children, over time, develop an internal feeling for the passage of time. They sense how long five minutes is or a half hour or a week. When you say we'll have snack in five minutes, they know that that is pretty soon. It's not enough time to become thoroughly engrossed in something complex that you love to do, nor is it long to wait if your stomach is rumbling. But a child with autism who does not have that time sense will not realize that that's enough time to finish writing that sentence or to do two more math questions. He might panic, thinking he's going to be told to put his things away when he's not finished. The teacher told him to do those ten questions, so that's the rule and now he's not going to be able to complete the work, landing him in trouble, or worse, having it for homework. So a tantrum may ensue due to his frustration over the impending time limit."

"So what can you do about it?"

"Lots, but it's a slow process. You need to work on a couple things together like building a relationship with the kid, so he trusts you and knows you're there to help. To start building a sense of time, you work on it constantly, pointing out how much time passed since you did the last thing, how much time we have until the next item on our schedule and using visuals."

"Visuals?"

"Kids with autism for the most part, take in what they see more easily than what they hear. So, instead of just talking about the passage of time, show it. I use something called a Time Timer® a lot. We have small, four-inch ones for a kid's desk, some in watch form for individuals, a twelve inch one on the wall and I use one on the interactive white board all the time."

"How does that help?"

"Say we're starting a new subject in ten minutes. The timer shows ten minutes in bright red and the numbers slowly count down, the red section getting smaller until the time is up.

"We also run our lives in my class, by a schedule. Some kids use the words on the schedule, others go by the pictures. Do you use some kind of daily organizer in your business?"

"Definitely. I used to keep this book but now I do it all on my phone. I'd be sunk if I lost it. I have listed there all the things I need to do in the day and which I need to do first. Otherwise, I might forget an important step in the morning that will have ramifications for that afternoon. Like what if I forgot to get the dough rising first thing in the morning and didn't have any fresh buns for lunch so Jeff can create his sandwiches."

"Kids with autism have trouble making sense of their world. They often feel that things just come at them unexpectedly. They feel that they can't prepare themselves and don't know what might be expected of them. A visual schedule gives them a sense of order, so they know what's coming next. They're not so on edge that way.

"I get it. Mel has these visual schedules all over their house for Kyle to follow. She says it cuts down on the amount of nagging parents have to do if they can just point the kid to the steps he needs to follow in the poster on the wall. At first, I wondered where she was finding the time to make all these charts but then I looked closely at them. Honestly, some of them just aren't pretty and look like she scrawled them on the spur of the moment. When I asked her, she laughed and said that's exactly what she did. Kyle doesn't care. As long as he understands what she means, he can follow it. And you know, Mel is not very good at drawing - not at all. She's actually pretty bad at it, but she says as long as she tells Kyle what it means, he gets it and follows it. I have noticed a couple places where Kyle has drawn over top of her picture though, to make it look better. Mel doesn't care and said that Kyle is making it his own, which is a good thing."

"So, you get this, and Mel gets this. My brother gets it and even I do to a certain extent. What was wrong with Ethan's last school? Why did he have so many problems there?"

"Just like parents, most teachers are doing the best they can at the time with the tools at their disposal. Some may lack experience with kids who learn differently or think differently. There may have been no one in their school to help, no one with some background in autism spectrum disorders.

"Pretty much every school nowadays has at least one special education teacher. But when most people took their university training, special education dealt with things like cerebral palsy, attentional difficulties, learning disabilities, intellectual disabilities. Little was known about teaching kids with autism even fifteen years ago. Since the prevalence rate for autism has burgeoned in the last decade or so, every teacher will encounter a student with autism and many are still unprepared for how to help. When the prevalence rate is one in every forty-two boys, every teacher can expect to have a student with autism.

"Look, most people who go into the teaching profession have strong verbal skills. We're talkers. At the older grades we tend to lecture, rightly or wrongly. Even in the younger grades where things are more visual and hands-on, we still tend to talk a lot. And when we get frustrated, most adults talk even more. We repeat ourselves, we raise our voices, and we use more words, and all this goes over the head of the kid with autism."

They turned the last corner, walking onto the semi-commercial street where the bakery resided.

Rob continued. "Most kids on the autism spectrum have trouble with auditory processing, making sense out of what they hear and knowing how to act on it. Their ability to process what they hear goes down at times of stress or when there's a lot of background noise. Think about the most difficult times in schools for these kids - in the gymnasium, the hallways, the boot rooms, all noisy, confusing places."

"Mel insists that they have a routine for everything they do at home."

"Exactly. That way Kyle knows what's expected of him. He doesn't freeze in uncertainly or have a meltdown out of frustration when he can't figure things out. It takes time to teach the routine, but it is well worth the time and effort for everyone concerned."

"But then Mel does things to purposely mess up the routine. At first Ben objected; he thought it was being mean to Kyle."

Rob laughed. "Yeah, I can see how someone could think that. But first you teach the rules and the routine. We always, always do it this way. Then you need to teach change because no matter how hard you try, life still throws curve balls and your nice little routine gets disrupted. If you don't teach a child how to adapt and live through that change, then they're hooped when it happens, especially if you're not around to guide them through it."

"Kyle has certainly had lots of disruptions to the routine Ben created - like a fire in their kitchen, cutting a gash in his head and going to the emergency room for stitches, getting lost, moving like three times in one year. And meeting a new father.

"But the best thing out of all that was that Kyle got to meet his new auntie - me!"

"I take it you see that as a good thing for him?"

Ellie's elbow dug into his stomach. "Jerk," she told him, but her smile told him she knew he was teasing. This was a different Ellie than Rob had seen before - a far different Ellie than the siren who'd launched into him in Mel's room that first day. This Ellie was more like the woman who bantered with Jeff and probably the Aunt Ellie that Kyle loved. She really wasn't as bad as he'd originally thought and tonight had been fun. He'd almost be sorry when it was over.

THE NEON SIGN for the bakery was visible just a block or so up ahead. Soon their walk would be over. Rob was surprised that that realization disappointed him. He was actually having a good time with Ellie, unbelievable as that seemed.

"Where exactly do you live from here?" he asked her.

Ellie withdrew her hand from his arm and pointed. "You take the first right after the bakery, then carry on for one and a half blocks."

When she lowered her arm, Rob grasped her hand and pulled it again through his arm. He kept his other hand over hers. She looked at him but didn't pull away.

"Do you have house, apartment or what?" he asked her.

"I live in the suite over my parents' garage. Years ago, that was part of the head baker's perks, getting free rent in exchange for less pay and horrendous hours. When he retired to go live with his daughter in Florida, my father tried taking over his duties and it was a disaster. Dad used to specialize in some of the bakery items, especially the donuts but little else. When he found that he was not that good at the other baking, he increased our output of donuts. He made great donuts, for sure, but as people became more health conscious, they ate fewer donuts and wanted more choices when they came into the bakery."

"So, what did you do?"

"It took a lot of work, but I convinced dad to let me try my hand at the baking. He didn't seem to realize that for years I'd been working under Clive, our former baker, and in his later years, I'd done it all. He really wasn't here more than in name only, but dad didn't know that. I worked hard and I…"

"And modest, too."

"I'm not bragging, just stating the facts. I love it and have studied hard to get better and better. Unlike dad, I'm responsive to the market and make what people like. Dad fought me every step when I tried to change this place into a bistro. He wanted coffee, plain old coffee, none of this latte, espresso kind of stuff. But that's what draws people in."

"It looked like business was thriving when I was there today."

"It is. It actually is, especially over lunch hour. Bringing in Jeff was the best move I ever made. He spent hours watching cooking shows on television, drinking in all that information. You may have noticed, but nothing is ever lost on Jeff - once he learns it, it's in there forever. Luckily for me, his knowledge of meats is extensive, and he cooks up something different every day for sandwiches. We keep it simple, but fresh and delicious."

"So, Jeff is a computer genius plus a cook? What did he do before coming to work for you?"

"Not much of anything, from what I gather."

"Nothing? How could that be? He looks like he's what, in his early thirties?"

Ellie nodded. I think he'd tried a few short-term jobs but didn't find anything that suited him. He attended college for a while but didn't stick with that either, until Mel found him mostly online programs, which he aced. I gather that his parents are pretty protective of him and were just as content if he remained in their basement, under their eye. Mel says they were afraid that the world would be hard on him or that he'd have trouble coping."

"How'd he end up at your place?"

"Mel's doing again. The day she helped Ben, Kyle and their housekeeper, Millie move into the penthouse, she arranged for Jeff to cook for them. Ben was so impressed with the food that he called me. Once I'd sampled what Jeff could do, I begged him to come help at the bakery. We needed something to pull in the lunchtime crowd."

"Was this something he wanted to do?"

"I'm not sure he was looking for a job, but what he really wanted to do was cook. His mother rarely let him use her kitchen. Occasionally he'd go to Mel's place to use hers but he wanted free reign over a kitchen every day. I provided that."

"How was it going from not working to working every day for you?"

"We had lots of discussions that first week and some things to work out. Once Jeff learned what *my* rules were, he added a few of his own and we've gotten along great ever since. He's reliable and creative. At first, I worried about the expense of the cuts of meat he chose but once his roasts were simmering in the oven and customers smelled the aromas, we sold out of sandwiches every day.

"I worried at first that Jeff really didn't care that much what the customers said they liked. He cooked what he wanted to cook. But there's variety and choice that everyone's happy and business has never been better."

"Your dad must have gotten over any of his old ideas then."

"Not really, but Mom's convinced him to come in less and less. Kyle has helped with that. He loves having a grandson nearby. Dad no longer asks to look at the books. Instead, I think he sees nearly all the tables full and that tells him enough.

"Another thing," Ellie continued. "When I first started selling different types of coffee, all I could afford was second-hand equipment. It broke down all the time. Well, some of it still does, but not for long. Jeff is a whiz at fixing anything and our equipment's never been in better shape."

"How do Mel and Jeff's parents feel about all this if they were over-protective and wanting to keep him at home?"

"I'm not sure that it matters. At first, they were definitely not in favor and came to talk to me about it. Mrs. Nicols explained to me that Jeff is not like other young men because he has autism. She wanted to make sure I would not take advantage of her son or treat him badly. As if!"

Rob smiled at her indignation. Now that he was getting to know Ellie, he could not imagine her treating anyone badly. Well, maybe anyone besides himself, he thought, remembering their first meeting.

"Mel, I gather, had been fighting with her parents for years, trying to get them to loosen their reins on Jeff. I guess Jeff had had a couple lousy experiences many years ago with a bad boss. But who hasn't had that happen to them? You learn and move on. At the bakery Jeff is getting to do what he wants to do. He's not keen on having to come in so early but once he realized that the meat had to be cooked and ready for the lunch crowd, he's never missed a day and is never late."

"It sounds win-win for both of you."

"Definitely for me and good I think for Jeff, too. Probably if it wasn't good for him, Jeff would just not show up anymore. I think his parents have relaxed about it, too. At first they came by almost every day, staying for hours, watching Jeff and how he was treated. I treat him exactly the same as I do the rest of my staff. Besides, he's family now. We kid around and give each other a hard time. The Nicols must have gotten that message because they're usually only here on Saturdays now, when Mel and Ben bring Kyle in."

. . .

They were in front of Ellie's house now. They'd walked right by Rob's car and he hadn't even noticed.

"How could I have done that? I meant to stop at my car and drive you the rest of the way home. We didn't have to walk all this way. I don't know how I didn't notice."

Ellie laughed. "Maybe you were having too much fun with the enemy?"

"Yeah, I guess that was it. I did have fun. After our shaky beginning, I never thought I'd say that to you."

"Me, too, after thinking you were being nasty and ruining Sara and Ethan's lives," she said, grinning back at him. "Want to come up for a few minutes?"

"Tempting. But I think I should be getting home. I have a lot of work to do prepping for the boys' group tomorrow."

There was an awkward pause, the first uncomfortable moment they'd had.

Ellie, ever forthright, said, "Maybe we should do this again some time."

"You mean you, me and Jeff?"

"Well that's not exactly what I had in mind, but something like that, sure."

"Can I call you sometime?"

"Sure. I'm in the book, but it's easiest to get me at the bakery. I'm there every day but I go to bed early. This is considered a late night for me."

"That must make dating tough."

"Who has time for dating?"

"Maybe I could convince you to make an exception."

"You know, you just might be one of the few guys who could. See ya.

"Night, and thanks for the good time."

CHAPTER 12

"Mrs. Fellows, may I speak with you a moment, please?" Sara looked at her son's teacher and hesitated. "We're in a bit of a hurry - errands to run and that sort of thing."

"This won't take too long and it's important." Rob could almost see Ethan's mother squirm, much like her son did when put on the spot. To make it easier for her, he added, "I need your help and advice."

Mel appeared at the door, standing aside as the last of Rob's students left the room. "Hi, Mrs. Fellows," she introduced herself. "I'm Mel Wickens, the kindergarten teacher and also a parent of one of Ethan's friends in this class. Rob asked if Ethan and I would spend some time together in my room next door while you two talked. Would that be all right with you? Ethan already knows me, don't you, big guy?" She ruffled Ethan's hair and he leaned in to her. Mel gave him a firm squeeze against her side.

Still reluctant, Sara relented. "Just for a couple minutes, then we have to be getting on our way. Is that all right with you, son?" Without responding, Ethan reached for Mel's hand and started down the hall.

Rob grinned. "None of my kids ever mind going to Mel's room. She has the coolest toys in there and six-year olds aren't that very different than five-year olds."

When they were seated, he began. "I really do need your help with something. You're the expert on Ethan; I'm only just getting to know him. I may know a lot about teaching and six-year olds and about autism, but each kid is unique and you're my best key to what makes Ethan tick.

"Today, he ran away," he continued then waited for Sara's reaction.

Her indrawn breath came quickly then her eyes flickered to the doorway where her son had stood moments ago.

"He's all right, you saw that yourself," Rob reassured her. "But I thought you should know. We caught him quickly and he was fine, but we want to make sure he's always fine. Tell me, is this the first time he's run or has this happened before?"

Sara hesitated. Rob could see a multitude of answers pouring through her mind. "We're all on the same side here," he reminded her. "We want what is best for Ethan, not just in this school year but in the future."

With her eyes on the desk between them, Sara admitted, "This is not the first time, no. At his last school it happened a lot. That's some of the reason they would ask me to come get him, when they were short-staffed and didn't have someone available who could run after him.

Then it started coming out in a rush. "But it wasn't just the school's fault. It happens with me, too. I'm in a panic half the time when we go shopping. What if I lose him? What if I can't catch him? What if my back is turned just for a half second and he bolts and I don't see which direction he took? What if some stranger sees this little boy alone and takes him? I don't know what to do."

"Okay, we'll work on this together. We have the same goals - neither of us wants Ethan to bolt and we all want to keep him safe." He pushed the box of tissues closer to Sara. Her tears had started, and her head remained down. "Can you tell me about when he runs?" he asked.

Sara started on a different track. "It's my fault. My husband tells me that all the time. I started it, he says and now I have to live with it."

Rob just waited. When she seemed to need encouragement, he asked, "How do you think it started?"

"When Ethan was little, I started this game. You have to understand how hard it was when he was small. Everyone dreams of this baby you'll sit with and cuddle. But Ethan wasn't like that. He didn't seem to like me when he was a baby. He didn't want to be held. When he cried, I couldn't make him stop. Every baby wants his mother to comfort him, doesn't he? But not Ethan, at least not with me.

"No," she corrected. "It wasn't just me he didn't like. When my mother-in-law came over, she couldn't comfort him either. The whole grandma-in-the-rocking-chair-thing didn't work with Ethan." She swiped at her wet cheeks with another tissue.

"Other mothers talk about what a bonding experience nursing was, gazing into their child's face during feedings. Well, it didn't work that way with us. Sure, I'd gaze into his little face but he didn't look at me. His eyes wandered around, or if they did look at me, it wasn't at my eyes. He'd seem to stare a few seconds at my nose, then at an eyebrow, or parts of my face but not into my eyes the way other babies would. And he tolerated my holding him just until he was finished eating, then he'd squirm and fuss until I put him down. He'd actually prefer lying in a crib alone to being in his mother's arms."

Rob opened his mouth to say that he'd heard this many times before from parents of kids with autism, but Sara rushed on.

"Before he was born, I signed up for this mothers and tots play group. You sit around in a circle, sing songs, chant nursery rhymes, play in the swimming pool, all things normal babies love to do with their mothers. But I cancelled. How could I go when I'd be the only mother there who didn't know how to make her baby stop crying? The only mother whose baby hated to be held? The only mother whose baby hated her? Babies are supposed to give you unconditional love. Even lousy mothers have kids who love them and want them, but not mine."

This was more than Rob had bargained for. He was good at analyzing situations, finding out the reasons that might be behind the behaviors and at making a plan. The touchy-feely, sensitive stuff was not his forte. But, this woman was hurting and they would not be able to get onto the planning stage before spending time on some of this. Right at that moment, he wished *he* was in the kindergarten room playing with Ethan and Mel was in here with Mrs. Fellows. Suck it up, he told himself. You can do it. At least you can try not to make her feel worse.

"Mrs. Fellows, I've seen you with your son and I've seen how Ethan reacts to you. He loves you - it's obvious. His face lights up when you come for him at the end of the day. He wants to share with you what he's done." He saw her about to disparage that last comment and put up his hand. "I know, I know, he may not show it in the same way as some of the other kids, but he does want to share with you. How his day went may not come out in a rush of words, but he'll fish around in his back pack until he finds some paper he's worked on and hold that out to you. He's communicating. Not all communication is about words; in fact we convey far more with our body language and our actions than with our words. Ethan wants to show you what he's done. And, he always looks for a hug. He may have not when he was young, but he's grown into it now. Did you notice how he even leaned into Mel for a hug just before they left the room?"

Sara nodded. "A couple years ago he'd never have done that."

"His nervous system has matured," Rob explained. Sara's forehead creased, so he explained. "Many kids with autism seem to be wired differently. Their sensory systems can be over active or under active. With some kids, it takes a lot more stimulation to arouse them to a level where they respond. Others seem hyper-sensitive and over-react to things like touch, sounds, smells, noises and other things in their environment. They can't seem to filter out all the input coming at them. A baby's too young to explain to you or to run away from it all so they do the only thing they can - cry. For some, the normal jiggling and hugging we do to try to calm a baby may not help and may even increase their sense of being overwhelmed.

"Sometimes too, we're gentle with a baby, very gentle in our touch. That light, feathery touch can be calming to some kids, but is like fingernails on a blackboard to others. Before they left this classroom, did you notice how Mel hugged your son? There was nothing soft and gentle about it - Mel hugged him firmly. Did you see Ethan's reaction?"

Sara nodded. "He sort of melted into her. I hadn't thought about the different kinds of hugs before. Maybe that's why Ethan hates my mother. She's a very gentle sort and tries to brush his skin lightly. Even as a baby, he'd arch away from her and scream. But he was better with my dad, who's more of a gruff guy and held him solidly across his chest.

"He could not stand my father-in-law either. When Ethan was a baby, my husband's father really didn't have anything to do with him. Women looked after babies, in his mind. But when Ethan began walking around, he took more of an interest. He'd build these towers of wooden blocks and Ethan would knock them down. That's how they played together. But it would all end in screams when Jack would suddenly pick Ethan up and toss him in the air. Most little kids love that, but Ethan would scream and scream. It's not that he was ever dropped, not even close, but he hated that game. It got so bad that whenever his grandparents would come over, Ethan would start screaming or hide. They complained a lot to my husband about how I was raising Ethan so badly and making a sissy out of him.

TRYING to get back on track, Rob asked, "You said that this started as a game. His running, I mean. What did you mean by that?"

"When he was little, it was so hard to relate to him or to get him to relate to me. What kind of a mother does not bond with her child? Well, that mother was me. I looked after him as best I could, but we didn't really have that kind of mother-child bond you see in movies or read about in books, or watch other mothers having.

"So, whenever Ethan did respond to me, I was elated. We started this game when I'd pretend to chase him. He'd run and giggle. He'd even look over his shoulder to see if I was coming, almost as if he wanted me to. It was one of the first things we ever did together, actually played together."

"Sounds like a pretty normal experience. Why do you sound like that's a problem?"

"Because it became a problem. My husband says that's where this whole running away thing came from, from me teaching him to run and having someone chase after him."

Rob contemplated a moment, trying to get the words right. "Mrs. Fellows, I don't have kids of my own but I'm around small children all day. On the playground, I'd say that half their games involve running or chasing. Kids do it all the time. When I visit my niece and nephews, I play chase games with them when I run after them, grab them and tickle them. They love it! So do I, for that matter. I bet most parents have played like that with their kids.

"The problem," he continued, "is that with kids with autism, they may not generalize in the same way. While my niece gets that this is just something we do in the house with Uncle Rob, I doubt she'd act the same way in a different setting with a different adult."

"That's exactly what Ethan has done. At his last school he ran the most from an Educational Associate he really liked."

"Why do you think he ran when he was at that school?"

"Sometimes he'd run, trying to play with her. But at other times he ran almost in a panic. They told me he'd run like demons were after him and have this terrified look. When they caught up to him, he'd be panting and sweating and his heart was racing, but it wasn't from the exertion because he never really did run that far. It was like he was scared and trying to get away from something."

"Most kids instinctively pick up the social rules, like when and where it's okay to do certain things, such as playing chase games. Children with autism spectrum disorders don't seem to automatically get these things and need to be taught the rules. And, when they do generalize on their own, they might get it wrong and not know how to self-correct that wrong perception, or even realize that it's wrong and that other kids don't act that way.

"Mrs. Fellows..."

"Sara," she interrupted. "Please call me Sara. You already know enough about me for us to be on a first name basis. One side of her mouth turned up as she said this. So, she did have a sense of humor and might be able to laugh at herself. Good to know. He might not need to tread so lightly.

"Okay, Sara. First, quit beating yourself up over playing a game with your son when he was younger. You've probably seen other parents play with their kid like that and maybe you even did it with your mother and father when you were his age. It's a normal thing to do. At that time, you did not know that Ethan had autism. There was no way you could have guessed that he might take and run with this one aspect of your lives."

When Sara smiled at him, Rob thought back over what he'd just said and caught the unintended pun. "Sorry. You know what I mean, he added, then continued. "So, what started out as a fun thing to do with mom became over-generalized, for whatever reason and has now become a pattern."

Sara nodded.

"A pattern we don't want. Look, here are the things that concern me. One, while this may be a fun game for a two-year-old, it's no longer an appropriate kind of play for a six year old, at least not in the way Ethan's doing it. Two, it's not safe. Even when he's trying to have fun with someone, looking over his shoulder while he runs into the street could have disastrous consequences."

Sara's tears started again. "I know, I know. That's constantly on my mind. And, if anything happened, it would be all my fault." Her spine straightened. "But that's why his previous school had a one-to-one aide with him at all times, to keep him from running."

Rob's left eyebrow rose just a bit. "Did it work? Did it stop him from running?"

"Well, no, but when he did run there was someone watching who could run after him." But when they were short staffed, they would call her.

"Is that what you want? Do you also want a fence? Do you want him tethered to the ground or to an adult? Maybe he just shouldn't be allowed outside at all."

"Look here, Mr. Sells. My son deserves fresh air and exercise just like any other child, even if he does have autism and even if he does complicate *your* life."

"Yep, you're right. I absolutely agree. But how do we do that and at the same time keep him safe?"

"Get another aide to be with him at all times!"

"Hmm. That might work right now, although you did say that he still ran at his other school. Let's think about this a moment.

"Remember how kids with autism get into patterns?" He waited for Sara's nod. "What patterns are we helping him develop if we glue an adult to his side, one who will chase after him every time he runs?"

Sara sighed. "We might be reinforcing the same game I set up with him when he was younger."

"Yes. I'm sorry, but yes, that is most likely what we'd be doing. But, there's more. Apart from teaching him that this is one way to interact with that adult and that it's supposedly fun, how long could we continue this?"

"As long as is necessary to keep him safe."

"You and I have a pretty good idea how fast a six-year-old boy can run, and we could both probably catch him. But Ethan is not going to stay six for long. Soon, he'll be ten then sixteen. Have you seen how fast teenaged boys can run?"

"But that's in the future. I'm worried about him *now.*

"Me, too. Remember about autism and patterns, though. When you and he started that chase game a few years ago, you were thinking about the fun you were having with your boy, not about the possible ramifications down the road." He watched Sara's face crumble. "I'm sorry. I don't mean to be hurtful, but it's the truth. You were doing what probably three-quarters of all parents do with their toddlers. The difference is in how Ethan internalized those actions. He got into a pattern and didn't get the part about that pattern only being appropriate in certain circumstances.

"Now, if we're not careful, we'll send him a different message - one that says we don't trust you. You're not like other kids. You can't handle yourself. You must have an adult glued to your side."

"If that's what it takes to keep him safe."

"Sara, there is another way, several other ways in fact, but they're not fast. Look. Here's another worry I have. The playground is an important social arena for kids. They learn a lot out there and practice much-needed skills like negotiation, compromise, cooperation, turn-taking and fair play. But kids won't play with that one child who has an adult beside him. A one-to-one aide would isolate Ethan. Not only would we be sending *him* the message that we don't trust him and don't believe he can learn to be like other kids, but we're sending that same message to every other student on the playground. It would be like pasting a big 'Don't Play With Me' sign onto Ethan's forehead. He'd be one kid standing alone with an adult while all the other children raced around and had fun without him."

Rob could tell by Sara's expression that she could envision this happening to her son.

"But he's not a bad boy. He just doesn't know. I want him to have friends. I want him to play with other kids just like any other little boy."

Rob pushed the tissue box closer to Sara once again. "Then we're on the same page. We both want the same things for Ethan. And, I, for one, believe that he can learn not to run away. There are certain ways kids comport themselves in schools and out in the public. Ethan can learn these ways. How about it? Are you up for working with me on this?"

CHAPTER 13

*R*ob pulled a piece of paper towards himself. "I'm a visual thinker and need to see, not just talk about it when I make a plan. Now, how should we start? Any ideas?"

Sara looked blank, so Rob suggested, "What about using an ABC to map it out?" When Sara still looked blank, he drew one horizontal line near the top of the page and created three vertical columns. At the top of the first column he wrote Antecedent. The middle column was titled Behavior and the last one Consequences. "Now, think of a time when Ethan ran. What was happening before? This might give us a clue as to why he ran."

"The last time I know about was last week at home. We were having company over, my husband's boss and his wife. Ethan had never met them before and I didn't know them very well either. He was pretty good while I was cooking and getting ready, but the Jacksons had only been at our house about ten minutes when we heard a thump, the door slammed, and Ethan was gone."

"What was happening about the time he ran?"

"I'm not sure. The only people in that room were Nona Jackson and Ethan. She was very distressed and said she was just trying to lift Ethan onto her knee to read him a story. She reached for him and when she tried to cuddle him, he went like a limp noodle and fell through her lap to the floor. She's positive he wasn't hurt but said he got up off the floor and ran."

"Was there anything about her you can identify that might have bothered Ethan?"

"She had on this frilly, starchy blouse that made scratchy sounds when she moved. I remember thinking it looked like those old, starched collars and must be awfully uncomfortable.

"Anything else?"

"She had on perfume. Not that cheap cologne, but obviously good quality scent. She must have really liked it because she wore a lot of it. A lot. When she entered the house, it was almost overpowering and made me wonder what the interior of their car must smell like."

"Ethan's not used to perfume?"

"No. When he was a toddler, he had eczema and we had to use scent-free detergents and soaps. Since scents bothered Ethan, I never wore perfume. His eczema's all gone now, but I never got back into the habit of wearing perfume. We don't light scented candles and those sorts of things either. We stopped, and then just never started again."

"Let's go on to 'B' for a minute and describe the behavior. What exactly did Ethan do?"

"I'm not positive since all I have is Mrs. Jackson's word for it. According to her, everything was fine although she was having some trouble lifting Ethan onto her knee. She said he was all stiff. She thought he'd warm up once she cuddled him and started reading."

"What happened next?"

"She said that he then made himself go limp and dropped to the floor. The sound we heard was his legs hitting the floor. Then he got up and ran for the front door. We heard it slam, then Ethan was gone."

"Where did he go?"

"Across the lawn and then down the sidewalk. My husband caught him pretty quickly."

"What did he do when he caught him?"

"He picked him up and carried him the way Ethan likes it - like a monkey. You know, chest to chest, Ethan's arms and legs clinging tight and his dad's arms around him. He's always liked this. He puts his head on your shoulder and relaxes."

"Okay. Let's go back a minute to 'A', the Antecedent. What do you think precipitated the running?"

"It could have been anything - the perfume, a strange woman trying to hold him, the stiff rustling of her blouse, unexpectedly having other people in our house, or anything else. Who knows?"

"Unexpected company?"

"Well, obviously I knew they were coming, and we prepared the meal but I don't think we told Ethan until the doorbell rang and they were here."

"Sounds like any one of those things could have upset Ethan then a couple piled on top of each other might have felt like too much and he needed to escape."

Sara nodded.

Rob pointed to the last column. "And what was the consequence to all this?"

"The main consequence was that it spoiled our evening. I stayed with Ethan up in his room while my husband tried to entertain our guests on his own. It was not the best evening for anyone."

"Anyone?"

"No, none of us had a good time."

"What about Ethan? What kind of a time did he have after the two of you retreated to his bedroom?"

"Oh, Ethan was fine, probably better than any of us. We watched a couple of his favorite videos, I read him a story, and we played with his Lego, that sort of stuff."

"Does he like having your attention all to himself?"

"Sure. What kid doesn't?"

"So what was the negative consequence to Ethan for running away?"

Sara hesitated. "Well, he got frightened. Is that what you mean?"

"Not exactly. I mean what was the consequence he went through for having chosen running as his means of getting out of a situation he didn't like?"

"None, I don't think."

"Maybe this isn't a good example. What consequence does he receive at other times when he runs away?"

"I'm not sure what you mean."

"Say you're out shopping and he doesn't stay with you in a mall. What consequence do you impose on him later? Some people might think of it as a punishment if you like that word better."

"We don't really do things like that. I don't generally spank him, and I certainly wouldn't spank a child who was frightened."

"Spanking isn't quite what I had in mind. I'll try to explain what I mean. There is a consequence for all our actions. Some consequences are good - we like them, and they get us what we want. Other consequences we don't find so pleasant, especially the consequences we experience after making a bad decision. Those are the kinds of consequences I'm talking about. What kind have you found are effective with Ethan?"

Still, Sara hesitated, so Rob gave her some examples.

"Do you give him a time out, send him to his room, remove a toy, not let him watch television, make him go to bed early? The kind of consequences parents often use to teach lessons to their child."

"You have to understand. Ethan is different. He's been difficult from the start, but then later, we learned that he has autism. The diagnosis explains some of the difficulties he's always had but we're of course saddened by it. And we feel sorry for our poor little boy."

"I understand all that. But," he tapped his pen on the paper under the 'C' column, "for our purposes now, we need to see what the consequences are of his actions."

Silence from Sara.

"Are we in agreement that running away is a bad thing, something we want stopped?"

"Yes, of course."

"And you're with me on finding ways to teach Ethan not to run away but to find other ways of handling the situations?"

"Yes," a bit more hesitantly.

"Well, in order to teach him effective choice-making, he's going to have to experience consequences – both good consequences and ones he doesn't like. Just like all of us. We're rewarded for making good choices and things don't go as we'd like when we make poor choices."

ROB GRABBED a second piece of paper. "Tell me what Ethan enjoys." He began writing the favorite activities Sara listed.

She asked, "Why do you want to know those things?"

"So we can give him appropriate rewards whenever he makes good choices."

"I thought a minute ago you were talking about punishments."

"I like to start with the positive. It's easier to give a child a positive consequence for making a good decision than giving a negative one for a poor choice. It's easier to get a kid to buy in to a plan when he likes the rewards he's working towards."

Rob put down his pen and looked at Sara. "I can try to do this alone here at school. That's not the best way, not by far, but I could do it. The downside to that would be what Ethan learns. I've seen many kids who learn to follow the rules and to make good choices at school but don't carry over the same skills at home. They seem to sense that the two environments are different and that the same rules don't apply.

"For Ethan's sake, it would be ideal if we worked on this together - you, your husband and me as well as the other staff at this school. If we surround Ethan, with everyone giving the same message, I'm positive we can at least seriously decrease his running away, if not make it disappear altogether. But to do this, we all need to agree to give pleasurable consequences when he does the right thing and consequences he won't like if he's run away."

"Are you asking me to be mean to my only son?"

"No, no, not at all. This is teaching him, just as you teach any other skill."

"Then are you telling me to bribe my own kid into being good?"

"Nope. That's not what I mean either. Look on the night you had the Jacksons over, Ethan likely felt overwhelmed by both the unexpectedness of those people dropping in and by sensory sensations. He ran away. That's a bad thing. Granted, Ethan was trying to get away from something he didn't like, but there are other ways he could have accomplished that. Safer ways and I think that's what you want. It's certainly what I want for him, both here at school and at home. As far as I can see, this is a crucial life skill, one he needs to learn for his own safety, to say nothing of his parents' peace of mind."

"We would feel a lot better if we weren't constantly in fear that he might run and get hurt or lost" Sara admitted.

"Let's get back to consequences. That evening at your place, how do you think Ethan felt when his dad carried him home?"

"Relieved. You could see it in his face. Relieved and relaxed. And he had fun. As they got closer to the house, Rick started jostling Ethan up and down. It's a game they play and by the time they got in the house, they were both laughing."

"From Ethan's point of view, how do you think this whole thing turned out?"

"He got scared, and then he wasn't?" Sara's statement was a question. She wasn't getting it. Rob was not doing a good enough job of explaining his point.

"Here's what I think went on in your son's mind. He was startled by the disruption to his routine when these strangers came over unexpectedly. He had no preparation for this."

"We don't exactly need our child's permission to invite guests over!"

"Of course not. But Ethan is the kind of kid who needs to know when things are going to happen that are different or unexpected. All it requires is a sentence or two. Or, grab a pencil and a scrap of paper and jot down a quick social story about having company. Anything will do, just so long as he has some warning, even a five-minute warning might have helped."

Rob continued. "Then these strangers arrived. One tried to touch him in ways he didn't like. Some people approach little kids with a gentle touch, one they think will be soothing to a child. But to kids with tactile sensitivities, that soft touch could grate on their nerves and might even be perceived as hurtful. A firmer touch would likely have been a better approach. Mrs. Jackson told you it was hard to get Ethan on her knee because he was stiff as a board."

"Yes, that's what she said."

"So, in nonverbal language, Ethan was resisting. He did not want to sit on her knee. But this woman didn't know him so didn't read his body language. Of course, it might have helped if Ethan had used his words."

"Yes, but he might have said something rude or offended the wife of my husband's boss."

"We don't want him being rude, but would a couple rude words have made the situation any worse than his running off did?"

Sara shook her head.

"So, Ethan doesn't like this lady or being touched by her, so he runs away. By running, he escapes the smells or touches he didn't like about that woman. So, that's a positive consequence for him, don't you agree?"

"Yes, I suppose so."

"When he runs, he probably doesn't experience near the fear that you and your husband go through. He's a little boy, not thinking about all the things that could possibly happen to him. In this particular case, his running was positively reinforced as a good thing because it got him away from that strange woman."

"I guess it did."

"Then when your husband went after him, Ethan got to ride home in his favorite position. That position conjures up fun in his mind because it's a way to play with his dad. He got to be held tightly, giving good proprioceptive feedback to his body, something he was probably craving. Again, this is a positive consequence for having run. Then, and probably best of all, he got to spend a lovely evening with his mom, doing all the things he enjoys and he had your attention all to himself. How could running away be a bad thing?"

"When you put it that way, I can't see any reason for him to not run the next time."

"Exactly. That's why we have to break this pattern and give him new tools to get what he wants, more appropriate tools that will keep him safe."

"BACK TO THIS incident with the Jacksons. I wonder, and this is just a suggestion. Do you think in future it might be a good idea to not leave Ethan alone with a stranger until they have gotten used to each other?"

"You're right, so right. This is all my fault."

"We're not talking about faults here. That does not enter into it at all. What we're doing is making a plan to help Ethan be more successful the next time he runs into an unpleasant situation."

"What do you want us to do?"

"Glad you asked." He flashed her a grin. "Homework for Mr. and Mrs. Fellows. You know your son well and he talks to you more than to anyone else. Make up a list of ways Ethan can politely tell people to leave him alone the next time he finds himself in a similar situation. Could he ask to go to his room? Could he say that he wants to play by himself for a while now? I don't know but you and Mr. Fellows will come up with ideas that work best for your family."

"We can do that."

"Next, from that list, pick the items that you think would work here at school and give the list to me. We'll work on using the same words you're using at home, reinforcing each other."

"Makes sense to me." Sara was starting to feel more upbeat about this planning business.

"Last, please give me two other lists - one of consequences Ethan would think of as rewards, things I can use when he shows good decision-making. Plus, I need a list of consequences he won't like, ones to be used when he makes a bad choice. These might consist of the removal of something he likes. Can you do that?"

Sara nodded but without enthusiasm.

"Do you think we're on the right track?"

"Mostly. It's just that it will break my heart to be mean to my little boy."

"You know Sara, I look at it the opposite way. I see it as being mean to not curb this behavior and to not teach him better ways of responding to unpleasant situations. I'd feel mean if Ethan ran and got hurt. It would have been cruel to do nothing to prevent that. Try as we might we can't always be with him - not you, not his dad and not anyone at school. There will be times when Ethan must make a wise choice all on his own. Now is the time to help guide him so that he learns those skills."

CHAPTER 14

*E*llie glanced out the bakery window. Rob Sells was coming down the street. Wiping her floury hands on her apron, she strode out the door and across the street towards him. "So, you were shining me on." Ellie's hands clenched, her lips were tight, and she leaned her face in towards Rob's. He thought she might spit the words at him.

Rob took a step back.

"What's the matter with you?"

"Nothing's wrong with me except I'm ticked at the indifference one human being can show to another, especially *you*."

"I don't know what's got your panties in a knot but you're looking at the wrong guy. I haven't even seen you in over a week. Whatever's happened to you, it wasn't me. So, back off." His hands went into his back pockets.

"Who said it was all about me? Some of us care about others too, especially those who can't defend themselves."

Rob was torn between wanting to walk away and learning what had changed the softer Ellie of the other night back into the shrew he'd first met. Ah, it wasn't worth it. "I'm out of here." Rob turned to walk away, back in the opposite direction from the bakery.

Ellie snagged his left arm as he turned. Rob looked pointedly down at her hand, then up at her face, but she didn't let go. "Not so fast, mister," she told him. "Not until I find out why you're not doing your job as a teacher."

"Are you out of your friggin' mind?" Then he added, "Get your hand away from my arm. I have things to do." Rob glanced around to see if other people were observing the scene they were making.

Ellie didn't budge, nor did she look around. "You know, the other night I thought I'd been wrong about you, that you actually were a nice guy - running a boys' group, trying to learn so you could help those kids. On our walk home, I was even starting to get some warm and fuzzy thoughts about you."

This gave Rob pause. "You were?"

"Forget that. I was wrong. I can be such an idiot sometimes."

"Can't say I've noticed," the sarcasm thick in his voice.

She gave his arm a shake. "So why are you refusing to help Sara?"

"How is my teaching or my student's mother any business of yours?"

Ellie's shoulder's drooped. "Once I had this friend. She needed someone to stand up for her and no one did. She killed herself." She looked up at Rob with defiance. "That's never going to happen to someone I know again."

Relaxing his stance just a bit, Rob turned back toward this quieter Ellie. "Why don't you start at the beginning and tell me what I'm supposed to have done or not done."

"Sara can't have a life. She spends every moment of her day by a phone, waiting for a call from the school."

"Did she tell you how often I've called her during the school day?"

"No, not exactly, but obviously enough times to keep her on the edge of her seat waiting for the next call. She's just so sad."

"Her being sad is my fault too?"

"Maybe for some of it. I didn't go into all the details of her life but I know that school stuff is a big part of it."

"You might want to check how much of this happens now and how much was at their previous school."

That gave Ellie momentary pause, but she carried on. "Here's what she says. She's overwhelmed. She loves her kid, but he's difficult. I know what she means, having seen some of what Ben's been through with Kyle. While Kyle's fits of screaming have lessened a lot over the past year, it does not sound like Ethan's are getting any better.

"Did you stop to think of why Kyle seems better?"

"Well, it's Mel of course. And a bit my brother. He might be a lug but he tries. When Ben learned how to do things differently, Kyle reacted by screaming less."

"So you're saying that the adults in Kyle's life helped him learn a different way of coping?"

"Something like that, I guess. Sara needs the same kind of help Ben got."

"You're saying Sara needs to marry Mel?" Rob tried to lighten things up a bit.

Ellie jabbed his side with her elbow. "She needs the help of someone like Mel, someone who knows kids with autism. You're his teacher. Couldn't you be a help instead of being the ogre who's adding to the stress?"

Rob shook his head at her. "I can't talk to you about Ethan or Sara. I can talk in generalities about autism and parenting." He continued, "Parenting any kid is not a cake walk but it's especially hard when your child has autism. Some of the instinctual, parenting things won't work in the same way they would with a typical kid. So, you have to learn different ways, different strategies. Is it harder? Definitely. It takes more patience, more repetitions, more time."

"Such as?"

"Has Mel talked to you about Kyle and auditory processing?"

"Yeah, I get some of it."

"How would you explain it to Sara?"

"Well, most of us are talkers. And, the more frustrated or tired or angry we get, the more we talk to kids. We lecture. We threaten. We cajole. We talk, talk, talk."

"And all that goes over the head of a kid with autism."

"Mel keeps telling us that talking can make things worse. The kid is already upset, unsure what to do and how to avoid the things that are bothering him. Then Ben would loom over him, yammering away, his voice getting louder, but the words made no sense to Kyle. This just increased Kyle's tension and then he'd blow."

"Mel was right to be worried. The problem with a kid getting in the habit of blowing is that he gets bigger and the tantrums turn to aggression. The longer the pattern continues, the more entrenched it becomes. A two-year-old may throw his cup or a stuffed toy. An older kid may overturn a desk or throw dishes at you. Someone could and will get hurt."

"I think that's happening to Sara now. She was crying when she showed me the bruise on her forehead from some toy Ethan hit her with. She says it makes her afraid to go near her own child when he's upset, even when she knows he needs a hug."

That gave Rob pause. "I'm sorry to hear it's gone that far with them." They were both silent a moment.

"So what happens now?" Ellie asked. "Does it just get worse and worse, a parent held hostage by her own kid?"

"It can go that way. Except for rare cases, it doesn't have to be like that. You can turn it around, although the younger you start, the easier it is."

"How? What can she do?"

"Think back to the things that Ben learned to do with Kyle. Name one thing he does that you might not see in other households."

Ellie was quick to answer. "Visuals. I'd never heard the term before and certainly never seen them plastered all over a house like that. But once Ben started using them and once Kyle caught on, it did make a difference. Kyle wouldn't be screaming, and Ben wouldn't be yelling and exasperated. Well, he didn't actually yell all that much, but he certainly felt like it. I could tell. And believe you me, my brother can yell. You try being his little sister and get into his precious stuff when we were kids."

Rob smiled. "I can imagine you doing that quite often."

"He was older and had interesting stuff. It was especially intriguing since I wasn't supposed to be in his room."

"I bet you were a real brat."

"If you listened to Ben, yes. But I'm quite sure he has that all wrong."

"Tell me more about the visuals that Ben learned to use."

"To begin with Ben was late for work every day and late getting Kyle to school. Ben absolutely detests being late for anything and he's usually an organized guy, but no matter how early he started in the morning, he could not get Kyle up and ready on time.

"Then Mel helped him make these pictures of what Kyle was supposed to do in the morning. It took a bit of time, but not long before Kyle understood what each picture stood for and then he followed them in order. When he'd get sidetracked and start to play with his Lego™ or watch a Dora the Explorer™ movie, instead of raising his voice and ragging on Kyle, Ben would tap on the picture strip and show Kyle. And, believe it or not, Kyle would follow what the picture said. It wasn't perfect, but they didn't end up leaving the house mad at each other and they mostly got going on time."

"Good. What else did Ben do?"

"I guess the other biggie was social stories. He learned that from Mel, too. At first Ben couldn't believe that they worked because instead of words, Mel often drew pictures of what was going to happen. She really *cannot* draw. Did you know that? Ben would look at what she'd made and not have a clue what it was supposed to be. Mel said it didn't matter. She'd tell Kyle what it was about and he'd believe her. Then they'd follow the pictures and it would be all right. Well, maybe not totally all right, but at least far better than it used to be. You should have seen the ruckus Kyle made originally when he had to go in the elevator. But the social story helped."

"Yeah, elevators can be scary places for some kids. They're small, enclosed spaces. The door closes, and you can feel trapped inside. Then this little box you're in makes strange clanking and whirring and then it starts to move. You're not used to feeling the ground beneath your feet rattle or move. For a kid with no sense of time, it could feel like being trapped forever and he'd have no idea when it would be over, if ever. Anyone with vestibular problems, unsure of their balance or where their body is in space would be disoriented in that moving box.

"Did Kyle ever get over his fear?"

"Not perfectly, but it got better and better. So much better in fact that one night he took off on his own and they lost him for a couple hours. Ben almost went out of his mind."

"What happened?"

"Kyle for some reason went to Mel's house. It was quite a walk for a little guy and it was night time. No one had any idea he even knew the way. He would have had to go through the park in the dark, and then a couple blocks the other side. They found him asleep on Mel's deck with her dog curled around him."

"Scary stuff. Has it only happened that once?"

"Yes. Kyle's never shown any want to go off on his own again. But then Mel and her dog now live with them so there's no need to go find them. I actually think the whole thing was more traumatic for Ben than for Kyle. My brother was a wreck."

They were silent for a moment.

"Hey, did you notice something?" Ellie asked.

Rob sighed. "What now? Have you found another way in which I'm evil incarnate?"

Ellie pretended to whack Rob's arm. "I was about to ask if you've noticed that we're not fighting anymore. But maybe we should revert back. That seems to be our default mode."

"Fighting? Me? Look lady, you're the one who attacked me. I was on my way for some good coffee, maybe something sweet and I'd had the faint hope of some pleasant conversation. Guess I was wrong on all accounts, especially the latter."

It was Ellie's turn to sigh. Her eyes remained on the toes of Rob's sneakers. "Look, I'm sorry. Ben's always telling me that I run too hot and I blow off without getting all the facts.

"But this time I really thought I did have all the facts. If you could have seen Sara yesterday, you'd know what I mean. It's not everyday someone comes into my bakery and cries. Actually, I can only think of it happening twice in the past year and both times it was Sara doing the crying. I don't think she has many friends and comes to me for a sympathetic ear."

"And what does your sympathetic ear tell your mouth to say to her?"

"She's obviously hurting and she needs someone to stand up for her."

"And you've appointed yourself guardian of sad mothers?"

"Are you saying there's something wrong with helping someone in need?"

"Nah." His face softened. "I don't know if I could tell you to quit it, even if I wanted to. It seems to be part of who you are."

Now Ellie looked uncomfortable. "Maybe because I was raised in a house with three brothers, I can't stand to see someone being picked on."

Rob bristled again. "For the last time, I am not picking on anyone and that includes Sara and her son. Geez. Get off it, will ya?"

"I didn't mean *you*, at least not this time anyway. It's just that in general I can't stand bullies."

"Bullies! Now you're calling me a bully. As I said before, you, lady are a piece of work." He turned to walk away but didn't get far. Ellie still had hold of his arm. "Do you mind?" he asked, looking down at her hand restraining his arm.

"Actually, I do. It's hard to hold a conversation with you when you keep trying to walk away."

"My attempts to walk away should send a message to you. What about it don't you get?"

"I know you're not really trying to get away."

"Short of creating a scene in public, yeah, I am trying to get away. In case you hadn't noticed, this is not my idea of a good time on my day off."

"Come off it. Anytime you wanted, you could have pulled away from me."

"Yeah? Says who?"

"Says me. Admit it, you like me."

He pulled back his head and looked at her. "*I* like the woman who accosts me every time I see her? The same one who accuses me of all manner of heinous crimes?"

Ellie nodded. Then she smiled, and Rob's body slumped. How could you stay mad at a being like Ellie? He returned her smile. "Maybe I do, just a little."

Her smile broadened even more. She tugged on his arm. "Come on. I'll buy you a coffee. I know a nice little place not far from here." They set off together for the bakery, Ellie chatting and Rob wondering how he had gotten himself into this.

CHAPTER 15

"*I* don't get it," said Ellie. "What is about people like Mel that make it look easy to raise a child who has autism?"

"Easy? I doubt that Mel would say that, or anybody else. I imagine that Mel finds it a bit harder now that she's a mother. Before, she was just a teacher and that made it easier. You can go home at the end of the day and concentrate on other things, although your students are always in the back of your mind.

"Someone like Mel has extra training in strategies for kids with special needs and for behavior issues. That was the focus of the graduate work that we both did. Still, you only learn so much from books and the real knowledge you gain is from the classroom, working with the kids and with their parents. Those two groups are the best teachers."

"That's fine for people like you and Mel who have the time to go back to school for this training. But what's the average parent to do?"

"People like Mel and I?" He was back to bristling, something Ellie brought out in him more than any other person had ever done. "When we did our master's degrees, we had full-time jobs. We studied evenings and weekends and spent our vacation time sitting in lecture theaters. Every spare penny we could gather went into tuition and books."

"So, why'd you do it?"

"To get better at our jobs. To learn more about what makes kids tick, especially kids who learn in different ways."

"And did you get better?"

"I like to think so. Yes, I'm pretty sure I did, at least for the most part. I get these kids in the fall and by spring they've grown physically, but also mentally and emotionally. They're more in control of themselves, they've acquired more social skills and they've come along academically. Not all of them progress at the same pace or in the same areas, but I have to admit that they all do make progress. So yes, I do think I'm a success when you look at those measurements."

"But a parent wouldn't have this fund of knowledge that you and Mel acquired. What can they do?"

"The knowledge about strategies and things to try is out there. You don't have to read ominous textbook tomes to get it, either. In fact, we have a lending library of such resources at school, available for any parent."

"Why don't some take advantage of it and why is this all so hard for Sara?"

"Sara is the parent of one of my students," he reminded her. "I cannot talk about any of my kids or their families with you. Does that sound familiar, ring a bell with you somewhere?"

"All right, I get it. Don't talk about her, just about parents in general."

"Remember, these things are just my opinions. I think that for parents, there is some guilt."

"What do you mean guilt? It's not like they purposely gave their child autism!"

"No, of course not. Guilt does not have to be logical, does it? Whether or not it makes sense, there is some guilt about things like, What if I did something wrong that caused this? Did I expose myself to some toxin that got into the baby? Did I have too many x-rays? Or not enough prenatal tests? I had a lot of late nights during my first trimester. Did that stress the baby too much? I had one beer before I even knew I was pregnant. Or, is it my genes? Some people spend hours going through their family genealogy trying to find signs of autism in one family or the other, so they can blame the other spouse's genetic line."

"Are they right? Did they do something to cause this in their child?"

"Maybe but most likely not. The cause of autism spectrum disorders is still not known. They've found over three dozen genes that might be implicated in autism, but twin studies find some of those gene abnormalities in both twins, but one has autism and the other doesn't.

"Then, we've all known of mothers who truly did not look after themselves during pregnancy and that baby is not born with any evidence of autism."

"So, accurate or not, some parents might blame themselves for their child having autism."

"Yes, autism or any other problem. Then there's the way people react to that guilt. Some feel that they have to make it up to their child. They see their kid suffering and they want that to stop so they cater to his every whim, trying to apologize for what they perceive as the hard life he leads."

"I can see that. I'd do the same thing."

"It certainly is tempting, but there's another way to look at it. For the child, this is the only life he's ever known. Unless someone tells him, he's not even aware when he's young that things are harder for him than for others his age. To him, things just are. I'm not convinced that feeling sorry for a kid does him any good. Sure, as adults we might feel badly watching him struggle, but keep that to yourself - that's your issue, not the kid's. Feeling sorry for him conveys the message that something is wrong with him, that he's a thing to be pitied. That's not good for anyone."

"Isn't that a little harsh?"

"Well, maybe. I don't mean it quite that way but feeling sorry for a child doesn't help him. Yes, that kid will have struggles, ones that his peers don't have and some that they do. Rather than feeling sorry for him and indulging him to compensate, I believe you should spend your time equipping that kid with the tools he's going to need to manage his life. There. That's my soapbox for the afternoon."

Ellie sat back in her chair and clapped her hands. "And a fine one it is. I couldn't have done better myself. But is that it? Do you have any more thoughts on this?"

"Thought you'd never ask. Okay, just like when grief can take different forms when someone close to you dies, there is a grief process when the baby you'd anticipated didn't turn out exactly as you'd imagined. We all have this dream of an angelic cherub nestled into our arms, smiling and responsive to our touch. But many kids with autism aren't like that. The initial parent-child bonding can be tough when the baby doesn't seem to respond to your gestures, when he doesn't gaze into your eyes, or relish your cuddling. Some kids with autism scream a lot, sort of like a baby with colic that lasts for years. In those situations, it must be hard not to resent that child at times with all the effort you're putting in being rewarded with still more screams. Then, you'd feel guilty for resenting your own child, especially when the kid is obviously in distress or he wouldn't be howling. So there's guilt over having a child with a problem and guilt over resenting all the care it takes to look after this kid. Guilt can be paralyzing."

A waitress stopped by their table with a pot in her hand. "More coffee?" she offered.

Ellie waited for Rob's response. "Thanks, but I'm all coffee'd out now."

"None for me either, thanks, Kim." She looked at her watch, then around the bakery. She saw that there were no customers left, the baked goods had been put away and the coffee machines dismantled and rinsed. "Sorry. The time got away on me. But I see that you have everything under control. Go grab any of the left-over baking that you'd like to take home and please tell the others to do the same. Thanks for tidying up; I appreciate it. Only, next time, yell for me. Don't let me be such a slacker."

"You? A slacker? That'd be the day. But, thanks and yeah, we'd love to grab some of your baking. Night."

"What about you?" Ellie looked at Rob. "Hungry?"

"A bit, but not for anything sweet. I think my stomach's saying protein is needed. I think I have a couple steaks in the freezer that I could grill. Care to come over and sample my cooking?"

"See, you do like me."

"Not particularly. It's just that I don't get that many opportunities to sound off on my favorite subjects. You asked, so I had a captive audience. I'm not finished, way not finished, so I don't want to lose my listener. And if you're going to have to listen for the next hour, I suppose I have to feed you."

"When you put it that way, how could a gal refuse?"

CHAPTER 16

"This is cute." Ellie looked around the yard.

"Cute?" Rob asked. Just what a guy wants to hear about his place.

"Seriously, it is cute. Cute in a nice, manly way."

"Hah, that's better. I rent the main floor and this patio comes with it. There's a suite in the basement, one above me and a tiny one in the attic space. We're all either grad students or working people so it's pretty quiet." They were stretched out on matching chaise lounges. Every once in a while, Rob would get up to turn over the baking potatoes and the corn on the cob. "Almost time for the steaks."

"I love a man who can cook."

Rob raised one eyebrow at her. "What's that supposed to mean?"

"Nothing. I just love it when a man can cook."

"So, I do have some redeeming charms after all."

"Actually, you have many, well probably, but I haven't had enough time yet to dig deep enough to find them all."

"Have I just been insulted or complimented?"

"Neither. Both. But you are intriguing enough that I'll have to take the time to do that digging."

"Again, I can't tell if that's a threat or a promise."

"Settle on the fact that you're an interesting guy." Before Rob could think more about that, she told him, "Tell me more. I want to know about this parenting and autism stuff."

"Okay. There's the guilt stuff that we talked about but on top of all that is the fatigue. All parents of young kids are exhausted, from the baby stage on up. It takes a lot of time and energy to raise a child. But when that child has autism, the demands are far, far greater and so is the energy required."

"What do you mean?"

"Take sleep for instance. Most babies sleep through the night before their first birthday. A child with autism may not do that until they're almost ready for school. Some sleep very little, just cat naps here and there. And when an overactive baby or toddler is awake, a parent must also be awake to oversee what's happening. Sleep is often an issue throughout the life of a person with autism, but when you have a sleep-deprived child, you also have a sleep-deprived parent. Think about how you function when you've had a number of late nights in a row. Probably you're not at your best, your problem-solving skills go down, and your frustration level rises. Now think about feeling that way all the time and pile that on top of the guilt we talked about earlier. How well would you stay one step ahead of your kid? How much time could you devote to studying about autism and mapping out careful plans? Yes, that is exactly what such a parent should do but often they're simply hanging on by their toenails and have no time to even sit and reflect."

"That sounds like how Ben was when he first got Kyle. And he got his son because Kyle's mother said she couldn't take it anymore and could no longer look after him."

"What did Ben do?"

"Took him, of course. What did you think he'd do?"

"Sorry. Geez, you're prickly. Your brother seems to be doing a good job with him now."

"Yeah, now he is. But it was pretty rough at first, rough on both Ben and on Kyle."

"So, what else is going on with parents?"

"They hunker down. When you feel that you're at the end of your rope, you're exhausted and there's no end in sight, you hunker down. You put one foot in front of the other as best you can, just to survive. There's no time or energy left to stand back and reflect or to contemplate doing things differently. Often people get caught in this loop. They try the same things over and over again, but those things aren't working for either the kid or for the parents."

"That's like, 'If you do what you've always done, you'll get what you've always got.' Who said that anyway?"

"Not sure. Was it Henry Ford? No, wait. It might have been Mark Twain. Dunno. But it always reminds me of this other quote - 'If you want to change the result, you must change the way you do things'. I have no idea who said that one, but I like it."

"But based on what you've said, these parents are too busy surviving to think about how to change things," said Ellie.

"Plus, making radical changes means admitting that what you were doing before wasn't good enough. Most of us have enough ego that it's hard to admit that we've been wrong or that we don't have the answers."

"That's hardly fair. What these parents are likely doing are the same things most parents do or that they watched their own parents doing. And, usually it all works out pretty well."

"Exactly. But raising a kid who is on the autism spectrum takes more. The normal stuff might not work or not be enough."

"I still say that's not fair," Ellie protested.

"Who said anything about fair? Is it fair for Kyle that he has to work harder than most kids to stay calm and regulated during the school day? Is it fair that his sensory system launches into overdrive at the slightest provocation? Nope, none of it is fair. But it is what it is."

"Sort of play the hand you're dealt, eh?"

"Yep. Feeling sorry for him or doing any of that woe-is-me stuff does not help Kyle or any other kid in his situation. All that is actually more about the parents and how they feel than about their child."

. . .

FOR A WHILE, their mouths were too full of steak and corn to talk much. Butter dripped down both their chins. Rob liked that Ellie didn't seem to care - she actually laughed at herself. When his cob of corn almost rolled off his plate, she yelled, "Three second rule", but he caught it before it hit the grass, sparing him from deciding if the rule that anything on the ground less than three seconds was still okay to eat should apply in this case.

Since Rob hadn't expected company, he only had one beer in the fridge, so they split it. They sat, quietly sipping from their glasses. Ellie remarked on what a beautiful evening it had turned out to be.

Rob sprang to his feet. "Evening. Evening! Shit! I forgot. This is the evening of our support group, the first night for this session." He glanced at his watch. "It starts in half an hour. Sorry, but I gotta run. He noticed the butter stains and the odd steak dripping on his shirt and swiftly pulled it over his head as he ran into the house. "Don't think you have to leave. Stay, stay and relax." His voice was muffled for a moment, and then his head popped out of a clean golf shirt. He heard the water running in the kitchen sink as Ellie began washing their dishes. "Just leave that stuff. I'll get it later. You don't have to clean up." Although his words said the right things, he was relieved to have her help. And he was pleased that she would even think of pitching in in this way. The woman he'd briefly dated a few months ago would never have considered risking her French manicure in dish water. Ellie was fun and low maintenance and relaxing to be around. Too relaxing. He had almost missed this meeting because he was enjoying his time with her too much.

"What's this important meeting about?" Ellie asked.

"It's a parent support group Mel and I run each semester. Tonight's the first meeting for this group."

"Parents, huh? Isn't it a little strange that you have no kids and Mel just acquired one, yet the two of you run a *parent* support group?"

"It's not just parents. Hey, why don't you come along? There are grandparents and other relatives who attend, not just parents. Everyone who comes is concerned about a child who is struggling in some way. You see Kyle a lot; maybe you'd even learn something. Or,

314

share with the group things you've found that work with your nephew."

Ellie looked skeptical.

"It's up to you. It's at the school at seven o'clock and only lasts an hour or so. Honestly, you're welcome. I know Mel would love for you to join us." Then, he was off.

CHAPTER 17

*a*s the group took their seats, Rob noticed the empty chairs left between most people. Only those who came as a couple sat beside one another. By the third session, Rob knew that there would be no blank chairs, that the participants would have come together as a group and formed friendships. They'd shove the empty chairs out of the circle on their own and join ranks, literally and figuratively. It happened that way every time.

"Welcome," he began and introduced himself and Mel as the coordinators of the group. "Next, I want you all to introduce yourselves. If you want, just give your first name. Or, *a* first name, just something we can call you when you're in this room." That brought a polite chuckle. "If you want to tell us a bit more about yourself, that's fine too. Some people prefer to tell us that you're here because you're a parent to a child who has a specific challenge, but that's up to you. Give us a one word, one sentence or one paragraph introduction."

As usual, no one wanted to go first. Rob smiled encouragingly at one mother he'd met a number of times. She was about to speak when a voice spoke up from the back.

"I'm here because I've only recently gotten to know my nephew.

He's a wonderful six-year-old. He has autism and I want to learn more about the things I can do to be a meaningful part of his life."

Ellie. Bless her, Rob thought. Yet another plus on the scorecard. He worried that the score was tallying far too high in his estimation. Yes, she could annoy the life out of him, but maybe putting up with some of that was worth the plusses he got from spending time with her. He reined in his thoughts as another woman spoke.

"We've recently become foster parents to three brothers diagnosed with fetal alcohol syndrome. We already love the boys but it's quickly become clear that we need help. We've fostered many kids before but we can tell that the things we normally do might not work this time."

Round the others went, some stating just a first name, others giving a glimpse into their history and the reason why they had sought out this group. The last to speak was Mel.

"I've run this group with Rob for the last few years. Never has it meant so much to me as it has this year. I got married last summer and am now the proud step-mother to an incredible little boy who happens to have autism. While I've taught kids with autism for many years now, it is different living with one. There's no turning out the lights and shutting the door at five o'clock anymore. I'm sure all of you know what I mean." The answering laughs showed that they did.

Rob took over. "First, I want to talk about the elephant in the room. We'll look at it, talk about it, and then tell it to get lost.

"I imagine that every parent in this room shares the same thought - one you might not voice very often, but one that has haunted your thoughts. Here it is - 'It's my fault my child has these difficulties. I did something to cause this.' Now, I'm going to be blunt. No. No, whatever struggles your child has, they are not your fault. You are not to blame. You might have some power, but I guarantee that you are not powerful enough to have caused this."

He paused and regarded each person, especially those who looked the most uncomfortable as if they were hiding their guilt. "Were you a perfect parent? Were you an exemplary mother while pregnant? Unlikely. But neither was your neighbor who has a child who has no disability. They made mistakes along the way, as did you. Whatever has happened to your child is not your fault. You didn't cause it to happen, you cannot fix it or make it go away. Are we clear on that?"

A number of people appeared unconvinced.

"None of that matters. What does matter is what we do from here on in. You *can* help your child. Life *can* get better for all of you. Not perfect, perhaps not totally typical, but better. I guarantee it and you must believe it possible too or you wouldn't be here tonight.

"By the way," he continued. "I know just what efforts you have gone to to make it here this evening. Mel and I will do our best to make this and every other meeting worth your while."

He glanced at Mel and she stepped forward. "Rob and I are not the experts - you are. While we've gone to school for extra training in working with kids with exceptional needs, you are the true experts of your individual children. You know them best. You've found things that work and don't work."

One fellow said, "You can say that again about the 'don't work' part." Some of the tension left the room.

Mel continued. "Think about what it's like your first days on a new job. Then think about doing that same job six years down the road. You've learned a lot. Most of you have had at least that much experience with your child. While no two kids are alike, you can learn a lot from each other in this group. When you're pulling your hair out because nothing's working, someone else here might have found a solution to that problem and has moved on to their own new concern. There are twenty-four of us here tonight. Twenty-four times six means almost a century and a half of accumulated experience between us. Surely that counts for something if we just share what we've learned.

Rob said, "Sometimes people have looked to us as the experts. Yes, Mel and I are teachers, teachers who specialize in kids with learning differences. But, as you well know, we leave the building and go at the end of the afternoon and the kids come back to you. I might know how to cope with twenty some students during the day, but you know how to live with one special child all the time. I worry about them for a short span of the ten months they're in my room; you worry about them all the time. I send them home to you at three o'clock every day. On the other hand, all of you cheerfully send them back to me to have for six hours each day. You may have them one at a time at home with you, but I have them a couple dozen at a time."

He added, "Good thing we love them, isn't it?" The laughing was a bit louder and a trifle less forced this time.

"NOW THAT WE'VE talked about the fact that you are not to blame for your child having challenges, we'll move on to the next big item. Guilt. If you believe that you were somehow at fault, you'll feel guilt. In those saner moments when you know that you could not possibly have caused this, you might still feel guilty. Why?"

"I love my daughter," a voice from the side of the room said. "But sometimes I get sick of being on the same treadmill, the constant trips to the doctor's office, needing to get time off work, never any time to myself. Sometimes I resent the way my life has turned out since she's been born, then I kick my butt from here to China over feeling that way about my own flesh and blood. She can't help the way she is. She didn't ask to be born." Others nodded and added their assents. This seemed a common thread as others gave similar examples. The group was loosening up after realizing they were among like minds.

One woman said, "Sometimes I'm impatient with my son. He's so demanding and I'm so tired. I have a job and other kids and the house and everything. Some days it seems like too much, and then when my son needs something that messes up my plans, I lose it. Sometimes I yell at him. Then I hate myself for doing that and try to make it up to him."

This was the opening Rob was waiting for. "You've made a good point," he told her. He addressed the whole group. "How many of you have felt impatient with your child then felt guilty and tried to make it up to him or her?"

Nearly every hand rose, including Rob's own. "We're human, so we make mistakes. Let's admit it and move on. But there is one part of this I'd like to talk about some more. From time to time we're all going to mess up, feel badly, and then move on. That's normal and our kids will forgive us. The problem comes when we can't get past the guilt and try to make it up with over-indulgence.

"We have more of an imagination than do kids. We can put ourselves in someone else's place and imagine how it must feel. We look at our children struggling and feel badly that life has handed them this path. So, maybe we try to be extra nice to the child. We buy things to make him happy. We let him have what he wants; we go out of our way to indulge him. Then, before you know it, you have on your hands a little tyrant. And the worst of it is that we've made him that way. Now, not only does our kid have some type of disability, but he's a brat as well."

The looks Rob was getting were no longer warm and fuzzy. "Yep," he continued, "I just called your little darling a brat. No, I don't mean necessarily that your particular offspring are brats, but can you see the possibility? That guilt could lead to spoiling a child?"

He waited. Many seemed unconvinced. "Trust me on this. Your son or daughter does not need you to feel sorry for him or her. They need your love and your care and your guidance, but not your pity. Pity won't help him learn the skills he needs to be as independent as he possibly can."

Rob felt the shift in the audience and realized he was coming on too strong. Time to tone it down a notch and take another tactic. He looked to Mel, but she was already stepping forward.

"What do you think the biggest impediment is to your child having a successful, independent life as an adult?" she asked.

"The fact that he has a diagnosis of autism," one dad said.

"His wheelchair," said another.

A mom offered, "Running away. He takes off the moment things aren't to his liking. He takes a year off my life every time he does that. At this rate, I'm not going to live to see him into his teenage years." A couple people laughed but several looked like they felt the same way.

"No," said Mel. "Well, at least not quite." She nodded at the mom what had just spoken. "Your example is likely closest."

So much for a gentler approach, thought Rob.

"Those things could be barriers, but we can get around them. We'll learn and the kids can learn. The biggest barrier any one of your children will face is in not being able to manage themselves."

"What's that supposed to mean?" asked a woman in the front row. Several others nodded.

"It means being able to handle himself, more exactly, to calm himself when he's upset. To remain calm enough to think through his options when he encounters a problem. To react appropriately to the size of the problem."

"Well, my kid either throws something, yells or takes off when he runs into a problem."

"Yes, that might be what he does now, but we can turn that around," answered Mel.

The father looked skeptically at her. "Believe me, lady, we've tried. It's not as easy as just wishing it away."

"You're right. It's not easy. I absolutely agree," Mel told him. "But it can be done."

Rob stepped in. "Look, it is human nature to fall into patterns. We all do it - that's how habits are formed. Anybody here ever tried to quit smoking?" Hands went up. "Well, you know it's hard and you don't lick it overnight. Our kids fall into habits as well. Maybe the first time or two that behavior got them what they wanted, whether that was an object, attention or they were trying to avoid something. So, a habit was formed. Whether or not that pattern of behaving fits every situation is another story, but kids don't often stop to analyze things in that way. Instead, they fall back on what they did the last time. And, if that behavior doesn't get them what they want, then they have to up the ante, increasing the behavior."

"How many of us have ever given in to a child's tantrum just to make him stop?" Mel answered her own question by raising her hand. Many of the parents joined her. "I'm not proud of it and in my ideal world, I'd never do such a thing again, but as Rob said, I'm human. My goal though, it to help kids not use those negative behaviors to control their world, but to find better, more appropriate ways to get what they want.

"Soon, we'll stop so you can stretch your legs. But, being a teacher, I have an assignment for you." Mel continued amid the groans. "This is *your* group. We want it to be helpful for you, worth your time and effort to make it here each week. There are a number of things we could focus on but we'd prefer to tailor these meetings to your needs.

"We're all here because we care about a child who is experiencing difficulties. Some of your kids share the same challenges. Talk to each other. See if you can find areas that worry several of you and we can focus on those issues."

"Like what?" someone asked.

"Some of the past groups have wanted to talk about things like getting a child to bed at night, getting everyone up and out of the house on time in the morning, hygiene, throwing things, tantrums, hiding, whatever seemed most pressing at the time."

Mel glanced at Rob. That was his cue to say, "Let's take a break for a few minutes. There's coffee and cookies at the table behind me."

"You're good," Ellie told Rob as she peered at him over the stiff, paper cup of coffee. "But your coffee isn't."

"No one can make good coffee with a thirty-cup percolator." He waited a second then asked, "You think I'm good?"

"Don't fish for compliments. You know that you are. There were a few times there when I thought the meeting was going south on you, but you pulled it back and got the audience to come with you."

"That part was mostly Mel's doing. We tag team pretty well and she's more of the sensitive type than I am."

"Mel! *My* Mel - sensitive? That truly is a hoot. I'd love to be there if Ben heard you say that. You should hear some of the stories he tells of how Mel treated him when they first met, when he was first learning how to manage things with Kyle. Mel had absolutely no patience with him." She giggled. "It was lovely to see. My big brother, the guy who's always so in control, always wants to be the boss, humbled by this little woman and obediently following her orders."

"He wouldn't have done that if her ideas didn't work, though."

"No, that's true. That's why he started to pay attention to her because when he tried even a few of her suggestions, it helped. And, believe me, he needed the help if he and Kyle were ever going to survive one another."

"They seem like a great family now."

"Oh, they are. Ben would move the earth for Kyle. At first this parenting thing started as a duty, his obligation. Then that kid wormed his way into Ben's heart and looking after him was no longer just something he was expected to do. It became his life."

"Yeah, kids can do that to you," Rob agreed.

Ellie looked at him curiously. "Why, do you have kids? Are you married? I never thought to ask that before."

Rob's brow furrowed as he looked down at her. "Don't you think that's something I might have mentioned? Do you think I stashed a wife in the hall closet when you came over for those steaks?"

"No, jeez, but some people are divorced, you know. You could have an ex-wife hanging around somewhere and maybe even a passel of kids."

"Passel?"

"You know what I mean. Just when I think you're an all right guy, you act like a jerk."

"Does that mean you're about to start yelling at me again? Or yanking on my arm? Because if you are, how be you grab this one? My left one is still recovering from the bruises you gave me the last time."

Ellie's look of concern made him grin. She was reaching for his arm to check when she saw from his expression that he was kidding. "Jerk!" She punched his arm for emphasis. Rob rubbed that spot. "Now how am I going to mark papers tomorrow with an injured arm?"

"How'd we get into this anyway?"

"I think the conversation started with you telling me I'm good."

"Now, that was a mistake on my part."

"How so? Does the truth hurt?"

"God, talking to you is so hard."

"I don't see anyone forcing you to stand here." He gestured with his coffee cup toward the parents clustered in groups around the room. "There are plenty of other people here to talk to."

"Somehow, at the moment, I don't think they'd be as interesting."

"Interesting? Wow, first I'm good, and then I'm interesting. Things are working in my favor."

Ellie scrunched her nose at him. She so regretted giving this irritating man any sort of compliment.

Then he said, "You know, I find you interesting, too. In fact, very interesting."

That was not what she expected to hear. "Yeah?"

"Yeah. Interesting enough that I'd like to get to know you better. Can I buy you a coffee after the meeting's over?"

"That sounds delightful."

CHAPTER 18

$\mathcal{M}$el called the group back together. "I have a confession to make. My husband says I'm not known for being subtle. I have a tendency to say what I think. Unfortunately for you, so does Rob. For now, though, you're stuck with us." She paused. "One advantage of this is that you'll get to know us, warts and all. We will be frank about what we think. We'll tell you about the mistakes we've made and how we've learned by trial and error. Some things we get right, others we haven't, but we try. And, we learn all the time. Sometimes we learn by studying but more often we learn from the kids and from parents like you. At times it may seem like we have a wealth of knowledge, and maybe we do, but we're lucky. We have the privilege of working with parents and teachers all the time, so we can soak up their knowledge and share that with you."

Rob's turn. "Since we're planning to be open with you, we hope that you'll feel free to do the same with us. Most likely all of you have had Ward and June Cleaver moments when you've been stellar parents. There are other times when you've probably screwed up. That's all right. Kids are forgiving, and you get lots of opportunities to try again. Can any of you remember a time when one of your parents did the less than optimal thing? See? You survived and lived to tell the tale. Most of us do the best we can at the moment. Our intentions are good, but we're not perfect. So, if you feel like it, talk about your Kodak moments and it's okay to tell us about those other times, too. I guarantee that there will be others here who will understand and have done the same thing or something like it."

Mel took a step forward. "Have you ever felt stuck in a rut? Or, you're on a treadmill, plodding along, doing the same thing but never getting anywhere?' All parents get tired at times because of their busy lives. But when your child has extra challenges, it can be even more wearying. Sometimes to just make it through the day, you fall into the pattern you've developed, whether or not that pattern is actually working for you. We all do it."

"That's part of the reason for this group," Rob explained. "What we hope to do here is to help you identify which patterns are working for you and which aren't. Then, we'll look at ways to mix it up."

A couple of people groaned. An older woman said, "Honey, my life is mixed up enough already. I don't think I could survive any more mixing."

"Bad choice of words, I guess. Sorry," Rob said. "I get that the thought of turning your life upside down is unappealing and not even doable. But what if you could change one thing, just one little thing that would make your life easier - make your world flow just a little bit more smoothly?" He let those words sink in.

Mel told them, "I guarantee that we can do this. All your problems will not go away, but if we work together, we can each pick one small area where we'll make some changes that will help both you and your child. Guaranteed."

"Yeah, how can you guarantee that?" someone called out.

"There are no written guarantees. Of course not. And we can't do it for you or for your family. But we do know some tricks - simple things that have worked for other families and will likely help yours. Look, wouldn't life be better if just one chronic hassle was gone? Or lessened? That can happen."

"And then when it does, and you get that new habit firmly in place, you can move on to the next issue that's really bugging you and make some improvements there. It will snowball until you find your life is getting easier and your child is calmer and more confident. That will give your whole family the courage to venture out and try more new things. The more successful experiences you get under your belt, the better you'll feel and the more you can tackle," Rob added. "So, at coffee, did any of you find a common theme, some problem you share that you'd like to work on?"

One father raised his hand and said, "My wife and I would love to be able to go out for dinner as a family. It doesn't have to someplace fancy, even just a pizza joint would be fine."

Mel asked, "How many of you feel this is a problem in your family as well?"

Hands went up all over but one woman said, "After the last time we tried, who would want to? We all ended up so mad at each other that I cringe every time I drive by that restaurant." Laughter came from various quarters. They could relate.

"Okay," Mel continued. "That's one thing we can work on. First though, how many of you have kids on the autism spectrum, or whom you suspect might have some of the characteristics of autism?" When a few people hesitated, she added, "It doesn't matter if they have an official diagnosis or even if that word, autism, scares you off. I'm looking more for characteristics here than an exact label." Almost everyone in the room raised their hand.

One couple said, "We had thought our daughter might have autism or Asperger's, but instead her diagnosis came back as Nonverbal Learning Disability."

Mel nodded then turned to the woman who had introduced herself as a foster mother. "You mentioned that you have three boys who have fetal alcohol syndrome. Is that right?"

The woman agreed.

"Close enough. We can use the same...."

She was interrupted by one mother. "What do you mean, 'Close enough'?" My Jack has autism, not FAS. You just finished telling us that it is not our fault. Well, I for one did not drink while I was pregnant, so I did *not* give my son his problems. I resent you lumping

me in with someone who did actual, intentional harm to their baby."
She crossed her arms over her chest.

Mel replied. "I said close enough because both autism spectrum disorders and fetal alcohol spectrum disorders have a neurological basis. They share many characteristics and pretty much the same strategies work with both groups.

"And yes, FAS is caused by fetal exposure to alcohol prenatally. And yes, that is a preventable condition. But I think it would be an extremely rare mother-to-be who gets up in the morning saying to herself, 'Today I think I'll harm my baby.' Some mothers drink before they even realize they are pregnant. Those with erratic menstrual cycles may not know for months that they are expecting and by then the damage may have been done.

"For our purposes, we're not looking into the causes or even the prevention right now. We're going to look at clusters of symptoms and how best to respond to them and the strategies that will likely help." She turned to the mom of the girl with a Nonverbal Learning Disability. "And, we can use some of the same strategies for kids with NVLD as well. In your case, you'll just have to remember not to rely on visual representations, but to use words, since NVLD kids are strong in the language area."

BEFORE MEL COULD CONTINUE, one father stood and called out, "You know lady, I resent having to tiptoe around my kid. This wasn't what I bargained for. Before we had Zeke, we said that any kid would fit into our lifestyle. We weren't changing; we would fit the baby into our household. I still stand by that. I'm the adult. I support this family, and I make the decisions. I resent that a kid who has not even reached puberty seems to run our lives." There were murmurs of assent around the room.

"I don't blame you. You're totally right that you're the adult and you're the one in charge. Does it feel that way most days though?"

"Hell, no," was the answer. "No! This kid has us by the short hairs and we're tiptoeing around, trying not to upset the apple cart because when it goes over, look out. We all suffer and it can go on and on and on. Just to have some peace, we give in and cater to the little bugger. Look, don't get me wrong. I love my son; he means the world to me. But he's running our lives, ruining our lives. And on top of it all, he doesn't seem happy either. We're about at the end of our rope."

"Isn't it strange," Mel said, "How a child can frustrate you so much, yet you love him so much? I think everyone here shares the same feelings you expressed from time to time. They just might not put those feelings into words as well as you did. Thank you. You've raised some key points."

Rob's turn. "That's a big part of why we started this group. We heard over and over how frustrated loving, well-meaning parents were. And, how frightened they were that their kids were not getting easier to live with but more difficult. We don't have all the answers, that's for sure. But what we do provide is a forum to talk about what's working for you, what isn't and gather ideas for you to try. We also try to help by breaking these strategies into useable parts, things you can actually do in the average home without requiring the services of a team of professionals or a boat load of money." He addressed the disgruntled father. "Is going to a restaurant a problem for your family?"

"It's gotta be at least two years since we last tried it. The whole experience was such a disaster that we just gave up. It's not worth the aggravation and time and wasted money. Not to mention the embarrassment. God, it was awful."

"What happened?"

"Well, we made a reservation. It wasn't exactly a posh place we were going to, just one of the better chains of pizza and pasta places. The reservation was an attempt to make sure we that we didn't have to stand in line. We anticipated that would ruin the evening before it had hardly begun."

"That was good thinking."

"Yeah, well, we patted ourselves on the back too soon. To get to our table, the waitress took us by this water fall. To some people that might have been a nice addition to the ambience, but it was the start of everything coming apart for us. Zeke wanted to stop and look. That wasn't a big deal; I'm sure many kids want to take a closer look. Hell, I did too. But looking wasn't enough. Zeke wanted to trail his fingers in the water. He has this thing about water, you know. When the waitress noticed we weren't following her, she turned around and saw what Zeke was doing. She told him to get his hands out of the water that it wasn't allowed and was bad for the fish. Until then Zeke hadn't noticed the fish in the water. I guess they avoided his fingers and just swam the other way. These were gorgeous fish, some of the biggest koi I've ever seen. The way the overhead lights struck them, they gleamed golden in the water." He sighed. "Zeke has always loved shiny things. My wife and I looked at each other and knew we were in for a hurdle. I tried to distract him with a light touch to his shoulder and a reminder that our table was ready. He ignored me. I could feel my wife's tension and when she's like that, her voice gets all funny. She got behind Zeke and tried to herd him in the direction of the table and I got in between Zeke and the water. He resisted. I mean he just planted his feet on the floor and wouldn't move. If my wife hadn't stopped, she would have bowled him over.

"By this time other customers were watching. If we'd been at home, I'd have picked my kid up and plunked him where I wanted him to be, the hell with his screams. But there were a lot of people around, I didn't want to disturb the whole restaurant and I really wanted to enjoy a nice meal with my family. For once.

"The waitress came back carrying this little treasure box with a shiny, golden lid. She held it out to Zeke and thank goodness, it snagged his attention. He followed her to the table. Inside were crayons, plastic fish, a little book of mazes and other kid stuff. Plus, the table cloth was torn from a roll of newsprint paper, so he could draw on it. Thank god.

"My wife and I were pretty pleased with ourselves. We'd handled the incident quite well, we thought so we settled down to read the menus. This place was a tad more upscale than the usual pizza we had delivered to the house, so they called things by classier names. It wasn't easy to ask Zeke what he wanted because of the unfamiliar descriptions. What seven-year-old knows what Catalonia sauce means? Hell, *I* don't know what that is."

"So, I tried to explain the choices on the kids' menu to him but even they were written in these flowery descriptions. I tried interpreting as best I could, but it was obvious he wasn't getting it. So, I said, 'I'll order you a pizza, bud.' He eats pizza all the time." He stopped and glanced over at Mel, who nodded encouragement for him to continue.

"Then, we waited. And we waited. My stomach was growling, and I could tell by how restless Zeke was that he must be hungry as well. Or bored. We hailed the waitress to ask if she could hurry up our food. We'd already been sitting here almost twenty minutes. How long could you expect a kid to be good? Plus, the place was starting to fill up, so the noise level was rising until it was getting on even my nerves. And, the louder the conversations got, the more they cranked up the music. We almost had to shout to be heard."

"Then our food arrived. When she put Zeke's plate in front of him, he reared back and stared at it. Can't say I blamed him - it didn't resemble any pizza we'd ever had before. The sauce on it was white, not red the way pizzas should be. And, there were bits of green all over it. I don't mean flakes of oregano or basil or stuff like that, but big, honkin' chunks of green that may have been spinach. Whatever it was, I gotta say it looked slimy. Zeke braced his hands against the table to push himself away from the offensive plate. His chair scooted back, caught on a metal divider bar on the floor and flipped over backward. The thunk was so loud everyone in the restaurant stopped talking. People were craning their necks to see what had happened. We picked Zeke up; he was fine - a bit shaken, but fine. That kid has good reflexes and hardly ever hurts himself when he falls. So, we finish checking for broken bones and get him back into his chair. A waiter walking by, trying to be helpful, I think, pushes Zeke's chair into the table, trapping the kid between his chair back and that damn pizza. You should have seen the look of horror on his face. My wife puts a hand on his leg to try to calm him but before she can get out a word, the waitress is back with this foot and a half long pepper mill.

"'Pepper?' she asks. Then before either of us can answer, she starts grinding away on our plates. I tell ya, someone needed to take a little WD-40 to that thing. The noise it made as it grated! And, she peppered my son's plate, without even asking. While Zeke hates green stuff, and slimy stuff, he absolutely detests black flecks on his food. That was the last straw and he let loose. God, his screams." He shook his head and looked up. Around him were sympathetic faces, some nodded, some grimacing in remembrance of similar experiences they'd had.

"What could I do?" he asked the group. "I slung my howling kid over my shoulder and headed out as fast as I could, threading my way through the people lined up waiting for a table. My wife threw money on the table, gathered our jackets and trotted behind. We didn't even stop to stuff Zeke into his coat, but just ran for the car." He paused a few moments. "And that is the last time we ever tried eating out."

CHAPTER 19

Mel organized the assembly. "In a minute, we'll break into three groups. If you came with someone, you might consider joining different groups, so you can hear more ideas then compare them later. On the table at the side are pads of chart paper and markers."

She grinned at them. "We're teachers, after all, so what do you expect? We'll use Zeke's experiences as an example since what his dad described hit an accord with so many of us. What I'd like you to do is draw two vertical lines on the paper, creating three columns. Under the first column, jot down what Zeke did - the way an objective witness might have observed him at the restaurant. In the middle column make notes about what you think might have been behind the behaviors - why he reacted in the ways that he did. And, in the last column write suggestions for strategies that might help prevent things like this from happening again. Rob and I will be the note taker for two of the groups. Ellie, would you do the honors for the third, please? Ellie, raise your hand so people know who you are. All right. Grab a chair and form groups over here, here and here." Mel pointed to corners of the room as she spoke.

Rob was at her side instantly. "Ellie?" he asked. "Is that wise? I'm sure one of the parents could do it."

Mel raised an eyebrow at him. "What's wrong with Ellie doing it?"

"Isn't she a bit too, too..."

"A bit too what?"

"Oh, never mind. I suppose it'll be okay.

ROB CALLED the group back to order. "Let's take a look at what you came up with in your first column. Describe what happened."

As each group read out their ideas, Rob wrote them on the board.

"He played in the water."

"He wanted to keep playing."

"He wanted to watch the fish rather than sit at a table."

"But, he did follow and go to their table."

"He probably got anxious when he couldn't understand the menu options his father was trying to explain."

"He didn't like the look or the smell of the food when it came and tried to back away from it."

"He pushed his chair too hard and it toppled over, taking him with it."

"He eventually started screaming.

ROB ASKED, "What do you think was going on in Zeke's mind?"

The answers came from all directions as the parents got into the discussion. "He didn't know what to expect."

"Maybe he had thought supper would be like it usually is, at home."

"My kid doesn't react well to surprises, either."

"He got stuck on the fish"

"Water probably calms him or he likes the way it feels."

"He was hungry."

"He was eating later than he was used to."

"The food was strange."

"It might have been too loud for him in the restaurant."

"Did he dress up in uncomfortable clothes?"

"Lots of kids don't like fancy foods."

"Falling off his chair must have upset him."

"I'm with Zeke. A pizza is supposed to look like a pizza. I can't think of anything green that belongs on any pizza I'd eat."

"I can picture this kid, getting hungrier by the minute. He's in strange surroundings and it's getting louder and louder. But he's hanging on to the promise that he's getting pizza. He likes pizza, and then this strange stuff is set in front of him."

"My wife sneezes every time someone waves a peppermill in front of her. You can really smell the pepper from one of those things. I can see that any kid wouldn't like black flecks on his food."

Rob stood back to look at what they'd written. "You know, this is almost like being a detective. You have to try to ferret out what might be going on before you can decide on possible solutions. You've described what happened, then you've come up with some ideas as to what might have been behind the behaviors.

"From a parent point of view, what was the most undesirable thing that Zeke did that evening?"

One woman said, "Screamed in the restaurant. That's always our greatest fear that our kid will start screaming in public. It's happened many a time. That's our worst nightmare."

Someone else offered, "He fell off the chair but that's not that big a deal. He's probably not the first child to overturn a chair and he wasn't hurt. It doesn't sound like he made a big fuss about it. Right?" she asked Zeke's dad.

"Right. That was the least of our problems," he agreed.

Mel said, "Now, let's look at strategies we could use so the next trip to the restaurant will be more successful. So, what did you come up with?"

"Choose a different restaurant."

"Pick one without a waterfall if your kid is fascinated with water."

"Or fish."

"Go early, before it gets crowded. You might get your food faster that way and it might not be so noisy if fewer people are there."

"Plus, if there's a scene, you'll be embarrassed in front of fewer people." Chuckles followed this comment.

"Tell the waitress that your son is hates the smell of pepper before she brings the food."

"Tell the waitress that your son has autism or special needs or something like that, but tell her quietly, not in front of the kid."

"Ask to be seated in a quiet area, away from traffic and distractions."

"Sometimes a booth is better for that than a table in the middle of the room."

"Bring along something he likes to play with, something quiet."

"Yeah, like a favorite toy or something that comforts him."

"My kid is always calmer in a strange place if we place this lap weight on his legs."

"Some kids like the feeling of deep pressure when they're anxious. So, if you're in a booth, you could sort of squish him in between you and the corner of the booth."

"Or pile all your jackets on top of him if it's winter and you have heavy coats." Then she added, "I don't mean bury him totally, just from his shoulders down. Geez, don't look at me that way. Or, better yet, if things get rough you can bury your own head in the coats. I've often felt like doing that."

"Good," Mel said. "Great suggestions, although I've never tried the one about burying my face in my coat. I'll keep that one in mind. Rob, would you care to add a few more?"

"Sure. How about using a social story? On one of the earlier lists someone mentioned that Zeke didn't know what to expect. A social story would give him some of that information. Is everyone familiar with the term social story? Most of you, but not all. Okay, we'll come back to that in a minute.

"This next idea takes a bit more work on your part, but it could lead to a happier ending. Go to the restaurant on your own ahead of time. Explain to the manager what you'd like to do, then take pictures of the place. Start with an exterior shot of the door you'll enter. Then of the interior. If there are any special features, snap a shot of them as well. Then add a photograph of the table you'll sit at. But be sure to arrange it with the manager that that particular table will be reserved for you at the appointed time. You could be in for trouble if you've told your son you'll be sitting at table X but once you get there you can't have it. That would be just one extra aggravation you don't need."

"Right," agreed Mel. "And while you're there, you could ask to look at the menu, so you would know which of their choices would work best for your child. Some restaurants will even let you order ahead of time, then your food will be brought to you quickly once you arrive."

A woman in the front row said, "All this restaurant business sounds good but how do you go out to eat when your kid is on a gluten-free diet?"

"Some restaurants have gluten-free items. If you spoke with the manager ahead of time, you might be able to get the okay to bring in your own pizza crust, made with ingredients from your son's allowed diet. Then ask the restaurant to add their toppings and bake it for you. If the diet you follow is gluten and casein free, bring along your own soy cheese or other cheese substitute and ask if the cook would put your pizza under his grill to melt the cheese. Then that pizza would be brought out with the other food. Your son might think he was getting a restaurant pizza just like the rest of you."

Rob paused for a moment to see how the audience was following him. Good. They were all. He worried when he talked too much, for fascinating as his words surely were, he had no doubt that he could go on and on ad nauseum. He looked to Mel to take a turn.

ON CUE, Mel returned to the topic Rob had alluded to earlier. "Social stories. The term 'social story' was first used by Carol Gray in the early 90s. Her social stories used pictures and/or descriptive words that would describe a social situation or a task. The story would let the child know what was going to happen, what he could expect and what would be expected of him. When the social story was about a task, it might break the overall task into smaller, more manageable steps.

"Kids with autism spectrum disorders have trouble making sense of their world. For other kids, over time they are able to make generalizations about situations and expectations. If they've seen or done something similar before, they can automatically generalize those past learnings to the new situation. They then have an idea of what to expect. But kids with autism have more trouble with this. Situations often have to be nearly identical before a child will relate the new one to something that has happened previously.

"When everything seems new and you don't know what to expect, anxiety can arise. On top of this, most kids with autism spectrum disorders also have some degree of sensory sensitivity where sounds, smells, tastes or touch can feel exaggerated and greatly aggravating."

The audience was rapt as Rob paused, then carried on.

"So, picture being flung into a new situation without any preparation. You don't know what is going to happen to you or what people will demand of you. You can feel your inner tension begin to rise. The sounds could be pressing in on you, these irritating, background noises piling one on top of each other. Then someone might touch you when you were not expecting it, startling you. A woman walks by, her heavy perfume wafting after her. The scent clouds your head until it's hard to think, let alone breathe. Then someone asks you a question. Huh? You were not paying attention because there were so many other things competing for your attention that you hardly knew where to rest your eyes. So much was going on that it was hard for anything to register. Then that adult asks you something else. You have trouble making sense of his words. What was he saying? The adult raises his voice and says it louder. The tone of his voice has changed so that you think he might be mad at you. But mad at what? You haven't done anything wrong, just trying to stand there and survive. When he asks you the third time, you know you need to respond, but how? What does he want? Then, you're in trouble. You know you're in trouble, but the noises still press in on you. The adults are looking down at you expecting something, but what? What do they want? The lights start to strobe; the sunlight flashes through the window blinds. Outside, a car horn honks. Then a hand sneaks up from behind and rubs your arm. OW! You hate to be touched like that! Your heart is racing, the panic builds, and they're all looking at you. A strange man walks up to you and no, no, no, no more. You can't take it. Your hands cover your ears to help block out the sounds, your shoulders hunch in a protective way, your face screws up into a grimace and you scream. You fall to the ground, huddle in a fetal position and scream and scream and scream.

"Does this sound familiar? Do you think this is what might have happened to Zeke? From an adult point of view, this was an inappropriate way to act in a restaurant. But from Zeke's point of view, did others behave towards him in an inappropriate fashion?"

Mel watched the group closely as Rob's words sunk in. She wanted them to get a feel for what it might be like to be Zeke, but she did not want them to dwell on it too long. For some parents, pity kicked in readily and they had trouble getting past the sadness of the fact of what it must be like to live in their child's skin. From there it was an easy step to feeling so sorry for the child that protection rather than parenting became modus operandi, doing neither the parent nor the child much good.

"I have a friend, Ellen, who is also a special education teacher. She has this saying that might sum up how Zeke felt at that restaurant. She holds up her thumb and forefinger about a half inch apart then says, "I have just one nerve left and you're getting on it." That broke the tension as the parents laughed.

Mel felt it was safe to move on now. "It's unfortunate, but we are not going to be able to change the world for our kids who have autism - not in this life time anyway. In many ways, things are foreign to them. Author and neurologist Oliver Sacks described Temple Grandin as 'an anthropologist on Mars'. That's actually the title of one of his books, an excellent one, _An Anthropologist on Mars_. Temple Grandin is likely the most famous person in the world with autism. She is a familiar lecturer on the subject and speaks from personal experience.

Nonverbal as a young child, she was diagnosed with autism. Currently she is a professor at Colorado State University and has made a name for herself in the cattle handling industry, designing innovative, humane methods of working with livestock.

"When you read Temple's books or listen to her speak, she's clear that the world will not change for our kids. Sometimes, we may be able to get it to bend a bit, but change? No. So we must help kids with ASD acquire the skills and the tools they'll need in order to survive and hopefully flourish. That's what we want for all of our sons and daughters, right?"

Mel turned to Rob and he took over.

"So, as annoying as some of the people in the restaurant seemed to Zeke, he is in the minority. Most of us aren't crazy about being in noisy, enclosed spaces, close to other people, but we tolerate it. We do it because of the trade-off- there is something we want or something we get from being there. Is that something Zeke can learn? I think so. There is a chance that that will never become a situation of his choosing. It just isn't fun for him. But he can learn the skills to tolerate it, to hold it together for a limited, defined period of time so that he can eat a meal there with his family. Isn't that what you'd like?" he asked Zeke's father.

"Amen, brother," was the reply. The group laughed.

As they settled down, Rob made one more announcement. "Homework time, homework," amid the groans. "It's not too onerous, I promise. Two things - first, go to You Tube and watch a short video called, *'I Don't Like Meltdowns'*. You'll find it at..." and he wrote on the board
http://www.youtube.com/watchv=eHx8CJOZTfU&feature=related.

Next, he handed out papers that had the website link at the top, then the name Temple Grandin. "Go to Temple's website. Do an internet search on her and on her views. Go to Amazon.com, search for Temple's books and browse a few, using the Search Inside This Book feature if you don't want to purchase any of the books right now. One I'd highly recommend is called, *The Unwritten Rules of Social Relationships*. If you look at that book, pay special attention to page

119. There she and her fellow author Sean Barron, another adult who has autism, list the ten rules they feel anyone with autism needs to learn in order to function.

"Okay, that's it for tonight. Thanks for coming out and we'll see you next week here at the same time."

CHAPTER 20

*W*hen most of the parents had begun gathering their
coats to leave, Mel approached Rob. Well, approached
might be a mild term; attacked would be more like it.

She turned on him. "So, what was that all about my sister-in-law?
What did you have against Ellie taking notes for a group?" Her
expression was fierce.

Taken aback, Rob was unsure of his words. "Well, it's just a feeling.
She hasn't exactly seemed stable many of the times I've met her and
we do try to keep these meetings calm, while still letting people
express their feelings. Having a hothead running around didn't seem
like a good idea."

"Ellie, a hot head. You actually see my sister-in-law as a hothead?"

"You have to admit that's how she comes across. Remember the
way she attacked me in your classroom the first time I met her? That
did not seem like the behavior of a rational woman. She went off half-
cocked."

"But she believed she was defending someone in need of help."

"Sure, and it's noble and all that, but she didn't bother to get her
facts straight before she went off on me. What if that had happened
tonight?"

"Well, it didn't, and it wouldn't. I know Ellie. You two have gotten off on the wrong foot."

"Do ya think?"

Just then Ellie joined them. Mel said, "Hey, there. I was surprised to see you here tonight."

"Anything to help me learn more about my favorite nephew is high on my list of things to do. Besides, I wanted to see how this guy handled himself in a group." She nudged Rob's stomach with her elbow.

Rob looked uncomfortable, the words he'd just said to Mel revolving in his mind. She wouldn't mention them to Ellie right now, would she? From the smirk she was giving him, yes, that's exactly what she was thinking. His look pleaded with her and Mel's eyes went from Rob to Ellie then back again. She seemed to take pity on him.

"I get it now." She continued to look searchingly at the two of them. "I'll trust you to look after Ellie and I'll be on my way. Far be it from me to impede the course of true love," she said as she walked away.

"What? What did she say? I don't think I caught that," said Ellie. "What was Mel talking about? Something about true love?"

"Forget it. It was probably nothing."

"I think she said something about the course of true love. She must have been referring to something about her and Ben. You should have seen them in the beginning - they couldn't stand each other, were always at each other's throats about something or other. Why would she be telling you about that?"

Good question thought Rob and one he didn't want to think about too deeply. Surely, she couldn't be drawing a parallel between her own marriage and he and Ellie, could she? Nah, that was totally different. So, he said, "Ignore it. You know how she is."

"Actually, no. I thought I knew Mel, but I don't know what you're getting at." Ellie's face had changed from friendly into her battle-ready mode. Oh, oh. She was about to fly to the defence of yet someone else, of Mel and Mel most definitely was not in need of defence from anyone.

Sheesh. Now he was getting himself in trouble with two women within as many minutes - first Mel was annoyed with him over remarks he'd made about Ellie and now Ellie was getting ticked over something he said, or even just half said about Mel. A guy couldn't win. He'd better get out of this hole he was digging. A new topic was what he needed. "What did you think of the meeting? And thanks for your help, by the way."

"You're welcome. What's left to do?"

"Stack the chairs and put them against the back wall, gather the chart paper and markers and put them in my classroom, then turn out the lights and lock the doors. Mel had to get home right away, so I'm on clean-up duty by myself tonight."

"No, you're not by yourself. I'm here and it'll go faster with two of us."

"You don't have to do that, you know. I can handle it." Then another thought occurred to him. "How did you get here? If you'd like me to walk you to your car, I can do that before I start putting things away."

"I don't have a car?"

"You don't have a car? Who doesn't have a car?"

"Well, I do have a car, sort of."

"What's a 'sort of' car?"

"It's the kind of car you have but don't drive."

"Come again?"

"Wax in the old ears there, Sells, or is this one of those cases of weak auditory processing skills?"

"Brat. Your brothers must have been in misery putting up with you when you were growing up."

"Nah, they loved me. Who doesn't?"

Rob held up his hands and proceeded to tick of names on his fingers. "Well, there's...."

Ellie grabbed his hand and stopped him. "All right. Here's the thing about my car. I hardly need it because I walk everywhere. I live close to the bakery. The grocery store is just a couple blocks the other way. I'm leaning over a baking counter so much of the day that I like to stretch it out and go for a brisk walk whenever I can. Besides, working and eating in a bakery is enough to make one lose one's girlish figure if you're not careful to get enough exercise."

"I don't think you've lost anything." He stopped his gaze from checking her out. How uncool would that be with her standing right there watching him check her out. Yikes. Control yourself, Sells.

"So how did you get here tonight?"

"I walked."

"And how did you plan to get home? It's dark outside now."

"I planned to bum a ride from Mel. But it looks like she's gone and left me high and dry. Wait. Do you think a ride is what she meant when she said that she trusted you to look after me? I'd have called her on that but she walked away. You know, Mel knows that I walk everywhere. It's not like her to not ask if I needed a ride home. I don't know what got into her." She turned to look into Rob's eyes. "I guess I have to throw myself on your mercy now. Do you think you can put up with me?" Ellie clasped her hands together and placed them under her chin. She tilted her head to the side, smiled prettily and batted her eyelashes at him."

"Ya goof," he said.

"Maybe, but I'm an endearing goof."

"I don't know if I can argue about that or not. The verdict's still out."

"Hah! A challenge. I loooove challenges. Oh, you so should not have said that. The game's on now and you don't have a chance. You'll be groveling at my feet in no time, hoping for a crumb of my attention."

"A crumb?"

"A crumb," Ellie confirmed.

"Did anyone ever tell you that it's hard to follow your conversations?"

"No. How so?"

Rob started to roll his eyes, and then caught himself. Likely she'd have something to say about it if he did anything so juvenile. Instead, he said, "Let's get back to this car business."

"Sure, but why are you just standing here flapping your jaws? Isn't there work to be done? Or, oh, sorry. I didn't realize." Ellie apologized.

She's lost him again. "You didn't realize what?" Rob asked.

"That you're one of those guys who can't do more than one thing at a time. Like walk and chew gum, you know. Or, talk and stack chairs at the same time. It's okay, I can be patient. What did you want to talk about next, but make it snappy? There are a few dozen chairs to pile here and I need to get my beauty rest."

Rob stared at her. In college he'd taken some neuropsychology classes and wondered now about the processes at work within her skull. Her mind did not operate like that of other people. In fact, Ellie was totally unlike anyone he had ever met before. Life with her could be annoying but it sure as hell would never be dull. That is, if he could stand being around her and withstand her attacks, he reminded himself. But, right now, she looked warm and approachable.

"Earth to Rob," she reminded him. "Why are you staring at me?"

"Sorry. My mind must have drifted."

"Hmm. My company is that boring, eh? I'll have to try to do something to spice things up a bit."

"No, oh no. One thing you definitely are not is boring. And I think you've added quite enough spice to my life in the short time I've known you."

"Is that good or bad? I know. I'll choose to take it as a compliment, and then we're all good. Right?"

God, this woman. They needed to get back on track and try to have a normal conversation, if that was even possible. His mind searched for the frayed end of what they'd been discussing. Oh yeah - her car or her sort-of car. "Tell me about this car that you have or don't have."

"Okay. You'd better sit down for this."

Cripes, she meant it. She actually meant it because she stood there, hands on hips, waiting until he placed the chair he was holding back onto the floor, then with a glance to find her still waiting, he placed his butt on the seat.

"Now, hold on to your hat."

"I'm not wearing a hat."

"Geez, that's a figure or speech, Sells. Do you have to take everything so literally?"

Did she do this on purpose? Did she enjoy keeping him in a tail spin?

But she was ready to continue now. "My car is a 1964 Gordon-Keeble."

Rob waited for the rest. She just looked expectantly at him. "Um, good. I mean is that good? You weren't even born in '66. Is the car even road worthy? Is it an antique or whatever the term is for cars? Are you trying to get someone to restore it for you?"

"Restore it for me! You ass. *I* restored it. I've worked on this for almost ten years. It was in lousy shape when I got it but it is impeccable now, with all original parts. You better believe they've not been easy to find."

"I admit I don't know a lot about cars, but I've never heard of Gordon whoever."

"Keeble. Gordon-Keeble. John Gordon and Jim Keeble teamed up in the early 60s in England, created a few prototypes, and then the company was sold. The new owner made a short production run, but only one hundred of these cars were ever produced. Only ninety are now in existence far less than that are running. Mine is one of these."

"I suppose congratulations are in order."

"Do you think? You obviously know nothing about cars."

"I have a car."

"I mean *car* cars."

"Car cars?"

She let out an exaggerated sigh. "There are cars - regular, old run of the mill cars, then there are *cars* - cars with special significance. Cars that are high performance, are glorious examples of an era, cars that smell of luxury and endurance. You know, *car* cars."

"Oh, yeah, now I remember. *Car* cars. Sorry. I was thinking more of a car that gets you from point A to point B."

"Mine does that, too."

"But obviously not tonight."

"No, and not most nights. A car like this is not the kind you use for casual driving."

"I'd never really categorized my driving as casual or formal."

He got a glare for that. "What I mean is this car is rare and valuable. I keep it protected in a locked garage. It's also not meant for our climate, being built in Britain. I only take it on the road in summer and never when a storm's coming."

"You mean it's not water-proof?"

"Hah, very funny. I don't want to risk anything happening to it, that's all. It's my baby."

"Can I drive it some time?" Rob asked.

"That'd be the day. And, it's right-hand drive. I don't suppose you've ever driven one of those?"

Rob shook his head, no.

"No one gets behind the wheel of my baby but me," Ellie continued. "Well, Ben did just that once but I was in a jam and really needed someone to move it for me. The ovens went down at the bakery and I couldn't get away. Ben knew he was risking his life if he'd let anything happen to her."

"Her?"

"Her," Ellie nodded. "She's a beaut."

"What do you do, just go look at it? Her, I mean."

"Sometimes." Ellie laughed at Rob's skeptical look. "Actually, I work on her - that's my hobby. There's always something to do, something to fine-tune, some swapped-out part to replace with an original. Then there's all the time I spend trying to track down parts. With only one hundred ever built, you better believe parts are rare. And expensive. That's why I don't have another car since all my money is tied up in this one."

"Why would you do that? Then you're left without a usable vehicle?"

"I love old things. I like taking something that's sad and neglected and turning it back to its original beauty. There's an online community of enthusiasts who feel like I do and we help each other sourcing parts, and things like that."

"What other old things do you like?"

"Why? Are you wondering if I'd like you?"

This woman was outrageous. Was she flirting with him? Hard to tell. But, wait. Old? Did she actually think he was old? They were probably about the same age, give or take a few years. "Old?" he asked. "Do you think I'm old?"

"Well, maybe not *old* old, but it's more in the way you act. You know kind of stodgy and all that."

"Stodgy!"

"Don't worry. Only sometimes. At other times you look like you might be able to have a bit of fun and I even saw you laugh at yourself a few times when we were with Jeff. So, maybe you're not that old. It's something you could work on, you know."

"Yeah, like my walking and chewing gum thing. I'll keep that in mind, thank you." With that, he got up and resumed stacking chairs.

"I guess that means our conversation is over now," Ellie observed.

"I think your parents didn't put you over their knees often enough. Or your brothers didn't pummel you enough when you were a kid. How the hell do they put up with you?"

"They love me. Most people do, you know, once they get to know me. I'm pretty easy to be around and I'm fun and I'm loyal."

"Don't have too high an opinion of yourself, do you?"

"Nope. Just an accurate one."

As Rob pushed the last of the chairs against the wall, he thought that she was probably right. She was fun. And he'd seen evidence of her loyalty in the way she leapt to the defense of friends. And with her easy manner, all kinds of people probably did love her. That made him wonder, "Are you married? Have a steady boyfriend?"

"Nope and nope and don't need one."

"What?"

"Come on, Rob. Catch up, will ya? Nope to your first question and nope, don't need one to your second question."

"Need?"

Ellie sighed. "Okay, I'll try to speak more slowly and dumb it down a bit for you. Geez, I thought that since you're just standing still and not stacking chairs that you'd be able to follow a simple conversation. But, my bad. I'll try again."

"That's okay. I think I got it. Why don't you have a boyfriend? I mean someone who looks like you..." His voice trailed off. He needed to think before letting things flow off his tongue. He did not need to give out that much information.

She flashed him a grin. "Thanks. Although you tried to pull it back in, I think you just gave me a compliment." When he opened his mouth to protest, she held up a hand in a stop motion. "Nope. Once it's out there, there's no taking it back. Besides, did you know you look cute when you blush?"

He had never felt so off balance with anyone before. He liked to think of himself as a self-possessed kind of guy, calm and unflappable in any situation. But when he was with Ellie, his world's axis tilted just a little too far. Trying to recover, he said, "Come on. Let's get these things back to my room then we can lock up and go." He gathered most of the chart paper into his arms and motioned for Ellie to grab the markers and pads of paper.

Their footsteps echoed in the silent building. There was something about a school after dark. You picture a school as teaming with life, either hundreds of little bodies laboring at their desks, or voices ringing in the halls or kids running and yelling on the playground. This silent, still, feeling didn't fit with most people's impressions of what a school was all about.

Ellie, feeling the eeriness of the place and not used to hiding her emotions, pressed up close to Rob's back as they trod down the hall. Not expecting the contact, Rob started, losing his perilous hold on some of the packets of chart paper. They fell to the floor, their sheets splaying out in all directions.

"Oh, sorry," said Ellie. "I thought you heard me coming. This place sort of gives me the creeps in the dark like this." Only the red emergency lights gave off a faint glow. She bent down to help Rob retrieve his fallen items. Their heads whacked together with a resounding clunk.

"Ow!" Rob was knocked back onto his butt. He had not been expecting Ellie's weight to bang into his. "Are you all right?" he asked as he rubbed his head.

Ellie, too, was now sitting on the floor. "Yeah, I think so. You have a hard head, you know."

"Me? I was minding my own business. I didn't expect to get a head butt from you."

"That's the thanks I get for trying to help out a klutz who drops his things."

Rob started his retort, and then remembered who he was talking to. He looked over to find her grinning at him.

"See? You're starting to lighten up a little already. I knew you had it in you," Ellie told him.

"And I suppose you're just the person to bring out my lighter side?"

"Who better?"

She had a point. He couldn't think of anyone better. Although, maybe that bump on the head had jarred his brains. But for the present minute, he couldn't think of anyone else. The world narrowed down to just her. And him.

Rob stood and held out his hand to her to help her up. He expected some resistance and anticipated pulling her weight up, but true to form, Ellie surprised him. She more sprang up than was pulled, and her momentum carried her into him. Good thing he was taller, or their heads might have cracked again. As it was, her forehead bumped into his collar bone. He had hold of her hand, so they didn't go down this time. Her face was against his chest, and to keep her there, his hand holding hers went behind him. His other arm went around her back, pressing her closer to him. Then he didn't have to hold that first hand any longer as he felt her fingers relax their grip and find their way onto the flat of his back.

For seconds, for minutes, they just stood that way. In the distance, the boiler kicked in and there was the sound of water running through the pipes. The lights were low and it felt like they were all alone, with the world far away. This felt good, Rob thought. Almost too good. Was it just him? Did she like this, too? She wasn't pulling away, which was a positive sign. He let out a breath and relaxed even more into her. Ellie responding by turning her head to the side and resting her cheek on his chest.

She felt so warm and pliable in his arms. Wait. Pliable? Ellie? There was not a pliable bone in her body, he thought. But on the other hand, this felt oh so right. Then Rob, the rational guy who always thought everything through to the last detail, did an impulsive thing. She was so close, and it felt so good that he put a finger under her chin to tip up her head. Then he brought his mouth down on hers, gently, ever so gently, tentative about how this might go and how it might make him feel.

He was right to be leery because that kiss, that one kiss shook him to the core. The intensity was almost too much, and he had to draw back. But, not too far back. He tucked Ellie back into his arms, his one hand pressing her head to his chest and stroked her hair. And, she let him. This spitfire was actually letting him hold her and she wasn't fighting back.

The fighting Ellie he was beginning to know how to handle, but this Ellie, this gentle one who responded to his kiss, he did not know what to make of.

What to do now? While he felt like he could go on standing here holding her all night, he knew he'd have to break apart from her at some point. What should he say to her then? Should he apologize for taking liberties? What would she do? Had that one kiss shaken her the way it had him?

Ellie lifted her head and looked into Rob's face. Her smile lit her eyes. "Wow!" she said.

Oh, hallelujah. Thank god for this outspoken, forthright woman. There was no need to wonder when you were with her. She said what she thought, and you'd always know where you stood with her. His smile was gentle and his words soft. "Yeah, wow."

Ellie lifted her face to his. "I want to see if that was just a fluke," she said and she moulded her lips to his.

In a few minutes, she decided, "Nope. It wasn't a fluke."

Rob agreed. The glow of his wristwatch caught his eye as he stroked her hair. "It's late," he said. "I guess I should get you home since you have to get up so early in the morning for work." Then he hesitated, searching for the right words. There probably were none and he'd just have to take his chances with getting shot down. "May I see you again?" he asked tentatively.

"Oh, good," said Ellie.

"Good?"

"Yeah, good. That saves me from having to call and ask you out, which could have been awkward if you said no since I'll run into you at the school here."

Rob's head went back in surprise. She would have asked him out? Really? His grin was almost cocky. Her call would almost have been worth waiting for, but then, the anticipation and worry would have been too much. What if she hadn't asked him? What if some other guy took her notice?

"When?" he asked.

"Hmmm?" her reply was muffled between his shirt and his hand.

"When can I see you again?"

"How about now? I'm not going anywhere in a hurry." She raised her face again. This time the kiss was less gentle, less exploratory. She was the first to break away. "Whew. I do really need to get going. This floor looks pretty hard to spend the night on and I need to be at the bakery before five."

CHAPTER 21

"*N*o!" I want the green bowl. I always have my cereal in the green one."

"But Ethan, it's in the dishwasher. This red bowl is from the same set and holds the same amount of cereal."

"No! It's not the right one."

What had started as a good day went downhill fast. When Sara reminded him that he needed to pack his bag to take to school, Ethan grinned. Then his mom started in, talking too fast and too much and acting all twitchy, like something was wrong. It made Ethan feel funny inside; he didn't like it. And then, to top it off, his favorite bowl was missing. His cereal just would not taste the same if he didn't have the right bowl.

It was Friday - a big day for the boys. After school Ethan was going home with Kyle and Mel for a play date and a sleep over, his first ever. They'd do neat stuff.

His mom packed and repacked his bag, fussing and giving so many instructions. What was supposed to be a fun time had Ethan in knots. This was *not* going the way it was supposed to.

Ethan checked the visual schedule on the fridge. There was a picture of his Spiderman suitcase on wheels. The photo was a picture of Ethan pulling it behind him. There was *not* a picture of his mom packing it, the opening it up, taking things out, putting other stuff in and messing around with his case.

"Mom!"

Sara didn't respond. She was talking to herself about what ifs and instructions for Mel.

"Mom." Still nothing. Ethan walked over to her. He took her chin in his hands and pointed her face at him. That's what she did when she wanted his attention.

Sara pulled away. "Not now, Ethan. Can't you see I'm trying to get things ready?"

Well, he'd given it his best shot. Back to the old ways.

"No! I'm not going. I'm not going and you can't make me." With a mighty shove, he threw the opened suitcase across the floor. Socks and underwear flew in a jumble. His Lego instruction book fell out and got caught under the wheel of the suitcase, tearing the cover nearly off. "No!" wailed Ethan. "It's ruined now."

Sara put her head to her hand. Oh, god. Whoever thought that this was a good idea? Okay, deep breath. Mel thought it would be all right; she trusted Mel. Ethan and Kyle played well together at the bakery and Ethan woke up excited about this sleep-over. Whatever had put him in this mood now?

MATH PERIOD WAS OVER; it had been easy stuff today. Ethan and Kyle huddled around the building blocks on the carpet at the back of the room; they got to play since they'd finished their work early and afternoon recess wasn't for another five minutes.

The knock at the door caught his attention. As the door opened, Ethan stiffened. His mother was there, talking to Mr. Sells and in her hand was his Spiderman suitcase. What was she doing here? She'd ruined his morning and now was she here to wreck things again. Just when he and Kyle were having fun.

He watched as Mr. Sells and his mother turned to look at him. Mom had that look on her face again, the one where her lips were all smucked together and those gouged lines grew between her eyebrows. That face always meant bad news.

Now Mr. Sells got those lines on his face as well. They were looking at him and Kyle. Did even Mr. Sells think that a sleep-over was a bad idea? What did they know that he didn't? He'd thought it would be fun, but he was a kid. What did he know? It must be bad to make the adults look like that.

The bell rang. Ethan and Kyle gathered up the blocks and put them in their bucket. The students put on their jackets and lined up to go out for recess. Ethan followed along; his brain full of all the reasons the adults might think that sleep-overs were a bad idea.

Outside, Ethan ignored Kyle's calls to come play and wandered around the perimeter of the playground. He had a lot to think about. When the other kids in the class heard that he and Kyle were having a sleep-over, they talked about how much fun they had on sleep-overs. They seemed to think they were good things. Then, why did his mom look like that and why did Mr. Sells look worried along with her?

Well, they were wrong. He could do this. He knew Kyle and he knew Ms. Wickens. It had to be all right. He was a big boy now.

"Ethan, Ethan." There was his mom on the playground, waving her hand at him. What did she want?

"Ethan," she called again and started towards him. She didn't have the Spiderman suitcase with her anymore. Maybe she'd put it back in the car. Maybe she was coming to tell him that he couldn't go to Kyle's after school.

Ethan backed away. In just a few steps his back hit the fence. Still, his mother kept coming and she was joined now by Mr. Sells. Were they all out to get him? Did everyone want to stop his fun? Or maybe they knew something he didn't, and things could get really bad if he slept a night away from home. Maybe Kyle didn't have Spiderman sheets. What if he didn't have the right kind of pillow at his house, the kind that was funchy, and you could push into the right shape?

Ethan took side steps along the fence as the adults kept coming.

Then there was nothing against his back. He'd found his way to the entrance opening in the fence. He looked over his shoulder and there they were. Both his mom and Mr. Sells were coming after him from different directions.

Run! Every instinct in Ethan's body screamed, "Run!" So, he did. Running is what had worked for him for years. When things got too bad, when he couldn't take it anymore, he ran.

Ethan headed through the opening and was onto the sidewalk. A quick look over his shoulder showed that the adults were in pursuit, running flat out now. Ethan took off. There. There was an opening between the parked cars and across the road, he could see the field. If he could just get there, he would be safe.

Sara's cries changed in pitch from yelling his name to pleas of, "Get him. Somebody, please get him quick."

They were trying to get him. His mom confirmed it. Ethan spurted forward.

Rob called on every bit of strength he had to lengthen his stride. Ahead, he could see the traffic. He calculated the height of Ethan's head and knew that oncoming cars would never see him darting out from between the parked cars.

A horn blew. There was a squeal of brakes. Rob reached with everything he had and caught the back of Ethan's jacket. He threw the child in an arc back toward the curb, he hoped. All at once he registered the scent of burning rubber, and briefly the sound of grinding brake pads, the howl of a child, then the thud, then nothing.

CHAPTER 22

*T*he light was too much. And, what were those intrusive beeps? He just wanted to sleep. It all drifted away.

THERE IT WAS AGAIN, that pressure on his fingers. Two of them felt the way they did when his hammer missed the nail and whacked his thumb. Ow! Something pressed on the one again. He moved his hand out of harm's way, but felt it tugged back again, along with that same squeeze. For the love of....

With effort, slowly Rob cracked open one eye enough to search for whatever ensnared his sore hand. Immediately, he squeezed that eye closed against the bright light. He didn't know if the pounding drums or the crashing cymbals in his brain hurt the worst. But the pressure on his sore hand didn't help deaden the crescendo.

Then a hand hit his face. Well, tapped probably, but its effects reverberated within his head. He let out a groan.

"Rob, Rob, can you hear me? Rob." There was that tapping on his cheek again. He groaned again, louder this time as something put more pressure on his hand. Warm breath brushed his face. And that scent – he knew it from somewhere and it meant something good.

He stretched his eyelids once again. Since when did that take so much effort? It must be because he was trying to do both eyes at once. There, it was sort of wavy, but surely that must be the face of Ellie. And then he was gone again.

WHEN NEXT HE SURFACED, thank god there was nothing mashing his hand. But, there was this weight on his right shoulder that had not been there before. Gingerly and oh, so slowly, he tilted his head, and then forced open his eyes to inspect his shoulder. Hair draped itself there, hair fine and silky. Rob reached up one hand to touch it. His arm felt like it weighed twice its normal weight. As he brought it into his line of sight, he saw that it was encased in a bright, purple cast. What! Maneuvering it closer into his narrowed line of vision was not easy and he clunked it into whatever was beneath that mass of hair.

The weight lifted off his shoulder. "Rob, you're awake." And, there was Ellie's face smiling down at him.

He paused just to soak in the reflection of that smile. He tried to answer it with one of his own and winced. Automatically, he brought his hand to his mouth to feel the problem but managed to clunk himself with that cast. He noted the color again. He turned his arm over. "What the hell?"

"You were unconscious, so I chose the color for you. I thought your kids would get a kick out of it." Ellie grinned, pleased with herself.

He decided to let that one go. For now. "Where am I?"

"In the hospital. Don't you remember?"

He mulled this over. "Not really. I remember being on the playground at school, then, well, just waking up here. With you." He looked at her some more. "What are you doing here?"

"Mel called me. After the ambulance took you away, she had her hands full with the boys and the parent. Someone needed to keep an eye on you since you seem prone to getting yourself into such trouble."

He raised one eyebrow at that. "What happened to me?"

"Don't you remember? Oh, right, the doctors said you might not." She brightened. "You're a hero. You probably saved Ethan's life. If you hadn't thrown him out of the way, he might have been killed by that truck."

"Yeah. I guess he let out quite the wail, but he wasn't hurt. Just a few scrapes and bruises."

"Jeez. I hurt a kid?"

"No, you saved his life. If you hadn't thrown him out of the way of the vehicle, who knows how badly he would have been injured. Instead, you got hurt."

"What happened?"

"I gather that you just had time to shove Ethan behind you before the truck was right there." Ellie grinned at him. "Too bad you didn't lead with your hard head, but your hip took the brunt of the impact and your head bump was only secondary."

Rob winced. "The way my head feels, there is nothing secondary about it."

"That's because you have a concussion. But I'm afraid that might pale in comparison to when you start moving around."

"What do you mean?" Rob tried to raise himself up in the bed. The movement jostled his pelvis, and every joint, everyone bone, every muscle and tendon in that area howled in protest. Rob closed his eyes and willed himself back into unconsciousness.

Ellie pressed a cool cloth to his forehead. "The nurse's instructions were to ring her as soon as you were awake. They'll talk about your pain meds with you."

Not cool to whimper like a baby in front of a woman you're interested in, but Rob did it anyway. Somehow, the choice was removed from him, along with his will, then his hold on consciousness.

WHEN HE NEXT AWOKE, it was better. Not great, or even good, but better. Maybe that was helped by Ellie.

"Still here?" he asked.

"Yep. It's hard to shake me once I've dug in."

"I'm more with it now. Wanna tell me about what's wrong with me?"

"Bit of a leading question, don't you think? But maybe we'll leave that until you're more of an equal sparring partner."

Rob raised an eyebrow.

"Oh, you mean your injuries. Well, to start with, you broke your arm." Ellie ticked the items off on her fingers. "Next, you smashed your right hip bone up real good. You dislocated some of the bones in your pelvis."

They both looked down at that area of his body. "Not much can be done about that," continued Ellie. "They don't cast it or anything. You'll just need to lie still until the bones start to knit. But, moving on – there's your head. The truck smashed into your hip first, sort of spinning you around. That's when your head shmucked the truck and you got a concussion. It's too bad you didn't lead with your head; it could have absorbed most of the impact then you wouldn't have all this hip and pelvis business."

Rob just looked at her.

"But I'm assured that you'll live. You'll even walk and all that, but maybe not for a while yet."

"Anything else?"

"Nope. All your other body parts seem to be functioning as expected." She put away her perky expression and took his hand again. "Rob, you were so lucky, and this could have been so much worse. We could have lost you." She blinked rapidly.

Was that moisture brimming in her eyes? "How long have I been in here?"

"Three days."

"And, how long have *you* been here?"

"Three days."

CHAPTER 23

"Sh. Wait. I need to see if he's awake first."

"But I want to see him now," a small voice wailed.

Rob recognized that whine, but not the gruffer voice that came next.

"We need to see if he wants to see *you*. Remember that he's here because of you."

"Jerrod, come on," said Sara. "Ethan's just a child. He didn't think that his teacher would get hurt. It's not his fault."

Jerrod just looked at her. "Still. You still say that. When are you and the kid going to learn to take responsibility for your actions? Yeah, Ethan didn't plan for this accident to happen but that's the problem. Like you said, he didn't think."

Rob signaled to Ellie to open the door and let the family in. He gingerly touched the button to slightly elevate the head of his bed, thankful that the slow speed gave him time to adjust to the pressure on his hips.

"Mr. Sells, Mr. Sells." A little body broke loose from his mom's hands and Ethan ran for the bed. He hit it with a thud and reached for Rob's arm. Rob squeezed his eyes shut and gritted his teeth against the groan of pain welling up from below his midsection to his eyebrows.

Sara jerked her son back and held him firmly against her body.

After two deep breaths in, Rob opened his eyes and pasted on a smile for Ethan. "Hey, bud. Nice to see you. What brings you here?"

"We brought you stuff." Ethan shrugged off his mother's restraints and dumped the contents of a plastic bag onto the bed. Thankfully the contents were light. "See? We made these cards for you, all the kids did." He rummaged none too gently through the stack. "Here's mine." He held it up for Rob to see, perching it just a couple inches from Rob's nose.

Rob made the appropriate comments on the six-year old's art work, and then raised his eyes to the man in the room. "Hi. I don't think we've met." He raised his cast to show that he couldn't shake hands.

"I'm Jerrod Fellows, this guy's dad." He nodded at his son, who was now sorting through the cards and talking to himself. "My wife and I want to offer you our thanks and apologize for the pain our son has put you through. We can't begin to express how badly we feel about this."

"Thank you for saying that, but it was an accident. I'm just relieved that I reached Ethan in time, eh bud?" He ruffled Ethan's hair. Ethan shrugged and moved a half step away.

"Ethan," his father corrected.

"No, that's all right. I know that he's not comfortable with light touches like that. I forgot." He gestured to his IV pole and the bags of fluid running through tubes into his arm. "I'm not doing my best thinking with this stuff flowing through me. On our better days, Ethan and I understand each other."

"Ethan, what do you have to say to your teacher?" There was a pause while Ethan intently studied the construction paper creations spread over the bed. "Ethan," Jerrod prodded.

A wee, small voice said, "I'm sorry."

"For?" His dad asked.

"I'm sorry for running away and making you get hurt, Mr. Sells."

"And..." Jerrod was not letting this go.

"And I won't run away any more."

Rob gave it a few seconds. "Hey, bud." There was no reply, but he waited. Jerrod started to nudge his son, but Rob shook his head no. Finally, Ethan glanced toward the head of the bed.

Rob continued. "I know you're sorry, bud and that you didn't mean for this to happen. But, it did. It could have been much worse, and you could have been hurt." Ethan studied the pillowcase by Rob's left ear. "Now, let's show your parents something. Remember your figure eight breathing?" Ethan nodded. "Show them how it's done."

Ethan took a big breath in, then using hand motions, drew a figure eight while he slowly let out his air. Then he did it all again. Turning to his mom, he said, "Now you do it with me."

"Oh, I don't really think...."

Ellie jumped in. "Let's all do it together."

"That was great, Ethan," Rob said. "And tell us why you would breathe like that."

"To calm myself and give me time to think when I'm upset."

"Can you tell us when would have been a good time to use this strategy?"

"Yeah, I know. Before I ran away."

"I think you'll remember next time." Ethan nodded. "But is that breathing enough to make everything better?" Rob asked.

"No. It just gives me time so that I can think."

"Think about...?" prompted his teacher.

Ethan looked into the distance and recited. "What is the problem? What are some ideas to solve it? What is my plan? Is my plan working?"

"You got it, bud."

Jerrod interrupted. "If you know all that, why didn't you use it? You could have saved us all a ton of trouble."

"Sometimes these things take practice," explained Rob. "Sounds like Ethan has a plan for next time though." He turned back to Ethan. "Are we good then, bud?" He held up his hand for a fist bump. Ethan grinned and gave a hearty bump. Then he leaned over and gave his teacher a quick hug.

Sara teared up. Jerrod muttered, "How often does he give *us* a hug?"

ROB CHANGED THE SUBJECT. "I've got something for you," he told
Ethan.

That perked Ethan up.

Ellie brought out the social story that Mel had created for Ethan
and handed it to Sara.

"Ethan, we're giving this story to your mom. You now have
homework. Your homework is to read this story with your mom
before you come to school every day. Then read it again when you get
home from school and again before you go to bed." He paused. "How
many times a day does that make?"

Ethan used his fingers, but he came up with the right answer.

"Wait, there's more. Don't you think it fair that we give your mom
some homework, too?"

Ethan giggled.

Ellie handed a second booklet to Sara.

Turning to the parents, Rob explained. "What we need to work on
is Ethan's self-regulation – his ability to manage the size of his
feelings and to know how to respond appropriately to situations.
We've been working on it at school, but the concepts need to be
reinforced at home. We don't want Ethan in the red zone where he
blindly flees. We've made some progress and things are generally
good in the classroom now, but obviously we need to do some more
work." His gaze went between Jerrod to Sara and back again. "Are you
willing to work with us on this?" There were nods all around.

Ellie watched with growing concern, her eyes on Rob's pallor.
"Okay, enough for one day." She began stacking the students' cards
into a pile. "Thanks, Ethan for bringing these for Mr. Sells. He'll look
at them all later, but right now, he badly needs a nap." She escorted the
family out of the hospital room, shutting the door firmly behind them.

By the time she turned around, Rob's eyes were already closed. She
resumed her place by the side of his bed, propped her e-reader on the
side of the bed and cradled Rob's hand in her own.

CHAPTER 24

"Mom, breathe." Ethan held up his arm, making an elongated figure eight. "Mom come on. Do it with me."

"Ethan, I'm busy. I'm trying to get your bag ready." The last time a sleep-over at Kyle's had been planned, the result was a disaster when Ethan ran, and his teacher was injured. Sara was determined there would be no mishaps this time. There better not be she muttered to herself as she removed the items from her son's suitcase, laying everything on the bed to check again that she had not forgotten anything.

There was a tug on her arm. "Ethan, can't you see that I'm in a hurry to get your things ready?"

Ethan tugged again. When his mom glanced at him, he held up a social story - the one Mel had given him about sleeping over at Kyle's house. "Read it with me mom, then we'll breathe some more."

Sara took a step back, looking at that earnest little face. Her anxiety notched down a level, then a couple levels more. Who was the nervous one here? Ethan with his fear of the unknown and tendency to be easily overwhelmed was calm. She let out a deep breath.

"Good one, mom. That's the way to breathe. Now, let's do it again." He sucked in a deep breath and held it as his arm traced the pattern in the air. Sara joined it, rewarded with a smile of approval from her little boy. "Now that we're calm, let's read this social story."

As Ethan read the story aloud an explained each of the photographs, Sara's attention wandered. Yes, the weeks of practicing had paid off, so much so that Ethan could recognize when his mom was getting stressed. He intervened and calmed her down. She thought back on the ways *she* had tried to calm her son in the past. Mostly they involved talk, lots of talk. And probably a raised voice. Had she made things worse? If she'd only know what a difference just controlling your breathing could make.

But she knew now - the whole family knew. They practiced together. They ventured into the public in situations she never dreamed they could attempt together. Oh, it wasn't perfect, not by a long shot, but it was better. Sara could see that their lives were improving. And now her little boy was the teacher, helping his mom to calm down.

CHAPTER 25

Tomas grabbed his pocket as his cell phone vibrated. A half second later the ring tone sounded that could indicate only one thing - his wife was in trouble. Again. He wheeled the skid-steer loader to the side of the warehouse, fishing the phone from his pocket. Finger on the answer button, he raised his eyes to meet those of his boss.

Mr. Humber didn't say a word.

Tomas raised an index finger in the signal for "just one minute". Even the warehouse noises could not mask the sounds of sobbing both he and Mr. Humbly could hear coming from the tiny speaker on the phone.

"It's my wife," explained Tomas. "Our son...."

"I don't care." Mr. Humber's face belied his words. He paused and his expression hardened. "We all have problems, but this is company time. Once or twice, maybe we can overlook it. But I've spoken to you before about this. I said that if you take that phone call, it's over. Either get that loader moving or come see me in my office. I'll be watching."

The sound of sobbing was masked by an unintelligible roar, the

368

smashing of glass and shrieks of "No!" Tomas hesitated only a microsecond then put the phone to his ear.

"Maria! Maria! Are you there?" He paused. "Maria, speak to me."

"Oh, Tomas, I am so sorry to bother you at work." Through practice, Tomas could make sense of his wife's broken words.

"It's okay, Maria. Take a deep breath. Try to calm yourself and tell me what's happening." As if he didn't know.

"It's Manny. He's mad again. I'm sorry. I don't know what I did. He just came at me. I thought we were all right, and then he just started in."

"I know, honey. It's not your fault." Tomas paused. How many times had he wondered the same thing himself? "Are you hurt?"

"I'm okay. It's just a bit of blood and it's stopping now, but Manny, he's so upset." In the background the sounds of yelling and pounding overrode her words.

"Where are you now? Where is he?"

"I'm in the bathroom, like you told me to do. Manny's on the other side of the door. I'm so sorry, but I think he's made new holes in the door and part of the door jamb may be off. He's pushing on the door, trying to get in. I'm not sure the lock will hold."

"Did you position yourself the way I told you to?"

"Yes. My feet are against the vanity and my back is to the door. It's keeping the door shut, but the door bounces each time he throws himself at it.

"And Tomas, I think Manny has broken many more things this time. He threw the toaster to the floor and I think some parts flew off. He's mad that I'm hiding in the bathroom, so he's throwing dishes now. It sounds like lots are smashed."

"That's okay. The main thing is that you're safe. Now, is Manny safe? Did you lock the hallway door so he can't get out of the apartment?"

More sobbing. "I, I don't know. I think so. Oh, Tomas, I just don't remember for sure. I try to always do that when you leave for work. Maybe I did but I'm not sure. Oh, what if he leaves? Maybe I should go out and check."

"No! Don't do that. Just stay put. Remember what happened the last time you went to check and I wasn't there? We can't afford any more hospital visits. And, we know he hasn't left. I can hear him in the background, so he's all right. Just stay there. I'll be home as soon as I can. I love you. Just wait for me. I'm on my way."

Tomas's mind flashed to an image of the deadbolt he'd placed on the door to their apartment. Just under the deadbolt was a chain lock. No, no, Maria would not have put on that latch. She'd only turned the door lock and the deadbolt. Otherwise, how would he get in to rescue his family?

TOMAS CLICKED OFF HIS PHONE, glancing up at the window overlooking the warehouse floor. Yes, as promised, there was Mr. Humber watching him.

Knowing what was coming, Tomas drove the loader to its parking spot, shut off the ignition and plugged the machine into the recharger. He did his usual walk-around to ensure that his area was safe and he'd left nothing in the way to harm a co-worker. If he was careful and precise, everything would be all right. They'd all be fine. Squaring his shoulders, he trudged up the stairs to knock on the door to his boss's office.

The muffled "come in" came sooner than Tomas hoped. Mr. Humber stood behind his chair, a tidy pile of cash precisely in the center of his desk blotter. The edges were exactly lined up. An envelope with the name Tomas Rodrigues typed in large block letters was just above the stack of bills.

Unsure whether to attempt an explanation, Tomas waited. So did Mr. Humber.

"You answered the phone."

"Yes, sir." What else could Tomas say?

"You made your choice."

He knew it was inevitable, but he needed this job to support his

family. Struggling to maintain his dignity, Tomas tried. "I felt I had no choice, sir. My wife, she was in danger. *Is* in danger."

"Tomas, we are not unsympathetic to your situation. It's tough. I know that. But we have a business to run here. We need workers we can depend on."

"I understand. And, I am a good worker."

"Yes, you are. No one disputes that, when you're here. But how often do these calls come?"

As Tomas started to answer, Mr. Humber held up his hand.

"No, don't answer. It doesn't matter. At first, we understood. Emergencies happen to us all. We didn't keep track. But then it became a regular thing. Once a month, maybe we could overlook, but this is the third time this week. And the final time."

"I know, sir. We are working hard to solve the problem. I..." As much as he'd like to, Tomas could not promise that it would never happen again. That drew his mind back to what was likely happening with his son and wife at that very minute. He calculated how long it would take him to run home. There were less people on the streets in the middle of the day, so he could be faster than when going home after work.

"I'm sorry, Tomas, but it's over. This has happened too many times for us to keep you. We need workers we can depend on."

Tomas winced. A man was to be trusted. He must live up to his responsibilities. If he took on a commitment, he would fulfill it. And now, he'd let down this company that had taken a chance on him when he first came to this country. He had failed.

Mr. Humber indicated the money on the desk. "Here is your severance pay. It covers the two weeks until the end of this month."

Tomas started to interrupt, but Mr. Humber held up his hand.

"No, this is the way we are doing it. To be blunt, you're fired. But we do recognize the good job you do when you are here, so we're paying you out to the end of the month."

Tomas waited a second then raised his eyes from the money to Mr. Humber's face. "What if...?"

"No, this is final." He softened. "Look, in six months or a year, if

your situation changes considerably, maybe we will talk again, but I'm making no promises. There are other men waiting to take your place who are dependable workers." He watched the way his words affected Tomas. "Go home and attend to your family. We wish you well." He gathered the bills into the envelope and passed it to Tomas.

Neither man offered to shake hands.

CHAPTER 26

*P*ulling out his phone to check the time, Tomas hurried out of the place that had given him and his family a good living almost since the day he arrived in this country. He'd advanced in both responsibility and pay through hard work and diligence. He took pride in doing a good job and being known as a stand-up guy. Now, his reputation was shot.

His steps quickened as he realized just how much time had gone by since Maria's call. Was she all right? Where was Manny and what was he doing?

Tomas retrieved the last call on his cell phone and pressed the buttons to check on Maria. No answer. Maybe in his worry, he did something wrong and it wasn't Maria he'd called. He slowed his pace and punched in the numbers one by one. It rang once, twice, four times, and then clicked over to voice mail. At least he heard the sweet voice of his wife, but she didn't pick up. Tomas slowed and checked the number printed on the screen. Yes, it was the right number, of course it was, and he'd heard her answering machine message.

The phone went into his shirt pocket and he ran. Maria would know how worried he'd be and answer the phone if she at all could. Or, she'd call him back if she hadn't gotten to the phone in time.

Tomas took the phone from his pocket to make sure he hadn't accidentally turned it off. Nope, it was on. His pace edged up from a jog to a sprint.

~

THE PUNCH CAME between his shoulder blades with a force that sent Tomas into a nose dive. His chin hit the sidewalk, followed by his nose and forehead. One hand scraped along the concrete; the other protected the chest pocket that contained his precious cell phone, his only link to what might be happening at home.

The blow stunned Tomas momentarily and he didn't know what had happened. He turned his head to glance behind to see what he'd tripped over. That was when he noticed the pairs of sneaker-clad feet surrounding him by the entrance to the alley.

Tomas braced his hands under his shoulders to push himself to his feet. It didn't work. A foot kept him on the ground, a foot that planted itself almost directly where the punch had landed moments ago. Instead, Tomas raised his head, trying to make eye contact with one of his attackers. His gaze skittered around his limited field of vision to see if help was coming. No one. By late afternoon this street would be teeming with commuters heading home from work, but now, well, it was deserted.

"Dios mio," he muttered. "Que Dios me ayude."

"Huh, there's no help for saps like you," was the only reply Tomas heard.

He tried again. "What do you want?"

"Your money, genius, what do you think?"

"I don't have any money. I just lost my job today. I'm broke."

"Riiight. That's what they all say." His buddies joined his snickers. "Now hand it over."

"I told you. I don't have money. I got fired, I'm telling you. I can give you my boss's name and you can go check. He's only a few blocks away."

"I feel a nap coming on and Joey here, well, he's got a thirst on. We need your cash and anything else interesting from your pockets."

The toe of the sneaker by Tomas's right ear tapped on the sidewalk. Its owner said, "Now we can do this nice and easy or we can do it the hard way."

"What do you mean?"

"Is he dense or what?" His buddies laughed with him. "You can nicely hand us everything that's in your pockets or we can take it from you. I figure we're being pretty big, giving you options here."

"I don't have any money."

"This is getting old. Have at it, guys."

Rough hands turned Tomas to his back. Unprepared for the move, the back of his head cracked on the sidewalk. One grimy hand felt the hard, rectangular shape in his shirt pocket and fished out Tomas's cell phone, waving it in the air.

"No, come on, guys. You gotta give that back to me. My wife, she's hurt. That's the only way I can keep in touch with her and my boy. I need that. She could be bleeding and unconscious. I *need* my phone."

"Ah. For a sob story, that's not bad, but we've heard better, right boys?"

Other hands continued their search through Tomas's pockets. One hand shoved the side of his face into the sidewalk while a booted foot kicked his hips over to follow his face. A fist dug out the envelope that was jammed deep into his back pocket.

There was the sound of paper tearing. "Well, looky, looky what we have here." The guy fanned the bills in the air.

"Please, that's my severance pay. I told you I just got fired. We need that. I have to pay the rent next week and without a job, that's all we have."

"Ah, you're breaking my heart, sucker. Here. The milk of human kindness and all that..." A five dollar bill fluttered to the ground by Tomas's shoulder. With one kick to his back, and one tromp on his hand, they left.

CHAPTER 27

They were celebrating Rob's recovery with cappuccinos and goodies at the bakery. He'd been released three days ago and ready to venture back into the world for short stints, anyway. Ellie had hardly left his side on the first two days, but she had a business to run. So Ben and Mel gave Rob a lift to the bakery where Ellie was working.

"You do realize she's a brat, don't you?" Ben reminded Rob.

"Yeah, I kind of figure that one out pretty quickly," Rob admitted. He automatically moved his abdomen out of the reach of Ellie's jabbing elbow.

"That being said, she is my sister and I've had to tolerate her all my life. I know it can be rough. But I'm warning you, if you do anything to hurt her, I'll have to kill you."

"Ben!" said Mel and Ellie together.

"Butt out," said his wife.

"You jerk," said Ellie. "Lay off the big brother act. When we were kids I was in danger of *you* killing me. As if I'd rely on you to protect me from anything now."

While their bantering went on, Rob had time to think. He realized that that saying about cutting off his arm before he'd hurt her was true. He could not bear the thought of Ellie ever being harmed by anything, let alone by him. He would do all within his power to protect her. Always.

Yikes! Where had that come from? He turned to look at Ellie, forgetting all about the others in the room and realized that it was true. Everything was true. He would guard this woman with his life and grow old keeping that promise. That is, if she'd let him.

CHAPTER 28

*T*omas grabbed his pocket as his cell phone vibrated. A half second later the ring tone sounded that could indicate only one thing - his wife was in trouble. Again. He wheeled the skid-steer loader to the side of the warehouse, fishing the phone from his pocket. Finger on the answer button, he raised his eyes to meet those of his boss.

Mr. Humber didn't say a word.

Tomas raised an index finger in the signal for "just one minute". Even the warehouse noises could not mask the sounds of sobbing both he and Mr. Humbly could hear coming from the tiny speaker on the phone.

"It's my wife," explained Tomas. "Our son...."

"I don't care." Mr. Humber's face belied his words. He paused and his expression hardened. "We all have problems, but this is company time. Once or twice, maybe we can overlook it. But I've spoken to you before about this. I said that if you take that phone call, it's over. Either get that loader moving or come see me in my office. I'll be watching."

The sound of sobbing was masked by an unintelligible roar, the

smashing of glass and shrieks of "No!" Tomas hesitated only a microsecond then put the phone to his ear.

"Maria! Maria! Are you there?" He paused. "Maria, speak to me."

"Oh, Tomas, I am so sorry to bother you at work." Through practice, Tomas could make sense of his wife's broken words.

"It's okay, Maria. Take a deep breath. Try to calm yourself and tell me what's happening." As if he didn't know.

"It's Manny. He's mad again. I'm sorry. I don't know what I did. He just came at me. I thought we were all right, and then he just started in."

"I know, honey. It's not your fault." Tomas paused. How many times had he wondered the same thing himself? "Are you hurt?"

"I'm okay. It's just a bit of blood and it's stopping now, but Manny, he's so upset." In the background the sounds of yelling and pounding overrode her words.

"Where are you now? Where is he?"

"I'm in the bathroom, like you told me to do. Manny's on the other side of the door. I'm so sorry, but I think he's made new holes in the door and part of the door jamb may be off. He's pushing on the door, trying to get in. I'm not sure the lock will hold."

"Did you position yourself the way I told you to?"

"Yes. My feet are against the vanity and my back is to the door. It's keeping the door shut, but the door bounces each time he throws himself at it.

"And Tomas, I think Manny has broken many more things this time. He threw the toaster to the floor and I think some parts flew off. He's mad that I'm hiding in the bathroom, so he's throwing dishes now. It sounds like lots are smashed."

"That's okay. The main thing is that you're safe. Now, is Manny safe? Did you lock the hallway door so he can't get out of the apartment?"

More sobbing. "I, I don't know. I think so. Oh, Tomas, I just don't remember for sure. I try to always do that when you leave for work. Maybe I did but I'm not sure. Oh, what if he leaves? Maybe I should go out and check."

"No! Don't do that. Just stay put. Remember what happened the last time you went to check and I wasn't there? We can't afford any more hospital visits. And, we know he hasn't left. I can hear him in the background, so he's all right. Just stay there. I'll be home as soon as I can. I love you. Just wait for me. I'm on my way."

Tomas's mind flashed to an image of the deadbolt he'd placed on the door to their apartment. Just under the deadbolt was a chain lock. No, no, Maria would not have put on that latch. She'd only turned the door lock and the deadbolt. Otherwise, how would he get in to rescue his family?

~

TOMAS CLICKED OFF HIS PHONE, glancing up at the window overlooking the warehouse floor. Yes, as promised, there was Mr. Humber watching him.

Knowing what was coming, Tomas drove the loader to its parking spot, shut off the ignition and plugged the machine into the recharger. He did his usual walk-around to ensure that his area was safe and he'd left nothing in the way to harm a co-worker. If he was careful and precise, everything would be all right. They'd all be fine. Squaring his shoulders, he trudged up the stairs to knock on the door to his boss's office.

The muffled "come in" came sooner than Tomas hoped. Mr. Humber stood behind his chair, a tidy pile of cash precisely in the center of his desk blotter. The edges were exactly lined up. An envelope with the name Tomas Rodrigues typed in large block letters was just above the stack of bills.

Unsure whether to attempt an explanation, Tomas waited. So did Mr. Humber.

"You answered the phone."

"Yes, sir." What else could Tomas say?

"You made your choice."

He knew it was inevitable, but he needed this job to support his

family. Struggling to maintain his dignity, Tomas tried. "I felt I had no choice, sir. My wife, she was in danger. *Is* in danger."

"Tomas, we are not unsympathetic to your situation. It's tough. I know that. But we have a business to run here. We need workers we can depend on."

"I understand. And, I am a good worker."

"Yes, you are. No one disputes that, when you're here. But how often do these calls come?"

As Tomas started to answer, Mr. Humber held up his hand.

"No, don't answer. It doesn't matter. At first, we understood. Emergencies happen to us all. We didn't keep track. But then it became a regular thing. Once a month, maybe we could overlook, but this is the third time this week. And the final time."

"I know, sir. We are working hard to solve the problem. I..." As much as he'd like to, Tomas could not promise that it would never happen again. That drew his mind back to what was likely happening with his son and wife at that very minute. He calculated how long it would take him to run home. There were less people on the streets in the middle of the day, so he could be faster than when going home after work.

"I'm sorry, Tomas, but it's over. This has happened too many times for us to keep you. We need workers we can depend on."

Tomas winced. A man was to be trusted. He must live up to his responsibilities. If he took on a commitment, he would fulfill it. And now, he'd let down this company that had taken a chance on him when he first came to this country. He had failed.

Mr. Humber indicated the money on the desk. "Here is your severance pay. It covers the two weeks until the end of this month."

Tomas started to interrupt, but Mr. Humber held up his hand.

"No, this is the way we are doing it. To be blunt, you're fired. But we do recognize the good job you do when you are here, so we're paying you out to the end of the month."

Tomas waited a second then raised his eyes from the money to Mr. Humber's face. "What if...?"

"No, this is final." He softened. "Look, in six months or a year, if

your situation changes considerably, maybe we will talk again, but I'm making no promises. There are other men waiting to take your place who are dependable workers." He watched the way his words affected Tomas. "Go home and attend to your family. We wish you well." He gathered the bills into the envelope and passed it to Tomas.

Neither man offered to shake hands.

CHAPTER 29

*P*ulling out his phone to check the time, Tomas hurried out of the place that had given him and his family a good living almost since the day he arrived in this country. He'd advanced in both responsibility and pay through hard work and diligence. He took pride in doing a good job and being known as a stand-up guy. Now, his reputation was shot.

His steps quickened as he realized just how much time had gone by since Maria's call. Was she all right? Where was Manny and what was he doing?

Tomas retrieved the last call on his cell phone and pressed the buttons to check on Maria. No answer. Maybe in his worry, he did something wrong and it wasn't Maria he'd called. He slowed his pace and punched in the numbers one by one. It rang once, twice, four times, and then clicked over to voice mail. At least he heard the sweet voice of his wife, but she didn't pick up. Tomas slowed and checked the number printed on the screen. Yes, it was the right number, of course it was, and he'd heard her answering machine message.

The phone went into his shirt pocket and he ran. Maria would know how worried he'd be and answer the phone if she at all could. Or, she'd call him back if she hadn't gotten to the phone in time.

Tomas took the phone from his pocket to make sure he hadn't accidentally turned it off. Nope, it was on. His pace edged up from a jog to a sprint.

~

THE PUNCH CAME between his shoulder blades with a force that sent Tomas into a nose dive. His chin hit the sidewalk, followed by his nose and forehead. One hand scraped along the concrete; the other protected the chest pocket that contained his precious cell phone, his only link to what might be happening at home.

The blow stunned Tomas momentarily and he didn't know what had happened. He turned his head to glance behind to see what he'd tripped over. That was when he noticed the pairs of sneaker-clad feet surrounding him by the entrance to the alley.

Tomas braced his hands under his shoulders to push himself to his feet. It didn't work. A foot kept him on the ground, a foot that planted itself almost directly where the punch had landed moments ago. Instead, Tomas raised his head, trying to make eye contact with one of his attackers. His gaze skittered around his limited field of vision to see if help was coming. No one. By late afternoon this street would be teeming with commuters heading home from work, but now, well, it was deserted.

"Dios mio," he muttered. "Que Dios me ayude."

"Huh, there's no help for saps like you," was the only reply Tomas heard.

He tried again. "What do you want?"

"Your money, genius, what do you think?"

"I don't have any money. I just lost my job today. I'm broke."

"Riiight. That's what they all say." His buddies joined his snickers. "Now hand it over."

"I told you. I don't have money. I got fired, I'm telling you. I can give you my boss's name and you can go check. He's only a few blocks away."

"I feel a nap coming on and Joey here, well, he's got a thirst on. We need your cash and anything else interesting from your pockets."

The toe of the sneaker by Tomas's right ear tapped on the sidewalk. Its owner said, "Now we can do this nice and easy or we can do it the hard way."

"What do you mean?"

"Is he dense or what?" His buddies laughed with him. "You can nicely hand us everything that's in your pockets or we can take it from you. I figure we're being pretty big, giving you options here."

"I don't have any money."

"This is getting old. Have at it, guys."

Rough hands turned Tomas to his back. Unprepared for the move, the back of his head cracked on the sidewalk. One grimy hand felt the hard, rectangular shape in his shirt pocket and fished out Tomas's cell phone, waving it in the air.

"No, come on, guys. You gotta give that back to me. My wife, she's hurt. That's the only way I can keep in touch with her and my boy. I need that. She could be bleeding and unconscious. I *need* my phone."

"Ah. For a sob story, that's not bad, but we've heard better, right boys?"

Other hands continued their search through Tomas's pockets. One hand shoved the side of his face into the sidewalk while a booted foot kicked his hips over to follow his face. A fist dug out the envelope that was jammed deep into his back pocket.

There was the sound of paper tearing. "Well, looky, looky what we have here." The guy fanned the bills in the air.

"Please, that's my severance pay. I told you I just got fired. We need that. I have to pay the rent next week and without a job, that's all we have."

"Ah, you're breaking my heart, sucker. Here. The milk of human kindness and all that..." A five dollar bill fluttered to the ground by Tomas's shoulder. With one kick to his back, and one tromp on his hand, they left.

AUTISM BELONGS

SCHOOL DAZE: BOOK THREE

Autism
BELONGS

Dr Sharon A Mitchell

PROLOGUE

*H*e flew against the door, causing it to burst open just slightly, and then slam shut again. He backed up and flung himself another time, with the same results. Next, he swivelled, attacking the door with his back instead of just one shoulder. This time the door bowed a few inches, before returning to the latched position.

The woman on the other side of the door alternated between soft sobs and low singing. She crooned a lullaby, sometimes in English, sometimes in Spanish, sometimes in a language incomprehensible. "My baby, my precious baby," she murmured. Tears flowed freely.

Her head smacked back against the door with each blow. With her back to the door and her feet braced against the edge of the vanity, she fought to keep the door closed, the only barrier between her and her attacker.

CHAPTER 1

CHAPTER 2

Tomas grabbed his pocket as his cell phone vibrated. A half second later the ring tone sounded that could indicate only one thing - his wife was in trouble. Again. He wheeled the skid-steer loader to the side of the warehouse, fishing the phone from his pocket. Finger on the answer button, he raised his eyes to meet those of his boss.

Mr. Humber didn't say a word.

Tomas raised an index finger in the signal for "just one minute". Even the warehouse noises could not mask the sounds of sobbing both he and Mr. Humbly could hear coming from the tiny speaker on the phone.

"It's my wife," explained Tomas. "Our son...."

"I don't care." Mr. Humber's face belied his words. He paused and his expression hardened. "We all have problems, but this is company time. Once or twice, maybe we can overlook it. But I've spoken to you before about this. I said that if you take that phone call, it's over. Either get that loader moving or come see me in my office. I'll be watching."

The sound of sobbing was masked by an unintelligible roar, the

smashing of glass and shrieks of "No!" Tomas hesitated only a microsecond then put the phone to his ear.

"Maria! Maria! Are you there?" He paused. "Maria, speak to me."

"Oh, Tomas, I am so sorry to bother you at work." Through practice, Tomas could make sense of his wife's broken words.

"It's okay, Maria. Take a deep breath. Try to calm yourself and tell me what's happening." As if he didn't know.

"It's Manny. He's mad again. I'm sorry. I don't know what I did. He just came at me. I thought we were all right, and then he just started in."

"I know, honey. It's not your fault." Tomas paused. How many times had he wondered the same thing himself? "Are you hurt?"

"I'm okay. It's just a bit of blood and it's stopping now, but Manny, he's so upset." In the background the sounds of yelling and pounding overrode her words.

"Where are you now? Where is he?"

"I'm in the bathroom, like you told me to do. Manny's on the other side of the door. I'm so sorry, but I think he's made new holes in the door and part of the door jamb may be off. He's pushing on the door, trying to get in. I'm not sure the lock will hold."

"Did you position yourself the way I told you to?"

"Yes. My feet are against the vanity and my back is to the door. It's keeping the door shut, but the door bounces each time he throws himself at it.

"And Tomas, I think Manny has broken many more things this time. He threw the toaster to the floor and I think some parts flew off. He's mad that I'm hiding in the bathroom, so he's throwing dishes now. It sounds like lots are smashed."

"That's okay. The main thing is that you're safe. Now, is Manny safe? Did you lock the hallway door so he can't get out of the apartment?"

More sobbing. "I, I don't know. I think so. Oh, Tomas, I just don't remember for sure. I try to always do that when you leave for work. Maybe I did but I'm not sure. Oh, what if he leaves? Maybe I should go out and check."

"No! Don't do that. Just stay put. Remember what happened the last time you went to check and I wasn't there? We can't afford any more hospital visits. And, we know he hasn't left. I can hear him in the background, so he's all right. Just stay there. I'll be home as soon as I can. I love you. Just wait for me. I'm on my way."

Tomas's mind flashed to an image of the deadbolt he'd placed on the door to their apartment. Just under the deadbolt was a chain lock. No, no, Maria would not have put on that latch. She'd only turned the door lock and the deadbolt. Otherwise, how would he get in to rescue his family?

❧

TOMAS CLICKED OFF HIS PHONE, glancing up at the window overlooking the warehouse floor. Yes, as promised, there was Mr. Humber watching him.

Knowing what was coming, Tomas drove the loader to its parking spot, shut off the ignition and plugged the machine into the recharger. He did his usual walk-around to ensure that his area was safe and he'd left nothing in the way to harm a co-worker. If he was careful and precise, everything would be all right. They'd all be fine. Squaring his shoulders, he trudged up the stairs to knock on the door to his boss's office.

The muffled "come in" came sooner than Tomas hoped. Mr. Humber stood behind his chair, a tidy pile of cash precisely in the center of his desk blotter. The edges were exactly lined up. An envelope with the name Tomas Rodrigues typed in large block letters was just above the stack of bills.

Unsure whether to attempt an explanation, Tomas waited. So did Mr. Humber.

"You answered the phone."

"Yes, sir." What else could Tomas say?

"You made your choice."

He knew it was inevitable, but he needed this job to support his

family. Struggling to maintain his dignity, Tomas tried. "I felt I had no choice, sir. My wife, she was in danger. *Is* in danger."

"Tomas, we are not unsympathetic to your situation. It's tough. I know that. But we have a business to run here. We need workers we can depend on."

"I understand. And, I am a good worker."

"Yes, you are. No one disputes that, when you're here. But how often do these calls come?"

As Tomas started to answer, Mr. Humber held up his hand.

"No, don't answer. It doesn't matter. At first, we understood. Emergencies happen to us all. We didn't keep track. But then it became a regular thing. Once a month, maybe we could overlook, but this is the third time this week. And the final time."

"I know, sir. We are working hard to solve the problem. I..." As much as he'd like to, Tomas could not promise that it would never happen again. That drew his mind back to what was likely happening with his son and wife at that very minute. He calculated how long it would take him to run home. There were less people on the streets in the middle of the day, so he could be faster than when going home after work.

"I'm sorry, Tomas, but it's over. This has happened too many times for us to keep you. We need workers we can depend on."

Tomas winced. A man was to be trusted. He must live up to his responsibilities. If he took on a commitment, he would fulfill it. And now, he'd let down this company that had taken a chance on him when he first came to this country. He had failed.

Mr. Humber indicated the money on the desk. "Here is your severance pay. It covers the two weeks until the end of this month."

Tomas started to interrupt, but Mr. Humber held up his hand.

"No, this is the way we are doing it. To be blunt, you're fired. But we do recognize the good job you do when you are here, so we're paying you out to the end of the month."

Tomas waited a second then raised his eyes from the money to Mr. Humber's face. "What if...?"

"No, this is final." He softened. "Look, in six months or a year, if

your situation changes considerably, maybe we will talk again, but I'm making no promises. There are other men waiting to take your place who are dependable workers." He watched the way his words affected Tomas. "Go home and attend to your family. We wish you well." He gathered the bills into the envelope and passed it to Tomas.

Neither man offered to shake hands.

CHAPTER 3

$\mathcal{P}$ ulling out his phone to check the time, Tomas hurried out of the place that had given him and his family a good living almost since the day he arrived in this country. He'd advanced in both responsibility and pay through hard work and diligence. He took pride in doing a good job and being known as a stand-up guy. Now, his reputation was shot.

His steps quickened as he realized just how much time had gone by since Maria's call. Was she all right? Where was Manny and what was he doing?

Tomas retrieved the last call on his cell phone and pressed the buttons to check on Maria. No answer. Maybe in his worry, he did something wrong and it wasn't Maria he'd called. He slowed his pace and punched in the numbers one by one. It rang once, twice, four times, and then clicked over to voice mail. At least he heard the sweet voice of his wife, but she didn't pick up. Tomas slowed and checked the number printed on the screen. Yes, it was the right number, of course it was, and he'd heard her answering machine message.

The phone went into his shirt pocket and he ran. Maria would know how worried he'd be and answer the phone if she at all could. Or, she'd call him back if she hadn't gotten to the phone in time.

Tomas took the phone from his pocket to make sure he hadn't accidentally turned it off. Nope, it was on. His pace edged up from a jog to a sprint.

THE PUNCH CAME between his shoulder blades with a force that sent Tomas into a nose dive. His chin hit the sidewalk, followed by his nose and forehead. One hand scraped along the concrete; the other protected the chest pocket that contained his precious cell phone, his only link to what might be happening at home.

The blow stunned Tomas momentarily and he didn't know what had happened. He turned his head to glance behind to see what he'd tripped over. That was when he noticed the pairs of sneaker-clad feet surrounding him by the entrance to the alley.

Tomas braced his hands under his shoulders to push himself to his feet. It didn't work. A foot kept him on the ground, a foot that planted itself almost directly where the punch had landed moments ago. Instead, Tomas raised his head, trying to make eye contact with one of his attackers. His gaze skittered around his limited field of vision to see if help was coming. No one. By late afternoon this street would be teeming with commuters heading home from work, but now, well, it was deserted.

"Dios mio," he muttered. "Que Dios me ayude."

"Huh, there's no help for saps like you," was the only reply Tomas heard.

He tried again. "What do you want?"

"Your money, genius, what do you think?"

"I don't have any money. I just lost my job today. I'm broke."

"Riiight. That's what they all say." His buddies joined his snickers. "Now hand it over."

"I told you. I don't have money. I got fired, I'm telling you. I can give you my boss's name and you can go check. He's only a few blocks away."

"I feel a nap coming on and Joey here, well, he's got a thirst on. We need your cash and anything else interesting from your pockets."

The toe of the sneaker by Tomas's right ear tapped on the sidewalk. Its owner said, "Now we can do this nice and easy or we can do it the hard way."

"What do you mean?"

"Is he dense or what?" His buddies laughed with him. "You can nicely hand us everything that's in your pockets or we can take it from you. I figure we're being pretty big, giving you options here."

"I don't have any money."

"This is getting old. Have at it, guys."

Rough hands turned Tomas to his back. Unprepared for the move, the back of his head cracked on the sidewalk. One grimy hand felt the hard, rectangular shape in his shirt pocket and fished out Tomas's cell phone, waving it in the air.

"No, come on, guys. You gotta give that back to me. My wife, she's hurt. That's the only way I can keep in touch with her and my boy. I need that. She could be bleeding and unconscious. I *need* my phone."

"Ah. For a sob story, that's not bad, but we've heard better, right boys?"

Other hands continued their search through Tomas's pockets. One hand shoved the side of his face into the sidewalk while a booted foot kicked his hips over to follow his face. A fist dug out the envelope that was jammed deep into his back pocket.

There was the sound of paper tearing. "Well, looky, looky what we have here." The guy fanned the bills in the air.

"Please, that's my severance pay. I told you I just got fired. We need that. I have to pay the rent next week and without a job, that's all we have."

"Ah, you're breaking my heart, sucker. Here. The milk of human kindness and all that..." A five dollar bill fluttered to the ground by Tomas's shoulder. With one kick to his back, and one tromp on his hand, they left.

CHAPTER 3

Tomas cradled his hand to his chest. Gently, he shook it. Bruised, but not broken. He used his other hand to help push himself into a sitting position. He rested his elbows on his knees and hung his head.

Now what? What was he going to do? A man's duty was to look after his family and he'd just lost the last bit of money they were likely to see for a while.

His family! How long had it been? He reached for his cell phone and reality flooded in. It was gone. What was he going to do?

As spry as a man at least twice his age, Tomas got to his feet. He held back a groan as he flexed his shoulder muscles and resumed his journey home. His urgency hurried his steps into a lumbering jog.

At the apartment door, Tomas realized with relief that the punks had not taken his keys. Thank God he kept just the two keys on a ring and they'd sunk deep into the corner of his front pocket. What if they'd taken his keys and he couldn't get inside to Maria and Manny? What if they'd found out where his family lived and paid a visit when he was not there to protect them?

Protect them. Yeah, right. A fine job he'd done of protecting himself. But what could he have done, he wondered, as he used the handrail to pull himself up the three flights of stairs to their apartment.

As he reached the top floor, all was quiet. There was no knot of fellow tenants huddled outside their door listening to the sounds of battle within. Once, elderly Mrs. Weymouth had even called the police.

Instead, all was silent. At least the door was shut.

It took only a few tries for Tomas' fingers to fit the key into the lock and turn the mechanism the correct way. As silently as he could, Tomas swung open the door just enough to get his head in. Carnage. Carnage and silence.

With a sweaty hand against the door, he pushed, still gently enough to make room for his head and shoulders. Not a sound. He entered fully, shutting the door behind him, all the while his gaze taking in the state of his apartment, the apartment his Maria tried to keep so beautifully.

His eyes landed on the couch and on Maria. There she was, her head draped over the arm of the overstuffed Goodwill find. Was she...? No, there was the rise and fall of her chest. These episodes with Manny left her so exhausted. But, her face. One eye was swelling shut. The trickle of blood over her eyebrow had slowed and was now drying in blobs and runs. Her cheek bone was swollen and he knew from experience that it would soon turn a plethora of rainbow colors. Oh, his poor, beautiful wife. She'd been hurt. Their son, the child she raised so lovingly, had hurt his mother. Again.

Manny! Where was he? Stepping farther into the room, he scanned the apartment. The space was small - a living room and kitchenette spot all in one, beside a galley kitchen just wide enough to allow two people to pass if they were back to back. Maybe Manny was in the over-size storage closet that housed the mattress where he slept.

Tomas started down the short hallway and there he was. Manny was asleep on the floor in front of the bathroom door. Drying tear tracks and mucous streaked his face. There was blood on some fingertips and bruising on his knuckles. One side of the bathroom door jamb was off, with its tip stuck into the drywall beside the doorway. Tomas cringed. He'd have to patch the sheet rock and somehow find paint exactly the right shade to match the wall, so the landlord would never know that their son had made a hole in the wall. *Another* hole in the wall. The jamb looked to be in one piece, so replacing that would be easier.

The open bathroom door allowed him to see the order and tidiness inside, telling him that Manny had not gotten to his mom while she hid, bracing herself against the door. Thank God. His Maria's injuries could have been much worse if the door had not held or if Maria had not braced herself sufficiently to keep the door closed against their son's attack.

It looked like Manny had exhausted himself and fallen asleep. When things had been silent long enough, Maria would have opened the door just a crack and peeked out, ready to slam it shut if Manny launched himself at her. Tomas winced at the thought. To think that a boy, *his* boy would hurt his mama. No child ever had a mama as good as his Maria. Where did Tomas go so very wrong to raise a son who could harm a woman, let alone his own mother?

Unwilling to wake Manny and risk an episode erupting again, Tomas tiptoed past. He noticed that the child was covered with a blanket. Ah, Maria. After being hurt and terrified by their son, she still looked out for him.

Gently, he leaned over the couch and pressed his lips to her uninjured cheek. She awoke with a start, hands up to protect herself, fear evident in her widened eyes, her mouth open to shriek.

"Sh, sh, querida." He placed a gentle finger over her lips. "It's all right. You're safe now. I'm home."

Maria raised herself up on one elbow. "Manny?" she asked. She tried to look over her husband's shoulder.

"He's fine. He's asleep on the floor in front of the bathroom."

"Ohhhh." Maria sank back onto the couch and closed her eyes. A tear trickled down her cheek. "I'm sorry about the mess, Tomas. I'll work on that in just a bit. I was so tired by the time Manny stopped that I needed to lay down for a minute."

"I know, I know. Sh. Stay where you are. We'll clean up together in

a little while. Right now, I just want to know that you're all right."
Maria moved over to make room on the couch for her husband. They
cuddled together, relishing this quiet oasis in the turmoil their lives
had become.

For a time, all was silent, and then Tomas asked, "We should talk
about it. Can you tell me what happened?"

CHAPTER 4

Maria's muscles spasmed in defensive mode.

"Sh, it's okay querida. I'm right here and Manny's still asleep. Tell me what went on."

"I'm so sorry. I didn't see it coming at all this time. I don't know what I did to set him off. I thought we were having a good morning. I was drinking coffee and reading a letter from my madre. Manny was at the table with me, eating cereal - dry, the way he likes it. He was picking up each piece with his fingers and seemed to be enjoying it. Then he stuck a piece in his ear - you know how he does that. I held his head, trying to get it out of his ear. Manny kept twisting his head and pulling away from me. He grabbed a spoon and started banging it on the table and hollering while rubbing the side of his head. He flipped over his cereal bowl, spilling it, which made him even madder. I couldn't figure out what was wrong.

"Then he yanked open the refrigerator door and started throwing things onto the floor. He grabbed the milk and tried to put it on the table. It landed partly on his overturned bowl and spilled. I caught the carton pretty quickly and set it down. I got a cloth and started cleaning up the mess. I kept telling Manny that it was all right."

Tomas nodded. Such incidents were not unusual.

"And then he ran to the cupboard, but tripped over some of the fridge stuff that he'd thrown on the floor. He bumped his head on the table leg and started yelling even more. Before I could get to him, he made it to the cupboard and got out the cereal. When I saw that he was heading back to the table, I righted his bowl and got ready to pour in the milk for him. That seemed to be what he wanted because once I poured from the box, he climbed back onto his chair.

"I thought the trouble was all over. He'd wanted milk with his cereal but didn't know how to tell me that. As he began eating, I put things back in the fridge and started cleaning up the mess." She looked up at her husband. "I'm sorry the place is still such a disaster."

Tomas pulled his arms more tightly around his wife and kissed her forehead just to the left of the rising bruise. "What happened then?"

"Manny took only a couple bites, and then got madder than ever. He threw his cereal bowl across the room, and his spoon. He yelled, and then he looked at me. Tomas, I know that look; I've seen it before. I braced myself like you told me to and got on the opposite side of the table. Still, this time that didn't help. He launched himself across the table at me. It happened so fast that I couldn't get out of the way. Plus I was worried that he'd fall and hurt himself. Falling on me would hurt him less than falling from that height onto the floor."

"Oh, my dear, I'm sorry I was not here for you."

Maria placed one palm along Tomas's cheek. "You were off making a living for us. It's my job to look after our home and child while you are out supporting us."

With Maria's words memories of that morning flooded back - the shame of being fired, then the indignities of being robbed. How would he tell this lovely woman who was doing so much for their son that he had lost his job? There would be time for that later. Now, he must be there for Maria. "Did he hurt you?"

"Oh, not so badly; I reacted quicker today. Honest, Tomas, I'm all right. It only bled for a while and the bruising, well, we know that that will go down. We do *not* need to go to the doctor or hospital this time. And, I think Manny is all right, although we should look at his hands. He pounded so hard and so long on the bathroom door."

"How did the two of you get from the kitchen table to the bathroom?"

Maria hung her head. "I ran." She met her husband's eyes. "I tried, really I did. I tried to talk to him. I tried to figure out what was wrong. I tried reasoning with him but he was just so mad. He kept hitting me and hitting me and yelling and punching, and then he tried picking up things off the floor to hit me with. I remembered what you said, how if Manny knocked me out, who would be here to look after him and what harm could he do to himself? So, I tried to get away from him and as soon as I could, I ran to the bathroom.

"Oh, did that make him mad. Remember the last time I did that? When he found that he could not get to me? Well, this time I think it was even worse because he remembered, I think. He used his fists on the door. It was so loud and so hard and the door actually moved when he pounded it. I was afraid that he was going to bust it open. He tried. He was so strong and he was furious with me.

"We need to check his nails; he may have hurt them. He tried to tear the jamb off the door to get in. He tried biting at the door knob when hitting it didn't work. I heard some splintering when he was kicking the door. That's when I called you. Sorry Tomas, but I thought the door was going to give and then what would I have done? I know that your boss does not like it when I call you at work but I didn't know what else to do. It felt like I was trying to block the door for hours."

"Querida, it is fine. You did exactly the right thing. We'll be okay."

Their conversation was interrupted by the sounds of blankets and clothing shifting against the hardwood floor by the bathroom.

Maria tensed and listened. The blankets settled down again. "Tomas, I am sorry to be such a poor mother to our son. I love him, but honestly, I wish he would stay asleep a bit longer. I don't feel ready to deal with him quite yet. Do you understand what I mean?"

"Yes, my Maria, me, too. I feel exactly the same way. Our Manny, he has become a difficult boy to live with. I do not know what we have done wrong. He has been a different child ever since he came into our lives, not what I imagined when we were expecting our baby."

"I am ashamed to say that sometimes I watch out the window and see the other kids there playing, or walking to school. They are the same age as our Manny or even younger. Yet, they talk. They can go outside and play. They go to school." Sadly, she added, "And maybe love their mamas. Maybe they don't beat them."

Tomas pulled back to look into his wife's eyes. He framed her face with his hands. "Maria, you are the best mother I know - wife and mother. Manny loves you, I know he does. We have some good times, don't we?"

Maria nodded, with some reluctance.

"Yes, we do. Our boy is not always like this." Although, it seems to be happening more and more often, Tomas thought.

They heard the sounds of Manny getting to his feet.

"Manny, my man, come and see your tata."

When Manny reached the couch, Tomas lifted him up to sit between his parents. Maria put her arms around him and their son nestled into her embrace. His warm, relaxed body fit snugly. Maria thought that anyone entering the apartment now would think they were the perfect family. But they weren't, she knew. Did other families hide such sad secrets as theirs?

MARIA MOVED her hands down her son's arms. Gently, she picked up one hand and inspected it, then the other. Discoloration was beginning and those knuckles had to hurt. But from experience, she and Tomas had learned that Manny seemed to have a high tolerance for such pain. One of Maria's fears was that Manny would seriously hurt himself one day without his parents even knowing that it had happened. He didn't cry with pain. He didn't talk to them. So, after each such episode, Maria tried to inspect her son's body just to make sure he was all right. Physically. Secretly, she worried that something else might be wrong with her young one, something somewhere people could not see. Somewhere inside was something that could send her sweet boy on rampages.

TAKING advantage of the mellow moment, Tomas relaxed with his little family. Why could not life stay just like this?

Manny squirmed and his parents released him from their arms. He started across the floor, almost sliding in the puddle of milk.

When Maria made to get up to clear away the mess, Tomas tightened his arm around her. "Soon. Soon we'll get up and start cleaning. But let's just rest here quietly for a few minutes. Manny seems okay now."

Indeed, he did. Looking at their beautiful child, you would never believe the tempest that had been Manny earlier that morning. It was always that way. He'd seem fine, then there would be a huge meltdown, then he'd fall asleep. When he awoke, it was for Manny as if nothing untoward had happened. But these episodes left his parents drained.

"Maria, I have to know. Did Mr. Toolan come? Did anyone call him or the police this time?" Mr. Toolan was the building's caretaker. Although initially patient once he realized that although he was nine years old, Manny did not yet talk, Mr. Toolan's tolerance wore thin with repairing the damage the child caused to the apartment. Months ago he had stopped fixing the things Manny broke; making it clear that the damages were the tenants' responsibility and Tomas must both pay for the materials and fix the damages himself.

"No. At least, I don't think so. I did not hear any knocking on the door or any yelling, but it was hard to hear above Manny's noise."

"Maybe none of the neighbors were home and there was no note on the door when I came in, so we're probably safe this time."

Maria snuggled back into her husband's embrace. Tomas hated to break this calm mood, but he had to tell her what had happened that morning.

~

MANNY NAVIGATED the obstacles safely to where his blocks lived on the floor. That was *their* spot; they must remain exactly there or the world as they knew it would come to an end. Maria only ever washed the floor under them when they were positive Manny was asleep. She and Tomas would memorize the position of the blocks, and then replace them exactly as they had been. From bitter experience, they'd learned just how precise their son's memory was. He could tell if an angle or a distance was even slightly off.

The blocks went tumbling as Manny knocked them over, only to begin his endless game again. As he picked up one to join the growing stack, his gaze caught the sun coming in through the window. Dust motes danced in the air. Soon, Manny's fingers joined in the waltz, moving and swaying in the glittering dust specks. He stood, his body swaying to music that only he could hear.

"There goes our maestro," said Maria.

"At least he's quiet about it." Tomas's smile left his face. "Maria, there's something I have to tell you. I have bad news."

Maria examined her husband's face and noticed, really noticed for the first time the bruising. "Tomas, what happened? Did I black out and Manny hurt you?" Her fingers gently, so gently traced the discoloration on his forehead.

"No, it was not Manny. He was sleeping when I came in. This is worse."

Watching their son's graceful movements of hand patterns in the sun, he continued. "I lost my job. Mr. Humber heard the phone ring and fired me. He said it was one too many times."

Tears slid down Maria's face. "Oh, Tomas, I'm so sorry. So, so sorry. I should never have called you. I should be able to handle Manny by myself."

"No, querida. You did exactly the right thing. That was our plan, remember? Manny could seriously hurt you or hurt himself. He's big now, too strong for you when he gets like that. You were supposed to call me."

"But what will we do now?"

Tomas sighed. "Mr. Humber gave me two weeks' pay. Firing me was not just because of today - it's been coming for a while. He had an envelope of cash all ready with my name on it, as if he was just waiting for the moment to come."

"At least we're okay for a while then. We can pay the rent when it's due next week."

"No, we can't." Tomas didn't know which was the more shameful part to recount - the fact that he'd been fired from a good job or the fact that he'd then lost the last of their money. "On the way home I was mugged." At Maria's intake of breath, he was quick to reassure her. "I'm fine. I got a bit of bruising but they didn't really hurt me." On his other side, out of Maria's sight, he tried flexing the hand that had been stepped on. "I told them I had no money but they searched my pockets anyway and found the envelope with my severance pay. They took it - all of it except for this." He pulled out the rumpled five dollar bill, staring as he folded it over and over in his hands.

Maria turned and wrapped her arms around Tomas's neck. "As long as you're safe, we'll be all right. You'll think of something. It's just money. What would Manny and I have done if we'd lost you?"

Indeed, what *would* they do, wondered Tomas.

CHAPTER 5

$\mathcal{F}$aint humming sounds came from near the window. This was Manny at his happiest. How could he go from pure, destructive rage, to being a cherub inside of an hour? His tantrums left his parents drained and tense and waiting for the next eruption, but they seemed to leave Manny relaxed and peaceful.

Although they didn't talk about it, Maria and Tomas each watched their son as they cleaned up the mess. Thank goodness Maria had moved their plates and glasses to the top cupboard shelf, making them harder for Manny to reach. They were down to just two plates, four glasses and three mugs; the rest had been smashed in previous episodes of Manny's anger. It would be harder to serve soup now that their son had broken their last bowl.

They worked quietly, or as quietly as a person could sweep up bits of broken glass and crockery. As soon as most of the shards were secured in the trash, Tomas grabbed his meager tool kit to see what he could do to repair the bathroom door. This time it was doubtful he could hide the damage from the caretaker's eyes.

At first, he tapped timidly with his hammer as he repositioned the door jamb, nervous that the sound of pounding might distract his son from the sun beams and start him up again. But Manny was so

engrossed in a world only he understood that he did not flinch at the
increasingly firm hits of metal on nail, or give any indication that he
even heard what his dad was doing. In fact, it was like he was the only
person in the room - possibly in the world, Tomas thought sadly.
What would it be like to have a little boy who would run over
excitedly whenever he saw his dad bring out the tool kit? He chided
himself for wishing for something that might never be. He loved his
boy, loved him exactly as he was.

As it tends to do, the sun moved in the sky. Tomas and Maria
braced for another explosion. Sometimes, if Manny was not ready to
move on to the next thing, losing his sun beams drove him
inconsolably mad. This time though, they dodged a bullet and Manny
left the window before the sun did. He wandered the room aimlessly.
His parents watched him with uneasy eyes.

They couldn't just sit here, waiting for the other shoe to drop.
Tomas needed to make plans; he needed a job. And, he needed to
make things better for his family. Maybe he couldn't give them money
right now, but perhaps he could do something to wipe that anxious
look from his wife's beautiful eyes.

Before he broached his idea, Maria stood and held out a hand to
him. "Come with me, love. I have something to show you."

Tomas let her lead him the few feet into the galley kitchen. Maria
reached above the sink and took down the sugar container stashed at
the back of the cupboard. It was covered with a thin film of dust;
neither he nor Maria took sugar in their coffee so it seldom saw the
light of day.

"Here," Maria said. "It's a surprise for you."

Tomas removed the small lid and inside was an assorted collection
of bills. They were mostly small bills, but real bills, cash, nevertheless.

"Where'd you get this?" he asked.

Smiling, Maria explained. "I saved it, bit by bit. You sometimes
give me too much money for groceries Tomas, so I save what we don't

use. It's good to have some savings, no? I don't know how much there is, but maybe it will help."

Looking closer, Tomas saw that there was more money in here than at first glance. The bills were folded small and tight, allowing many more than you'd think would fit into that one, little sugar bowl.

"How should we celebrate?"

Maria watched their son. "Dare we?"

CHAPTER 6

"*L*et's go for a walk." Tomas knew that his wife had been cooped up in the apartment for far too long. When Manny was younger, she used to take him out often, but as he'd grown bigger and stronger and more unpredictable, it was no longer safe for her to go out alone with him.

Maria's face lit up, but then caution crept into her expression. "Are you sure?"

They both turned to look at Manny who was sitting on the floor spinning pot lids. "There are two of us. How bad could it be?" Tomas grinned at his wife. Yes, they both knew just how bad things could be.

"Why not? Do you want to tell him or should I?"

GETTING him out of the house was easier than anticipated. Sometimes it went well, other times an abrupt change in routine was just not worth the effort. Manny was particularly sunny and cooperative right now.

Although dust motes were invisible outside, Manny still turned his face up to the sun's warmth. Fall was here and there would not be too many more days like this.

Tomas and Maria strolled along, careful where they placed their feet. From past experience they knew that the sound of crunching leaves sent their son off the deep end. They did not need to tell Manny; his footsteps automatically missed the fallen leaves, even when he seemed to be peering upward toward the sun's rays.

They walked the same route every time - had to. Any deviation bothered Manny so badly. When he was younger, he'd throw himself to the sidewalk, flailing and wailing if they tried taking a different street. Tomas would simply hoist the screaming child over his shoulder and they'd head home. Now that Manny had some size on him, this was harder to do. Plus, strangers looked at a tantruming two-year-old in one way, but a half grown child doing the same thing was an entirely different matter.

Once, when struggling with Manny in front of a house, the people inside called the police. The woman told the emergency dispatcher that a man and woman were trying to snatch a child. Two police cars roared up, lights and sirens flashing and parked in a V formation half on the sidewalk, surrounding Tomas and his family. At the noise and sudden appearance of armed men in uniform, Manny stopped his struggling and instead clung to his father desperately. Tomas stopped grappling with his son to hold him close, rubbing his back and saying soothing words over and over. It was Maria who tried to explain to the cops. When one policeman then another tried to get some sense out of Manny, they realized something was different with the child and backed off. After asking for identification, the procession followed the threesome home, one policeman coming up the stairs to check that all was as Maria said it was. As Tomas set Manny on his feet inside the door of their apartment, Manny ran for the couch, picked up the remote, and settled in to watch TV with the waiting blanket wrapped around him. He looked like a boy who had done those exact actions over and over again and the officer left satisfied that the couple was not abducting some strange child.

~

BUT, today the sun was shining, and Manny seemed content. It would be a good walk, one of those they'd look back on and remember fondly. One without incident.

~

THEIR NEIGHBORHOOD WAS SHODDY-GENTRIFIED, an area not quite in transition. It was a mixture of single family, white-picket, small homes, older, low-rise apartment buildings and shops with owner-apartments overhead.

Although it never appeared that Manny paid any attention to where they were, he knew. Oh, he knew. The last few times they'd headed down this street, he had been transfixed by the display in the bakery shop window. Each time, it seemed harder and harder to get him to move on. Now, what to do, what to do? Should they continue on this street, knowing that they'd soon have to pass the bakery, or attempt to turn left at the next corner, *not* a move on their regular route?

At the corner, Tomas angled his body to make the turn. Immediately, Manny's arms came up at his sides, his hands elevated and that keening noise started in the back on his throat. His parents knew what this meant. Manny might not speak, but he communicated, for sure. At least, sometimes.

"All right, son. I understand. Papa made a mistake is all. We'll go straight." He pointed down the way they had originally been heading. Manny's noises stopped and he walked ahead of his parents on what he knew was the correct path. Tomas grabbed Maria's hand and gave it a squeeze. "Just hang loose and it'll be all right. Show him we're relaxed and we'll walk right on by."

Nope, not gonna happen. That's what Manny's body language said. He planted himself firmly in front of the bakery window and pressed his nose to the glass. He made little noises but not the ominous ones that forewarned of an eruption. These were more like happy noises, contented ones. If all their son wanted was a quick peek in a bakery window, then Tomas and Maria would oblige.

How long can you wait, nonchalantly regarding bakery goodies? Is it seconds or minutes before passersby notice or the bakery owner comes out to ask what you're doing?

Now Manny's hand rose and his fingers planted themselves on the window. His other hand came out of his mouth to join its partner. The pristine window became smeared.

"Okay, bud, it's time to get moving," said Tomas.

No reaction.

"Manny, let's go."

Still nothing. It was as if his son had not heard.

Maria scanned the street, checking to see how many people might witness the oncoming tsunami. Luckily, the street was deserted except for one couple, hand in hand, closing in on them fast. "Tomas..." Maria warned, with a nod toward the man and woman.

"I know, babe." He tried to put an arm around his son's shoulder to steer him away. Manny would have none of it and squirmed back into position. A glance over his shoulder showed Tomas that they were no longer alone.

"Hi," the woman said. Without waiting for a reply, she walked up to stand beside Manny. "Like what you see?" she asked him.

Manny ignored her. She didn't seem to notice or care.

"See that one over there?" The woman pointed in the direction of the cream puffs. "That's my favorite."

Still no reaction from Manny.

"But, when I'm feeling in the mood for chocolate, those éclairs really do it for me." She pointed to a lower shelf.

This time, Manny angled his body in the direction of her point.

The woman turned to survey Manny. "Let me see, young man. I wonder which one you like best. Hmmm. I have a nephew about your age and he, well he likes them all, but he especially likes the gingerbread cookies - the ones over there."

This time, there was no mistaking that Manny was paying attention. His eyes lit up and his fist banged on the glass.

The woman laughed. "Yeah, me, too. I get excited just thinking about eating one. It's just as well, since I'm here so often."

Tomas's distress was increasing by the minute. He gave a polite smile to the talkative woman then said, "We must be on our way. Manny, come." He hoped that he'd inserted just the right amount of assertiveness in his tone - just enough to get his son to comply but not enough to make him freak out. Tomas tried to wedge his body in between his son and woman. In case Manny pitched a fit, a stranger should not get caught in the cross-fire.

The woman was not good at taking a hint. Instead, she turned to Maria. "Are you his mom? Did you know that this bakery gives a free cookie to every child who comes in?"

As this sentence started to unfold and Maria could see where it was going, she tried to frantically signal the woman to stop, to be quiet, to run away, anything other than say what she just said.

Manny heard. Of course he did and oh, he definitely understood what he heard. He turned to his parents with a grin. One hand remained flattened on the window and the other commenced flapping in the wind. His body tensed and his heels left the ground, then lowered and repeated the exercise over and over.

Maria and Tomas exchanged deer-in-the-headlight glances. What to do now?

PAYING no heed to the body language of the parents and surprisingly, ignoring Manny's posturing, the strange woman bent, nudged Manny's shoulder with her own, then headed towards the door of the bakery. Looking at him over her shoulder, she said, "Come on. There's a cookie with your name on it in here." She held the door as Manny walked toward her.

So far, her companion had hung back but now he stepped forward. Addressing the parents, he said, "She's quite a force, but I can assure you, she's harmless. Honest. And, she likes kids. For some reason, she's good with them and they don't mind that she just blunders on in."

Tomas and Maria were like stone statuaries planted on the sidewalk, watching in horror as their son, their unpredictable son entered the bakery with a stranger. Shaking himself out of the reverie, Tomas glanced inside and cringed. The place was filled with tiny, glass tables and curved, wrought iron chairs. Visions of the shattered crockery in their apartment filled his mind.

The gentleman was still holding open the door. "You'd better go in," he said. "You might want to rescue your son from Ellie before she talks his ear off."

Inside, Ellie and Manny were crouched together in front of the counter display cabinet. Three of Manny's fingers were back inside his mouth, a good sign that meant he was relaxed. He always pulled them out before letting out a shriek. Ellie was pointing and naming each different piece of confectionary and Manny appeared to be paying rapt attention. Ellie finished with, "So which do you want?"

Maria stepped forward. "I'm so sorry. Everything looks good, but I forgot my purse at home. We'll have to come back another time when we have our money."

How brave his wife was, thought Tomas. She knew that denying Manny a sweet would bring about a doozy of a scene and still she waded in. "Querida, I think I have a few dollars in my pocket. We can get a small something for our little man." He'd pocketed a bit of money from the sugar bowl, just for emergencies.

The woman interrupted. "Oh, it's free for kids."

Maria looked from her to the man, checking if this could possibly be true.

The woman ignored Maria, her attention on the child as she followed Manny's gaze. "Got it. I see which one you want. Hang on a sec and I'll be right back." She lifted up the part of the counter that separated the customers from the staff and walked through, plunking the board back down in its place. She went to the sink to wash her hands, and then donned an apron.

As if it needed an explanation, the man pointed at her said, "That's Ellie. She owns the place.|"

Ducking down behind the counter to reach for Manny's treat, Ellie raised one hand in a sort-of wave.

The man raised his eyebrows heaven-ward then stuck out his hand. "I'm Rob. I try to follow along after Ellie and keep her out of trouble."

Tomas shook his hand and introduced himself and Maria. He indicated his son. "That's Manny. He, ah, doesn't talk much."

Maria looked at him. Much?

Meanwhile, Ellie came through another door with a plate in hand. A paper doily on the plate held a gingerbread man whose arms and legs splayed off the edges. Manny followed her with his eyes, bouncing on his toes. Ellie waved an arm. "Come one. Have a seat here." She placed the goodie on one of those fragile, glass tables and held out a chair for Manny.

He clambered onto the chair, bracing himself on the table for balance. The table started to tip, but Ellie caught it with her hip as if she did it every day. She slid Manny's chair closer to the table and placed a napkin beside his plate.

Maria followed along, worried. "Maybe he should not sit there. The table looks breakable and he can be, well..."

"Oh, nonsense," Ellie interrupted. "He's fine. My nephew sits at these tables all the time and if they survive Kyle, they'll survive any kid. Besides, they're safety glass. Come on and have a seat."

When Tomas and Maria warily sat down, they kept their eyes glued on their son, ready to spring into action if needed.

"What'll you have?"

Tomas realized that Ellie was repeating her question. "Just a cup of coffee for me please, and for you, Maria?"

When Ellie brought them their drinks, she included a malted milkshake for Manny. With a straw, in a tall, heavy, crystal glass. Manny's hands reached for it. Before either of his parents could make the save, Ellie swooped in. Prepared, she grabbed it and put it back in the center of the table. "Nope, that's for after your cookie. You finish everything on your plate, and then call me. I'll show you how to drink this." She paused and looked Manny in the eye sternly. "Got it?"

Manny's eyes drifted from Ellie to the milkshake then back again. He held her gaze.

Ellie gave him a thumbs up and smiled. "Remember; let me know when you're ready." Then, she was off.

Both Maria and Tomas sat with their hands on the table, at the ready to grab if things started to go flying. Neither took their eyes off their son or that milkshake.

Maria whispered, "A *glass* container? What was she thinking?"

THE BELL over the bakery door chimed. Running feet and a boisterous, high pitched voice announced, "Munchkin's here!"

Wiping her hands on her apron, Ellie hustled from behind the counter to catch the eight year old boy who sprang at her. "Hello, Munchkin. Just what did you do with my nephew, Kyle? I was hoping he'd drop in."

"I *am* Kyle, silly. You just call me Munchkin sometimes."

"Oh, you're so right. You do resemble Kyle. Did you bring your mom and dad along or did you drive over by yourself?"

Seriously, Kyle regarded her. "I don't know how to drive, you know. I don't think dad would let me try. The rule is that you have to be sixteen before you can get a license."

"You're right. I was just kidding you."

Kyle looked puzzled at that, but went to the pastry counter to peruse today's selections.

Giving Kyle's parents, Ben and Mel a hug, Ellie asked, "The usual?" Without waiting for an answer, she walked away to inspect goodies with Kyle.

Mel and Ben shrugged and shared a smile. They hung up their coats and sat at a round table with seating for three. After great deliberation, with input from both Ellie and Rob, Kyle slow-stepped his way to his parents table carefully carrying his precious cargo of his usual plate of giant gingerbread cookie. No matter how many times he visited the bakery and no matter how much deliberation went into his choice, he ended up choosing the same selection he had made the very first time he came here.

Rob brought over their drink orders, with a latte for himself. He drew up another chair to join them. "Well," he informed Ben, "your sister's done it again." He nodded to the trio at the other table that included a boy solemnly nibbling off the leg of a gingerbread man. "They were standing outside, minding their own business, when Ellie charmed the kid, leaving the parents no choice but to follow." He stirred some golden, coconut sugar into his latte. "Mel, you might be interested in the boy...." He left the rest of the words unspoken, but Mel got his meaning. They'd been teachers in the same school for several years now and had similar affinities to kids who learned differently.

Peace reigned as everyone applied themselves to their food or drink. The sounds of teaspoons clinking against cups and low murmurs of conversation floated around the bakery. The smells of cinnamon and fresh yeast breads overlaid that of the slow-roasted brisket that would yield sandwich meat for the supper crowd.

A howl broke the calm. Then the sound of a chair rocking on its legs.

"No, Manny, shh, shh, shh." Tomas was instantly behind his son, trying to prevent him from rocking the chair either over or into the glass table that was oh so close to his son's face. "Manny, stop. No!"

And, Ellie was there. "Well, I told you to let me know when you finished your cookie, didn't I? I neglected to tell you how to notify me though. Never mind. Your way worked just fine and here I am." She looked at Tomas and asked, "May I?" With her hip, she gently pushed the father out of her way.

"Here's the way we do it, Manny," she said as she leaned over him.

At her action, Maria drew in her breath. How many times had she been head-butted by her son when she got too close like that? She looked to Tomas and saw that he had the same fear.

But, Ellie carried on regardless of their looks or sputtered words.

"Now, we move your plate out of the way and bring the milkshake closer."

When Manny reached for it, she said sharply, "No, not yet."

There was a sharp intake of breath from Maria. You did *not* say no to Manny when there was something he wanted.

"Now," continued Ellie. "We scoot your chair back a bit like this to give you room. Now, hold out your hands." When Manny did as she asked, she placed the milkshake on his lap and folded his hands around it. "You have to use both hands, like this, or it will spill." She came around to the side of his chair and squatted down. "Here. I'll move the straw the first time for you, and then you have to do it yourself next time." She positioned it next to his bent head. "Now, sip."

Manny didn't move his head. He stared at the frothy drink with longing.

Ellie glanced at his parents. "Does he know how to use a straw?"

"I don't think he's ever tried one before."

Rob, watching the interchange had hustled over the counter and returned with a second straw for Ellie. She smiled her thanks at him. What a guy.

Ellie inserted her straw into the milkshake, took a big breath in, then, with exaggerated cheeks sucked in a big gulp of malted milk. Swallowing, she smiled at Manny. "Now, you try."

It took a few seconds of chasing the straw around with his lips, but Manny got the hang of it. His first gulp was so big, that the malt spilled out of his lips. Ellie grabbed a couple napkins and mopped him up. "My fault. I should not have shown you how to take such a big gulp. Try again, taking just a small sip this time." She imitated taking a little drink through a straw.

This time Manny got it right and the look on his face told the story of what he thought of his first malted shake. Ellie removed her straw and, wrapping it in a napkin, took it with her. "Enjoy!"

Peace settled again into the bakery, with the addition of slurping and sucking sounds from time to time from Manny's straw. Maria and Tomas allowed themselves to relax. Maybe this would turn out all right after all.

CHAPTER 7

The last possible dregs of the malted milkshake slurped into the straw. Manny stared into his drink. He used his fingers to swirl the straw into the remaining bubbles, then brought the straw to his mouth to lick the final drips.

Maria and Tomas braced. Now what? It had been a nice outing so far, but how would they get their son out of the bakery without a scene. The place was filling up with people.

Manny looked around the place. His gaze didn't linger on the other customers, but flitted from object to object. His head turned faster as he took in the bustle and confusion around him. He began to rock. A low sound started in his throat and his hands rose from his sides to wave in the air.

Tomas and Maria froze, knowing what was coming, but helpless to stop it in this room full of strangers. Manny's low keening rose in pitch and volume becoming audible to everyone in the room.

Mel appeared at their table, kneeling on the floor beside Manny. She put a device on the table in front of him and rubbed her finger over the glass surface. The picture of the bakery that appeared snagged Manny's attention. Although he continued to rock, the noises stopped.

Quietly she spoke. "See, this is the bakery. You're at a table just like this one. Here's the way it goes." She looked up at Maria and smiled, then touched the right side of the screen. A view from the door appeared. "You come in the bakery. Then you walk up to the counter. You place your order." With each sentence, another picture showed on the screen, illustrating her words. "Then you sit at your table. Someone brings you something to eat or something to drink. You sit quietly and eat nicely. Then, when you are all finished, it's time to go. You get off your chair and walk out the door with your mom or dad. You can wave good-bye to Ellie. You will come back another time."

Manny watched the whole thing intently. By the time it was over, the rocking had ceased. The screen went blank and Manny got down from his chair. He held out his hand to his dad, and then walked to the door. Outside, he stood beside his astonished father, while his mama talked to the woman, the woman who had saved them.

Maria asked her, "What did you do?"

"Sorry. Are you upset with me for interfering?" asked Mel.

"Oh, no. We are grateful. We had no idea how we were going to get our son out of the bakery without a big ruckus." Then, Maria thought about what she'd said. "I mean, our Manny, he's a good boy, but sometimes he gets upset when things don't go the way he thinks they should."

"I understand."

"You do? I'm not sure. You see, our Manny is different. I noticed your little boy. Manny is not like him." The sadness was clear in her voice.

"I'm not so sure that our boys are that different. We have our challenges with Kyle as well."

Maria forced a smile. "Kids will be kids." She held out her hand. "Thank you for your help."

"Wait! Don't you want to know what I showed your boy?"

"Si. I noticed pictures on your computer and he paid attention to them."

"That's called a <u>social story</u>. A woman named <u>Carol Gray</u> came up with the idea and it really works. I made that one for our son. He used to have trouble transitioning from one thing to another. If he liked something, he never wanted it to end. And, he really likes this bakery. So, we made a story for him. We'd read it before we'd come to the bakery and again when we got here. Then, I'd pull it out just before we were ready to leave. It worked and he got better. We don't need to use that particular one any more, but it's reassuring to have it just in case."

"We don't have a fancy computer at our house, but thank you for using yours with us."

"You don't need a computer, fancy or otherwise. You can write out a story on a piece of paper," Mel explained.

"Our Manny, he does not read."

"But he looks at pictures, I noticed. You don't need words to write a story. You can draw stick figures to illustrate what's going to happen. Just tell him what the figures mean and what is expected of him."

Maria looked skeptical that something so simple sounding could make any difference.

Mel tried to explain. "Kids with autism take in things that they see easier than things that they hear. That's why a story like this helps - the child does not just listen to what we're saying but they see the visual of what is happening."

"Kids with autism? Oh, that's not our Manny."

It was Mel's turn to look skeptical. She raised one eyebrow. "Where does he go to school?"

"He is not in school. He stays home with us."

"May I ask why?"

Maria thought it was quite obvious. "He is not like other children. He gets upset and he, well, he doesn't talk."

"Yes. So?"

Maria backed up half a step. "Pardon me?"

"I understand that he does not speak and that he might get upset, but that does not mean he can't go to school."

"No. We keep ourselves to ourselves. Manny is our responsibility. We will look after him."

"But..."

"Thank you again for your help. I must go now." And Maria left to join her husband and son to finish their walk.

MARIA WAS quiet on the way home. Tomas thought she was just tired after the emotional turmoil of the day.

After supper, Manny dug out his favorite movie, passed it to his papa and took his mother by the hand to the couch. As he settled himself, Tomas inserted the movie and started it playing. Manny waited until Tomas sat beside him, and then shifted his dad's arm so that it was around his shoulder. Manny snuggled in between his parents, holding Maria's hand, stroking it and playing with her fingers. Part way through the movie, Manny shifted so that his head was in his mom's lap and his legs sprawled across Tomas' thighs. He moved Maria's hand onto his head so that she could stroke his hair the way he liked. Soon his breathing deepened and he slept, resting contentedly in the arms of the people who loved and cared for him. For a time, his parents enjoyed the peace of normal family life and the beauty of their trusting, slumbering child.

After Tomas carried Manny to bed, Maria let loose with the thoughts that had been plaguing her since their outing that afternoon. "Do you know what that woman said to me?"

"Which woman? You mean the one who showed that story to Manny?"

"Yes. She asked me why our son was not in school. After I told her that he did not talk and that he got upset, she still asked why."

Tomas slanted his head at his wife. "She seemed like an intelligent enough woman. Why would she even think that a child like Manny could be in school? She must have misunderstood you."

"I don't think so." A few minutes later, she added, "Maybe things are different here."

They watched television for a while. When the next advertisement came on, Maria said, "It's a <u>social story</u>. That's what she called the pictures she showed Manny about the bakery. She said she made that for their son."

"I noticed their boy. He did not seem like our hijo."

"She called her boy Kyle. She said he used to have trouble with transitions and didn't want to leave the bakery because he liked it there. They would show him the story and he got better at leaving when they wanted him to go."

"Well, it sure helped us out today. I was in a panic about how we were going to get him out of there. All those glass tables...."

Maria hardly took in the show they were watching, her mind churning over some of the things Mel had said. "She told me that kids with autism like to look more than listen, or something like that."

"Autism?"

"That's what she said."

"Wonder why she'd say the word autism if you were talking about Manny, or about her son?"

CHAPTER 8

"*D*are we try it again?" It was another gorgeous fall day, with crisp air, yet the sun still held hope in its rays. It was not a day for remaining cooped up in an apartment.

"Do you mean going for a walk or to the bakery?"

Tomas grinned. "Are you up for trying both?"

So far, it had been a good day - a good few days, actually. There had been no major upsets. Of course, there had been many smaller ones but they'd been able to head those off before any true damage was done. Maybe it helped to have both of his parents home as they could tag off with each other when one started to lose patience with their son's demands.

THE WALK to the bakery was a tad more challenging this week as more and more leaves littered the walkways. But, Tomas and Maria were diligent; they knew what would happen if they scrunched just one too many times. Manny remained a step ahead; he knew the route.

At the bakery, he again plastered his hands all over the glass. Maria murmured that the next time, she'd bring a cloth and cleaner and wipe her son's handprints off the glass. They gave Manny ample looking time, before holding open the door.

"Now remember son, you have to be good. Be quiet and treat the things in here gently. And, no running..." Tomas spoke to the air. Manny was already inside, scrunching down in front of the display counter.

"Well, look who's here." Ellie came around the counter to greet them. "Give me five, man." She held up her hand expectantly to Manny. He turned from the goodies, regarding her with solemn eyes. "Don't you know how to give five?" She waited. "Here," she said, grabbing for Manny's forearm.

There was an intake of breath from Maria. Tomas leaned forward, ready to intervene before his son could hurt this friendly, naive woman. Manny did *not* like to be touched, especially when he wasn't expecting it.

"Like this," Ellie continued. "See?" She raised Manny's palm to meet hers in a gentle slap. "Now, try it again." She raised her palm, holding it there expectantly. Manny did not move. Ellie raised one finger in the air and said, "Hold that thought."

"Kyle, buddy," she called. "Get over here. I need your help for a demonstration." When her nephew jogged over, she said to him, "Give me five."

With a grin, Kyle gave her hand an exuberant slap. Then he turned to the rest of the group. "Anyone else?" he asked with a raised palm.

"Sure, I'll do it," said Tomas. They slapped hands.

"And, me," said Maria. Gently, she met Kyle's hand.

Kyle turned to Manny with his hand raised. "Give me five," he said.

Manny lifted his hand to meet Kyle's. The touch was fleeting, but it happened.

Ellie looked over at her brother and sister-in-law and winked. Mel gave her a thumbs up.

Maria and Tomas stared at each other and at their son. What had just happened here?

Kyle gave a "See ya," and returned to his gingerbread cookie.

ELLIE HELPED Manny make his choice and then served him his gingerbread cookie. As they sipped their warm, fragrant drinks, Tomas and Maria commented on the way Ellie hustled around. While chatting non-stop to customers, she flew between tables, loading used dishes into a plastic tub, taking payments at the till and placing orders. Her pace made Maria uneasy. When Ellie paused to see if they wanted anything more, Tomas commented on how busy she seemed.

"I'm short-staffed. Sal's off with sick kids, so I'm bussing tables as well as the rest. Sal has five kids and they get this flu one after the other, so it looks like she'll be gone for a while. Oh well, it's not forever." Then, with a smile, she was off.

Maria watched a bit longer, then stood. "I can't stand it any longer," she told her husband. "I'm going to give her a hand. I'm just sitting here when I could at least be clearing tables for her. She's been good to Manny."

It took a while before Ellie noticed Maria quietly working away. She did notice though that she didn't need to run quite as much. Then Maria was beside her. "Where can I wash these dishes?" she asked.

"Oh, you don't' need to do that. Thank you so much for bussing tables though. Here, I'll take that." she reached for the tub of dirty dishes.

"No, I don't mind. You've been good to my Manny and he likes it here. I can help you."

"Well, if you're sure. I can definitely use the help. The dishwasher's through here."

MARIA DIDN'T NOTICE the passage of time. It was good to feel useful and the hustle and bustle of the bakery was exciting. She felt like she was contributing and part of the team.

Carrying the dishes into the kitchen, Maria stopped short when she spied a man working at the counter. Walking with a full tub of clattering dishes, she had not entered the room silently, but he showed no sign that he sensed her presence. He gave off such an aura of concentration that she was hesitant to interrupt him. The man neither turned nor spoke. Maria hesitated, unsure if she should intrude. As she turned to back out of the room, his voice startled her.

"Well, are you going to stand there all day holding that tub?" he asked, without looking at her.

"Um, no. Ah, Ellie said the dishwasher was in here."

The man pointed to his left at the stainless steel door built into the lower cupboard. When Maria still didn't move, he looked over his shoulder at her. With no expression on his face, he returned to the dough he was punching.

Maria waited a few moments more, then eased out of the room. She saw Ellie polishing the glass of the display cabinet. "Ellie," she said. "There's a man in the kitchen."

"Oh, yeah. That's Jeff, Mel's brother. He's our main cook here. Could you smell the sauerbraten he's had roasting all day?"

Sauerbraten? "Um, he looks pretty intent on what he's doing and I didn't want to disturb him."

Ellie straightened. "That's Jeff doing his thing. When he cooks, he gets into the zone and blocks out everything else. Come on. I'll introduce you."

When Maria hesitated, Ellie linked arms with her and strode towards the kitchen.

"Jeff," she called. No response. "Jeff," she said a little louder. "Turn around a minute, please."

Jeff turned, or half-turned, his hands buried in dough.

"Jeff, I'd like you to meet Maria. She's helping us out here today. Maria, this is Jeff."

Jeff held out his sticky, dough *encrusted* hand for Maria to shake.

When Maria hesitated, he asked, "Do you have problems with social skills? Did anyone teach you that you're supposed to shake hands when you're introduced to someone?"

Maria attempted to shuffle the tub of dirty dishes so that she could get a hand free.

"Nope, not this time, Jeff," said Ellie. There are exceptions to that rule and when your hands are full of streusel dough is one of the exceptions."

Jeff shrugged. "Well, suit yourself." Then he turned back to his work.

Maria's glance at Ellie questioned if she was expected to remain in the same room as this man.

"Dishwasher's right over there." Ellie pointed.

Over his shoulder, Jeff said, "I already showed her where it was."

With a squeeze of Maria's shoulder and a hasty, "Thanks", Ellie returned to the front of the bakery.

Tentatively, Maria approached the counter and set down her load. Casting glances at Jeff, she inspected the dishwasher then began the loading process. She tried to handle the crockery without any clanking so as not to disturb Jeff's concentration. Eventually she gave up on stealth when she noticed that it didn't matter anyway. Jeff's focus was intent and he seemed able to ignore her presence. She found it spooky, although not unlike being home with Manny sometimes. He, too, could concentrate so hard on what he was doing that he paid no heed to his mama, no matter what she said or did. Actually, once she got past the worry that she needed to make polite conversation to this strange man, it was soothing to be able to work in silence with her own thoughts.

When she returned to the dining room for another load of soiled dishes, Ellie explained that Jeff mainly stayed back in the kitchen, cooking. He'd occasionally step out front, especially if one of the computers was down and his skills were needed to get it operational again. But, he said he preferred to make his own chaos and liked the freedom to create food without the bother of other people.

Meanwhile, Manny was getting restless. His gingerbread man was devoured and the last slurps of his malted milkshake were history. Tomas was surprised things had remained calm for this long. When was the last time he'd been able to enjoy two peaceful cups of coffee in a row. He'd thought he was pushing his luck when he accepted a refill from Ellie, but Manny had been content.

Now, Manny's right and left legs alternately came up and toed the underside of the glass table. Tomas placed his elbows on either side of his cup to weigh the glass top down, just in case. Then, Manny started rocking - gently at first then harder as two of his chair legs left the floor at a time.

Tomas swivelled his head around the room. Where was Maria? They could not stay here much longer. And, would they be able to leave as easily as they did yesterday?

No Maria still, but instead, Ellie came by. "It's getting close to dinner time," she said. "Would Manny like to come see the options?"

Tomas quickly shook his head. Although their budget might allow them to splurge on coffee for he and Maria and a milkshake for Manny, eating supper out would take far too much of their cash. "No, thanks. We really should be going."

"I'd really like you to stay and have supper with me. My treat. I don't know how else to repay Maria for helping out here. I already offered to pay her for her time, but she declined."

"You were good to us and to our Manny, so Maria wanted to give a hand. She saw how hard you were working. She's good at these things is my Maria. In the village where we are from, people help each other."

"Well, she saved my life this afternoon all right. Now please, let me serve you a meal. I guarantee it will be delicious. Jeff is a skilled chef." She held out her hand to Manny. "Come. I'll show you your choices."

Before Tomas could formulate a polite refusal, Manny had jumped down from his chair, taken Ellie's hand and was standing on a stool to see the top of the counter. Ellie kept one steadying hand on his shoulder and one at the small of his back. And, Manny let her.

Soon he returned, walking oh so carefully heel to toe, both hands tightly strangling a china plate, balancing steaming sauerbraten on a fresh ciabatta bun with a side of mixed green salad. Behind him came Ellie with two identical plates. With a flourish, she set the two on their table and rescued the third from Manny's hands. "Your son chose the meal for you. He wanted all of you to have the same thing." Turning to look at his son, she said, "Oh, we forgot the cutlery. Do you remember where they are?" Without answering, Manny took off for the counter where three sets of utensils were wrapped snuggly in cloth napkins.

Tomas rose from his chair. "We don't let Manny handle knives or forks. They're too sharp."

"Looks like he's managing this time." And, sure enough, he did. "I'll go round up Maria to join you. And, thanks for loaning her to me. I can't tell you how much her help meant today. You know, if she ever has some spare time and wants a job, we'll take her. Any hours she could give us would be welcomed."

Maria flushed as she took her seat, head down and beaming at the praise. "It was nothing. I enjoyed it."

Tomas did not look as pleased. "Maria has all she can do being a wife and mother to us. We don't leave her much free time on her hands. We need her at home."

TOMAS WAS UP EARLY, consuming too strong, too hot coffee and perusing the help wanted section of the paper. The pickings were pitiful. The last three warehouse jobs he'd called said they only took applications in person and to come over and get in line. He'd done just that. For one, the highest paying job, the line of hopefuls snaked outside the building and around the corner. That was over a hundred guys vying for two openings. Nonetheless, Tomas had waited, shuffling ahead a few steps every ten minutes or so. When he worked his way up to the building's entrance, the shout passed down the line, "Position's filled. Head on home the rest of you."

The next two he tried for didn't have quite as much competition, but he had no luck with either. There were guys with more experience who got the jobs.

Today, Tomas' plan was to find the best possibility and be there long before the doors even opened so he'd be first in line. But the choices in the paper were meagre.

Maria was so hopeful for him. She just knew that a fine man like Tomas would find a grand job; anyone could see what a good worker he'd be. Although she said all the right things and smiled for him at the right times, he had caught her counting the money in the sugar bowl when she thought he wasn't looking.

What kind of a man would let his wife worry like that? What kind of a man did not look after his family?

But today, today would be different. It had to be.

AND, it was different. The position at the janitorial supply warehouse did not have a line-up of would-be employees. Tomas was pleased that he seemed to be the first person there. Mr. Blakely interviewed him, then said that they had never given a man a job without first trying him out. That gave them a chance to see what they think of Tomas and Tomas time to see if this was the kind of place he'd like to work. They considered this time as training, sort of a non-paying apprenticeship. Tomas wouldn't mind working for a day on a volunteer basis, so they could get an idea of just what kind of worker he was, would he? Look at it as an investment in his future, in a company where there was room to grow.

Certainly, Tomas wouldn't mind, especially when they said it might be just for the morning.

So, he moved crates, unpacked boxes and shelved items. When a truck drove in for a load of certain cleaning supplies, Tomas loaded the cartons. It was warm in the warehouse, without the type of ventilation Tomas had been used to at Mr. Humber's shop. But, despite the sweat streaking down his face and the way his shirt clung to his aching muscles, Tomas did his best to demonstrate his worthiness.

Lunch time came and went. No one came near Tomas to check on his work or see how he was doing. No one told him where the break room was or what hours he'd have free for lunch. So, Tomas worked on. And on.

Finally, at four-thirty, Tomas noticed some of the lights in the office out front going out. Then the warehouse lights dimmed. He waited a few minutes, but none came back on. In fact, the hallway lights turned off. Quietly, Tomas walked in that direction, searching for Mr. Blakely or anyone to tell him what was going on. The front offices were dim with only the setting sun's light from the grimy outside windows. He did not see a soul. Hesitating, he climbed the stairs to the office where he'd been interviewed so many hours ago. Timidly, he knocked on the closed door. A muffled, "Yeah" sounded.

Tomas turned the knob and poked just his head through. "Excuse me, Mr. Blakely," he said. "I wondered what hours I should be keeping. The lights went out and I don't see anyone else around."

"Well, Tomas, is it? Around here we're not partial to clock watchers. This is generally quitting time, as long as the work is done. Did you finish putting away all the load that came in on that semi-trailer?"

"Almost all of it, sir."

"So, you're telling me the job's not done yet?"

"Not quite. I worked non-stop sir, as quickly as I could."

"Hmmm." Blakely frowned and waited.

"But, I can finish up before I leave today."

"Good, good. That will be good." He returned to his paperwork.

"Excuse me, but should I return tomorrow? Did you find my work satisfactory during this training?"

"Let's say that the verdict is still out. How be we give it another try tomorrow and see what we think of each other?"

"All right. I'll just finish up that load then be here early tomorrow morning."

IT HAD BEEN dark when Tomas reached home the day before. All that physical work, plus not eating all day left him famished. He was never so grateful to tuck into a plate of Maria's tamales. He was tired, but confident that he'd found a job. He explained to Maria about the temporary volunteering that would soon turn into a permanent job, one with room for advancement.

The next day he left home even earlier, determined to make a good impression. When he arrived, the doors were locked. Almost fifty minutes later, Mr. Blakely arrived and slapped Tomas on the back. "Good to see an eager worker," he said, ushering Tomas back toward the warehouse. "I see you brought your lunch today. That's the sign of a man prepared to work."

Today progressed much as had the day before, but this time with two semi-trucks unloading and even more boxes to be stored away, all the while filling orders for arriving pickup trucks. If this was a fall day and it was this hot in the warehouse, Tomas wondered fleetingly what it would be like in the summer? Still, he worked as if his life depended on it. Periodically he'd glance around, expecting to see an observer or even partially hidden cameras so someone could check on the quality of his work. Certainly, no one came into the warehouse to watch him. Just as he'd think he had made it through the list of tasks, he'd notice another one tacked to the hanging clip board.

Tomas put even more effort into the job today than the day before. This would be his last trial day. Tonight, he and Maria would celebrate his new job.

When the lights turned off this time, Tomas inspected the tidy warehouse one last time and was satisfied with the job he'd done. He climbed the stairs to knock on the door to Mr. Blakely's office. "Excuse me, sir," he said. "I've finished for the day. Are there some papers you would like me to sign to get onto the payroll?"

"I was meaning to come down and talk to you about that today, but as you can see, this mound of paper has kept me at it all day."

Tomas waited expectantly.

"It looks like you picked up your pace a trifle today."

"Yes, sir."

"We're still not sure you have what it takes to make it in our organization. Our standards are high."

Tomas frowned.

"Let's say we give it one more day, and then we'll have a deal. Shake on it?"

Tomas hesitated then came forward and shook the man's hand.

"So, we'll see you then tomorrow morning?"

Tomas nodded.

"You know, I think you just might make it here."

WITH THOSE ENCOURAGING WORDS, Tomas walked home with a lighter heart. Tomorrow. Just one more day, then he'd have a job and be able to provide once more for his family. What was two days' work for free compared to a permanent position and room for advancement?

"MARIA, let's celebrate. After supper we'll head to the bakery for a treat."

"Do you think we should? You haven't been paid yet, and we've never taken Manny there in the evening."

"Querida, you worry too much. I have proven my worth as a worker to Mr. Blakely. What would his warehouse look like without me? He has no one else to do the job."

"But, Manny..."

"Manny's been an angel in that bakery every single time. He likes it there."

"And, they like him."

"Yes, they do seem to like our son. Let's go."

IT WAS dusk as they donned their jackets. Manny was fine until they reached the outside door of the apartment and he saw that it was no longer bright daylight. Manny only left the house during the day. He balked, not responding to their, "Come on son", or the pull of his hand. His shoulders reached for his ears, one hand rose to his side and the other fingers entered his mouth. A low, keening sound began. Tomas' voice rose as he sternly ordered his son outside.

"Wait," said Maria. "Let me try something." She rummaged in her purse until she found a scrap of paper and a pen. "Manny, we're going to the bakery. See?" She drew a sketch of three stick figures walking - one smaller, holding the hands of the two larger figures on either side of him. "This is you, me and papa walking down the sidewalk to the bakery." Then she drew the same stick figures sitting at a small table. "We'll have a snack there and something to drink and then come home."

Manny's flapping hand stilled and he used it to hold the paper with his mother. When he stared intently at the drawings, Maria recited the whole story again, and then waited. It took seconds, seconds in which Maria feared that her son was mulling it over, trying to decide whether or not to comply, and then he stepped through the door his father was holding and waited.

Now what, thought Maria? Manny remained in that fixed position, hands out to either side, staring straight ahead. "What? What is it, Manny?" Part of her wondered why she even asked. Never, not even once in his whole nine years had Manny ever given her a response. She walked in front of her son and turned to look at him.

Manny turned his face toward her and held out his hand. She took it. He remained fixed with his other empty hand stuck out. His dad stepped forward and took that outstretched hand. As soon as Tomas completed his grasp, Manny's footsteps started down the sidewalk toward the bakery, leaving his parents staring at each other over his head. "It worked!" mouthed Maria.

INDEED, it did and the visit went smoothly. Ellie was still on duty, which made Maria wonder at the hours she kept. As always, Ellie dropped what she was doing to high-five Manny, and then inspect the display case with him. Despite the array of goodies, Manny always chose the same thing.

But tonight, with the job prospect securely in his pocket, Tomas wanted to splurge on a treat for himself and his wife as well. Maria chose a cream puff bulging with piped whipping cream and topped with snowy confectioners' sugar. Tomas had a gooey chocolate éclair.

Without many customers in the bakery, Ellie pulled up a chair to join them.

"This pastry is muy fantastico," Maria told her.

"Thanks. I make them myself. And how's yours?" She turned to Tomas.

"Heavenly. I feel like a kid who wants to lick his fingers."

"Have at it. I certainly do," Ellie said.

Maria asked, "Aren't you going to have one?"

Ellie waved her hand. "No. Definitely not. Do you have any idea how many of those I've consumed in my life? Or how I so do not enjoy them anymore after baking them every day? They're favorites with my customers, but to be honest, I'm sick of them."

"You should taste some of my wife's churros," said Tomas. "There are none better."

"Churros? I'm not sure I've ever had one of those."

"They're a piped, fried dough laced with anise and vanilla and sprinkled with cinnamon and sugar," explained Maria. "They are common where we come from."

"Do you have any? I wouldn't mind tasting one some time."

"The next time I make a batch, we will bring you some."

Ellie paused a minute, then turned to look at both Tomas and Maria. Then, she addressed Maria. "You know, variety is good and it's nice to change it up. This bakery was floundering before Jeff came on board. He brought in new ideas and new dishes. Now, our food menu changes daily, but our pastries remain about the same.

"Do you think you might ever consider making some churros that I could sell here? I could front you the initial ingredients, then you could work out what you'd need for your time and labor."

Tomas had stiffened. "My wife cooks for our family and

sometimes for our friends. She has her hands full looking after her family."

"Tomas, this I could do at home. It would not take away from the time I give to you and to Manny. I like baking, you know that. But we can only eat so much, the three of us." Her eyes pleaded with her husband, trying to see past his stern look. "Why don't we try just one batch? I could make it and you bring it to Ellie to see what she thinks."

"We'll see," was his reply.

Maria gave Ellie a tentative smile.

"Well, I'd sure appreciate it if you could see your way through to help me out," replied Ellie, catching Maria's eye.

Without many customers in the bakery, Ellie pulled up a chair to join them.

"This pastry is just delectable," Maria told her.

"Thanks. I make them myself. And how's your's?" She turned to Tomas.

"Heavenly. I feel like a kid who wants to lick his fingers."

"Have at it. I certainly do," Ellie said.

Maria asked, "Aren't you going to have one?"

Ellie waved her hand. "No. Definitely not. Do you have any idea how many of those I've consumed in my life? Or how I so do not enjoy them anymore after baking them every day? They're favorites with my customers, but to be honest, I'm sick of them."

"You should taste some of my wife's churros," said Tomas. "There are none better."

"Churros? I'm not sure I've ever had one of those."

"They're a piped, fried dough laced with anise and vanilla and sprinkled with cinnamon and sugar," explained Maria. "They are common where we come from."

"Do you have any? I wouldn't mind tasting one some time."

"The next time I make a batch, we will bring you some."

Ellie paused a minute, then turned to look at both Tomas and Maria. Then, she addressed Maria. "You know, variety is good and it's nice to change it up. This bakery was floundering before Jeff came on board. He brought in new ideas and new dishes. Now, our food menu changes daily, but our pastries remain about the same.

"Do you think you might ever consider making some churros that I could sell here? I could front you the initial ingredients, then you could work out what you'd need for your time and labor."

Tomas had stiffened. "My wife cooks for our family and sometimes for our friends. She has her hands full looking after her family."

"Tomas, this I could do at home. It would not take away from the time I give to you and to Manny. I like baking, you know that. But we can only eat so much, the three of us." Her eyes pleaded with her husband, trying to see past his stern look. "Why don't we try just one batch? I could make it and you bring it to Ellie to see what she thinks."

"We'll see," was his reply.

Maria gave Ellie a tentative smile.

"Well, I'd sure appreciate it if you could see your way through to help me out," replied Ellie, catching Maria's eye.

CHAPTER 9

*C*onfident that he now had the job, Tomas did not set his alarm clock any earlier than he had the day before. Still, he was again the first person to arrive at the warehouse. He pulled the collar of his jacket up against the damp, morning air as he waited, shifting from foot to foot. At the loading dock sat a semi-truck and an impatient driver. Tomas could do nothing but apologize to the trucker; he had no keys to raise the door to help the guy unload.

Mr. Blakely approached on the sidewalk, with his shoulders hunched, eyes on the ground. He jerked his head up at Tomas' greeting, as if startled to see him there. Preoccupied, thought Tomas.

With a nod, Blakely said, "Looks like it's time to get at 'er for another day." He unlocked the door, and then headed up the stairs to his office. Tomas watched his retreating back for a few seconds then headed to the warehouse to fire up the fork lift.

It was a few minutes before one o'clock when Tomas entered the break room to grab a bite of lunch. He stood, his mouth full of sandwich when Mr. Blakely entered, accompanied by another man, of about his age.

"Good to see that you're almost finished your lunch, Tomas. You can pack up your things and be on your way. Your replacement is here now. Wish things could have worked out better."

Tomas' eyebrows lifted and he stared. The new guy didn't meet his eyes. Blakely only held his gaze fleetingly. "You heard me," he said. "Go on, get out of here now. Better luck at your next job."

"Next job? I thought I had this one. Mr. Blakely, this is my third day working for you and I have done everything you asked of me. I know I've done a good job."

"That might be your opinion but I disagree and I'm the boss."

"But you said that the first day was training to see how we liked each other and then you told me to come back. I did." He pointed down the hall. "Go look at the warehouse. I bet it's never been in better shape."

Now Mr. Blakely faced him. "Don't make this any harder on anyone than it has to be. Surely this is not the first job you've been sacked from. Now, go on. Get out. Guys like you are a dime a dozen."

Tomas drew himself up and faced his former employer directly. "I see. I'll go as soon as I get my pay."

"Pay, what pay? You were here as a volunteer trainee and it didn't work out. Get off my premises."

The other gentleman had stood in the background, trying to be invisible. Now, he and Tomas exchanged glances. To Tomas he asked, "Did you agree to volunteer for a day as a trainee?"

"Yes. That was the arrangement."

"And what happened after that?"

"This man," and Tomas pointed at Mr. Blakely, "told me he was unsure of my work and to come back the next day. I worked my butt off, sweat pouring off me all day in that stuffy warehouse and I didn't stop once for a break. I stayed late and finished every item on the task list. And, that was just the first day. The next day I arrived an hour earlier, before the doors were even opened and did the same thing. No one came back to help or to check on me."

The new guy turned to Mr. Blakely. "Is that right? Is that what you plan for my volunteer training day? And the next?"

The guy pivoted to face Tomas. "Hi. I'm Paul." He stuck out his hand. "I've heard of scams like this. Employers too cheap to hire help run these ads to get free labor. Then, before the guy wises up to what's going on, he gets 'fired' and another newbie shows up to do the sweat labor."

"Can they do that?" asked Tomas.

"Not legally. And not morally, but guys like this have no ethics." He took two steps towards the door. "Hey," he said to Tomas. "Can I buy you a coffee?"

"Wait!" said Blakely. You're not leaving, are you? We had a deal. You're starting work for me today."

"As if I'd work for a scum bag like you."

"But who's going to unload the trucks?" Blakely hollered.

Tomas looked over his shoulder and pointed at Blakely. Paul didn't bother turning his head, but gave him the finger over his shoulder. "I know of this coffee shop," he told Tomas. "It's not that far and the food is worth the walk."

∼

Soon, Tomas realized just where his new acquaintance was taking him for coffee. "Do you know Ellie?" he asked.

"Yeah. She went to school with my little sister and I played football with her brother, Ben. Madson's not that big of a place and this bakery has been in their family since I was a kid."

Paul and Tomas walked directly to the counter to place their orders, intent on their conversation. Not until he turned around to find a table did Tomas really look around. His eyes lighted on his family. Maria and Manny shared a small table, Manny intent on dismantling his gingerbread man, Maria reading a book.

Just then Manny raised his head and spied his father. His eyes got large, his mouth opened and a word came out. Just one word, but oh, such a word. One he'd never uttered before. "Papa!"

Maria's head came up. She stared at her son. Did that word come out of his mouth? "What? What, Manny?"

"Papa." He didn't blink. His eyes never left his father's face.

Tomas was frozen. Had his son spoken? Had he said what he thought he'd heard?

Maria turned to follow Manny's gaze and saw her husband staring agape at their son.

"Say it. Say it again," Maria instructed Manny.

Manny began rocking and his attention returned to his cookie.

Tomas slowly approached on wooden legs, his eyes full of wonder. "Maria! Did you hear? Did my Manny call me Papa?"

"I, I think so. He said it twice even. Oh, Tomas!" She leapt up and threw her arms around Tomas's neck, sloshing his coffee onto them both. "Oh, sorry. I'll get a cloth." And, she was gone, leaving Tomas regarding their son with such pride.

He ruffled Manny's hair and gave him a hug. "How is my little man?" This was the typical greeting he gave, never expecting nor ever receiving a response. This time, though, he waited, afraid that if he even moved, the spell would be broken and Manny would retreat to silence. He waited and waited some more. The gingerbread man seemed to hold more interest for Manny than did his father's presence. The moment seemed gone, but both he and Maria had heard that one special word, so it must be true.

Tomas looked around the room to see if anyone else was in awe of the miracle. One person watched and celebrated with him. Mel, the woman who had drawn them that story observed the incident. She knew just what this meant for the parents and more importantly, for Manny. She grinned and gave Tomas a thumbs up. Then, while she held his attention, she pointed to herself, moved her tips of her fingers across the table in a walking motion and then held up her index finger. Tomas nodded his head like a bobble doll.

Maria was back with paper napkins, wiping off her husband and the table, bubbling over with excitement. "He did it! He really did. Manny spoke. Oh, Tomas do you know what this means? Maybe he'll do it more and more. Maybe..."

Tomas hugged her to him and kissed the top of her head. Then he remembered where they were. He'd forgotten himself. He and Maria did not show affection in public; that was for private times. He turned and noticed Paul waiting behind him, blowing on the foam and sipping this latte.

Ellie came by with their pastries and greeted Paul with a kiss on his cheek. "How's it going? How many rug rats do you and Sue have now?"

Paul gave her shoulders a squeeze with his free hand. "Just two and most days they are more than we can handle."

Maria followed this quizzically. And, why was Tomas even here? He was supposed to be at his new job.

"Paul, I'd like you to meet my wife, Maria and my son, Manny." They nodded and smiled at each other. "Let's sit down." He pulled over an empty table to join theirs. "Maria, I have some bad news." He and Paul related the scam that Tomas had fallen into.

Cleaning tables around them, Ellie piped in. "I've heard about that, too."

Jeff's hand was deep in the innards of a computer along the back wall. "The United States Supreme Court in Walling v. Portland Terminal Co. serves as a landmark case on employer treatment of trainees," he informed them. He continued in their silence. "They call it the Walling Factors, the criteria used to determine if a trainee or intern should be paid." Jeff looked up at the group. "You know all this, don't you?"

All four adults shook their heads side to side.

"Basically, if the trainee is gaining the same skills or experience he would at a vocational institute, he can go unpaid because he's not an employee. The training must be for the benefit of the trainee and the trainee can't be taking the job of someone who should be paid for that work."

When his audience continued to stare, he tried to explain more fully. "Look, it's simple. If the training is mainly for the benefit of the trainee, he does not have to get paid. If the work done is mainly for the benefit of the employer, then the trainee needs to be paid. Look it up in the Department of Labor website." Jeff returned to beefing up the RAM in the aging computer.

"What kind of job are you looking for?" Tomas asked Paul.

"I used to be a realtor, but you know what's happened to that business since the recession. The company I worked for folded. I'm good with my hands and have a strong back, so I'll try just about anything."

"That's about where I'm at, too," Tomas said.

"Why don't we help each other out? Most places are looking to hire more than one guy." He walked a few steps over to nab a discarded newspaper. Thumbing through until he found the classified section, he gave half to Tomas. "Why don't we both look and let the other know when we see something promising. Here." He scrawled his phone number on a napkin and passed it to Tomas. Tomas did the same for him.

They sat back to enjoy their fragrant brews, and eat churros. Churros? Tomas looked at the warm, sweet and spicy cinnamon treat. These tasted just like the churros Maria made.

Maria sat there beaming at him. She nodded. "Yes, I made a batch so Ellie could see what churros are. She ate one, then two and asked if she can serve them to her customers. And, look," she gestured around the room. "Some people even went back for seconds."

"*You* made these?" Paul asked. "My compliments to the chef. Tomas, you're one lucky man."

❧

THEY WATCHED Ellie fly around the room; it was hard to miss her non-stop motion. There were customers standing by the door, waiting for a clean table. Others entered the bakery, but upon seeing a line-up, retreated and walked up the street. The strain on Ellie was obvious.

Maria stood. "Tomas, I have to help her. Will you stay here with Manny for a few minutes?"

"With a boy who calls me Papa? Anytime."

Paul finished his coffee and left for home. He had to meet his kids after school; his wife was working late that week.

Tomas had downed the last of his coffee and finished off Maria's, too. Manny had nothing left to eat or drink and was tiring of playing with his fingers. Tomas glanced around for Maria, who was nowhere to be found.

Ellie noticed him searching and stopped by to explain that his wife was in the kitchen helping put together the calzones for the supper crowd. She searched his face then made a decision. "Tomas, I'm really strapped here as you can see. With Sally out there is just too much work here for Jeff and me to keep up. I have another worker coming in at six o'clock, but until then, do you think there's any chance that Maria could stay and give us a hand? I can't tell you how grateful I'd be. She's such a help and I'm desperate. As you can see, I'm losing customers when I can't keep up and I can't afford to turn away business."

"What does Maria say?"

As he said the words, his wife appeared behind Ellie. "Please, Tomas, I'd like to stay and help Ellie if you think you could handle Manny on your own this afternoon." Her black eyes pleaded with him.

"Is this what you want?"

Maria nodded, her eyes not leaving his.

"You are helping out a friend?"

Again, Maria nodded.

Even a stranger could read the misgivings on Tomas's face. But, it was hard to refuse Maria anything she wanted and she asked for so little.

Reluctantly he gave one nod.

The smile Maria returned made it worth it. He'd do just about anything to have her beam at him that way.

"Please come back and have supper here. It's the least I can do," said Ellie.

Manny, meantime, had lost patience with all the adult talk. He'd sat long enough and roughly pushed his chair away from the table. From long experience, Tomas' and Maria's hands were there to catch the table, just in case. Manny walked to the door. When only his dad followed, he scanned the room for his mother. Tomas opened the door and took Manny's hand. Manny's feet were rooted to the floor.

"Come on, son. Mama's staying here. We'll come back for her later, after we go for a walk and play a bit."

Manny rose to his toes and sucked in a deep breath.

Oh, no, thought Maria. It's going to happen. He's been so good and now they'll never want us back in the bakery again.

The keening sound rose to a shriek. The flapping hands knocked against the closed, glass door.

Then, Mel approached. In her hand was the iPad she'd been working on. "May I?" she asked Tomas, raising her voice to be heard above Manny's wails.

Ashamed to admit he needed a stranger's help managing his son, but remembering the magic she'd worked the last time, he said, "Please. If you can help, go ahead."

Mel knelt on the floor beside Manny, dodging out of the way of his waving arms. She set her iPad on her lap and placed a hand on each of Manny's shoulders. Tomas could see that she was pressing down hard. Harder than he thought she should for a little boy. He was stepping forward to intervene when she spoke to his son.

"See Manny? Here's the story we read last time about the bakery." And she read it to him again. Gradually, the shrieks decreased, the flapping slowed and he came down off his toes. His attention focused on the pictures of the bakery on the iPad. "See? There's you sitting at the table. And there's your mom and your dad. Now, it's time to go.

"But it's different this time. We're changing it a bit. This time, Manny and Papa are going home for a little while. Mama has to stay here and help Ellie. See? Here they are working in the picture. And, here is Manny and Papa going out the door to walk home. In a little while, you and Papa will come back here to get Mama. You'll eat supper together, and then all of you will go home." Her voice dropped on the last words with a tone of finality. She stood. "See you later." Then she turned her back and walked back to her table. She stopped once to wave.

Manny responded to the tug of his father's hand and left the bakery to the words of Tomas. "We'll go home and play with your blocks, then later we'll come back to get Mama. Won't that be fun? You get to go to the bakery twice in one day." Tomas prayed that his words were true and the afternoon would be fun.

CHAPTER 10

*M*el came over to where Maria and Ellie were standing. The tension had not yet left Maria's shoulders but she gave Mel a weak smile.

"Thanks," she said. "Thank you very much. That could have been so much worse. You could not imagine what Manny can be like when he gets going."

"Oh, I have a fair idea," Mel told her with a grin. "I'm in a profession where I can say I've almost seen it all, at least where kids are concerned."

"You're a nurse?"

"No, I'm a teacher."

"She teaches kids with special needs," Ellie explained. "Her specialty is kids with autism."

"I am sure you have never seen a boy like our Manny. He can be a handful." She thought a minute. "Does that always work? I mean that story thing on your iPad?"

"Well, is there anything that works every time with all kids? No, it doesn't work as often as I'd like, but yeah, it often does work. Some kids with autism have a difficult time making sense of the words they hear. If you *show* them what you want them to know, it can make it easier for them to understand. Some of the unwanted behaviors are because the child is anxious and not sure what's coming next or what will be expected of him. Transitions are especially hard for them and a story like this can help."

"We don't have an iPad."

"Doesn't matter. Paper will do just fine."

"I'm not sure why it helped Manny, because he doesn't have autism; I've heard about autism and Manny's not like that. But I'm glad your story worked this time. Thank you again for helping us. You were so kind." With a smile and nod at Mel, Maria picked up the nearby tub and began clearing tables.

Ellie asked Mel, "Why does she say that Manny doesn't have autism?"

⁓

"I SAW WHAT HAPPENED OUT THERE," Jeff told Maria when she came into the kitchen to load the dishwasher. "You should let Mel help you."

"We did. Her story helped Tomas get Manny out of the bakery without a fuss. Or, at least without much of one."

"My sister knows what she's doing. She's really good with kids who have autism."

"Why does everyone assume Manny has autism? My son is not autistic!" Despite her defiant words, Jeff was unruffled.

He continued, "If you want to say so," and turned his attention back to his mixing bowl. A minute passed, and then he thought better of it, but spoke with his back to Maria. "Why do you say he doesn't? It's plain to everyone else that that kid has autism. What do *you* think it is that makes him different?"

"I have heard of autism. Those kids are far, far worse than our Manny. They are in their own world. They just rock and bang their heads. Some never talk. They are hopeless. That is *not* my son."

"Hmm. I think I've seen Manny rock. Does he ever bang his head? And, I haven't exactly noticed him chatting up a storm when he's here. But maybe he saves all his chatter for when he's home. Right?"

Maria could honestly say one thing. "He spoke. Right here in this bakery. He said 'Papa'".

"That's great. It's encouraging. But is that normal for someone his age? You and Tomas acted like it was a big deal, not something that happens every day. I'm not good at reading facial expressions, but I'd say that both of you guys looked shocked."

Maria looked down but had to be honest. Her voice low, she said, "That was the first word he has ever said." Fists gripping both side of the tub, she stared at the assortment of dirty utensils. "We have been terrified that he will never talk. How would he get by if he can't talk? And then, he said 'Papa'. You don't know what that meant to us."

"No," agreed Jeff. "But I might have a better idea of what it meant to Manny."

"I don't understand."

"No, you might not. It's an autism thing."

"I would be happier if you would not talk about autism. That is not Manny."

"Why are you so against your kid having autism?"

"Because then what would happen to him? Now, we have hope but if he had autism we would lose all that." Shaking her head, Maria said, "It cannot be true. What would become of him if ever he had autism?"

"Maybe he'd be a baker or a chef like me."

Ruefully, Maria shook her head. "I have tasted your cooking. That is not something someone with autism could do."

Jeff turned to look at Maria. He waited until she stopped rattling dishes and faced him. "I have autism," he informed her.

THE FISTFUL OF cutlery Maria clutched clattered to the floor. She gaped at Jeff.

"You should close your mouth. That's not a good look on you," Jeff told her.

Maria's bottom teeth came up to join their partners. "What did you say?" she asked.

"You heard me. So from now on, you'd better watch what you say about autism. No slams, no stereotypes and no denying."

"Denying?"

Exasperated, Jeff placed his wrists on his hips, dangling floury hands to the side. "Just why do you think everyone keeps mentioning the word 'autism' in your presence? Or more correctly, in the presence of your son?"

"I don't know. I honestly can't figure that out. No one has ever said that before we started coming to this bakery."

"Maybe that's because we're like family here and in our family, we understand about autism. Ellie's boyfriend Rob teaches kids who have autism. My sister Mel is likely the best autism specialist you're ever going to find. Her son Kyle has autism. I have autism. Maybe that's why we talk about it and why we can spot it in someone else, too. Like your son."

Maria loaded the dishwasher in silence. Wiping her hands on her apron, she shook her head and told Jeff, "No, I don't think so."

Before Jeff could reply, she grabbed her tub and left the kitchen.

TWENTY MINUTES LATER, Maria returned to the kitchen. Rather than heading straight to the dishwasher as was her habit, she perched the overflowing tub on the counter and watched Jeff baste the garlic chicken breasts. "Can I ask you some questions?"

"Don't you mean, 'may'?"

"Pardon?"

"It's 'May I ask some questions', not 'can'. Of course, you physically *can*, but I think you were asking for my permission. Yes."

Maria, slightly baffled by Jeff's grammar lesson, asked, "Yes?"

"Aren't you going to ask me something?"

"You say you have autism?" Her voice rose at the end of the sentence.

"We're already established that."

"But you're not like those people I've seen in movies."

"When you've met one person with autism, you've met one person with autism. Look, everyone's different, has different skills, abilities and challenges. Are *you* the same as every other Spanish speaking women?"

"Of course not."

"How do you think it's any different with people who have autism? Look, I have autism. It's one of my characteristics, just like one of yours is that you have dark hair. Autism does not define who I am, it's just a part of me and might affect how I think and do some things."

Maria had to mull this over, so she worked at cleaning up the countertop. "And you think this is why my Manny can't talk?"

"You'll have to ask Mel. She knows more about that kind of stuff. This is what she studied in her Master's degree."

Quietly, Maria asked, "What makes you think Manny has autism?"

"Have you seen how he rocks when he gets upset or bored? Flaps his hands? The sounds he made when he had to leave the bakery with just his dad because that was unexpected? And, what does he do every time he comes here? He spends ages looking over his choices, then picks exactly the same treat each time."

"I didn't know you were watching."

"I may hang out in the back cooking, but I see what goes on in here.

Jeff continued. "I bet he doesn't like it when you change things up. Like he always leaves the bakery with both his parents. Do you have to walk the same route to get here each time?'

"Yes, we do. You should see what happens if we try to take another way."

"Yep, I get it. Been there, done that."

"But now you change things yourself. You cook something different every day."

"I'm older now and I've learned strategies that help me. I can't say that I don't prefer things to be the same way, but I'm way more adaptable now than when I was a kid."

"Do you think Manny will become that way, too?" There was so much hope in Maria's voice.

"Depends. He'll learn some things on his own, but he'll need help."

"What kind of help?"

"The kind experienced people can give; people like Mel."

"Do you think my Manny could ever be like you?"

"Nope. Those would be pretty big shoes to fill, don't you think?" Jeff grinned at her. "Manny can find his own way and he might just surprise you."

THEY WORKED IN SILENCE, Maria washing and putting away the cooking pots Jeff had just finished with. Then, she helped him prepare the panini sandwiches, ready for grilling for the customers' orders during the supper time rush.

Washing his hands, Jeff asked over his shoulder, "So, why isn't Manny in school?"

CHAPTER 11

For Maria, the afternoon had flown by. This was work? Why did people grumble about having to go to work? For her, this was fun. She had not realized how much it would mean to her to get out of the house, to meet other people and to not worry intensely about Manny every second of her waking day. Several times she felt nasty twinges of guilt when it crossed her mind to wonder how Tomas was doing with Manny. He was a good dad and they'd be fine, but he was not used to being home alone with their son. Still, if Manny got violent, Tomas was better able to subdue him than was she.

The way people complimented her on her work warmed Maria's heart. This was basically the sort of housework she did at home daily, but here, well, here people appreciated it. She felt bad for letting that thought enter her mind. Of course, Tomas appreciated what a good homemaker she was, but somehow, here it was different. She was part of a team working to make the bakery a success. It was exciting and fun. Was it all right though to be enjoying herself so much when her family was at home?

The next time the bell over the door tinkled, Maria was too busy to look up. But, as she turned with a loaded tub of used dishes, a whirlwind grabbed her around the waist and squeezed. Tomas was there to catch the tub and steady his wife with one hand. Maria looked into the smiling face of her son. Manny. She grabbed him tightly and rocked back and forth with him before giving him a kiss on his dishevelled head. She rubbed their noses together and he giggled. Actually giggled. Wow. This was the sweet Manny, the memories they held dear to their hearts against the times when things got tough.

If this was the kind of greeting she got after not seeing her son for a few hours, she should go out to work more often.

IT WAS a few minutes before six o'clock. Maria was secretly just a little disappointment to see her replacement enter the bakery, wash her hands and don her apron. With a flourish, Ellie brought over three steaming plates of dinner for Maria, Tomas and Manny. She told Manny to come find her after he'd finished eating everything on his child's size plate and she'd help him pick out his treat. Manny's eyes followed her retreating back. Sensing this, Ellie turned around and pointed to his plate. "*First*, eat that. *Then*, the treat." Her tone brooked no argument. She shared a wink with Mel. "See," she mouthed to her sister-in-law, "I can learn." The first....then.... strategy was one she'd seen Mel use often with Kyle.

It worked with Manny, at least this time. Deep in conversation, his parents had not noticed that he'd cleaned his plate. What drew their attention was the rocking of the table as Manny pushed back to get down from his chair and go find Ellie. The room was small enough and his parents were now not as apprehensive about this behavior so they let him go, confident that Ellie would pay attention to Manny, as promised. Even that worked well.

Mel gathered up her used dishes and took them to the bucket on the counter. Returning, she pulled up a chair at Maria and Tomas' table and asked, "Mind if I join you for a minute?"

Maria and Tomas shuffled their chairs over to make room. Once settled, Mel took out her iPad. "Would you like me to leave this here with you in case you need to go over the story before you leave? It's getting dark outside."

Perplexed, Tomas said, "We know the way and there are streetlights."

Mel laughed. "I wasn't thinking about you. No, it's Manny here I wondered about. It's different walking home in the dark from what he's used to in the daylight. If he's only ever been here in the day, you may find that he's startled to see that it's dark outside."

She had a point. They'd never walked with their son after dark.

"Thanks, but no. We've never ran one of those things."

"I'll show you. It's simple. You press this round button at the side to turn it on. Then this bar and the words 'Slide to Unlock' appear. Take your finger and slide in the direction of the arrow." She passed it over to Tomas.

"Which finger?" he asked.

"Doesn't matter. Just not the one covered in jelly, please, although the screen's washable. Kids use these all the time."

Tomas slid the white bar and a picture of Manny in the bakery appeared. He held it up for his son to see. "See Manny? It's you."

Manny continued to crunch one leg of his gingerbread man, but watched the screen.

Mel leaned over. "Now, see this arrow in the middle of the picture? Touch it with your finger and the story will start."

Sure enough, it did. They all sat and listened and watched as the story of Manny at the bakery unfolded.

"Thank you very much. It's an amazing machine," said Maria. "Manny likes his story."

Mel stood up. "When you're done with the iPad, just leave it behind the counter. Ellie will get it to me or Ben when we're back tomorrow or the next day."

"Don't you need it tonight?"

"Nah, we're good. Keep it with you just in case you need it." She circled the table to where Manny was digging off the gingerbread man's icing eyes. "High five, buddy." She held up her hand.

Maria and Tomas watched, fearful that their son was going to be rude to this helpful woman. But Mel just crouched there patiently, her eyes not leaving Manny's face.

Tomas made to reach for Manny's arm to guide his hand to meet Mel's. Mel turned her face just a fraction towards Tomas and shook her head no.

Another few seconds passed. Manny did not look directly at Mel, but raised his hand to lightly tap hers.

Mel grinned. "Good boy." To his parents, "See you guys."

IT WAS a few minutes before six o'clock. Maria was secretly just a little disappointed to see her replacement enter the bakery, wash her hands and don her apron. With a flourish, Ellie brought over three steaming plates of dinner for Maria, Tomas and Manny. She told Manny to come find her after he'd finished eating everything on his child's size plate and she'd help him pick out his treat. Manny's eyes followed her retreating back. Sensing this, Ellie turned around and pointed to his plate. "*First*, eat that. *Then*, the treat." Her tone brooked no argument. She shared a wink with Mel. "See," she mouthed to her sister-in-law, "I can learn." The first....then.... strategy was one she'd seen Mel use often with Kyle.

It worked with Manny, at least this time. Deep in conversation, his parents had not noticed that he'd cleaned his plate. What drew their attention was the rocking of the table as Manny pushed back to get down from his chair and go find Ellie. The room was small enough and his parents were now not as apprehensive about this behavior so they let him go, confident that Ellie would pay attention to Manny, as promised. Even that worked well.

Mel gathered up her used dishes and took them to the bucket on the counter. Returning, she pulled up a chair at Maria's and Tomas' table and asked, "Mind if I join you for a minute?"

Maria and Tomas shuffled their chairs over to make room. Once settled, Mel took out her iPad. "Would you like me to leave this here with you in case you need to go over the story before you leave? It's getting dark outside."

Perplexed, Tomas said, "We know the way and there are streetlights."

Mel laughed. "I wasn't thinking about you. No, it's Manny here I wondered about. It's different walking home in the dark from what he's used to in the daylight. If he's only ever been here in the day, you may find that he's startled to see that it's dark outside."

She had a point. They'd never walked with their son after dark.

"Thanks, but no. We've never ran one of those things."

"I'll show you. It's simple. You press this round button at the side to turn it on. Then this bar and the words 'Slide to Unlock' appear. Take your finger and slide in the direction of the arrow." She passed it over to Tomas.

"Which finger?" he asked.

"Doesn't matter. Just not the one covered in jelly, please, although the screen's washable. Kids use these all the time."

As Maria helped their son into his chair, Tomas slid the white bar and a picture of Manny in the bakery appeared. He held it up for his son to see. "See Manny? It's you."

Manny continued to crunch one leg of his gingerbread man, but watched the screen.

Mel leaned over. "Now, see this arrow in the middle of the picture? Touch it with your finger and the story will start."

Sure enough, it did. They all sat and listened and watched as the story of Manny at the bakery unfolded.

"Thank you very much. It's an amazing machine," said Maria. "Manny likes his story."

Mel stood up. "When you're done with the iPad, just leave it behind the counter. Ellie will get it to me or Ben when we're back tomorrow or the next day."

"Don't you need it tonight?"

"Nah, we're good. Keep it with you just in case you need it." She circled the table to where Manny was digging off the gingerbread man's icing eyes. "High five, buddy." She held up her hand.

Maria and Tomas watched, fearful that their son was going to be rude to this helpful woman. But Mel just crouched there patiently, her eyes not leaving Manny's face.

Tomas made to reach for Manny's arm to guide his hand to meet Mel's. Mel turned her face just a fraction towards Tomas and shook her head no.

Another few seconds passed. Manny did not look directly at Mel, but raised his hand to lightly tap hers.

Mel grinned. "Good boy." To his parents, "See you guys."

CHAPTER 12

S oon, the gingerbread man was demolished and even the crumbs licked up by damp fingers. Full and satisfied, they got ready to depart. Maria set Mel's iPad behind the counter confident that all was well.

"Don't you need it?" asked Ellie.

"No, we played it for Manny a before he ate his cookie. He liked it. Thank Mel for loaning it to us, please."

TOMAS HELD the door open for his family. Manny, holding his mama's hand went first. Then, he froze. The familiar street looked different. While they ate, a sprinkling of rain had come down, making the asphalt glisten in the street lights. Seen through Manny's eyes, yes things did look different.

But, they'd walked this route many a time, and he'd listened to the story on the iPad. It wasn't like they were asking the little guy to navigate the route home on his own.

Tomas used the hand not holding the door to push between his son's shoulder blades.

Manny's little sneakers were Crazy-Glued to the ground.

"Come on, son. It's time to go." Tomas pushed harder while Maria gave a gentle tug to his hand.

Nope, Manny was having none of it.

Sighing, Tomas realized that this approach wasn't going to work and he so did not want everyone in the bakery to witness a tantrum. He crouched on the ground behind Manny, balancing on his toes. Maybe they could get out of this gracefully. Gently he put his arms around his little boy and whispered softly, his breath tickling his son's ear.

He barely got out his soft, encouraging words when he sensed the rising tension. He heard Marie's indrawn breath as Manny's hand turned in hers, raking his nails across the thin skin on the back of her hand.

Manny rose on the balls of his feet. He raised his elbows and pushed them forward. Then with a whoosh, he pulled both his arms and head back with a force that knocked Tomas off his feet. His arms reflexively let go of his son to cradle his nose where Manny had head-butted him.

Tomas toppled and rolled on the ground holding his face; Manny perched on his toes, keening in time to his hand flapping; Maria tried ineffectually to get through to her son, while keeping a safe distance from his arms. Mostly, she blocked the street. Once, Manny had panicked and ran off in a grocery store, causing his parents minutes of heart-stopping terror before they found him.

Ellie and Jeff appeared by Tomas's side. Ellie offered Tomas a handful of napkins as Jeff helped him to his feet.

"Wow, your kid sure packs a whollup," said Jeff with admiration. "I wasn't half that strong at his age."

Tomas just looked at him. He used the napkins to wipe away the blood trickling onto his lip from his nose. There wasn't really a lot of blood, but his nose sure hurt like blazes.

Ellie pushed past the men to crouch near Manny.

"Wait," said Tomas. "Don't get so close to him." He so didn't want anyone else to get hurt by Manny.

Without looking at him, Ellie waved Tomas off. "It's fine. I'm fast," she assured him.

"Manny, look," she said. "I've got your story." Ellie had pressed the start button as she walked over and the story was already almost done. But that was enough to snag Manny's attention. He stayed on his toes and his hands still flapped, but his noises reduced in speed and decibels.

Now that she'd snagged Manny's attention, Ellie held the iPad out to Maria. "Here," she said. "Play it again for him."

Maria wedged herself between Ellie and Manny, just in case. Holding the iPad close to her son, she pressed play.

Manny's heels came down and he stilled as he watched the short video play out. When it was over, he removed two fingers from his mouth and pressed the play button.

"Here, you hold it now," Ellie told Tomas. "Mel used to make sure Kyle knew that instructions came from both she and Ben."

Tomas did as instructed, grateful to Mel for thinking to revise the story to add an ending about walking home by the light of the streetlights with his parents. When the story came to an end, Manny seemed less tense, but his feet were still rooted half in, half out of the bakery.

"Play it again," suggested Ellie.

They did and one more time and yet another. Manny relaxed visibly. When it was over, he faced in the correct direction of home, gripped his mama's hand and, without looking, held out his other for his papa. Tomas gratefully passed the iPad to Ellie with a heartfelt, "Thanks."

IT WAS peaceful walking through the darkened streets and Manny seemed content. It took his parents far longer to release the tension in their bodies.

"Well, that went well," quipped Maria.

"All but one little blip at the end. Still, it could have been much worse."

"Far worse." She reached her free hand over to brush the side of her husband's face. "How's your nose?"

"It's fine. Although now I have more appreciation for what you went through the time Manny broke your nose. I know how mine feels and it's definitely not broken."

"But really, what happened there was small potatoes compared to what might have happened. Do you think if we'd played that story again for him before we hit the door, he might have been more prepared?'

"Who knows? Well, Mel must have suspected that there might be problems."

They walked another half block before Tomas said, "Kind of makes you wonder why we haven't done things like this before, you know, gotten out and met people. We basically holed up in our apartment for a good part of Manny's life."

They both thought about the reasons why they'd stuck to themselves, afraid of going out in public in case their son created a scene, the kind that had become all too frequent.

A scene. Other than today, when had the last one been? They used to come almost daily, but this week? Well, the last one was the day Tomas lost his job due to Maria's call for help. Sure, there had been smaller blips along the way, but nothing that erupted into major violence. And the incident today was actually minor in comparison to the upsets they'd lived through.

Maria remarked on this. "Manny's been good lately, better, don't you think? Was your afternoon with him all right?"

"Fine. Or, mostly fine. He got frustrated when his tower toppled too many times, but nothing we couldn't manage. You're right. Things have been better lately. I wonder what's made the change."

"We haven't been cooped up in the house so much. Do you think that could make a difference to him?"

"Maybe it makes a difference to us, especially to you. You were stuck inside far too often. I know you had no choice when I was at work and it's been rough on you."

"We were fine, Tomas, although I admit that this is much nicer, these walks and going to the bakery and talking to people. Do you think Manny likes it, too? Is that why he's calmer because he's getting out and doing different things?"

"I never thought of it before. Do you think it's possible that a kid like Manny could get bored?"

WITH A SLEEPY MANNY BATHED, cuddled and tucked into bed, Maria and Tomas had time to themselves. In bed, with the lights out, Maria broached the subject that had been on her mind.

"Tomas, what do you know about autism?"

"Not much. I saw that old movie, *Rainman* when I was a kid. I think on television I've seen scenes of people who rock back and forth, bang their heads, and are lost in their own worlds. Why?"

"Because several people now have mentioned autism and Manny. I think they think that he's autistic."

"No, that can't be. No. They don't know our son. He's not hopeless like those people."

"You know Jeff - the guy at the bakery who cooks and fixes computers?"

"Yeah, didn't they introduce him as Mel's brother?"

"Yes. He has autism."

"No, that's not right. He can't."

"He told me so himself today. He seems definite about it. And, he says that Kyle, Mel's son has autism also." Maria shifted her head on Tomas's shoulder so she could look at his face in the moon light. "He says that all people with autism are different and that that view I had of autism is only one part, a small part of autism. Jeff says that autism is just one of his characteristics."

"I've seen Kyle there. He seems like every other kid."

"According to Jeff, he's a kid who has autism."

They were silent for a while. Then, Tomas asked, "What makes him think that Manny could have autism?"

"Jeff asked me why I thought Manny rocked and flapped his hands, didn't talk and made noises."

Tomas digested this information. "Why *do* you think he does those things?"

"I don't know. I never thought about the why of it. I just thought that that was Manny and he was different than other kids. I hoped that he'd grow out of it."

"But, he isn't, is he?"

Maria sighed. "No, I so want to believe that he is, that he's getting better and will soon be just like the children I see out the window. But, he's not. He's just not. And, I can't seem to make him better."

Tomas pulled her into his arms. "Querida, you are the best mother any child could ever have. This, this problem with Manny, it's bigger than both of us. We're doing the best we can."

"I asked Jeff that if Manny did have autism, would he ever be like Jeff. He said that Manny will need help - special help. It sounded like more than we can do for him, but stuff that people like Mel know.

"Then, he asked me why Manny is not in school."

CHAPTER 13

Maria hovered. She was never a dithering sort of woman and the way she hovered just out of arms reach of their son got on Tomas' nerves. She trailed after Manny, looking more like a timid mouse than his Maria. Her hushing sounds and hesitant vibes were making both the males in her life edgy. They'd had a few rough days with Manny. Maybe they'd grown complacent and let their guards down. Now, they were back to walking on tenterhooks.

THE FIRST OF the month was almost here. Tomas, usually a most patient man, was short-tempered at home. When several of Manny's blocks escaped from their teetering tower, toppling onto the newspaper, Tomas snapped at his son to, "Get those blocks out of here and leave me alone!" With a shake of the paper, he returned to his study of the want ads.

Unused to that tone from his parents, Manny stiffened. Maria feared that he was going to shriek back or even attack. Maria approached gingerly, but placed her hands on her little boy's shoulders and squeezed softly. Manny raised the blocks and let them fly with a yell. Maria ducked, but then pressed down firmly on his shoulders, as she had seen Mel do. The reaction was not immediate, but some of the tension left the child's body and his arms lowered. After staying that way for a minute, she helped Manny gather up his blocks and move them to his favorite spot in front of the window. The sun beams wouldn't appear until later in the afternoon, but for now, this might let Tomas read the paper in peace.

For the past several days, Tomas and Paul had showed up at a day worker place. How it worked was that men looking for a job registered at the office, then as jobs opened up for an hour or two or for the day, those at the front of the line would pile into the waiting truck and get a ride to wherever they were needed. The jobs were always menial and physically demanding but Tomas did not mind that. What he did mind was that it was temporary. When you showed up, you never knew where you might work, what you might be doing, the hours, or worse, even if you'd get work that day. The latter was unacceptable to a family man with responsibilities.

Today had been one of those bad days - one where there was little call for day workers and most of the men in line had been sent home. Tomas was just a few behind the lucky ones who had gotten work. Now, he was home, searching for some sort of job, anything to apply for. His concentration was broken by the telephone.

Maria hurriedly got it, giving a soft, "Hello" into the receiver. She smiled when she heard who was on the other end of the line, but her smile turned into a hesitant frown. "I don't know," she said, "I'd like to help you, but there's Manny. I'll have to see what Tomas says. May I call you back?" She took down the number.

Their apartment was too small for Tomas to not have heard Maria's side of the conversation. He waited for his wife to explain.

"That was Ellie." Maria was hesitant. "She called for help. She says it's crazy at the bakery and the lunch crowd has not even started yet. She asked if I could come in to help, even if it's just for a few hours. I told her I'd have to ask you."

Tomas' face had darkened as he listened to his wife. He wanted to thump his chest and do the 'I am the man of this house and I will support my family' routine. But, looking at Maria's nervous, hopeful face, he swallowed his words. She knew how he felt about the man providing for his family and the woman's place in the home. But, lately, he had not been doing such a good job of that, had he?

Ellie was a woman and she worked, but she was unmarried, with no man to look after her. Mel worked and she had Ben to support her, but Ben didn't seem to mind that his wife worked. Ellie had told them that her parents used to own the bakery, with their dad baking and their mom running the front of the shop. Growing up, all the kids had worked in the bakery, under their mother's direction.

Ellie had been good to Tomas' family, welcoming them when venturing out into public with Manny was still new to them. And, not just Ellie but the rest of her family and staff had greatly helped Tomas, Maria and Manny.

While Tomas let his thoughts wander, Maria awaited his answer. She watched the thoughts flitter across his face and knew the cultural dilemma he was facing. It was the man who went out to work, not the woman. Yet, there was an obligation to help out a friend. Maria prayed that the latter would rise to the surface as her husband weighed the issues. This was not a permanent thing, just a once-in-a-while job until Sal returned to work. Besides, it was fun. And, much as she adored being a wife and mother to her family, it felt good for the first time ever, to financially contribute to their home.

Tomas studied the paper a moment more, then his wife's expressive, black eyes. "When?" he asked.

Maria's brilliant smile was his reward. "Soon. Now. Right away," she said. "And, Ellie suggested that we all come down for lunch."

"She seems to be feeding us quite a bit."

"I don't mind. It's a break from cooking."

Surprised, Tomas asked, "I thought you loved cooking?"

"Generally, but not all the time. Sometimes it's nice to sit down to something that I didn't make myself. Jeff's a good cook and it's always different."

All this was news to Tomas. "Shall we go, then?"

"Wait. I want to try making a story for Manny." Maria drew a large stick figure, a small one in between then a shorter adult on the other side. Two lines served as a sidewalk. Then she drew these same stick figures sitting at a round table. Well, kind of sitting, if you stretched your imagination. She was not much of an artist and this was pretty hasty sketching.

But, Manny was an uncritical audience. When she showed him the pictures and explained that they were going to the bakery for lunch, he did not look at her nor respond. Instead, he stood, opened the closet door and tried to pull his jacket down off the hanger.

His parents watched in amazement. This was the first time he had ever gone for his coat. He understood! He had honestly understood what his mama was trying to convey. And, he responded appropriately and cooperatively.

Money might be tight, Tomas might be worried about his job prospects, but the hearts of the mother and father soared as they held their son's hands on the way to the bakery.

MARIA BARELY HAD time to finish her prosciutto, Swiss cheese and cornetto sandwich before the lunch crowd enveloped the place.

"Saturdays are usually busy, but not like this," explained Ellie as she topped up Tomas' coffee. "Look," she said, "the crowd doesn't seem to bother Manny."

And, it didn't. Manny was too preoccupied trying to scoop up every crumbled piece of his rich, cornetto bread. He'd never had such a delicacy before. Neither had Tomas nor Maria. The cornetto resembled a croissant, but was not quite the same. Ellie explained that this was another of Jeff's experiments. He'd tried it out on a few people Thursday, then when it passed muster, they'd set out a sign that the Saturday special would be served on cornetto rolls.

Maria was nervous about leaving Tomas and Manny alone at the table, unsure how her son would act. It had been fine last time, but with Manny, you just never knew. And, he had never been here when there were so many people milling around.

A rattling sound approached, and then a large plastic bin plunked onto the table. It was a bucket of building blocks, carefully carried over by Kyle. Reflexively, Tomas angled his body so he could interfere in case Manny lashed out at this little boy.

"Hi," said Kyle. "Wanna play?"

It wasn't totally clear who he was speaking to. He made direct eye contact with none of the table's inhabitants, but seemed to address the air above their table. Ellie, more used to her nephew, asked him, "Who are you talking to?"

Kyle raised his eyes to his aunt. His expression said what he thought of that question. "Him," he said, pointing at Manny.

"Do you know that *him* has a name?" asked Ellie.

"Aunt Ellie, you are silly sometimes. Of course, he has a name. Everyone has a name."

"But do you know what his name is?"

Kyle shook his head.

"Kyle, I'd like you to meet Manny. Manny, this Kyle." Then, to Kyle, she asked, "Can you give Manny a high five?"

Kyle raised his hand and waited and waited and waited without flinching. Manny finally moved his hand into position and made contact. Although the adults heard the slap, they were impressed with the accuracy of a child who could find the hand without looking directly at it or its owner.

As Kyle stood on his toes to open the bucket, Tomas and Maria held their coffee cups in the air to make more room on the minuscule table.

"Whoa, there. Do you think there's enough room on this table top for any of the creations you build?" asked Ellie.

That gave Kyle pause.

Ellie nodded to the carpet in the corner, the one with roads and city blocks printed on it. "Why don't you guys go over there to play?"

"Okay." And, Kyle was off.

Tomas protested. "I don't really think..."

At the same time, Maria, "This is not a good idea." Tomas let his wife finish. "Manny does not play with other children."

"Doesn't he like blocks?" Ellie questioned.

"It's not that," said Tomas. "He's never played with other kids."

Tomas looked up as Mel joined their group. "Maybe this is a good time for him to start, then," she said.

Maria said quietly, "You don't understand. Sometimes Manny can be rough. We would not want him to hurt your son."

"I don't want my son to be hurt either, but I think Kyle can hold his own," said Mel. "Look. Would it help if I stayed with the boys while they played?"

"We do not want to impose," started Tomas. He was thinking that he didn't want this nice lady to get hurt either.

"Oh, it's nothing. I'll enjoy it as much as the boys." Mel stood and held out her hand to Manny. "Want to come play?"

While Tomas was still forming his protest, Manny climbed off his chair, and taking Mel's hand, followed her to the floor mat in the corner where Kyle had already dumped out the bucket of building blocks.

MANNY LOOKED at the blocks that were so familiar to him. Never before had he seen these colorful blocks outside of his own home. And, at that home, *he* was pretty much the only person who ever touched them. His parents knew better than to interfere with Manny's blocks and tower building. Now, here was this other child taking control of the blocks.

"Here," said Kyle as he swept an arm through the middle of the pile, shoving half towards Manny. "These are for you and these are mine."

Manny's one fist entered his mouth, while the other hand rose and flapped. His body began to rock back and forth and a low sound came from his mouth. Observing this, Tomas brought his coffee cup over to Mel's table by the carpet. "May I?" he asked, gesturing at one of the vacant chairs.

"Sure. Worried, are you?"

"Manny has those blocks at home and doesn't like anyone touching them."

"This is a good experience for him then."

Tomas sighed. "You don't understand. My son can be unpredictable. He gets upset."

"He's a kid."

With his eyes not leaving his son's swaying body, Tomas confessed. "Sometimes he lashes out. You can't always tell when it's going to happen." There. He'd said it.

Mel reached over and gave his forearm a quick squeeze. "It's okay. I understand. And, I'll watch the boys closely." Her eyes said that she did get it, but Tomas was doubtful. How could she? He had to try to make her see what could happen, what might well happen.

Painfully, eyes on the carpet, shoulders slumped, he started. "He hurts, well, sometimes he has hurt his mother." He could not meet her gaze. "It's not Maria's fault - she is a wonderful, loving mother. I do not know why he does it. And, sometimes it goes on for a long time and she can't make him stop. When it's really bad, she had to call me at work and I'd come home to rescue her. That's why I lost my job; I had to leave too many times."

"That's tough."

"But what could I do? He's getting bigger and a couple times he really hurt his mama. Once we had to go to the hospital to get the bleeding stopped."

"You're right. Safety comes first."

Now that he'd started, the dam burst and he couldn't contain the words burbling out of his mouth. "It's been better these last few weeks, or at least mostly. Maybe it's because I'm home more now. And, we've been getting out more, coming here and going for more walks."

Mel nodded. "A change of scenery can help all of you. And, Manny's been good at the bakery."

"We never thought we could do something like this with him. It got so we avoided going out in public with him in case he'd make a scene. But, that also meant that Maria was trapped in the house most of the time."

"Do you know what it is that upsets him?"

"No! If I knew what it was, I'd make it go away!"

"Make it go away? Well, it would be nice if we could smooth the path for our children that way, but it's not very practical, is it?" When Tomas didn't respond, she continued. "Sometimes, the best we can do is teaching our kids how to handle frustrations because we can't follow them around in life, fixing their problems for them."

This woman didn't get it. "But that won't work with Manny. I can't talk to him."

"You can't? Kyle doesn't seem to be having a problem talking to your son."

Their attention turned to the boys.

Their play had started out with Kyle building a car out of his share of the blocks and running it down a street on the carpet. Manny, after watching Kyle and then inspecting every square inch of one particular block returned to his usual stacking. His tower now teetered precariously. Tomas tensed, ready to spring into action if Manny let loose when his stack invariably toppled over.

Just then, Kyle's car, accompanied by the engine noises Kyle was making, plowed into the base of Manny's tower. "Kerpow!" bellowed Kyle triumphantly.

There was a moment of silence. Manny stiffened. Tomas braced for action. Across the room, Maria tensed, cradling a bin of dishes to her side. Her grip bent the plastic. Mel readied herself to intervene if necessary.

The silence was broken by Kyle's delighted giggle. He threw himself to the floor on his back, rolling both ways on the floor, laughing. His next roll pushed him against Manny's legs. Kyle's swaying arms reached out, wrapped around Manny's waist and pulled him to the ground to roll with him. Kyle was having a jolly old time.

Tomas stepped forward to disentangle the boys in case Manny lashed out. Mel watched intently. She put out a restraining hand. "Wait," she whispered to Tomas.

In a few more seconds, they both heard it, low and soft under Kyle's rambunctious laughter, but it was there all the same. A rarely-used laugh came from Manny's half squished body. He no longer resisted the rolling from Kyle, but participated in swaying them back and forth. As the boys turned toward the adults, they glimpsed Manny's face. His mouth was wide open, his head thrown back and his clear brown eyes sparkled. He was happy!

Tomas waved to Maria to come over. He had seen his son serene in sleep. He'd seen him angry. He'd seen him cuddle sleepily with his mom. He'd seen him content or engrossed in his own play. But never, ever had he seen him take such enjoyment in being with another person. After all he and Maria had tried to do for their son, it took one small boy that they hardly knew to bring out this side of their kid.

Maria rested one hand on Tomas' shoulder and stood behind his chair, astounded at the spectacle in front of her. There was her son, rolling on the floor, playing with another child. At that moment, he looked just like any other kid.

Suddenly, Kyle let go of Manny and sat up. "Let's do it again," he said, and proceeded to stack Manny's blocks.

Maria sucked in a breath. Kyle was touching the blocks that Manny had been using. She knew what usually happened when *she* touched Manny's blocks.

Manny righted himself to a sitting position. With a scowl and fingers in his mouth, he watched Kyle. The "ah, ah, ah" sound came from his throat and he bounced himself up and down on his knees. Before he could work himself up too badly, Kyle said, "Here." He handed Manny the wheeled vehicle he'd built out of the blocks. "Your turn." When Manny didn't take the car, Kyle thrust it farther into Manny's space. "Take it," he instructed.

Manny reached out for the car. He turned it over and over, and then raised it over his head with one hand. The fingers of his other hand came out of his mouth and his index finger delicately spun the front wheels. And spun them and spun them.

Kyle, meanwhile, grew impatient. "Come on, you knock it down now." When Manny didn't comply, Kyle grasped Manny's outstretched arm, and lowered it to the carpet. He made a pretend motion with his other hand, urging Manny to take down the tower.

Again, Tomas rose to assist his son. Ben, Kyle's dad had come over to see what Mel was watching so intently. In a low voice, he said to Tomas, "Hang on a sec. Let's see how this plays out. We can separate them fast enough if things get out of control, but the boys might figure it out on their own."

And, he was right. Kyle ran an imaginary car back and forth across the carpet, racing up to the tower, but stopping just short of a collision, all the while making zoom, zoom noises.

Manny placed the car on the carpet and imitated Kyle's motions. Kyle grinned at him and instructed, "Okay, now!"

Manny let loose the car with enough force to explode the blocks across the carpet. Once again Kyle's giggling and rolling started, capturing Manny in a bear hug of joy. This time, Manny hugged back, and then the game began again.

"AMAZING," said Tomas when he felt he could breathe again.

The lull in the bakery crowd allowed Maria to observe up close for a few moments. She and Tomas entwined hands under the table. "I dreamed, but never thought I'd see the day when Manny played, actually played with another child."

"We celebrate our successes where we find them." Mel and Ben shared a smile. Then she raised an eyebrow at her husband, with a nod toward the boys. "Sure," Ben mouth back as he lowered himself to the carpet with the kids.

Mel motioned Tomas and Maria to a nearby table. "You can still see Manny from here, and Ben will watch them." To Maria, she said, "Looks like the crowd has slowed down for a bit."

As they settled in the chairs, Mel faced Tomas. "You mentioned that while things have generally been better lately, there are still some rough patches." He nodded. "Do you mind if I ask you about them?"

Tomas's back straightened. "We handle it and we look after our son."

Maria intervened. "I think that Mel is saying that she might have some ideas for us to try. Right?"

"Look, if you don't mind my interference, I might have some suggestions that could help you and help Manny. I've been through this myself as a parent and I've had lots of experience with kids."

"You have been most kind to us. Certainly, we would like to hear what you have to say." Tomas became stiffly formal when he started into his defensive mode.

Mel studied him carefully. "Well", she began, "life can be especially frustrating for kids who don't talk. They have no way to make their wants and needs known. Often, it's up to the parents to play a guessing game; sometimes we're not very good at it, frustrating the kid even more. That's when he might lash out. Does Manny ever seem to want something and you don't know what it is?"

"Oh, yeah," said Maria. "Sometimes I'd give him anything, anything at all, if I could just figure out what it is he's after." She turned to Tomas. "Remember yesterday? He must have been hungry and fancied something, but every snack I offered just seemed to make him madder."

Tomas nodded. "We see this often, but don't know what to do. If only he'd just say what it is he's after."

"Sometimes we use pictures with kids who can't speak to us. Look, here's what I mean." Mel pulled up some pictures on her iPad. "This is just a very simple choice board, but pictured here is a glass of milk and a glass of orange juice. The child can point to the drink he prefers." She quickly scrolled through more pictures. "Here's one that shows three kinds of cereal." She scrolled some more. "This one's not about food, but gives the child a choice of either wearing a blue shirt or a green one." That may not seem like a big deal, but so much of life is out of the control of these children; having even a small say, such a choice in what he wears can be empowering."

Maria moved her finger through a few more choice boards. "Some of these have like ten different pictures to choose from."

"Yes, and some have many more than that. But when we're first getting a child used to the idea, we usually just stick with two or at the most, three pictures."

"This is very nice, but we do not have a computer or an iPad," said Tomas.

"You don't need either. What you do need are pictures. In fact, I wouldn't recommend starting with pictures on an iPad. Who wants to have to carry this thing around all day? Instead, you might want to put a couple pictures on the fridge. Or, start a book of pictures, sort of like a choice book."

Maria and Tomas sat mulling over the possibilities.

Encouraging them, Mel asked, "What does Manny like to eat? You mentioned snacks. What are his favorite snacks?"

"Grapes," said Maria.

"Green ones," added Tomas, "definitely not the purple kind. We made that mistake once. We learned that our son is for sure not color-blind."

"I think Ellie has some grapes in the display case," said Mel and she left with her iPad. At the counter, she asked to borrow a cluster of grapes and, placing them on a white, paper napkin, took a photo of the fruit.

"What else?" she asked.

"Crackers," said Maria, "but only this kind." She pulled a small package from her purse. "I always carry some, just in case."

Mel smoothed out another napkin and took a shot of the crackers. "Now, I'll just print these for you." She fiddled with her iPad, mumbling something about air printing, and then went to find her brother, Jeff.

In minutes, the printer in the corner spit out two color pictures of Manny's favorite snacks. Mel thanked Jeff who complained that she really needed to take the time to learn how to do some of these things on her own.

Mel, like a practiced sibling, ignored him. "Now, you can tape these to your fridge or put them someplace handy when you want Manny to choose a snack." Then, she added a caution. "But, you can't expect him to just know what this is all about. You have to teach him."

"Thank you, but we are not teachers."

"Parents are their kids' first and their best teachers. What I mean is, you are going to have to practice with Manny, show him over and over what these pictures mean and how to make choices. You might need to place actual grapes on top of the picture so he makes the connection. Maybe give him a cracker as you show him the corresponding picture. Do this over and over. You might need to hold up both a cracker and a grape and ask him which he wants. He might catch on to the picture representations, but you might need to begin with the actual objects, and then move on to the pictures. Over time, he'll come to see that he has some power and the ability to make choices.

"Later, we can add in more and more pictures and of more things than just food."

"I appreciate your time, but we do not want our son spending his life pointing at pictures. We do not want him to rely on such things. What we really prefer is that he just talk."

"Definitely! That is the goal. Please believe me that using pictures will not prevent or delay your son from speaking. Talking is so much less work, that if and when he does begin using words, they are so much faster and easier, that he'll leave these pictures behind.

"In the meantime, having a communication system can decrease some of the frustration and powerlessness he might feel – you know, those kinds of feelings that can lead to aggression." Mel regarded Maria and Tomas steadily. "Manny will only get bigger. And stronger. The more you can do to reduce his frustration and his aggression, the better off he'll be and the better off you'll all be. Believe me, been there, done that."

"Kyle seems like such an easy child," Maria said with a note of wistfulness.

"Huh," said Mel. "You might not have said that a couple years ago."

The three adults shifted their attention to the ruckus in the corner, their spider senses now alert to the slight change in timbre. Ben moved from the sidelines to the middle of the excited fray.

Mel's look was rueful. "I don't want to burst your bubble, but I think our good times are almost over."

Ben said over his shoulder to them, "I recognize that tone in Kyle's laughter. He's about to turn from sweet to over-stimulated."

Tomas and Maria looked confused.

"Kyle's good for a certain amount of time but when he's tired that time is shorter and he had a restless night last night. I think we'd better pull the pin on this." He looked at Mel. "Do you want to do the honors, or shall I?"

"But the boys are having fun," protested Maria.

Mel nodded at Ben to interrupt the boys' game while she explained to Manny's parents. "When Kyle gets too wound up, he can't easily calm himself. We can tell by the sound of his laughter - it becomes shrill. Then, instead of winding down, he gets going faster and harder until the laughing turns into screaming and things aren't fun at all for him. Or us. It takes much longer to get him into a calmer state if we let this go on for too long."

"How do you stop it?"

Mel laughed. "Sometimes, not easily. It depends. If we catch things soon enough, we can often distract him and get him going on something else that quiets him. Today, I'm not sure. It might be harder since he's not at home. Also, he was genuinely enjoying himself with your son and may not want to stop. Brace yourself; this might not be pretty."

"If he protests, will you let him continue playing some more?" She was hoping Manny could continue to play this wondrous game with this miracle boy.

Mel looked quizzically at Maria. "No, if we tell him it's time to stop, then it's time to stop."

Tomas said, "If that was Manny and we tried to make him stop something he wanted to do, we might have a tantrum on our hands."

"Yes," agreed Mel. "That's a possibility. Then what would you do?"

"We'd likely leave him for a bit then try again later," said Maria.

"That's usually what we do when we want to get him into bed at night."

Mel leaned forward, resting her bent elbow on the table and her chin on her fist. "How does that work for you?"

Tomas laughed. "Well eventually he gets to bed every night."

"I hope you don't mind my asking. It's the teacher in me, please understand. So, what do you think Manny learns from that?"

"I guess that if he waits us out, he can play a bit longer, but eventually he'll have to go to bed." Tomas thought a moment more. "Sometimes he falls asleep on top of his blocks, and then we undress him and put him to bed."

Ben walked up with a giggling, but more subdued Kyle firmly clamped and slung upside down over one shoulder. "Huh," he said. "Been there, done that. I used to do *anything*, anything at all, not to have this kid scream. At least, that was before Mel came into our lives. Now the screaming is rarer and Kyle knows the rules and the routines."

"Most of the time," added Mel. "We're all still part of a work in progress."

Ben twisted Kyle around so that he rested against Ben's chest. "I think we'd better get this young man home. I see a bath, hot chocolate and a bed time story in his immediate future."

"Hot chocolate," mumbled Kyle from the vicinity of his dad's neck.

Mel pushed back her chair and grabbed the bucket of blocks the boys had cleaned up with Ben. She squatted down to eye level with Manny. Quietly, she said, "Kyle had fun playing with you. Maybe you can come to our house one day to play with him again. Will you give me a high five?"

While she spoke, Manny's rocking stopped. His eyes did not move from a spot on the carpet, but he held his hand aloft. Mel gently slapped his palm, and then gave his hand a squeeze. "See you," she said.

"Are you going to work some more?"

"No," answered Maria. "I think Ellie's okay now that things have died down. It was pretty hectic there for a while."

Worriedly, Tomas asked, "Was it too much for you? You don't have to do this, even if she is a friend."

Maria hurried to reassure him. "Tomas, I love it. It's fun to be part of the team making things happen here. It is work I can do and it's interesting and I like meeting the people who come in here."

"Well, if you're sure you're not getting over-tired. But, this was a one-time thing anyway."

Maria frowned. "Yes, she just asked me to come in today, that's right. But Sally will be off for a few more weeks. I know you don't want me working, but it's just a few hours a day for the next couple weeks and it would really help Ellie out. I don't know how she would have coped if I had not come in. There would not have even been clean dishes for the customers to eat from."

Watching the carpet, Tomas changed gears. Manny gently swayed back and forth in his sitting position, sucking on his fingers, with his eyes at half-mast. "Let's talk about this more tomorrow. For now, I think we have our own young man to get home."

Although Manny sometimes did not want physical contact, tonight he didn't object when his papa hoisted him up, cradling his gangly frame. Manny's head rested on Tomas's shoulder, his arms limp at his side, his legs dangling. Tomas shifted the weight to get a better grip and settle his son more comfortably.

Quietly, Maria and Tomas waved good-bye to Ellie and Jeff and went out into the night.

Both parents were pensive for the first part of the walk home. Then, Maria asked, "What did you think about what Ben and Mel were saying about Kyle getting over-excited?"

"Yeah, Manny does that, too. But with him it's not from playing with anyone, but from some game he has going with himself."

"Do you think you can tell when he's going to get out of control?"

"Maybe sometimes, but not always."

"Do you think we could stop it when we notice the signs?"

"We've never really tried, have we?"

Maria admitted, "I'm always afraid of making it worse or having him lash out at me."

"We're in a bad position. If we don't do anything and let things build up, then he gets really going and his world just erupts. If we tried to interrupt things and head it off, would we be any better off than if we let him be?"

"I guess we could try, but I'd rather do it when the two of us are there with him," said Maria.

Tomas squeezed her hand. "I want both my wife and my son safe." They walked on another half block. "That was interesting what Ben said about how he used to do anything to keep Kyle from screaming."

"I can hardly picture that in the Kyle we see at the bakery."

"You know, I think I get the point Mel was making. What Manny is learning is that when we tell him to do something and he kicks up a fuss, then he gets his way."

"You're right. If he yells or throws things, we don't make him take his bath or come for lunch if he doesn't want to. We wait until he's ready."

"*If* he's ever ready."

Maria laughed. "You're right."

"Maybe we can talk to Mel about this another time. She's a teacher and teachers are used to handling bunches of kids, where we just have experience with this one."

"Did you hear what she said to Manny when she knelt on the carpet with him?"

"No, I didn't catch that. I was talking to Ben."

"You won't believe this. She told him that Kyle had fun playing with him and said that maybe Manny could come to their house to play with him."

CHAPTER 14

"Here goes," said Maria. She held up a picture green grapes in her left hand and red grapes in her right.

"Manny," called Tomas. "Come see what your mama has for you." When Manny didn't glance up from his blocks, Tomas went and took him by the hand, gently pulling him to his feet then to the kitchen.

At first Manny stood beside his papa, fingers in his mouth, eyes roving about the room. Instructions to look at the pictures had little effect as Manny's glance slid by them.

Maria knelt down, placing the picture directly in front of her son. "Manny, would you like some grapes? Which ones do you want?"

Manny tilted his head back to get a better look. Maria moved them not quite so close to his face. First Manny studies the photo of the green grapes. His finger left his mouth and started to approach that picture. Then his gaze moved to the other picture. He shrieked and his wet fingers stabbed at the offending red grape representation. And, the melt-down began.

"SO MUCH FOR THAT IDEA." Tomas sighed and collapsed on the couch. "We will not do that again. Why not just give him the green grapes? We'd have saved ourselves half an hour of grief."

"I wonder if we should have used pictures of just things he likes, maybe green grapes and crackers?"

"Are you up for trying it again?"

"Nope, not me!" At least not now, Maria thought.It could be avoided no longer. The first of the month announced itself and the rent was due. Tomas was almost silent during breakfast, girding himself to go talk to their landlord. Pleading for extra time to come up with the full rent money so went against his principles and his pride. Never had they been late before. And, so far his prospects of getting full-time work were bleak.

He looked around their apartment. It was small, yes. Was it ideal? Far from it. A child needed room to play outside in the fresh air and sunshine, but that just was not possible in their third floor walk-up. Sure, Maria kept the place spotless and decorated it as prettily as she could on their budget. And, the neighborhood was good. Tomas need not worry about the safety of his family when he was gone.

If he had trouble coming up with the rent money this month and next, would they be evicted? Then what? While this place was tiny, at least they had two bedrooms. Well, not exactly two, but Manny's bed was in the large walk-in storage closet, plenty big enough for a small bed and dresser. If they had to move, it would be to a smaller place still. Manny would have to sleep with them or in the living room. Could Tomas go to work, leaving his family alone during the day if the lived in some of the more questionable neighborhoods? Maria would truly be a prisoner in the apartment.

But, wasn't she now? She was afraid to take Manny out of the apartment by herself, and with good reason. There was that time when she took him to the store for some milk. She never knew what upset him, but suddenly he threw himself to the floor in a full-on yelling, shrieking, kicking tantrum. His hands snatched items from the nearest shelves and threw them. When his mama bent to him, Manny grabbed the jug of milk from her hands and tossed it. Landing on the edge of a shelf, the container broke, spewing milk all over the floor, the stocked shelves and Manny. The feel of the cold liquid on his face momentarily silenced the child, then he let loose with sounds that dragged in customers from all over the store. Maria could not make him stop. She could not pick him up. She could not get him to stand up and walk out of the building with her. Dragging him by one arm along the floor occurred to her desperate mind, but she could not do that in front of all these people. So, she continued to plead and soothe, all to no effect. She'd intersperse this with attempts to restock the shelves but nothing helped. When Manny got like this, there was nothing to be done but let him wind himself down. Maria suffered the accusing stares of the onlookers and all their unsolicited advice.

By the time he wound down, he was exhausted, as was his mother. He did eventually allow Maria to lead him out of the store. She half walked, half carried her tired boy the three, oh so long blocks home.They never did get the milk and never again did Maria enter a store alone with Manny.

His wife was too often trapped inside this apartment. But she was not even safe there. Tomas had lost track of the number of times Maria had phoned him for help when Manny attacked her. And, there were countless more times that he'd come home to find fresh bruises or cuts on his beautiful wife when Manny had hurt her.

MARIA INTERRUPTED HIS REVERIE. "Tomas, you're so quiet. What is it?"

Looking into her eyes hurt. It was his duty to protect and care for his wife and child and he had failed. First, he had failed to instill in their son the values of respecting women, in particular your mother. He had not taught his son well and he had not protected his wife from their son's rages. Then he had failed to provide for his family. He lost his job and could not find another. Now, he would have to admit that there was not enough money to cover their rent. What kind of a man would get into this position?

He took Maria's soft hand in both of his. "I am so sorry, querida. I have let you and our son down. Today our rent is due and I do not have enough money to cover it."

Maria stood up and walked toward the kitchen counter. "How much are we short?"

As Tomas named the sum, Maria withdrew the sugar bowl from the cupboard and brought it to the table. She dumped it upside down and began smoothing out the crumpled bills. "I bet we have enough in here."

Tomas had forgotten the stash that Maria had been saving. While he helped stack and count the bills, Maria took off for the hall closet. She dug in her coat pocket and came back with an envelope containing more bills, these ones carefully folded.

"What's that?"

"It's my pay!" Maria was so excited. "I told Ellie I would just help her out as a friend, but she would not let me lift a plate without agreeing that I'd be paid for the work, the way she pays everyone who helps there. She said it's not much, just minimum wage, but is it enough to help with the rent?"

Tomas's face darkened. *He* was to provide for his family. That was the man's job, not the woman's.

Maria's words rushed in. "Ellie said to consider it fun money, just a little something for extras and to compensate for my time." She looked to see her husband's reaction. "I know I can't make the kind of money you do and could never support anyone, but maybe I can help out just a little?" Her voice rose at the end of the sentence.

Tomas's emotions warred within him. A wife working for pay went against every chivalrous value he'd been raised with. It made him less of a man if he could not provide for the family he'd created. But looking at Maria's pleading, shining eyes, he bit back the angry, insulted words that were percolating too close to the surface. He needed to think before saying something too quickly. How could he wipe that hopeful expression from Maria's face?

"Tomas, I want to help, too. Will you please let me?"

Things were different here. Ellie working didn't count since she wasn't married and had no man to look after her. But, Mel worked and Ben didn't seem to mind. Many women held down jobs in this country. But, it was not his way and not the way he'd been raised. Still....

Maria shoved the sugar bowl stack of money closer to Tomas. "This is your money, bits that I saved from the housekeeping money you gave me. Sometimes you were too generous and we did not need all of that so I stored it in here."

His beautiful, smart wife. He took the envelope she offered. "We only need to add some of this to what I already have to make the rent. Thank you, querida."

"Wait! There's more." Maria left the room and came back with her purse. "I know this isn't much, but it is payment Ellie gave me for selling the churros. I thought we'd use this for a treat for ourselves."

"A treat at the bakery?"

"We'd be fools not to."

SINCE IT WAS SUNDAY, there wasn't much Tomas could do to further his job hunting, other than checking Saturday night's classified ads. So, it was a good time to go spend their treat money.

As they walked, Tomas asked, "Did you expect to get paid for making those churros?"

"Not initially. I thought I was baking them to show Ellie what churros were. But once she and Jeff tasted them, they wanted to offer them to their customers. Oh, Tomas, people liked them so much. Ellie said she'd pay me any time I wanted to make them."

Tomas squeezed her hand before responding. He needed to gather his thoughts. "Do you want to do it again?" he asked carefully.

"Sure, when I have time. I love to bake and we can only eat so much of the stuff. Why? Do you see a problem with it?"

"Noooo, I guess, as long as you're not overtaxing yourself."

"I'd only do it when I feel like it or when I'm not busy with something else."

The bakery was not yet within sight. Maria slowed her steps.

"Tomas, what would you like me to do if Ellie asks me to help out again? It may not happen if she's not busy, but what should I say if she does?"

"What would you like to say?"

"I know how you feel about your wife working. But this is just a little bit of work and I would only do it when you're here to be with Manny. I do not want to work all the time - when would I get my housework done? But just sometimes, yes. And it feels good to help a friend."

"I'll leave the decision up to you then. I will have a job soon, so money will not be a problem. But if you want to work a little, I guess it's all right with me."

"Oh, Tomas, thank you, thank you." The words were muffled as her arms squeezed his neck. Giving her husband a hug in public was not something Maria usually indulged in, so Tomas knew he did the right thing.

THE BELL tinkled over the door to the bakery. When he saw who was entering, Ben waved them over, pulling in another table to make room for Tomas, Maria and Manny to join them. Ellie came from behind the counter to high five Manny and take him to the counter to choose his treat. This time Tomas and Maria followed after giving Ben and Mel the 'one minute' sign. Today, Manny was not the only one looking forward to a treat, but they were opting for something cream filled, rather than Manny's perennial gingerbread man.

When Maria reached for the plate containing Manny's cookie, Ellie moved it back out of Maria's reach, instead passing it down to Manny. "He can do it," she told Maria.

Manny oh so carefully followed his mother over to the Wicken family's table. Once he'd deposited his precious cargo, Mel gave instructions. "Come here, Manny, and give me a high five." Maria and Tomas held their breaths, thinking that their son would ignore this woman who was being nice to him. Mel waited without moving or speaking. It was almost ten seconds before Manny's feet moved around the table towards Mel. He did not look at her, but raised his hand. Mel gently tapped his palm, giving his fingers a gentle squeeze. "It's so nice to see you, Manny." She moved her chair back a bit to allow Ben a turn.

"Give me five, Manny," instructed Ben. Manny complied.

"And, me," said Kyle with more exuberance. Manny, standing between Kyle and Ben, had only to turn his body slightly to meet Kyle's hand. There was a resounding slap and an accompanying, "Hi, Manny!" from Kyle.

As he lowered his hand, Manny turned his head and glanced at Kyle out of the corner of his eye. He uttered a very low, "Hi."

Maria and Tomas gaped at their son and at each other. Manny had spoken. Again! That was twice now and both times in this bakery. It must be a charmed place.

Watching them, Mel said, "It'll happen more and more often now. You'll see."

As Tomas helped Manny into his chair, pushing it close to the table, Maria asked Mel how she knew this.

"I've seen it before. Sometimes other kids are the best speech therapists of all and have a way of drawing language out of each other."

"Thanks for inviting us to join you. When we walked in, you looked like you were having a serious conversation and we didn't want to interrupt."

"Mommy's worried," explained Kyle. "Mr. Tinsdale's sick and the school's dirty."

"Kyle. That's not quite right," corrected Ben. "Mr. Tinsdale's the janitor at Mel's school. He's off work indefinitely with some health problems and they're having trouble finding a replacement. They've had a couple day workers but that's not really the way to go."

Mel explained, "The way we run our school, all the adults in the building develop relationships with the kids. It doesn't work to have a different janitor there every day. We need someone we can get to know and someone to rely on. It has to be a special person too, because sometimes we have students work with the janitor."

Tomas and his wife exchanged glances. "What does a janitor have to do?"

"The usual that you'd expect - clean the floors and bathrooms, wipe off desks, do minor repairs, call in trades people when more is needed, cut the grass and clear snow at different times of the year. Kids stuff too much toilet paper down the toilets and they get clogged, so that needs to be taken care of. Little fingers leave prints on the windows. Their shoes track in dust and mud. The janitor should remind kids of the rules and doing their part in looking after the school, without getting mad at them. *That* was a problem with a guy who subbed in last week.

"Plus, as part of the school staff, a janitor must be there for the kids," said Mel. "That latter part is crucial. I'm the staff rep on the hiring committee and that last part was the stumbling block for our last two candidates we interviewed."

"Mel's second guessing herself, wondering if she was too stringent in her requirements, because now they have nobody," explained Ben. "They have kids with allergies to dust and stuff like that so they need someone to be looking after the place."

Trying not to look too eager, Tomas asked, "What qualifications does a person need?"

"There's no particular course; it's mainly on-the-job-training, spending a bit of time with a more experienced person in another building to learn the ropes. Of course, the person needs good all-round instincts when it comes to repairs. Having a steam engineering or boiler certificate would help, but it's not crucial. Our furnace system is pretty good and the district has a supervisor we can call in if there are problems."

Tomas, trying to hold in his excitement, attempted to portray calm confidence. He didn't want to impose on this new friendship, but this job sounded perfect for him. "Where I come from, there was no need for furnaces, so I have no experience with boiler systems. But the rest of what you describe, I can do and do well."

"My Tomas can fix anything. Even the caretaker of our building comes to get Tomas when he has trouble with some repairs," said Maria.

"Seriously?" Mel asked. "Are you saying you're interested in the job?"

"Si. Very interested."

"Would you need to give much notice before you could begin? We're looking for someone who can start quickly so we don't have to rely on a different sub each day."

With dignity, Tomas explained, "I have recently left my last position and am looking for another now. I am able to begin anytime."

"All right, then. Give me your contact information and I'll give it to the committee. You understand that because I know you, I can't be in on your interview, but I can give a recommendation. I've seen you with your son and you have the kind of patience we're looking for." When none of them came up with a piece of paper, she passed Tomas a clean napkin to write on.

CHAPTER 15

By the end of the week, Tomas was ensconced in Madson School as the replacement janitor. It was not a permanent job; he was only there until Mr. Tinsdale's return, but the job would for sure last the rest of this school year. Then, depending on Tinsdale's health and the possibility of long-term disability, the position could turn into a permanent one for Tomas.

Although nervous, Tomas had survived the interview and thankfully, his former boss, Mr. Humber, must have given him a good recommendation. Tomas was honest about his reason for leaving his previous job, explaining that there were difficulties with his son and he had had to take time off to go help his family. Truthfully, he could say that the circumstances that caused him to need time off work had changed. He admitted that he could not guarantee that it would never happen again, there had been no incidents for several weeks now and he was hopeful that things were settling down. Luckily, there was some flexibility in his janitorial hours and if he had to leave during the day, he could return later to finish up his work.

Tomas liked working independently and felt that was his strength. He also liked order and cleanliness. Doing repair work was an interesting challenge, not a chore, so for him, the job was ideal.

~

EARLIER IN THEIR MARRIAGE, Tomas had looked forward to being a father. He believed himself to be good with children and liked being around them. At first, he delighted in being a dad. Manny's lack of responsiveness was just an aspect of his independent personality, a sign of early maturity, his parents felt. They had a self-possessed sort of son, who was marvellous at entertaining himself. But, as he reached the toddler then preschool ages, his lack of speech grew more worrisome. Maria finally gave up on the ideal of toilet training because Manny took no interest in the process whatsoever and became increasingly upset at her efforts to get him into the bathroom.

The more Tomas and Maria compared Manny to other children they saw, the more their anxiety blossomed. Would he be one of those children who grew up in the confines of their parents' homes, growing into dependent adults, hidden away from the eyes of others? There had been a young man in their village that was that way, seldom seen or heard of, but everyone knew he was there in the back room of that one house. People there looked after their own. And, it was more protection than shame that kept such helpless people within the confines of immediate family. Yes, that was the reason he remained hidden, it must be. But their Manny would not grow up to be like that. And yet....

~

MANNY SNUGGLED against Maria on the couch, watching one of his favorite movies. He kept his mama's hand between his own, gently stroking her fingers. Maria kissed the top of his head and thought about some of what Mel had said about frustrations and communication.

This was a good day. Would it be a time to have another go at that choice board business? No, not when their morning was so peaceful with her little boy cuddled next to her, almost asleep. She rested her head on the back of the couch and joined Manny in a nap.

~

IT WAS Manny's stirring that woke her, then his cry of irritation. Maria looked at her watch. It was almost time for Tomas to come home for lunch and she had nothing prepared. Now, Manny was fussy, just when she needed to get some food prepared.

When Manny was hungry, he did not seem to understand the concept of waiting until it was ready. His irritation was growing; if this turned into a meltdown, she would not be able to make lunch.

She glanced at the top part of the fridge where they had placed the pictures Mel took. Dare she try it now?

"Come on, son." She took Manny by the hand and led him to the fridge. She moved the pictures of the green grapes and the crackers down to the child's eye level. She knelt beside him. As his annoyed sounds grew in intensity, Maria moved her head out of range. Standing behind Manny, she took his hand and pointed at first the photo of the grapes, then the picture of crackers. She touched his hand to each picture as she labelled the food. "Which do you want, Manny? Green grapes or some crackers?"

No response. Maria touched his hand to the choices again as she named the food. Again. And yet again. He just didn't get it and was getting more impatient by the minute.

"Hang on a minute, little man." Quickly, Maria got out one cracker and one grape. She held them on top of each picture and again gave him the label for each food. As Manny started to reach for the cracker, she moved it slightly out of his reach and placed it above its picture. She restated his choices.

Manny's hand slapped the picture of the cracker. "Good boy!" Immediately, she gave him the cracker. Within seconds, it was devoured. Manny stood there waiting.

"Would you like more?" Maria held the grape and another cracker above their pictures. Manny's hand came out of his mouth and left a moist trail on the picture of the cracker. "Yes, Manny, you can have a cracker."

The next time, Manny chose the grape. Wow, thought Maria. My son can even mix it up. But, this was a one-off. The next time he went back to his crackers.

$$\sim$$

THE CLICK of a key in the lock signalled Tomas' arrival. He stopped on the threshold, listening to his son's giggle and Maria's laugh. Manny stuffed yet another cracker into his mouth.

"Watch, Tomas, watch!" Maria reached for another cracker, and asked Manny if he wanted a grape or a cracker. Manny's hand slapped the picture of a grape this time. "He gets it!"Maria's grin was huge. "It's a slow way to feed him, but he actually gets it. He can tell me what he wants!" Then, looking at the clock on the wall, "We were having so much fun. Sorry, but I forgot about making lunch." She moved the cards from the fridge to the table and handed Tomas the next cracker and grape. "Here, you try this with him while I make some sandwiches."

$$\sim$$

A BOY CAME WHEELING down the wet hallway floor his hands driving the wheels almost a blur. "Hey," he called. "Who are you?" He glided up to where Tomas stood with his mop and pail, cleaning up the evidence of hundreds of little sneakers entering the school building that morning. The child applied the wheelchair brakes unevenly, causing the chair to swerve slightly, sliding half around Tomas. Tomas reached out to steady the chair, fearful that this boy would fall out.

"Nah, I'm okay. Don't worry about me. I know how to handle this beast," the kid assured Tomas. "Hi. I'm Jordan. I'm in grade 4. Who are you?" Jordan held out his hand, a hand that didn't quite lay flat. His wrist was cocked at a ninety degree angle, with his thumb out straight and his fingers pointing back toward his inner elbow.

"Hi. I'm Tomas Garza. I'm taking Mr. Tinsdale's place as the school caretaker." He was unsure if he should shake Jordan's extended hand. Did it hurt the kid to have it bent like that? Since Jordan just waited,

Tomas gingerly wrapped his around the boy's smaller hand. He was surprised at the firmness of the grip Jordan gave him.

Jordan grinned. "I'm strong, aren't I?"

Despite the fact that he was in a wheelchair, this was still a kid, Tomas realized. "Yep, you are."

Before he could admonish the child about driving his chair on wet floors, Jordan was off with one hand flap over his shoulder, and a "See ya."

ALTHOUGH OF COURSE he knew what a wheelchair was, Tomas had never before met a person who used one. At all other past encounters, Tomas had politely averted his eyes, so as not to be seen staring at the person or the contraption. Where he grew up, wheelchairs were rare; he couldn't think of when he'd ever noticed one.

Now, this child, Jordan, had not given Tomas time to feel awkward in the presence of someone with a handicap. He'd been in his face and confident.

"I see you've met Jordan," called Dr. Hitkin as she walked down the school hallway. "He's quite a force, isn't he?"

"I don't think he should be using that thing on wet floors. He was not very careful. He could have fallen."

"Yes, he could have and he likely will sometimes," she agreed.

"But shouldn't we stop him from doing that? He should not be allowed..." Tomas stopped. This was his first day on the job and here he was telling the principal how to run her school. Way to get fired. "I am sorry. I was worried for his safety."

"And well you might. In this building, I make the rules, but I only make rules that I can enforce. I can't stop Jordan from being a child, nor would I want to. You're quite right that he might fall out of his chair; that's a very real possibility with an energetic kid like Jordan."

"He might get hurt."

"True, he might. All boys run the risk of getting hurt in their play. Have you never fallen out of a tree when you were a kid?"

"Off a roof, in my case. But I wasn't handicapped."

"I'm not sure Jordan realizes there's a difference. He sees himself as a kid."

"Don't we need to protect him?"

"We protect each and every child in this school to the extent that we can and that it's good for them. But we encourage every student to be a child and to be themselves despite any differences they may have."

Tomas looked unconvinced.

"Dr. Hitkin said, "You'll have to come watch one day. Our OT, occupational therapist that is, comes a couple times a year and gives the kids lessons on falling. We spread out the mats in the gym and the whole class practices how to fall."

Tomas' head drew back and his eyes widened. "Not children like Jordan."

"Especially kids like Jordan. She pays extra attention to the kids who use wheelchairs, walkers or braces. They need to know how to protect themselves as best they can if they fall. Then she works with them on ways they can get back into their chair or walker with or without help. Because, we know it's going to happen, don't we? Falling is inevitable in life."

"I don't think I could allow that if Jordan was my boy."

"Mel mentioned that you have a child with special needs."

Tomas stiffened. "I have a son, yes. His name is Manny."

Dr. Hitkin smiled encouragingly. "How old is he?"

"Nine."

"What school does he go to?"

"He is not in school." Dr. Hitkin waited. With quiet dignity, Tomas explained, "He is not like other children."

"Exactly how is he not like other children?" asked Dr. Hitkin.

"Manny is fine. He is at home with his mother and we look after him." Tomas squeezed out the mop in the bucket. "Now, I must get back to my work. I will do my best at this job." And, it pays the rent, he thought.

CHAPTER 16

"Sure, he'd have fun," assured Mel as she watched Manny and Kyle demolish their gingerbread cookies, one appendage at a time.

Maria was not convinced. "I don't know."

"He and Kyle are friends now. They do well together. Manny could sit with him and his class." At Maria's look of alarm, she amended, "Or, he could sit on a chair at the side between you and I."

Next Friday a touring company was bringing a puppet show to Madson School. Mel thought it would be a nice way of introducing Manny to the school and being around other kids.

"We don't really take him out in public. We've had some unpleasant experiences." Maria hated to make the admission but she'd grown more comfortable with Mel over the past weeks.

Mel looked around the bakery pointedly. "Isn't this a public place?"

Maria laughed. "But it's different. We're used to it now and Manny's comfortable here. He knows the routine."

"He could get used to school and the routine there as well."

"Attending one puppet show wouldn't really make him used to anything."

"It's a start."

~

AT SCHOOL, Dr. Hitkin sought out Tomas. "Have you seen the posters?" she asked.

Since he was standing right beside one, Tomas indicated it. "The kids are buzzed about it. Jordan came wheeling by yesterday, to tell me how great it's going to be."

The principal laughed. "That boy has really taken a shine to you."

"He's a good kid."

"You seem surprised."

"No, it's just that I've never known anyone handicapped before."

"I don't think Jordan sees himself as handicapped. He's a kid who just happens to get around in a wheelchair."

"But his parents must worry all the time."

"As do all parents. Yes, he could get hurt the way he uses those wheels, but how many kids are daredevils?" She raised her eyebrows. "I dare say *you* did a thing or two you didn't want your parents to find out about when you were Jordan's age."

Tomas chuckled. "I can think of a time or two or three. But that's different. I was a normal kid."

"Ouch. Don't ever let Jordan hear you say that he's not a normal kid. Can you imagine what that would do to him?" Her tone softened. "Look, I know his parents and yes, they do worry. But do they have the right to prevent him from discovering all that he can be? Do any of us as parents?"

There was silence between them for a moment, then Dr. Hitkin continued. "The reason I stopped you was to invite your wife and son to the puppet show. I think your little boy would enjoy it."

"Thank you very much, but I don't think so. Manny's never been in a school before."

"Then it's high time he was. We would love to have him and this is a great show. They come every year and we've never had a student not love it. The show's open to our students and the families of staff members. That means you."

507

~

THE NEXT DAY AT SCHOOL, Mel sought out Tomas. "Hey, I heard that you might bring Manny to the puppet show. I wondered if he'd like a story about it."

Cautiously, Tomas explained that he and Maria had not decided yet if it was a good idea for Manny to come to school. Not wanting to appear ungracious, he added, "But he does like your stories."

"Good. In case you wanted it, I've made him a story about the puppet show." She handed him a stapled booklet.

On the cover was a picture of Manny grinning with his hand raised. The title of the book was *Manny Goes to the Puppet Show*. Tomas opened the book. Each page held a large picture with a caption. The first was of Manny and Maria holding hands and smiling. The next was the outside of the school building, with the shot focusing on the entrance door. Then there was a shot of Tomas standing in the hall, waving. The facing page said, "We walk down the hall to the gym" with an angled shot of the hallway plus the gym door. From previous assemblies, Mel had added a picture of students sitting in the gym. The story explained that "Other children will be sitting on chairs in the gym, waiting for the puppet show to start. I will sit with Mama and Mel and Kyle." The next page showed a picture from last year's puppet show and the words, "The lights will be dimmed, everyone will be quiet and the puppet show will begin."

Tomas turned the page. So Manny would know what was expected of him, there was a photo of children watching the show in the dim light, laughing. "I will sit quietly and watch the show. Sometimes the puppets do silly things to make us laugh." Then, "When the show is over, we clap. The lights will go on and I will leave the gym with Mama. We will wave good-bye to the kids and to Papa. Then Mama and I will walk home. Papa will meet us at home after he finishes work."

Tomas didn't know what to say. It was easier to focus on the trivial than on the fact that this new friend had taken the time to make a booklet for his son. "Kyle? Won't Kyle be sitting with his class?" he asked.

"Just this once, it will be all right for Kyle to sit at the side with us. It might make Manny feel more comfortable since this will all be new for him and he might mimic how Kyle behaves. Kids make good models for each other."

"I don't know what to say. Thank you for going to all this work. I'm sorry but we do not know if we should bring Manny or not, but we will think about it."

"Take the book anyway."

LATER, Tomas and Maria talked about the puppet show. They hated to deprive their child of anything but what if he behaved badly? Things had been calmer for the most part this past month or so, but not perfect. There had been no *major* incidents of Manny attacking Maria but there were still smaller things like scratching and pinching and throwing things. Plus, Maria had gotten good at dodging

Although neither wanted to distress the other, their minds each replayed scenes from the past - scenes in the grocery store, the doctor's office, the hospital emergency room - all places where life had gone badly awry for their family.

"It's just that he's so unpredictable. I can't always tell when things are going to go badly," said Maria.

"It's been okay at the bakery, though. He's not done anything more there than would any other kid. He even plays all right with Kyle."

"Yeah, that's nice to see."

Maria frowned. "But in the past, I've had some short trips to the supermarket that went all right as well. That's what worries me; I can't guess when things will be fine and when they will be just awful.

"What if he freaked out during the puppet show with all those kids around? What if the people you work with saw how he can be?"

"If the principal saw Manny at his worst, would she think I'm not fit to be around other people's children if I can't even control my own?"

Tomas was still new to his job. What if they brought Manny and he hurt some child? Or even if he turned on his mother? It had become second nature to Tomas to position himself between his son and wife at home just in case Manny attacked her, but at school there were so many children and adults around. What if he wasn't in the right spot to intervene? How could he face these kind people at the school if his son, his own flesh and blood hurt someone? Would he lose his job? It was probably too much to risk.

"Tomas, are they just being nice to you because you're new? We love our son, but why would they want a child like Manny inside their school?"

"I don't know. There seems to be all kinds of children in Madson Elementary School. In the girl's bathroom, there's this area the size of several cubicles put together. There's a change table in there that can be raised and lowered and shelves for diapers and supplies. The girl they use it with is not a baby - she's ten and they change her diapers. There's even a ceiling lift. The EAs use it for a little girl who's in a wheelchair. They told me she has spina bifida. She talks but she can't walk. There's this other boy who wheels around in his chair like a maniac. I even saw him pop a wheelie when he thought no one was watching. What kind of a school allows that?"

CHAPTER 17

*T*he day of the puppet show dawned and Tomas and Maria still had not made their decision when it was time for Tomas to leave for work. "I'll call you at noon to see how things are going, and then we'll decide whether or not you should bring him. All right?"

MANNY WOKE UP LATE, after a restless night. He'd been fitful the evening before, so they skipped his usual bath in favor of just getting him into bed. In the long run, his bedtime was pushed back anyway, and then he was in and out of bed for the next several hours. The neighbors were fighting again and although Tomas and Maria could usually ignore it, Manny seemed particularly affected by the sounds. The fights weren't often, but when they started, Manny was guaranteed a poor night.

Manny's routine was out of whack. He'd woken up too late to have breakfast with his papa. Now he prowled the apartment restlessly, unable to settle to anything. Yearning for a break, Maria watched the clock until Manny's much-loved television show came on. On cue, Manny buried himself under the couch cushions to watch.

Maria gratefully reached for another cup of coffee and a book. She'd have at least twenty minutes of peace.

Not so. While the show usually mesmerized her son for almost a half hour, today he stirred at the first commercial and would not go back to watch, despite all her coaxing and cajoling. He resumed his restless pacing, flicking his fingers at the drapes and lampshades.

"Stop that, Manny. You're going to knock over the lamp."

Crash. Did he do what she'd just warned about on purpose, or was that a coincidence?

As Maria retrieved the broom to clean up the broken shards, Manny's fingers sought other flickering possibilities. He settled on the living room window drapes. At least they won't shatter, thought Maria.

Restlessness drove him on. The day was overcast, so no sun motes came in to entertain him. His travels took him in a circuit around the room, bouncing on his toes as he went. Manny's bare heel found one tiny shard that his mom's broom had overlooked. Small, narrow and sharp, it easily penetrated his skin. He went one step further, and then another before his full weight rested on that heel, driving in the shard.

Maria never knew what caused her son's shriek, but then, she often never knew the reason behind his outbursts. His howl erupted just as she emptied the dustpan into the trash can. Dropping her implements, she ran to her son, but could see nothing attacking him, nothing to account for the ferocity of his yells.

"What, what is it Manny?"

His head was upturned, his hands were flapping, his mouth open in a screech. He jumped up and down on his toes. To calm him, Maria took one hand and tried to guide him to the couch where she hoped to cuddle her son. Manny allowed himself to be led one step, then two, but the third brought his heel once again in contact with the floor. His scream became piercing. In pain, he lashed out. His first blow struck Maria's cheek bone with force that moved her back a step.

With one hand protectively against her cheek, Maria once again came nearer to try to see what was wrong. Putting her face close to get his attention was the wrong move. Manny arched back, but the movement caused his heel to touch down again. Reflexively, his head came forward fast, butting into Maria's nose. Off balance as she was, this blow sent Maria backwards to the floor.

Still, Manny wailed, spinning in circles, hands flapping, hopping on his toes. Maria brought her hand to her face, pulling it away, bloody. While her cheek was likely just bruised, blood gushed from her nose. From experience, she knew that her nose bled freely but this did not necessarily mean it suffered any permanent damage. Still, her head reeled from the pain. Gathering her hands and knees under her, Maria attempted to stand. Her vision spun and for a few seconds she feared she might black out. But, she couldn't. There was no one else here to look after Manny.

Gingerly, she righted herself, and then tried gathering the quivering, fighting mass of nine year old boy into her arms and towards the sofa. It didn't work. He resisted, lashing out blindly. Maria pulled back, trying to regroup. She had to get him to the sofa. Sometimes, he was calmer sinking into the cushions, especially if she threw a heavy quilt over him or even squished him with the extra cushions.

This time, Maria stooped low, trying to come in under his flapping arms, hoping to push him toward the sofa. Only about six feet, she thought. If I can at least get him close, maybe I can pull him the rest of the way, and then drag him up.

Her bear hug attack did get him closer to her goal. Together, they fell backwards. The surprise cut off his shrieks and he caught his breath noisily. Then, Manny's heel dragged on the floor. In panic, he fought in earnest. One hand connected with Maria's sore cheek, the nails dragging down her face to her neck. Usually, she and Tomas waited until Manny was asleep before trying to cut his fingernails. But lately, they must have forgotten. Keeping his nails short was a survival tactic they'd learned after both being scratched innumerable times.

Things had been better over the last while, so they'd grown lax. She regretted it now.

He was down on his side with Maria partially on her hands and knees beside him. Now, Manny was angry. An angry Manny usually meant bad news for his mother. His eyes turned toward her, the object that he believed had caused his latest hurt. As Maria rose up on her elbows to approach her son, he lashed out. His forearm connected with the side of her head. Crack. The blow toppled Maria to her side. Manny lay on his back, beating his fists on the floor, wailing. Then his feet got into the action. Unfortunately, he hit his heel in just the wrong spot and the shard pierced in farther.

This time when Maria attempted to approach, Manny again linked his pain with the presence of this other person. His hand fisted where his mama's hair hung over one shoulder. He yanked with all his strength. Maria gave an answering yelp as her body was pulled over top of her son's chest. The added weight stilled Manny momentarily, and then Maria tried to move herself off of her son. Now his other hand reached for a better purchase in her hair.

Maria's, "No, no, no, Manny," had no effect. Her son was beyond reason.

The ringing of the phone startled them both into stillness and silence. The phone rang once, twice, then three times before Manny became accustomed to the sound and launched himself at his mother, all the morning's frustrations coming out in this release of energy.

Maria rolled, trying to protect her face from the onslaught of fury that her son had become. Her initial panic was overtaken by her reasoning powers. The plan. The plan when this happened was for her to get to the bathroom and barricade herself in. The cell phone remained on its charger beside the vanity so that she could call Tomas for help.

Struggling to evade Manny's fists and nails and teeth and flailing legs, Maria edged her way across the floor toward the hall. When she got her torso far enough away, she half crawled, half ran to the bathroom and slammed the door.

Manny the battering ram was right after her. The door opened about two fistfuls wide before Maria got her feet braced against the side of the vanity, the way Tomas had shown her. First, she craned her neck to make sure that none of Manny's body parts poked through the opening. Then she used her leverage to push against Manny's pounding weight and got the door closed. She knew from past experience that just locking the door would do little good. She needed to keep her back and shoulders against the door and her feet flat against the side of the vanity to have enough strength to hold the door shut as her little boy threw his body against the door.

His sobs broke her heart, but she knew that they'd be in even worse trouble if he got to her. He was big enough to do her serious damage. Her greatest fear was that somehow she'd be knocked unconscious in one of these confrontations. Then, what would become of Manny? Anything could happen and he had no sense of danger.

Maria was certain that her son loved her, of course, he did, but when he was in one of these rages, it seemed like he did not even know who she was. All vestiges of the sweet child who cuddled with her were gone. Every motherly instinct in Maria yearned to go comfort her child, take him in her arms and rock him until all the anger and sadness melted away. But, she'd tried that, too many times to count, and the result was never the one she desired. Tomas was clear that she was to keep herself safe, not only for her own sake but for Manny's. The second thing she was to do was to phone Tomas.

Tomas had cobbled together an extra-long piece of wire so that the cell phone charger could remain plugged in at all times and Maria could reach the phone from her protective position against the door. She only had to release one shoulder from its hold to grab the phone and bring it to her.

She reached. Her hand came up empty. She moved one foot from its perch on the vanity long enough to allow her to lift her head to peer at the phone holder. Empty. The phone was not in its assigned place on the charger.

When had they last used it? Its permanent station was here in the bathroom just for such emergencies as this. They *always* left it here.

But the past few weeks had been calmer. They had grown less vigilant because Manny seemed more settled. He'd behaved well in public at the bakery and when out walking with his parents. He'd seemed a happier child and any upsets were mild compared to how things used to be.

How could they become so careless? They'd been lulled into thinking that the worst must be over and let down their guard, no longer checking each morning that the bathroom refuge was all set up, just in case. Now Maria remembered. Her cell was in her purse. She'd put it there the last time she worked at the bakery, so that Tomas could contact her if he and Manny needed anything. She'd forgotten all about it being there and never returned it to the charger. Now it must be dead; she was sure Tomas would have tried that as well as their main phone.

In the other room, the phone rang again, rang ten times without an answer. Maria could picture that phone on the end of the kitchen counter. It would be within easy reach if she was preparing supper. It was one step away for anyone sitting at the kitchen table and only a half dozen paces from the sofa. But from here, barricaded in the bathroom, it was a chasm away.

After only a minute, the ringing started again. Tomas. It must be Tomas trying to reach her. No one else would keep phoning so often. When he received no answer, he would know that there was only one reason Maria did not answer either their land line or her cell phone.

Oh, Tomas. He liked his new job so well. It suited him. He was good at fixing things, liked everything looking nice and he was good with kids. Her Tomas would rush home to save his family, but what if this meant he'd lose this job, too?

CHAPTER 18

*H*is toe tapped. Tension was evident in every muscle, every fiber of Tomas' being. Maria would not leave the house on her own with Manny. Even if she thought things were better now and she did venture out with their son, she would take her cell phone. Sure she would, just in case she needed help.

But why didn't she answer? Her cell gave the message that the cellular customer was away from the phone. She always left it on, but maybe she'd forgotten to charge it. That did not explain why she wasn't answering their land line. She knew that he would call by noon; they'd discussed it over breakfast that he'd call and they'd decide if she should bring Manny to the puppet show.

There was only one reason Tomas could think of that Maria would not answer either phone. Because she couldn't.

What of their plan? If Manny had a very bad day and the aggression came out again, Maria was to secure herself in the bathroom where her cell phone lived so she could call Tomas for help.

No answer on either phone and no call for help from Maria was bad, very bad in deed.

Dropping his phone into his pocket, Tomas ran to the office. Dr. Hitkin was just on her way out when she saw Tomas' face.

"Tomas, what is it?"

"It's Maria. My family. I think they're in trouble. I told you...."

"Go, go. Yes, you told me this might happen." She made shooing motions with her hands. "Go. You're needed. Call and let me know how things are."

Stashing his broom in the closet, Tomas thrust his arms into his jacket as he ran. Down the steps of the school, across the grass that he'd just cut that morning and onto the sidewalk. Twelve blocks. Twelve long blocks. Walking to work this past week, those blocks seemed short. In the morning, he was eager to get to work. In the late afternoon, he was anxious to see his wife and son. Now, each block stretched like an endless border, keeping him from protecting those he loved.

It was fine, he told himself. Everything's just fine. Maria and Tomas went to the park and she simply forgot to take her cell phone with her. He'd be home in a few more minutes and find the apartment empty. He'd make a pot of tea and sit down to wait. Soon, he'd hear Maria's laughter coming down the hallway, then she and Manny would burst in the door, their cheeks ruddy from the cool air and their hair windblown.

Worst case scenario, Maria would be barricaded in the bathroom with Manny asleep on the hallway floor. Everyone would be safe and sound once they calmed down when he opened the door and walked in. Their plan would work. The only hitch might be the door.

Manny's launches at the door came less frequently now and each one less ferocious than those in his initial frenzy. Maria tried talking to him through the door, keeping her voice low and even and soothing. She reassured him of her love and she longed to open the door and hold him in her arms.

From past experiences, she knew that although every motherly instinct urged her to do just that, it was not a good idea. If she showed herself too soon, before he was sufficiently calm, just her presence could escalate things again and he'd attack.

Her son would attack her. What had she ever done to make her little boy hate her so? When he was like this, he bore no resemblance to the sweet child she held while he slept. She loved the way his long, butterfly lashes lay on his cheeks when he slumbered. He looked so innocent, so gentle, nothing like the enraged child she's witnessed this past half hour.

But his tantrum was winding down. She'd had enough experience with them to know that. Still, it was too soon to venture out, but eventually Manny would sleep, utterly exhausted by all the emotional and physical energy he'd spent.

From the sounds on the other side of the hollow door, Maria could picture the scene. By now, Manny would be on his back, on the floor. The current thumps were from the back of his heels hitting the door as he lay with his hips wedged close to the wall and his legs up against the door. Every so often, he'd give a kick but by now Maria no longer had to exert all her strength to keep the door from bowing in on her.

Gingerly, she got to her feet, using as much stealth as possible so as not to disturb her son and risk his ire starting up again. Soon, it might be safe to open the door a crack and take a peek.

And, soon, Tomas would be home. When he got no answer on either phone, he would surmise what was happening with his family and come home to rescue them. Sad, so sad for a papa to feel he had to stand between his son and his son's mama. Maria knew that it hurt her husband's soul, the things that happened to them in this house. Raising a hand to a loved one was so foreign to Tomas' nature. How had this started with Manny? Where did he get such ideas that it was all right to attack his mama? Tomas gave the example of nothing but respect and gentleness when dealing with their family.

Tomas! How would he get in?

Okay, think, Maria, she said to herself. Think. Did she put the chain on the door when Tomas left for work this morning? Tomas always told her to and it was her habit, but had she remembered this today? Things were out of sync that morning, with Manny sleeping in so late and not joining them for breakfast. Maria remembered sitting at the table after Tomas left, relishing the silence in her home and the indulgence of a third cup of coffee while she read the paper in peace. But, did she get up from the table to engage the chain on the door?

It mattered. It truly did. While Tomas, of course, had a key to their apartment locks, that chain could keep him out. It was an especially stout one, high up beyond Manny's reach, designed to keep their family securely inside and intruders out.

WHILE SHE STRAINED HER EARS, listening for the sound of her son's deepening breaths, Maria tried to visualize her morning. No, she could not recall getting up from the comfort of her coffee and going to the door before Manny awoke. No, she had not fastened the deadbolt then.

But later? Oh yes, now she remembered. She was sweeping up the debris from the smashed lamp. With the dust pan balanced in her hands, she walked past the door on her way to the trash bin. Her eye caught the door, noticing the chain swinging from the door frame. She had carefully fed the ceramic lamp remnants into the garbage, then, clutching the dustpan under one arm, fastened the lock.

Oh, dear. Now, there was no way for Tomas to enter the apartment. An integral part of their safety plan was for Maria to make her way to the door, even if she had to keep the kitchen table between herself and her son - even if it meant picking up one of the kitchen chairs and using it to ward Manny off, anything so that she could get to the door and unlock it so that Tomas could come in to help his family.

But, she'd forgotten. Only once before had she not remembered. Now what?

She glanced at her watch, or where her watch should be, but it was gone. A quick glance around the bathroom sink and floor told her that it was not with her. She inspected the long nail scrapes along her forearm, some with drying trails of blood. When Manny scratched her, he must have scraped off her watch.

How long had it been since Tomas's phone calls? Her sense of time was so off when these incidents happened. In the throes of the attacks, they seemed to stretch on for hours, even days, but usually they were no longer than a quarter hour, maybe up to an hour at the worst. But the aftermath, the cool-down part could take varying amounts of time. In truth, Maria had no idea how long it had been since Tomas tried phoning.

But, he'd be here soon. She knew her husband and knew that when she did not pick up the phone, he'd be leaving the school building as quickly as possible and racing home. He'd get home and be stuck out in the hallway, imagining all sorts of dreadful things, like the time she'd had to spend the night in the hospital due to the concussion their son had given her. That was before they'd perfected their plan.

Okay. It had been a while since Manny produced any thumps on the door. Soon, soon now, he'd relax enough to fall into exhausted slumber. Maria knew that once that happened, nothing, not a thing would wake him. It would be safe to sneak by and undo the deadbolt

But, if she left the safety of the bathroom too soon and Manny was still in his aroused state, his rage could return in an instant and he'd be on her. In the close confines of the hall, she'd never be able to get away, or even to drag herself back into the bathroom without slamming the door on any of Manny's body parts.

She needed to time this just right and do it before Tomas got home. If Tomas pounded on the door to be let in, the sound would upset Manny and his anger would elevate into attack mode once again. Then Maria would really be hard pressed to escape from the bathroom refuge to let Tomas in.

It was difficult to gauge the passage of time without her watch, but it had been a while since her son's last desultory thump. She lay down on the floor and pressed her ear to the crack under the door to see if she could hear Manny's breathing. That might give her a clue as to how close to sleep he was, or if mercifully, he was already out. The breath sounds she detected were deep and even.

She stood, looked about the room that had been both her refuge and her prison and took a deep breath. With both hands, she grasped the doorknob, pulling it toward her stomach before turning it. Slowly, ever so slowly, she inched the knob to the right, until the latch cleared the striker. Then, with another deep breath in and out, she held the next one in an attempt to be silent. Maria positioned herself so that her left eye, the good one, the one Manny had not punched, was peeking out the crack of the door.

It felt strange to recognize her apartment when she felt like she'd been in a foreign battlefield for the past half hour. But, there was the broom leaning beside the front door where she'd left it when she turned the deadbolt. Casting her eye down, she saw Manny's jean-clad legs strewn sideways where they'd fallen from their vertical perch on the door. They didn't so much as twitch.

Good. Manny must be asleep. Maria opened the door another inch. Now, her eye and part of one bruised cheek peeked out. She could see her son's torso now and the gentle rise and fall of his chest. Another indication that he was likely asleep. Poor Manny. He needed a blanket and pillow so he could rest more comfortably. She'd get that for him just as soon as she unlocked the door so Tomas could come in.

But now, to get over there. Maria remembered to lift the door slightly on its hinges so that they didn't squeak. Manny hated that sound at the best of times and, so close to his ear, it would surely wake him and send his mood back into the badlands.

Made it so far. The door was not open enough for Maria to slip through. She slipped off her sneakers and tiptoed on sock-clad toes past the twisted legs in the hallway. She stopped, let out her breath and consciously lowered her shoulders and unclenched his fists. Relax. The incident was over now and they'd all be fine.

She continued, gently placing one foot then the other beside Manny's waist, then his shoulders, then by his sweat-plastered head. The hallway didn't allow much room for maneuvering, filled as it was with the sprawled body of a hefty nine year old.

She made it. She was now past her little boy without waking him. She paused to regard his sweet face, serene in sleep. How could this gentle creature turn into a monster bent on harming his mother? What was it that drove her son at such times? Much as she loved him and would give her life for him, it was hard not to resent Manny during the times that he brought such havoc into the lives of his mother and father.

Tomas! That reminded her. She should get that cell phone back on the charger. If only it had been where it was supposed to be, then maybe Tomas would not have had to leave work. She could have kept in touch with him by cell, letting him know when Manny was winding down and that neither of them was seriously hurt.

Now, where had she left it? Likely it remained in her purse, which was beside the bed. Maria turned to head back down the hallway. She'd made it once passed the sleeping Manny, so he should be even more deeply snoozing now. Carefully placing each foot in the angles left by his sprawled body, she made it. Rummaging through her bag, yes she found it. Pressing the button, she saw that it was indeed dead and badly needed to hook up with its charger.

Tiptoeing, Maria made it back to the bathroom, reassured by the tiny click sound of her cell phone making contact with its charging receptacle. Now, to let Tomas in.

Maria grasped the knob of the bathroom door to slide on by just as a frantic pounding started on the door to their apartment. Tomas was there, yelling and pounding to be let in. In her haste to get to her husband, Maria yanked on the bathroom door, causing the hinges to squeal.

Manny stirred, restlessly at first, then with more intent as Tomas's knocks continued. He could hear his dad's voice, even if the words were muffled.

Maria stepped over her son, less cautiously this time, trying to get to the door quickly. But, it was harder to circumvent Manny's body now that it no longer remained inert. He squirmed in that half-sleep, half-awake state of confusion. He bent his knees, resting his feet flat on the floor. Oh, wrong move. Jamming his heel onto the floor brought back a flood of pain and Manny to full consciousness. At his howl, Maria leaned over him in concern.

Another bad move. Manny's eyes opened at the pain to see his mama's nearby face with her glossy hair hanging low within his reach. Every time she came close, he hurt, his senses told him. Rather than trying to get away from him though, his hand reached out and latched onto her hair. His shriek, his pull and Maria's yelp all coincided. The unexpected pull yanked Maria off balance and onto Manny. She attempted to swing her body to the side so as not to crush her son, but was only partly successful. While her head remained at his shoulders, the rest of her body fell onto Manny's legs, her shin flattening Manny's bent leg against the hallway floor. His heel connected with the wall, causing the shard to again dig in.

Manny began rolling from side to side, howling, his fist clenched in Maria's hair. From the hallway came Tomas' yells and pounding, both with his fists and the flat of his hand. Above Manny's shrieks, Maria could hear the desperation in Tomas' voice.

Maria knew she had to do something to get this situation under control. Think, think, she told herself. Logically, she needed to release her hair from her son's grip so that she could cross the apartment to open the door for Tomas. But, how do you extract a sweaty, panicky, little boy fist from multiple strands of long hair? She could cut her hair but there were no scissors within her reach. She could ask him to let go, but knew how effective that would be when Manny was hysterical and beyond reason. She could not remain half crouched with her hair being yanked with each twist of her son's body.

So, she did the only other thing she could think of. Taking a deep breath, she ducked low under his swinging arms, ignoring the painful pull on her hair. With both hands, she grasped under his arms and holding his body tight to hers, raised Manny to a sitting position. She rested there a minute, catching her breath. When had this child gotten so heavy?

But, she was only part way there. With one knee on the floor and the other foot firmly planted, she placed both arms around Manny's body and hoisted him to her and up. Or, that was the plan. They would have both ended up sprawled in a tangle of arms and legs if the hallway had not been so narrow and the wall she fell against held them both up. Rest just for a second, she thought, and then try again. She yelled to Tomas that they were coming, doubtful that he could hear her over Manny's yells and the racket that the man himself created.

Now, another heave with all her might and they were up. Or, rather she was up with Manny leaning heavily against her. At least squeezing him tightly had somehow stopped Manny's tugging on her hair. For the minute, he was limp in her arms, all sweaty, drooling little boy.

Maria gave him a hug and kissed the top of his head. No matter what, he was her son and she loved him.

Next, her plan was to edge them toward the door, that is, unless she could extricate her hair from his grasp. If that was possible, she could cover the distance between here and the kitchen door much more quickly.

Nope, his fingers were wound too tightly around some messy strands to get away without ripping the hair from her scalp. Now that Manny seemed a bit quieter, Maria turned her head to holler to Tomas that they were coming. She hoped he heard.

Keeping one foot braced against the wall, Maria shuffled her other into the hall, towards the kitchen table. Shifting her weight to her forward foot, she pulled Manny's body along, and then brought her rear foot under her shoulders. She took several steps this way, struggling to support Manny, but at this rate, the sun would be up the next day before they made it. Neighbors would have to lend Tomas a blanket and pillow in the hall.

"Manny, Manny, stand up. I can't support you. You have to stand on your own." She gave him a slight shake to get his attention when he didn't respond. "Manny." As he seemed to find his balance, at least partially, she removed her hands from under his armpits and placed them on his shoulders. As she started to rub gently, she felt him tense up, then remembered to instead press down firmly. "Easy, son, it's all right. You're fine. Just relax. Mama's here." She pressed even more firmly to get him off of his toes and flat on his feet.

As Manny rested his weight on his foot, the shard attacked him again. His scream was one of pain and answering volume came from outside in the hallway. Manny's arms flew in the air, flapping wildly.

His hands released the grip on most of his mother's hair, but not all. Some hairs were so entwined between his fingers that they remained glued there. Manny's sudden and rapid flapping caught his mother by surprise and her head was not quick enough to follow his hands. Maria felt the strands tear from her scalp and her scream joined Manny's.

After the initial shock, Maria realized that she was free, free to run to the door. She turned and took off for the kitchen table, intending to round it to reach the door and her husband.

But Manny had other ideas. There she was again, this person who was there every time his foot hurt so badly. He lunged after her. Driven by pain and hysteria, Manny was fast and strong. His hands grabbed the back of his mother's sweater with a jerk, pulling her back off her feet. Maria crashed backwards, into her son, tumbling them both to the ground.

Maria heard the breath rush out of her little boy when she landed on his chest. As swiftly as she could, she rolled off of him, checking to see that he was all right. His panicked eyes stared at her, his mouth moving in an attempt to suck in air. There was no rise and fall to his chest.

He wasn't breathing! What should she do?

Tomas's shouts through the door had been joined by several other voices that had not registered on Maria until now. Tomas was here. Help was here. Surely they'd know what to do for Manny.

CHAPTER 19

*H*alf crawling, half sprinting, Maria lunged the half dozen steps for the door, turning the deadbolt and catching her shoulder on the door as it burst open. She fell into Tomas' arms and his tight squeeze. He held and rocked her for seconds as his eyes scanned the room for their son. "Manny - where is he?"

Then the waiting group heard the harsh indrawn breath as Manny was finally able to suck in air. That first big breath was let out in a howl of fear and rage.

Tomas gave his wife a final squeeze and ran to bend over his son. "Hey, little man. How's my big guy? Papa's home. Are you all right?"

From the other side of Tomas, a heavy blanket appeared and was laid gently over Manny. Then hands, feminine hands, smoothed the blanket over him, to conform to his shape. Sitting back on her heels, Mel smiled a hello.

On the other side of the kitchen, Dr. Hitkin was inspecting Maria's face and head as she handed her tissues for the flood of tears the young mother was producing.

ONCE SHE SAW that Manny was all right for now, Mel came around the kitchen table to enfold Maria in her arms. Maria remained there, sobbing quietly while Tomas picked up his son, blanket and all and sat with him on the couch. Once again, Manny was becoming drowsy and would soon return to sleep. These episodes left him exhausted.

Maria raised her head. "Mel, what are you doing here?"

Dr. Hitkin stepped forward and held out her hand. "Hi, I'm Delora Hitkin, the principal of Madson School. When Tomas said he had to leave for an emergency at home, I went for my car to see if I could help out."

Maria's questioning eyes turned to Mel. "Dr. Hitkin asked me to be in charge of the school while she left, but when I heard that it was Tomas' family, Rob stepped in and I came along since I know Manny."

"We're a family at Madson and when one of our own is in trouble, we all band together.

"But the puppet show..." asked Maria.

"It's going on right now. I'm sure the kids are having the time of their lives and that next time, Manny will enjoy it as well."

Maria asked, "Don't you have to be there? You're the principal."

"I'd be a poor administrator if I had to be present every second. I have competent staff who will all step forward when needed. The school can get along fine without me for a few hours. Now, let's see to your little boy.

From the couch, Tomas called, "He's asleep now. He seems all right." Carefully, he rose to his feet with his boy in his arms, turned around and deposited him on the couch. "Maria, querida, how are you?"

"I'm fine." Then she remembered her manners. To the others, "Would you like some coffee or tea?"

"Sure, that would be lovely. But, let me make it. Tell me where things are and you sit down," offered Mel. "You've had a rough morning."

With Manny softly snoring on the couch, Tomas righted a fallen chair and straightened the skewed draperies before joining the women at the kitchen table. "The lamp?" he asked his wife.

"Gone. It fell over when Manny's arm hit it."

"I'm sorry." Tomas knew how she had loved that lamp. They'd found it in a flea market shortly after moving into this place. Maria liked the way the etched glass cast shadows.

"Care to tell us what happened?" asked Dr. Hitkin once they were all seated.

Maria looked at Tomas. "I'm not sure. Manny was restless from when he woke up."

"And last night, too," added Tomas. "We had trouble getting him to settle and to go to sleep."

Mel asked, "Was there anything different in his routine? Something that may have upset him?"

"We didn't bathe him last night because he was so off. It was all we could do to get him into his pajamas and into bed. It took him ages to fall asleep, and then he slept in this morning. He's always up in time to have breakfast with us before Tomas leaves for work. Today, by the time he got out of bed, his papa was already gone."

Mel reached into her bag for a piece of paper. "Let's do an ABC."

"A what?"

"ABC stands for antecedent, behavior and consequence. It's a way that we can look at incidents to see if there is a pattern. If we can find patterns, we can sometimes prevent these things from happening again.

"So, under antecedent, or things that happened before, we'll put down these things:

- unsettled evening
- missed his usual bath
- trouble falling asleep
- woke up late
- missed breakfast with his dad
- restless this morning

"Was there anything else? Anything different from how he usually is?" Dr. Hitkin took over while Mel wrote down what Maria said.

529

"Well, this isn't so different, but he did lots of walking on his toes and flapping. He used his fingers to flick at his ears and he kept shaking his head."

Mel and Dr. Hitkin looked at each other; they'd seen this before. "Has he been sick?"

Neither Maria nor Tomas had noticed anything. Manny hadn't thrown up, he didn't have a runny nose or a fever, but he had been quieter than usual and restless. None of his usual pursuits had interested him for more than a few minutes.

"Let's get back to that in a minute," said Mel. "Now for the behavior part. Maria?"

Maria and Tomas looked at each other. They did not air their dirty laundry in public. Problems at home remained private; they looked after their own. Plus, what would these women think of them if the learned that their son would become violent and attack his mother? What kind of parents could not control their own child? If they thought Tomas was not good with children, might Tomas lose his job?

Watching their hesitation, Dr. Hitkin covered Maria's hand with her own. "You love your boy, we can see that. But you're having some problems with him right now. We understand. Between Mel and me, we have over thirty years of experience with children who have special needs. Will you let us help?"

These were proud people, placing loyalty and self-reliance high at the top of their list of priorities. They were private, sticking to themselves in a culture they were only beginning to understand. But, so far, they had had only good experiences branching out. The people they'd met through the bakery had all been fine individuals. Manny had improved over the past months and had never misbehaved when they were there. So far, Tomas liked his new job. He felt accepted and welcomed by the people at the school. Dare he risk losing that? What would they think of him if they learned the things his son had done? Did these people genuinely want to help and could he dare trust them?

Tomas took a big breath. They had to start somewhere. While protecting his family came first, he had to work to support them. That meant leaving Manny home alone with Maria. He needed them both to be safe. Manny was getting bigger and stronger.

Maria watched her husband's face, understanding the warring within him. She felt the same way. This decision she would leave up to him.

"Manny gets angry," he began. "It's unpredictable; we never know when it might happen. Sometimes it happens when we are both here, but most often it is when he is just with his mama." He put his arm around Maria's shoulders. "A child could not ask for a better mother than my wife. We do not understand how he can turn on her like this." He brushed aside Maria's hair and ran a gentle finger down her bruised cheek. "Once, our Manny lashed out and broke his mother's nose. We had to go to the emergency room."

Tears overflowed Maria's eyes. "I do not think he means to hurt me. At other times, he is affectionate and we play together. But something comes over him sometimes and he becomes a different child. When he was smaller, I could just hold him in my arms until the worst had passed. But now that he is bigger, he is so strong when he is angry."

"I understand," Mel told her.

"But you have never seen Manny when he is like this."

"True, but I have seen other children, including our son, Kyle."

"Kyle? Surely not."

"No, it has not happened in a long time, but when he first came to live with Ben, it was common. We had a few incidents when he was in my kindergarten class."

"At school?" Maria could not imagine such as thing.

"We're prepared and have enough people around to help and to keep everyone safe. And, the more time we spend with the child, the better we get at reading him and hopefully heading things off before they get this far."

Maria confessed, "We try to be good parents."

"Of course, you do. And for a typical child, you would likely be perfect parents. But some children are just more difficult to raise and the usual things may not be enough. Parents of kids with special needs may need to learn more strategies and have a wider bag of tricks at their disposal."

"What do you mean by strategies?"

"Some things are simple," Mel explained. "Like the social stories we used with Manny at the bakery. Things like this help prepare a youngsters for what will happen and what will be expected of him. Then there are other strategies that can help calm the child, like pressing firmly on his shoulders, holding him snuggly, and using things like a weighted blanket." She pointed at where Manny lay sleeping on the couch.

Maria got up to inspect the blanket. "It is quite heavy. We just had a light sheet over him last night because he seemed so restless."

MEL DIRECTED them back to her sheet of paper. "Let's look at the C column now for consequences." She turned to Tomas. "You mentioned that this happens when you're home too, but maybe not as severely. Tell me, what do you do after Manny gets upset and things start to escalate?"

"I'm bigger and stronger than Maria, so I can hold him. I pick Manny up, bring him to that couch and hold him tightly with my arms around him. Maria brings us a blanket and fits it snuggly around us and I just hold on tight until I can feel him start to relax. Maria sits close by and strokes his hair. Sometimes she sings to him. It might take a while but he calms down and sometimes falls asleep."

"Ah," Dr. Hitkin observed. "You're applying pressure with your hug - a good strategy. That's the same principle behind using a weighted blanket. Weight and pressure can have a calming effect."

Mel continued. "So, a consequence that Manny receives is a deep pressure hug from his dad. That would help settle him. It also may be a sensation he's craving and he's learned that if he raises a fuss, someone will give it to him."

Tomas had not considered this. "But he goes to such extremes, especially with his mother."

"Did Maria used to provide such tight hugs when he was upset?"

"When he was smaller, yes, I used to," admitted Maria. "But I can't now."

"I wonder if he's trying to get that deep pressure hug and when you don't supply it, he ups the ante to get you to respond in the way he wants, the way he always used to. When you don't, he must get frustrated."

"Does he ever."

Dr. Hitkin asked, "Would it be all right with you if we tried to come up with other ways for Manny to get what he might feel he needs?"

"At this point, we'll do anything," said Tomas.

"To start with, I have a weighted blanket at home that you can try. Kyle doesn't use it anymore."

"You'd do that for us? Thank you," said Tomas.

Mel continued. "It's tough for kids who are nonverbal. They can't tell us what they want or need, so we have to become keen detectives, watching their behavior and using trial and error.

"It's frustrating not to be able to make your basic wants and needs known. The child may be trying to communicate, but we don't understand. Can you imagine how you'd feel in that position? How angry you might become? I'm not excusing what Manny has done and no one has the right to hurt another person. But there is something behind his behavior. It's our job to figure out what."

It was Dr. Hitkin's turn. "One of the first things we like to do is check if there is a physical reason behind the negative behavior. You'd be surprised how often we learn that a child has a bladder infection or a sinus or ear infection that we could not discern, but made the child feel restless and grouchy. While other kids might tell their parents that they have a headache or a stomachache or their ear hurts, kids who are nonverbal don't have that luxury."

Maria's eyes met those of her husband. Was it possible that their child was sick or in pain and they didn't know it?

"When was his last medical checkup?"

Neither Tomas nor Maria could remember. They only took him

when he was sick, which rarely happened. Besides, visits to the doctor were expensive.

"You're aware that you now have medical benefits, don't you? That's part of your contract with us."

"We had no benefits at my last job. Do these benefits cover all of my family?"

"There are limits, like with any plan package, but yes, if you take Manny to the doctor, the cost of the visit and basic procedures are all covered. Your health card may not have arrived in the mail yet, but we'll have your policy number at the office. As long as you have that, you'll be covered."

"I think it's worth taking him to the doctor," Mel said. "The fact that he was restless last night and this morning may indicate that he's not feeling well. You said that he was flicking at his ears and shaking his head. There's a possibility that he could have an ear infection or something else. Having an infection can alter a child's behavior, making him irritable and out of sorts. For some kids, their frustration with this may lead to aggression, especially when he has no way of letting you know what is wrong."

Maria said, "There's a clinic just a few blocks over. Maybe we could take him when he wakes up."

Mel had another thought. "Before you go, you might want to stop by my house to pick up that weighted blanket Kyle used to use. Doctors' offices can smell funny to some kids and they don't like it. They have to get up on this high, narrow table which can be scary if they think they might fall off. Then, this strange person starts touching them and using instruments like the stethoscope or a tongue depressor, sticking things in their mouth and nose and ears. This stranger will want the kid's clothing removed and it can be chilly. All these things can be upsetting and you don't know how Manny will react."

Tomas was ready to back out of the whole thing. They'd just gotten Manny calmed.

"It'll be okay," Mel assured him. "There are some things you can do to help. Take along the weighted blanket and use it both while you're in the waiting room and during the examination. Only remove as much clothing as you need to for the doctor to examine that part of his body at a time. Keep the weighted blanket on. For part of the exam, you can hold Manny on your lap, hugging him tightly."

Somewhat reassured, Maria nodded.

"And, if you stop by our house, I'll give you a story that I made for Kyle about going for a check-up at the doctor's office. No guarantees, but it might help.

"You know, if you used the same doctor, the pictures would even be accurate. And, Dr. Finley understands kids with autism. His office is across from the park. Here, if you have a phone book, I'll get the number for you."

"But Manny doesn't have autism."

Dr. Hitkin and Mel looked at Tomas without comment.

Mel stood. "Anyway, here's my address. Millie, our housekeeper is there now and she knows where this stuff is. I'll give her a call to let her know that you're coming by. The doctor story is in a green binder. There are lots of stories in it, but look on the tabs for the one that says doctor. We keep a bunch of stories for when they're needed. If you find that this one helps Manny, I'll make a photocopy for you."

As they left, Dr. Hitkin told Maria, "And you might want to get yourself checked out, too. That's a nasty bruise you have."

Mel poked her head back in the door. "When you pick up the blanket and story, you might consider telling Manny that this is where Kyle lives and that on the weekend, he could come over to play."

CHAPTER 20

*M*aria shut the door and leaned her back on it. "Did I hear that right? Was Mel actually inviting Manny over to play with her son after she heard the things he can do?"

"That's what it sounded like to me. But let's see how this doctor thing goes first."

While Manny slept, Tomas called the number Mel had given him. He explained the problem and that they wondered about an infection. The answering receptionist asked if Manny was complaining. Uncomfortably, Tomas admitted that his son did not speak.

"That's all right. We have several patients here who have autism and other developmental disabilities. With kids, we don't like to leave suspected ear infections too long. Come on in around three o'clock."

THEY STARTED GETTING Manny ready as soon as he stirred. He wasn't interested in lunch, despite their coaxing. Usually, he had a healthy appetite, even if he did insist on sticking to his few, chosen foods.

Then, he needed a bath. That sweaty boy smell was something

only a parent could love. Manny's diaper and clothes needed changing before they could leave.

Checking the slip of paper in her hand, Maria confirmed that this old, two-storey Victorian house matched the address Mel had given. While Tomas waited in the car with Manny, she rang the ancient door bell. Its distinctive peals were audible through the heavy, lead glass door.

Soon, an older woman opened the door. "You must be Maria. I'm Millie. Is Manny in the car?" She peered past Maria, spotted Tomas and Manny and waved. "I look forward to meeting him. Mel said that you might bring him over to play with Kyle on the weekend."

"Um, well, we'll see. Manny has a doctor's appointment this afternoon and we want to see how he is first." She accepted the laminated papers from Millie and thanked her.

ON THE WAY to the doctor's office, Maria sat in the back of the car with Manny and read him the story, over and over. Although his parents were getting tired of it, once his focus turned to the pages, his attention did not waver. Self-consciously, Maria went over it again in the waiting room. There was only time for one repetition though, because the nurse came to put them in an examining room almost immediately. She explained that she knew kids with autism found the waiting room difficult and he'd be calmer during the examination if he had time to become accustomed to the room and the examine table first. She bustled away before Tomas could explain that his son was not autistic.

They only had time to reread the story twice more before a tap on the door signalled that the doctor had arrived. He introduced himself, shaking hands with first Tomas, then Maria and squatting down to greet Manny. He did not seem put off by the little boy's wandering gaze. Firmly, he reached for Manny's right arm, placed the child's hand in his own, larger one and gave a firm squeeze.

"He has to get used to me touching him," he explained to the parents. Then, he asked Tomas to sit up on the examining table, ignoring his protest that he was not the patient. He reached for his otoscope, inserting a fresh probe. He showed it to Manny and asked him to watch while he looked in his dad's ears. Then, it was Maria's turn to have her ears checked, but this time, he asked Tomas to lift Manny onto the table beside his mom so that Manny could have a look as well.

Next, the doctor asked the parents to each sit on either side of Manny on the table, sandwiching him in closely. His hope was that this would make the child feel more secure and that with parental arms around him, he was in no danger of slipping off the table. "Squeeze him in nice and tight," the parents were instructed.

After looking in Manny's ears, nose and throat, the pronouncement was made. "Your son has acute otitis media with effusion. That means he has an infection in his middle ear. His ear drum is red and slightly bulging. Have you noticed Manny pulling at his ear or flicking them or shaking his head?"

When the physician learned that it had been years since Manny had a physical examination, he started in right away. "We need to check for other signs of infection as well." As Manny lay on the table, his mom covered him with the weighted blanket, glancing nervously at the doctor.

He nodded. "Good idea. We'll only undress him as much as we have to. While I examine him, do you think you can distract him?"

Maria picked up the story and began reading. As she started, the doctor looked over and smiled but waiting until she'd finished to comment. "I recognize that. Is Mel your son's teacher?"

"No, we're just friends. She loaned us this story for this afternoon's visit."

"You're lucky to have her as a friend. She knows a lot about autism. Madson's a great school for kids with special needs."

The doctor warmed his hands before the examination, working his way down Manny's body quickly but thoroughly. He knew he had limited time. "His lungs sound clear. The infections seems confined to his ears and sinuses. This is likely a hold-over from that cold you said he had a month or so ago."

He held up Manny's arm and said to him, "Watch. I'll show you a trick. I bet I can make your arm jump." He tested the reflexes in each elbow and was rewarded by a tiny giggle. Next, he bent Manny's knees up and tested the reflexes there. "Do you think your foot will bonk your daddy?"

The next reflex to assess was the one of the sole of his foot. As he lifted the first foot, Manny flinched and pulled away. The doctor paused and moved on to the other foot. No flinching there. He squatted down to take a look at the sole of Manny's foot without touching it. "Ah, ha." He called Maria over and pointed. "See that area there? Look by his heel. There's that area of redness with a lighter part in the center. Wait until I get my light." He shone a bright, magnifying light on the spot and the splinter came into view, the thin shard glittering reflected light. "That has to come out. It looks pretty sore."

"How do we do that?" Maria was frightened for her son and for how he'd react to any procedure.

"Simple. This is not a big deal." First, he gently swabbed the area with a non-stinging disinfectant and blew on it to dry it. Manny gave a laugh and moved his foot. "Tickles, eh?" Next a numbing substance was sprayed to dull the sensations on his skin. "I want to freeze the area in case I have to probe deeper to extract whatever is in there. Then I want to thoroughly cleanse the area to prevent infection. If I numb the area first, then Manny won't feel when I insert the needle to freeze the area."

While Tomas kept his son amused by reading a children's book, the doctor froze the area. He explained that he'd give it time to take effect, and then be back in a few minutes.

When he returned he tested the effectiveness of the freezing by running a pin alongside the splinter. The child never moved. Maria watched as the doctor made a small incision with a scalpel, then used long tweezer-like things to probe the open wound until he found the splinter and removed it. Using the magnifying light, he inspected the area but didn't see anything else. The cut was so small it didn't require any stitches. Instead, more antiseptic went on, then a butterfly bandage. Soft cotton was the next layer, with a larger bandage over that. "This should make it easier for him to walk on it, but I think he'll have much less discomfort now that that sharp little piece is out of there. It must have dug in at every step. No wonder he walked on his toes when he came in here today."

Neither Maria nor Tomas mentioned that their son frequently toe-walked, but they had both noticed how often he did it this afternoon.

"Between a splinter and an ear infection, this young man's had a rough day," the doctor continued. "By the way, for our records, when and where was your son diagnosed?"

"Diagnosed?"

"Who first told you that he has autism?"

"Autism? But, he doesn't. No one has ever diagnosed him with anything."

"And why is that?" the physician wanted to know.

Flustered, Tomas said, "Well, no one ever has. Manny stays home with us and we look after him."

"Do you mean he doesn't go to school?"

"Sir, our son is not like other children. You noticed that he still wears diapers. He can't learn."

"Whoa. I don't think you'd want to let your friend Mel hear you say that. She'd take a strip off you. All kids can learn. They might do it at their own pace and maybe learn different things, but they can learn."

As Dr. Finley wrote a prescription for an antibiotic, he urged Tomas and Maria to get Manny in school. Mel was a good person to talk to about it. "He really should be in school. You'll be surprised at the progress you'll see in him. And, take this with you as well. I'm making a referral to a developmental pediatrician. My guess is that this is an autism spectrum disorder but I'm not a specialist in this area. You need to know what you're dealing with so that you can find the right strategies and therapies that will help your son be all that he can be."

Then, he took Maria's chin in his fingers to inspect the injuries to her face.

~

THANKFULLY, Manny approved of the taste and texture of the liquid antibiotic and gulped his spoonful without complaint. He was subdued for the rest of the day, complying with his parents' requests to eat a bit of supper then get ready for his bath. Tomas taped a plastic bag around the sore foot so it would not get wet. With his back against the corner of the tub and his foot resting on the tub's top edge, Manny sat slumped, relaxing in the warm water until he became drowsy. He was asleep by the time he was dried off, pyjama-clad and tucked tightly into bed.

He wasn't the only exhausted one in the family. Both his parents had spent too much emotional energy, plus Maria was sore from her confrontation with Manny that morning. A lot had happened that day.

"Tomas, what did you think about your boss and Mel coming here this morning?"

"I don't know what to think. At first I was embarrassed to have someone else see the problems we have in our family. I still feel that way, but they didn't make me feel ashamed. I'm not sure they understand just how awful things can get, but they had a glimpse. And, they saw your poor face."

"Somehow, I didn't feel quite so alone with them here, like there were other people on our side. Dr. Hitkin didn't accuse us of being awful parents. Instead, she tried to help."

"And, they weren't scared off. Can you believe that Mel still mentioned Manny coming to play with her son?"

When they were in bed, before drifting off to sleep, Tomas mused about Madson School. "You should see it, Maria. There are kids there with disabilities - kids who don't walk, kids who don't talk, and even a couple who remind me of Manny."

"Like Manny? But he can't learn like other kids."

"Maybe not, but I don't think he's any worse off than these other kids I saw there. And everyone seems to think it's normal that they're in school."

"What would they learn?"

"I don't know. I don't see them carrying books, but they're in the classrooms. They seem to move around a lot, sometimes in one room, then in another."

"They have these other people there too, people who aren't teachers but sort of like helpers. They work with these kids or sometimes with the class while the teacher does things with the special needs kids."

"You said that Dr. Hitkin asked why Manny was not in school, even though she knows that he's different."

"Yeah, she's mentioned it a couple of times. And when she invited him to the puppet show, she called it 'a start'."

Tomas thought that Maria had fallen asleep when she asked, "Do you think it's possible that Manny could go to school?"

CHAPTER 21

*A*fter considerable debate, Maria and Tomas decided to brave taking Manny to the bakery Saturday morning. Maybe the antibiotic was taking effect or maybe their son was just ebbing into another up cycle where life would run more smoothly for a while. Regardless of the reason, they thought they should take advantage of the relative peace and get out of the house, their first venture since that bad, bad day.

Ellie met them at the door and followed her usual routine with Manny. They took up right where they left off as if the stressful week had not occurred. If Ellie knew that things had been rough for Manny, she didn't let on.

As Manny munched his gingerbread man, his parents began to relax. Maybe this would be all right. This place had become almost a sanctuary for them, a public refuge where they could go when they'd been cooped up too long inside, and a place where they and their son seemed accepted.

Maria glanced around uneasily as the bakery started filling up. She watched Ellie's practiced speed, greeting customers, serving orders and clearing tables. Should she help? Ellie hadn't asked her to and really, she should not leave Tomas and Manny alone.

Tomas' shoulders stiffened. He couldn't help it. Maria turned toward Tomas' gaze and heard Ellie's, "Hey Munchkin," signaling the arrival of her nephew, Kyle. Maria turned away from the door. Like Tomas, she was embarrassed to see Mel, this woman who now knew the shame of their family problem. How would Mel react?

Soon, Maria had her answer.

"Mind if we join you?" Ben asked. Without actually waiting for the okay from either Tomas or Maria, he lifted another table over to join theirs, sat down and hooked two chairs with is foot to drag them to the double table for his wife and son. He nodded to the counter. "They'll be forever there with Ellie, discussing the merits of all the choices, and then Kyle will end up with the same thing he always chooses." He nodded at Manny's plate. "Hmm. I see a pattern here."

"Hey, Manny." Mel knelt beside Manny's chair with her hand raised. And waited. And waited. He needed more of a cue. "It's been a while, hasn't it? Can you give me a high five?" One, two, three, four, five, six seconds passed, then Manny raised his hand to slap Mel's, possibly with more force than necessary but it was hard to grade your movement without looking directly at the target. Still, Manny was unerringly accurate considering he gave Mel no more than a sideways glance. "Look, here comes Kyle. Kyle, come greet your friend."

With both hands clutching his cookie-bearing plate, Kyle carefully deposited his cargo on the table, then joined his step-mom beside Manny. A little shy, he leaned into Mel, looked at Manny's legs and said a barely audible, "Hi."

Manny gave no sign that he'd heard and made no noise. Fearing that his child was being rude to these nice people, Tomas opened his mouth to prompt his son. Before a word came out, he watched Manny raise his hand in the air to Kyle. Kyle knew the drill and high-fived the other boy. Mel squeezed a shoulder of each boy, and then sat down, as if this was an every-day occurrence.

The boys ate silently while the adults chatted. The awkwardness Tomas and Maria had feared didn't happen and they began to relax. When both boys had thoroughly dismantled their gingerbread men, Mel guided the kids to the play area in the corner. Maria gave her permission reluctantly, scared of what might happen. Mel invited her to join her at a table beside the boys, with a reassuring, "It'll be all right. We'll stay by them and watch, but I'm sure they'll be fine."

She was right and the boys resumed the game they'd played the week before of tower building/tower destroying.

"Wouldn't you think they'd get tired of doing the same thing over and over?" asked Maria.

"You don't know Kyle well if you'd say that. He can repeat something over and over if he's intent on the game. But we don't let things go on too long because he can stim on it."

"Stim?"

"Yeah, he can get too involved in a repetitive action, doing the same thing over and over and over. Sometimes it gives him comfort, but we're careful. Sometimes it can get him over-excited and agitated, almost like he can't stop even when he wants to. If this game goes on too long, I'll play with them and try to change if up a little. It's good for Kyle to learn to be flexible and that there's more than one way of doing something. He may not like it, especially at first, but over the years we've expanded his repertoire of play by doing this."

"Manny likes to do the same things all the time, too. Like he flicks our living room drapes. Or, he plays with his hands in the sun beam coming through the window. He can stack blocks for hours, too."

"Hmm. Do you think it's good for him?"

Maria sat back in her chair. "I never really thought about it. It's just something he does. And when he's doing those things, he's quiet. Sometimes I really appreciate that quiet."

"No kidding. I know what you mean. It's good to give kids with autism time to themselves; sometimes they need to just veg out and relax because often things are tough for them. There's a fine line between adequate time to do exactly what they want and getting too caught up in repetitive actions. It's hard to find that fine line, isn't it?"

Maria was puzzled. "We've always just thought that this was Manny. And, autism. His doctor mentioned that word, too. But Manny doesn't have autism. I've heard of kids with autism and they sit in the corner and rock and bang their heads and are in their own little world. That's not Manny. I saw that old movie, *Rainman* too and that's not Manny either."

"You're right that some kids with autism are like Dustin Hoffman's character in *Rainman*, but that's rare and there are some kids so affected by the autism symptoms that may seem locked in a world of their own, but again, that's rare and might be only for a portion of that child's life. Even though it doesn't appear that way, the child may be far more aware of what's going on that we give him credit for. We know so much more about autism these days and how to help kids regulate their emotional state and learn."

Hesitatingly, Maria said, "Manny's doctor is making a referral to a developmental pediatrician for us. He thinks we should find out if Manny does have autism." She stared at her son before raising her eyes to this friend. "And, he said that Manny should be in school."

$$\sim$$

"He's right," agreed Mel. "He should be in school."

"But you've seen how he can be! Well, you didn't actually see it, but you heard us talk about it and you saw my bruises. He can hardly be around other children."

Mel regarded the boys and the mixture of their giggles as yet another tower collapsed in a mess of blocks. She looked at Maria. "He's around my son."

"Yes, but you're here and I'm here."

"True, but are we interfering in their play?"

Maria tried a different track. "Manny's different. He can't learn like other children."

"Nope, he probably can't. Neither does Kyle. Kyle certainly learns but his learning style is different than that of some of the other kids in his class. In fact, most of us learn differently."

Maria shook her head. "You know what I mean. Obviously something is wrong with my son. He doesn't talk, no matter how much I've tried to make him. Have you ever heard of a nine year old who does not talk? And he's still in diapers. No school would want a child like that."

"I would. Madson School would. I can guarantee you that Manny is welcome at our school. He would be well taken care of and once he's been there for a while, he'll learn and grow and you'll be surprised at the changes in him."

"He's so big. I've seen kids walking to school, kids who look like they're in kindergarten. What would happen if Manny was in with them and he got mad? He could seriously hurt those little kids."

"He wouldn't be in with the five year olds. If you bring him to school, he'll be with kids his age or close to his age."

"How could that be? He doesn't read or write. I know what other nine year olds do and Manny would not fit in."

"No, not right now. He's not ready to sit at a desk and work on math problems. But we don't know just what he *can* do. We have kids in all our classes who are not doing grade level work but who benefit from spending some time with children their age. Kids are good role models for each other. You'd be surprised how much they watch each other and model their actions on what they see going on around them."

"That's just it. Manny pays little attention to anyone around him." She watched the boys and amended, "Except for maybe Kyle. Look, he's watching Kyle and waiting for him to run the car into the blocks."

Mel nodded. "That's what I mean about kids being good for each other. Remember the first time my little hellion of a son ruined Manny's tower? There was always the chance that Manny would get mad, but he looked at Kyle, saw Kyle laughing and that made him think. Now, the kids are actually playing together."

"Just say that Manny went to school. I mean, I love my son, but I am aware of his limitations. What would he learn?"

"I don't know what he'll learn down the road; I don't think anyone can predict that. But for now, we'd start with basics. I like to start where kids are, look at them from a developmental viewpoint and go from there." At Maria's quizzical look, she explained. "By developmental, I mean the stage of development he's at and that will vary. Take play, for instance. Small children go through a stage where they are solitary in their play. Then, as they mature, they may play alongside another child, but not really play *with* the other kid. Then they develop the skills to actually play together." She nodded at their boys. "It looks like Manny's entering that phase now."

"As nice as it is to see Manny playing with another boy, his play is not really what concerns us. There are other things that are priorities for us. Things that will help him in life."

"Play is the primary way young children learn. While Manny's playing, he's learning all sorts of things. If you watch, he's learning patience. He has to wait until Kyle does his part in breaking down the tower. And, Kyle must wait for Manny to rebuild the tower. They're also learning turn-taking. Both are important skills in life."

"I hadn't thought about the wait part. Manny is *not* good with waiting; when he wants something, he wants it right now. Learning to wait would be a good thing. What else would he learn in school?"

"While we're still on play, he'd learn that other people have ideas and wants that differ from his. He may not like it, but sometimes he'd get his way and sometimes he'd need to follow someone else's lead, just like he did the first time Kyle smashed up the tower he was building. Manny compromised, another good skill to have.

"In order to compromise and follow someone else's ideas, you have to watch. Play is one of the ways that kids learn to read the body language that other people give off and to understand those non-spoken signals. He'll learn how to have fun with others and that being in the company of other people is pleasurable."

"He's always been pretty solitary, only letting Tomas or I play with him in a limited way. We try, but he seems to prefer his own company much of the time."

"There's nothing wrong with that to a certain extent, but too much time alone does not allow him the opportunities to gain social and coping skills."

"And, in school....?" Maria asked.

"He'd have more opportunities to learn how to tolerate other people. No matter who we are, or where we are, life is a group affair and we have to be able to rub shoulders with other people, even when we don't feel like it. Sometimes others annoy us or we just want to be left alone, but we can't be by ourselves. We need to learn coping skills for those times and how to tolerate the presence of others."

"That makes sense but those aren't the things I think about when I consider school. No one taught me stuff like that when I was in school, but that was in another country. It must be different here."

"No, likely it's not that different. These things are all part of what's called the 'hidden curriculum', important parts of school that are not taught. Most kids pick this stuff up automatically on their own, but with some children, we need to explicitly teach these things.

They watched the demolition of yet another tower. Then, Mel continued. "These are things like how to follow along in a group. How to share a laugh with other people, when to wait and when to forge ahead."

"And, you think Manny could learn these things in school? Couldn't we just teach them at home?"

"It's possible," Mel admitted. "But, has he learned them so far?" She paused. "I didn't mean that to sound unkind. It's just that these things while not impossible are tough to teach at home with one child. Lots of this learning lends itself to group situations more than when a child is alone or with just one adult."

"I don't know. I get what you're saying and these things would help Manny, but he's so different than other kids his age. I see them walking down the street and much as I'd wish it were otherwise, I can't see him joining them."

Mel reached over and squeezed Maria's hand. "No, not right now he can't. He's not ready. But who knows what is in his future?"

The two women watched their sons who did not seem to tire of playing the same game over and over again. Mel continued. "Manny does not have to be just like other kids to be around other kids. At

Madson School, we have kids of all skills and abilities and there's a place for each and every one."

Maria turned and put her elbows on the table. "Tell me exactly what Manny would do in school. I can hardly see him sitting still for a history lesson."

"That depends on the lesson. If it's a lecture, no, he would not like it. Too many words and terminology would make it hard for him to relate to and to pay attention. But some lessons are more hands-on and he may be able to participate on some level. He may not get out of the lesson each and every point that some kids would soak in, but he could still benefit from the exposure and the activity and being with his peers."

"When Manny gets bored or restless or upset, bad things happen. You saw the after-math of one episode, but I'm ashamed to say that it happens more often than we'd like." She rethought what she'd said. "Actually, we'd prefer that they never happen but that seems to be out of our control." She raised her chin and looked Mel directly in the eyes. "I've been hurt by our son, hurt enough to go to the hospital. I'm a lot bigger and stronger than school children are. I could not live with myself if our son hurt a child. That is a big reason to keep him out of your school or any other school. He could hurt someone."

"Yep, that is a possibility."

Maria had been so hoping that Mel would not agree with her. Her shoulders slumped. "So I guess we should continue on as we have been."

"Not necessarily," Mel told her. "I don't want to paint a picture for you that things will be all rosy at school. Just the opposite may happen. This would be a big change for Manny and the initial period of adjustment can be rough.

"But, I'm confident that he'll come through it - we'll all come through it, and things will get better after that. Look, if he stays home the way he has been, he'll likely continue down the same path he's headed now. He's getting bigger and stronger. When he's frustrated, the chances of hurting someone are high and that someone is likely you. It's not just you I'm worried about, but what if you fall in a skirmish and knock yourself out? What would happen to Manny then?"

"That's what Tomas worries about, too."

"I don't see things changing a lot for the better if Manny continues to remain at home. But, if he's in school, we have a greater chance of teaching him other ways to manage his frustrations."

Maria sort of agreed. "Maybe."

"Another thought. Sometimes kids act out because they're bored. Being in the same apartment day after day, with the same toys could get boring. Just like we need to get out every so often, so do kids, even kids with special needs. They get bored, too. He would be less bored at school because there are more people around, more going on and he'd be learning new skills."

"I don't really think of Manny as being bored, but possibly he is. It's hard to know when he can't tell us."

"That's another thing we'd work on at school," said Mel. "A communication system. Sometimes kids get aggressive when they're frustrated because they can't make some need or want known. Can you imagine what it must be liked to want something, really want it, but be unable to convey that to the very people who could help you?"

"We've seen that with Manny. Like when he wants something to eat and we can't figure out what it is he wants. He's torn cupboards apart looking for something that we're probably out of, but we can't figure out what it is he's after. If we knew, we'd run out and buy it, but we just don't know. He gets so worked up and mad."

Mel nodded. "It must be awful for him. But, there are things that could help."

"You mean you'll teach him to talk?"

"That, of course, is the ultimate goal and the easiest form of communication. Some kids who are on the autism spectrum come to spoken language later than other kids. Some may develop a limited vocabulary, some will eventually speak as well as their peers, while some may never acquire the skills to speak."

Maria slumped. More discouraging news.

Mel held up a finger. "Wait. Even if the latter is the case for your son, there are other ways he can communicate. Some kids use dedicated communication devices, or iPad apps. Others use a simple picture system. We would likely start with a few pictures for Manny, and then build up from there. We would experiment to see which system he takes to.

"You should see the look on a child's face when they first make the connection that by giving someone a picture of something, they actually receive that thing that they want. What power! Kids just blossom. Suddenly they have control. If they give their mom a picture of orange juice, then they get a glass of juice. No whining, no tantrums, just a simple pointing to a picture then presto, they get what they want."

CHAPTER 22

D r. Hitkin stopped Tomas in the hallway. "Does Manny eat
pizza?"

"Yes, certainly. Why?"

"This Friday is pizza day at our school. I thought Manny might like
to join us for lunch. Maria, too of course."

Tomas went with his reflex response. "I don't think so. Manny's
not a group kind of kid and he's never been in a school before." He
picked up his mop. "But, thank you very much all the same." He
moved toward the outside doors to remove the evidence of hundreds
of dusty little foot prints in the entryway.

Dr. Hitkin moved along with him. "This might be a nice
introduction to school for him. He could come a bit early to see where
his dad works. He and Maria could sit with Kyle and Mel to eat. I hear
that those boys get along well."

"Yes, they have played together at the bakery." Tomas paused,
unsure if he should say more. But his fatherly pride would not let him
hold it in. He beamed. "You should see my boy. He plays, actually plays
with Kyle, playing little kid games and he giggled! We had almost
given up hope of seeing such a thing."

"I understand how you feel. I hear that from a lot of parents as their children acquire new skills. This is just the start for your son. Wait until you see the progress when he's around other kids every day."

Tomas closed off again. "My Maria and I, we have not made any decisions about that yet. It is a big step." And, what would happen if Manny got angry here? He could hurt someone. Would they blame it on Tomas and he'd lose his job? He did not dare voice that worry to his boss. "We are waiting to hear what the doctors have to say about the assessment."

"No matter what the assessment results are, Manny is welcome here as a student and if he just wants to come have some pizza with us on Friday." She started to walk away, then turned back. "You might want to stop by Mel's room. She said she had something to give you for Manny."

~

WHEN TOMAS ENTERED THE APARTMENT, Maria was at the table, papers spread around her, a frown on her face.

In Tomas' experience, important-looking papers were not good news. "What is it? Are we being evicted? The rent's up to date but have too many people complained about Manny's noises?"

Maria rubbed the side of her husband's face. "No, it's nothing like that. Our home's safe. The assessment report on Manny came today but I can't understand what it says. Look, there's eight pages, all about Manny, but the words...."

Tomas sat down to start reading. He opened the drawer that held his reading glasses, hoping that would help. He got some words, the smaller ones, but there were too many foreign terms. Since English was a second language for both of them, they assumed the fault was with them.

"Do you think we should make an appointment with the doctor to ask him to tell us what all this means?"

"Doctor appointments cost money. Our insurance only covers so many a year. But I'm having trouble getting past the second page here.

Look at the words they use - 'pervasive developmental disorder'. I get the last one, even if I don't like them using it to refer to my son. But the rest?"

"I wonder, Tomas, what about Mel? Do you think we could ask her to take a look at this letter? She's a teacher, I think some special kind of teacher."

"This letter probably says things about us, about our family and our son. And, it might not be good. Do we want to jeopardize her friendship by having her read this?"

"She's already seen us at our worst and still talks to us. Ben, too. He didn't see the things Manny did, but he likely heard about it."

"We have to trust someone and I'm not sure who else to turn to for help."

WHILE BEN SAT with the boys as they played in the corner, Maria, Tomas and Mel huddled over the report. As soon as Mel saw the thick sheaf of papers, she sighed. "I see why you were having difficulties. They often write these reports in jargon." As she peered at the first page, she muttered, "Why can't they use plain language?

"Okay," she continued. "Here's how you tackle these things. See the first paragraph here? That usually says why the patient was referred, his age, height, and stuff like that. These next pages talk about the various tests they used during the assessment, and then they go on to talk about how he performed on each measure and how they drew their conclusions. It's interesting, but might not mean as much to you just yet. You probably want to know the bottom line.

"When I'm in a hurry, I just read the opening bit, then flip to the back." She thumbed through the pages. "Here. See where it says summary? This is where the good part starts." She read silently to herself, her finger skimming across the lines. "Yep," she said.

Two anxious faces peered at her. "What?"

"Yep, just as we thought." She looked up. "He has autism."

Tomas grabbed the papers. "Where? Where does it say that?"

"Here." Mel pointed to the words '...diagnosis of a pervasive developmental disorder."

"Where does it say autism? I don't see that."

"Oh, dear." Mel sighed. "This gets tricky. There are a couple systems used for diagnostic criteria. The previous system was from a manual called the DSM-IV. In the DSM-IV, there was sort of an umbrella term of pervasive developmental disorder. Under that umbrella came categories such as Autistic Disorder, Asperger's Syndrome, etc. Under that system, Manny would likely have met the criteria for a diagnosis of Autism Disorder. But the DSM is revised every so many years and the last version came out is the DSM-V. Based on the DSM-V his diagnosis is Autism Spectrum Disorder with accompanying intellectual and language impairments, Level 3."

Maria and Tomas looked blank.

"Although many diagnosticians switched over to using the DSM-V when they diagnose, the team who saw Manny mention terms from both the DSM-IV and V; I guess they were trying to cover all bases. But either way, they say Manny has autism.

"Let's look at this part here." She pointed to a sentence. "Do you mind if I mark on this? "She pulled a highlighter from her purse. "This is the important part where is says, 'confirms a diagnosis of Autism Spectrum Disorder with accompanying intellectual and language impairments, Level 3.'" She underlined those words with the highlighter.

"It's saying that my son has *more* than just autism?"

"Only sort of. He has autism, yes, both going along with the autism is a language impairment; he doesn't talk in comparison to other kids his age."

Tomas and Maria looked at each other. Well, yeah, they had noticed that. It hardly seemed necessary to write that fact down.

Mel continued. "The middle part of the sentence says he has an intellectual impairment as well. His ability to acquire, retain and use information is not the same as other kids his age."

It was quiet around the table as the trio digested the information.

"Can the doctor's fix it?" asked Tomas.

Mel shook her head. "There is no cure for autism. It is a lifelong disorder."

They studied the boys playing in the corner. Every once in a while, two separate giggles could be heard.

Tentatively, Maria tried. "But, Manny, he's changed. He's playing with Kyle and he's never done anything like that before. And you say that Kyle's changed, too."

"Definitely," Mel agreed. "And both boys will continue to change as they grow and acquire new skills."

With hesitation Tomas asked, "Is there a pill?"

"There is no pill that will make the autism all go away. Sometimes some kids are helped by some meds that allow the child to pay attention better or remain calmer so that they are better able to learn, but it is definitely not automatic that if a child has autism, he will take medication."

"What do we do now?"

Mel returned to the report. "After the summary, there is usually a list of recommendations or suggestions. Ah, here they are." She read for a couple minutes. "Pretty standard stuff - exposure to other children, follow the recommendations of a speech/language pathologist, referral to an occupational therapist for follow-up on sensory strategies, social skills training, maintain a language-rich, structured environment, support routines with visuals and work closely with your school."

Looking up, she caught the expression on her friends' faces. "Sorry. Jargon stuff again, but this is stuff I'm comfortable with, stuff we do every day at school. You're in luck. There is not one thing listed here that we don't do at Madson School and do well. You won't need to take time off work to run Manny to appointments; the therapists will come right to the school. And when they're not there, the school staff will carry on with the programming these specialists lay out."

"Who are these people?"

"An occupational therapist is a professional trained in things like life skills and sensory sensitivities. You've already found some sensory strategies that work, like hugging Manny tightly, pressing on his shoulders, using the weighted blanket, etc., but the OT will help you learn more about the parts of Manny's nervous system that might be over- or under-aroused and things you can do to help him stay calm. As he gets older, he'll learn how to regulate himself more, without needing to rely so much on the adults around him.

"The speech therapist will work on a couple things. One is Manny's ability to understand what is said to him. Another is his skills at making his wants and needs known. Some kids show negative behaviors out of frustration when people don't understand what they want. Maybe Manny will eventually talk; we can't know that yet, but in the meantime, the speech therapist will help us work on other ways for him to communicate."

"And all this would happen at school."

"Definitely. All this and much, much more." Mel's encouraging expression contrasted with that of the anxious mother and father in front of her.

∾

WAVING plates of gingerbread men under the noses of the boys did the trick. They abandoned their blocks and followed Ellie to a table.

Ben's knees cracked, announcing that he was he rising to his feet. As Ellie started to giggle, he pointed a finger at his sister. "Not a word, you. Not one word." Ellie hid her mouth behind a napkin as she munched on a gingery leg with the little boys.

Ben joined his wife at Tomas' and Maria's table. "Ah, for some adult conversation. What are we talking about?"

"I was just telling them about some of the things we work on at school," replied Mel.

"School is not the way it was when you and I were kids," Ben told Tomas. "I made an ass out of myself with some of the assumptions I had when Kyle started school." Mel nodded emphatically.

"What happened?" asked Tomas.

"What didn't? I hardly know where to start." Ben glanced at his wife. "I bet you can list a whole bunch of things, but I'll recite my sins on my own, thank you." Turning to Tomas, he said, "For one thing, I couldn't get Kyle to school on time. Oh, I'd start way early in the morning, but somehow, it kept not working out and we were late each day, no matter what I did. Mel finally stepped in and her suggestions helped. Still, it wasn't easy.

"Then I made assumptions about some of the kids in the school. I didn't think my son should be around kids who were different. Hell, I didn't want to think that Kyle was different from the average child. I kept denying that he had autism. I know, I know, all the evidence was right in front of me, but I didn't want it to be true.

"I thought that the school was too poor to provide proper desks and chairs, not understanding that they purposely use different types of seating and furniture to benefit some kids. Mel had to explain everything to me, sometimes over and over again. But, she was patient - not! Sure, she has the patience of a saint with the kids, but with me, that's a whole other story."

"Could it be that the kids learn more quickly?" Mel asked sweetly.

Ben pretended to give her a noogie then squeezed her shoulder. "The worst was one of the tantrums Kyle had. I was even there to witness it when my kid ran up to his teacher and kicked her in the shins." Ben ran a hand over his face. "I was getting interested in this woman and trying to make a good impression when my kid attacks her. It's hard to recover from a move like that. But, she forgave me, forgave us, and we moved on."

Maria looked back and forth between Mel and Ben. "Mel was Kyle's teacher?" she asked.

"Yep, that's how we met. Kyle had just come to live with me and I was new to this whole parenting thing, let alone autism. She had to teach both of us."

Tomas was a few sentences back. "Are you saying that Kyle attacked his teacher?"

"Well, I don't know that I'd call it 'attacked'," said Mel. "He was frustrated and he took it out on me. He tended to lash out physically a lot back then."

Tomas turned in his chair to look at his son, Kyle and Ellie. "He seems so calm now."

"Yeah, yeah, but he can still be a little hellion sometimes. He's a kid. But, he's a pretty good kid. It took a while to work out the kinks of how we'd live together, but it's mostly good now."

Maria and Tomas traded glances. They were certainly not at a 'mostly good' stage.

EPILOGUE

The principal had a suggestion. "Why don't you take an early lunch and go home so you can walk your wife and son here for the pizza party?"

Gratefully, Tomas headed home. He and Maria still weren't sure about this decision. So much was uncertain when it came to their son.

As he turned the key in their door, he could hear a woman's voice he recognized, but it was not that of his wife. Maria and Manny sat at the table with their heads together, staring intently at the borrowed iPad screen. As the voice died away, Manny's finger pressed the triangle to make it play again. Mel's voice came through and Tomas recognized pictures of Madson School. Manny was watching the story Mel had made about Manny going to the pizza party.

"Well," Maria stood up. "We're about as ready as we'll ever be." In answer to Tomas's unspoken questions, she said, "It's been a good morning. He's been settled and the sun graced us with the dust motes, so he's nice and relaxed."

As the video ended, Tomas instructed, "Time to get your coat, Manny. We have to leave now if you're going to eat pizza with Kyle."

Marie whispered in his ear, "I'm so nervous, I won't be able to eat a thing."

"Good. That means we'll both have our hands free to jump in, just in case," Tomas whispered back.

They started out, but had only gone half a block when Maria remembered the iPad. It only took Tomas minutes to run back for it. They didn't dare not have it handy, remembering that one incident at the bakery.

Once outside the school, they stopped, showed Manny the door and played the video for him again. Then, taking big breaths, they each latched on to one of their son's hands and entered the building.

The first face that greeted them belonged to Mel. She knelt down to eye level with Manny, gave him a soft hello, and then said, "Give me five." She never let on that her knees were killing her as she waited, then, ever so slowly, Manny's hand rose to brush hers.

Just a tiny bit of tension left Maria's shoulders.

They started down the hallway, bound for Mel's classroom. The sound of rapidly spinning wheels approached them. Tomas' heart sank. As fond as he'd grown of Jordan, he did did not want to see him right now. He remembered his initial reactions to Jordan's wheelchair and feared that the apparatus might upset Manny. Before he could interfere, Jordan was there, in all his exuberant glory.

"Hey, Mr. G., watch this!" And Jordan executed his signature wheelie, but with some added flare this time. "Cool, eh?" As his tires touched down, Jordan spun to regard Tomas' family. "Is this your kid?" He wheeled closer, almost on top of Manny's toes. "Hi, I'm Jordan." He held up his hand for a high five.

Manny, who had been mesmerized by the shiny, chrome, spinning spokes of Jordan's chair, didn't move.

Mel stepped in. "Jordan," she called. "What about me?" She held up her hand.

Jordan smacked her hand and grinned.

Mel placed one hand on Jordan's chair to keep him still as she explained. "Manny's new to the school. Let's go easy on him until he gets to know you." She again crouched down to Manny's level. "Jordan wants to meet you," she told him. "Can you give him a high five?"

Jordan, not known for his patience, held his hand suspended.

Come on, come, thought Tomas. We only have so long before things can go south on us. The quicker they got this over with and Jordan went on his way, the safer they'd all feel. He moved to reach for Manny's arm, but didn't need to. Manny raised his eyes from Jordan's entrancing wheels and turned his head. Looking out the side of his eyes, he peered at Jordan and raised his hand. Jordan gave it a resounding smack, then with a, "See ya," wheeled away.

Phew. Another bullet dodged.

Then, a small head ducked out of the next classroom. Kyle. "Manny, come on, aren't we ever going to eat? We're waiting for you."

Would you like a free story?

Anything For Her Son is a tale about a mother's love for her autistic child. Grab your free copy at https://dl.bookfunnel.com/a27d9uzou0

Come back and see how Kyle, Ben, Mel and their friends are doing, and meet more students of Madson School. You'll find them in the next four books in the series.

Autism Goes to School
Autism Runs Away
Autism Belongs
Autism Talks and Talks
Autism Grows Up
Autism Box Set
(the first 5 books in the series)
Autism Goes to College - Jeff's Coming of Age Story
Anything For Her Son

If nonfiction plus autism is your preference:

DR. SHARON A. MITCHELL

Autism Questions Parents Ask & The Answers They Seek
Autism Questions Teachers Ask & The Answers They Seek

Try the psychological thriller series **When Bad Things Happen**:

Gone
Trust
Selfish
Instinct
Reasons Why
Mine
Young Anna (short story free at https://dl.
bookfunnel.com/xrj0h5wef9)

DEDICATION

To those unique individuals who are autistic and the families who love them.
To the dedicated and talented people at Autism Services.

And to M.E.A.L. - the most wondrous beta readers ever. This book owes a *lot* to you.

Turn the page to read GONE: A Psychological Thriller.

And yes, autism is part of this story, too.

EXCERPT FROM AUTISM
TALKS AND TALKS

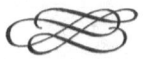

SCHOOL DAZE: BOOK FOUR
Autism
TALKS AND TALKS
Dr Sharon A Mitchell

EXCERPT FROM AUTISM TALKS AND TALKS

*L*ori's back was to the door as she put away the last of the staff coffee cups. Everyone was supposed to clean up after themselves, but that didn't always happen. The kitchen needed to be tidy before the kids arrived.

"Who are you?" a strange man asked from the doorway. In his hands were bulging plastic grocery bags.

"I'm Lori Nabaker. Who are you supposed to be?" Although school was over for the day, the doors off the parking lot were open for kids to arrive. But, anyone could walk in.

"Supposed to be?" The guy just stared at her, the bags dangling from his fingertips. "What do you mean 'supposed to be'? I am who I am; there's no supposing about it." He looked at her some more. "Are you *supposed* to be here?"

Lori's weirdo meter rose. What was with this guy? Who was he and how'd she get trapped in this room with him? Never show fear and maybe she could bluff her way out. "Excuse me. Let me pass." His large body still blocked the doorway. Then he stood aside, taking a step into the room and pivoting so that the back of his hips pressed against the counter's edge.

As she scurried out the door, away from this strange man, she heard him mutter, "Mel should have warned me about the odd people here. At least she'll be out of the way before the kids show up."

Lori stopped. "Kids? Mel?"

"You know my sister?"

"Mel's your sister?"

When the guy nodded, the tension in Lori's shoulders dropped noticeably. She came back into the room with her hand extended. "You must be Jeff - Mel's told me about you. I'm the EA who works in her classroom sometimes." Jeff looked blankly at her, so she explained. "EA. You know, Educational Associate. I help out with the kids."

There was no recognition in his eyes and his expression didn't change. Come to think of it, his expression hadn't changed since he arrived. But his next words were gentler. "Oh, yeah, Mel told me that someone from the school would assist me."

"Assist you? I thought *I* was running the Little Chef's club and that Mel's brother was supposed to assist me."

"There you go with that suppose thing again." Jeff looked away from her as he laid the things from his grocery bags on the counter. Each item was lined up precisely, equal distance from each other and from the edge of the counter. Concentrating on his task, Jeff asked, "Are you a chef?"

His words were muffled partly because his back was to her and partly because he was dragging packages along the counter, getting their placement just right. "Pardon," she asked. "What did you say?"

"I said, 'Are you a chef?'".

"I just told you I'm an EA."

"Well, then..."

"Well, then what?"

"Well, then, I *am* a chef. That's why Mel asked me to volunteer my time to run the Little Chef's club. You can help me though, that is, if you know how to act and don't scare the kids. If you stay you're going to have to watch your language."

"My language!" Lori's indignation made her voice rise on the last syllable. She most certainly had not used any profanity during this whole unpleasant encounter.

"Yes, your language. You'll have to watch how you talk around the kids. No more of this "suppose" stuff. You have to speak plainly and say what you mean. Some of the kids who'll be here have autism, you know. They won't like your imprecise way of talking."

As Lori's mouth opened in retort, there was a flurry of rustling plastic as Mel came through the door carrying far more bags than the two Jeff had arrived with.

Mel dropped the bags on the floor and smiled at both of them. "Oh, good," she said. "I see that you've already met."

Her smile froze as she looked from Jeff to Lori and back again. "Hey, guys, is everything all right?"

Jeff reached for the bags and continued the tedious process of unpacking and lining up the contents perfectly on the counter.

"It's a good thing the counter's long," Lori said, the sarcasm sneaking into her voice. Mel gave her a sharp look, but Jeff simply agreed. "Yep."

Sensing the tension, Mel asked, "What's going on?"

Her brother answered, "We were just getting a few things straight. We've established that Lori's an EA and I'm a chef."

Mel continued looking from her brother to her friend. "So, why is that a problem?"

"No problem," Lori hurried to reassure her. "We're good."

Sneakers squeaked and slapped on the hallway floor, accompanied by high-pitched voices. The kids had arrived for Little Chef Club.

"Well, this is it," said Lori.

"What is it?" Jeff asked.

"The beginning of Little Chefs."

Jeff stared at her. "What did you think it would be?" Then, turning to his sister, "Are you sure she's the right person to be helping us with this? She seems unclear about a number of things."

Mel squeezed his shoulder. "Wait until you see her with the kids. You'll see that she's perfect."

Jeff didn't look convinced but the kids burst through the door, overtaking any conversation the adults had begun. The students' enthusiasm was admirable but needed to be toned down to match the size of the school's kitchen. Mel had them line up against the wall. She waited for silence before reminding the group who she was, then introducing Lori and Jeff.

"How can you be a chef?" one boy asked. "Where's your chef's hat?"

"Right here." Jeff pulled it out of the last bag and settled it on his head. Next, he donned his apron, pulling the string ties from the back and fastening them in the front.

"Wow! Just like on TV," said Matt, the smallest child in the line.

"Not necessarily," said Karen, a grade six student. "It depends on the restaurant and on the show. There are all kinds of aprons and several kinds of chef hats. First, there's..."

"Thanks, Karen," Mel interrupted. "We might have time to go into that later, but right now we need to begin our chef's session. Jeff will be leading our group since he's an actual chef"

Over Mel's head, Jeff grinned at Lori. To the kids he said, "Who washed their hands before coming here?"

Of the eight kids, two put up their hands.

"Good for you. Now, we're going to do it all over again."

Groans came from several kids, along with "Do we have to?" "Again?" "Mine look okay already."

"Anyone who touches anything or eats in my kitchen must first wash their hands," Jeff announced. "Ms. Nabaker will show you how."

When Lori hesitated, he asked Mel, "She does know how, doesn't she?" This made the kids laugh, Jeff look at them quizzically and Lori glare at him before herding the kids in a line towards the sink.

Standing beside his sister, out of the way of the line-up, Jeff said, "I think this is starting off all right."

"Mostly. Except for Lori. You're being a little hard on her, aren't you?"

"What do you mean? She has to wash her hands just like everybody else. She wants to help lead, so I thought this was something she could be in charge of." He waited a minute then asked, "Why aren't you getting in line?"

While Mel waited her turn, she listened to the kids. One voice rose above the others, both in volume and frequency. Karen was explaining to anyone who would listen, the different hand washing techniques. She was currently at the sink demonstrating how a surgeon would wash, counting off the number of scrubs for each finger. Except no one was paying any attention to her monologue.

A grade six boy, Jim said, "Come on, Karen. We're never going to get to cook anything if you hog the sink the whole time." Lori intervened and got the line moving again.

When Karen's voice continued to rise above the others about this hand washing business, Mel intervened. "You certainly know a lot about hand washing, Karen. Thanks for your input, but we're moving on now to the cooking part."

Karen paused then switched topics. "Chateaubriand is made from the most expensive cut of beef. It's cut from the tenderloin and is about four inches thick." The other kids just looked at her as she continued. "Because of the thickness of the cut and how expensive the meat is, it has to be cooked just right."

Again, Mel interrupted. "Thanks, Karen, but we're not talking about Chateaubriand this week."

"But it's a classic chef dish," Karen protested.

Jeff took over. "Right. It is and it's something I make at the deli. But we don't have enough time today or the budget for that kind of meat. Today, we're starting with the basics."

"Basics? But I'm not a basic kind of girl. I know a lot about this stuff already," protested Karen.

As if he hadn't heard her, Jeff continued. "First, we'll learn about safety in the kitchen. Washing your hands and keeping utensils and surfaces clean is key. That comes before anything else, even tasting the food."

"We do get to taste some stuff, don't we?" asked another boy.

"Definitely. It's a poor chef who doesn't taste what he's cooking. How else would you know if it's any good?" The kids looked relieved.

"Who has used a knife before?" Jeff asked. Most kids raised a hand. Jeff pulled a foot long knife from the drawer. "Who has used a knife like this?"

"That's a cimeter and used for butchering, but not normal kitchen use," Karen informed them. "Sometimes it's used for cutting steaks and tenderloin, the kind used in Chateaubriand."

Jeff looked at her. "Are you here to learn or to teach?"

Lori moved to Karen's side and placed an arm along her shoulder. "Karen reads a lot and stores her knowledge. Cooking shows are her passion, so she has a lot to offer this group." She smiled at her warmly.

"I watch a lot of cooking shows too, and study this area. But we're not here to spout off our knowledge. We're here to learn how to cook certain items that I've chosen. If you want to discuss some aspects of cooking with me after class that will be fine." Jeff's words were blunt, but only Lori seemed uncomfortable.

Over Karen's head, Mel grinned at Lori. She mouthed, "It's okay," then nodded at Karen. Mel was right; Karen did not look upset or show that she might have felt snubbed.

A PSYCHOLOGICAL THRILLER

GONE

WHEN BAD THINGS HAPPEN BOOK 1

SHARON A. MITCHELL

GONE: A PSYCHOLOGICAL THRILLER

CHAPTERS 1 - 4

PART I
MONDAY

CHAPTER 1

*J*ackson sipped his morning coffee - just the temperature he liked it, creamy and the best coffee beans Gevalia offered. At least Elizabeth got that right. He turned the newspaper to the next page. Behind his paper screen was the murmur of his wife's voice. You'd almost think she was there alone.

Well, time to get moving. He had stuff to do, a life to get on with and plans to make things even better. He let the paper flop onto his plate of congealing eggs. Straightening his suit, he stood and checked that his cuff links were properly seated.

Elizabeth placed a kiss on their son's forehead and rubbed noses with him. Four-year-old Timothy remained focused on plucking Cheerios off his highchair table.

Irked, Jackson thought he'd try once again. "Isn't he a little old to still be using a highchair? For God's sake, he's almost ready for school and could sit in a chair."

Elizabeth looked up, frowning. "I've explained before. He's much safer strapped into his highchair. He could fall off a chair and get hurt."

Jackson sighed. Turning, he picked up his briefcase in one hand and his suitcase in the other. That was another thing Elizabeth did right - she always had his case packed with exactly the items he'd need to wear during the week.

Elizabeth came to the doorway. She adjusted her husband's tie and brushed the lapels of his suit. Perfect, as always. She looked up at him. "Are you sure you can't come to the neurologist appointment with us this morning?"

"We've been through this. I have to work, you know that. Someone has to pay the bills and keep a roof over our heads." He didn't meet her eyes. "Besides, it'll be the same old, same old anyway."

"But things have changed. They're getting worse."

Of course they are, Jackson thought. And if you wouldn't baby him so much, he'd have a chance of being normal. He glanced over at his son who was oblivious to their conversation, the tension in the air or their very presence, he thought. "Anyway, gotta go." He leaned toward Elizabeth to place the obligatory peck on her cheek.

Behind Elizabeth, a bumping and rattling started as the highchair legs skittered across the floor. She rushed over to their son, wrapping her arms around his head. "He's having a seizure!"

Well again, of course he is, Jackson said to himself. When does he not? He loved his son, he really did, but for just a little while he'd like to have a normal boy, a boy he could play with, take places and be proud of. He shook his head. He was proud of his son, an appealing tike. When out in public, people commented on how good looking he was, but when they tried to engage him, Timothy's eyes slid away. Elizabeth would step in to explain their son's lack of interest, saying he was ill and not feeling well. Partially true; he was ill. That was just it. This was not what Jackson had signed on for. Still, the kid would probably be better if his mother would stop this over-protective bit. Every guy knew that when a baby entered your life, the mom's focus would be on the child for a while. Understandable. But should that baby remain the center of her universe for four whole years, with no end in sight?

He watched a few moments longer as the highchair shook with the violence of Timothy's spasms. Then the odor of urine filled the kitchen. Figures. Kid pissed himself again. If he would not be toilet-trained, he wished Elizabeth would keep the kid's diaper on. At least when he was home, rather than going through this farce of toilet training. He shook his head and went out the door. Outside, he said to the air, "Be back Friday night. See you then." Or not.

ELIZABETH CRADLED TIMOTHY'S HEAD, protecting it from bruising and bumps on the back and arms of the highchair. Although the seizures rarely lasted more than a minute or so, they could seem to take forever when you held your writhing child in your arms, praying for it to be over, praying for him to be undamaged by this assault on his brain.

Finally, the thrashing stopped, and Timothy slumped to the side. The seizures took so much out of him. He'd sleep for the next hour, at least, and awaken groggy and disoriented. She liked to remain near, providing comfort and whatever security she could offer.

Unstrapping him from the highchair took a while because of the five-point harness and double locking system. Once, before all that was in place, a seizure had thrown him right out of the chair, adding a minor concussion on top of all his other problems.

With her nose that close, Elizabeth could smell the urine. Looking under the chair, she saw the puddle forming. She grimaced, knowing how much Jackson hated that. Well, so did she, and she was sure Timothy felt the same way. It was just that he had no control. None of them had control over this. Timothy actually smiled at her when she dressed him in his big boy underwear this morning. Was it just half an hour ago? She cherished moments like that, when he would look right at her and share his enjoyment. Even if he didn't say it, she knew he was proud to have that diaper off. So much for today's toilet training session.

Lifting a limp forty-pound child out of a snug-fitting highchair was no simple task, but Elizabeth honed this skill over the many times she had to do this on her own. Getting him into her arms, she felt the wet soaking into the sleeve of her new blouse. Another one for the dry cleaners.

She glanced up at the doorway toward her husband. Gone. Out of habit, she schooled her expression so her disappointment wouldn't show, then remembered that there was no one there to pretend for. Jackson was gone; Timothy was sleeping the sleep of the unconscious, as he always did after a major seizure.

It was Monday and Jackson was gone. Another long week of basically single parenting until Jackson returned home Friday.

CHAPTER 2

D r. Muller's office was familiar, sadly familiar. What Elizabeth wouldn't give to have never had reason to enter such a place. Or even if this visit was a one-shot deal. Or their last visit.

Set up for kids, there was a section in the corner with a low wall separating the waiting room chairs from the kids' play area. Meant to be easily climbable by the average child, a startling number of the small kids entering this office needed to be lifted over the barrier to sit in the ball pit or helped to reach for the toys. While some young patients obviously wanted their parents' help in getting to the play area, Timothy showed no such reaction. He appeared neutral to his surroundings, neither clinging to his mom, burying his head against her legs nor clambering to go play. Elizabeth assumed that he was more mature than other preschoolers, already above such things as a ball pit, and so self-possessed that he was content with his own thoughts. At least this meant he wouldn't be one of those kids who screamed when lifted away from the toys to have their turn with the doctor.

Instead, Timothy sat quietly beside his mother, playing with his hands. Jazz hands, she called them; he could twist them into such intriguing shapes and seemed content to do this for hours. Thankfully, Elizabeth thought that he had fewer seizures when quietly occupied. Maybe.

~

THE RECEPTIONIST CALLED Timothy's name. In the doorway to the hall stood a smiling Dr. Muller. Elizabeth stood, said her son's name softly. When there was no response, she gently took his upper arm and guided him off his chair toward the physician. Dr. Muller squatted to be closer to Timothy's height and held out his hand. "Hi, Timmy. It's good to see you again."

"Timothy," reminded Elizabeth. "His name is Timothy." She gave a soft nudge to her son's shoulder, hoping he would respond to the extended hand. She had practiced this with Timothy at home. While he would shake hands with her, he could not seem to generalize that action with anyone else.

The doctor straightened, unrebuffed and led the way to his office.

~

"So, how has it been going, young man?" Dr. Muller directed his question to Timothy.

As always, his mom answered for him. "Not well, not well at all."

The neurologist tried again with Timothy. He called his name, waited then called again, watching for a shift in Timothy's attention, a glance his way or some recognition that he had heard his name called. Nothing.

"He's never comfortable in any place but home," Elizabeth explained. Then she started to describe that morning's seizure.

"Wait." Dr. Muller held up his hand. "I'll get the nurse in here to take Timothy away to play. Then we can talk."

"Oh, he won't go with anyone but me."

"I'd prefer not to talk about your son in front of him. If we had some privacy, you can speak more freely."

"That's not a problem. Timothy doesn't talk."

"I'm aware of that. But that doesn't mean that he isn't listening and understanding what we say."

"I only wish that were true. My husband and I talk all the time, and about our concerns over him and he never pays any attention."

"As you wish, Mrs. Whitmore. You are his guardian."

"Yes. As I was saying, the seizures are worse."

"Frequency? Intensity?" he asked.

"Yes, to both. And they're not just absence seizures, or at least we don't notice many of those anymore. Maybe they're still happening, but the major ones take up our attention. Remember those he used to have, the kind where his upper body would stiffen when he was lying down, and he'd sit up?"

"Jackknifing. Are those occurring more now?"

"They do, but it's not just those. Sometimes one arm will rise in the air, straight up, and stay that way for maybe half a minute. You can't bend his arm down when that's happening. He's clunked both Jackson and I in the face several times. At first Jackson got mad, thinking Timothy was doing it on purpose to be funny. But he's not - I swear he is not."

"How often is this happening?"

"Several times a day. And that's not all. Over the last week or two, he's having tonic-clonic seizures. I looked it up on the internet. He seems to lose consciousness, then his body is twitching and moving. If I don't protect him, he hits his head. Hard. I try to keep him by me at all times, because he just drops to the ground when it happens. Once he got this huge bump on his forehead." She brushed Timothy's bangs back, showing the remnants of what was a nasty contusion. "What I need to know is when this will end."

Dr. Muller leaned back in his chair. "I know this isn't what you want to hear, but the honest answer is that I don't know. There's a chance never."

Elizabeth's body moved to the edge of her chair. "But before you called this Infantile Spasms. He's not an infant anymore. I thought that most kids grew out of this."

"West Syndrome," he began.

"But Jackson told me it wasn't West Syndrome."

"Mr. Whitmore did not want it to be West Syndrome." He sighed. "West Syndrome, although we sometimes don't know why it occurs, is a genetic disorder passed down from men to their sons."

"Jackson did not have seizures. Ever. I asked his mother."

"It can be recessive in a man, but still passed on to his son."

"That would mean…".

"Yes, I'm afraid that that's how your husband saw it, that if Timothy had West Syndrome, then the fault or blame lay with the father. There is no blame; it sometimes just happens."

"This is something babies get. I think we first noticed it when Timothy was about six-months-old. It's been three and a half years. Shouldn't he be growing out of it by now? It's getting worse and the seizures are changing."

"I understand. Since he first started having them, we've noticed abnormal EEG patterns. They were consistent with what we often see in West Syndrome. But they do seem to be changing. I think he might be developing a different variety of seizure disorder."

"Okay, that might be good, one you can do something about."

Dr. Muller shook his head. "I'm afraid that what we might be seeing is Lennox Gastaut. It's a rare form of epilepsy that begins in childhood."

"When does it go away?"

"It doesn't, or at least it rarely goes away."

"We can treat it, can't we?"

"We have medications that can help to keep it under some degree of control."

"He's already on anti-epileptic meds!"

"Yes, and he'll remain on some, but we'll tweak the doses, the timing and the exact meds until we find the optimum level of control with as few side effects as possible."

"Side effects?"

"We'll aim for a balance between dampening down the seizure action without overly sedating Timmy."

"Timothy." Elizabeth's voice rose. "It's Timothy. If we had wanted him called Timmy or Tim or some other variation, we would have named him that. We chose Timothy. It's a strong and solid name."

"Sorry." Dr. Muller glanced at the child. "Timothy, I didn't mean to get your name wrong."

The child seemed not to care either way. He fixated on the play of his hands in the sunbeam coming through the south-facing window.

ELIZABETH TOOK a minute to absorb this news before composing herself. She grasped her son's hands, pulling them tightly to her lap. "What about his development? There was some question about that when you thought it was Infantile Spasms."

"You're right. There is often some degree of cognitive impairment with IS. But, when the child was meeting all development milestones previous to the onset of the seizures, there is a greater chance of development closer to typical."

"Closer." Elizabeth held on to that word. It meant good things. Sort of. "He seems fine now. I mean, just look at what he can do with his hands. He has more dexterity than do kids a year older than him. He can pick up the tiniest speck that I can hardly even see. But he knows it's there and goes after it."

Dr. Muller nodded.

"And he's far more content than most four-year-olds. He hardly needs any entertaining; he can amuse himself for long stretches where other kids plague their parents."

Again, Dr. Muller nodded, encouraging Elizabeth to continue. When she didn't, he asked the one question she did not want to discuss. "How is his speech?"

She looked away. "It's not there. Or, hardly at all."

"Hardly? That you would say that is encouraging. What words does he say? Momma? Daddy? Please? Me? Does he respond to his name? Go get the item you ask for?"

"No, none of those. Not once that we've ever heard. But when he says something, he can go on and on for sentences." Her voice became more enthused. "He can recite long speeches from some of his videos. He loves them and watches them over and over. And he's so smart he can run our DVD player all by himself. And he can find the things he wants to watch from You Tube on the iPad".

They both watched Timothy wave and contort his hands in the air, smiling as he did so.

"He's a beautiful child," Elizabeth whispered.

"Yes, he is a good-looking boy. Mrs. Whitmore, I wonder if there is something else we're seeing here."

"This Lennox-Gastaut?"

"Well, that and possibly something else as well."

"Something you can cure? Something that will go away?"

"I'm afraid not. We are likely talking about a lifelong condition. Conditions, to be exact."

ELIZABETH PUSHED BACK her chair and reached for her son. She swept him into her arms. "Thank you, Dr. Muller. Anything further will have to wait until my husband is with us. He was really not pleased about the possibility of West Syndrome, and I doubt he will like the sounds of what you are insinuating now." She took several steps toward the door. "We'll call to make an appointment when Jackson can be here."

"Just a minute, please." Dr. Muller held up a piece of paper. "Here are your prescriptions for the new medications. You remember how we weaned him gradually off the current medication by going from three times a day to two, then one, then giving one day of rest before beginning the new one. The valproic acid waChapters not giving as much control as we'd like, so we'll see what a combination of Lamictal and Clobazam will do. Begin with the Lamictal first, just one before bed then by this weekend, add one Clobazam first thing in the morning. We'll see what that does."

"We'll see? Aren't you supposed to *know*?"

"I wish I did, but medicine is not an exact science. Everyone's metabolism handles compounds differently. We'll need to play around with this until we find the best combination to give him some relief."

Clutching her son tightly, Elizabeth fled, prescriptions in hand.

Behind her, the receptionist called. "Mrs. Whitmore, don't you want to make your next appointment? Dr. Muller said he wanted to see you in two weeks."

"Later. I'll call you later when I know my husband's schedule. I want him here the next time."

CHAPTER 3

*A*fter securing Timothy in his car seat, Elizabeth sat behind the
steering wheel, hands in the ten o'clock and two o'clock
position, clenching and unclenching her fists. Okay, breathe, she told
herself. In through the nose and out through the mouth. Calming
breaths. She glanced in the rearview mirror at her son. Timothy was
content, playing with his fingers, two of which found their way into
his mouth. Elizabeth grimaced. She always cleaned his hands
immediately after leaving a doctor's office. You never know what
germs were floating around such places and Timothy could not afford
to get any sicker than he was. Upset at the possible negative prognosis
Dr. Muller hinted at, she had completely forgotten about cleansers
when she fled his office.

Why did she have to do this alone? Why couldn't Jackson have
taken even just an hour off work to go with her? Part of her brain
knew that he was already halfway across the State by now and had to
travel for his job, but still.... This felt too much like single parenting,
something she had not signed on for. She wasn't one of those strong,
independent women; she needed a man to rely on. A man like her dad
had been would be ideal. But those were rare commodities, and it
wasn't fair to Jackson to compare him to her pretty much perfect dad.

Well, he would still be perfect if he hadn't ended up dead, leaving her alone.

I'm not alone, she reminded herself. I have a beautiful son and a loving husband. We're fine.

~

ELIZABETH UNCRUMPLED the papers still locked between her fingers. She spread them out - yes, the prescriptions were still readable. And yes, she knew the routine of weaning Timothy off one medication, while gradually increasing the dose of a new one, recording side effects, and efficacies. She could do this. She had to.

~

SHE MADE the drive to the pharmacy on autopilot. Great. Looked like Timothy was just falling asleep. He'd be cranky if she woke him. Sighing, she began loosening the straps on his car seat.

"Come on, big guy. We have to go see Mr. Rexton." A groggy Timothy leaned on his mom, the back of his head pressing into her neck. She hefted him up a little higher and with one arm firmly around his bottom, reached into the front seat for her purse, slinging it over her shoulder. Since she became a mother, there were no more clutch purses for her - only shoulder bags that would leave her hands free. This whole business was easier when Timothy was younger. Toting a forty-pound child was tougher than one might think. Who needed to go the gym when she did this all day?

~

MR. REXTON'S warm eyes greeted her. He always served Elizabeth himself rather than relying on his assistants. He took a special interest in Timothy. Elizabeth discovered that pharmacists held a wealth of knowledge and could help explain things she was too overwhelmed to ask her son's specialists, or didn't get the first time she heard them.

She handed over the new prescriptions. Sam Rexton raised his eyebrows. "Let's hope that these just might do the trick. How has the little tike been?"

"Obviously not well or well enough," Elizabeth replied, nodding at the prescriptions.

"Let me pull up his chart." After perusing the screen a minute, he asked, "Shall we go over the protocol for weaning him off of the valproic acid?" As they discussed the approach Dr. Muller laid out, Timothy stirred in her arms. It was one thing to hold a sleeping forty pounds, but another to keep a good grip on a squirming forty pounds. She slid him down her legs and steadied him until his feet seemed firmly planted, holding his right hand.

"We have a bit of a back-log right now, so it will take about twenty minutes for me to fill these. Do you want to wait?"

Timothy was pulling at her hand. "No, I think we'll come back. I have a bit of shopping to do then I'll fill the car with gas. We should be back within an hour or so."

The pharmacist pointed to the jar on the counter containing suckers. Elizabeth shook her head. "Still low carb so we're avoiding sweets. But thanks, anyway." Besides, such treats made such a sticky mess.

"See you soon," he told Timothy. "When you come back, I'll have a better treat waiting for you."

SHE DIDN'T NEED MUCH, just a few things at the grocery store. Some nuts, cheese and avocados. They didn't last well so she liked to buy them fresh a few times a week. While it had at first seemed daunting, the ketogenic diet wasn't that difficult to maintain once she had firmly in mind which foods to have on hand. The worst part was eliminating breads. Sandwiches were a quick meal for a child, but they'd learned to make do. Mostly, she and Jackson stuck to the diet as well, and they'd each lost a few extra pounds. While it had helped them, she was not so sure that the diet was having any effect on their son's seizures. But, as Dr. Muller said, maybe they'd be worse without this low-carb diet. She grabbed her insulated bag out of the trunk, and they went to pick up their groceries. This would be a fast trip because she had a surprise in mind for Jackson so would need to make time for an extra stop. No, it wasn't his birthday or their anniversary; she just wanted to do something nice and keep it in the freezer for when he got home Friday. She had placed an order for a Dairy Queen Ice Cream cake - his favorite Reeses-Pieces kind and would pick it up after she got groceries, then gas, then Timothy's prescriptions. And Jackson thought that all a housewife did was sit at home watching soaps.

JACKSON LIKED to tease that she was such a creature of habit. Maybe that was true, but she found it easier to get chores done when she kept to a schedule. She filled the car with gas every Monday. When she first got her driver's license, her dad had drilled it into her to never let her gas tank get below half full because you just never knew. Only driving around town she used little gas, certainly not like poor Jackson who put thousands of miles on his car each month. The life of a traveling salesman. Elizabeth often wondered if Frankfurt Electric knew just what a gem of an employee they had in Jackson. She wasn't sure his take-home pay he showed her reflected his real worth. Despite the long hours he worked, they'd have a hard time living off just his wage. Good thing her father had the forethought to prepare a trust fund for her and bought their home as a wedding gift.

ELIZABETH PULLED into the gas station, the same one she always went to. Sticking with the familiar made life easier - just one more thing that she didn't have to figure out during her day.

As she started the pump running, she watched her son's sleeping face through the side window. He looked so at peace. But she knew that even in his slumber a seizure could attack. Thankfully, there had been just one today.

When the nozzle clicked off, she placed it back on the pump, then shut her gas cap. She reached in the compartment in the driver's door for her hand sanitizer. You never knew who had last handled these gas pumps and what germs they might carry that she might pass on to Timothy. The seizures were far worse when he got sick.

After rubbing for the required thirty seconds, she replaced the sanitizer, grabbed her purse to head in to pay for her gas. Crossing the pavement, she felt the sun on her hair and wiped her forehead with the back of her arm.

She hated perspiring; it was not her thing. Goodness, it was a blistering afternoon.

Hot. She glanced back at her slumbering son. The temperature inside a closed car could rise quickly, and Timothy had already been in the car almost five minutes while she pumped the gas. Getting overheated was one condition that brought on seizures. Should she wake him up and carry him inside with her? He was such a dead weight when he didn't want to awaken. She'd just be a few seconds inside and he would be in plain sight all the time.

Elizabeth returned to the car, slid in and started the engine, cranking up the air conditioning. It was the right thing to do; it was already uncomfortably hot inside. In the rear-view mirror, she could see that Timothy hadn't stirred. That neurologist appointment this morning must have taken as much out of him as it did out of her.

"Just a few more minutes, baby, then we'll head home and relax." Leaving the engine running, and leaving the door unlocked so she could get back in, Elizabeth went to pay for her gas.

She timed it poorly, and there were two people ahead of her in line. But then it was finally her turn. "I'm on pump five, please." She placed her purse on the counter to rummage through to find her wallet. Her purse was cavernous. Who would have known you had to carry around so much stuff for one small child?

The gas station attendant repeated the price. "Yes, I just need to get my credit card," Elizabeth mumbled, face pointed into the cavern of her shoulder bag. Opening her wallet, the first thing she saw was the picture of her son, taken on his fourth birthday. It always warmed her heart, that picture. Timothy with his arms around his parents, all wearing silly party hats.

Pulling the wallet out, she glanced at the car where Timothy sat, oblivious to the world.

She froze like a mannequin posed in a catatonic position. She could not take in what her eyes were seeing.

What? Who was that? There was a man, and he was opening the driver's door. Wait! He was getting in. "Hey!"

Elizabeth took off, yelling. Whereas the gas station had been full when she pulled in, but now it was void of people - except for this strange man getting into her car.

The guy shut the door. She could see his hand go to the gear shift. He was going to take off!

She sprinted the last few steps, turning her ankle on the concrete lip, breaking off the heel of her shoe. The car crept forward. Her left hand grabbed for the rear door handle, latched on and pulled. The car was already moving and picking up speed. She threw herself inside, her torso sprawling atop Timothy's car seat, her legs dangling outside. As she attempted to right herself, her left shoe flew off as they bumped over the curb. She yanked her legs inside just as the car's momentum swung the door shut.

CHAPTER 4

"*H*ey! Stop! Are you crazy? This is my car!" Elizabeth worked at righting herself, checking to see that she had not squashed Timothy when she dove into the car. No, he was fine and still asleep. "Stop this car right now and get out!"

"Not gonna happen. I need a car."

"Well, you can't have this one."

"Could have fooled me, lady. I seem to be the one driving."

Her hand went to her chest as if that would stop her racing heart. More quietly she asked, "Why are you doing this to us? We haven't done anything to you. This is kidnapping. You'll go to prison."

"I'm not kidnapping anyone. What do you take me for? I started driving, and you slammed yourself into the car. While it was moving, even." He glanced in the rear-view mirror. "Right on that kid. What kind of mother does that?"

Elizabeth's head whipped from side to side, checking all the windows. Surely someone had noticed what was happening and called the police. Any second now, cops and rescuers would surround them. She just needed to buy some time. "Look, just slow down a bit and drive carefully. There's a child here. What is it you want from us?"

"I don't want nothing from you. I need a car. I didn't plan on you tagging along."

"But you were driving off with my son!"

"How'd I know someone would leave a kid sleeping all alone in a car?"

Elizabeth grimaced. He was right. "Look, just pull over and let us out, all right? You can have the car."

"Are you kidding? You can identify me and the car. How soon before you're screaming away to the police? You made your choice, so now you're coming with me." He thought a moment more. "Or you could jump out, the same way you jumped in, but I'll keep the kid as insurance that you'll keep your mouth shut."

"I'm not leaving without my son!"

"We could do this another way. You leave the kid on the street while you stay with me."

"I can't abandon my child on the street. Anything could happen to him." Anything *did* happen to him, she thought. And while under her care. Jackson called her an over-protective and hovering mother. And still this had happened. But it was her fault; she had done the unthinkable and left her son alone.

The initial panic was tamped down a bit now. Their lives were not in immediate danger, at least not at this moment. Although they were on the freeway heading south, at least this lunatic was not driving wildly. "Where are we going?"

*"A*RE *you sure you gave me the right schedule? We can't find her." Impatience was in his voice.*

"It's Monday, isn't it? You can absolutely count on her to be where she's supposed to be. The only deviation would be if the kid got sick. That happens, but she never keeps that information to herself. There would be calls for sure and there's been none."

"She's not where you said she'd be."

"Shit, man, she even follows the same route. Look, she was home for the

morning, then had a one o'clock appointment with the neurologist. Maybe there was some hitch there, and she's running late because he overbooked his appointments again. Anyway, since his meds were running low, next she'd go to the drugstore. While the prescription's being filled, she'll go get groceries. Next, she'll fill the car with gas. She always does that Monday afternoons. If you just hung out there, you'll see her."

"We did. I got a guy there now and one at the pharmacy. I'm at her house. None of us have seen her. She's gone."

"Not possible. No one is more boringly the same than Elizabeth. Find her! That's what you're paid for."

ELIZABETH RUBBED her son's knee. He slept peacefully, so the touch reassured her more than him. Only then did she realize that her hand still clutched the credit card she'd pulled from her purse. Thank god. She may need it. She hunched over slightly, slipping it inside her bra, out of site of the maniac who had kidnapped them.

Her purse! All her ID was inside it and she'd left it on the counter at the gas station. Relief washed over her. They'd know who she was, her address, her car registration information. Next of kin info was all over her cards, so they'd have called Jackson by now. Although there had been no other cars in the lot while she paid, surely the kid who worked there would have watched her run for the car and known she'd been car jacked. The place was likely swarming with cops even now. She just needed to sit tight for a bit longer then the rescuers would be here. Now, to keep this crazy man calm until then. Calm she could do. If nothing else, Mount Holyoke College had honed her skills at presenting as calm and self-assured. Act like a lady, she told herself. Decorum was everything.

"EXCUSE ME, SIR." Sir? She winced. Maybe that was a bit over the top. She asked again, "Where are you taking us?"

"I'm not *taking* you anywhere. You chose to come along. Since you're here now, it can't hurt for you to know. Bathinghurst."

Bathinghurst was hours away, and it was just a little town. "Why Bathinghurst? Is that where you're from?" Maybe she could do a reverse Stockholm syndrome and get him to like her, to like them.

"My granny's place is there."

"Oh. Is she ill? Do you need to visit her?"

"She's dead." The car sped up. The tension in his voice was palpable.

Okay, wrong way to steer the conversation. But she had to go with it now. "I'm so sorry to hear that. Was it recent?"

"Eleven days ago, so they said."

"I guess you didn't get to go to the funeral then?"

"They wouldn't let me out."

~

Get your copy of *GONE* at
https://Books2Read.com/GoneAPsychologicalThriller

Psychological Thriller Series "When Bad Things Happen":
Gone
Trust
Selfish
Instinct
Reasons Why
Mine (coming December, 2021)
Young Anna (free at https://dl.bookfunnel.com/xrj0h5wef9)

Read the rest of the autism series:

Autism Talks and Talks
Autism Grows Up

Autism Goes to College - Jeff's Coming of Age Story
Nonfiction:
Autism Questions Parents Ask
Autism Questions Teachers Ask

Get your FREE short story about a single mom and her autistic child
Anything for Her Son at https://dl.bookfunnel.com/a27d9uzou0

www.ingramcontent.com/pod-product-compliance
Lightning Source LLC
Chambersburg PA
CBHW030740030726
47497CB00001B/60